The
MX Book
of
New
Sherlock
Holmes
Stories

Part XXXIII – 2022 Annual
(1896-1919)

The MX Book of New Sherlock Holmes Stories

Stories

Part XXXIII
2022 Annual
(1896-1919)

SOUTHAMPTON STREET

359

EDITED By David Marcum

OFFICES

TRADITIONAL HOLMES ADVENTURES COMPILED FOR THE BENEFIT OF THE RESTORATION OF UNDERSHAW

First edition published in 2022
© Copyright 2022

ISBN Hardback 978-1-80424-013-7
ISBN Paperback 978-1-80424-014-4
AUK ePub ISBN 978-1-80424-015-1
AUK PDF ISBN 978-1-80424-016-8

Published in the UK by
MX Publishing
335 Princess Park Manor, Royal Drive,
London, N11 3GX
www.mxpublishing.co.uk

David Marcum can be reached at:
thepapersofsherlockholmes@gmail.com

Cover design by Brian Belanger
www.belangerbooks.com and *www.redbubble.com/people/zhahadun*

Internal Illustrations by Sidney Paget

CONTENTS

Forewords

Adventures

(Continued on the next page . . . .)

(Continued on the next page . . . .)

These additional Sherlock Holmes adventures
can be found in the previous volumes of
The MX Book of New Sherlock Holmes Stories

(Continued on the next page . . . .)

(Continued on the next page . . . .)

PART V – Christmas Adventures

(Continued on the next page . . . .)

PART VI – 2017 Annual

(Continued on the next page . . . .)

The Unwelcome Client – Keith Hann
The Tempest of Lyme – David Ruffle
The Problem of the Holy Oil – David Marcum
A Scandal in Serbia – Thomas A. Turley
The Curious Case of Mr. Marconi – Jan Edwards
Mr. Holmes and Dr. Watson Learn to Fly – C. Edward Davis
Die Weisse Frau – Tim Symonds
A Case of Mistaken Identity – Daniel D. Victor

PART VII – Eliminate the Impossible: 1880-1891
Foreword – Lee Child
Foreword – Rand B. Lee
Foreword – Michael Cox
Foreword – Roger Johnson
Foreword – Melissa Farnham
Foreword – David Marcum
No Ghosts Need Apply (A Poem) – Jacquelynn Morris
The Melancholy Methodist – Mark Mower
The Curious Case of the Sweated Horse – Jan Edwards
The Adventure of the Second William Wilson – Daniel D. Victor
The Adventure of the Marchindale Stiletto – James Lovegrove
The Case of the Cursed Clock – Gayle Lange Puhl
The Tranquility of the Morning – Mike Hogan
A Ghost from Christmas Past – Thomas A. Turley
The Blank Photograph – James Moffett
The Adventure of A Rat. – Adrian Middleton
The Adventure of Vanaprastha – Hugh Ashton
The Ghost of Lincoln – Geri Schear
The Manor House Ghost – S. Subramanian
The Case of the Unquiet Grave – John Hall
The Adventure of the Mortal Combat – Jayantika Ganguly
The Last Encore of Quentin Carol – S.F. Bennett
The Case of the Petty Curses – Steven Philip Jones
The Tuttman Gallery – Jim French
The Second Life of Jabez Salt – John Linwood Grant
The Mystery of the Scarab Earrings – Thomas Fortenberry
The Adventure of the Haunted Room – Mike Chinn
The Pharaoh's Curse – Robert V. Stapleton
The Vampire of the Lyceum – Charles Veley and Anna Elliott
The Adventure of the Mind's Eye – Shane Simmons

PART VIII – Eliminate the Impossible: 1892-1905
Foreword – Lee Child
Foreword – Rand B. Lee
Foreword – Michael Cox
Foreword – Roger Johnson
Foreword – Melissa Farnham

(Continued on the next page . . . .)

Part IX – 2018 Annual (1879-1895)

(Continued on the next page . . . .)

(Continued on the next page . . . .)

Part XII: Some Untold Cases (1894-1902)

PART XIII: 2019 Annual (1881-1890)

(Continued on the next page . . . .)

PART XIV: 2019 Annual (1891 -1897)

(Continued on the next page . . . .)

(Continued on the next page . . . .)

Part XVII – Whatever Remains . . . Must Be the Truth (1891-1898)

Part XVIII – Whatever Remains . . . Must Be the Truth (1899-1925)

(Continued on the next page . . . .)

Part XIX: 2020 Annual (1882-1890)

(Continued on the next page . . . .)

(Continued on the next page . . . .)

Part XXII: Some More Untold Cases (1877-1887)

(Continued on the next page . . . .)

(Continued on the next page . . . .)

Part XXV: 2021 Annual (1881-1888)

(Continued on the next page . . . .)

(Continued on the next page . . . .)

Part XXVIII: More Christmas Adventures (1869-1888)

(Continued on the next page . . . .)

Part XXIX: More Christmas Adventures (1889-1896)

Part XXX: More Christmas Adventures (1897-1928)

(Continued on the next page . . . .)

The following contributions appear in the companion volumes:
Part XXXI – 2022 Annual (1875-1887)
Part XXXII – 2022 Annual (1888-1895)

Dedicated to
these friends of the
MX Anthologies who
recently crossed over
the Reichenbach:

Carole Nelson Douglas
Greg Hatcher
Carl Heifetz
William "Bill" Lawler
Mark Levy

R.I.P.

Editor's Foreword:
"We can but try."
by David Marcum

Some approach the Sherlockian Canon, that small batch of just five-dozen original Holmes adventures, as if that number – *Only sixty stories!* – is unalterable. They're quite firm: *Verily, verily, the Canon shall be sixty stories – No more, no less!* But then the exceptions creep in . . . .

Sixty may be absolute – *No more, no less!* – but then there's *The Apocrypha*, that extra-Canonical material that maybe ought to be included too. "How Watson Learned the Trick" and "The Field Bazaar", though not full-length adventures, are important slices-of-life from the famed Baker Street sitting room. And if one accepts those, then there are the Canonical plays – all by way of the First Literary Agent: *The Crown Diamond* and *The Speckled Band*. Then onward to the lesser-known (and most confusing) play *Angels of Darkness*. And don't forget the two stories which clearly feature Holmes in an off-stage setting, "The Man with the Watches" and "The Lost Special". So already the pure Sixty-story Barrier has been breached.

And then there are those absolute purists who make other exceptions. "*Sixty adventures – No more, no less!*" they cry, prepared to defend that idea to the death. But then, a moment later, they follow with, "Well, except for these two or three pastiches written by a friend of mine, or by the person whose attention I'm seeking or whose celebrity favor I want to curry with my praise." Thus, their conviction of The Immaculacy of The Canonical Sixty is already cracked and compromised.

Along the same lines, some insist that The Canon be insulated from the bigger picture, keeping Holmes's world a cozy little place solely defined by only what is found recorded in the "official" sixty tales. If it isn't recorded there, they insist, then it didn't happen. But there's a loophole for that: The Canon mentions over one-hundred-forty "Untold Cases" in addition to the Told Sixty, and the details of these are often so vague that they are very much open to infinite interpretation. It's a bold concept, and too much for some to assimilate: Holmes and Watson are doing things off-stage that we don't get to witness in the Canonical Sixty.

I haven't done the math, but it would be a good project for someone to make a solid estimate of just how much time accrues in just the events of The Canon that we actually see recorded and presented. For instance, the bulk of "The Five Orange Pips" – around 82% – consists of just an hour or so in the Baker Street sitting room on a late September 1887 night, either hearing the client's story, or discussing it after he leaves to go be murdered. The rest occurs in a short breakfast scene the next day, followed by another concluding conversation that evening.

It would be interesting if someone were to calculate the amount of time that is actually recorded in The Canon – either passing from the beginning of a case to the end, or simply what's shown "on screen", against how much total time that passes within the forty years between Holmes's first *recorded* Canonical case, "The Gloria Scott" (in Summer 1874) and the last, "His Last Bow" (in August 1914). I'm certain that it would be stunning for some just how much unrecorded time there is, wherein Holmes and Watson live all those other parts of their lives beyond the lens of the pure Canon that so many defend.

And in that recorded time, there are historical events occurring all around them. Many don't want to acknowledge those either. They like the idea that Holmes and Watson interact with anonymous folk like Jabez Wilson or Hall Pycroft, or others that no one has never heard of before or since. They don't want to hear about Holmes actually functioning in *The World*. But he does. In some of those Canonical Untold Cases, there are references to Holmes's interactions with historical figures, so it isn't a total impossibility, even for the Defenders of the Sixty, that he had contact with others. Holmes assisted the Pope (Leo XIII, whose Papacy ran from 1878 to 1903) in two Untold Cases, that of the Vatican Cameos, and also the death of Cardinal Tosca. He assisted the Royal Family of Scandinavia (as mentioned in "The Noble Bachelor" and "The Final Problem"). He was hired by the King of Bohemia (although such title was rather flimsily moribund by the late 1880's), and he assisted the British Prime Minister (whose name was changed for security's sake.)

So when Canonical purists dislike those post-Canonical stories wherein Holmes is involved with recognizable historical figures, they really don't have a Canonical leg to stand upon. The door for this was thrown open with the publication of Nicholas Meyer's Game-changing 1974 work, *The Seven-Per-Cent Solution*, wherein Holmes and Watson meet Sigmund Freud. Before that, in Canonical adventures which had been prepared for publication in *The Strand*, Watson and the First Literary Agent had pointedly changed names to protect identities. But not so in the document that Meyer uncovered. And when it was understood that Watsonian manuscripts could be published without the need to cross the First Literary Agent's desk, such editorial protections were no longer honored – or necessary.

The list of historical figures that Holmes and Watson have encountered who appear under their own names in latter-day post-

Canonical adventures is staggering, and many show up multiple times: The Queen of England and the Prince of Wales (and later the King). Gladstone and Disraeli and Lord Salisbury (and other Prime Ministers). Actors like Ellen Terry, Henry Irving, Lillie Langtry, and Basil Rathbone. Writers such as Bram Stoker, Henry James, Charles Dickens, H.P. Lovecraft, H.G. Wells, and F. Scott Fitzgerald. Inspector Abberline and Montague Druitt. The Dalai Lama and Henry Ward Beecher. Dr. Joseph Bell and Dr. Cream and Dr. Joseph Lister and Dr. Crippen. Both of my grandfathers, William Marcum and Ray Rathbone. Bismarck and Kaiser Wilhelm and Winston Churchill. Theodore Roosevelt and Franklin Roosevelt. J. Edgar Hoover and Adolf Hitler.

The list is overwhelming – although the *School and Holmes* website has made a good start at cataloging various figures encountered by our heroes in post-Canonical adventures. Here's the link for the letter *"A"* – Dive in, and like Jabez Wilson in "The Red-Headed League", you can progress through that letter, and *"with diligence [you] might get on to the B's before very long. . . ."*

https://www.schoolandholmes.com/charactersa.html

Many who try to limit Holmes to the Canonical Sixty are unwittingly limiting what makes him the greatest detective. If we only accept what's presented in The Canon, then we find that a good many of Holmes's cases are small affairs indeed, giving the impression that Holmes is a very skilled *but very small-time* problem solver. Of course, he loved the problem for the problem's sake, no matter its size or seriousness, and to him it didn't matter if a client was a pawn-broker or a king, a stockbroker or a banker or baronet. Yet many of the recorded Canonical cases are rather insignificant in the great scheme of things. If not for being memorialized in The Canon, for example, no one would have ever known or cared about the existence of Jabez Wilson or Hall Pycroft.

Holmes was involved with so many people over the course of his career, and his reputation grew and grew through the decades. Therefore, it's certain that even though a sizeable percentage of his clients were those who lived *small* lives, there were also just as many who lived *big* lives. And if Holmes was interacting with these historical *figures*, then he was interacting with *history* as well.

Many Canonical limiters don't want that. They *want* Holmes to be a shabby small-timer who mopes around the sitting room in brown studies, getting in the dumps at times and not opening his mouth for days on end, until he's consulted by an otherwise unimportant figure who has a curious vexation – five orange pips, for instance, or a blue jewel in a bonny goose container. Granted, there are the occasional cases of greater importance – stolen naval treaties and that irksome Napoleon of Crime – but many stories presented in The Canon are much smaller in scale. Yet just because that's what's on the "accepted" Canonical stage doesn't mean that it's the whole story.

In 1989, one of my few heroes, Billy Joel, released "We Didn't Start the Fire", a nearly-five-minute long song detailing the events from 1949 (the year of his birth) to 1989. He wrote it after speaking to a twenty-one-year old who told him that things were much rougher in 1989 than it had been when Joel was in his twenties. Joel responded by pointing out all of the historical events – some quite grim, like the Korean War – which occurred in those bygone days, all just as rough as what the young man was facing in the present. The chorus states, *"We didn't start the fire – It was always burning since the world's been turning. We didn't start the fire, No, we didn't light it, but we tried to fight it."* The implication of this is that these historical challenges have always been with us, but that one can meet them as they appear and do one's best to succeed.

And this, believe it or not, is rather like Sherlock Holmes's own creed.

In both "The Problem of Thor Bridge" and "The Creeping Man", Holmes makes a statement that's easy to slide over too quickly, but which, in fact, is something well-worth remembering:

"We can but try."

In context, Holmes first makes the statement in "Thor Bridge" when explaining that he has a theory, but it might be wrong:

> *[Y]ou have seen me miss my mark before, Watson. I have an instinct for such things, and yet it has sometimes played me false. It seemed a certainty when first it flashed across my mind in the cell at Winchester, but one drawback of an active mind is that one can always conceive alternative explanations which would make our scent a false one. And yet – and yet – Well, Watson, we can but try.*

"Thor Bridge" was first published in February and March 1927. The next Canonical tale to be published was "The Creeping Man", a full year later (in March 1928, just a little over a year before Watson's passing). In that, Holmes is suggesting that he and Watson bluff their way into seeing an antagonist, to which Watson replies:

4

"We can but try."

"Excellent, Watson! Compound of the Busy Bee and Excelsior. We can but try – the motto of the firm."

The motto of the firm indeed! Even though this statement only appeared in the fifty-fifth and fifty-sixty published Canonical adventures, it was certainly Holmes's philosophy long before that. It served him well as he carried out his investigations, and also as he lived his life – for besides encountering many historical figures, Holmes encountered a great deal of challenging history as well.

Holmes was born in 1854. Watson's birth was two years earlier. We can look at the world around us now and bemoan all that is legitimately wrong – and it truly is wrong in so many ways! – but the challenges people faced in those days, while different, were also quite grim indeed. Disease and genocide – different forms then and now, but still the same human suffering under different guises. Wars and starvation on all levels – they had it, and we have it. Societal unfairness, foul corruption, and evil injustice and from top to bottom, with the haves always greedily clutching at theirs while the have-nots scramble – some surviving and others not.

Google, that amazing tool undoubtedly brought back from the future to this time by some as-yet unborn time-traveling Prometheus, provides an instantaneous way to find out this or that fact. It is truly an amazing thing. A quick check shows that between 1854 and 1900, there were nearly *three-hundred wars* around the world! Eight of those were in the year of Holmes's birth. And while that seems like a long time ago, and they might have been small compared to the World Wars and possible Nuclear Wars and Cold Wars that we've been conditioned to in our lifetimes, they were very real and devastating and disruptive and deadly for those who were involved. Lives were ruined or lost.

During that same period, there were several dozen pandemics and endemics and plagues – fevers and cholera, influenza and bubonic plague, malaria and smallpox.

The world was a dangerous place. It *is* a dangerous place. It always has been. It isn't just bad now. This – the history we're living in right now – is just a different kind of bad.

We didn't start the fire. It was always burning since the world's been turning.

But we can be strong and face it.

Like Sherlock Holmes . . . .

We can but try.

5

I had the idea for *The MX Book of New Sherlock Holmes Stories* in early 2015 as a way to have more stories about the *True Canonical Holmes* – a hero, and not a modernized broken sociopathic murderer who had stolen Holmes's name, a version that was insidiously creeping into the world's perceptions of him. The idea for volumes of stories about the True Holmes was more popular than I could have ever imagined, as so many people still need *Heroic Holmes*. My 2015 hope for possibly a dozen or so new stories grew and grew over that year to become the first MX three-volume set with over sixty new adventures – the largest Holmes anthology collection of its kind ever produced. (We've since regularly surpassed that.)

It quickly became obvious that both authors and readers wanted more, so the series was established as an ongoing venture. From nearly the beginning, it was decided to direct the royalties from the books to a school for special needs children that was located at Undershaw, one of Sir Arthur Conan Doyle's former homes in Hindhead, England. The school was originally called *Stepping Stones*, but it has since been renamed to match the building where it resides, *Undershaw*. As of this writing, this series, by way of the incredible contributions from over 200 authors and the amazing support of countless fans around the world, has produced nearly 700 new traditional Holmes adventures and has raised nearly *$100,000* for the school. That's nearly *One-Hundred-Thousand Dollars!* That number will almost certainly be exceeded by mid-2022. (And I'm told that even more important than the money has been the spread awareness of the school around the world and its valuable work.)

When COVID-19 came upon us in early 2020, I was worried about this series, and how everyone's suddenly upside-down lives might be affected in terms of contributing new Sherlock Holmes stories. While some people found it more difficult to write when conditions became unfavorable, most rose to the challenge, and the books continued as before, with multiple volumes of high-quality traditional Holmes adventures. There were six volumes in 2020, and six more in 2021. Now as I write this, the world watches as a vile Beast has invaded Ukraine, and still the contributors have done an amazing job, and I continue to receive stories for the next set of books, *However Improbable . . . .* planned for Fall 2022.

I cannot express my admiration and gratefulness enough for those who have provided stories under ongoing challenging conditions.

Each and every contributor who has added to this series with stories, poems, forewords, and artwork are the finest kind of people, and they are heroes of the first order, and should all be incredibly proud of what we've accomplished. And as conditions still prove to be challenging . . . .

We can but try.

"Of course, I could only stammer out my thanks."
– *The unhappy John Hector McFarlane*, "The Norwood Builder"

As always when one of these sets is finished, I want to first thank with all my heart my incredible, patient, brilliant, kind, and beautiful wife of nearly thirty-four years, Rebecca – every day I'm luckier than the day before! – and our amazing, funny, brilliant, creative, and wonderful son, and my friend, Dan. I love you both, and you are everything to me!

In late 2020, I was fortunate to obtain my dream job, working as a municipal civil engineer for the city whose specific infrastructure had inspired me to go back to school in my thirties to be an engineer. It's the best job I've ever had with an amazing group of people – and the learning curve has been amazing in its own way as well. I knew the engineering, but learning things from the municipal side is a new challenge. On top of that was family time – most important – and also the various Sherlockian efforts that I've pursued.

In 2021, through the new job, I found time to write a number of new Holmes pastiches and essays, and also to edit and get published twenty-two different books. (These included six of my own books, six MX anthologies, five Holmes anthology volumes for Belanger Books, the remaining four volumes in *The Complete Dr. Thorndyke* collection, and a book of Holmes stories by Nick Dunn-Meynell.) Then, in late 2021, the boss I was hired to replace retired, so my work responsibilities increased exponentially.

Thus, the editing of the *2022 Annual* took on new challenges as it fit in around my real life. Thankfully, the various contributors were wonderful as usual, and I can't thank them enough for their patience, and for the stories that they sent, even as they worked around their own ever-more-complicated lives.

For the *2022 Annual*, some contributors simply couldn't join the party this time, due to all sorts of reasons – too busy or too stressed. Perhaps there were health- or job-related issues, or burnout. Several experienced tragic deaths of their loved ones over the past few months. I completely understand, and cannot express my gratitude enough for their past participation, and I hope that they'll be back in the future.

Other authors found that Watson was whispering to them much more urgently than before, and they ended up with more than one story to submit. Some had two or three, and in a couple of cases, a full half-dozen tales. In these trying times, I was incredibly grateful to receive them, and they are invaluable additions to the latest set.

Back in 2015, when the MX anthologies began, I limited each contribution to one item per author, in order to spread the space around more fairly. But some authors are more prolific than that, and rather than be forced to choose between two excellent stories, I began to allow multiple contributions. (This also helped the authors, as their stories, if separated enough from each other chronologically, could appear in different simultaneously published volumes, thereby increasing their own bibliographies.)

Hal Glatzer and David MacGregor each contributed two stories this time. Dan Rowley, Tim Symonds, Arthur Hall, and me (your editor) provided three, and the indomitable Tracy Revels wrote an amazing six of them.

Also of note are the six stories contributed by the late Terry Golledge. In early 2022, I received an email from Niel Golledge, Terry's son, with a sample story, "The Addleton Tragedy". Terry had written it, along with nine others, in the 1980's, but they were never published. Niel had recently approached another editor about them, but that chap felt that it would be too much work to prepare the original typewritten manuscripts for modern publication. That was his big mistake, for it was absolutely worth the extra editorial work, as Terry Golledge's stories are wonderful and Watsonian. Niel graciously agreed to let me edit and include six of them for this collection, and later in 2022 they, along with the remaining four stories, will be published in their own separate volume, to the delight of Sherlockians like me who can *never* have enough tales about the *True Sherlock Holmes*. (An interesting side-note: Terry Golledge's mother worked as a governess for Sir Arthur Conan Doyle for several years in the early Nineteenth Century, so these tales have a bit of extra associational history.)

I can never express enough gratitude for all of the contributors who have donated their time and royalties to this ongoing project. I'm constantly amazed at the incredible stories that you send, and I'm so glad to have gotten to know so many of you through this process. It's an undeniable fact that Sherlock Holmes authors are the *best* people!

There is a fine group of people that exchanges emails with me when we have the time – and time is far too rare for all of us these days! I don't get to write back and forth with these fine people as often as I'd like, but I really enjoy catching up when we do get the chance: Derrick Belanger, Brian Belanger, Mark Mower, Roger Riccard, Denis Smith, Tom Turley, Dan Victor, and Marcia Wilson.

There is a group of special people who have stepped up and supported this and a number of other projects over and over again with a lot of contributions. They are the best and I can't express how valued they are: Ian Ableson, Hugh Ashton, Derrick Belanger, Deanna Baran, Andrew Bryant, Thomas Burns, Nick Cardillo, Chris Chan, Craig Stephen Copland, Matthew Elliott, Tim Gambrell, Jayantika Ganguly, Paul Gilbert, Dick Gillman, Arthur Hall, Steve Herczeg, Paul Hiscock, Mike Hogan, Craig Janacek, Susan Knight, Mark Mower, Will Murray, Tracy Revels, Roger Riccard, Jane Rubino, Geri Schear, Brenda Seabrooke, Shane Simmons, Robert Stapleton, Tim Symonds, Kevin Thornton, Tom Turley, DJ Tyrer, Dan Victor, I.A. Watson, and Marcia Wilson.

Next, I wish to send several huge *Thank You's* to the following:

- *Jeffrey Hatcher* – I missed my chance to meet Jeff in person at *From Gillette to Brett V* in October 2018, although I very much enjoyed his presentation. I was already aware of him for the incredible work that he had done in bringing a rather grim Holmes novel with a remarkable lack of hope, Mitch Cullin's *A Slight Trick of the Mind* (2005) to the screen in the form of *Mr. Holmes* (2015). My deerstalker and I were at the theatre on the film's opening day, having just re-read the book in preparation, and I wasn't sure what to expect. An elderly Holmes's life in the book is very bad, and it only get gets worse, with more bad piling high with each new chapter. Still, I normally defer to the printed version of things as the "true" version – especially when changes are made for a film. In this case, I happily made an exception to my rule.

    My own father had passed away in 2011 after struggling for several years with both Parkinson's and Alzheimer's, and to see Holmes's decline on screen was almost too vivid to bear – but Jeff's deft handling of the script, and the wise changes he made to the original plot in order to give Holmes a happier better future than shown in the book, were exactly what was needed.

    When Steve Emecz interviewed Jeff for the MX Publishing Audio Collection and then put me in touch with him, I was very pleased, and this was exceeded when Jeff agreed to write a foreword for this collection.

    Jeff, thanks very much for all your work, and the contribution of your time to these books. It's very much appreciated!

- *Steve Emecz* – As I've explained elsewhere, Steve works a way-more-than-full-time job related to his career in e-finance. MX Publishing isn't his full-time job – it's a labor of love. He, along with his wife, Sharon Emecz, and cousin, Timi Emecz, *are* MX Publishing. In addition to their very busy real every-day lives, these three sole employees take care of the management, marketing, editing, production, and shipping, and they absolutely cannot receive enough credit for what they accomplish.

Some people have a picture in their minds of a publishing company with several floors on some skyscraper, hundreds of employees running around like ants, with vast departments devoted to management, marketing, editing, production, shipping, etc. That is not always the case. Those old giant dinosaur publishers are still around, and they might squeeze out a Sherlockian title or two every year for those readers who foolishly think that there are only one or two Sherlockian titles every year (thus cheating themselves of some really incredible stories), but those publishers don't represent the modern way of doing things. MX has become the premiere Sherlockian publisher by following a new paradigm: Avoid the sucking whirlpool of traditional publishing and get books to readers as soon as possible. And they manage to get all of this done with a truly skeleton staff.

From my first association with MX in 2013, I saw that MX (under Steve's leadership) was *the* fast-rising superstar of the Sherlockian publishing world. Connecting with MX and Steve Emecz was personally an amazing life-changing event for me, as it has been for countless other Sherlockian authors. It has led me to write many more stories, and then to edit books, along with unexpected additional Holmes Pilgrimages to England – none of which might have happened otherwise. By way of my first email with Steve I've had the chance to make some incredible Sherlockian friends and play in the Holmesian Sandbox in ways that I would have never dreamed possible.

Through it all, Steve has been one of the most positive and supportive people that I've ever known.

With his and Sharon's and Timi's incredible hard work, they have made MX into a world-wide Sherlockian publishing phenomenon, providing opportunities for authors who would never have had them otherwise. There are some like me who return more than once to Watson's Tin Dispatch Box, and there are others who only find one or two stories there – but they also get the chance to publish their books, and then they can point with pride at this accomplishment, and how they too have added to The Great Holmes Tapestry.

From the beginning, Steve has let me explore various Sherlockian projects and open up my own personal possibilities in ways that otherwise would have never happened. Thank you, Steve, for every opportunity!

- *Brian Belanger* – Over the last few years, my amazement at Brian Belanger's ever-increasing talent has only grown. I initially became acquainted with him when he took over the duties of creating the covers for MX Books following the untimely death of their previous graphic artist. I found Brian to be a great collaborator, very easy-going and stress-free in his approach and willingness to work with authors, and wonderfully creative too.

   Brian and his brother, Derrick Belanger, are two great friends, and several years ago they founded *Belanger Books* which, along with MX Publishing, has absolutely locked up the Sherlockian publishing field with a vast amount of amazing material. The dinosaurs must be trembling to see every new Sherlockian project, one after another after another. Luckily MX and Belanger Books work closely with one another, and I'm thrilled to be associated with both of them. Many thanks to Brian for all he does for both publishers, and for all he's done for me personally.

- *Roger Johnson* – I'm more grateful than I can say that I know Roger. I was aware of him for years before I timidly sent him a copy of my first book for review, and then on my first Holmes Pilgrimage to England and Scotland in 2013, I was able to meet both him and his wonderful wife, Jean Upton, in person. When I returned on Holmes Pilgrimage No. 2 in 2015, I was so fortunate that they graciously invited me to stay with them for several days in their home, where we had many wonderful discussions, while occasionally venturing forth so that they could show me parts of England that I wouldn't have seen otherwise. It was an experience I wouldn't trade for anything.

11

Roger's Sherlockian knowledge is exceptional, as is the work that he does to further the cause of The Master. But even more than that, both Roger and Jean are simply the finest and best of people, and I'm very lucky to know both of them – even though I don't get to see them nearly as often as I'd like, and especially in these crazy days! (The last time was in 2016, at the Grand Opening party for the Stepping Stones School (now called Undershaw) at Undershaw in Hindhead.

In so many ways, Roger, I can't thank you enough, and I can't imagine these books without you.

And finally, last but certainly *not* least, thanks to **Sir Arthur Conan Doyle**: Author, doctor, adventurer, and the Founder of the Sherlockian Feast. Honored, and present in spirit.

As I always note when putting together an anthology of Holmes stories, the effort has been a labor of love. These adventures are just more tiny threads woven into the ongoing Great Holmes Tapestry, continuing to grow and grow, for there can *never* be enough stories about the man whom Watson described as *"the best and wisest . . . whom I have ever known."*

David Marcum
April 5th, 2022
128th Anniversary of
"The Empty House"

Questions, comments, or story submissions
may be addressed to David Marcum at

thepapersofsherlockholmes@gmail.com

12

Foreword
by Jeffrey Hatcher

I've never written a Sherlock Holmes pastiche. At least not in prose. I've written the plays *Sherlock Holmes and the Adventure of the Suicide Club*, *Sherlock Holmes and the Ice Palace Murders*, and *Holmes and Watson*. I also wrote the screenplay for the film *Mr. Holmes*, based on Mitch Cullin's novel *A Slight Trick of the Mind*. But I've never attempted a classic short story or novel of the sort Arthur Conan Doyle excelled at. The reasons are two-fold:

I've never had the stamina to write prose fiction, be it the short story or a long form narrative. There's something about the density of the words and the requirement to depict a complete world with both exterior action and interior thought that defeats me. When I was in junior high, I started writing a shorty story – maybe it was going to be a novel, I can't remember – and around that time I'd read Dashiell Hammett's *The Maltese Falcon*. Its opening is devoted entirely to a description of what Hammett's private eye hero Sam Spade looks like:

> *Samuel Spade's jaw was long and bony, his chin a jutting v under the more flexible V of his mouth. His nostrils curved back to make another, smaller, V. His yellow-grey eyes were horizontal. The V motif was picked up again by thickish brows rising outward from twin creases above a hooked nose, and his pale brown hair grew down – from high flat temples--in a point on his forehead. He looked rather pleasantly like a blonde Satan."*

So, I figured that's what a writer's supposed to do. Start with your main character and describe him in laborious, infinitesimal detail. So that's what I did. I can't remember who my main character was or if he even had a name, but I was onto my third page and hadn't gotten below his upper lip. And he wasn't going to be the only character in the story. I was going to have to do this with all the characters. Then I'd have to describe the rooms they inhabited, their homes and offices, their cars. Not to mention the outdoors. It came down to this: I don't like having to describe what the tree looks like. I never finished that story or novel or whatever it was supposed to be. It was properly abandoned. Instead, I turned my interest to dramatic story telling: Plays and screenplays, the first fully executed

13

one being a one-hundred-forty page film adaptation of Ian Fleming's *Moonraker*, five years before the Roger Moore movie. (Mine was better.)

The second reason I've never attempted a Sherlock Holmes story is that although the form seems simple enough, schematic even, the content, tone, and style that Conan Doyle mastered with such apparent ease is actually very hard to impersonate. The joy in a familiar form such as the Holmes stories lies in the reader experiencing the changes the writer rings within the form.

I wrote a few *Columbo's* in the 1990's and each classic *Columbo* episode had the following structure:

Act One: *Meet the polished, sophisticated murderer and watch him or her commit the ostensibly perfect crime.*
Act Two: *Columbo investigates, discovers a clue that tells him the perfect crime isn't so perfect.*
Act Three: *Columbo and the murderer play cat and mouse as more mistakes are uncovered and more chess moves take place.*
Act Four: *The murderer finds the means to save himself.*
Act Five: *Columbo tricks the murderer into incriminating himself or reveals the final damning clue that closes the case.*

The fun was in watching the form reenacted in different settings with different characters, clues, twists, and surprises.

Similarly with Holmes, we start a story expecting a scene in Baker Street, the arrival of a client, a mystery posed. "Will you help me, Mr. Holmes?" Then Holmes and Watson set forth into the streets of London or the Great Grimpen Mire to investigate the case. They meet increasingly desperate and malevolent characters. Another crime is committed or foiled. Finally, the culprit is captured. Throughout the story Holmes will reveal his deductive powers, his psychological perceptions, his wit, his courage, his humanity – along with those of Dr. Watson's. Yes, there are occasional departures from the form, but, with rare exceptions, the departures are not what we crack the spine for.

Enjoy the stories you're about to read. Think of them as an old and dear friend who's come to visit you – and he's got something terribly new and exciting to tell you.

Jeffrey Hatcher
March 2021

"These little narratives"
by Roger Johnson

Younger readers – and writers, for that matter – may not be aware that it's not so very long since the choice of new Sherlock Holmes stories was very limited indeed. If you were lucky, you might find a copy of *The Misadventures of Sherlock Holmes*, edited by Ellery Queen and published in 1944. There were two printings before the Conan Doyle family's lawyers spotted a copyright infringement in another Ellery Queen anthology and used it as a reason to have *The Misadventures* withdrawn. Sir Arthur's sons could never be persuaded that the non-canonical stories might encourage readers to seek out and read the great originals.

The occasional new story did get published. In 1945 J.C. Masterman, a distinguished Oxford University academic and wartime intelligence chief, contributed "The Case of the Gifted Amateur" to *McKill's Mystery Magazine*, and S.C. Roberts, the no less distinguished Cambridge University academic who became the first President of the Sherlock Holmes Society of London, included a short story, "The Adventure of the Megatherium Thefts", in his classic 1953 book *Holmes and Watson: A Miscellany*. The specialist Holmesian journals occasionally published good new stories, but until 1974 the only book of consequence was *The Exploits of Sherlock Holmes*, comprising twelve tales written by Adrian Conan Doyle and John Dickson Carr, and published in 1954. (Adrian had made himself so intensely disliked among American Sherlockians that Edgar W Smith, head of the Baker Street Irregulars, dismissed the book as "Sherlock Holmes Exploited". In fact, the stories are never less than good, and several are excellent.)

1974 was the year of wonders, beginning with the Royal Shakespeare Company's hugely successful new production of William Gillette's play *Sherlock Holmes*. Adrian Conan Doyle had died in 1970, predeceased by his brother Denis, and, despite some subsequently dubious handling of Sir Arthur's estate, the attitude towards sincere fictional tributes to his most celebrated creations was now more relaxed. The first novel-length pastiches had only recently appeared, derived from the scripts of successful movies: *A Study in Terror* and *The Private Life of Sherlock Holmes*. More would come, but the real breakthrough was Nicholas Meyer's *The Seven-per-Cent Solution*, which would itself become a notable film.

The floodgates were not yet breached. That would come with the expiry of Sir Arthur's British copyright in 1980 – and would be followed by problems when copyright in all countries of the European Union was extended to seventy years after the author's death. Freedom was finally declared in 2000 – except in the U.S.A., whose copyright laws are unlike any other nation's. Nevertheless, it was now legal to write and publish new Holmes stories almost everywhere, and, as long as publication was a matter for the professionals, we could be pretty confident that the result would be of at least reasonable quality. But fashions in the book world change, and even Sherlock Holmes doesn't always appeal to the professional publishers.

What actually destroyed the floodgates was the rapid development of the home computer and the world-wide web. Self-publishing became much easier and cheaper, and in time the authors didn't even have to produce a printed version of their works, as the internet made it possible to post them online for anyone to read. One result is easy access to stories created with admiration and affection. Another, alas, is that the good stuff is vastly outnumbered by the less good – often poorly constructed and badly written, sometimes actually offensive.

Fortunately, it isn't hard to find new Sherlock Holmes stories of genuine quality. The book you're reading now is evidence of that. This series began in 2015, with the publication of three volumes, whose editor, authors, and publisher generously donated all their royalties to the restoration and maintenance of Undershaw, the house that Arthur Conan Doyle had built in the Surrey Hills for himself and his family. The fact that *The MX Book of New Sherlock Holmes Stories* continues, six years on, is heartening. That it now exceeds *thirty* volumes is amazing!

The apparently indefatigable David Marcum ensures that the standard remains high, and the proceeds still go to the upkeep of Undershaw, which since 2016 has been home to the Undershaw School, providing care and education for children aged 8 to 19 with Autistic Spectrum Disorder and associated learning needs.

Could there be a better recommendation?

Roger Johnson, BSI, ASH
Commissioning Editor: *The Sherlock Holmes Journal*
December 2021

An Ongoing Legacy
for Sherlock Holmes
by Steve Emecz

Undershaw
Circa 1900

*T*he *MX Book of New Sherlock Holmes Stories* has grown beyond any expectations we could have imagined. We're very close to having raised $100,000 for Undershaw, a school for children with learning disabilities. The collection has become not only the largest Sherlock Holmes collection in the world, but one of the most respected.

We have received over twenty very positive reviews from *Publishers Weekly*, and in a recent review for someone else's book, *Publishers Weekly* referred to the MX Book in that review which demonstrates how far the collection's influence has grown.

In 2022, we launched *The MX Audio Collection*, an app which includes some of these stories, alongside exclusive interviews with leading writers and Sherlockians including Lee Child, Jeffrey Hatcher, Nicholas

Meyer, Nancy Springer, Bonnie MacBird, and Otto Penzler. A share of the proceeds also goes to Undershaw. You can find out all about the app here:

https://mxpublishing.com/pages/mx-app

In addition to Undershaw, we also support Happy Life Mission (a baby rescue project in Kenya), The World Food Programme (which won the Nobel Peace Prize in 2020), and iHeart (who support mental health in young people).

Our support for our projects is possible through the publishing of Sherlock Holmes books, which we have now been doing for over a decade.

You can find links to all our projects on our website:

https://mxpublishing.com/pages/about-us

I'm sure you will enjoy the fantastic stories in the latest volumes and look forward to many more in the future.

Steve Emecz
March 2022
Twitter: *@mxpublishing*

The Doyle Room at Undershaw
Partially funded through royalties from
The MX Book of New Sherlock Holmes Stories

A Word from Undershaw
by Emma West

Undershaw
September 9, 2016
Grand Opening of the Stepping Stones School
(Now *Undershaw*)
(Photograph courtesy of Roger Johnson)

I am delighted to bring you news of Undershaw . . . from Undershaw. Since September 2021, under our new name, vision, and values, our wonderful school has been focussing on Undershaw community pride. To that end, we have focussed on recruiting, retaining, and upskilling a talented staff cadre, each one a specialist in their field, experienced with SEND education, and each one an innovator of new teaching and learning practices.

We have fortified our school life with robust qualifications and have strengthened our relationships with exam boards to ensure our students leave us with the qualifications they deserve, and of which they are eminently capable. Our school is awash with academic, artistic, and musical talent, and we feel privileged in our role of unleashing that potential in a way that works for our learners.

Our traditional classroom learning is complemented by a variety of other techniques. For example: Our outdoor learning area, for which we are currently fundraising. A Fire Pit shelter will double as an outdoor

20

classroom, and will enable us to continue our learning in nature all year round and in all weathers. We know that learning outdoors amidst nature does wonders for well-being and contentment. We have such a beautiful and inspirational campus and, as much as it is our *raison d'etre* to equip our provision for all our learners, it is also our role as caretakers of Undershaw to nurture and improve the campus for the generations to come.

It is only through our relationships with benefactors such as MX Publishing, and the wonderful authors who support its charitable giving, that we are able to thrive through 2022 and beyond. The culture at Undershaw is an extremely positive one, and we're delighted that you are joining us on our journey. For up-to-date news about our school and our work within the Special Educational Needs sector, please see our website at www.undershaw.education. Our newsletters carry a vast array of student activities and daily goings on, while our news articles take a deep dive into some of the ways Undershaw is redefining opportunities for our young people.

As ever, my heartfelt thanks to you all for your unrelenting support. Our students, staff, and families are full of pride at belonging to #teamundershaw, and I look forward to writing to you again soon with more tales from the Surrey Hills.

Emma West
Acting Headteacher
March 2022

"Undershaw" Hindhead Conan Doyle's House.

Editor's *Caveats*

W hen these anthologies first began back in 2015, I noted that the authors were from all over the world – and thus, there would be British spelling and American spelling. As I explained then, I didn't want to take the responsibility of changing American spelling to British and vice-versa. I would undoubtedly miss something, leading to inconsinstencies, or I'd change something incorrectly.

Some readers are bothered by this, made nervous and irate when encountering American spelling as written by Watson, and in stories set in England. However, here in America, the versions of The Canon that we read have long-ago has their spelling Americanized, so it isn't quite as shocking for us.

Additionally, I offer my apologies up front for any typographical errors that have slipped through. As a print-on-demand publisher, MX does not have squadrons of editors as some readers believe. The business consists of three part-time people who also have busy lives elsewhere – Steve Emecz, Sharon Emecz, and Timi Emecz – so the editing effort largely falls on the contributors. Some readers and consumers out there in the world are unhappy with this – apparently forgetting about all of those self-produced Holmes stories and volumes from decades ago (typed and Xeroxed) with awkward self-published formatting and loads of errors that are now prized as very expensive collector's items.

I'm personally mortified when errors slip through – ironically, there will probably be errors in these *caveats* – and I apologize now, but without a regiment of professional full-time editors looking over my shoulder, this is as good as it gets. Real life is more important than writing and editing – even in such a good cause as promoting the True and Traditional Canonical Holmes – and only so much time can be spent preparing these books before they're released into the wild. I hope that you can look past any errors, small or huge, and simply enjoy these stories, and appreciate the efforts of everyone involved, and the sincere desire to add to The Great Holmes Tapestry.

And in spite of any errors here, there are more Sherlock Holmes stories in the world than there were before, and that's a good thing.

David Marcum
Editor

Sherlock Holmes (1854-1957) was born in Yorkshire, England, on 6 January, 1854. In the mid-1870's, he moved to 24 Montague Street, London, where he established himself as the world's first Consulting Detective. After meeting Dr. John H. Watson in early 1881, he and Watson moved to rooms at 221b Baker Street, where his reputation as the world's greatest detective grew for several decades. He was presumed to have died battling noted criminal Professor James Moriarty on 4 May, 1891, but he returned to London on 5 April, 1894, resuming his consulting practice in Baker Street. Retiring to the Sussex coast near Beachy Head in October 1903, he continued to be associated in various private and government investigations while giving the impression of being a reclusive apiarist. He was very involved in the events encompassing World War I, and to a lesser degree those of World War II. He passed away peacefully upon the cliffs above his Sussex home on his 103rd birthday, 6 January, 1957.

Dr. John Hamish Watson (1852-1929) was born in Stranraer, Scotland on 7 August, 1852. In 1878, he took his Doctor of Medicine Degree from the University of London, and later joined the army as a surgeon. Wounded at the Battle of Maiwand in Afghanistan (27 July, 1880), he returned to London late that same year. On New Year's Day, 1881, he was introduced to Sherlock Holmes in the chemical laboratory at Barts. Agreeing to share rooms with Holmes in Baker Street, Watson became invaluable to Holmes's consulting detective practice. Watson was married and widowed three times, and from the late 1880's onward, in addition to his participation in Holmes's investigations and his medical practice, he chronicled Holmes's adventures, with the assistance of his literary agent, Sir Arthur Conan Doyle, in a series of popular narratives, most of which were first published in *The Strand* magazine. Watson's later years were spent preparing a vast number of his notes of Holmes's cases for future publication. Following a final important investigation with Holmes, Watson contracted pneumonia and passed away on 24 July, 1929.

Photos of Sherlock Holmes and Dr. John H. Watson courtesy of Roger Johnson

The MX Book
of
New Sherlock Holmes Stories
Part XXXIII – 2022 Annual
(1896-1919)

Of Law and Justice
by Alisha Shea

Miasmas drift through lamplit streets
While stealthy shadows crawl
'Cross cobblestones uneven.
Footsteps echo off the walls

Of grimy, gritty storefronts
Bricked in stone that once shone white.
Dim figures cloaked in secrecy
Now infiltrate the night.

They pause beneath a sagging awning
Which shields them from clear view
Of a passing bobby, diligent
Buttons polished, clearly new.

Unwittingly, he passes on
Whistling off-key down the street.
His billy club swings jauntily
As he strides off on his beat.

Sitting in their shelter,
Releasing relieved sighs,
One voice whispers to another,
"You keep watch while I apply

"My set of gleaming lock picks
In assault against the door.
That by entering this venue
We may gain the truth, afore

"Our client suffers shipwreck
Of honour and career
Which fortune will bestow
Lest we are successful here."

Presently the lock gives up,
Resistance overcome.
Inside a velvet darkness

31

Bids invaders be welcome.

A sudden spark, a gentle glow
Shows faces dear, revealed.
Not simple thieves, nor hooligans
But men who aide and heal

The weary and the hopeless,
Those who suffer loss
Of goods or reputation
Though others count them dross.

Stretching high and stooping low
And lying on the floor,
Proof of innocence is found.
A future is secured.

Returning home, a meal is had
Beside a crackling flame.
A glass of brandy, ounce of shag,
Shared peace in their domain.

A sleepy protest questions
Abuse of strict legalities.
The reply steeped in great wisdom
Declares with certainty.

"All issues are not black and white.
Such assumptions are absurd.
There are times when one must break the law
For justice to be served."

The Crown of Light
by Terry Golledge

It was a close and humid day in the August of 1896. Holmes and I were returning on foot from an expedition to Bradley's the tobacconist where I had replenished my supply of Arcadia mixture and Holmes had obtained a fresh stock of the abominable black shag whose fumes he inflicted on all and sundry. We were in no hurry, the oppressive atmosphere making the slightest exertion a labour, and as we rounded the corner into Baker Street a cab was seen to be standing before our door.

"I say," I noted, "we appear to have a visitor."

He paused to look at me sardonically. "An excellent deduction, Watson, and worthy of further exposition,"

"Really," I said acidly, "I fail to see what other inferences are to be drawn from the mere fact of a hansom waiting before our chambers. Perhaps you will be good enough to enlighten me."

He moved on slowly and I hastened to catch up with him. "Well, I would suggest that it has been there more than a few minutes. The horse has provided its own evidence of that, and since the beast is munching contentedly on its nosebag and the jarvey isn't in view, it seems that the caller is the cabbie himself, either on his own behalf or as a messenger for a third party."

"Of course, but that is so obvious that it scarcely warrants comment."

"Then, my dear fellow, it must be equally obvious that the cab is there, so why mention it if you aren't prepared to take the matter to the end?"

I knew from experience that when my friend was in a disputatious mood there was nothing to be gained by verbal fencing, so biting my tongue, I preceded him to our door to use my key. On our entering the hall, a man who could only be the cab driver sprang from the wooden chair on which he was sitting and looked from one to the other of us,

"Mr. 'Olmes – Mr. Sherlock 'Olmes?" he asked eagerly.

Holmes stepped forward. "I am he, and this is my colleague. Dr. Watson. Pray tell me in what way I may be of assistance to you."

"I need 'elp, Mr. 'Olmes, desperate 'elp, and I can't think of no one else to turn to! I took the liberty of coming 'ere, 'oping you can advise me."

Holmes gave the man an appraising look, then gestured to the stairs. "Come, I shall hear what you have to say, but I promise nothing at this stage."

He led the way to our sitting room and, divesting himself of his coat, sat down with his back to the window with our visitor facing him. The man was agog to begin his story, but Holmes wasn't to be hurried. "Fill the briar which protrudes from your waistcoat pocket. I think you will find the good Doctor's special blend both soothing and stimulating at the same time."

Taking the hint, I brought out my newly replenished pouch and passed it to our guest. Holmes filled his cherry-wood with his own pungent shag while I, on retrieving my pouch, selected the inscribed silver mounted briar presented to me by my brother officers of the 66th.

"Now, my good fellow," said Holmes when our pipes were drawing, "I beg you to state your problem, and I promise to listen with all attention. The doctor will make notes against the unlikely event of my memory being at fault, then I shall decide if you can be helped."

The man took a deep breath and loosened his neckerchief. "Well, Guv'nor, it's like this. My name is Pritchard, Lewis Pritchard, and I'm the owner of the cab standing out front. I do very nicely at my trade, and live out Deptford way in as neat a little two-up, two-down as you could wish for. A few weeks back, I was asked if I'd be interested in buying the house at a very fair figure and I said I was. As I said, I make a good living from my cab and it's a poor week indeed when I clear less than three pounds after all expenses, although it means being out in all weathers."

"A man of industry," Holmes murmured as Pritchard paused to relight his pipe. "Proceed, I pray you."

"I married about three years ago, and although to our sorrow we as yet have no children, we are both young and pray that time will be kind to us."

Here my companion interrupted him. "I take it you purchased your cab on your discharge from the Royal Artillery?"

Pritchard looked startled. "Why, yes sir, I did. But how do you know my regiment when I said nothing of it?"

Holmes waved a deprecatory hand. "Your bearing indicates you have seen military service, almost certainly overseas, and when you reached for Watson's tobacco pouch, I observed the regimental crest tattooed above your wrist. The tattoo is of a style common to India. May I also venture to suggest that as you chose to drive a cab on your discharge and your horse looks particularly well-cared-for, you were most probably a driver."

The man eyed Holmes with new respect as he nodded. "Right on target, Mr. Holmes, and if I say it myself, no finer lead driver ever took a gun into action. But if I may continue, you will have gathered that I made a very happy marriage, and all was well until some four months back, when I found on several occasions my wife was absent when I returned home at night. At first I paid little heed, until I noticed these absences took on a regular pattern of occurring every Tuesday and Thursday. I sought an explanation, but beyond saying she had been visiting friends, she offered nothing. When I pressed her, she became agitated and accused me of base suspicion and lack of trust. I protested strongly, yet her very words aroused in me those very feelings of which I stood accused."

At this juncture Holmes, who had been listening intently with closed eyes, leaned forward and spoke sharply. "Tell me, sir, why do you represent yourself as something you are not?"

For brief moment the man looked confused, but recovered quickly. "I don't understand. What do you mean?"

"Come now," said Holmes with some asperity. "I beg you, don't take me for a complete dunderhead. You are a man of some education which was probably acquired at a minor public school, although you didn't reach university. Why present yourself as of the labouring classes? You play your part well, but to one who has made a study of philology, your deception is apparent. I warn you, Mr. Pritchard – or whatever your name is – I'm not to be trifled with, and unless some very good explanation is forthcoming, I must bid you good day." He rose to his feet and looked down sternly at the man who had the grace to look abashed.

"I crave your pardon, sir," said he. "You are in the right, although what you see as a deception was in no way intended to fool you. If you will allow me to tell something of myself, you might understand the reason for this masquerade."

Holmes surveyed him keenly, and apparently satisfied resumed his chair. "Very well." He nodded curtly. "Pray proceed."

"I will not affront you by asking for a pledge of secrecy," said our visitor. "I have every confidence you will appreciate my position when I tell you that I am the youngest of three sons from a prominent and well-respected family. My father and one brother hold important posts in the Civil Service. Not in the public eye but working, if I may put it so, behind the scenes. Whatever administration is in power, they are there to guide and advise the government to the best of their ability. My other brother is a lawyer with a leaning towards politics and a lot of ambition. When young, I led a wild and dissolute life, often causing my family acute embarrassment, and this culminated in my father disowning me completely, cutting me off without even the proverbial shilling.

"This shocked me into realising the dangerous path I was treading, and I sought to redeem myself by enlisting as a private soldier in the Royal

Artillery. As you may well imagine, the lot of a gentleman ranker isn't an easy one, and very early on I found it expedient to adapt my manner and speech to that of my comrades. I confess I never quite succeeded in mangling the Queen's English as did some of my fellows, excellent chaps though they were. When I took my discharge the same considerations applied, and thus I came to you as that which I in fact have become. Does that explain my little deception?"

Holmes smiled faintly. "It is understandable in the circumstances, but what of your wife? How much of this does she know?"

Pritchard rubbed the bowl of his pipe against his cheek before answering slowly. "She is aware that I was once a gentleman, but of my family she knows nothing. She is a person of some education herself, her father being a wealthy clothing manufacturer who – although a self-made man – ensured that she and her older brother had the advantages denied him. As with a number of men who rise above their humble origins, Joe Smithers is still something of a rough diamond, but hoped his children would move up the social scale, and when his only daughter announced her intention of marrying a common cabman – to say that he disapproved is to understate the case. As Freda, my wife, was of age, he couldn't forbid the match, but from thence on he has neither spoken nor made any effort to contact her in any way. In all fairness," added the man, "I must make it clear that he settled the very handsome sum of two-hundred pounds a year on her, which is more than my father did for me. Of course, the money is hers to use as she sees fit, and I lay no claim to any part of it. Yet it is that very money that has precipitated the present crisis and brought me to your door." His voice broke and he hung his head to recover his composure.

Holmes's pipe gave forth a chorus of obscene gurgling noises and he laid it aside reluctantly, spilling ash down his waistcoat in the process. "Continue, Mr. Pritchard – if that is indeed your name."

"It's the name I've been known by these ten years past, so I can fairly call it my own. As I said, I was given the option of buying the house in which we live, and yesterday the offer was put on a firm footing and a price quoted which was more than fair. The present owner is advanced in years and is to spend the remainder of his days with a daughter in Sussex, so he requires a quick decision from me. Freda and I have often talked of owning our own home, and I was keen to get back to talk it over with her. As it happened, I picked up a fare who kept me darting hither and thither until quite late, and in consequence it was past ten o'clock before I'd seen to the nag and made my way home. Freda was home, but I knew she had been out as her boots stood in the passage showing signs of damp from the summer shower that had fallen earlier that evening."

"A piece of deduction worthy of yourself, Holmes," I chuckled.

He flung me an impatient look and urged our visitor to continue.

"I was too full of my news to make an issue of it then," Pritchard went on, "but when I announced our good fortune, I was disappointed at her lack of enthusiasm. It wasn't that she raised any objections, but neither did she seem to have any joy from it. It was when I came to speak of financial matters that things came to a head. As I mentioned, she has her own income, paid monthly through her father's solicitors, and I have never inquired how she disposed of it. She isn't prodigal or extravagant and I assumed she invested it safely, so when I suggested that a small portion of her money should be loaned to me to effect the purchase of the house, I was floored by her reaction.

"At first she was evasive, then when I pressed her for an answer, she became extremely agitated, and eventually refused point blank to lend me a penny. In vain I pleaded, pointing out that it would be a loan on strictly business terms, but she was adamant. I was set on having the property and with my own modest savings short of my needs, my only other resource was to obtain a loan for the remainder, but why should they have the interest when she might do so? Her response was to say that I must do as I saw fit, and at that I lost my temper, using harsh words that only served to reduce her to tears, with the result that for the first time in our marriage we retired to bed in an atmosphere of anger and hostility. I spent a restless night and rose well before dawn. I knew Freda was awake, for I heard her sobbing into her pillow, but I was still angry and went to prepare my breakfast without a word to her."

The unhappy man paused and shook his head sadly before proceeding.

"It was while searching in the kitchen drawer for a knife that I came across this pamphlet." He pulled from his inside pocket a creased piece of paper and held it out.

Holmes took it and unfolded it. Looking over his shoulder, I saw a cheaply-printed sheet headed *"The Crown of Light Mission"*, exhorting those in need of spiritual comfort to seek solace and guidance at the above on Tuesdays and Thursdays with Mr. and Mrs. Lester Burton, followed by an address in a less salubrious part of Bermondsey. Holmes perused it with an expression of distaste, then laid on the arm of his chair and sat back with a sigh.

"Apart from what we are meant to read," he said, "it tells us little. It was produced on a small hand-press, not by a firm of commercial printers. The paper could have come from one of a hundred stationers and was cut to size by a pair of not over-sharp scissors, so I suggest it wasn't intended for mass distribution, but run off as required to be given to selected persons. Did you ask your wife if she had knowledge of it?"

37

Pritchard nodded. "I went to her at once. At first she feigned ignorance, but when I pointed out that I hadn't seen it before, and as she and I were the only people in the house, it followed that she must have put it in the drawer. Again she resorted to tears, saying I was determined to make her unhappy, but I still insisted on an answer. At last she said, not very convincingly, that it had probably been pushed through the door and she had put it away without reading it. At that I flung out of the house and went to my work a bewildered and unhappy man. As I prepared my cab for the day's work, I fell to brooding on her conduct and decided that her refusal to be frank with me was in some way linked with her absences from home and that piece of paper.

"I left the mews and, ignoring any prospective fare who tried to hail me, I drove at my best pace to the address in Bermondsey to see if any clue might be gleaned. The place was an old warehouse, and as I entered the gate, I was accosted by a rough-looking character reeking of beer whom I took to be the caretaker. I attempted to question him about the mission, but all I got was foul abuse and told if I didn't push off I'd be out on my ear. I saw no profit in trying to reason with the lout so I left, and it was then that your name came to mind. I thought there was nothing to be lost by entreating your help, or at least advice, and here I am. It may seem a trivial domestic matter to you, Mr. Holmes, but I'm at my wits end and know not where to turn for relief."

Holmes raised his eyes broodingly to our caller. "As you say, it may well be a trivial matter, but my instincts warn me that there are deeper waters and bigger fish than may be apparent to us now. If you will give your consent to let me take whatever steps seem good to me, I shall be most willing to attempt to throw some light on to your problem. I believe your wife to be in grave trouble – so grave that she feels unable to confide in you, and may be driven to desperation if the matter isn't resolved quickly."

Pritchard blanched under his tan. "What can it be, Mr. Holmes?" he cried. "Freda is as pure and honest as the day is long. How could she be in serious trouble?"

"That we must discover, sir," Holmes replied austerely. "I can make no judgement until I'm in possession of all the facts. There is nothing more you can tell me?"

"I have told you all I know. What must I do now?"

Holmes stroked his long nose. "Do nothing and go about your business as usual. Above all, put no further pressure on your wife, for I fear she is near breaking point. Leave me your address and that of the mews where you keep your equipage and I will be in touch. Now, good day to you, Mr. Pritchard, and be of good heart."

The door had barely closed on our client before Holmes had vanished into his own room, reappearing ten minutes later as a completely different person. He wore a decrepit billycock hat and a shabby buttonless coat secured at the waist by a length of frayed string. He carried an old carpet-bag which clanked as he put it down, and a straggly moustache adorned his upper lip. I marvelled at his facility in changing his whole appearance and personality with a few simple accessories and to become the very essence of the character he purported to be.

"Come, Watson, we must move apace," he cried. "Be so good as to secure a four-wheeler for our journey. No self-respecting cabbie will stop for such as I."

Resigning myself to another missed lunch, I preceded him down the stairs and was lucky enough to find a growler discharging its passengers on the other side of the road. The driver looked askance at my disreputable companion but offered no objections, and on a muttered word from Holmes I directed the man to Bermondsey. Holmes slouched pensively in a corner, only rousing himself as we rattled over London Bridge, when he turned a quizzical eye on me.

"Well, what is your reading of the case?" I, too, had been pondering, but was forced to admit that I had no substantial theory to offer. Nevertheless, I made the effort.

"Obviously there is some threat hanging over Mrs. Pritchard, but on the present information I cannot conjecture what it can be. Apart from marrying in defiance of her father's wishes, she seems to have led a blameless existence, and even her father wasn't so uncaring as to cut her off completely. In fact, her allowance is very generous – as much as my wound pension from a grateful government. By Pritchard's account, they are a loving couple and hitherto have had no secrets between them,"

"Excellent, my dear fellow. So we need more data to build upon, and perhaps it may be found in this squalid neighbourhood. Ah, we approach our destination, and that unprepossessing iron hut is the address we seek. Continue for two-hundred yards that I may alight unremarked, and wait where you can see without being seen."

I rapped on the panel with my stick, and as the cab slowed, Holmes slipped nimbly on to the cobbles, his carpet-bag clinking in his hand. I told the driver to take the next turning and stop and, handing him a half-sovereign as earnest of good faith, bade him wait upon my return. I walked back to the corner in time to see Holmes shuffle up to the iron gate of the mission and enter. Crossing the road, I strolled in the same direction and, on coming level with the gate, I paused to fill and light my pipe, keeping a covert eye on the entrance. Less than a minute passed ere I heard the sound of voices raised in altercation. Then Holmes came into view, pursued by a large uncouth-looking figure uttering threats of violence bestrewn with some of the foulest oaths it has been my misfortune to hear. He slammed the gate behind Holmes, who retaliated with a shake of his fist, and to my dismay added his own comments in language that matched that of the other man. Never in the whole course of our association had my friend inclined to coarseness of expression, and to hear it now was a shock to my sensibilities. I excused him now on the grounds that it was in keeping with the character he was presenting and that he must deplore it as much as I. So reflecting, I turned back to where I had left the cab, throwing a quick glance over my shoulder to ascertain that my companion was following. On entering the cab, Holmes delved into the depths of his carpet-bag to produce a loosely-wrapped parcel from which he took a pair of boots and a light jacket.

"I fear the trousers must do," he said, peeling off his moustache. "The absence of a hat can be accounted for by a gust of wind from the river. Have the cabbie drive to the nearest police station and we shall see if they have any useful facts about this so-called mission." As we went, he told me of his encounter and its outcome. "I posed as an odd-job man seeking work, and found our repellent friend drinking beer in a back room. I recognized him at once as a notorious bully-boy from the Elephant and Castle, and I know for a fact that he has several counts against him for violence and petty thieving. It owes more to the constitution of his victims than his own restraint that he hasn't faced a more serious charge than assault and battery. However, I asked fairly enough if there was any work to be had and I was told to push off, but I began to walk round and point out that the place could do with a few touches here and there. At that he became aggressive and offered to throw me out if I didn't 'sling my 'ook', and I became equally offensive with the result that you observed."

"Good Heavens!" I gasped. "You could have come to serious harm at the hands of that brute!"

"Really, Watson, have you so little faith in me that you fear I couldn't hold my own with such a crude rascal as he? You have remarked on my mastery of the noble art on more than one occasion. But here we are at the bastion of law and order. Be good enough to keep me company and be ready to stand surety for my respectability, dressed as I am."

We entered the police station where a sergeant was writing laboriously in a ledger. He laid his pen aside with the air of one glad of the excuse to be relieved of his task and greeted us civilly.

"Good afternoon, gentlemen," then a surprised look came to his face. "Why, it's Mr. Sherlock Holmes and the Doctor! What brings you to this part of the world?"

I remembered him as the constable who had discovered the body of Enoch Drebber on that memorable first occasion when I had been privileged to see Holmes display his remarkable powers, and although unable to put a name to him, I recalled my friend anathematizing him as a blundering fool who would never rise in his chosen profession. I was human enough to be mildly gratified that the sergeant's stripes proved my colleague to be even so slightly fallible. He could have read my thoughts, for he gave me a rueful grin before addressing himself to the sergeant.

"Rance, is it not? John Rance?"

"That's so, sir. Sergeant Rance these two years past, thanks to you."

Holmes looked mystified. "I recall nothing I have done to advance your career, pleased as I am to note it."

"Not directly, Mr. Holmes, but I knew you thought I should have recognized that drunk in Lauriston Gardens that night as the murderer, so I got to thinking about smartening up my ideas and this is the result, while Harry Murcher still pounds a beat down Brixton way, so it's you what takes the credit."

"Then I congratulate you, Sergeant, and perhaps I may draw a little on that credit by asking you for some local information."

"Anything I can tell you I will, sir, and perhaps there may be a good word in it for me. I'll not presume to put myself alongside of Inspectors Lestrade and Gregson, but a favourable mention in my record can do no harm."

At the mention of the two Scotland Yard inspectors, Holmes smiled sardonically and contented himself with a non-committal grunt. "What do you know of The Crown of Light Mission along the road from here?"

Rance sucked on his moustache and pondered the question before answering.

"Well," said eventually, "I know nothing that gives us any concern – except for that caretaker they've hired."

"You mean Bert Carver?" Holmes put in quickly.

"That's him, and I give a lot to feel his collar, but since he come out of Pentonville last spring he's had that job and never a sign of old ways. The job was found for him by a prison visitor and he reports to us once a week. Not very willingly, I may say, but so long as he don't give no bother, there isn't much I can do about him."

"What of the minister, or whatever he calls himself?"

"All I know is what I hear from the beat man. This bloke turns up with a woman said to be his wife about six o'clock every Tuesday and Thursday and leaves just after nine. Where they live I've no idea, and I've had no call to ask. That's all I can offer, Mr. Holmes, and I wish it could be more."

41

"Ah, well," sighed Holmes. "Not as much as I had hoped, but I shall remember your willingness to help, Sergeant." A couple of florins slid across the desk to vanish quickly, and with Rance's expression of goodwill echoing in our ears we made our exit and returned to Baker Street.

Over our belated lunch, my companion was taciturn, paying little heed to the handsome pork-and-veal pie provided by Mrs. Hudson. Eventually he pushed his plate to one side with the meal barely touched and went to the window, where he stood for some time gazing broodingly down at the street. I observed his back for some minutes before venturing to break in on his thoughts. "I say, if you aren't going to finish that pie, I see no point in letting it go to waste."

He turned to stare at me blankly for some seconds. Then, like a dog ridding itself of fleas, seemed to shake himself into the present.

"By all means, my dear fellow, make of it what you will, but be hasty, for we must go out again."

My surprise was evident and he explained impatiently.

"Don't you see, Watson?" he said irritably. "This is Wednesday, and tomorrow there is another meeting of this so-called mission. I feel it to be imperative that we prevent Mrs. Pritchard attending, and indeed to put a stop to its activities once and for all. I intend to see the lady and induce her to lay her trouble before me, that it may be lifted completely."

"Do you think she will confide in you?" I said through a mouthful of pie. "If she will not trust her husband, why should she trust you?"

"It is possible. I'm a stranger to her and she has no reason to fear my censure or disapproval. I think that fact may persuade her to unburden herself if I can convince her that I can hold out hope of relief."

"Can you promise her that?"

"There is blackmail involved, and you know my views on that. I will strain every nerve and sinew to bring to book those foul predators on human frailty. Now do hurry. I wish to talk to the lady before her husband returns home."

Still chewing, I pursued him down to the street, and soon we found ourselves crossing to the south side of the river for the second time that day. Our journey took us through a succession of mean streets to Rotherhithe, and thence to the outskirts of Deptford where our driver halted to ask directions of a patrolling constable.

As we approached our goal, Holmes bade the cabbie stop and, after alighting, we watched the vehicle out of sight before we proceeded on foot. Holmes looked approvingly at our surroundings, and indeed the district was less sordid than those we had just traversed. It hadn't yet lost the battle against the ever-encroaching octopus of London, and there was still a rural feeling to this little corner. The house we approached had gleaming brass-work on the newly painted door and gay curtains hung at the windows, evidence of the loving care lavished on this humble dwelling, The door was opened by a woman in her late twenties, as neat and tidy in her person as the exterior of the house, yet her eyes showed strain and worry foreign to the pretty features.

Holmes raised his hat. "Mrs. Pritchard?" he asked on her look of inquiry.

"Yes, that is my name. What can I do for you?"

"I am Sherlock Holmes, of whom you may have heard, and this is my friend and colleague, Dr. Watson." He indicated me, and I in turn raised my hat.

Her face took on a guarded look, but Holmes continued ere she could speak.

"I beg of you to forgive our intrusion, and rest assured we wish to cause you no distress. If you permit us to enter, I shall explain our business."

After a momentary hesitation she stood aside. Then, closing the door behind us, led the way into a small but comfortable parlour.

"Be seated, gentlemen," she said. "I know of your reputation, Mr. Holmes, but I'm at a loss to understand your interest in me."

"I will be quite open with you, Madam," began Holmes when we were seated. "I can but hope you will be as frank with me, for only the truth will serve to raise the shadow of anxiety from which you suffer."

"I fail to see – " she began, but Holmes held up an admonitory hand.

"Hear me out, I pray you, if not for your own sake then for the sake of your husband. My reasoning leads me to believe that you are being blackmailed, and the source of the blackmail is The Crown of Light Mission. If you will give me your complete confidence, I pledge myself to the downfall of the villains who batten on the fears of such unfortunates as yourself. I have no connection with the official police, and whatever you tell me will be safe with the good Doctor and me."

She stared at him in amazement overlaid with fear and anguish, but my companion wasn't to be diverted.

"You are being bled white by these people, and unless you confide in me, there can be no end to it until you are penniless and your marriage destroyed. Is that what you desire?"

Mrs. Pritchard had turned a deathly pale, her eyes fixed on the stern features of my friend. At length she made a gesture of resignation and spoke in a tone of great bitterness.

"How this came to your notice I don't know, but you are correct in your assumption of blackmail. Not through any fault or misconduct on my part, but because of one who is very dear to me. I refer to my brother."

She paused to take a deep breath, and then the words spilled out from her as water from a broken pitcher. "It began some four months ago when I received call from a man who purported to be collecting on behalf of The Crown of Light Mission. I have little time for these mendicants who seem to divert the larger part of the offerings into their own pockets. I refused instantly, but the creature had his foot in the door and said if I wouldn't contribute on my own behalf, it would be to my brother's advantage to do so. Of course, this held my attention and I demanded an explanation of his words." She paused and looked at us defiantly. "Perhaps I should tell you something of my family to make the subsequent events clear,"

"I know you to be the daughter Joseph Smithers, a clothing manufacturer," Holmes interposed. "I also know that you have an older brother, and that you married in defiance of your father's wishes, but nevertheless he settled a generous allowance on you and that allowance is being filched by this so-called Crown of Light. Pray continue with your account, Madam."

"Very well, Mr. Holmes." She moistened her lips. "This person told me that Marcus, my brother who virtually runs the business now, has been embezzling large sums of money from the firm and spending it in dubious pursuits, and unless I wished my father to hear of it. I would be wise to contribute to their poor mission."

Holmes frowned. "Surely in that case there would be more profit in going to your brother?"

"That was my first thought, but the man forestalled me by saying my brother was being taken care of and my small contribution was but a make-weight. I was bemused and near collapse, but I told him I had no money in the house. He smiled – oh, what a terrible smile! He told me to attend the next meeting of the mission and bring fifty pounds in gold. I was almost out of my mind and to get rid of him I acceded to his demands. Little did I know what it was to lead to, for since that day I have been paying three pounds at each and every meeting of that evil mission, twice a week."

"Good Lord!" I exploded. "That's more than your whole allowance!"

"You are well informed, Doctor," she said bitterly. "I'm rapidly reaching the end of my resources, and what will then ensue I fear to contemplate."

"What does your brother say of this?" asked Holmes. "Have you told him?"

The lady shook her head vigorously, "I was forbidden to tell him that I was also being made pay on the threat of the whole matter being exposed. What induced him to commit such folly is entirely beyond my comprehension."

44

Holmes rose abruptly, taking me by surprise, but I could sense from his attitude that he was steps ahead of my thoughts.

"Thank you, Mrs. Pritchard. I think it safe to say that you have made your last payment to these leeches, and I may even offer some hope that you will see the return of at least part of your money. Come, Watson, time presses."

He paused in the doorway to add almost as an afterthought: "Where might your brother be found at this hour?"

She hesitated. Then, convinced of my colleague's integrity, she spoke. "He has his own establishment at Blackheath overlooking Greenwich Park. He is unmarried, but prefers to live away from home. My mother is a strong-willed woman who terrorises even my father so that he spends as much time as he can at the Walworth factory for the sake of peace and quiet." She gave her brother's address, which I scribbled into my notebook.

"Then be of good heart, Madam," said Holmes. "Say nothing of this to your husband at this juncture, although I feel you would have been wise to confide in him from the first moment."

We had the good fortune to find a cab-driver willing to take us up the steep incline of Blackheath Hill to the Heath, but it was a painfully slow journey. Dusk was falling as we were deposited at the gate of a neat little villa commanding a fine view over the park to the twinkling lights beginning to appear on the river beyond. Holmes pull on the bell was answered by an elderly woman of upright carriage. She took Holmes's card and conducted us into an anteroom. We weren't left to kick our heels for long before the door opened to admit a pleasant-looking fellow whose features proclaimed his kinship with Freda Pritchard.

"Mr. Sherlock Holmes?" he asked, twisting the card in his fingers.

"I am he," my friend replied.

"Then this other gentleman can only be your biographer, Dr. Watson, whose accounts of your exploits I devour avidly. I'm honoured to meet you in the flesh, but I am at a loss to divine the reason for your presence. But be seated, I beg you. I usually indulge in a small drink at this hour and I hope you will join me."

Once we were seated with a generous measure of Scotch whisky in our hands, Holmes came straight to the point.

"First of all, Mr. Smithers, I'm going to ask you a question that you will find insulting and impertinent. Please bear with me and take no offence, for once I hear the answer I expect to hear from your lips, I will reveal the purpose behind it."

45

Smithers looks mystified but inclined his head in acknowledgement. "Fire away, Mr. Sherlock Holmes. I know you do nothing without good reason, and you have fairly set my curiosity afire."

"Very well, I will be blunt. Are you being blackmailed?"

Our host's mouth fell open and he stared at Holmes in amazement. "Blackmailed?" he stuttered. "Why should I be blackmailed? My life is an open book, and though I have all the minor vices of most men of my age and position, there is certainly nothing that I'd pay to have hushed up."

"Thank you, sir," said Holmes. "That is as I thought, and now I can tell you the reasons behind my offensive question. Before I do so, I must ask for your assurance that I shall be left to deal with the matter in my own way, and that you will not try to take matters into your own hands."

His grave tone impressed itself on the other who nodded a grudging consent, and Holmes went on to lay all the facts before him. Smithers listened with growing horror that quickly changed to rage and indignation as Holmes described the pitiful state to which Freda Pritchard had been reduced. At the end of the recital he sat pale and tight-lipped, his fists clenching and unclenching as the full enormity of the situation sank in.

"Good God, Mr. Holmes, why did she not come to me at once? I could have set her mind at rest and showed her the falsity of the charge."

"That was the cunning part, sir. She was told that you too were paying for silence, and if she let it be known that she also was paying, all would be revealed. It was a plot to keep you apart, and that is why I came here tonight, certain that you were an innocent party. Who would know enough of your family circumstances to be so convincing?"

Smithers left his chair and paced rapidly back and forth, his brow corrugated in concentration before stopping to face Holmes.

"Tell me, sir, does the name Lester Burton strike a chord?"

Holmes looked up sharply, his eyebrows raised. "It does, but where did you hear it?"

Our host resumed his seat and laid his head back as if to collect his thoughts. Then he began to speak in a low voice.

"What I have to say is in the strictest confidence, which I'm sure you will appreciate. When my sister declared her intention of marrying Lewis Pritchard, it wasn't the most welcome news to my father, but for all his faults he loves Freda and desires her happiness. The main opposition was from my mother, and you may think me lacking in proper respect when I say she not the most lovable of women, but it is a fact. Even my father fears her. She was a machinist in his first factory and was astute enough to see that he would rise in the world with the right encouragement, so she married him." He grinned boyishly. "I was born five months after the wedding, but she wouldn't thank you for reminding her of the fact. She

46

has aspirations to be the great lady and saw Freda and me as stepping-stones into society, and you can imagine her chagrin when my sister remained obstinate and I showed no interest in the girls paraded before me."

He sat up and fixed us with a firm look. "Don't misunderstand me, gentlemen. I'm not averse to the company of the fair sex, but I prefer them to be of my own choosing."

"We hadn't thought otherwise," said Holmes. "Proceed, I pray you."

"Well, when Freda wouldn't submit, my father forbade her the house – on my mother's orders, of course – but to salve his conscience, he secretly made her an allowance. Mind you, I thought she could have done better, but for all I know he may be a most worthy fellow,"

"Doubt it not, sir," my friend put in. "Until this business cast its shadow, they were the happiest couple alive. But forgive me, I interrupt."

Smithers continued. "A few months ago I was at Croydon races, where I made a bit of a killing. I threw a celebration party at a nearby hotel, and among those present was Lester Burton, He seemed a stout-enough fellow and we travelled back together somewhat the worse for wear, as happens on these occasions. I must have found him a good listener, for I later recalled bemoaning the rift with my little sister. By morning it had gone from my mind until shortly before lunch, when who should turn up at the office but this Burton on the pretext of asking after my health. We went out for a steak pudding and a glass of porter, and out of the blue he asked if I would like to be reconciled with Freda and offered to act as intermediary.

"Against my better judgement I became interested, but had to point out that I knew nothing of her whereabouts except that it was in these parts. He waved my objections aside and I agreed to let him see if he could trace her. A week later he approached me again with the story that he had spoken with Freda and the message she sent was that she wanted to neither hear nor see anything of me nor of the rest of the family, and would I please leave her alone. Does that fit in with your theory, Mr. Holmes?"

"As I surmised, the idea was to prevent any communication between you. But now that the truth is out, we can bait the trap to catch our rat. Time is of the essence. Your sister cannot tolerate the strain much longer, and there are others in like situation."

"What can I do, Mr. Holmes? I place myself at your disposal and will follow your instructions to the letter." Holmes studied the man before giving a nod of agreement. "Your aid would be invaluable, but do nothing on your own initiative or the consequences may be dire. Be at my chambers at eight o'clock tomorrow morning. Do you know where this man Burton has his quarters?"

"Not the actual address, but although he was very close about himself, he did make a rather bad joke about having a fine view of Smithfield, Barts, and Newgate from his window."

"That narrows the field. Now we must go, and we shall see you in the morning."

"I'll send the boy for a cab to take you to Blackheath or Maze Hill – whichever station is your choice." Smithers rang the bell and gave the necessary orders, and ten minutes later we were on our way. At London Bridge, Holmes made straight for the all-night telegraph office, then mystified me by taking a cab to the General Post Office in St. Martin's-le-Grand, where he disappeared for twenty minutes. He returned humming tunelessly to himself and spoke not a word for the rest of the journey. At Baker Street he jumped from the cab, leaving me to pay, and by the time I reached our sitting room he had gone into his own room, closing the door firmly behind him, and that was the last I saw of him that night.

Over an early breakfast he was more forthcoming. "Mr. Marcus Smithers will be on our doorstep shortly, as will our client, whom I telegraphed last night. I rely on your down-to-earth common sense, Watson, to see that the two get along together, for I hope that some part of the family feud may be settled out of this sordid affair."

"That sounds like one of them now," I said as a cab stopped outside.

The doorbell pealed faintly and my friend looked at me with a roguish smile.

"Would you venture to say which?"

I shrugged. "As I cannot see through walls it could be either, but no doubt you know differently."

"It is certainly Smithers. If it was Pritchard arriving in his hansom, he would take time to settle his horse before leaving it. The gentleman whose tread is now on the stairs paused only long enough to pay the driver, who immediately drove away. Come in!" he called as a knock came on our door.

Smithers entered. "Good morning, gentlemen," he said. "What's afoot?"

"Pull up a chair, my dear sir," said Holmes, "Allow me to pour you some coffee while we await another guest. In fact, I believe he is even now below.

A few minute elapsed before Pritchard appeared, pausing on the threshold at the sight of our other visitor, but Holmes waved him to a chair and supplied him with coffee. He raised an eyebrow in my direction before taking a seat for himself and stuffing tobacco into his pipe.

I cleared my throat. "I think, gentlemen, this meeting is long overdue. Mr. Marcus Smithers, this is your brother-in-law, Mr. Lewis Pritchard." I sat back to watch the conflicting emotions chase across the faces of the pair.

Smithers recovered first, getting to his feet to thrust out his hand. "My dear Pritchard!" he cried. "As Dr. Watson says, this is a long overdue meeting, and I'm delighted to make your acquaintance at last!"

For the merest fraction of a second our client hesitated, then he rose to clasp the proffered hand. "You are right, sir. This is a long-delayed meeting, but through no wish of mine. Your sister would have welcomed a sign from you, but alas, it never came." He turned to me. "However, I fail to see how this concerns the matter in the forefront of my mind."

"I think I do," said Smithers, turning to look at Holmes and myself.

"It does indeed," I said in my role of mediator. "You both have Mrs. Pritchard's welfare at heart, and neither of you has the slightest cause to feel antipathy towards the other."

Holmes intervened brusquely. "Please, gentlemen, let us proceed to the matter in hand, and explanations can come later. You will make your way to Deptford, where Mrs. Pritchard may have comfort from the knowledge that her conflict of loyalties is over. You, Mr. Smithers, know how all this came about and can lay the whole story before Mr. Pritchard and your sister. I enjoin all three of you to remain at Deptford until I telegraph, you, and above all you must convince the lady that she has nothing to fear. Now away with you. Watson and I have our own furrow to plough."

As soon as our visitors had left, Holmes sprang to his feet and, ignoring the coffee cup he overset in his sudden access of energy, threw off his dressing-gown.

"Come. Mr. Lester Burton is due a visit from us. I think we can be certain of finding him at home at this hour."

"I may be obtuse, Holmes, but do we know where to find him? The casual description he gave Smithers of the view from his window is vague enough and there must be a goodly number of locations with such a view."

Holmes chuckled. "What do you imagine I was doing at Post Office headquarters as we came home last night?"

A light dawned on me and I could have kicked myself for not deducing the reason for my prolonged wait, but his tone piqued me.

"I didn't think you to be bribing Crown servants to betray their trust and duty," I snapped.

"Neither was I," he snapped back. "It so happens that the authorities have cause to be grateful to me for a service I rendered them some months back, and they aren't averse to aiding in the downfall of any miscreants if it's in their power to do so."

He chattered inconsequentially as we trotted along Oxford Street in a growler, but said nothing of the matter in hand until I asked who would be paying his fee in this messy case.

He smiled thinly. "I'm hopeful that Lester Burton will be persuaded to make a significant contribution once I have him in my grasp. I see by the set of your coat that you aren't armed, but no doubt our sticks will serve if it comes to it. Ah, I think we may alight here."

The sight of Barts Hospital revived memories of my first meeting with the man with whom my life was to be so involved, and divining my thoughts he clapped me affectionately on the shoulder. "Much has happened since that January day long ago, old friend. I shall never cease to be grateful to young Stamford for bringing us together. But come, the weather is about to break and we have no waterproofs with us."

The sky had assumed a leaden hue presaging the imminence of heavy rain. Holmes hurried us down Old Bailey and into a doorway, the entrance to a block of service flats. He approached the porter ensconced in his cubbyhole and, after a few quiet words, a coin changed hands before the man resumed his perusal of the racing pages in his newspaper. We then made our way up the stairs to stop before a door on the second floor. Holmes pulled at the bell, then leant on his stick until the door partially opened and a plump face surrounded by side-whiskers peered out at us.

"Mr. Lester Burton?" said my friend ingratiatingly.

A wary look came over the suety face and the man licked his lips nervously. "Who are you? What do you want?"

"My name is Sherlock Holmes, and I wish to have a few words regarding The Crown of Light Mission. Ah, no you don't!" Holmes thrust his stick into the gap in time to prevent the door slamming on us, then applying his shoulder to it burst into the apartment, forcing its occupant back several paces. I followed Holmes inside and shut the door behind me, leaning my back against it to preclude any escape.

"This is an outrage!" spluttered Burton, for I was sure it was he. "Leave at once or I shall call the police!" He retreated as Holmes advanced on him menacingly.

"Yes, by all means call the police, and a pretty story there will be to tell them. They take a very poor view of blackmail."

"I have no idea of what you are talking about," the man blustered, but his eyes were filled with fear as he edged back, followed inexorably by Holmes.

"Don't trifle with me," said Holmes, "At this very moment, a lady is on her way to lay information against you, but her husband and her brother, suitably equipped with horsewhips, will precede the minions of the law."

Sweat beaded the plump features and Burton began to speak, but his words were drowned by a violent clap of thunder following the lashing of rain on the window. He began again and the pause had given him back some confidence.

"I refuse to bandy words with you, sir. I have heard of you as an interfering busy-body, and I can only conjecture that what little notoriety you have achieved has gone to your head. Withdraw at once, or I shall call the porter to eject you."

Holmes glared at him with loathing and contempt. "How dare you attempt to outface me, you despicable cur!" he almost snarled. "I'm here to break you and ensure your evil trade is brought to an end. I'm not bound by any rules that may prevent the police treating you as you deserve."

"And how do you propose to do that?" Burton sneered.

"That is your choice: Either surrender all the material that gives you power over your unhappy victims and sufficient funds to make at least some restitution, or be prepared to have me beat it out of you."

"You wouldn't dare. Even were your wild accusations true, what proof can you have?"

"All that I require." Holmes loomed menacingly over the cowering figure. "Come, accept that the game is lost and you may yet take flight before the police arrive."

The blackmailer put on a show of bravado. "Threaten all you will. You will find nothing here that you want. Get out!"

Taking a pace forward, Holmes grasped Burton by the shirt-front and shook him until his teeth rattled. Rarely had I seen my friend in such a cold rage and I feared that he would lose control entirely, but at last he flung the wretch into a chair where he huddled, his breath coming in shallow gasps. Holmes took a grip on himself and cast an eye around the room.

"Watson, do you go through that coat that hangs behind the door and see what you may find."

My search produced a bunch of keys, a small diary, and a pocket book containing a number of bank-notes. I passed it all to Holmes who made a cursory assessment of the money then threw the keys back to me.

"See if you can match one of these to the safe that stands in the corner. I suspect its contents will prove illuminating."

Burton made to protest, but a threatening gesture from Holmes made him subside fearfully in the chair.

The safe was an early model by Chubb, and the second key I tried allowed me to swing the door open. I was faced by two large ledgers, a bundle of papers, and a leather bag which on being opened revealed a considerable sum in sovereigns and half-sovereigns. Holmes pounced on the ledgers and swiftly turned the pages for several minutes before slamming them shut with a grunt of satisfaction.

"This is what we need," he said grimly. "The bank-notes and gold will provide some recompense for such victims as can be traced and furnish my fee into the bargain. As for the papers – well – "

"You can't do that!" Burton screeched. "That's theft!"

"Then tell the police," Holmes replied contemptuously, turning away in disgust.

With a speed born of desperation Burton sprang from the chair and snatched at the pocket-book which Holmes had laid on the table. I leapt to stop him and he aimed a blow that caught me on the shoulder that sent me cannoning into Holmes. By the time we had recovered, our blackmailer had grabbed his coat and was halfway through the door. With a frantic lunge I tried to hold on to his arm, but he slipped through my grasp and ran for the stairs, leaving me staring at the pocket-book which was all that I retained of him.

"Let him go," said my colleague. "We've drawn his teeth, and you did well to hang on to the money. If Mrs. Pritchard can be induced to lay information against him, he will not get far."

I admit yielding to the temptation to keep to myself the fact that my rescue of the pocket-book was less deliberate than he assumed, but no harm was done by that. I went to stand beside my friend at the window to look down at the street. The rain had stopped and people were hurrying to get their business done before the next downpour. Suddenly, Holmes gripped my arm and sucked in his breath.

A running figure dashed into view at the very moment that a brewer's dray lost a wheel immediately below us. The loaded cart tipped over, shedding its load, and the running man disappeared from sight beneath the heavy casks. The cries of horror from the horrified onlookers reached us through the closed window, and as the crowd congregated Holmes turned away.

"I think we would do well to leave before we are implicated," he said quietly, and taking the ledgers and papers he pushed me towards the door. Pausing only to collect my stick, I followed him down the stairs and through the entrance hall, where the porter had deserted his post to see what was happening in the street. Crossing into Newgate Street we found a cab, and stopping only at the Strand telegraph office to send a wire to the Pritchards, proceeded back to our rooms.

I stopped suddenly as we entered the sitting room. "Holmes!" I gasped.

"The bag of gold!"

"Really, Doctor, do you think me so careless?" He threw the leather purse on to the table. "We have an hour before lunch, which I shall occupy by going through these books while you count the money."

We applied ourselves thus, and the total sum staggered me. The pocketbook yielded £2,400 pounds in notes of various denominations, while there was a further £120 and ten shillings in gold coins. When I reported the amount to Holmes, he nodded his satisfaction,

"It seems Mr. Burton had no faith in banks, which is fortunate. At least a hundred-and-fifty of it belongs to Mrs. Pritchard, but it will be the deuce of a job to apportion the remainder. It seems that no sum was too insignificant for that creature to reach for, and his accounts show amounts a small as five shillings from more than one of his victims. I hope that some can be induced to come forward at tonight's meeting if they can be persuaded they have nothing to fear. I shall enlist Mrs. Pritchard' aid in that, as they may trust her as one of themselves."

"But what hold could he have over all these people?"

"Who knows? If a duchess wished to conceal an indiscretion, she would be no more anxious than the wife of a market porter to pay for silence. It is a matter of degree. Where one would find five-hundred pounds, the other would struggle to raise five shillings. I'm not interested in the details. Blackmail is a dirty business whatever the sum involved, and I rank it as more evil than a murder committed in a moment of passion."

"What of the papers?" I ventured.

"I shall destroy them unread. I've no desire to have people's weaknesses laid before me, and whomever cannot be traced through the ledgers will have no more demands made on them. A prominent advertisement in the newspapers announcing that The Crown of Light Mission has sufficient funds for its needs should be enough to relieve the minds of most contributors."

We didn't linger over lunch and, as we hailed a cab, Holmes took a paper from a passing newsboy.

"I say, look at this," he chuckled, passing the paper to me."

The headlines shouted at me. *"Man Killed by Falling Beer-Barrels"*. I read on:

> *A man identified as Mr. Lester Burton was killed in an accident in Old Bailey when the wheel of a brewer's dray collapsed and dislodged its load as a man ran by. He was killed instantly. Alfred Huggins, the porter at his residence, said Mr. Burton was a quiet gentleman who gave no trouble.*

53

It is believed that the deceased had two callers shortly before he met his death, but no trace of them can be found.

"No more than he deserved," Holmes said, then leant back with closed eyes until our cab dropped us at the Pritchards' house. Pritchard himself admitted us, and before he conducted us in, Holmes handed him the newspaper.

"It's all over, then?" asked our client.

"Apart from some loose ends, but your wife has nothing to fear and never did have, as I expect you now know. However, with your permission I will ask a small service of her."

"Ask what you will, Mr. Holmes. Anything to repay our debt to you. But come, she is waiting on you."

With the advent of Holmes and myself, the small parlour seemed very crowded. As well as the Pritchards and Smithers, a thick-set elderly man stood squarely in the middle of the room, his ruddy face glistening with perspiration.

"So you're the famous Sherlock Holmes," he said before anyone else could speak. His eyes latched on to my friend's lean figure, "I'm Joe Smithers, and a confounded old fool I've been."

Holmes inclined his head. "Most of us are at times, even my friend Dr. Watson," he said urbanely, obviously not including himself in that and ignoring my splutter of indignation."

We disposed ourselves on the chairs brought in by Pritchard and the assembly looked expectantly at my colleague.

"You had something to ask my wife," Pritchard said tentatively.

"I have indeed. Now the threat to your happiness is lifted, Mrs. Pritchard, do you have the courage to attend at the Mission tonight and help me do likewise for those others who were in the same situation? I have a number of names, and if you will identify those whom you know, I think they will trust you rather than myself."

"There is no more danger?" the lady asked fearfully.

"None. Burton is dead and all his records are safe from revelation."

"Then I will do it gladly. A number of poor wretches will have as much cause for gratitude as I. You understand that none of us knew any of the other's secrets and we all went in fear of exposure, and also we had been threatened with physical violence if we talked between ourselves or failed to meet that man's demands."

A steely glint came into Holmes's eye. "Ah, our friend Carver. I promised a police sergeant a good turn, and I found an interesting piece of information among Burton's papers. He also had a hold on Carver over the matter of a night watchman who was killed in a robbery at a bonded warehouse. He deserves to be thrown to the lions, and Sergeant Rance will take great pleasure in feeling Carver's collar, as he so elegantly puts it."

He thought for a moment. "One loose end remains, and that is the woman calling herself Mrs. Burton. What do you know of her?"

"She hasn't appeared these three weeks past," replied Mrs. Pritchard. "I doubt she was his wife, for she seemed as cowed as the rest of us."

"Then you have anything against her should she appear?"

"Nothing."

"Then let us give her the benefit of the doubt." Holmes cast his eye benignly on the gathering. "Can it be that I have also effected a family reconciliation?"

It was the elder Smithers who replied. "You have, Mr. Holmes. That is what I meant when I said I had been an old fool. Freda has chosen well, and all that I can do now is to make up for the lost years as best I can. One thing has come out of this, and from henceforth I shall be master in my own house. Too long have I been weak and skulked in my works for the sake of peace and quiet, but no longer. Freda and her husband will always be welcome in my home, and I hope I can persuade Marcus to return until such time as he finds a wife of his own choosing."

Holmes rose to his feet. "Then we shall meet at Bermondsey at six o'clock tonight."

There was but a limited response to Mrs. Pritchard's attempt to return as much of the money as possible, the majority of the victims being happy to slink away, relieved to know that they were no longer menaced. Even Holmes was unable to trace all of Burton's victims, and eventually a well-known charity received a handsome anonymous donation.

What fee Holmes awarded himself I don't know, but some weeks later I was astonished to have in the post my not insignificant bookmaker's account marked "*Paid, with thanks*". I knew better than to raise the matter with my friend, for he can be very touchy at times.

It was several years later that I saw an item in *The Daily Telegraph* that raised my eyebrows. It announced the purchase of Lewis Pritchard's cab firm by Tilling's, the gigantic cab company. No mention was made of the price that was paid, but the paper's business correspondent seemed to think that Pritchard had done very well out of the deal.

When I showed the paragraph to Holmes, he responded by pointing to the obituary column where I read of the death of Sir Charles Richards, a high-ranking official at the Foreign Office. My expression remained blank until Holmes gave me a hint.

"Richards? Pritchard? Come, Watson, I knew who Pritchard was right from the beginning. I thought even you could put two and two together and come up with the right answer."

The Case of the Unknown Skull
by Naching T. Kassa

My friend, Mr. Sherlock Holmes, has been part of many a strange case in his illustrious career. And though the reader may be familiar with those accounts concerning the Devil's Foot, the Dancing Men, and the Speckled Band, I fear there are unpublished cases which may rival even these. It is only recently that I was permitted to publish the account of the following recollection, one which occurred on 8th February, 1897.

The bitter cold of January had bled into February of that year, frosting the windows of Baker Street, and causing a great deal of discomfort to my old wound. I wish I could say that I had stayed by the fire to assuage the pain, but the activities involving my patients and those of my companion kept me far from home. It was an unusual evening that found us together in the sitting room when Mrs. Hudson entered, bearing a card upon a salver. She carried it to Holmes, who, after studying it, bid her admit our visitor.

"Have you heard of the Honorable Josiah Merridew, third son of the Earl of Albermere?"

"I cannot say I have."

"Then you shall meet him soon enough. That is his step upon the stair."

Seconds later, a tall man with a round and florid face entered our rooms. His small eyes peered out from behind large spectacles, and his silk hat lay tipped up on his head.

"Mr. Sherlock Holmes?" the man asked.

"I am he," my friend said rising from his chair. "Pray be seated, Mr. Merridew, and tell us why you are visiting me instead of attending tonight's performance of *Tristan and Isolde* at the Royal Opera House as you had planned."

The man, who had seemed much agitated upon his arrival, froze and stared at Holmes with widening eyes. "However do you know that?"

"A simple deduction. You are dressed for the opera, when no one wears such evening-wear for a simple dinner, and the tickets are still in the pocket of your waistcoat."

Merridew glanced down and then back at my companion with a rather sheepish grin. "For a moment, I thought you might have followed me from my home."

"I haven't been to Park Lane since last week," Holmes replied. "And I assure you, you weren't the subject of my investigation then."

The young man's eyes grew wider.

"You may wish to inform your maid that the bottom of the shoe requires as much attention as the top," Holmes continued. "There are several dried bits of mud common to Park Lane on the sole."

"It is true," Merridew said, dropping on to the settee. "You are the very man I seek. Mrs. Chester was right to send me to you. Please, allow me to collect my thoughts and I shall explain the terrible events which have brought me to your door."

While we waited, I poured the fellow a small brandy which he accepted with a grateful nod.

"I know this is a matter for the Metropolitan Police," Merridew began, "but there would be a tremendous scandal should the newspapers become involved."

"Watson is nothing if not discreet, and I give you my word, Mr. Merridew, the papers shall learn nothing from us."

An expression of relief flickered over the fellow's face. "You have my thanks. I don't think my poor mother would survive the shame. She is a sensitive creature. It is partly on her behalf that I have come."

"Then by all means," Holmes said, resuming his seat and leaning back, legs extended before him. "Give us your account."

"My strange story begins with the death of my father, the sixth Earl of Albermere, this past October. Prior to his marriage to my mother, he had been married to the Duke of Salisbury's daughter. She died soon after while giving birth to their only son, William. As the eldest child, my half-brother would've succeeded my father, but he vanished while on an expedition in the heart of Africa and hasn't been seen or heard from since. Efforts were made to locate him upon my father's death, and when those efforts failed, my elder brother Thomas assumed my father's duties. I was bequeathed the house in Park Lane, one which I'm afraid had fallen into some disrepair due to disuse. I decided to alter the home and hired a reputable builder to affect the changes.

"My mother, learning of my plans, asked that she might come with me to London. She had been rather ill since the passing of my father and so I agreed, thinking that the change might do her some good. I brought her up from Hampshire, intending to stay in the more habitable parts of the house while the work was done.

"My mother was in good spirits when we arrived in London, and for a good part of the first week, she seemed her old self. It wasn't until the second week, when the workmen were to arrive, that her disposition took a dark turn.

"One morning, she came down to breakfast looking rather pale and drawn. I inquired as to what was the matter and she confided that she had not slept all night. Apparently, there were rats in the wall. She could hear them scurrying. I told her I would tend to the matter at once. Mrs. Chester, our housekeeper, had accompanied us to London, and I charged her with finding a suitable rat-catcher.

"I gave no more thought to the matter, as the group of workmen had arrived and assembled in my study. All seemed attentive to my instruction, save one. The fellow, a rather brash man of forty, stared into the hall the entire time. I could not see the hall from my desk, but upon shifting my point of view, I soon found the object of his interest. It was my mother who stood in the hall outside. Upon seeing me, she hurried by.

"You must know, gentlemen, that my mother was at one time an actress of some stature and a great beauty. Even now, in her advancing years, she still attracts attention, and I am much accustomed to this. I reasoned that the fellow had simply recognized her and thought little of it. It was only when he vanished from the study, and I had inquired as to where he had gone, that I was met with a rather frightening answer: None of the laborers had ever seen him before. They believed him to be one of the servants.

"A sudden premonition of evil overcame me, and I hurried back to my mother's room. To my horror, I found the fellow standing outside, holding her gently by the arm. They spoke earnestly for several seconds, in tones so low that I could not hear them until I drew nearer.

"'I will always be of service,' said he.

"'Thank you, Bob,' she replied.

The fellow looked away then, and upon seeing me, released my mother. He tipped his hat and set off in the opposite direction.

"'Who was that man?' I asked when I reached her.

"'He is the rat-catcher,' she replied. 'He has been searching the house for signs of the vermin. I told him about the sounds I heard last night.'

"'He seemed rather familiar for a rat-catcher. How do you know his name? Why did he have you by the arm?'

Her face grew flushed. 'He introduced himself and I felt rather faint. Like a true gentleman, he steadied me.'

"Her expression and this false reply were as a needle to my soul. The fact that it came upon the heels of my father's death increased my ire. I could not contain myself.

"'You did not seem faint this morning. Really, Mother. Can you not consider your station? You should not encourage the attentions of such persons.'

Her eyes blazed. 'You suspect me, Josiah? I, who have sacrificed all for you?'

"'Sacrificed? What have you ever sacrificed for me?'

Her face took on an expression of such sorrow that I instantly regretted my words.

"'*How sharper than a serpent's tooth it is to have a thankless child,*' said she. Then she turned and shut the door, leaving me in the hall.

"I'm ashamed to say that my temper got the best of me that day. I did not speak with my mother that evening, though now I wish I had."

Holmes opened his eyes. He regarded the gentleman with a curious stare.

"I retired early that evening, and by quarter-of-ten, had slipped into my bed to sleep. I awoke to a horrible scream, such as I have never heard in my life."

"What time was this?"

"Eh?"

"What time did you hear the scream?"

"Around three perhaps? I heard the clock toll the hour shortly after."

"You may continue."

"Very well . . . Where – Ah yes. Lamp in hand, I rushed down the hall. The scream sounded again, and I realized it had come from the west wing of the house. I rushed in and found – "

The young man paused and withdrew a handkerchief from his pocket. He blotted his brow and then continued. "My mother lay upon the floor, a figure dressed in black leaning over her. When I appeared, he fled. I would have pursued him, but my mother called me back.

"'Josiah!' she cried. 'No!'

"Her face, Mr. Holmes! I shall never forget it if I live to be a hundred. It was ghastly white and her eyes – they looked as though the last shred of sanity might flee at any moment.

"'I will send for the police, Mother. This man will pay for his assault on you.'

"'No . . . no police.'

"'Was it the man who came today?'

"'No police! Swear to me, Josiah!'

"I did not wish to give my word, but she begged me. Begged me until I could no longer refuse. The words I uttered gave her little peace, however, for she suddenly clutched at her breast, her face contorted in agony. Within seconds she was senseless.

"I chafed her wrists, but to no avail. She would not rouse. I called for Mrs. Chester, who had been a nurse in her youth, and hurried to fetch the doctor myself.

"When I returned with the physician, I found my mother awake but quite weak. After examining her, the doctor announced that she was in a grave condition due to her heart and prescribed complete bed rest. She was not to be moved, nor was she to be excited in any fashion. I sent the builders away and informed my brother of the situation. Mrs. Chester has been caring for mother ever since. That was a fortnight ago, and she has only just begun to show improvement.

"Mr. Holmes, I did not see the face of the man who attacked my mother, but I am sure it was the one who came to see her that day. Mrs. Chester told me the fellow couldn't have been a rat-catcher, for the simple reason that she did not send for one. In fact, it was her plan to take care of the rats herself. I don't know who he could be."

"You haven't contacted the police?"

"I gave my word I would not."

"Then you have taken other precautions to protect your mother?"

"We have. My brother has hired several individuals to watch the house and repel anyone who might do her harm."

"Then this fellow is not the reason you have come to me."

"No, though I fear he has some hand in what has happened this evening."

Holmes rose in his chair and leaned forward.

"For the last three days, Mrs. Chester has complained of strange sounds within the walls. She has been awakened by the soft squeal of rodents on no less than two occasions, and it was her opinion that rats had invaded the space by way of the more ruined parts of the house. Being a somewhat ingenious woman, she decided to trap the beasts where they lived and save us the trouble and embarrassment of hiring a rat-catcher. She came to me this evening, just before I was to leave for *Tristan and Isolde*, her face flushed and eyes wide. She held something wrapped in her apron, cradling it as though it were made of glass and might shatter if she dropped it."

"'Mr. Merridew, sir,' said she, her voice just above a whisper. 'You mustn't go to the opera, sir.'

"'Whyever not?' I asked.

"'I've found something, sir. Something you must see.'

"'I've no time for riddles, Mrs. Chester.'

"'I found it in the wall, sir.'

"For a moment, I thought she'd found a dead rat within the wall and brought the creature out to see. But it wasn't a rat. When she uncovered it, I found it was something far worse."

Merridew paused and reached into the pocket of his cloak. He withdrew a bundle and held it out to Holmes. My companion accepted the package and carefully unwrapped it.

I have seen many horrors in my life, both as a medical man and as a colleague of Sherlock Holmes. But I must admit, the revelation of the thing wrapped within the apron cloth filled me with an unreasoning dread, one I still feel to this day.

Holmes held the skull in one hand. There was a gap in the jaw where two teeth had once been, but otherwise, it appeared to be intact.

"I was horrified by her find, Mr. Holmes," Merridew continued. "And I must confess, I nearly fainted when I first saw it. We have no clue how it might have come to be in the wall, though I am of the mind that the man who attacked my mother is somehow responsible. I was at my wit's end as to what to do, but Mrs. Chester, wise woman that she is, counseled me otherwise. She said I should take it to you and trust to your discretion."

"Were there other remains?" Holmes asked, pulling his glass from his pocket and studying the object with great care.

"I must confess, I did not go to the space in the wall and search myself, though Mrs. Chester gave me her word there was nothing save the skull."

"How long has the house been in the possession of your family?"

"My grandfather, the fifth Earl of Albermere, had the house built in the summer of '32, I believe. My father inherited it fifteen years ago, but as I mentioned before, we seldom used it unless on a visit to London."

Holmes finished his examination and then set the skull upon the table. "You were right to bring this to me, Mr. Merridew. This is unquestionably the skull of a murdered man. I should like to see the place where it was found. Would our presence disturb your mother?"

"I had hoped you would come tonight. I have a carriage waiting. As to my mother, the doctor has prescribed a sedative, one she often takes before bed. Nothing will disturb her."

"Very well then. We shall leave at once," Holmes said. He moved to wrap the skull and hand it back, but Merridew held up a hand.

"Would you keep it, Mr. Holmes?" he said with a shudder. "I would rather not bring that thing back into my house."

"I should be glad to. And, when the time comes to inform the police, I shall take the matter in hand."

"I am indebted to you."

A brisk carriage ride through the gaslit London streets took us to Merridew's home in Park Lane. Though not as opulent as those houses around it, the building possessed an air of nobility. From the outside, it seemed well-kept.

Merridew led us inside.

Having procured two rather ancient oil lamps, we entered the west wing of the house. As our client had related, the space was in some disrepair. Perhaps it had been poorly and hastily constructed, or the materials had been of inferior quality. Whatever the reason, we found ourselves forced to avoid piles of crumbling brick, peeling paper, and rotted flooring. Holmes kept his eye upon the dusty floor as we walked, his eyes gleaming with interest.

"I found my mother here," Merridew said, pointing to the mouth of a hallway. "She is loathe to speak of the incident. She will not even tell me why she was here."

Holmes fell to one knee and studied the spot for several moments, both with his glass and eye. When he had finished, we continued on.

Merridew led us to the door of what might have been a servant's bedroom. Here he paused, and in a whisper cautioned us.

"We must be quiet from here on. My mother's bedroom lies adjacent to this room, and I don't wish to wake her." He opened the door and led us inside.

The room was quite small, but large enough to accommodate a bed and other sundry furniture. Merridew indicated the wall on the left. Much of the plaster had fallen away, leaving a large hole. Holmes examined it for several minutes, both inside and out, going so far as to crawl halfway inside. He then turned his attention to the floor and the plaster which lay about it.

"Was this room ever connected to your mother's?" Holmes asked.

"Not to my knowledge. Why do you ask?"

"If you peer inside the hole, you will see a door in the opposite wall. It has been sealed and – "

Suddenly the door to the room we occupied flew open and a man stepped inside. Though not as tall as Mr. Merridew, the fellow bore many of the same features, including the small eyes and spectacles. He held a candle in one hand and the flame's light flickered over his bearded face.

"What is the meaning of this, Josiah?" the man asked. "Why have you invited these persons into this house?"

"Thomas?" Merridew said. "I didn't expect you here so soon, Brother. Have you heard – "

"Mrs. Chester has informed me of all your foolish doings. You should have spoken with me before running off to find consulting detectives. I could have given you the solution to this problem without resorting to those outside our family."

"And pray, what is that solution?" Holmes asked blandly.

The seventh Earl of Albermere frowned. "That is a private matter, sir. Not for your ears, nor the ears of your companion."

"This is Mr. Sherlock Holmes," Merridew said. "He believes the skull

63

belongs to a murdered – "

"Murder?" the Earl's laughter rang out throughout the room, a cold and mirthless sound. "How dare you, sir! Leave this house at once, or I shall be forced to call the constabulary."

"A capital idea," Holmes replied. "I'm sure they will be happy to accompany me to Baker Street where they will take possession of a certain skull found on these premises."

"You took it with you?" The Earl cried, glaring at Merridew.

"I thought it the best course of action," the larger man replied, quailing beneath his elder brother's gaze. "Mr. Holmes promised secrecy that the police will not."

The Earl shook his head and then turned to Holmes, somewhat resigned. "Very well. I shall tell you how the skull came to be in the wall. It is a stage prop – one used by my mother's theater company. My brother may have told you she was once a rather famous actress before she married our father. Her Ophelia was without compare, and the skull belonged to the production of *Hamlet*. It was gifted to her upon her retirement. You see, the skull belonged to a rather obscure actor named Robert Reed who, upon his death, bequeathed his skull to the theater company. My mother and he had been engaged sometime prior to his death and the company manager thought she might like to keep it as a memento. Unfortunately, she caught me playing with it as a child, and so she hid it in the closet. The rodents must have transferred it from there into the wall. It is all quite logical, gentlemen."

"And not particularly scandalous," Holmes continued in his bland tone.

The Earl's frown became a firm line. "My mother is unwell, Mr. Holmes. According to my brother, she has only just begun to recover from an incident wherein a man stared at her. Even the smallest hint of scandal may send her into relapse. I am sure you wouldn't wish to have her death upon your hands?"

Holmes lowered his eyes contritely and shook his head.

The Earl's countenance took on an expression of triumph, delighting in my friend's discomfort.

"As you can see, Mr. Holmes, there is no murder involved."

The man's contemptible behavior infuriated me. Earl or no, I might have given him a piece of my mind, had Holmes not taken hold of my arm.

"I must apologize to you and your brother," Holmes said. "It appears I have been mistaken. However, I promise you, I shall not make such an error again." He started for the door, then paused. "I hope you do not mind if I keep the skull. It shall be a reminder to me of this incident from this day forward. Good day, gentlemen. We shall show ourselves to the door."

Neither the Earl nor Merridew accompanied us from the room, and when we entered the foyer, a strange and tragic sight met our eyes. A woman stood before us in her nightdress, her hair disheveled, and feet bare. She gazed at us with haunted eyes, her face sallow, lips pale. It took me several seconds to recognize the renowned actress she had once been.

She rubbed her hands together as we approached, and I realized they were red and chafed. Before Holmes or I could speak, she rushed away and vanished into the east wing of the house.

The sight of Lady Albermere in such a state left us both silent as we stepped out the door. I hailed a cab, and when we were on our way to Baker Street, his demeanor changed. A grin spread over his face, and he laughed in that silent way so peculiar to him.

"What is it?" I asked. "Surely you do not find her ladyship's condition humorous?"

"Forgive me, my dear fellow. It is the Earl who amuses me. If he is half the actor his mother is purported to be, she is a great one indeed," he replied. "If I hadn't had the facts within my grasp, I might have believed him myself."

"He lied?"

"I am not as yet convinced he has ever set eyes upon it. I believe he is more interested in family reputation than in the truth. Careful study of the skull contradicts much of what he said."

Holmes reached into his pocket and withdrew his cigarette case. "Unless this Robert Reed was himself murdered, the skull did not belong to him. I found fractures which could only have come from several blows to the head, one of which would have assuredly killed the owner. It is also a well-known fact that skulls used in the theater consist of only the cranium. The mandible is always removed. This, in addition to a small section of desiccated flesh I found upon the crown, proves that our skull was never used in a theatrical performance.

"Further examination of the skull also revealed that the bone bore marks of rodent teeth, more consistent with the stripping of flesh than with simple transferrence. There is also the matter of the closet."

"The closet?"

Holmes lit a cigarette and gazed thoughtfully out the window. "There was none. The rooms had been connected at one time in a rather peculiar way. A large space existed between the two doors, large enough to accommodate the body of a man under six-foot. The door of the room we visited had been removed at sometime in the past, boarded up and covered with plaster – none of which decayed by itself. Rather, it was carefully removed to appear ruined. I found evidence of chisel work around the edges of the hole and on several pieces of plaster. No doubt, this work was done with the utmost care, for Mrs. Chester mistook it for the sound of rats in the walls."

"For what purpose?"

"You know my methods. What does the evidence tell you?"

I grew silent, considering all that he had told me.

"Someone destroyed the wall on purpose – to get to the body hidden inside!"

"Excellent," Holmes said, leaning back against the seat of the cab. "Our culprit removed the rest of the body, leaving only the skull behind. Why, I do not yet know. Perhaps he was interrupted in his work and intended to return for it later. All that I can tell you of him is that he stands six feet tall, walks with a limp, possesses black hair, and wears boots with a hole worn in the left sole."

"That is why you studied the dust on the floor. You found his footprints."

"And the hair trapped in the edges of plaster. Invisible save to me, who was looking for it. His were the only footprints which led to the room, aside from those of a woman. As you recall, only Mrs. Chester had been to the room before Mr. Merridew and ourselves."

"Why remove the body?"

"Mr. Merridew had decided to renovate the home. The body would be discovered. I believe the murder was committed some six years ago. Judging by the undisturbed dust in the room, I'd say no one had visited it in at least that length of time."

"The Earl must be the perpetrator," I said. "He certainly knows of the crime. And he wasn't pleased when you suggested you would keep the skull. To whom do you think it belongs?"

"It is a grave mistake to theorize without facts. This evening I pretended to err. I have no intention of actually erring now. Again, I can only supply a description. The victim stood less than six-feet tall, had lost two teeth sometime before his death, and was a guest in the home of the Merridews six years ago. I believe his skull is the single thread which may unravel the entire tapestry. The Earl cannot allow me to keep it. I'm sure he will come for it soon."

Unfortunately, Holmes's statement proved erroneous. Two days passed with no word from the Earl. For those two days, he remained in our rooms, consulting his commonplace books, pacing the floor, and playing the violin. I stayed with him, forgoing my patients and waiting for a visitor who never came.

On the third day, Holmes tossed the morning papers aside and bade me return to my work.

"I require data, Watson," said he. "And I must leave these rooms to

66

have it."

"Let me take the skull," I said. "I will safeguard it until this evening. No one would think to look for it in a medical bag."

"Very well. But don't let anyone know you have it."

"Will you send word if the Earl comes?"

"You will be the first to hear of it."

I took the precious cargo with me on my rounds, glancing over my shoulder whenever I stepped into the street. Fortunately, no one of import seemed to follow me and time passed without incident. When the afternoon grew long and my old wound made it impossible to continue, I decided to return home. I took a cab to Baker Street and hurried up to our rooms.

What I found there, chilled my blood.

The sitting room was a shambles. Papers lay strewn about, glass littered the floor, and furniture had been overturned. The sight which caused me to drop my bag, however, was a pair of legs lying in the doorway of Holmes's bedroom. I rushed forward and found, not my friend as I had feared, but a stranger dressed in the garb of a laborer. A tall man of perhaps forty, he possessed black hair and a large hole marred the sole of his left boot.

"He is stronger than he looks," a voice said.

I turned to see Holmes standing behind me. He seemed a bit disheveled, and his lip had been bloodied, but otherwise, he seemed none the worse for wear. He leaned down and withdrew something from the unconscious man's hand.

"As I surmised," he said, hefting the strange, metal object. He slipped his fingers through four metal rings and gripped the object in his palm. "I believe it is called a 'knuckleduster'. An American invention."

The man on the floor groaned.

"See if we've some rope," Holmes said. "We must secure our prisoner before turning him over to the police."

Twenty minutes would pass before he came to consciousness. His eyes grew wide, and he struggled against his bonds until Holmes and Inspector Stanley Hopkins stepped before him.

"They call you Bob Reed, do they not?" Holmes said.

I turned to Holmes in some surprise. Our captive's eyes grew wider, but he didn't reply.

"Come, come. There is no need to keep silent. I have spoken with those who know you at Covent Garden. You are a set maker by trade."

"What of it?" Reed said at last.

"This is Inspector Hopkins of Scotland Yard. If you confess to your crimes, he will do all he can to make things easy for you – and for the other person involved."

The man seemed to falter for a moment. "There is no one to blame but me. I killed him and stuffed him in the wall. When I heard the house was to be renovated, I came to recover the body. I knew the Lady in the past, but she knew nothing of my doings. She caught me there in the room a fortnight ago and I pursued her when she ran. That's all there is to it."

He would say no more after that, and at last, Hopkins led him away. We were left alone in our rooms.

"I had hoped to avoid it, Watson," Holmes said. "Though there is blame involved, I do believe the punishment has already been enough."

"What do you mean?"

"I know to whom the skull belongs. After you took it from our rooms, a visit to the Royal Geographical Society provided the answer. The gentleman matched our description exactly. Not only is he five-foot-eleven inches tall, but he also lost two teeth during an attack in Egypt. His disappearance was much discussed six years ago, though it was believed he had gone to Africa and vanished there. He is William Merridew, noted explorer and eldest son of the sixth Earl of Albermere."

"Good heavens! The older brother!"

"And true heir to the title. I sent my findings to 428 Park Lane, and that's why Mr. Reed appeared on our threshold. However, I believe that when Reed's arrest becomes public, we shall have another visitor. We have only to wait."

This time, Holmes was not mistaken. Less than an hour after the evening papers had reported the attack on Sherlock Holmes by an unidentified man, a soft knock sounded on our door. Mrs. Hudson entered with a solemn expression on her face.

"You may show her in, Mrs. Hudson," Holmes said.

Seconds later, a woman dressed in black entered our rooms. When she wrung her gloved hands together, I knew her immediately.

"Will you sit, Lady Albermere?" I asked.

She accepted my offer and sank down upon the settee.

"Do your sons know you have come?" Holmes asked gently.

"My sons know little of my deeds," she replied. "But it is on their behalf that I have come. Your note reached me this morning. You blame my son, Thomas. That is why I sent Bob to you. He was to reclaim the skull."

"And to kill me, if need be," Holmes said, his lips a thin line. "Is that what you have come to do too, my Lady?"

"No," she said, softly. "I am tired of blood and death. Please, do not blame my son for what I have done, nor for how he has protected me. Neither of my sons know the whole truth."

Her gaze grew distant then and she commenced to rubbing her hands together once more.

"What is the truth?" Holmes prodded.

"The truth?" She laughed in the same mirthless way as her son. "I am a murderess, gentlemen."

Before we could respond to this outburst, the Lady rushed into her story.

"I thought it would be easy . . . I never accepted William as my son. He was crass and believed I held an interest in him. His father favored him . . . though he never deserved it. One day, he would be the seventh Earl of Albermere. I couldn't let that happen. Couldn't allow him to take everything from my children . . . I had to protect their inheritance . . . had to protect *them*. It was I who planned it, who brought Bob into it. He's always loved me, has my Bob. Strange how I couldn't stomach the sight of him after . . . after the blood.

"I thought the house in London would be best. Because of the need for repair, no one ever used it. I led William to believe that I wished an assignation with him, and he was most eager to comply. It was I who baited him to the servant's room while Bob hid in the room between. When William embraced me, Bob crept up on him. He never turned – not even when Bob brought the club down upon his head.

"I think it would've been all right if William had died then. But he didn't . . . he didn't die . . . and he just keep groaning there on the floor. I couldn't stand the moaning. He wouldn't stop . . . Bob couldn't hit him again. He lost his nerve. So, I took the club and I . . . ."

She wrung her hands together, over and over. "The blood . . . I can never quite wash it out."

"Mr. Reed hid the body in the wall, did he not?" Holmes said in a mild tone.

She nodded. "For six long years, the secret was safe. And when my husband died, the inheritance of my sons was secured. Unfortunately, Josiah decided to repair the house in Park Lane, and I knew drastic action must be taken. Bob agreed to help me. He came to meet me that day."

"You secreted him in the house and joined him in the servant's room later that night. Together, you broke into the wall."

She nodded. "It seems I have severely underestimated you, sir. Yes, it is as you say. It took several hours, but we broke into the wall and . . . the rats . . . they came pouring out. Then I saw the bones and it all came back . . . all the blood. I suppose I lost my reason when Bob pulled the bones from the wall, for I swear I heard William's moaning and felt the slick of his blood upon my hands. I fled from the room and Bob followed. He must've left the skull in the wall . . . he must have."

69

She fell back on the settee. "I am not long for this world and have no right to wish for mercy. I will face God's judgment soon enough. All I ask is that you keep this secret from my children until I have gone. They already think so little of me. They would never believe I loved them not wisely, but too well."

The week following Lady Albermere's funeral, a messenger delivered a thousand pounds and five rubies of inestimable value to Baker Street. The money had been sent at the request of the Honorable Josiah Merridew, while the rubies were sent with the compliments of the seventh Earl of Albermere.

Holmes accepted the thousand but declined the rubies. These, he sent back to their owner.

"Vengeance is often confused with justice, Watson," said he, as the messenger took his leave. "The Earl seems to think I kept the secret of the Merridews because I wished a reward. I kept the secret because justice had been served. The Lady has paid for her deeds, and the one who loved her will soon face the hangman's knot. There is nothing to be gained by sullying the Albermere name."

"I hope you don't mind if I take some satisfaction in your returning the rubies to the Earl and keeping his brother's payment."

"You may take all the satisfaction you wish. Though in a way, I must thank the Earl. The lies he told to protect the family reputation led me to the murderer."

"Such a tragic circumstance," I said shaking my head. "The Lady was a great actress. I saw her once upon the stage, not as Ophelia but as Lady Macbeth. Strange how her life reflected her art."

"It is indeed unfortunate," Holmes said with a nod. "And worse still that nothing in her life became her like the leaving it."

The Strange Case of the Man from Edinburgh
by Susan Knight

"I tell you, gentlemen, someone is trying to kill my wife!"

To say Holmes and I were taken aback at this blunt outburst would be putting it mildly. The bearing and sober dress of Mr. Ramsay Ballantyne, for that was how the man had introduced himself, spoke of one not given to wild imaginings. He was a stern-looking Scot in the cast of a Presbyterian minister, tall and lean, almost entirely bald, and yet not elderly by any means.

"If that is so, then surely it is a matter for the police," Holmes remarked, but his nostrils quivered as if already scenting an interesting case.

"My wife is adamantly against such a procedure," Mr. Ballantyne replied, in the lilting accents of an Edinburgher. "She will not take the threats seriously and claims the whole thing is a prank played by one of her friends or relations."

"A strange sort of a prank," Holmes said. "But pray explain the nature of the supposed attempt on her life. And please do sit down, Mr. Ballantyne. We will all be more comfortable."

The man took a seat reluctantly, staying poker-upright in the hard chair he had selected, as if fearing any concession to comfort might detract from what he had to say.

For his part, Holmes stretched out in his usual armchair, as if ready to be entertained. I took a seat across from him, also facing our visitor.

"I have to confess that the matter did at first seem to be some sort of a twisted joke," he began. "The letters she received being of such a ludicrous nature, so badly spelt, and with such a mangled syntax." He shook his head in disgust.

I began to think: Not a minister, but a teacher. I could well envisage Mr. Ballantyne in front of a class of boys, keeping their grammar and spellings in order with a switch.

"I trust you have brought the letters to show me," Holmes said.

There was a pause. "Alas no. They are destroyed. Before I could stop her, Hélène, my wife, tore them up and tossed them in the fire."

"All of them? I think you have one at least with you."

Mr. Ballantyne looked surprised, but reached into his inside jacket pocket and brought out a missive.

"I will not ask how you knew it, Mr. Holmes," he said. "I have heard of your methods. I suppose you noticed that, at the first mention of the letters, my hand made an involuntary movement towards my breast."

Holmes nodded and smiled. Clearly this Ramsay Ballantyne was a person of no little perception. For my part, I hadn't noticed the gesture. He now handed the said letter to Holmes, who scanned it and then passed it to me. In a cursive hand, in red ink, it read as follows:

Hélène you have been worned. You cannot escape the fate. Your days are short. Blud must to be spilled for your duplicite.

"To the point," I said. "Though I see what you mean, sir. The writer is not an educated person."

Holmes held up his hand to silence me.

"On the contrary, Watson, we can make no such assumption."

"You think the note has been written that way deliberately in order to mislead us?" Mr. Ballantyne asked.

"Perhaps." Holmes leant even further back, making a steeple of his fingers. "However, might I assume that your wife isn't British, sir? She is perhaps French? Belgian?"

Ramsay Ballantyne now evinced astonishment. He nodded.

"French. But how – ?"

"Tut tut, sir. Not a difficult deduction. The way you pronounced her name is one clue. And see how the writer has placed the accents correctly over her name. There are many signs that he, or she, isn't a native speaker of English. '*Warned*' and '*blood*' are misspelt as if transcribed by someone who has only heard them spoken aloud and has guessed at the spelling. However '*duplicity*', a more unusual word, is correctly spelt, apart from the final letter. And that is how the word appears in French, though usually with an accent *aigu* over the final '*e*'."

Mr. Ballantyne nodded. "Of course. I should have noticed that, too."

"And then," continued Holmes, "there is the handwriting itself. You see how it flows to the right with many looped letters. I have made quite a study of graphology, and can tell you that the note is written in the calligraphic style taught in French schools."

Mr. Ballantyne took back the letter and studied the handwriting. "It is indeed an educated hand," he conceded. Definitely a teacher.

"However, that raises an interesting question, does it not?" Holmes said. "If the writer is French, writing to your French wife, then why write in English?"

"He knows she will show it to me, who cannot speak the language."

"Hmm." Holmes was thoughtful. "But I am sure, Mr. Ballantyne, that this crude little missive cannot comprise the sum of your concerns. What else is there?"

Again our visitor paused, looking solemn: A man who liked to underline the significance of his actions.

"This," he said at last.

He produced a box from an outer pocket and laid it before us. Holmes reached towards it.

"Stop!" Ramsay Ballantyne exclaimed. "It must be opened with the greatest of care, Mr. Holmes. You will understand why in a second."

He first drew on to his right hand a grey leather glove, and then slowly lifted the lid. Holmes peered in.

"Ah," he remarked with satisfaction. "Yes, indeed."

I, however, could see nothing of the contents, being at too great a distance. However, I hadn't long to wait for the horrid revelation, for Holmes straightway reached into the box, and drew out a huge and hairy spider, placing it gently on the back of his other hand.

"Mr. Holmes," whispered Mr. Ballantyne, as if fearing to disturb the monster. "It is deadly poisonous."

"That is something of an exaggeration," Holmes replied calmly. "*Steatoda nobilis* can indeed give a nasty bite, but very seldom does it prove fatal. Still, I will put her back in her box. For now . . . Indeed, you may leave the little lady with me if you wish, Mr. Ballantyne, for I am sure you aren't comfortable carrying her around with you."

"I should be much relieved, Mr. Holmes. But tell me, is the creature indeed less dangerous than I understood it to be? I thought it a tarantula."

"No, no – As you may imagine, spiders have been yet another of my fields of interest. *Steatoda nobilis* isn't harmless, far from it, but its venom is unlikely to cause more than the pain you would get from a bee or wasp sting. Still, it is an unpleasant gift to receive. How did it arrive?"

"In a package addressed to my wife. Luckily, I was with her when she opened it, and was able to prevent the creature escaping from its box and biting her."

"This box?"

"The very one."

"Nothing distinctive," Holmes said, examining it. "And the package itself?"

"Nothing distinctive either. Just my wife's name and address inscribed upon it."

"You didn't bring the wrappings with you."

"I didn't think to."

"A pity. Did you notice the handwriting? Was it perhaps the same as in the threatening letter?"

Mr. Ballantyne thought for moment, frowning.

"No," he replied finally. "It was printed in capitals. I am sure of it."

"Nonetheless, I should like to see it," Holmes said.

A slight smile of relief lightened the man's grave face.

"Of course. I should like nothing more than for you and Dr. Watson to accompany me home, to convince my wife, as I have failed to do, that this is no trivial matter."

The three of us took a cab to Paddington Station, whence we boarded a train to Wimbledon, and then another cab carrying us thence up the steep hill to Mr. Ballantyne's residence, a solid Georgian house on the edge of the Common. At first, I took the person who came forward to greet us to be Mrs. Ballantyne, a tall, stately woman in a black dress, quite the counterpart to the husband. However, this turned out to be the housekeeper, a Mrs. McDuff.

"Your wife is in the library," she told Ramsay Ballantyne in answer to his query, thereby revealing herself, in case her name didn't, to be a Scot like her master. "She is reading, I believe."

Why her tone should express disapproval was strange. Surely reading was a most acceptable pastime for a gentlewoman, particularly in a library. Perhaps she thought her mistress should be occupied with something more practical – like sewing, for instance.

"Thank you, Margaret," Mr. Ballantyne replied. "Please arrange for some refreshments to be brought us."

"To the library?" Again that disapproving tone. "Would the withdrawing room not be more suitable?"

"We will take it in the library, thank you, Margaret," he replied, somewhat impatiently. I suppose such domestic details seemed irrelevant under the more urgent circumstances.

Mrs. McDuff nodded, unsmiling, and withdrew. She was evidently as dour as those of our race are often reckoned to be.

Hélène Ballantyne, on the other hand, wasn't at all like that, and not, I have to confess, as I had imagined her. Her husband being so upright and stiff, I had thought his wife must be of a similarly serious character, as well as slender, elegant, and restrained, in the typical way of French ladies. But Hélène was round and bubbly, with mischief in her eyes. And very young. Laughing aloud and merrily at the sight of the three of us, so solemn and concerned, she put down the book she was reading. Its yellow cover revealed it to be far removed from one of the classics, which perhaps explained the housekeeper's tone of censure. The lady's taste was clearly for sensational reading matter.

Mr. Ballantyne introduced us.

"Mr. Holmes, the great detective!" She smiled broadly. "What an honour! But my dear Ramsay," she continued, "you have brought your friends here to chase the wild goose, I think." She possessed the lightest and most charming of French accents. "The more I consider it, the more sure I am that it is my cousin, Adolphe, who is sending the letters. He is a silly boy who would think he is being funny."

"But the spider? That is no joke, Hélène."

"Did it bite anyone? No. It is probably quite harmless."

She shook her head and her dark curls quivered as if they shared her mirth. I noticed that she missed off her "aitches", so that Holmes became "'Olmes", and the spider, somewhat comically, "'armless" (Eight legs but no arms!). I shall not, however, attempt to reproduce her accent here for fear it might prove tedious for my readers.

Holmes coughed. "Not quite harmless, Mrs. Ballantyne. As I have informed your husband, though seldom fatal, that particular spider's bite can be very painful."

She shrugged. "But who would want to hurt me? You know well, Ramsay, there is nothing true in these silly accusations. You know that, my dearest." She took his hand and pressed it to her lips. Then she turned to us. "You can see, gentlemen, just what a very old fogey my husband is . . . ." She laughed again. Ramsay Ballantyne was, I guessed, barely forty. "He married me when I was sixteen, five years ago. Since then, I have lived a life without blame in Edinburgh and here. And before my marriage – *Mon Dieu!*" She threw her little white hands up in the air. "What evil can a young girl from Lille do in a convent school, that years later causes someone to want to kill her? No, it is a joke. In bad taste, yes certainly, but nothing to worry about. See, I am not worried."

At that moment, Mrs. McDuff entered, every line of her face expressing discontent.

"Please take care not to spill anything," she said, setting the tray down on the desk, from which papers had swiftly to be moved.

"Coffee, Ramsay! In here?" Mrs. Ballantyne looked wide-eyed.

"It's tea, actually, Madam," the housekeeper said.

Mrs. Ballantyne laughed merrily. "Of course it is. You British and your everlasting tea-drinking! A cup of Darjeeling, and all is well, is that not so?" She turned to the housekeeper. "A big coffee with cream for me, please, Margaret." Her warm smile wasn't returned, the woman merely nodding and stepping out of the room.

"I will be *maman*," our hostess then said, holding a pretty porcelain jug over matching cups. "Milk, Mr. Holmes? Dr. Watson?"

I nodded. "Just the merest amount," I said, for I like it strong.

Holmes shook his head with impatience. He wasn't here to drink tea.

"This cousin of yours – Adolphe?" he asked. "Where does he live, Mrs. Ballantyne?"

"As far as I know, he is still in Lille." She passed me my cup.

"But the last letter sent had a London postmark."

"You kept one of the letters?" Hélène asked her husband. "I thought we had burnt them all. Well," she shrugged again, "maybe not Adolphe, then. It must be someone else. Unless . . . ." A smile burst over her face as if the sun had suddenly emerged from behind a cloud. "I have it! He is come to London to surprise us! Ramsay, there will be a knock at the door one of these days, and it will be Adolphe!"

"My dear girl . . . ." There was an unmistakably patronising tone to Ballantyne's voice, "that is too great a leap of the imagination, even for you."

"Not at all. It is just what he would do, the silly boy."

"I suppose," Holmes drawled, "it is too much to hope, Mrs. Ballantyne, that you still have the wrappings in which the spider was delivered."

A charming little frown appeared on her forehead. "I think . . . I think . . . ." She rang a bell, and a young maidservant soon appeared. The two women spoke in French for a few seconds, and then the maid withdrew.

"Claudine has gone to look. I think maybe you will be in luck, Mr. Holmes."

Indeed, shortly after, the maid returned with a pot of pungent-smelling coffee, as well as a quantity of brown paper on which was clearly printed, as Mr. Ballantyne had told us, the name and address of his wife.

"Margaret forgot the cream. No matter, I will take milk."

Holmes was examining the wrapping paper closely. As far as I could tell, there wasn't much to see, but then, of course, I am not gifted with his powers.

"I thought it was the lace collars I had ordered," the lady remarked.

"Well," he said finally, "I will retain this if I may. And Mrs. Ballantyne, although you are convinced there is no real threat involved here, I beg you to stay alert and not to open anything that looks in any way suspicious."

She nodded, a little smile trembling on her lips.

"I promise, but really, Mr. Holmes – "

"As for you, sir," Holmes turned to her husband, "the same instruction. Open nothing if you don't know the source. And please keep me informed of any developments."

He stood up.

"You are leaving so soon?" the lady cried. "But Mr. Holmes, you have had neither tea nor coffee. And the poor Dr. Watson hasn't had time to drink his."

Holmes turned to me. I knew that look.

"I am ready to go," I said, draining the cup, which anyway contained little more than a thimbleful. "Thank you, Madame." I too stood up, and inclined my head.

"Another time then, gentlemen," she said smiling, "I hope."

Little did we realise how soon and under what circumstances our return would take place.

Mr. Ballantyne accompanied us to the door.

"What do you think, Mr. Holmes?" he asked. "Can it all be just a silly prank?"

"You were right to consult me. It may well be as your wife thinks – that her cousin is behind it all. On the other hand, there is certainly enough here to cause alarm. I beg you, please be very very careful."

He agreed that he would.

The early spring day that had started misty when we first set out had by now turned into a pleasant and sunny afternoon. As we walked down the drive-way, I looked back at the house. Mr. Ballantyne was still standing in the doorway. I raised a hand to wave farewell, but he seemed lost in thought and didn't reciprocate.

"A fine house for a teacher," I remarked. "He is doing well at it."

"A teacher?" Holmes chided me. "Whatever gave you that idea? Surely you could tell instantly. Did you not observe the handsome stick pin in his cravat."

I had not particularly.

"It was in the form of a thistle – the insignia, of course, of the Caledon and Dunedin Merchant Bank."

"Of course," I replied sourly. Neither a minister nor a teacher, then, but a banker – and a prosperous one at that.

Holmes grinned at me.

"And of course, his position was indicated on the card he sent up this morning. I am sorry, Watson, for teasing you. Even I, sometimes, have the need for concrete information, you know."

I laughed with him, though still somewhat peeved.

We were strolling down the hill towards the station. Already the leaves of the plane trees lining our route were unfolding, dressing the bare branches in pale green.

"Do you think Hélène Ballantyne's life really is in danger?" I asked after a while.

"As to that – Well, what did you make of the lady?"

77

"Quite delightful. And not 'French' at all!"

He smiled. "Your eye is so easily turned by a pretty face, my friend. I suppose by 'not French', you mean that she is not aloof and proud. But you know, that is just a prejudice based on the manners of certain Parisian ladies. Mrs. Ballantyne is a provincial. It is quite a different matter."

"Whatever caused her to marry Ramsay Ballantyne? They appear such an ill-matched pair. And yet, she seems happy enough."

"I am flattered you would ask me that," Holmes replied, although my question was, in fact, a rhetorical one. "However, on the subject of matrimony, and indeed on the general nature of relationships between the sexes, you are in a much better position that I to speculate."

I was silent. Although it was some years since my dear Mary had passed away, I considered his remark insensitive, recalling as it did my lost, happiest times. However, I couldn't expect him, whose heart had never been so engaged, to understand.

It was barely a week later. Holmes and I were sitting over breakfast when Mrs. Hudson appeared holding a telegram which had just been delivered.

"You take it," Holmes said. "I find I have butter all over my fingers."

I opened the grey envelope and almost turned that colour myself.

"Good Lord! What terrible news!"

"What is it?"

"Ramsay Ballantyne is dead!"

Buttery fingers notwithstanding, Holmes snatched the message from my hand, as if to find other words written there. "Sent by Mrs. McDuff," he said. "Oh, I am very much remiss. I should have stopped it."

"I don't see what more you could have done."

He was already on his feet.

"Come. There is no time to be lost."

"Where are we going? To Wimbledon?"

"Of course. Put down that slice of toast, man, and hurry."

I would not even be permitted to finish my breakfast.

The door was opened to us by the French maid, Claudine, looking pale and anxious. She showed us into the withdrawing room, already occupied by three persons, two of whom we recognised. The third, a thin young man, stared wild-eyed as we entered. Beside him stood Mrs. McDuff, who nodded a grim acknowledgement to us, while poor Mrs. Ballantyne, reclining on the sofa, looked utterly distraught, her curls a-tumble, her face swollen and pink from weeping. She was wearing a loose robe, a tea-gown in a pale blue, silky fabric, the sort of garment my own dear Mary would have worn in the morning before dressing to go out. It was, even under the sorry circumstances, most becoming.

"Thank goodness you are here!" she exclaimed, and, jumping up, threw herself into Holmes's arms.

I had almost to smile, my friend looked so discomfited. He patted her back and gently withdrew from the embrace.

"You will find out who did this terrible thing, Mr. Holmes," she stated rather than asked.

"My dear Mrs. Ballantyne," he replied. "It will be for the police to do that. I see Inspector Lestrade is already on the case. You can ask for no one better than him."

The same man was now approaching us.

"I might have guessed you'd turn up, Mr. Holmes," he said genially enough, "given the extraordinary nature of the crime."

"It is a crime then, and not an accident?"

"It was supposed to be me. *Me!*" Mrs. Ballantyne cried, and then again subsided into grief. Luckily, I caught her before she fell, and kept firm hold while leading her, staggering, back to the sofa. She looked up at me with eyes the colour of forget-me-nots, and clutched at my hand.

"Thank you, Dr. Watson," she said. "You are so kind."

"It seems a parcel arrived for the lady," Lestrade explained. "However, it was her husband who opened it. The box contained a venomous snake. The enraged creature shot out, biting him, and he succumbed almost instantly."

More sobs from the sofa. "It was so terrible," she muttered. "Poor Ramsay!"

Holmes shook his head. "The foolish, foolish man. I told him to be cautious."

"Did you, now?" the inspector asked. "When was that, then?

"Mr. Ballantyne consulted me recently regarding some threats directed at his wife," Holmes explained, continuing, "I trust you have caught the snake. I should not like to think it is lurking around here somewhere."

"Yes, thankfully, it is dead," Lestrade replied. "The servant – Claudette?" He consulted his notebook. "Claudine – a most resourceful young person, ran into the room on hearing the lady scream out. She seized a poker and succeeded in smashing it over the head of the creature."

"May I see?"

"The thing is in the breakfast room where the tragic event took place."

We followed him out.

"The – er – victim is still there, too."

The breakfast room turned out to be pleasantly airy, east-facing, and so chosen no doubt for the sake of the morning sun that was even now streaming through the window. Remains of a breakfast very like our own still lay on the table, toast and eggs and a pot of coffee. However, the porcelain cups and saucers lay smashed, and the milk jug had toppled over, spilling its contents across the damask tablecloth, the stain dark from the wood beneath.

Between the table and the window lay the body of the unfortunate Mr. Ramsay Ballantyne, his face frozen in a contortion of horror. I recognised the man who crouched beside him as Dr. Merry, a colleague who was frequently called upon to assist the police in their investigations. He looked up at me, shaking his head.

"A bad business, Watson," he said. "Once bitten, the poor man didn't stand a chance."

"There's the guilty party," Lestrade said, gesturing to a box on the sideboard, presumably the same which had held the living snake. Holmes crossed over to it and drew out the dead reptile.

"A-ha!" he said. "You will recognise it at once, I think."

Its speckled markings indeed looked familiar.

"Is it swamp adder?" I asked, recalling a previous occasion when another such was employed as a fiendish agent of death.

"Indeed, it is. And here is the paper that wrapped the box. Inscribed, as you will see, by the same hand that sent the spider."

"What spider?" asked Lestrade.

Thereupon, Holmes had to expand on the matter as we knew it.

"Hmm," said the inspector. "A nasty business altogether. Sending poisonous insects and snakes through the post! That's a first in my experience. Whatever next?"

"Might I examine the body?" Holmes asked.

"Of course, though there isn't much to see."

Dr. Merry made way for Holmes, who crouched down beside the corpse.

"Look here," he said, raising his head. "Is this not rather strange?"

He pointed to a pair of puncture marks on the victim's neck, evidently the snake bite.

"What's strange about it?" I asked.

"Perhaps nothing," he replied. "However, I am imagining Mr. Ballantyne opening the box. Surely the snake would have gone for his hand, his wrist. The nearest uncovered piece of flesh."

"Unless he was wearing gloves as before."

"As you can see, he is not, which is strange in itself. He was so careful before."

"Perhaps he was bending over the box to see what was in it," I suggested.

Holmes clapped his hands. "Of course. Sometimes your voice of common sense cuts through my suspicious imaginings. Mr. Ballantyne bent his head low over it. Well, all that remains now is to track down who sent it."

"This 'Adolphe' you talked about?" put in Lestrade.

"Hmm," Holmes muttered. "Yes, by all means try to track down Adolphe, though . . . Well, we'll see."

"Since Mrs. Ballantyne was the intended victim, should measures not be taken to protect her?" I asked.

"I have already spoken to the housekeeper, and more especially to the lady's personal maid about it," Lestrade put in. "This Claudine is utterly devoted to her mistress, and has promised to exercise the greatest caution until we discover the callous villain who has done this deed."

"Did the girl have anything to add to what we already know?" I asked.

"Not really," Lestrade replied. "The box arrived by special delivery first thing. Claudine brought it in to her mistress, who had just come down, as you can see, to breakfast with her husband. The maid left the room. Shortly after, she heard the scream and rushed back in. Seeing the snake on the table, she seized the nearest implement, a poker, and managed to batter it to death."

"I see."

That accounted for the broken cups and saucers.

"And Mr. Ballantyne?"

"By that time, Mrs. McDuff, the housekeeper had arrived on the scene. She could tell that her master was already in his death throes. Nonetheless, she sent for the family doctor as well as the police."

"Is that the young man in the withdrawing room?" Holmes asked.

"No, the doctor left when we arrived with Merry. That young fellow is Mr. Ballantyne's secretary. Name of – " Lestrade again consulted his notebook, "Mr. Frederick Page."

"How does he come to be here?"

"He was bringing Mr. Ballantyne some papers for them to work on this morning."

"Was he indeed? Interesting, interesting. . . . Shall we rejoin the others for now?" Holmes said, adding, "I hope you will permit me to pursue the investigation, Lestrade. Since Mr. Ballantyne had commissioned me to do so, I feel I owe it to him."

"I am always grateful for your help, Mr. Holmes," the inspector replied, a little drily, adding, "Well, almost always."

The scene in the withdrawing room was much as before, although now Mr. Page was standing by the window, looking out. He was a pale young man with fine light hair. His appearance, along with the dove-grey suit he was wearing, gave the impression of a shadow, rather than of a full-bodied individual, and one, I suspected, who at that moment would have liked to be able to dematerialise altogether. Meanwhile, Mrs. McDuff still stood by, motionless as a statue, while poor Mrs. Ballantyne remained prostrate on the sofa.

"It is all my fault!" she was saying as we entered. "I shouldn't have dismissed it as a joke. It should have been me, who died, not Ramsay . . . My poor, poor Ramsay!"

Lestrade shook his head. "A tragic business," he said. "But you, Madam, are in no way to blame. You couldn't have known."

"I am amazed," Holmes added, "that he opened the box so carelessly after my warnings."

"He snatched it from me," Mrs. Ballantyne said. "I told him not to touch it, but alas, he was too curious." She collapsed in tears, her whole body racked in shudders.

"I wonder if the lady might go to her room to lie down," Holmes said. "It is clearly all too much for her. Perhaps there is something she can take to calm her."

Lestrade nodded.

"A good idea."

Mrs. Ballantyne stood and took a step, but nearly fell again.

"Claudine," she said. "Please send for Claudine."

"You go with her," Holmes said. "I should like a word with the maid."

Somewhat surprised at this instruction – to which, however, Lestrade made no objection, I offered the lady my arm and, she leaning heavily on me, we ascended the stairs to her room. As a doctor, I am, of course, well used to visiting ladies in their bedrooms. On the present occasion, I was, however, unaccountably uncomfortable. It was instantly clear that Mrs. Ballantyne didn't share sleeping quarters with her husband. The room was entirely feminine in its appurtenances, with pretty throws and cushions in delicate colours, and I felt I was intruding on the lady's private domain. Perhaps my confusion showed on my face, for she explained, "Ramsay sleeps fitfully, and often reads late into the night. He kindly decided to spare me his restlessness, and stays in the adjoining room."

The poor woman, speaking as if her husband were still alive!

She threw open a side door to show me. It was a different world, a monk's cell in its austerity. A single iron bedstead stood against a wall, a small table beside it on which lay a Bible.

She laughed through her tears at the expression on my face. "Despite what you might conclude about this, Dr. Watson, my husband and I loved each other dearly. He was one of a kind. There can be no one else like him."

"I am sure of it," I said, seeing she was about to break down once more. "But please, rest now."

We returned to her room, but instead of lying down, she crossed to the window. I followed her.

"What a wonderful view," I remarked. We were at the rear of the house, its fine garden backing onto Wimbledon Common.

"I love to look at the trees in all seasons," she said. "They calm me. See how the leaves begin to unfurl. Spring is such a wonderful season, is it not? A time of new beginnings. *Oh, God!*" She clutched at the window sill.

To distract her thoughts I asked, "How long have you lived here?"

"Only just over a year. Before that we were in Edinburgh. Then Ramsay was asked to take over the London branch of the bank. I thought . . . ." She smiled sadly. "You know, Dr. Watson, in Edinburgh we lived in the New Town. There was always lots to do, to see, people to visit."

"Yes, I know Edinburgh well," I replied. "I have family there." I regarded her tear-stained face. "So you are lonely here, I think."

"A little. But I am getting used to it."

She must have imagined life in London would be the same, or more so, as life in the busy Scottish capital. Instead, she found herself far from the centre, in this remote place. Her husband had his work, but she would know no one, would have nothing to do.

Five years married and no children, I thought but didn't ask. Most women in her position by now would have one or two little mites to care for.

She sighed deeply, her words echoing my suppositions.

"Now I have no one at all." Again she took my hand. "Promise me you will stay my friend."

Taken aback at the intensity of her tone, I replied in some confusion, "I promise. But your cousin – "

She flared up. "If Adolphe did this, then a thousand thousand curses upon him! But no, I cannot believe it. I cannot. Oh, Dr. Watson, please find out who killed my husband."

I stammered that Holmes would undoubtedly get to the bottom of the matter.

"I pray to God he will. Now, I will rest. Leave me please." She subsided on to the silken coverlet of the bed.

"Can I fetch you anything?" I asked. "I have no potions with me, but perhaps I could ask Mrs. McDuff to send up a soothing cordial."

She shook her head and buried her face in her pillow. I left the room quietly and descended the stairs. Holmes was no longer in the withdrawing room.

It turned out he had been talking to the same dour housekeeper.

"It was like trying to squeeze water from a stone," as he told me later.

"Even though it was she who summoned us to the house?"

"Yes, that is interesting, isn't it?" He paused. "From what she said, it became clear, finally, that she was utterly devoted to her master, and rather less to her mistress."

"I think that even I could have deduced that much," I said. "To be sure, she was in love with Mr. Ballantyne."

"Ah, you are ever the romantic. But what of Mr. McDuff, then?"

"Is there such a person?"

"There is, indeed." He looked at me quizzically. "The lady's father. Currently resident in Fife."

"I see. The 'Mrs.' is a title of convenience."

"Yes, but she is considerably older than her employer. Perhaps her feelings might be said to be more maternal than amorous."

"Still, she heartily dislikes his wife."

"That might be putting it too strongly. I get the impression that she considers young Hélène a silly goose, far too frivolous for such a man as Mr. Ballantyne."

"Perhaps that was what he liked about her, Holmes. Given the strange ways of the heart and all that."

"Again, I bow to your better wisdom on such matters."

He was teasing me again.

"Unforthcoming as she was in general, however, she was happy to tell me that the couple have separate bedrooms." He looked at me. "As you must have noticed just now."

"Yes. That's true." I described the arrangements, adding Mrs. Ballantyne's explanation as to why it was like that.

Holmes made no comment.

"What of the secretary?" I asked. "Does he come into the picture at all, do you think?"

Holmes regarded me with even more amusement. "You are determined that he should be in love with Hélène Ballantyne, and that perhaps the strength of his feelings led him to an extreme. Let me see . . . Ah, yes. Either to kill the woman who had rejected him, or the husband who stood in his way?"

I had to admit that such thoughts had indeed crossed my mind, the young man's arrival that morning being rather too much of a coincidence.

"But what a dangerous proceeding in that case," Holmes continued. "The plan might have misfired terribly, with the wrong person slain. Still, we won't rule out Mr. Page entirely. There is something about him that raises questions in my mind. I don't think he has been completely honest with me."

"In what way?"

"He claims to have arrived with papers for Mr. Ballantyne to go over this morning, and yet did you notice what the corpse was wearing?"

I tried to remember: Nothing out of the ordinary, surely.

Holmes cut in on my musings somewhat impatiently. "He was dressed as if preparing to go out. In addition, Mrs. McDuff had been quite taken aback at the arrival of the secretary, which occurred shortly after the terrible event, for Mr. Ballantyne had said nothing to her about it. This, she said, would have been most unusual, for he was generally very precise in his arrangements. She had assumed that he was preparing to set out for the office after breakfast as was his custom. When I challenged Mr. Page on the matter, he mumbled that there must have been a misunderstanding. He showed me the papers he had brought, as if they proved anything, except to give him an excuse to be there."

"Then you think he came to see the lady."

"Or perhaps the maidservant, Claudine. Surely it hasn't escaped your notice that the maid is quite as fetching as her mistress."

"Ah."

"Perhaps you are too smitten with *la belle Hélène* to notice." He waved a dismissive hand in the air. "In any case, we will leave Lestrade to pursue the matter for now. Let us go home and finish our own breakfast, for I find I am suddenly very hungry."

Time passed, as time is wont to do. Lestrade seemed to believe that cousin Adolphe was the key to everything. However, the boy was nowhere to be found, neither in London, nor Edinburgh, nor even at his home in Lille, his very elusive nature, in the eyes of the inspector, underlining his guilt.

"If he is innocent, then why is he hiding, Mr. Holmes?" Lestrade remarked, standing one morning in front of our fireplace. "I am inclined to Mrs. Ballantyne's view that it was a prank that went disastrously wrong – for why would young Adolphe want to hurt his cousin? And now the lad is terrified out of his wits."

"Hmm," Holmes said. "You may be right, Lestrade." He drew on his pipe as if utterly bored with the subject.

Meanwhile, I was keeping my promise to Hélène Ballantyne to be a friend to her. It wasn't an onerous undertaking by any means. There was, after all, something in Holmes's earlier insinuations, though to say I was "smitten" was going too far. I enjoyed her company, especially when she forgot her troubles and shewed herself to be the lively young woman of our first acquaintance. To distract her from her sorrows, I would meet her in Wimbledon to take tea (or coffee in the lady's case) in one of the delightful establishments in the village, or if the weather was fine to go for walks on the Common. She had a true love of nature, explaining that, growing up in an industrial city, she now revelled in the delights of the countryside.

"Yet you miss Edinburgh," I said.

"But in Edinburgh, you always have nature nearby. The times I have climbed Arthur's Seat or taken a turn in the Meadows or even in the Botanical Gardens!"

Another time I asked how she had met her husband. For an instant she looked stricken at the painful memory, then rallied.

"My papa has business interests in Scotland. I accompanied him one time and liked it so much I prevailed upon him to let me stay on there to learn English. Don't you think I have a 'fine wee Scots accent'?" Her face lit up. "The nuns in the school were horribly strict, but we were occasionally allowed to go out to cultural events – the theatre and so on. Oh, how I love the theatre!" She clapped her hands together. "I was even thinking of becoming an actress, though papa would have been terribly shocked! But I took part in some of the school plays, you know. It was such fun. I was Helen in *Women of Troy* once." She smiled at the memory. "But you asked about Ramsay. I met him through one of papa's associates at a reception in the French Consulate. It was quite the whirlwind romance, as they say."

Perhaps the fact that I found it hard to reconcile such a whirlwind with the serious gentleman I had met shewed on my face, for Hélène, as I had come to call her at her request, laughed merrily.

"Oh, but you have a saying in English, do you not, that still waters run deep." We were walking on the Common at the time, and she took my arm. "Ramsay was like that, and I think it is the same with you, Jean."

Good heavens! I admit that I was much attracted to her, but she was a widow of only a month or so, still in the black weeds that suited her so well. On the other hand, I mused, she was French.

Let me state now that I remained, and remain still, devoted to the memory of my dear late wife. However, Mary would have been the last person on earth to begrudge me happiness. One day I might expect to remarry and maybe even to raise a family, although I wasn't anticipating anything of the sort so soon and in such a way. Now I was conscious of Hélène's closeness, the light scent of her lavender water, the touch of her little hand on my arm, the faintest pressure of her breast. My heart started to beat faster. Was this then what was meant by a whirlwind romance?

"You are silent," she said. "I hope I haven't offended you, Jean."

"Not at all," I replied, a little shakily, and we talked thereafter of more inconsequential matters.

I hadn't divulged to Holmes the extent of my involvement with the lady, but no doubt he suspected it.

"A good thing you are looking after her," he said one day. "It is strange, though."

"What is?"

"Well, since the death of her husband, Mrs. Ballantyne has not, to my knowledge at least, received any further threatening letters, nor indeed any unpleasant parcels. It is possible, of course, that she has simply omitted to inform us. You might ask her about it, the next time you meet her. I hardly think the danger can have passed so completely."

To tell the truth, that she might yet be attacked had quite escaped my mind, and I chided myself for the oversight. When I put the matter to her at the earliest opportunity, she became thoughtful. We were sitting in Wimbledon's pleasant little Cherry Tree Café, with its flowery wallpaper and pretty cups, a favourite place of hers. She particularly loved their cakes, and was daintily partaking of a slice of Victoria sponge, using a small two-pronged fork to carry each bite to her lips.

"Mr. Holmes is right," she said finally, putting down the fork. "It is indeed strange. Of course, if Adolphe or another is behind it all, they are possibly too shocked at the fatal outcome to pursue their vendetta."

"So now you think Adolphe may have had a sinister motive after all?"

"Oh, Jean, I don't know what to think any more." She pushed her plate away. "My appetite is quite spoiled."

Of course, I apologised profusely. She forgave me, and even finished her cake. I forbore to tell her of the tiny blob of cream on the corner of her mouth, it looked so charming.

A few days later I called back to the house as arranged. The lady had taken a fancy to go on an excursion to the famous windmill. I confess that I was rather neglecting my medical obligations, and Holmes too, who, however, seemed caught up in some new study, for he was preoccupied with his Bunsen burner and stinking vials, and hardly acknowledged my frequent departures.

On being shewn into the withdrawing room by Claudine – and yes, I could agree that she too was very pretty – I found Hélène still in her blue morning robe.

"Oh, Jean, I am so lazy this morning. Forgive me."

"Of course," I said. "We can postpone our outing."

"No, no. I will get dressed in a moment. But, Jean dear, I was delighted to receive your gift. Thank you so much. How did you know they are my favourites?"

My gift? I had sent no gift. I espied an open box of chocolates upon the table. A sudden shiver went through me.

"I hope to God you haven't eaten any," I said.

"No, my dear. I was waiting for you." She picked up the box and offered it to me.

"Hélène, they aren't from me. I didn't send them."

She stared at me in shock, dropping the box. The confections rolled over the carpet.

"Oh, *mon Dieu*," she cried. "They are from *him! – The killer!*"

I started to pick them up, carefully, replacing each one in its little paper bed.

"We must get them analysed," I told her. "It's very possible they are poisoned. Where is the wrapping in which they came?"

She called for Claudine and gave her rapid instructions in French. The girl nodded and disappeared off, soon returning with the papers. The address had been printed as before, though the hand and ink looked to be different, no doubt to avoid raising suspicions in the lady's mind.

"Why did you think they were from me?" I asked.

She shewed me a card. It read simply, "*Sweets to a sweet, J.*" Far too sentimental to be something I would ever have written.

Of course, there was no more talk of windmills that day.

"With your permission, Hélène," I said, "I will take all this to Holmes. He has the means to analyse the chocolates. Let us hope we are fearful for nothing, and that they are harmless."

"Perhaps." She looked very small and vulnerable, and I longed to be able to comfort her further.

I instructed her to stay home and told Claudine to keep an eye on her. The girl had been promoted to housekeeper, since Mrs. McDuff hadn't wished to stay on after the death of her master. In any case, I don't think Hélène would have let her.

Instead of looking concerned, Holmes surprised me by rubbing his hands together gleefully, exclaiming, "Ha! I expected as much!"

He set to immediately to analyse the chocolates, cutting each one in half carefully, extracting a small crumb and placing it into a vial containing clear liquid. He then added a drop of another solution from a pipette, shook it and observed the reaction. The first six so tested proved to be unadulterated, and his good humour waned somewhat.

"I have better hopes of this one, Watson," he said at last, examining the seventh. "See, there's a tiny puncture mark underneath."

Surely he shouldn't hope to find anything. Still, Holmes had his notions and I kept silent. At last, his investigation done, he turned to me in triumph, holding up the vial. The liquid within had turned bright red.

"Cyanide."

"My God."

"Of course, no one was meant to eat it."

I looked at him, uncomprehending.

He sighed. "I have to apologise to you, dear friend."

"Why, Holmes? In what way?"

"I am afraid I have used you cruelly."

"I don't understand."

"Of course, I suspected the woman from the start. But how to prove it? I had to make use of your affections, in order to trap her."

A chill of fear overcame me.

"Hélène?"

He nodded. "It was almost unforgiveable of me, I know. But the woman is a monster. She and her accomplice."

"Frederick Page?"

"Not at all. That poor fool was another dupe, summoned, not as he thought, by Ballantyne but by his employer's wife, in a crude attempt to confuse. No, her accomplice was her sister, Claudine Dutoit."

I suppose my mouth dropped open, for Holmes couldn't help but chuckle.

"Oh, my poor Watson. How I have left you out of things. The women thought they were being so clever, but Claudine didn't even use a false name. An application to Lille soon revealed that Hélène and Claudine are siblings. Indeed, did it not strike you that they look very alike?"

"But how could you know about the chocolates?"

"I deliberately mentioned the lack of further suspicious packages to you because I knew it would get back to the lady, and that she would be likely to act quickly to avoid, as she would think, suspicion falling upon her. I therefore commissioned young Wiggins to activate the Baker Street Irregulars and keep an eye on both Mrs. Ballantyne and Claudine, which they did admirably."

The Irregulars were a gang of street urchins whose ability to blend with the crowd had enabled them frequently to assist Holmes in his investigations.

He popped a chocolate into his mouth. I started.

"Fear not. It is one I have already tested and found harmless. He pushed the box towards me, but I shook my head, shuddering.

"You will have noticed the name on the box, that of a well-known chocolatier in Piccadilly. Wiggins followed Mrs. Ballantyne there and observed her purchasing it, getting a clout on the ear by the doorman for his trouble." Holmes chuckled. "A necessary hazard for which I reimbursed the lad well. Anyway, the lady returned home and, early the next morning, Claudine was followed by one of Wiggins's foot soldiers to the General Post Office near Charing Cross, where he observed her posting a parcel of a similar size to the box of chocolates. You see the animal cunning of the pair, acting out the charade far from home."

"They poisoned the chocolates themselves and then sent the box to themselves?"

"Precisely."

"But how did you come to suspect them? Hélène seemed so genuinely upset at her husband's death. Indeed, it might have been she who was bitten by the snake. As you said before, a great risk to take."

"Another charade, my friend. Did you not tell me of her predilection for amateur dramatics? I strongly suspect that Ramsay Ballantyne didn't die of a snake bite at all, but, as I think a full autopsy will discover, of the same cyanide used in these chocolates. The symptoms being similar, the doctor would have had no reason to doubt but that the swamp adder caused the victim's death, particularly given the mark on the neck, probably made while the man was dying by something like a small two-pronged fork. I noticed such an item on the breakfast table."

I felt sick to the heart, and sank into my chair. A two-pronged fork – just like the one with which the cold-hearted woman had used to eat her cream cake.

Holmes continued. "To be sure, I prevailed upon Lestrade to let me examine the snake more thoroughly, and found it was certainly already dead before its head was smashed in."

I was angry with Holmes, though I supposed I could understand why he had kept me in the dark. He wished to use me to trap the murderers but couldn't trust me, if I knew all, to act out my part convincingly.

"But why should she do it? She had been married to the man for five years. Why now?"

"Life in Edinburgh was gay. No doubt a merry round of parties, dinners, concerts, theatres, of flirtations even, while the older husband, immersed in his work, indulged his pretty bride. Then they move here, where there is nothing to distract her. She is bored to death, with a man who has turned out to be far from the passionate lover of her favoured reading matter. I imagine she only married him to escape from the strictures of the convent school."

That thought had occurred to me too.

"She starts to think that life would be better as a rich widow," Holmes went on, "no doubt again getting ideas from the sensational novels to which she is partial. She calls for her sister to come over from France to pretend to be her maid, and eventually share the loot. Did you know that Claudine only started working for her recently, after the couple moved to London? They hatch the plan, thinking themselves terribly clever. I can only imagine the shock when you and I turned up, though the lady disguised it well. She had thought only to be dealing with plodding London policemen, and not the foremost private detective in Britain."

Preening himself, he took another chocolate. I hadn't known him to have a sweet tooth before, though I understand that particular brand of the confection is highly valued by connoisseurs. At that moment, to tell the truth, I felt so darkly about the whole business that I could have almost wished he would take a poisoned one by mistake. Not to die, of course, but to be sick. He had used me very badly.

"My heart is broken," I said.

"Nonsense. Your heart is perfectly intact. Anyway, the baggage would have thrown you over as soon as you had outlived your usefulness." He laughed. "You know I am right. If you really want a new wife, find yourself a nice comfortable woman, nearer your own age, one you can trust. One who won't put poison in your cup of Darjeeling. Or preferably, stay a contented bachelor, like myself."

Was he contented? It wasn't an adjective I should readily apply to him. Only sometimes, when he played his violin, did I guess him to be perfectly at one with himself and with the world.

We conveyed our discoveries to Lestrade, and duly accompanied him and his team to Wimbledon where we found the sisters blamelessly playing cards together.

"Jean," Hélène said, rising up, and looking in puzzlement at my companions. "I fear you have found something amiss with the chocolates. Is it so? Thank God, neither of us ate any of them."

How she was transformed, moments later from the sweet, pretty young woman before us. When faced with the truth, she became a snarling maenad, and cursed me and Holmes in a French which I imagine would never be found in school books. Claudine, for her part, shewed no sisterly solidarity, but tried to make out that she had nothing to do with the affair, that she was as astonished as the rest of us. But soon the pair of them turned on each other, each maintaining her own comparative innocence. They were taken away still screaming.

"You know, Watson, what first alerted me, by association of ideas, to the lady's involvement," Holmes said, that evening as we sat over glasses of a fine port wine. I had decided to forgive him, for after all a friendship like ours is to be cherished above a passing fancy. "It was," he said, "the arachnid."

I waited for him to expand.

"*Steatoda nobilis*. Known in English as the 'False Widow Spider'. Cheers."

He laughed, and we clinked glasses.

The Adventure of the Silk Scarf

by Terry Golledge

Sherlock Holmes was never an easy person to persuade that, although his powers of observation and deduction were far superior to those of most other people, his body was subject to the same laws as were lesser mortals. It was therefore to my relief and satisfaction that he gave in to my urgings to spend the night at a very comfortable hotel in the pleasant Kentish town of Sevenoaks. He had brought to a successful conclusion the gruesome murder of the Hopfield murderer, thereby saving Inspector Griffin from a mistake that could have blighted the remainder of his career.

We were sitting in the smoking room over brandy and cigars, having enjoyed a most excellent meal, with Holmes more relaxed than I had seen him for many weeks, He was chaffing me over my concern for his health and well-being, and I was happy to have him in such good spirits.

"I do vow, Watson, no mother hen clucks more assiduously over her chicks than do you over myself," he observed.

"Ah, but you must understand that I have a double responsibility. Firstly as a medical man and then as a friend, so I must be doubly watchful."

"And thirdly," he said with a chuckle, "should anything happen to deprive you of my company, you would be unable to afford to remain at our present address on your own."

"Really, Holmes!" I exploded. "That is a most outrageous remark, and not a matter for levity."

He was instantly contrite and spoke in a conciliatory tone. "Forgive me, my dear fellow. I do appreciate your concern and know your advice is of the best, even if I do not always follow it. But wait – I see we have a visitor,"

I turned my head to see the solid figure of Inspector Griffin bearing down on us. He was out of uniform and, in his suit of heavy tweed, he looked the very model of a country squire.

"Good evening, gentlemen," he said as he neared us. "I hope I don't intrude?"

"On the contrary, Inspector," smiled Holmes. "Your arrival is most opportune. I fear that without your advent, the good Doctor was about to consign me to bed for my health's sake. I count you a veritable saviour."

"Pay no attention to him, Inspector," I said when he looked blank. "He is in a puckish mood tonight and will take nothing seriously. Let me get you a glass of this fine brandy, for I see you are off duty."

I rang for the waiter and Griffin sank back into a deep armchair across from Holmes and me. He said nothing until our order had been fulfilled, and even then seemed to take an inordinate time to get his cigar drawing to his satisfaction.

Holmes eventually gave him an opening. "I divine, Inspector, that your visit here isn't just for social purposes?"

Griffin fingered his moustache and spoke apologetically. "Well, sir, I must confess to an ulterior motive, and I hope you will not take it amiss or think me presumptuous in seeking your counsel."

Holmes waved his hand. "Feel free to speak, I beg you."

"The fact is I have been asked to find a missing person, but as the person concerned is of age and seems to have disappeared of her own free will, there is nothing I can do in my official capacity."

"Then what is your problem?" Holmes asked with a frown,

"Let me put the whole story to you. I was approached this evening by Major-General Romney, who resides at Brent Croft, Foxford. That is about four miles from the town off the London Road. He bought the property some six years ago on his retirement from the army." Griffin took a sip from his glass. "The household consists of the General and his wife, his daughter Ellen, and the usual complement of servants, among them his former batman Ted Lennard, who is valet, groom, orderly, and self-appointed bodyguard. The daughter is a handsome girl of twenty-three, engaged to a Mr. Peter Witham, whose grounds of Witham Court adjoin the General's. I should add that Mrs. Romney is the General's second wife, and is some years his junior." Here the inspector paused as ash from his cigar dropped on to his waistcoat. He brushed it away and proceeded with his account.

"Some time after tea yesterday, Miss Romney took it into her head to vanish from home, leaving only a short note for her father. In it, she stated that she needed to be alone to resolve a problem, and he wasn't to worry about her. Her fiancé knew nothing of this until late last night when the General's man was sent to make inquiries of him, and also in the village, all to no avail. General Romney waited throughout today for some news or communication, and having neither, he called on me late this afternoon to obtain my help, I pointed out that the girl was of age and therefore a free agent, and as there was no evidence of foul play or coercion, I could take no official steps. Being an old soldier, he understood I was bound by rules and regulations, but he is an influential man, being a magistrate and a member of the police committee. I knew that if I could help him it would do my career no harm, and I hinted that I might be in a position to give him unofficial assistance. To be blunt, sir, I had you in mind, knowing you to be staying here tonight. If I have presumed too much on such short acquaintance don't hesitate to reprimand me, but if you can see your way to speaking to the General, I shall be eternally grateful and forever in your debt."

Holmes studied the policeman thoughtfully before replying.

"As you are aware, Inspector, although I'm a professional man and look to my fees for a living, I only accept cases with intriguing or unusual features, which your problem doesn't obviously have."

Griffin's face fell, but before he could speak Holmes continued.

"However, in view of our pleasant and fruitful association of the past few days, and taking into account the fact that Watson will be more than pleased if I spend more time away from the polluted atmosphere of London, I see no reason to turn down your request. Who knows – we may find more meat on the bone than is apparent at first sight." The inspector leaned across to grasp my friend's hand.

"Bless you, Mr. Holmes!" he said fervently. "You have taken a weight from my mind, and I appreciate it."

"Do not count your chickens, Inspector Griffin. There may be no more to the matter than appears on the surface, but at least I shall breathe more of your sweet country air while keeping my mind active, eh, Watson?"

I knew any objections I might make would be brushed aside, and I contented myself with a grunt as Holmes at once became business-like.

"Have you given me all the facts as you know them?" he asked.

"I have related all that passed between me and the General not two hours since. I cannot vouch for the General telling me every detail."

"It is too late to do much tonight," Holmes reflected. "Can you arrange for us to meet General Romney in the morning? I prefer it to at his house, as the trail must begin there." Griffin nodded and my friend went on. "Meanwhile, if you will be good enough to impart all you know of the Romneys, I shall have something on which to ponder."

The inspector looked round to ensure we weren't overheard and began slowly as he arranged his facts.

"As I said, the General came to Brent Croft on his retirement, which I understand was hastened by the death of his first wife. The present Mrs. Romney was the widow of an officer killed in the Zulu Wars, and is a good thirty years younger than the General. They were married soon after his retirement, and as you may guess, the marriage gave the local gossips a field day. If Miss Ellen had any feelings towards a much younger woman taking her mother's place, she gave no sign of it, and they have always appeared to be on the best of terms." Here the inspector paused to take out a stubby pipe, accepting the pouch offered by me with a nod of thanks. We all lit up and a blue haze soon hovered over our heads.

Griffin took up his tale again. "The indoor servants number four: A cook-housekeeper, a housemaid, a parlour maid who also attends Mrs. Romney, and the General's man Ted Lennard, of whom I spoke earlier. He occupies a privileged position, having served his master since the war in the Crimea, and subsequently during the Mutiny and all the other campaigns in which the old man was involved. Rumour has it that he isn't overly fond of the present Mrs. Romney, but naturally, the General wouldn't countenance any show of disrespect from him,"

"You are remarkably well informed," Holmes put in.

Griffin smiled and permitted himself a wink. "I owe that to George Izzard, the village constable. I allow him a certain amount of discretion on his patch, but I insist he keeps me posted on events in the village. I don't use him as a spy," he hastened to add, "but I do like to be forewarned of any likely trouble. Not that we have much, apart from the occasional bout of fisticuffs outside The White Horse on a Saturday night, and a little not-too-serious poaching."

"You have said nothing of the missing girl's fiancé, Peter Witham," remarked Holmes. "Is he well-thought-of in the neighbourhood?"

"He inherited Witham Court on the deaths of his father and older brother from typhoid." Inspector Griffin's tone was neutral. "Until then, he lived in chambers in London, and I understand he was regarded as something of a Champagne Charlie. He looks to have settled down since coming in to the estate, although he still spends a considerable amount of time in London. The General seems to accept him as a potential son-in-law, having shown marked disapproval over a previous suitor for his daughter's hand. That was John Paxton, a not-very-successful writer who lives with his mother on the edge of the village. As for Witham, my private information is that Ted Lennard has little regard for him, but my belief is that in Ted's view there is no man good enough for Miss Romney."

Holmes stood up and rubbed his hands. "Thank you, Inspector. You have painted a very clear picture of the situation, and I assure you that it will receive my very best attention. You will arrange for us to meet General Romney tomorrow morning?"

"Indeed I will. A message will be sent to him first thing, and I shall await you with a wagonette at nine o'clock if that suits."

"Excellent. Is accommodation available at Foxford?"

"Tom Rudge at The White Horse keeps a good house, and his wife is renowned for her table."

"Then Watson and I will bring our bags, and should it be necessary to spend another night in your pleasant countryside, we shall stay there. Now we will bid you goodnight."

We watched the inspector's departing back and my companion turned to me with a smile.

"The very best type of police officer, Watson," he said. "Would that we had more of the same kind. Now I shall seek my room and over a pipe or two reflect what may be drawn from this apparently mundane affair. Sleep well, old friend."

Holmes was in a pensive mood at breakfast, but later as we stood on the hotel steps to enjoy the first pipe of the day he turned to me.

"You have more experience of the fairer sex than I, Watson. Here we have a young lady whom to the best of our knowledge has a happy home and is engaged to an apparently worthy gentleman of her own choice. Why does she suddenly take it into her head to disappear, leaving only a brief note to her father indicating that some problem is exercising her and no word to her fiancé?"

The same thought had occurred to me as I lay in bed trying to apply my friend's methods to such information as we had, and I could only arrive at one conclusion.

"It could be that she is having some doubts in respect of her prospective marriage, and wishes to review her feelings with no pressure being brought to bear upon her."

"Quite so. Your reasoning is faultless as far as it goes – but what has encouraged such doubts? Are they newly risen, or have they been harboured for a period? If the former, what recent event is responsible? If they are of long standing, is there a connection with her previous suitor, the one discouraged by the General? Did she – ?"

"Steady on, Holmes!" I protested. "One question at a time. You have chided me often enough on the folly of speculation unsupported by facts."

"Indeed I have, and rightly so, but my questions are rhetoric and merely indicate that they must be asked and answered before we can begin to proceed to a theory. But here is the inspector, and it may be we can think of further questions during our journey."

On arriving at Brent Croft, a trim parlour maid conducted us to a large comfortable study, book-lined and smelling of leather and cigars – obviously the old soldier's retreat. The General, a broad upright figure with a closely trimmed white moustache standing out in his mahogany features, rose from a deep armchair to be introduced to us by Griffin.

"Of course I have heard of you, Mr. Holmes," he said in a clipped voice. "I gather Dr. Watson is an old frontier campaigner, as well as being your chronicler and confidant." He invited us to be seated. "I'm grateful for your interest in my daughter's disappearance, and you will not find me ungenerous toward your efforts."

Holmes frowned. "Let us be quite clear on this, General: My fees reflect the time spent and the difficulty of the task and aren't variable, unless I decide for my own reasons to waive them altogether."

The General flushed under his tan. "I crave your pardon, sir," he said stiffly. "I had no intention of patronising you, but this matter is disturbing for me, and I spoke thus out of anxiety."

Holmes acknowledged the apology and came straight to the point, his tone brisk as he asked his questions.

"Tell me, General, what positive steps have you taken to trace your daughter's movements since Sunday night?"

"When she didn't return yesterday, I sent a telegram to my sister in Surbiton inquiring if she had received any visit or communication from Ellen. They are very fond of each other and my daughter stayed with her aunt for some months after the death of her mother. The answer was negative, and having no other relatives or close friends to whom she might have gone, I could think of nothing further than to consult the good Inspector Griffin. He explained the official position, but thankfully he prevailed on you to offer your services."

"I understand you made inquiries of your daughter's fiancé, and also in the village, without success."

"My first steps. Now Lennard, my factotum, has on his own initiative taken the dog-cart to ask at the railway stations if she had been observed on Sunday evening. You may be aware that we are distanced almost equally from two stations, and she is well-enough known to have been noticed if she had purchased a ticket from either."

Holmes stroked his chin and looked at the older man. "Tell me, General, did anything suggest to you that your daughter wasn't in her usual spirits?"

The General considered this for a few moments before speaking, frowning as he strove for recollection,

"Let me see," he said slowly. "On Sunday she went to evening service at the village church. We had all been to morning service, but I'm sorry to confess that I find one helping of our vicar as much as I can digest in one week. I had retired to this den of mine where I was putting the finishing touches to my memoirs, which I hope to publish next year. The time was well past nine when my eyes told me I had done enough and I went to the drawing room just before my wife came in. She said it was such a beautiful night that she had taken a walk in the grounds, and the maid told me that Ellen had gone to her room directly after coming in from church, and that was the last time she was seen by any of us."

Holmes steepled his fingers, his eyes narrowing in thought. "Tell me, sir, exactly what steps you have so far taken, in the greatest detail. There is another point which may prove to be vitally important: How was it possible for her to leave the premises unbeknown to anyone?"

"Her room is in a passage to the left of the stairs, while the rooms of myself, my wife, and my man are to the right. When she failed to come down to dinner, I sent the maid up to see if she had fallen asleep, but her room was empty."

"What time was that?"

"We dine at seven, so it would have been a few minutes after that. A back staircase leads to the yard and stables, and if the servants were busy in the kitchen, it would have been easy for her to slip out unobserved had she so desired."

"Has she done that before?"

"Not to my knowledge. Why should she?"

Holmes shrugged the question aside. "Then the hours between four o'clock and dinnertime at seven must be our starting point. The sun sets a few minutes after seven, so it is reasonably light for half-an-hour after that. Inspector Griffin tells me that you made some inquiries as to whether she had been seen in the village, or by Mr. Witham."

"That is so, but with no result. Young Witham was as much in the dark as the rest of us. It wasn't until later that I found this note addressed to me. It was on my dressing table."

The General took an envelope from his pocket, passing it to Holmes, who inspected it closely before removing the single sheet of paper within.

"There is no doubt that this is Miss Romney's hand?" asked Holmes.

"I would recognize it anywhere," the General said firmly.

My companion began to read aloud the brief note:

Father Dear,

I must go away for a short while to consider a problem that only I can resolve. Please do not worry. I shall return very shortly.

All my love,
Ellen

Holmes produced his magnifying glass and subjected the letter to an intense scrutiny before passing the paper and lens to me.

"What do you make of it, Watson?" I looked at him reproachfully, knowing that whatever deductions I might make he would turn inside out.

However, I tried do my best not to seem too obtuse and applied myself to the task.

"Well, what do you see?" Holmes spoke sharply.

I passed the items back him. "Beyond the fact that it was written with a fine-nib pen on good quality paper, it tells us very little."

"Little enough," agreed Holmes, "As you say, it was written with a fine steel nib by someone who was under great stress and was acting on impulse. I would suggest that the ink used was Valkden's blue-black."

We all waited on further revelations and he quickly obliged.

"The type of nib is obvious, but if you examine the paper closely, you will observe that sufficient pressure was applied to cause parallel grooves on the down strokes. The users of fine pens are invariably light of touch. It is undated and the last line is paler, showing the use of blotting paper, which indicates haste and impulse, while the pressure of the pen leads me to deduce emotion and stress."

"That's all very clever," growled General Romney. "I concede that the paper and ink is ours, and the pen is of the kind favoured by my daughter, but does that bring us nearer to finding her?"

"Would you describe your daughter as an impulsive woman?"

"Indeed not. Neither would she procrastinate if a decision had to be made."

"Then it is reasonable to assume that something occurred just prior to her departure to precipitate it, and if we discover that occurrence, we have made a step forward,"

At this juncture, there was a knock on the study door and the pretty parlour maid entered hesitantly. Behind her loomed the burly figure of a police constable, ruddy and perspiring, his helmet under his arm.

"Please sir," said the girl, "George – Mr. Izzard – says he must speak to the inspector. I told him he was engaged with you, but he won't take no for an answer."

Griffin rose with a word of apology and glared at the constable. "This had better be important, Izzard. Out with it, man."

"Beggin' your pardon, sir, I think I should speak to you alone."

Izzard fixed his superior with a hard look.

The inspector hesitated, then turned to us deprecatingly. "Will you excuse me, gentlemen?" He followed the policeman from the room, returning some few minutes later with a sombre expression. When he spoke it was as though a bomb had exploded in our midst.

"A most terrible thing has occurred," he said tightly. "Mr. Peter Witham has been found dead in the woods adjoining his estate, almost certainly murdered. I know nothing beyond that, but Miss Romney must be found and apprised of the tragedy. I can now take official action in the search for her, but I hope I may still look for your co-operation, Mr. Holmes?"

"Most certainly," replied my friend. He turned to the General who was sitting rigidly in his chair. "When do you expect your man to get back from his inquiries, sir?"

The old soldier took a grip on himself. "If he had news from Shoreham, he would have been back half-an-hour since. I assume he drew a blank there and went on to Otford. We may expect him soon. He drives the dog-cart at a fair clip."

"I shall await him," said Holmes. "Proceed to your duties, Inspector, but disturb nothing until I join you."

Griffin gave my companion a hard look. "As you say, Mr. Holmes. You will find the place? It is on the path near the stile where a hedge divides the Witham estate from the General's."

"Someone will show me, but I reiterate, nothing must be disturbed before I arrive, do you understand?" As the door closed on Inspector Griffin, an angry snort came from the General.

"Damnation, man, you take a cavalier attitude towards Griffin. Were I in his place, I would consign you to Hell."

Holmes eyed him coldly. "General Romney, I wouldn't presume to question your military judgement. Pray extend the same courtesy to me. What was a domestic inquiry has now become a criminal matter in which my expertise has been sought, and I must apply my own methods."

The old man bowed his head. "I beg your pardon, sir. I have a high regard for Inspector Griffin and wouldn't otherwise have spoken thus. You must proceed in your own way, of course." He looked up. "I believe I hear the dog-cart outside. Perhaps Lennard has some news for us."

Very shortly a perfunctory knock on the door was followed by the entry of a stocky well set-up man. He ignored Holmes and me and spoke directly to the General.

"Otford, sir. Eight-thirty-four to Holborn Viaduct. Could have changed at Bromley for Victoria. Sunday night, that was."

"Thank you, Lennard. You have done well. Meanwhile we have had some terrible news. Mr. Witham has been found dead in the woods between our properties – murdered, by all accounts. I have only the bare facts. These gentlemen are Mr. Sherlock Holmes and Dr. Watson, who were asked to help find Miss Ellen and now assist Inspector Griffin in his investigation in finding the perpetrator of this foul crime." The manservant's leathery face was expressionless, showing no sign of shock or even surprise at the news. He stood waiting for the General to issue instructions.

"Mr. Holmes wishes to question you," said the latter. "Answer him as truthfully as you would me."

The man turned to look at Holmes with eyes that bordered on insolence.

"Ask away, Mister, if the General says so, but I don't know nothing about Mr. Witham."

"We shall see," said Holmes, clearly nettled by the man's attitude. "You say Miss Romney caught the eight-thirty-four from Otford. Who told you?"

"It was Bert Carter, the booking clerk. He remembers the time, as he'd just bagged up his small change and Miss Ellen had nothing smaller than a sovereign, so he had to count it all out again."

"What condition was she in? Composed? Agitated?"

"Bert noticed nothing amiss, but she was heavily veiled."

"How would she have reached the station? Obviously you didn't drive her, and nothing has been said of any carriage being taken."

"She must have walked. Taken her about an hour or so. She had a small travelling bag with her, so Bert says."

"Where were you between tea and dinner on Sunday night?" Holmes's voice was suddenly sharp.

"Me?" Lennard scowled. "I saw to the mare and washed the trap, then went to the kitchen for a cup of tea and a chat with Mrs. Hodge, the cook. At six or just after, I brought the General a whisky-and-soda water in here. Then I went up to lay out his mess-kit for dinner. After he'd dressed and I'd tidied up, I went back to the kitchen for my own dinner, and it was about half-after-seven I first heard Miss Ellen was missing."

"Were you surprised?"

"Worried and surprised. It was never Miss Ellen's way to be less than considerate towards others, She'd never give no one trouble. Anyway, I had a word with the General, and he sent me off to ask Mr. Witham if he'd seen her, He said he'd brought her home from church in the morning and didn't expect to see her until he come to dinner Tuesday."

"That is correct," the General affirmed. "He was going to London yesterday morning and expected to stay overnight."

"He still intended to go despite his fiancé's mysterious absence?" My friend sounded incredulous. "He made no further effort to ascertain if she had returned or sent a message?"

"No doubt he had his reasons." The old soldier sounded unconvinced by his own utterance and looked at Lennard appealingly.

"I called at Witham Court yesterday afternoon," said the latter quickly. "The housekeeper said she'd seen neither here nor hide of him since early morning when he went to catch the train."

"So you saw him on Sunday night, but not since?" The man nodded and Holmes continued. "You didn't think to inquire about him when you visited the stations?"

"Why should I? I was only concerned with Miss Ellen."

Before more could be said, we were joined by Inspector Griffin who exhibited a certain amount of impatience. "Mr. Holmes! How much longer must we wait? I have Dr. Marsh standing by to officially confirm death, although there is no question about it. He is a busy man and has living patients to attend to."

"A few minutes more, Inspector," my friend replied soothingly, then broke off as the door opened to admit a pretty fair-haired woman whom I adjudged to be some thirty years of age.

"Edward!" she cried with an edge to her voice. "Will you kindly tell me what is happening? You have been closeted with these people for more than an hour, and there is a policeman clumping about in the hall." She paused for breath. "I'm entitled to know what is going on in my house."

The General advanced to take her by the hand. "Inspector Griffin you know. These other gentlemen are Mr. Sherlock Holmes and Dr. Watson, who came to assist in finding Ellen. Brace yourself, my dear. We have lately received some terrible news."

"Not Ellen?" she gasped, wide-eyed.

"No, thank God, but tragic enough. Peter has been found dead in the lower wood – murdered."

As her husband finished speaking, the lady's face blanched and giving a low moan she crumpled to a senseless heap on the floor. I knelt down beside her and took one of her hands. It was cold and clammy, with the pulse shallow and rapid, as was her breathing.

"She is in a state of shock," I announced. "Have her put to bed and kept warm, with hot drinks when she regains consciousness, and send for her own doctor."

With the assistance of Lennard, I got her to her room, where we left. Mrs. Hodge and the parlour maid to get her into bed. When we came out, we were met by Holmes at the head of the stairs.

"General Romney has given me permission to inspect Miss Romney's room and any other parts of the house that I may so wish," he said to Lennard. "Will you be my guide?"

The man gave a surly nod and led us along the corridor to throw open a door at the opposite end. "This is Miss Ellen's," he said grudgingly. It was a light and airy chamber, feminine without being fussy. Holmes stood in the doorway before entering, his keen eyes taking in and recording everything. He then went to a small escritoire under the window and picked up a leather writing case which he examined under his lens.

103

"This is the only occupied room this side of the staircase?" he asked Lennard, who stood glowering at us suspiciously.

"The others are guest rooms. Miss Ellen did have the one corresponding to this on the other side, but when the new mistress came she took that, and Miss Ellen moved into here."

"Now show me the other rooms – without disturbing Mrs. Romney."

We went back to the other corridor, stopping at the third door. The end room, from which I had lately emerged, was Mrs. Romney's, and the chamber we now entered was obviously the master's. Holmes looked around and raised his eyebrows.

"I see there is no communicating door to Mrs. Romney's room," he said mildly.

"That's right," Lennard said sourly. He pointed. "That door there leads to the Guv'nor's dressing room, and another beyond to my billet."

Beyond a cursory glance around, Holmes showed little interest in the bedroom or dressing room, but on reaching the man's quarters he stared curiously. "You are snug enough here," he offered. "I don't think the other servants are so well provided for."

"They haven't been with the General for thirty-six years, nor campaigned over three continents with him," said Lennard proudly.

"I'm not criticising," smiled Holmes. "He is fortunate to command such devoted loyalty. I see you have some mementoes of your adventures." He indicated a collection of trivia displayed about the room.

"They've all got a story," said the man, his animosity falling away. "That lump of lead we found in the General's map-case at Inkerman – Major Romney he were then – and that wicked looking knife gutted his horse in the Ashanti fight in '73."

Holmes picked up a length of silk from beneath a chair and ran it through his hands. "Indian, of course."

Lennard's scowl returned as he nodded. "Took it off a Pandy at Meerut in '57. Mind you, I had to take his head off first. He come at us waving a *tulwar* with no good intentions." He took the scarf or turban from Holmes and draped it over two pegs on the wall.

"One last thing," said my companion. "Is it possible for anyone to pass along this corridor without you knowing, if you are in here?"

"Absolutely impossible. There is a floorboard that creaks whenever anyone passes, and I hear it, awake or sleeping."

Holmes frowned. "I didn't hear it. Did you, Watson?"

I shook my head. "Not a sound."

The manservant explained. "That's because a weight on the board in the passage makes it creak this end, right under the head of my bed. Let me show you." So saying he walked out into the passage and took a few steps in either direction. Sure enough, when he reached a certain point a faint creaking came from where he had described.

"Your own private alarm system," remarked Holmes as we joined Lennard outside. "Who knows of this?"

"Just me and the General, and now you two gents. I hope you'll keep it so. I don't want no one else in on it. I'd do anything for the Guv'nor, and for Miss Ellen too. Anything," he said passionately. "You don't think any harm has come to her, do you?"

Holmes looked him straight in the eye. "Not in the physical sense, but something occurred to worry her enough to make her need to be alone while she thought it over. If we knew what that was, we might know where to start looking."

The man's face was expressionless as he turned away. "Then if that's all, I must get back to the General. Do your best to find her, sir."

We followed him down the stairs where he turned into the study, and as the door closed on him, Holmes looked thoughtful.

"That man knows more than he is saying, Watson. I wonder what he's hiding? But come," he went on briskly. "The inspector grows restless."

The latter was indeed edgy and hurried us incontinently to the location of the crime, passing on the way an old and abandoned stone cottage. The stolid Constable Izzard stood on guard, and beside him a bearded man whom I at once recognized as a member of my own calling. Hovering in the background was a foxy-faced character wearing a corduroy jacket and moleskin trousers, both items which would have benefited from a wash, as indeed would have their wearer.

"Dr. Marsh," said the inspector in an apologetic tone, "I crave your pardon for the delay, but Mr. Sherlock Holmes," he indicated my friend, "is assisting me in this matter and was adamant that nothing should be disturbed until his arrival,"

"The blame is entirely mine, Dr. Marsh," Holmes put in smoothly. "It is imperative that I should examine the ground ere it is trampled over."

"I know you by repute, Mr. Holmes," replied Marsh stiffly. "No doubt this other gentleman is Dr. Watson. I hope I shall not be detained unnecessarily, for I'm a busy man."

"That I appreciate," said Holmes. He stood motionless, scanning the surroundings keenly before taking his lens and bending his lean frame to scrutinise the ground leading to where the body lay sprawled on its back, partly hidden in the undergrowth.

On reaching the dead man he dropped to his knees, his beaky nose inches from the corpse, all the while muttering under his breath.

Presently he stood up and beckoned to the police surgeon. "Make your examination, Doctor, but be good enough to follow precisely in my footsteps. Will you permit Dr. Watson to view the body with you?"

"Of course. Anything to hasten matters."

We approached cautiously to find ourselves gazing down on the corpse of a well-nourished man whose ghastly features and protruding tongue gave unmistakable evidence of the manner of his death.

"Not much doubt there, eh, Watson?" said Marsh as he set about his task. "Strangulation. Dead about twenty-four hours or a little over." He rose to his feet and brushed the knees of his trousers, eager to be about his rounds. "Nothing more you want from me, Inspector?"

"No, Doctor, except to ask you to look in on Mrs. Romney. I fear that this news on top of the mystery of her step-daughter's absence has been something of a shock to her."

Marsh had obviously been made aware of Ellen Romney's disappearance, and without comment gave us a curt nod and took his leave.

"Do you agree with the findings, Watson?" asked Holmes.

"As far as it goes," I said cautiously, not wanting to openly criticize a professional colleague, and earning myself a sharp look from Holmes.

"Who found the body?" he asked, "Was it you, Izzard?"

The constable shook his head. "No, sir. It was Joe Bennett here." He bent a dark look on the rough-looking man who stood nearby. "Says he was out for a walk and saw a boot sticking out from the bushes. More like he was up to no good setting snares. Tell the gentleman about it, Joe, and no nonsense."

Bennett looked as if to deny the accusation but thought better of it.

"Well, sir," he said in an injured tone, "like George says, I were just taking a morning stroll when I sees this boot. I grabbed hold and pulled, and out 'e pops. I could tell 'e were a goner, so I runs to get George Izzard afore he started 'is beat."

"You moved nothing after that?" Holmes queried, and got a shake of the head in response. "I didn't touch nothing neither, sir," offered Izzard. "Just took a quick look and came straight to the Croft where I knew Inspector Griffin was."

My companion nodded his approval. "Good man. Now, Watson, take a closer look at the body, and tell me truthfully what you see."

I knew he had detected my previous reticence, and this time I made pretence of a more thorough inspection, even though I knew what I had seen. I looked up to meet his sardonic eyes.

"Dr. Marsh's findings were correct as far as they went," I said slowly. "The man most certainly died of strangulation, but there is no evidence of finger or thumb marks that would have been apparent if it had been done manually, although there are signs of bruising around the front and sides of the neck. Therefore I deduce some other means was employed."

"You mean a rope or cord?" Griffin hazarded.

"I doubt it," said I, shooting a meaning look at Holmes,

"It's your body, Inspector," the latter put in. "What do you make of it?"

Inspector Griffin look mildly shacked by my companion's flippant tone, but collected himself and spoke thoughtfully. "Well, sir, the man was obviously strangled, and we have the word of two doctors on that. As Dr. Watson says, there is no evidence to suggest an assault with bare hands and rules out choking from internal sources, the bruising must be significant. If not a cord or rope, then what?" He paused and snapped his fingers. "I remember now! Some years ago when I was at Gravesend, I dealt with the case of a Spanish seaman who was strangled by one of his mess-mates using a length of window-cord. 'Garrotting', I believe they call it, and that left a distinct weal, just like a red necklace."

"Excellent!" cried Holmes. "You are right in every detail, except for the points you haven't yet had brought to your notice. Bear with me just a while longer, Inspector," he added as Griffin's face darkened. "I shall hide nothing from you, that I promise."

"We haven't searched his pockets," said the inspector. "Perhaps robbery was the motive, although I confess I find it hard to believe that any footpad would be here on the off-chance of finding a victim."

"Quite," said Holmes. "Nevertheless we may learn something from the contents that is of use, but not just yet."

He took his magnifying glass and commenced a systematic examination of the surrounding area, gradually widening his circles, pausing now and then as his eye was caught. Once he stooped to retrieve an object from the ground to slip into his pocket, and again to produce a pair of tweezers with which he delicately removed something invisible to us from a low branch of a bush. He returned to where we stood with an air of satisfaction and took Griffin by the arm. "There is nothing more to be discovered here, Inspector. Let me draw the picture for you," He led the other over the ground he had covered.

"We know that the killer was a fairly powerful man. Witham was of good physique, yet he made little attempt to defend himself. Just here on our right, as you will observe from the trodden state of the turf, is where the assailant lurked in wait, probably for more than a few minutes. He allowed his victim to pass, springing from behind to do his terrible work. When his object was achieved, which I deduce was very quickly, he dragged the body to where it was partially hidden before making off along the path, which is too well used to afford us any clue as to direction."

"But you discovered more than that," Griffin stated flatly.

"Indeed, but first let us see what the poor fellow's pockets may tell us, if anything."

The inspector set about the task, which yielded a sovereign case containing nine sovereigns and three half-sovereigns. There followed a cigar-case, a silver box of wax vestas, an assortment of silver and copper coins, and a small bunch of keys. In the corner of a waistcoat pocket, wrapped in tissue paper, was a handsome diamond ring, and from another came a slim silver watch which showed the correct time.

Holmes seized on the last item, opening the back to reveal the inscription *"To Peter with all my love"*. His face darkened, but he made no comment. Finally the inspector brought out a pocket-book, the only contents being a couple of bills and a letter. Griffin, after slowly reading the letter, stared at my companion open-mouthed. The latter took it from him, and over Holmes's shoulder I was able to read the few lines inscribed thereon. It was dated for Sunday and began without salutation or preamble:

> *I deem from this moment our engagement to be terminated. Your scandalous and despicable conduct has made it impossible for me to ever meet you again. You will not need me to specify the base conduct to which I refer, nor can I expose you without bringing pain and anguish to the one I love above all others. I pray that your sense of shame tells you to avoid meeting any of my family again, and that you have sufficient honour remaining to repent and mend your ways.*
>
> *Ellen Romney*

"That explains why she left in such a hurry," observed Griffin sagely.

"Not quite," Holmes demurred, "What was the scandalous conduct that led her to write the letter, and how is it connected with Witham's death?"

"So you think we must find the girl to get these answers?"

"Not necessarily, although she must be found sooner or later." He lapsed into deep thought, chin on chest and hands clasped behind him, only roused when the inspector asked if the body could be taken away.

"What? Oh, yes, of course," said Holmes absently.

Griffin had a whispered colloquy with Constable Izzard before joining Holmes and me, and then addressing my friend with an edge to his voice.

"Now, Mr. Holmes, you hinted at information which I don't share. If you will be so good as to let me in on it, I may possibly be bright enough to make something of it off my own bat. I welcome your co-operation, but I don't want to be made a fool of."

Holmes looked shocked. "My dear Inspector! Nothing is farther from my thoughts, but first I would ask you to examine this." He took out his pocket-book to reveal a yellow filament, so fine that a breath would have taken it away. "I removed it from a low bush adjacent to the body. What do you see?"

"Why, a thread of silk. Has it significance to our matter?"

Holmes fished in his pocket and produced a rough pebble, somewhat smaller than a golf ball. "And this? It was also close by, and the only one to be seen on the leafy mould."

Inspector Griffin stared at it, then shook his head despondently.

"Perhaps I'm not so bright after all. Explain, I beg you."

"Do not blame yourself. I may have missed the point had I not already had my wits jogged at Brent Croft. Tell me, Inspector: What do you know of *Thuggee*?"

Griffin removed his cap and scratched his head. "Very little, except that it was a form of murder once practised in India and we now apply the term of '*thug*' to any brutal and violent character,"

"Quite so. Strangulation was the Thugs' method, achieved by throwing a strip of cloth round the victim's throat to thus cut off his breath. A turban was the instrument employed and it could then be wound back on the head leaving no sign of a weapon. A few coins in the end of the cloth gave it weight so that when lashed at from behind the victim's throat was encircled as with a whip. Watson will bear me out, I think."

"That's true," I agreed. "But surely the sect was eliminated years ago? Are you suggesting a gang of Indians is operating here?"

The inspector's face lit up. "I think Mr. Holmes means that whoever did this employed the same tactics, and that pebble was the weight. It also implies that the silk thread was from the other part of the weapon, and the killer had some knowledge of this *Thuggee*."

Holmes didn't reply and Griffin stopped short to stare at him aghast.

"Good Lord!" gasped the latter. "Do you mean you suspect the General of this? Why, it's unthinkable! What reason could he have?"

"Reason enough if what I think is correct, but no, he isn't the only one who is familiar with the subcontinent,"

"You mean Lennard? But why? I know he had little regard for Witham as Miss Romney's fiancé, but surely he'd not take such drastic action?"

"I shall say no more until I have all the facts. You will see for yourself shortly. Then, if you have an alternative theory, don't hesitate to voice it. I have been wrong before. Norbury – eh, Watson?"

We strode on in silence until we once more stood in the entrance to Brent Croft. Our arrival coincided with the appearance of the station fly, from which alighted an elegantly dressed young woman carrying a small travelling case.

Griffin at once strode forward and addressed the woman sharply.

"Miss Romney! Wherever have you been?"

She drew herself up to look at him coldly. "I see no reason to account to you for my movements, Inspector. Have I committed some crime by making a journey without your permission?"

Griffin flushed. "I beg your pardon, miss, but your father has been extremely concerned by your unexplained absence and came to me for assistance. I in turn enlisted the help of this gentleman, Mr. Sherlock Holmes, who was aiding me in another matter. I'm sorry to say that since then events have taken a more tragic turn."

She reached out to grasp his arm. "My father!" she gasped.

He hastened to reassure her. "The General is quite well, miss, but it is bad enough. May we go into the house?"

She led us into a drawing room where she threw back her veil and looked at us from dark-shadowed eyes that showed signs of stress. Before she could ask the questions trembling on her lips, Holmes spoke.

"I think your first consideration, Miss Romney, must be to relieve your father of the anxiety engendered by your absence. He will doubtless make you aware of the other reason for our presence here. Afterwards, Inspector Griffin and I would have a few words with you."

She nodded. "Of course I must see my father." She gave us a hard look and turning on her heel went out.

"A 'determined young woman'," my companion murmured. He looked found a bell cord which he pulled, and shortly the parlour-maid came in.

"Do you know where Mr. Lennard may be found?" Holmes queried.

"Yes, sir. He's in the kitchen having a cup of tea along of Mrs. Hodge."

"Then pray ask him if he will be good enough to join us at once."

Holmes turned to the inspector. "Will you trust me to conduct this interview in my own way and not intervene until I give the word?"

"I hope you know what you are doing, Mr. Holmes. I'm content to give you some leeway, but I remind you that I shall be the one to get it in the neck should things go awry."

"Be easy. We are too near the truth for things to go wrong now. Ah, Lennard, I wonder if you will oblige by giving us another sight of your room? Inspector Griffin wasn't with us earlier, and I'm sure he will find much to interest him."

The man looked at us steadily for a few seconds. "If you must," he said ungraciously, turning to lead the way upstairs.

On entering the room, Holmes went to the length of silk that still hung on its pegs. Taking it down, he handed it to Griffin, then produced the thread from his pocket-book for the inspector to compare. Next he took out the pebble and held before Lennard, who blanched at the sight.

"Well, Lennard?" said Holmes quietly. "Your silence will serve no purpose now, except to cause more distress to those you would protect."

The man eyed us stonily. Inspector Griffin's brow was creased in a frown as his eyes darted between Holmes and Lennard, while the former waited for a reaction from the manservant. I began to see the pieces fall into place as Lennard looked straight at my friend, defiantly at first, then his shoulders sagged in resignation.

"I suppose it had to come out sooner or later," he said at last. "I've no regrets for what I done. The blighter got no more than he deserved."

"Are you confessing to the murder of Peter Witham?" said Griffin in his most official voice. "If so, I must caution you – "

"Save your breath," replied the unhappy man. "Yes, I killed him, swine that he was."

"Why?" asked the inspector.

"If you don't know, then I'm not about to tell you." Lennard sat on the edge of his bed, obstinacy written in every line of his face.

"Ah, but I think I know," put in Holmes, "and I'm pretty sure that Miss Romney also knows, although she may be unaware that it was your doing." He went to stand before the man. "Have you considered that it may be that she suspects her father?"

"That's impossible!" Lennard stood up agitatedly. "Why, the General'd never be capable of doing what I did, and in any case he don't know why I done it, and I pray that he never finds out."

"Inspector Griffin stepped forward. "Edward Lennard," he intoned solemnly, "I'm charging you with the murder of Peter Witham. Have you anything to say?"

There was no reply, and Holmes shook his head.

"Then let me reconstruct events leading up to the murder," he said. "I think it was on Sunday that Miss Romney came into possession of evidence that made her aware that her fiancé wasn't an honourable man. It was more than the revelation of some minor peccadillo that might be readily overlooked and excused. We can be sure of that from the tone of the letter in which she renounced her engagement to Witham, and from the phrase she used to indicate that if the facts were made public it would give distress to the one she loved most. That could only be her father, so I asked myself what it implied.

"She was in turmoil, unable to face her family with the secret locked inside her, so she decided to go away to compose her thoughts in some privacy. Unbeknown to her, what she had discovered was also known to Lennard, and had been for some time. He was fiercely loyal to the General, and when Miss Romney fled, he divined that she too had become aware of the situation."

At this point, Holmes paused and looked at Lennard sadly.

"Witham was having an illicit relationship with Mrs. Romney, was he not?" he asked. "You knew of it, but couldn't bear to see the General hurt and humiliated. Am I correct?"

The wretched man nodded. "Aye, that's about it. I've seen 'em in that old cottage together behaving like a couple of animals, night after night when the Guv'nor was shut away in his study. I never knew Miss Ellen'd found out, though. Not 'til she went off, leaving that letter for her dad."

"So you took matters into your own hands, hoping that with Witham's death, she would have no cause to make her father aware of the matter,"

Not waiting for a reply, Holmes continued, addressing himself now to Inspector Griffin. "Lennard knew from his inquiries that Witham was taking the early train to London and, from his local knowledge, that his intended victim would take the path between the two properties. Taking that scarf," he indicated it, "he went to lay in wait, probably picking up the pebble from the drive where they lie in profusion along the edge."

"And he knew of this Indian business from his time there with General Romney," Griffin chipped in.

Before Holmes could continue the door burst open to admit Ellen Romney. She was pale but composed, and stopped to survey the solemn group gathered in the room.

"Father has told me of Peter's murder," she said icily. "What steps are you taking to apprehend his killer, Inspector?"

"That is done, miss," Griffin replied with some embarrassment. "Lennard has confessed to the crime and is now under arrest."

"No!" she burst out angrily, "That is ridiculous! What reason would Ted have for committing such a crime?"

"The same reason that sent you away, Miss Romney, and caused you to break your engagement," said Holmes, "He has been aware of what was going on for much longer than you, and feared that your discovery of it would force you to confide in the General."

The young woman swayed on her feet and I took her arm to lead her to a chair. She collapsed limply and looked dazedly at Lennard,

"Is this true, Ted?" she whispered. "You'd known all along?"

"That's right, Miss Ellen. I was hoping you'd realise he weren't good enough for you and give him the shove afore the truth come out." His eyes showed some animation. "John Paxton – he's the one for you, even if he ain't got much money,"

"Oh, Ted," she sobbed, the tears running down her cheeks. "It wasn't needed. I'd never have told Father what that woman was doing." She turned her face up to look at us angrily. "I'll deal with her in my own way and Father will never know of her shameful deceit." Her anger turned suddenly to fear. "He needn't know, need he? He mustn't!"

"That depends on what Lennard says in court, Miss Romney," said Holmes. "He's admitted the murder, but if he refuses to give reasons, well – " He shrugged. "I think if Inspector Griffin is prepared to take a fresh statement covering the bare facts of the murder, it may well be seen as personal animosity." He carefully avoided the inspector's eye.

"I shan't say nothing to damage the Guv'nor, rely on that, miss," said Lennard stoutly, seemingly uncaring for his own predicament, "You go on and tell him old Ted's blotted his crime sheet at last."

Inspector Griffin jerked his head, and the still-sobbing Ellen Romney ran from the room, only to return within minutes with a wrathful General Romney on her heels.

"Griffin, you oaf!" he roared. "What in God's name has got into you? And you, Mr. Sherlock Holmes – whatever reputation you had is shot to pieces by this stupidity!"

"I beg your pardon, General," said Griffin with dignity. "I must do my duty, whatever the circumstances. Lennard has admitted to killing Mr. Peter Witham, and I have no choice but to take him into custody."

"That's true, sir," said the accused man. "I done him in, all right."

"Nonsense!" boomed the General. "You've been bullied into saying this!"

The inspector looked outraged and Holmes intervened coldly.

"With all deference due to your age and former rank, sir, I assure you that is no room for error. The matter is quite clear, and if you would help your loyal servant, I suggest you procure for him the finest legal advice that you can. Your opinion of me I discount, but the aspersions you have made regarding Inspector Griffin's integrity do you no credit."

For what seemed minutes the old man simmered, finally speaking in a more composed manner. "So it's true, then? But why, Ted, why?"

"It were for Miss Ellen, Guv'nor. He were never right for her and would only have made her life a misery." Lennard was speaking calmly and with confidence. "I think she guessed it, but was too much of a lady to face him with it."

The General snorted, "If she had something to say she'd say it, lady or no lady." He swung to face his daughter. "Wouldn't you, girl?"

"Perhaps." Her eyes fell, but already the General had turned away.

113

"Inspector, I spoke unjustly and in haste. Will you accept my humble apologies? And Mr. Holmes, will you also be so generous?"

Holmes smiled faintly, while Griffin inclined his head gravely.

"You were shocked and under a strain, sir," said the latter. "Now I must ask Lennard to accompany me to the police station."

General Romney gnawed at his moustache. "What will be the outcome, Griffin?" he asked.

"There can only be one, sir. Unless," Griffin added, "he can make a plea of insanity which the court will believe."

"I'm as sane as any of you lot," Lennard said furiously. "I knew what I was doing and why, and I ain't going to snivel for no one."

The General seemed to have aged a decade since entering the room. Now he turned almost pleadingly to the inspector. "I know this is irregular, but will you allow me a few minutes alone with Ted? I give my word he will make no trouble, and you may post a man outside my study door and on the terrace." He turned to his servant, "You'll not let me down?"

"Never have done yet, have I, sir?"

With the briefest hesitation Griffin agreed, "Of course, General, and I'll not insult you by placing sentries. Ten minutes, sir?"

The two old soldiers, both holding themselves rigidly, made their way down to the study, leaving Ellen Romney to gaze tearfully after them until Holmes sought her attention.

"One point I would clear up, Miss Romney," he said. "Will you be so good as to tell us when you first became aware of your step-mother's involvement with your fiancé?"

She looked at him dully before speaking in a low husky voice.

"It was on Sunday evening. Peter had brought me back from church and I had gone to my room feeling unwell. Soon afterwards I went to open the window for air and I saw Charlotte – Mrs. Romney – hurrying down the drive. Although I maintained a superficial show of amity towards her for Father's sake, I was never comfortable in her presence for reasons I was unable to explain to myself. On a sudden impulse, I decided to follow her. Nobody saw me leave and I was some thirty yards behind her when I saw her enter the old cottage. Have you seen it?"

We murmured assent and she went on.

"I was intrigued enough to approach cautiously and peer through one of the glass less windows. What I saw horrified me! She and Peter were locked in a passionate embrace, and even as I watched they displayed such abandonment that my senses reeled. I began to feel physically sick, yet I was mesmerised, unable to drag myself away from the ghastly sight."

She shuddered at the memory and Holmes laid a hand on her arm.

114

"Do not distress yourself, Miss Romney. We follow your meaning. Pray tell us of your subsequent actions."

"At last I forced myself to flee back to the house, shamed and disgusted by what I had witnessed. That my father's wife should give herself so wantonly to the man to whom I was promised was unbelievable, yet I had the evidence of my own eyes. My first thought was to denounce her to Father, but the idea of inflicting pain and humiliation on him gave me pause.

"I knew I couldn't face her without my anger betraying my knowledge, so as I became calmer I decided to go away until I could make up my mind as to a course of action. I wrote a note to Father, which you will have seen, and also a letter to Mr. Witham in which – "

"We have seen that also, miss," put in the inspector. "From the contents of his pockets, we deduced that the affair was of long-standing."

"There isn't much more to tell," said Ellen Romney, "I sneaked out down the back stairs like a thief, and caught the train to London, where I spent two nights at an hotel for ladies before coming back to this."

"What decision had you made?" asked Holmes, ever anxious to have a story complete.

"I was going to confront her with what I had seen, and warn her that unless she mended her ways I must tell my father. Whether I could ever bring myself to do so I know not, but be assured, gentlemen, I shall use all my wiles to bring her to heel," she concluded grimly.

There was a period of silence before Griffin moved towards the stairs.

"Then the case is closed," he said heavily, "I can feel pity for the man whose loyalty drove him to extremes, but the law must be upheld. I think the General should be left in the belief that Lennard was actuated by concern for his master's daughter and last his self-control through an excess of zeal."

Holmes made no sign of agreeing or disagreeing, and we arrived at the lower floor just as the General came out of the study, closing the door behind him. His shoulders were bowed and his eyes spoke of unshed tears. He came towards us and with an effort straightened up to become the very picture of the gallant old campaigner that he was. He looked at his daughter for a moment, then spoke in his usual crisp voice.

"Go to your room, my dear," he said in a tone that brooked of no argument. "I have something that must be said to these gentlemen before the final act."

"Where is Lennard?" Griffin asked sharply.

"Have no fear, Inspector. He remains in my study with pen and paper to write his statement." The General gave the travesty of a smile. "He knows his duty and will do it."

115

Even as he spoke there came the sound of a shot, muffled by the heavy door, but nevertheless unmistakable. With an oath Griffin sprang forward and flung open the door, Holmes and I crowding on his heels.

"God d--- it!" roared the inspector, stopping in his tracks. "This is an outrage!"

I wasn't unprepared for the sight that met our eyes. Lennard sat at the desk with the muzzle of a revolver in his mouth and the back of his head completely blown away, the window behind him spattered with blood and brains. Inspector Griffin stared at the macabre sight before turning to face the General, who stood calmly beside Holmes. "Confound it, General!" he cried furiously. "You connived in helping this man evade justice. How could you abuse my trust so?"

"I sir?" said the General with dignity. "I merely left him here to write his statement. He must have found my old service revolver in the desk drawer and decided to take this way out. I cannot pretend regrets that you were baulked of your prey, though."

"He was my prisoner and it will reflect on me!" Griffin almost snarled.

"I shall see no blame attaches to you, Inspector," replied the General soothingly. "We value you too highly to see your career ruined." He sat down heavily on the nearest chair. "The real tragedy is that it need never have happened. You see, I knew all about my wife and Witham and had the matter under control."

"You knew?" Griffin and I stared at him, but Holmes showed no sign of surprise whatsoever.

"Gentlemen," said General Romney patiently, "I may be older than you, but I'm not blind, and neither am I in my dotage. Very early in my marriage, I knew I was mistaken in taking a wife very near my daughter's age, but I had enough pride and self-esteem to keep it to myself."

"She knew that you were aware of her unfaithfulness?"

"I was about to confront her with it when Ellen's disappearance took precedence in my thoughts. When Witham came to dinner on Tuesday, I was to present my ultimatum."

"Which was?" This from Holmes.

"He would break off his engagement to my daughter. Charlotte would have a reasonable but not overgenerous allowance provided she left my roof and didn't reside within ten miles of Foxford. Ellen is a mature woman and would be capable of taking events in her stride when told the true facts. Witham was never but second choice for her, thanks to my meddling in her life." He dropped his head into his hands and sighed.

I jumped as my companion touched my arm. "Come, Watson, old friend," he whispered. "There is no more for us to do here, and the General and Miss Romney have the strength of character to survive this tragedy. If only he had confided his knowledge to her and Lennard earlier."

We crept out unnoticed, and it wasn't until we had retrieved our luggage and settled in the train to London that he referred to the matter again.

"We shall hear more of Mrs. Romney, Watson. She will not sink into obscurity, mark my words."

"And perhaps under another name," I said, my contempt showing in my tone, at which he laughed and resumed his study of the evening paper.

Barstobrick House
by Martin Daley

Chapter I

As I reflect on the many thousands of cases I associate with my friend Sherlock Holmes, I am aware that many cannot find their way into print due to their particularly sensitive or confidential nature. Holmes himself has forbidden me to publish certain investigations, and there have been other occasions when I have given a pledge to a client that I would only consider publication if those involved were to pre-decease my friend.

In recalling the surprise telegram I received from Holmes, encouraging me to tell the story of what he called "The Cornish Horror", my mind strayed to another case later that year that I, *myself*, deliberately withheld. It is only now, many years later, and having considered how others have permitted me to recount their own strange and curious problems, that I feel it only proper that I should publish a case that arguably had such great effect on me personally. It began upon receipt of a letter from a dear friend, three days after my forty-fifth birthday.

As I have chronicled elsewhere, Holmes's health had suffered at the start of the year through overwork, but his inability to rest had resulted in him keeping up a relentless pace that had shown no signs of abating as the year had progressed. Up to that point, he had already been involved in cases that had seen him journey, not only to Cornwall, but to Kent and Staffordshire, as well solving mysteries involving Colonel Carruthers, the Dowager Lady Isobel, and the disappearance of the one-legged Hurdy-Gurdy man on Bond Street.

Finally, as we entered mid-summer, his workload had eased somewhat, and by August he found himself either wandering restively around our apartment, or curled up on the sofa under a cloud of blue pipe-smoke.

His mood wasn't lightened by the usual summer temperature. August was its regular oppressive self. An airless heat was trapped within the streets of the capital while the bleached buildings opposite our rooms in Baker Street reflected the mid-morning light upon our windows as if someone was playing a spiteful trick with a giant magnifying glass.

"Anything of interest, Mrs. Hudson?" asked Holmes as our landlady entered with the morning's post.

"Not for you, sir. I'm afraid," she replied, causing my friend to slink back into his languid position on the sofa. "Just something for the good Doctor."

"Thank you, Mrs. Hudson," I said, taking the letter from her, while feeling secretly contented that for once it was I that was the centre of someone's attention. "Good heavens!" I cried upon opening it, "it's from Jeannie!"

"Attracting the fairer sex once again, Watson?" asked Holmes from the sofa with a mischievous expression.

Ignoring my friend's impish comment, I explained, "Jeannie is a childhood friend whom I haven't seen in – " I paused to recollect. " – Good heavens, it must be over twenty years." She wrote:

Kirkcudbright, Scotland

My Dearest John,

> *It has been almost ten years since we last corresponded and more than twice as long since we were together. Your birthday prompted me to write and make two requests of you.*
> *Firstly, it is my own fortieth birthday next month and my parents are insisting that we hold a small celebration. As darling Hugh is unable to attend, and as we haven't seen each other in so long, I would love it if you would consider coming home for a short stay and join us. There is plenty of room here, and it would be wonderful to see you again. My second request – regardless of your availability for our celebration next month – is that we can see a little more of each other in the future. As I get older, I think more and more of our childhood and the wonderful times the three of us spent together.*
> *My father is still the gamekeeper on the Queenshill Estate where you used to visit. It would be wonderful to see you again. Please write and say you will come.*

Affectionately yours,

Jeannie

"Well, I never," I said to the room in general. I appraised Holmes of the letter, more out of courtesy than anything else, not believing he would be remotely interested.

119

"You should go," said Holmes as he blew pipe-smoke upwards, dispersing the blue rings that were attempting to reach the ceiling.

"Oh, I don't know," I said, turning back to the letter. 'It's been such a long time."

"Yes, it will do you good to take a break from the heat of London. I shall come with you."

My eyes shot up from the page, my expression of incredulity obviously speaking volumes.

"Don't look so surprised," said Holmes, clearly amused. "You have supported me all these years, friend Watson. I have a feeling that you may need a little support of your own, once you start delving into your past."

As I hold my pen today, with the rather unsteady hand of recollection, it was as if Holmes was anticipating the profound affect the trip would have on me.

"Are you sure?" I asked.

"Of course," he replied, as if taking a casual leisure trip to the country or the seaside was the most natural thing in the world for him. "When is it?"

"Jeannie's birthday is on a Sunday, so it would mean travelling up the day before. We would then stay for a few days afterwards, I suppose."

"Perfect."

For the remainder of the day, I couldn't help myself from glancing over the top of my newspaper at my friend as I tried – like I had on countless other occasions – to fathom the workings of that great mind.

The following day, after composing my reply to Jeannie, I paused as I went to post my letter. "Are you *sure* about going to Scotland?" I asked.

"Of course," my friend looked up with a smile, "I would love to see where it all began for my trusty biographer."

We spoke little of the matter during the following month until a few days before we were due to leave, I raised the topic again with Holmes and found his apparent enthusiasm hadn't abated. The day before my friend's birthday, we set off from Euston on the long journey.

There was little conversation between us as our train rattled north. As usual on such a journey, Holmes spent most of the time in a meditative state while I struggled to concentrate on the various newspaper stories, I found myself reading and re-reading. Anticipation, excitement, and a strange feeling of foreboding combined to make my journey uncomfortable, and it wasn't until our train sat breathing heavily in Carlisle Station, prior to the final leg of our journey, that Holmes sought to assuage my feelings.

"You seem troubled," he said from beneath his drooping eyelids.

"I suppose I am. I never thought such a trip would affect me so."

"What are you afraid of?"

"That's the thing – I don't really know! It's just been such a long time. I haven't been home – if it is appropriate to call it home – since I left for medical school over twenty-five years ago."

"I sense you are concerned about raking up old memories."

"They do say that some things from the past should stay in the past."

"And yet you seemed happy with the arrival of your friend's invitation."

I knew that Holmes had already deduced the reason for my discomfort.

"Yes," I replied, "Jeannie is a dear friend of ours from childhood."

"Ours?" Holmes let the word hang there.

"Indeed. My mother was childhood friends with her mother, Elen. When Aunt Elen met William McFadden of Kirkcudbright, she moved east along the Galloway Coast from Stranraer. He was – and still is – the gamekeeper on the Queenshill estate near Kirkcudbright. It is owned by the Neilson family, steel magnates from Glasgow. While Elen and William had Jeannie, my parents had Hugh and myself and we would go on family holidays to visit them every year. It's a beautiful place."

"And I take it that your friend and your brother were particularly close?"

I smiled thinly at Holmes's perception.

"Indeed. Even though Hugh was seven years Jeannie's senior and I am closer in age to her, it was the two of them who became closer as we all grew. As I left to travel south, I believed and hoped that there would be a happy ending for them both."

"But alas, your brother fell on hard times."

"Yes," I replied, somehow finding a kind of catharsis in speaking of my brother, "I always maintain he was the cleverer of the two of us, and could have been a doctor himself had he put his mind to it. But he went to Edinburgh and seemed to drift from one job to another, unable to find what he was looking for. I'm ashamed to say I gradually lost touch with him as I launched my career and went abroad."

"And it was your friend Jeannie who sent you his watch upon his passing."

"Yes. I didn't realise that the two remained so close and when Hugh died, his goods and chattels were sent to Jeannie."

"Don't torture yourself, old friend. However much we care for others, everyone must take responsibility for the paths they choose."

I knew Holmes's summary was perfectly logical, but I couldn't help thinking about our carefree childhood days when Hugh would look after his little brother. This led to the inevitable feelings of guilt at being oblivious to the extent of his troubles in adulthood, and being unable to offer the help he no doubt craved.

I did feel a little better, however, after articulating my feelings, and as we crossed the border, I found myself looking forward to our journey's end.

Chapter II

Kirkcudbright's tiny station was as pretty as I had remembered it. When we stepped down from the train, it was as though I had been transported back in time to my childhood. The large round clock still hung above the westbound platform, which was furnished with gas-lamps that stood like sentries at twenty-yard intervals. From their posts hung decorative baskets, flush with brightly coloured chrysanthemums and wisps of heather.

"*John! John!*"

My reverie was broken by the familiar Galloway accent, calling from the other end of the platform. Jeannie looked as lovely as ever, her beautiful chestnut-coloured hair peeping out from under her bonnet. We rushed towards each other.

"Jeannie, it's so wonderful to see you again! It's been so long."

"Thank you for coming, John. It means a great deal to me. I've been so looking forward to your stay."

"How are your parents? The estate? What have you been up to?"

I was giddy with excitement at the sight of my dear friend and had completely forgotten about Holmes, who had followed me along the platform at a more reserved pace. Jeannie however, looked past me and gave a slightly embarrassed cough.

"Oh, I'm so sorry!" I said to them both, "Jeannie, this is Mr. Sherlock Holmes, my friend from London. Holmes, this is Jeannie McFadden."

"Miss McFadden," Holmes touched the brim of his hat, "it's a pleasure to meet such a dear friend of the doctor. Thank you for inviting us to share in your special celebration."

"Thank you for coming, Mr. Holmes. It's lovely to meet you. Now, let's get you both to your lodgings. You must be exhausted after such a long trip."

We followed her to a carriage that had clearly doubled as a working vehicle over the years.

"Thank you, Robert," Jeannie said as the driver climbed down to help us with our bags.

Queenshill Estate was four miles inland from the little harbour town. It consisted of a large working farm and acres and acres of forestry. The nearest property to the road was the large farmhouse in which Jeannie and her parents lived. Further along the driveway was the original gamekeeper's cottage, which was too small for the McFaddens and so was now occupied by Mr. Neilson's butler and his wife. Then further still was Barstobrick House, named after the large hill that towered above the estate, and the family home of Neilson and his family.

Elen and William McFadden were just as I remembered them – it was if time had stood still in this idyllic place. I had to stop myself from calling Jeannie's mother *Aunt* Elen and attempted Mrs. McFadden before both she and her husband insisted on me using their Christian names. That didn't stop William from instinctively lapsing back to his use of the adjective 'wee' when referring to me, as he had when my brother and I were children. Every time he used the term 'wee' John, I swear I saw the hint of a smile pluck at Holmes's lips.

Elen made a wonderful meal from the produce of the farm and, after some further reminiscing over a dram, Holmes and I made our excuses and retired early to our rooms, shattered after such a long day. Before I turned in, I peered out of the window at the black sky, another feature of this wonderful part of the country. I thought how I'd missed this, and yet on the other hand, of all the adventures I had experienced instead. There was almost an innocence about this place – untouched by the war and villainy I had encountered since leaving all those years ago. Uncertain as to whether I had made the right decisions, I turned out the light and let myself be engulfed by the blackness and the silence.

I enjoyed a wonderful night's sleep and awoke to an autumnal sunshine filtering through the curtains. Unaware of the time, I prepared my toilet, dressed, and went downstairs in search of some breakfast. To my surprise, the house was deserted, until Elen appeared into the kitchen from the rear entrance, carrying a bowl full of eggs.

"Morning, John. Sleep well?"

"Good morning, Elen. I did, thank you." Then looking around, I asked, "Where is everyone?"

"Oh, you must have been sleeping like a log, because there was all sorts of activity during the night. There has been a fire at the big house. William and Mr. Wallace – that's Mr. Neilson's man – managed to put it out before it took hold. Thankfully there isn't much damage. Jeannie's up there helping clear up the mess, and Mr. Holmes followed them when he learned of the excitement."

"That's dreadful news," I said. "Hopefully no one was hurt?"

"No, thankfully not. The house is virtually empty, as Mr. and Mrs. Neilson are visiting family in America. Apparently Mr. Wallace discovered the fire quite early and raised the alarm. No major damage done."

"Good heavens! I'll go along and see what I can do."

"Would you like some breakfast before you go?"

"No. That's very kind, Elen, but hopefully I can get something later."

I hurried along the sweeping, tree-lined drive to what those on the estate and throughout the area referred to as "the big house". I found William and another man removing sodden sheets from the building through a large sunroom that was attached to one side of the building. Some of the glass panes had broken and others were blackened with soot. Fortunately – as Elen had suggested – the main body of Barstobrick House appeared undamaged.

"Ah, morning wee John!" called William as he saw me approaching.

"Good morning, William. How did it happen? Why didn't you wake me?"

"*Argh*, there was no need. Once Mrs. Wallace woke me, I hurried along to help Mr. Wallace here, and between us we managed to dampen it down before it got started." William then realised that I hadn't met the man to whom he was referring. "Oh, by the way, this is Mr. Wallace. This is John Watson, a friend of Jeannie's who used to come and stay, along with his brother when they were wee boys."

"Pleased to meet you," I said, "although it's a pity it is in such difficult circumstances."

"Yes, well at least there was no great damage done," said Wallace, "and no one was hurt." I wondered if the sad expression he wore was permanent, or had simply been prompted by the night's events.

"I suppose the fact that the house was empty is both a blessing and a curse," I suggested. "On the one hand, there was no one there to get hurt, but on the other – had the fire taken hold – the whole house could have been destroyed."

"Well, the cook and her daughter stay at the other end of the house," said Wallace, "but, as you say, they were unharmed, as the fire was virtually confined to the sunroom."

"Jeannie's helping them to clean up," added William.

I looked past him to see the three blurred figures through the damaged glass, sweeping and gathering up damaged items. Before I could resume the questioning, an approaching voice cried out from behind me.

"Good morning, Watson! I trust you slept well?"

"Holmes!" I exclaimed, turning around. "Where have you been?"

"It would seem adventure has even followed us to this little tranquil corner of the world," he said, ignoring my question.

124

He had obviously met Mr. Wallace earlier, as – without further hesitation – he began questioning the man.

"You said that your wife heard something shortly before you discovered the fire?"

"Yes," said the butler. "My wife's a very light sleeper, and our bedroom faces the drive. She woke me, telling me that she thought something was wrong – just instinct I suppose. When I went out to investigate, I looked back and saw the flames in the sunroom taking hold. It was then that I asked my wife to fetch Mr. McFadden, and between us, we managed to get water from the byre and douse it down."

"What exactly had caught fire?" I asked.

"Excellent, Watson!" said Holmes before Wallace could answer. "I was just about to ask that myself."

"While Mr. and Mrs. Neilson are away, they are taking the opportunity to have the house decorated," explained the butler. "The painters had delivered their equipment only yesterday and stacked most of it in the sunroom in preparation to start work tomorrow. There were pots of paint, dustsheets, cleaning fluids – any of which could have caught fire."

"Does your master have any enemies, Mr. Wallace?" asked Holmes.

"Not that I particularly know of, sir," he replied after a little thought. "I suppose there is always the type who are jealous of other people's success, but I'm not aware of any great feud with anyone."

"Yet someone may have known that the house would be empty."

"Everyone knows each other's business round here, Mr. Holmes," said William, a little confused by my friend's question. "It would have been common knowledge that they were away."

"Do you mind if I take a look at the sunroom door?"

"Yes, by all means. Be careful, as there is quite a bit of broken glass, but certainly you can have a look if you like."

"Thank you," said my friend.

I followed him to the entrance where we almost bumped into Jeannie, who was exiting with a box of breakages.

"Good morning, Miss McFadden," said Holmes, "and a very happy birthday."

In all the excitement, I had completely forgotten about the reason for our visit.

"Jeannie, I can't apologise enough – I'm mortified!" I cried. "Many happy returns."

"Don't worry, John," she said with a characteristic gentleness. "It isn't uppermost in my mind either right now."

She put down the box and we hugged.

"I do have a card and a gift for you back at the house," I added apologetically.

Holmes meanwhile had taken a small lens from his inside pocket and was examining the lock of sunroom door. Although the upper pane had been blown out, the lower, timber part of the door was still intact, if a little blackened. The annex itself was about fifteen feet wide and led to the side door of the main house. Beside *it* was a small window. Holmes addressed the two staff who were still sweeping up shards of glass.

"Good morning, ladies. Could I ask if either of you heard anything prior to Mr. Wallace raising the alarm?"

"No sir," said the elder of the two.

"And this door was locked, I assume?" he asked pointing to the large side door.

"Yes sir, that's always locked, as is the tradesman's door round the back while they were away. Mr. Neilson gave the painters permission to use this entrance."

"May I see inside?"

"Yes, sir."

I followed Holmes into a small hallway that led into the main entrance to the house. It occurred to me that in all my visits to the estate as a child, I had never set foot in the big house until this moment. There was further evidence of the work that was about to commence as scaffolding was stacked on the floor awaiting construction. William and the butler had followed us in and joined us at the foot of the grand staircase that was the centrepiece of the entrance hall. Holmes addressed the butler.

"Mr. Wallace, has anything of note recently come into Mr. Neilson's possession?"

"Yes, as a matter of fact, there has," he replied. "Mr. Neilson has recently purchased a painting by the famous local artist, Edward Hornel. You've probably heard of him."

"No – and this painting is of great value?"

I was both amused and a little embarrassed by Holmes's dismissal of the artist.

Wallace was a little taken aback but continued anyway, "Oh, well, Hornel is thought to be one of the best artists in the world. Mr. Neilson successfully bid for one of his most famous works at an auction house in Glasgow last month."

"Was this widely reported?"

"Yes. The story of this major work returning home, as it were, was in the local paper for a few days running."

"May I see the painting?"

"Yes, I suppose so," said Wallace, a little confused. "If you just follow me, it will be in Mr. Neilson's study."

Wallace took a set of keys from his pocket and opened one of the three doors that opened directly from the entrance hall. We followed him into the room.

"That's the one, sir," said the butler, pointing to a large, rather abstract oil in pride of place behind a large walnut desk.

"Ah," said Holmes softly to himself, and then he added to everyone. "Gentlemen, there may be more to this unfortunate incident than meets the eye." But he refused to elaborate.

Chapter III

Amidst all the disruption caused by the morning's events, I felt sorry for Jeannie, whose big day had almost been completely overlooked as a result. Generous soul that she is, however, she never made a fuss and continued helping clean up the mess.

"There have been plenty of birthdays in the past, John," she said with a smile when I raised the point. "Hopefully, there will be plenty more in the future."

As she and the others got on with restoring the big house to its condition of twenty-four hours earlier, her mother continued in her kitchen, making a cake and preparing the rest of the food for that evening's celebration.

The day progressed and I commented to William that the official services were conspicuous by their absence. The gamekeeper laughed.

"Aye, there isn't much round here, son. There's only two or three part-time policemen and a similar number of volunteer firemen. Once we got on top of the fire, there was no need to bother them. Besides, being slightly out of the way up here, I don't know how long it would have taken them to get here – the whole place would have been up in flames!"

"Still, I think it should still be reported to the authorities as a matter of course."

"Aye, I'll have a word with Mr. Wallace and next time he's in town, he can pop into the police station and let them know."

It was typical of the slow, *laissez-faire* attitude that pervaded among the people of the Galloway Coast, and not for the first time, it was as though I was taken back in time to my childhood, and how things used to be in that simpler time.

The day passed without further incident and, as afternoon turned into evening, people gradually started to gather for Jeannie's party, oblivious to the morning's events. Friends and neighbours from farms and hamlets around the area enjoyed the night's festivities, dancing to the music produced by a couple of young men skilled on the fiddle and squeeze box. When she wasn't being dragged onto the make-shift dance-floor by various friends, Jeannie spent most of the night going from table to table, laughing, joking, and generally sharing stories about her forty years amongst these good people. I watched her from afar and was pleased that she enjoyed the life she had chosen. I also felt proud and privileged to know someone so gentle and kind.

Holmes spent most of the evening sitting in the corner with his pipe, observing those present. Although it was lovely to be part of such an event, it was neither mine, nor his, idea of a relaxing evening, and we made a polite exit earlier than most. Before I retired, Jeannie said we would spend the following day together on the estate, as we hadn't had an opportunity to properly catch-up. I agreed it was a splendid idea and went to my room. I imagined Holmes propped upright for most of the night smoking endless pipes as he contemplated the events of earlier that morning. Either way, it was almost certain neither of us would enjoy a good night's sleep with all the raucous activity downstairs.

I must have fallen to sleep sometime in the small hours and I awakened around nine o'clock. As I descended the stairs, I heard Holmes in conversation with Jeannie.

"You can come with us, Mr. Holmes. John and I are going to spend the day walking on the estate."

"That's very kind, Miss McFadden, but I shall politely decline. I intend to visit the beautiful little town you introduced us to upon our arrival.

"Ah, Watson, good morning," he continued. "I trust you slept well? I'm sure you will have a fine day in this wonderful Scottish air. I shall see you both later."

With that, and a touch of the brim of his hat to Jeannie, he left, leaving our host somewhat bemused.

"Don't worry," I said. "He can be very unpredictable at times."

Like Jeannie, I had no idea exactly where my friend was going or what he was up to. My curiosity gradually dissipated as we enjoyed a wonderful day idly wandering round the vast estate and catching up on old times – in one respect they seem like a lifetime ago, while in another were so vivid, they could have been only yesterday – none more so than when we climbed to the top of Barstobrick Hill. The panoramic view was spectacular, with Kirkcudbright in the distance and the sea beyond, glistening like a vast field of diamonds in the low sun. The autumn colours of the fields and valleys in between were equally as stunning. As the sun moved round, violet turned to russet browns, to orange, and then to yellow.

At the bottom of the hill, Barstobrick House stood, seemingly unharmed from the accident the previous day. I couldn't stop smiling at the scene. Jeannie must have read my mind.

"Do you ever see yourself returning, John?"

"Oh, I don't think so, as beautiful as it is. I've been in London now for almost twenty years. I probably have more roots there than anywhere else. When Mary passed away, I thought about moving and making a fresh start. But where to? I had built up my practice. I had my patients and whatever friends I had left there. Present company excepted, of course," I added with a smile.

"And not forgetting your adventures with Mr. Holmes," said Jeannie, teasingly.

Again, I smiled with slight embarrassment, "It's true. Holmes was away for a few years and when he returned, we resumed our friendship – and if I am honest, I would have to say that filled a rather large void in my life." I resumed taking in the view, "Having said all that, I would love to visit here again sometime. I'd forgotten how beautiful it is here."

"Well, you're always welcome," said Jeannie, linking my arm. "Remember, I asked for two things in my letter."

We left it at that and made our way back down the hill, where we were met by Jeannie's father, who was wheeling an empty barrow.

"What are you two *bairns* up to?" he asked, much to our amusement.

"We've just been catching up on old times," said Jeannie. "I've been reacquainting John with the estate."

"I'm just off to the garden to pick some vegetables if you want to come along."

"Yes, I haven't shown you the walled garden yet," she said, turning to me.

We walked further along a path that led from the big house to a high wall, with what seemed like a disproportionately small wooden door at its centre. William opened the door, wheeled his barrow through, and we both followed. Inside, I could see that the wall formed a perfect square approximately two-hundred yards in each direction. Uniform rows of plants and produce covered the ground in front of us and led to a long, elegant glass house at the far end of the garden.

"What a beautiful place," I exclaimed.

"Yes, it's probably my favourite spot," said Jeannie, "I come here quite a bit."

"It wasn't here when I was a boy."

"No, it was built about fifteen years ago. Hugh paid for it."

Jeannie's words didn't register at first and I looked at her for clarification, "My Hugh?" I stammered.

129

"Aye," said William. "He was a generous laddie, was wee Hughie."

Jeannie added, "Hugh's fortunes fluctuated wildly and he came to stay often. Dad wanted somewhere to grow produce and develop plants for the estate – but Mr. Neilson was never interested – " she added under her breath. "Anyway, when Hugh was down here one time, he had had a particularly successful period and insisted on having a walled garden built. He paid for it all."

"I didn't want anything as big," explained William, "but he insisted. He had a local builder come 'round and build it for us."

As Jeannie helped her father harvest some of his produce, I sat on a bench and contemplated the beauty of the place – the colours and birdsong, and above all else the revelation that my brother had financed the whole space. My reverie was broken by the clanking of the iron ring that opened the door.

"Holmes! What are you doing here?"

"Good afternoon," said my friend, also touching his hat in the direction of Jeannie and William, who remained on the far side of the garden. "I arrived back at the farmhouse and Mrs. McFadden said I might find you all here."

"What have you been up to?"

"I must say I'm beginning to really enjoy our little sojourn. I have spent a very informative day in Kirkcudbright."

"It's a beautiful little town, isn't it?"

"I can't say I really noticed. I was more testing a theory than taking in the sights."

"And what theory was that?"

"That the little incident the other night wasn't the innocent accident that everyone believed. It may well have been an accident, but the fire didn't start by itself. It was caused by the clumsiness of someone breaking in."

I suddenly realised to what he was referring. "The painting," I said.

"My first suspicion that it was no ordinary accident came on Sunday morning, immediately after the break-in." Holmes broke off from his narrative and lit a cigarette.

"Among all the footprints on the soft drive were a distinctive set. Whereas most were heading towards the house, these were deeper but showed no showed no heel, and were heading in the opposite direction away from the house. Inferences? Someone was either on tip toes, or more likely –"

" – Was running away!"

"Precisely. My suspicions were confirmed when I found the marks of a dog-cart which had been standing for some time on the soft ground outside the entrance to the estate. The tracks made by the wheels and its horse were quite distinct from any other vehicles that had made continuous and uninterrupted tracks as they passed by. The running man's footprints finished at the dog-cart and it pulled away.

"I believe it was the sound of this man running past the butler's cottage that disturbed Mrs. Wallace from her slumber.

"When I inspected the lock on the sunroom door, it was clear it had been tampered with. The burglar must have forced the lock. He wouldn't have known that the decorators' equipment was stacked just inside, and he almost immediately disturbed it and inadvertently started a small fire in the process. Then he panicked and ran."

"What did you find out in town?" I asked.

"I spent the morning in the library, leafing through the back editions of the local newspaper." He drew on his cigarette and exhaled lengthily, "I must say that *The Galloway Gazette* is an excellent publication. It's such a pity that the authorities never read it. Had they done so, they would have discovered that no fewer than three significant burglaries have taken place in the last four months, as far east as Dumfries, as far west as Stranraer, and as far north as Ayr.

"What they all have in common, of course, is that they are all less than three hours train journey from Kirkcudbright, which may well be a little unassuming town which attracts little attention, but is also the busiest harbour in the area."

"So it's from Kirkcudbright that the thieves have been shipping their booty?"

"I believe so. It's the perfect, inconspicuous location."

"But where are they shipping it to?" I asked.

"To the Continent – or France, to be more precise."

"How do you know that?"

"If my theory is correct that the little town is used as a distribution point, shipment can only be made by either rail or sea. Given that towns like Dumfries and Ayr have mainline rail links, I worked on the hypothesis that sea travel would be the more likely option.

"I didn't know the destination, however, until I visited the harbour. Among the many boats that were quite obviously local fishing vessels was moored a slightly larger boat – the *SS Alsace*. Beside the name on the rear of the boat, someone had crudely tried to erase the French tricolour – without much success, I might add. There was no sign of life on the vessel. I looked across at the shabby little building on the dockside, over which hung a sign that stated rather optimistically that it was the Harbour Master's Office."

I chuckled at Holmes's disparaging remark. He failed to see the humour and carried on his narrative.

"The occupant of the office was standing in the doorway, enjoying a pipe.

"'Good morning,' I said, indicating towards the dozen or so vessels bobbing gently and at the glinting sea beyond, 'A beautiful sight.'

"'Aye,' he replied. 'I never get tired of it.'

"'You've been here quite some time then?'

"'Ye could say that – thirty years next year.'

"'Good heavens, thirty years! No doubt most of these boats have a similar length of service.'

"'Aye, one or two, but ye always get the odd one who turns up.' He nodded towards the *Alsace*."

"'Really? I must say I was admiring that boat earlier. In fact, I am just visiting the area and was thinking about hiring a boat for the day to explore the coast a little more. You don't know if she's for hire, do you?'

"'I would'nea think so. She's docked a few times over past couple of months, but is just normally moored for the night. It was supposed to be the same this week, but apparently there's been a change of plan.'

"'Oh dear,' I feigned disinterest and, much to my satisfaction, the garrulous Harbour Master carried on with his indiscretion.

"'Aye, she was supposed to sail yesterday morning, first thing, but now y'r man came in only this morning and told me she will set sail on Wednesday.'

"'Wednesday? That means it would be free tomorrow. I wonder if Mr. – ?'

"'Ross. Duncan Ross.'

"'Yes, Mr. Ross, I wonder if he would be receptive to taking me out tomorrow?'

"'Ye can always ask, I suppose. He's staying at the Selkirk Arms with his two crew.'"

"It was at that very moment that all the links fitted together and the matter appeared as clear as crystal. The name the man gave me took a little while to register, but I suddenly realised what – or should I say *who* – we had stumbled upon."

The name sounded familiar to me as well, but I couldn't quite place it.

"'Ah, Mr. Ross,' I said to the Harbour Master," Holmes continued. "'I think I have seen him, as I, myself am staying at the Selkirk Arms. He is the tall chap with an olive complexion.'

"The Harbour Master took the pipe from his mouth and looked at me. "No, no, you've got the wrong man, sir. He's a wee fella with bright ginger hair. There's no mistaking his nationality,' he said with a chuckle to himself. 'Has a very well-spoken Edinburgh accent.'

"'Ah, I must be mistaken,' I said. 'Not to worry. No doubt I can make other arrangements.'

"With that, I bid the man a good morning and found the local police station."

"What did you do there?"

"There are no official detective policemen in the area, so I asked the uniformed officer to notify the nearest force. The man was a complete imbecile, but he got finally through to the Chief Constable at Dumfries, who said he was would send a man through to help."

"Help with what?" I asked.

"With preventing the attempted burglary that will take place at Barstobrick House tomorrow night."

Before I could question Holmes further, William and Jeannie came over and we all returned to the farm house. Along the way, Holmes asked if Mr. and Mrs. Wallace, the cook, and her daughter from the big house could join us. When they were all assembled, he repeated his story to his spellbound audience.

"Well, I never," exclaimed William. "Who would have thought something like this could happen here?"

"You said yourself, Mr. McFadden – everyone knows each other's business in a small community like this, and when the thief learned that Mr. Neilson had purchased the valuable artwork of – " Holmes gestured, trying to recall the artist's name.

"Hornel," I prompted.

"Indeed. And then learning that the Neilsons were out of the country, he saw it as the perfect opportunity for his next job."

"Little did he know that the owners were having their house decorated in their absence," I said. "Had he not caused the fire, he would most likely have got away with the painting from under our noses."

"But now he thinks he has a second chance. The incident was reported in this morning's local newspaper. It stated that Barstobrick House was undamaged and there was no suspicion of any wrongdoing. The thief therefore knows that the valuable painting is still intact, and I believe that temptation has gotten the better of him. He has held the French vessel back from sailing, and it can only be with the intention of making a further attempt, believing that his failure has been undetected and knowing that the house is still empty."

"Why would the thief go to the trouble of sailing to France, Mr. Holmes?" asked Jeannie.

"It is much easier to dispose of valuables on the Continent than it is here, Miss McFadden. The other burglaries I referred to include pieces of diamond jewellery, a coin collection apparently worth thousands, and an ancient artifact initially owned by one of the Mughal Emperors – all small enough to carry and make off with, and all valuable enough to profit from if a buyer can be found. Sadly, the Continent is full of such unscrupulous characters."

"What can we do in the meantime?" asked Mr. Neilson's man.

"Other than wait, Mr. Wallace, not very much, I'm afraid. The policeman is arriving from Dumfries at noon tomorrow." He turned to the cook. "Madam, I think it would be wise if you vacated your rooms and stayed here with Mrs. McFadden for the next two nights."

Elen put her arm around the elderly lady, who was obviously shaken by what she had just heard. "I'll come and help you pack some things."

Chapter IV

The policeman who arrived from Dumfries the following afternoon was a large, gruff individual with a shock of auburn hair and matching full beard. He identified himself Malcolm Fraser, a sergeant in the local detective force.

"The Chief Constable asked me to come down and help you capture this baddie," he said with great enthusiasm. "The Chief had spoken with Inspector Lestrade of Scotland Yard, who said you'd helped him on a couple of occasions."

Typical of Lestrade I thought to myself. Holmes saw my expression and smiled.

"Yes, one or two," he said to Fraser.

Holmes, Fraser, and myself, joined by the two local constables, took up our positions in the big house shortly after six o'clock. While four of us secreted ourselves in various places in Neilson's large study, one of the uniformed officers remained hidden in the hallway – Holmes's theory being that if the thief somehow evaded capture in the act of the theft, the constable outside would still be able to apprehend him on the way out. Knowing it would be after midnight – if at all – that the thief would appear, I settled down for a long wait.

"We must sit without light," said Holmes, turning down the lamp. Then he added, "And try not to fall asleep, Watson."

The grandfather clock in the hall outside signalled each excruciating hour. Although I would never admit it to Holmes, I felt my eyelids drooping when I was awakened by the clock striking two. Shortly afterwards I heard a noise, distinct from anything else inside the house. It was the sound of the door to the glass annex opening and shutting. When it was shortly followed by the noise of the small window beside the door leading into the house being jemmied open, there was no doubt that this was it. I instinctively looked across at Holmes, but couldn't make out his features in the pitch darkness. The sound of slow, soft footsteps could be heard in the hall outside, and I hoped that the constable stationed there didn't get too enthusiastic in his duty to arrest. I heard the sound of the doorknob to the study turn and sensed the large door opening. My heart pounded in my chest with excitement and anticipation.

Peering through the darkness, my pupils struggling to focus, I saw the vague outline of a diminutive figure. He seemed to stand for a moment, as if sensing something was wrong, but then moved forward towards the desk. I dared not breathe.

"*Now!*" cried Holmes, turning up the lamp and almost causing me to jump out of my skin.

Within an instant Fraser and the uniformed constable had hold of the little man who was literally in the act of reaching up towards the painting. The look of horror and surprise on his face was something to behold. The other uniformed officer rushed into the room and also took the arm of the prisoner.

"Alexander Murray, I presume?" said Holmes, "Also known occasionally as Duncan Ross, William Morrison, and no doubt several other aliases as and when required?"

The man was now being held by the two uniformed officers, but neither prevented him for drawing himself up straight and assuming a haughty, authoritative air. "And who the devil are you?"

"My name is Sherlock Holmes."

Even the dim light of the study couldn't conceal the colour from the prisoner's face draining away, as he slunk down again and adopted a demeanour of abject defeat.

"Ah, I see my name is familiar to you," added my friend. "No doubt your erstwhile partner in crime alerted you to me, following his apprehension – in not-so-dissimilar circumstances, if I recall – some years ago. His detention didn't stop you from carrying on your career in thievery however, I see – the only difference being is that you have replaced the rich pickings of the big city banks with the rather easier pickings of your rural homeland.

"The game is up, Murray." Holmes's tone was cold and unforgiving, "This particular crime route, leading to your unscrupulous foreign market, is well and truly closed. And no doubt will be for some time as with any luck, you will find yourself under lock and key for some time to come."

Murray looked up. "I hope you rot in hell, *Mister* Holmes."

"No doubt I'll see you there," said Holmes, casually, and with a clipped nod to the policemen, Murray was yanked away and led to the police wagon that had been secretly parked in one of the cow sheds.

"It's been a pleasure working with you, Mr. Holmes," said Fraser.

"The pleasure was all mine, Sergeant. If you go down to the harbour in town in a couple of hours' time, I'm sure you will also be able to apprehend Mr. Murray's accomplices aboard the SS *Alsace*."

"Will do, sir." With that, the policeman followed in the direction of his colleagues.

As we watched the wagon disappear into what was left of the night, I turned to Holmes. "How on earth did you know who this man was?"

"Later, my dear fellow," was his infuriating reply. "I think it's time we got some sleep before our own long journey."

With the blood coursing through my veins following all the excitement, I slept only fitfully over the few hours before what could be decently described as morning. We breakfasted before Jeannie accompanied us back to the station for our return journey.

"It's been wonderful to see you again, John" she said with a warm embrace on the platform. "And you too, Mr. Holmes," she added, offering a hand.

"Thank you for hospitality, Miss McFadden. It has been a most enjoyable stay."

I promised to keep in better touch with my childhood friend and made tentative arrangements for a return visit the following year. With that, our train pulled away and it was off back to the capital once again. As there were several hours to pass, I broached the subject again of the unexpected events of the previous night.

"I don't understand who Murray is – and what on earth put you on to him?"

"You may remember, Watson, our adventure some years ago that was brought to our door by Mr. Jabez Wilson."

"Certainly. What started off as an amusing practical joke ended with a serious attempted robbery."

"Precisely. We apprehended John Clay in the cellar of one of principle London banks. His 'pal' as he described him – Archie Nichols it turned out, if my memory serves me – was also arrested as he tried to escape through Mr. Wilson's shop next door. But there was a third man in Clay's gang, if you recall, and he got away: Our friend from last night."

"I do remember now – He went by the name 'Duncan Ross'. Mr. Wilson met him when being interviewed for a position in The League. I thought it sounded familiar, but that was nearly seven years ago."

Holmes nodded. "The villains had hired offices at Pope's Court, to get Jabez Wilson away from his pawn shop where the gang was spending time in the cellar, digging a tunnel into the bowels of the nearby bank. The man Wilson met in Pope's Court was Murray – or as he called himself then, *Duncan Ross*, a beneficiary of the so-called Red-Headed League.

"Upon learning that Clay had been arrested, Murray fled back to his homeland, where he has spent the last few years perpetrating low-risk burglaries for high rewards. I had noticed various stories in the newspapers over the months and years reporting periodic burglaries of valuable artifacts from remote areas of Scotland – the Highlands, the Borders, even the Isles of Skye and Arran were victims at various times. What they all have in common is that they are rural locations with minimum policing. Why risk capture in the big cities of Edinburgh and Glasgow when there are such rich, unguarded pickings elsewhere?"

"And the remote areas of the southwest also fitting the bill perfectly," I added.

"Precisely. Murray and Clay were from well-to-do stock and had contacts in high places, both at home and abroad. Murray therefore had a developed the perfect scheme of perpetrating these robberies and shipping the spoils over to the Continent, where they would be sold, while he disappeared back to Edinburgh to lay low for a few months before selecting his next location."

"John Clay is from the other end of the island," I said, perhaps naively. "They seem an unlikely pair."

"Not particularly," countered my friend. "The two met at Eton. I have a theory that like-minded people tend to gravitate to one another, whether they be good or bad. Moving in mutual circles, it was almost inevitable that the two would end up collaborating."

"And when Clay was captured," I concluded, "Murray decided to continue alone."

"Yes. I was a little chagrined that he slipped through our net that night and thought we would never see him again. Reading the newspapers all these years, I often suspected it could be Murray who would be perpetrating these thefts. Little did I know that I would encounter him personally, four-hundred miles away from my own hearth!" Holmes chuckled.

Our train arrived on time under the darkening September skies. We took a cab from Euston Station back to our lodgings. As it turned onto Baker Street, I had an overwhelming feeling of being home. I'm not sure, when I left a few days earlier, that I had been looking for the answer of where *home* was, but as Mrs. Hudson welcomed us at the door, I assuredly found it.

137

Our ever-obliging landlady had prepared a blazing fire on what was now a sharp autumn evening, and on the table was a steaming pot of coffee and a plate of buttered crumpets. I smiled at her thoughtfulness and the squeaking of my chair as I sank into it gave me a further feeling of comfort. I sat staring into the flames thinking about the events of the previous few days.

"I am completely worn out," said Holmes, "I feel as though I could sleep for a week!" He paused, as he headed towards his bedroom and put his hand on my shoulder, as if reading my thoughts, "You aren't only a gentleman, Watson – you are a gentle man. Don't torture yourself unnecessarily, my dear fellow. I know something of elder brothers choosing their own path. One has to let them decide for themselves which one they should tread."

He left me to stare into the fire and contemplate family and friends, past and present.

The Case of the
Abstemious Burglar
by Dan Rowley

"I have been wondering how long it would take the Metropolitan Police to consult me about these burglaries where nothing has been taken."

Settling into a chair, Inspector Gregson gave a start. "How did you know that's why I am here? There has been no public report that the burglar – or burglars – haven't stolen anything."

"Gregson, I'm simply applying logic to the facts. Even the scantiest newspaper reports allow some deductions. By my count there have been four break-ins to date, commencing a little over three weeks ago. Each has received a short notice in *The Times*, in none of which is there any mention of items removed from the site. That absence suggests nothing was removed, given *The Times*'s commitment to full reporting. Four such incidents are too much for coincidence. Your presence here indicates the Yard's efforts are stymied, and you need my help."

It was early afternoon in the fall of 1897, and we were in our sitting room in Baker Street. The sky was dark with clouds, and the air had turned rather chill. Holmes had been updating his indices in which he stored clippings and other materials that could be relevant to his inquiries, and I had been reading the newspaper when Mrs. Hudson ushered Inspector Gregson into the room. At Holmes's invitation, Gregson lowered his tall frame into a chair and clasped his square, pudgy hands in his lap. Before he could speak, Holmes had interjected about the burglaries.

Running a hand through his light hair, Gregson smiled. "I should have known, Mr. Holmes, that you would know why I had come. I always feel more confident when I have your assistance, so I hope I shall have it now."

"The affair promises to have some interest, but before I decide, I need more information. Please give me the details, and leave nothing out."

"Well, the first burglary was twenty-three days ago. It was at the offices of a merchant in Leadenhall Street. His name is George Linacre, and he deals in exportation of a variety of dry goods. The break-in happened at night. The perpetrator (or perpetrators) pried open the door with what appears to have been a crowbar."

"Do you have reason to believe there was more than one? That is the second time you have used both a singular and plural form."

"No, we aren't sure."

"Then pick one form, and we will assume it includes both."

"Very well. When Linacre's assistant arrived the next morning, he saw the marks on the door and called in a patrolling officer."

"How frequent are patrols during the night?"

"A bit irregular, but generally every ninety minutes or so. In any event, when Linacre arrived, he and the assistant searched through the office and could find nothing missing."

"Are you confident the search was thorough?"

"Yes. Linacre is quite intelligent and said he would know if anything had been taken."

"Let us hope so. Any evidence or trace is long gone, especially as your people and others undoubtedly have been mindlessly tramping through the site." Holmes leaned back and closed his eyes. "Continue with the second one."

"That was sixteen days ago, a stockbroker named Mathew Crofts. His office in Lombard Street was broken into during the night. The burglar again entered by forcing the locked door, likely with the same type of implement. The next morning Crofts discovered it and called us in. He also did a thorough search and couldn't identify anything as missing.

"There was a longer period until the third incident, six days ago. A solicitor's chambers in Carey Street were forcibly entered by similar means. The next morning the solicitor, Richard Kebell, alerted us but felt nothing had been taken."

"Finally, three days ago, Robert Placett, a doctor in Harley Street, notified us his office had been burgled. When we arrived, we found the same marks on the door. Placett swears not one item, even the drugs he stores, is missing."

"Watson, do you know this Placett?"

"Not personally, but he has a good reputation, especially with wealthy patients."

"All right, Gregson, a few questions: Were the patrol patterns the same in the last three cases roughly the same as in the first?"

"Yes, I would say so."

"When did the Yard decide the cases were connected?"

"We began to have our suspicions a day ago. While the first two were in the same police division, the second two were in different divisions. So only recently did we start to realize we might be dealing with one set of criminals."

"I thought the new structure where the divisions report to districts was to avoid this type of thing."

"It is. But the local officers didn't immediately report to their division and, because nothing was taken, the divisions didn't think to report to their district. Doctor Placett is an acquaintance of my District Superintendent and called him about the situation. The Superintendent assigned me, and I sent out an inquiry to all divisions and districts. When the reports came in, I realized there might be some connection."

Holmes smiled. "Good work, Gregson. I'm confident Inspector Lestrade will be annoyed by your diligence."

"That may be so, Mr. Holmes, but beyond the method of entry and the fact nothing was taken, I see no pattern here. The four victims all have different professions – merchant, stockbroker, solicitor, doctor. The crimes aren't centered on any geographic location. The first two are relatively close, but the second is west of them, and the fourth is even further west and to the north. Nor is there any pattern in the spacing of the break-ins. From the first to the second is seven days, from second to third ten days, and from third to fourth three days. And I'm at a loss as to any plausible motive."

"This has been helpful, Gregson. I will help you, but of course you may have all the credit. I would like to visit the four scenes in the proper order and interview the relevant parties. I would prefer that your people perform some preliminary work. Once that is done, we can commence in the morning. Do you have a list of the exact addresses?"

"Yes, I knew you would want that. Here it is." Holmes then gave him some further instructions, and Gregson retrieved his hat and coat and left us.

"Watson, I assume you would like to accompany me. Gregson may be the brightest inspector in the Yard, but I suspect he has missed some important clues. Even with a cold trail, we hopefully will discern more than the police."

"Of course I would be delighted to assist you, as always. However, I believe I detect the odor of a roast, so it seems we will eat well shortly." And indeed we did, afterwards enjoying sherry and cigars before turning in for the night.

The next morning, after a hearty breakfast of eggs, a rasher of bacon, and toast with jam, Mrs. Hudson arrived at the door with an envelope in her hand. "A policeman just delivered this for you."

"Thank you, Mrs. Hudson." Holmes opened it and perused the contents. "As I instructed Gregson, the policeman who went to each establishment determined that all the doors have been repaired or replaced and that none of the victims knows any of the other three. Let us be off to Leadenhall Street to see our merchant, Mr. Linacre."

We donned overcoats to ward off the fall chill, descended to the street, and hailed a cab. The driver went south on Baker Street and turned left to go east on Oxford Street. I took time to admire the various shops and fine emporia along the way, all presenting a delightful variety of goods and services, virtually everything Her Majesty's Empire had to offer. Among the delights were haberdasheries, tobacconists, stationery of the finest type, clothing for men, women, and children, coffee and sweet shops, and exotic offerings from the Caribbean, Egypt, India, and the Far East. One could probably even find beautifully crafted goods from Hong Kong and tea from our enclaves in China.

We finally arrived at Leadenhall Street. Pulling up to the address Gregson had supplied, we alighted, paid the cab driver, and entered the offices of George Linacre through a nondescript door with no indication of what lay within. The first thing we found was a large room with several clerks working busily on a variety of documents. There was bustle as they handed envelopes to runners, who rapidly left for their destination as if their very life depended on speed.

Holmes approached the closest clerk. "I am Sherlock Holmes, and this is Doctor Watson. I believe Mr. Linacre is expecting us."

"Yes, an officer was here earlier. Please come this way." He led us through the large room to a doorway in the back. We went through that into a small antechamber containing a writing desk at which stood a young man of about medium height with black hair, brown eyes, sharp features, with an eager look on his face.

We again introduced ourselves. He shook our hands. "Hello, I'm John Humphries, Mr. Linacre's assistant. He's expecting you." With that he ushered us into a much larger office, containing a desk, comfortable chairs, a sofa, a safe, and several cabinets against the walls. A husky man in his mid-forties with sandy hair and a blue waistcoat barely containing his ample girth rose from behind the desk to great us.

"I take it you are Mr. Holmes, and you must be Doctor Watson. I recognize you from the descriptions in *The Strand*. How can I help you?"

Thankfully Holmes didn't respond to the reference to my reports of our exploits, which he believed I dramatized too much. Instead he replied, "We would like to ask you a few questions. If Mr. Humphries is the person who first discovered the break-in, I would prefer he remain with us."

"Yes, he is. John, stay here."

"Let us start with you, Mr. Humphries. About what time did you arrive the morning after the burglary."

"I normally try to get here by nine o'clock, and that day was no different."

"Describe for us what you found."

"The outer door had been forced open. The wood by the lock was splintered, and there were gouges on the door itself. I hesitated for a

142

moment for fear someone might still be here, but decided that was unlikely. So I came into the outer room where the clerks work."

"Was anything disturbed out there?"

"No, sir. The clerks lock everything away at night, and there was no sign of anyone trying to force their way into any of the storage units. The outer door to my alcove is unlocked at night because I store my papers in the outer locked units when I depart for the day. I went into my alcove and noticed that the door to this office, which is locked at night, had been similarly forced open. The marks on the jamb and door looked the same to me. I immediately went outside and summoned an officer. He came in and I explained what I had found. I showed him the two doors and started to explain about the outer office and my alcove. About that time, Mr. Linacre arrived and joined us here in his office."

"Fine, Humphries. Very concise." Holmes repressed a sigh that he couldn't inspect the damage. "Mr. Linacre, you may continue with what you found."

"The only damage was to the door. Because it was locked, we don't lock my desk or these cabinets. The safe hadn't been tampered with. John and I went through all the cabinets and my desk. Nothing was missing."

"You're positive?"

"I couldn't be mistaken. The materials in the cabinets are arranged alphabetically, and John keeps a meticulous index that lists not only the folders, but also the contents of each one. He and I checked the cabinets against the index and confirmed that everything is there."

"And the contents of your desk?"

"A few personal items such as address and appointment books, all of which are intact. And what I was working on the day before, so that I have a clear recollection of what that was. Again, nothing missing."

"What do the cabinets contain?"

"Mostly commercial materials such as purchase orders, invoices, receipts, bills of lading, and so forth. Anything truly valuable, such as sensitive intelligence, reports from my factors, or letters of credit, we keep locked in the safe."

"If you don't mind, I would like to make an inspection of the cabinets."

"By all means, go ahead."

With that, Holmes spent the next hour minutely examining the folders and their contents. Periodically I would also take a look, but they were exactly as Linacre described and meant next to nothing to me. Holmes finally finished and looked at Linacre.

"Thank you for your time. Come, Watson, let us move on."

After putting on our overcoats and going back outside, we hailed another cab. Holmes gave the address on Lombard Street. As Gregson had noted, it wasn't very far from the first location to the next. The address was a much older building than the first, one of weather-worn brick and small windows. We entered and went up the stairs to Crofts's office. Unlike the merchant headquarters, there was only one room here. If anything, this location had more hectic activity. In the center of the room, a stock ticker noisily clattered and spat out a stream of tapes. Young men were tearing them off, rushing over to one of many books on shelves around the room, hurriedly examining one or the other, and then going to the back of the room for a quick consultation with a thin, wiry, and energetic red-haired man in his mid-thirties, dressed in his shirt-sleeves and grey pants. He would then hold a whispered conversation with the younger men, who then ran out of the room, presumably on their way to the nearby Exchange.

Holmes walked over to the red-haired man. "I assume you are Mathew Crofts. I believe that the police told you to expect me."

The man nodded. "Yes, I'm happy to help, as I'm mystified by this entire affair."

"You were the one who discovered the break-in?"

"I'm normally the first one here. I have no idea what they were after. There is no money here, and we lock all papers in our desks at night. There was no attempt to force any of those locks."

"What's in the books that line these shelves?"

"We collect private information about many of the companies traded on the exchange. When a quotation comes in on the ticker, one of my people checks the relevant information in the proper book and then consults me about whether to execute a trade."

"Were any of the books missing?"

"No. As you can see, the shelves are full. I ensured there were no gaps between the books, and I had my chief clerk double-check that nothing was missing."

"And the contents of the books?"

"That would take too long to search each one, and of course I don't have the manpower to do that and run my business."

"May I look at the books?"

"I'm sorry, but you may not. They contain information that is very closely held by us. You may walk around the room if you like."

Holmes then spent some time wandering about the room, apparently at random. When he concluded, he stood there for a while gazing off into the distance, clearly deep in thought. He suddenly started and walked out. I made our apologies and hastened after him. We procured a cab and retraced our route, this time in a westerly direction, on Cheapside and Holborn, until we turned left on Chancery Lane, then right on Carey Street to the chambers of the solicitor, Richard Kebell.

We entered a venerable old grey building, the masonry of which was blackened with London's soot and grime. There were large bay windows on each floor, and the entry door was of heavy oak with a huge brass knocker. We went upstairs to the second floor and passed again through a door into a large room with several clerks sitting on high stools before writing desks. The walls were lined with shelves containing folders and boxes, presumably filled with paper, the inevitable weapon of the legal profession. One of the clerks directed us to Kebell's office, which was the third door on the left.

The door was open, and as we entered, a tall thin man arose from the desk where he had been reading what appeared to be a legal tome. He was in his sixties, with hair that had once been black, but now turning white. He was dressed in a morning coat and peered at us through a *pince-nez* tied by a ribbon to his button hole. "Ah, you are Sherlock Holmes, I presume. The police alerted me you likely would show up."

"Yes, and this is my colleague, Doctor Watson. I have a few questions for you."

"I only have a short time, as I must leave to discuss a case with a barrister. I have heard of you, and at times have need of a detective, if that is of interest to you."

Holmes disregarded this last remark, as he normally didn't care to do work through a lawyer. He insisted on direct contact with the client so that he could make his own independent assessment of the client's character and trustworthiness. "I will not take too much of your time. Other than the outer door, is anything else locked up at night?"

"I do lock some papers in my desk, depending on their nature. But that is relatively rare. We have no money or other valuables here, so nothing else is secured."

"How are you sure nothing was taken?"

"It was a tedious process, I assure you. We keep a master file of all the materials we have. My chief clerk, with the assistance of other clerks and a few junior solicitors, went through everything to ensure it was all there. They just finished that two days ago."

"What types of matters do you handle?"

"Nothing criminal. But otherwise virtually any type of civil matter – real estate, trusts, wills, domestic issues, contracts, personal injury, and so forth. Our clients are quite varied, from the humble to the well born."

Holmes asked, "May I look at the files?"

"You may know that a good bit of the material is covered by legal privilege, so I'm afraid I cannot allow you to look in the files. In fact, some of them are so confidential I cannot permit you to open the drawers, which would allow you to see the names of my clients. I have to leave for my meeting, and my chief clerk is out. I might be able to arrange something." He went to the door and said to the clerk right outside, "Tell Jonathan and Benjamin to come in here." Turning to us, "These two can be a bit slow-witted at time, so I'm going to have them both supervise your inspection. In this case, two heads are hopefully better than one."

At that point, two young men entered. Both were roughly the same height, had brown slightly unkempt hair, and appeared nervous in Kebell's presence. He gave them detailed and strict instructions about how to supervise our inspection, then bade us goodbye.

With Jonathan and Benjamin in tow, Holmes walked around the main room, looking at labels on files and boxes that he was permitted to see. Every so often he would pause at a particular drawer he wasn't allowed to open and stare at it for several minutes. The two young men were perplexed by his actions, but of course I was familiar with his methods and ratiocinations. When he was satisfied, he thanked them and we left to return to Baker Street, as it was likely past Doctor Placett's visiting hours. I was delighted to find that Mrs. Hudson was preparing a succulent leg of lamb with new potatoes and salad for our evening repast.

The next morning, as we were having coffee, Inspector Gregson appeared in the doorway. "Mr. Holmes, there was another break-in last night. This time it was the Rector's office at Saint Bride's Church. I thought you would want to visit the scene before anything is disturbed. I have ordered a man to guard it and let no one enter."

"Capital, Gregson. We shall go at once."

We hastily donned overcoats and went down to the cab that Gregson had left waiting at the kerb. We quickly went back to Chancery Lane, turned left by Temple Bar, and were soon on Fleet Street. As always, I was impressed by the magnificence of the church. It had a beautiful spire that rose above the surrounding buildings, first in a plain square shape with a single round window, then a more ornate structure with a large arched window surrounded by pillars. This was capped by four successively smaller octagonal shapes with arched windows, finally ending in a wonderful steeple. While it could be seen from many vantage points around the City, up close it made one humbled by a true masterpiece, which of course one expects when seeing the work of the inimitable Christopher Wren.

We entered the front door, passed through the vestibule and then continued down the nave with its high walls and barrel celling. We located

146

a door to the right of the altar and, assuming it would lead to the Rector's study, Holmes led us forward. Sure enough, at the end of a corridor stood a constable guarding a door. He immediately straightened his back when he saw Gregson.

"Good work, Constable. No one has entered, correct?"

"No, sir, not a soul."

The door and the frame were splintered, and the lock was partially misaligned. Without a word, Holmes began a minute inspection. He peered at the door, lock, and jamb for quite some time. Then he got on his hands and knees and began picking up splinters and scrutinizing them with a magnifying glass he'd retrieved from his inner pocket, it being one of the items he habitually carried. Straightening up, he looked at both of us. "From the disturbance of the material on the floor, I detect two different types of shoes: One has leather, the other gutta percha soles. The sizes appear to be different, so that would seem to answer our question about whether there is only one burglar. Gregson, does the damage to the door look to you to be similar to the other four cases from the descriptions you've received?"

"Indeed, it does."

"Let us talk to the Rector then." At a nod from Gregson, the constable hurried off and shortly returned with a man wearing clerical garb. He was plump, in his late forties, rapidly balding, with squinting eyes and a habit or wringing his hands vigorously. "Hello, I'm Oliver Faber, the Rector here. How can I be of assistance?"

"I'm Inspector Gregson of the Metropolitan Police. This is Mr. Holmes and Doctor Watson, who are assisting me. Mr. Holmes would like to ask you some questions."

"Do you always lock this door at night?"

"Yes. I have some quite old vestments and altar items that I keep stored in a closet. Also, we have some manuscripts and Books of Common Prayer that range from one- to two-hundred years old – or more."

"Is there anything else of value?"

"No, just copies of my sermons, liturgical materials, and my various reference and similar books, such as commentaries on Scripture, convocation minutes, and directives from the Bishop and Archbishop."

"Is anything missing?"

"I don't believe so, but I cannot be positive until I've had an opportunity to do a more thorough examination. Of course, I immediately checked the closet, and everything seems to be there. The other materials are all on the shelves placed vertically. If anything had been removed, I would notice."

Naming the other victims, Holmes asked if the Rector knew any of them. He said that Linacre, the merchant, periodically attended services there.

Holmes then strode into the office and began walking by the desk in the center of the room. He looked at the shelves and into the closet. To the Rector's bewilderment, he abruptly left without a word. I again made apologies for his behavior, and Gregson and I hurried back through the church to find Holmes standing on Fleet Street, hailing a cab. It was there that Gregson left us there to pursue another case, while Holmes and I traveled back to Oxford Street, turned right onto Regent Street, went left through Cavendish Square, and emerged onto Harley Street. Throughout the ride, Holmes was silent but seemed impatient to make our last stop. The look in his eyes was instruction enough not to interrupt him.

We arrived at a typical Harley Street surgery, a narrow red brick building with front steps leading to a plain door with windows on each side. A brass plaque next to the door proclaimed this was the surgery of Robert Placett, M.D. The door was opened by a servant who politely informed us that consulting hours had ended for the morning, but Holmes presented his card, and within a moment we were ushered inside.

We found ourselves in a narrow corridor stretching back to a window overlooking a small courtyard. There were two doors on each side. From where we stood as we removed our coats and hats, we could see that the first on the left was a patients' waiting room with various comfortable chairs and small end tables. Across from it was the consultation room, with a small desk and wooden chairs where the doctor could converse with his patients in privacy. Further along on the left was the examination room, with the usual table and cabinets with various instruments. In the back on the right was a closed door – presumably the doctor's office. It had a small alcove at the entrance for a nurse to work on records, and there were locked cabinets presumably containing various medicines. On the right wall of the alcove was an obviously new door.

We were led back to the closed door, where the servant knocked. The door was opened, and there stood a man in his mid-fifties, of average height and weight, and with a full head of luxurious brown hair. His gleaming eyes took us in, and he said, "You must be Sherlock Holmes." Disdainfully glancing me, he smirked. "And you're Watson, the writer, I take it."

No doubt Holmes found this amusing. Before I could object, he replied, "Yes, We have just a few questions."

"I'm glad my calls finally are producing some action in this infernal matter. Proceed."

"At night, is this the only door other than the front one that is locked?"

"Yes. As you can see, the only thing of value in the alcove are the medicines, and they are separately stored and locked with the finest devices. Obviously there is nothing kept in the waiting room or consulting room. And my instruments in the examining room are kept in locked drawers. None of the other locks have been tampered with."

"I see. And what is kept in your office? I see there appear only to be those filing cabinets, these shelves with books and journals, and your desk."

"What deductive abilities. The cabinets contain my patient files, including my notes, test results, and so forth. My desk has working and personal papers. The shelves merely contain materials any decent library would have. And before you ask, I thoroughly checked and nothing is missing. I would know."

Holmes ignored his supercilious manner and continued. "What type of medicine do you practice?"

"I'm a generalist taking care of any ailments my patients may have. I take it from the questions that I was asked when the police informed me you were coming that there have been other incidents."

Holmes ignored his question. "May I examine your files?"

"Don't be absurd! Absolutely not. They contain sensitive patient information."

Nodding as if expecting that answer, Holmes turned and left. I made no apology and followed him out.

"What an obnoxious specimen. I hope he treats his patients with more kindness."

"I doubt it. You go back to Baker Street. I must go trace some things. I may be absent for a while, so don't concern yourself."

Resigned to his habits, knowing it useless to inquire what he was going to do, I returned home. The next few days I tried to amuse myself by reading the newspapers and a new military history of the Afghan campaign, and reorganizing some notes on cases including a matter in Reigate earlier that year, and also a case Holmes had solved by measuring the lengths of shadows in a garden at different times of the day.

When I wasn't so occupied, I reflected on what we had learned. It wasn't clear to me that nothing had been taken. The broker hadn't examined the contents of the books, which seemed odd given his stress on the value of those contents. The Rector wasn't positive because he hadn't had time to look carefully. And while their explanations for not allowing Holmes to do a more thorough examination was somewhat plausible, the refusals of the broker, solicitor, and doctor made it impossible to determine what the burglars might have been after in those instances. I agreed with Gregson there was no geographic or chronological pattern to the break-

149

ins. The fact that the Rector knew Linacre might be suggestive, but I couldn't fathom what it meant, given the lack of connection of any of the other victims.

Then late one chilly afternoon as darkness descended, there was a knock on the door. Gregson stood there, holding a scruffy individual by the collar. The man was short with disheveled hair, an unruly goatee, and a bent nose. He was wearing wire-rimmed glasses and a workman's cap and clothes. Gregson explained, "I received a message from Mr. Holmes to meet him here at this time. When I arrived, this disreputable character was lurking in the street. He refused to answer any questions, so I took custody of him and asked Mrs. Hudson to summon a constable. I didn't want to leave him alone with her."

"Quite commendable, Gregson. I particularly appreciate your solicitude for our landlady."

Startled at the sound of Holmes's voice, Gregson was disconcerted to discover the stranger had grown half-a-foot and was smiling at him."

"What on earth, Mr. Holmes? What is going on?"

"No time for that, Gregson. I'll remove this disguise and explain everything later." He left us and, emerging from his bedroom in a moment in his normal attire, Holmes commanded, "Watson, retrieve your service revolver from the desk. Where we're going, you may need it. Gregson, you're welcome to come as well. We're meeting a special squad from the Yard in thirty minutes." We put on our overcoats and hats to ward off the fall chill, descended to Baker Street, and quickly found a growler. Holmes whispered directions to the driver and we took off at a rapid pace, going through a maze of streets in an easterly direction. It became increasingly dark with less street lighting, so I wasn't sure exactly where we were, other than to divine we were somewhere in rabbit warren of streets in the East End.

When we finally stopped and got out, I was able to get my bearings and realized we were in notorious Whitechapel, where Jack the Ripper had committed his atrocities nearly a decade earlier. Motioning to us, Holmes silently led the way to a corner. A fog had begun to descend, exacerbating the chill, and I noticed we were near an establishment named The George Tavern.

A shadowy figure emerged from the fog and beckoned to Holmes, who went over and had a murmured conversation. He returned. "That man is the leader of the squad conducting the raid. Our target is on the first floor. One group will proceed through the public house on the ground floor to block the stairway exit. We'll follow the other group, which will take an external staircase in the back alley up to the room where our targets are holding a meeting. Follow me and stay alert. These men are dangerous."

We made our way around the building to a narrow, dank alleyway. There were pools of water on the stones, and garbage was scattered here and there, wafting unpleasant odours. I could hear the scurrying of what I could only assume were rats. Holmes motioned us silently toward the foot of the external staircase. The men ahead of us carefully ascended the stairs until they came to a door. On finding it was locked, their leader looked at the largest man and pointed at it. The large man easily crashed through, and we could hear the commotion of shouting and scuffling inside. Several shots were fired. Then there was silence. The leader came to the doorway and said, "You may come in now."

We entered a room that ran the width of the building and was approximately ten feet deep. Cheap chairs and tables were strewn about amidst the debris of broken ale bottles and glasses. There were eight men, all in working clothes similar to what Holmes had worn earlier. Several were panting, and showed cuts and torn clothing.

The leader of our group turned to his men. "That's the lot. The wagons should be downstairs to take them away."

"You aren't as clever as you think," one of the captives snarled. "Henderson, our key man, isn't here. And you'll never find him."

Holmes smiled. "You are quite wrong. *I'm* Henderson. I know all your plans, and they are thwarted."

Suddenly the captive broke free, pulled out a wicked looking knife, and lunged at Holmes. Fortunately I was holding my revolver and got of a shot that hit his thigh, bringing him down writhing in pain.

As I began treating his wound, Holmes said, "Good show, Watson! We'll leave our companions to put these miscreants where they belong. Gregson, let us repair to Baker Street for a well-earned repast."

"And I surely hope an explanation, Mr. Holmes."

On our return, Mrs. Hudson had already laid out a cold collation of meats, cheeses, condiments, and breads. Once we'd finished, Holmes lit his pipe and looked over at us. "So now we may have an explanation."

"I don't see how you determined this, and I certainly cannot fathom who any of the men were tonight – either the ones we were with, or the scoundrels in that room."

"Gregson, you actually provided a key clue when you stated there was no pattern to the burglaries."

"I'm afraid I don't understand."

"The absence of any pattern was in fact the pattern: A merchant, stockbroker, solicitor, physician, and Rector that were geographically dispersed, had no connections with one another other than the merchant periodically attending the Rector's church, and apparently had nothing taken from their offices after a physical break-in. Although I couldn't ascertain from physical inspections that nothing was taken, the victims seemed honest and had no reason that I could fathom to lie about anything not missing. From the beginning, I suspected that most of the burglaries were a diversion to put the police on a false trail, hiding the true target."

"But how could you tell what the true target was?" I asked.

"There was one commonality of all the offices: Even though nothing physical was removed, each office had information of some type – information the burglars could read and take away with them, leaving no physical trace. I therefore concentrated on the type of information in each office.

"Let us take a step back and reflect on possible motives. The apparent lack of pattern suggests someone attempting to conceal the motive. Although there are many motives, the most common are greed, anger, jealousy, revenge, and pride. Greed could be a factor in the first two burglaries because the merchant and the broker had valuable commercial information. The solicitor could have something of that nature as well, but I seriously doubt criminals trying to misdirect the police would be after such information. And the break-ins at the doctor and the Rector confirm that, as there is no commercial advantage there. Yes, Gregson, before you interrupt, a doctor could have information about a serious illness of a captain of industry, but the Rector would have nothing. So I eliminated greed.

"Pride, revenge, and jealousy also would be unlikely. Those typically are intensely personal motives, and we have no evidence here that would indicate that."

"But, Mr. Holmes, we don't know that. There could be something in the past of one of the men that triggered such a motive."

"True, and the police might spend months combing through the past histories of each victim. There is one connection: The Rector and the merchant. But that leads us to nothing – the mere fact of attendance at a church is just that, an isolated fact that indicates nothing concerning motive. It would require thousands of interviews and searches to determine what other connections, if any, there might be. I don't think that is necessary because there is a much simpler solution in terms of motive: *Anger*.

"The target was the solicitor's office. He clearly was well-to-do, with an equally lustrous set of clients. And recall that, among other matters, he dealt with what he delicately referred to as 'domestic' issues. That of course would include marital difficulties, and – " His face grimaced with disdain. " – divorce. You recall that he mentioned he uses so-called detectives. While I couldn't see the more sensitive clients' names, I could see invoice records that allowed to confirm that indeed he handles divorce and often hires individuals, presumably to follow wayward spouses to collect evidence. While I don't engage in such activity, I'm aware of its existence."

Gregson interjected, "Are you suggesting someone angry about an infidelity broke in? It wouldn't be the spouse who hired the solicitor. I suppose it could be a third party harmed in some way by the adultery, such as another spouse. But would such a person construct such an elaborate scheme?"

"Ah, you would if you wanted to discover the secret trysting place of a woman and her paramour. You see, it has nothing to do with the husband or the wife. It is the paramour and the secret location that the burglars were after. And the logical conclusion is that they want to harm the paramour when he is vulnerable and least protected."

"What do you mean 'least protected'?"

"Gregson, let us assume, for purposes of argument, that the paramour usually has bodyguards accompanying him, but not when he secretly meets the wife of another man. There are a number of individuals who might utilize bodyguards, such as the wealthy and certain criminal elements. But think for a moment about our burglars and the type of anger that might motivate them.

"An important type of anger is political anger. If you wanted to assassinate a prominent political figure, what better way to do it than when he is without protection and distracted by the attentions of his paramour."

"Holmes, do you mean to suggest a member of the Royal Family!"

"Capital, Watson. You have followed my logic precisely. The burglars are a group with a political agenda they conceive can be facilitated by killing one of our Royals."

"Are you talking about the Irish," asked Gregson.

"No. Anarchists."

Silence filled the room as Holmes continued. "I began to keep an eye on them some time ago, as did my brother Mycroft in his duties with the government. You'll remember the plot to blow up the Greenwich Observatory in 1894. In February of that year, police found Martin Bourdin severely injured near the Observatory with explosive materials on his person. It was discovered that he had connections to anarchist groups.

"They believe in what they call 'propaganda by the deed'. As you both know, using bombs against political targets has become all too frequent." He of course was referring to what had become a world-wide phenomenon, with bombings in Chicago, Barcelona, and Paris. "I worry that the ever-increasing availability of dynamite will be something we come to regret – allowing mass murder of civilians on an unprecedented scale. There is scheduled to be an international conference next year to deal with this threat, but I'm not optimistic.

"In any event, I went to Mycroft with my deductions after we visited the physician. He confirmed that the Home Office was conducting surveillance of several groups. He and I met with the appropriate official, and, after some discussion of the tactics of our burglars and the suspected target of the assassination plot, we determined the most likely group. Luckily, the Home Office had been able to infiltrate the group with a member of Scotland Yard. We communicated with him, and he introduced me to the group as an expert in explosive construction. That's where I have been the past days, in the disguise in which you saw me. I ingratiated myself with them. My chemical knowledge made it easy to persuade them of my bona fides. I learned of the meeting tonight, alerted the Home Office to set up the raid, and you know the rest."

"Mr. Holmes, that is astounding as usual. I never would have imagined that a series of unrelated burglaries could turn into a plot against a member of the Royal Family."

"There's one more thing, Gregson: You may want to have a word with your superiors. I believe the member of the Yard who was undercover participated in the burglary at Crofts, the stockbroker. He was bragging to me that he'd received an inheritance from an aunt, but he was quite nervous and shifty-eyed when telling me. And he had a large amount of cash, which wouldn't be the normal way of receiving a bequest, as he claimed. The more likely explanation is that he memorized some of the information in the books in Crofts's office and sold it, probably to another broker."

With a bemused smile, Gregson left us. We had a nightcap and retired for the evening.

Late the next day, we were in the sitting room, where Holmes was inspecting some samples of bee pollen and I was reading an article on a new medical procedure. There was a knock on the door, and Mrs. Hudson entered. "This package just came for you, brought by a fancy coach."

Thanking her, Holmes unwrapped it. Inside there was a handwritten note. I couldn't see the entire note itself, but was fairly certain I caught a glimpse of the Royal Seal and that it was signed '*I am in your debt. E*'."
Holmes threw the note onto the fire. With a slight upturn of the corners of his mouth, he showed me a box of beautiful cigars. "I believe this is his usual brand. Shall we partake, old friend?"

The Blackfenn Marsh Monster
by Marcia Wilson

The Inspectors

"**S**tanley Hopkins." Inspector Lestrade closed his eyes and pinched the bridge between his nose, hard. The glower in his pale face matched his meagre office window, for a sudden gust sent dirty grains of snow and cinders against the glass. "Only last week I had to take tea with Mr. Baynes. D'you remember him?"

The younger Scotland Yard inspector was a fundamentally polite fellow, so he made the effort to do as requested, even as his shivers threatened to shake Lestrade's guest chair apart. Lestrade had buried him under their coats over the weak floor vent from the Yard's coal furnace. How could he have been so single-minded as to buy a billet back to London in this weather? It was childish – but, no, Hopkins was an adult and prone to the foolishness that only grown men knew. There was probably a lot more of Hopkins that Lestrade saw in himself than he liked to admit, but he took comfort in the fact that Hopkins was (unlike himself, he thought with satisfaction) an optimist.

"I – Isn't he . . . rather tall? Stout about the middle like John Bull, and wheezes, and doesn't look like he could do much, but he's strong as a bear and can climb a roof like a cat?"

"Yes . . . ." Lestrade had not opened his eyes. "We have a balance of favours that we must regrettably pull from each other, and that means we tolerate each other every two or three months. Usually, I drink the tea and listen to him tell me, 'We stagnate here in the provinces,'" The imitation of the man was convincing. Lestrade was possibly exaggerating the rolling pomposity that dripped out of every syllable. "And every time, Hopkins, *every single time* he says this, I think to myself, 'You don't know Hopkins and what I've seen on his desk.'" Lestrade leaned back and stared at the plaster ceiling. "Have you . . . angered someone in the Home Office?"

"Not knowingly . . . ?"

"Hmph. Put your hands around that teacup, man. Mine are chilblained just looking at you." Lestrade continued reading through Hopkins' files. Hopkins' face twisted in a poor approximation of a smile (his lips were numb) and complied.

"I know you don't like country cases. I'm sorry." Hopkins winced at stating a fact so blatant it insulted. Lestrade hated country cases because

155

he liked the country very much, if only it was nothing but countryside. Nothing spoiled his joy in quiet pastoral gardens and butterflies so much as corpses and killers, and legend had it that if any rusticating old copper would bumble into the only unlawfully deceased for a hundred leagues, it would be surely Lestrade, who was either the luckiest of unlucky policemen, or vice-versa. Even Gregson, the Yard's standing expert on All Matters Lestrade, was stymied to which. "Lestrade . . . there aren't many men I can consult right now . . . ."

"Just . . . stop, Hopkins." Lestrade straightened in his chair, a movement that sent the wheels squeaking back on the polished floor. His dark eyes glittered. "Did the world change so much since yesterday? Did I somehow sleep through a complete shift in administration, through which the hard-working country copper faced a grisly case and saw it plucked off his desk and into the interfering, meddling, condescension of the Yard?" The little man waved Hopkins' notes in the air. "Am I reading this true? Can it be possible that there is a nasty murder that affects a quiet little village, and this village is happy that an outsider is coming in to take over? Is this what happened?"

Hopkins took a deep breath. "Not . . . happy, so much, Lestrade, but . . . relieved."

"Relieved," Lestrade repeated flatly. "Oh, this is a nice one, is it?"

Hopkins groaned. "'Nice' is the last word we shall ever hear attached to this death."

"Just how nasty was this? You've left out an awfully lot of detail, which I've only just realised now that I agreed to help,"

Hopkins mumbled at his shoes. "I beg your pardon?" asked Lestrade.

" . . . 'n bnmnsdr," Hopkins repeated, no more intelligible.

"What did you say?"

" – s"

Bang! Lestrade sank backwards into his chair, each eye-socket plugged with his palms. "A *swamp monster*?"

"Could you repeat that, only louder?" Hopkins snapped testily. "I'm not sure Croggins heard you down in archives."

"You've put me on another monster hunt!"

"I've never put you on a monster hunt! It wasn't really a monster, though, eh? Just a very large dog wrapped in a dogskin with phos – " Hopkins coughed to a stop at the wild-eyed-savage-out-of-the-jungle look on the other's face.

"You do realise," Lestrade strangled, "we need Mr. Holmes and Dr. Watson equally badly for this investigation." Hopkins could have melted from gratitude. Lestrade had said "we", and that was a certificate of solidarity.

"I went to Baker Street first, but Mrs. Hudson said he and the doctor were unavailable, being as they were on holiday."

Lestrade jeered. He had a good face for it. "And how often does Mr. Holmes go on holiday?"

"Out of free will? I thought that was a cypher for . . . something else?"

"Oh, dear. No."

"You mean they really are on holiday?"

"No. One is." Lestrade sighed. "I daresay the other is sneaking out at night to solve puzzles while his attending physician sleeps. This is why you came to me, eh? Because you hope I might know where our private consulting madman and his guardian ang – guardian *doctor* – have gone to ground?"

Hopkins grumbled. "Mr. Holmes hardly ever turns down one of your cases these days. He says they're more entertaining."

"Hopkins . . . We need to have a little talk someday about your candor. Anyhow . . . your report orbits around your disagreement with the country doctor who says it was a natural death? If you're disagreeing with the verdict of the coroner, you may request another examiner provided you have a good cause, but you have to find one on your own . . . and I'm not any sort of medically qualified certifier for an unusual death."

Hopkins had been under control until this point. Lestrade saw his throat work around a tight swallow. "There's a law still on their books down there," he began carefully. "Dating to the Roundheads, and was writ to discourage the angry public from attacking Crown-approved engineers from draining the swamps, marshes, lowlands, and other 'unproductive lands' to make them arable to tenant crops. If we are to believe the descendants of the families who witnessed this original contention, there was much anger between the common folk and the landed outsiders. The law is clear: Anyone who has served the Crown and dies within a day's ride within the original town boundary-stones is granted a professional examination to rule or out-rule foul play."

Lestrade winced. "Mayn't I have another look at your file?"

"Oh, do. I've stared at it until my eyes quit." Hopkins slumped, exhausted in the uncomfortable wooden chair. The soft whisper of papers moving back and forth under Lestrade's hands sent him, without warning, into a deep sleep.

"Hopkins!" The policeman jumped. Lestrade was looming over him – never a sight for sore eyes. It was enough to send any Yarder awake and alert for whatever trouble that inevitably followed. Such as the time.

The little shelf-clock on Lestrade's desk gave horrifying news. "You let me sleep!" Hopkins squeaked.

"Might as well until the wire returned." Lestrade handed him his coat and hat and donned his own, ushering him out the door with bewildering speed. "Come! We'll grab a hot supper at The Fool's Cup before the train."

"But . . . shouldn't we find Mr. Holmes?"

"I daresay he'll meet us at the Marsh . . . ."

"What? Why? How?" Hopkins clutched his briefcase with the fervor of a mother holding her newborn child. "He can't be found! You said so!"

"I didn't look for him." Lestrade grinned. It was terrifying. "I looked for Dr. Watson. And he's never outside the range of his *locum*."

Dr. Watson

My friend Sherlock Holmes often needs restoration after an exhaustive case. Under events that shall remain private, Holmes had stretched himself too thin, and I took it upon myself to set him to recovery. Thus, we closed our rooms in Baker Street and rented a small cottage by the seaside, for Holmes usually found the lap of waves and wind soothing to his nerves.

After three days, he complained there were no more little puzzles to keep his mind obedient. By the end of the first week he paced fretfully on the floors for diverting news. Upon the end of the second week, I was fast becoming a self-made expert on deflection and diversion. I began to contemplate a secondary career for this talent should my profession fail and send me to the destitution of spying for wages.

On the third week, we were half-finished with Holmes's medically induced purgatory. It wasn't a second too soon that our breakfast was interrupted with an express packet delivery.

"A problem with a patient?" Holmes inquired. From what little I could see of myself in the silver teapot, my expressions must have been a feast for his deductions. "Or shall I venture something unexpected?"

"You're right. This is an urgent letter from Lestrade, wrapped inside Barrows' correspondence. He is begging for my assistance, and I confused – " I froze in midsentence, for a name from the past had leapt upon me. "Good heavens!" I passed the paper to Holmes.

My Dear Dr. Watson,

I normally consult your friend, but an odd matter has fallen to the Yard that falls within your discretion. My colleague Inspector Hopkins was assigned the investigation of a death in Blackfenn Marsh. The dead man was Captain James G. Baxter of the Northumberland Fusiliers. The

158

coroner, Dr. Alain Rennels, insists he died of natural causes, but there is a queerness about the facts that roused Hopkins' suspicious. The old laws of the province demand a more thorough investigation than Rennels is qualified to perform.

I know that Hopkins has learned much from Mr. Holmes and if he feels something amiss, a man should take a second look at the crime, if only to err for the side of caution. The next course of action would be to find a second professional to confirm or deny Rennels' decision.

I thought of you, as I presume the passing of a fellow Fusilier would be of interest. I realise I am taking liberties, for I am drawing conclusions based on o photograph of Captain Baxter and he is wearing a Fusilier's medal on his lapel. Should you be interested in taking this case, we are authorised to pay you as a consultant, and to approve what resources and assistance you might require in settling this matter. I have attached further details below.

Yrs Sincerely,

G. Lestrade
Scotland Yard

"Hmm," Holmes exclaimed. "My condolences, Watson. Your reaction is hardly that of an impartial acquaintance."

"As you know, I was in the process of joining my regiment when the war broke out. We barely docked in Bombay when half of us fell from the foreign climes. An error in the new rails had halted even the delivery of the mail and we were technically marooned. Baxter ran our station house (really, a rajah's mansion), and though he was recovering from his own illness. he took charge of our troops. The discretionary officer was insensible with the same puerile fever that had struck us. Thanks to Baxter, we reached Candahar by maritime rail, and I'm not certain everything he did would have been approved were the need not so great."

"An expedient thinker."

"Precisely. We were in his care a fortnight, but I remember him a cheerful fellow, ever ready with a prank designed to make the victim laugh. There was no evil to him that I saw – he was the type of trickster that would steal your boots and then return them polished with a bill of services from the brownies demanding cream.

"A most intelligent man," I added, "but he was a dreadful patient. Utterly loathed conventional treatment because it took away his time from

159

his studies. He was forever reading or taking notes of the wild animals. The cooks dreaded him. He haunted their kitchen to loot the larder for interesting fish and game." The brief memory had warmed me, but remembering the letter's purpose cast me down. "I cannot refuse. A Fusilier should attend."

"And I offer my services. I am no certified cutter, but I know my way about an examination room as well as the next."

"I should be glad for it. Lestrade's letter gives me a broad definition of privilege."

"Broadness is needed. This case is more than a little odd if Lestrade and Hopkins are both set upon the trail – their rails rarely cross." Holmes sipped his coffee, eyes half-shut for thought. "Blackfenn Marsh . . . Well!" Without warning, Holmes began to chuckle. I didn't follow this train of thought and said so. "Oh, some ridiculous rumours about a monster, some sort of serpent or wyrm in the marsh – as if a large reptile could thrive in our frosty clime."

"I try not to underestimate the credulity of men, Holmes."

"Oh, of course. A pity that is so difficult."

The Inspectors

Hopkins and Lestrade packed their notebooks with information that hadn't made it into the written reports. The plan was to give all this to their consultants and possibly save some time and fruitless searching.

"The public hasn't yet been made aware of anything more than the death of the captain," Hopkins recited the facts as Lestrade short-handed his speech. "'*Captain James Baxter, N.F., Alnwick Academy, was an excellent researcher and publisher of scientific articles. He gathered regard (plus gratuities and gifts) from influential patrons. He may have been the only man in England capable of competing with James Edmund Harting in his expertise for British wildlife . . . .*'" Hopkins was cautiously quoting from the peerage books. It would never do to imply sub-standard perfection for the English Naturalist's golden child.

Lestrade grunted. "Can't pick up anything printed about wildlife without Harting somewhere under the cover."

"He's written six books in six years."

"Baxter hoped to match that?" Lestrade was stunned.

"Not just he. Trying to out-write that prodigy is the new Holy Grail. Honestly, Mr. Holmes and Dr. Watson probably know a lot more about either gentleman than we two. They move in those circles: Hunting and fishing and leisurely pasttimes such as that. Didn't Watson write Holmes's family are squires?"

160

"Tell me more about the legal knots."

"Right. To be plain, the local doctor – Rennels – is Blackfenn's unofficial Lay Coroner. It's a convenient duty for him, as he is paid for every death he signs, but he isn't obligated to give every corpse on his table an autopsy. That is reserved for specialists. Even he didn't know about the old law about an in-depth death report for former veterans."

"Lovely. How did this turn up?"

"The keeper of the tavern is the fifth-great grandson of the last specialist."

"And the duty wasn't invoked since? This is a dull place! Is that why this Rennels retired here?"

"He claims to have moved here to enjoy the country airs without the crime of city life."

The policemen stared at each other. It never ceased to amaze them that educated, intelligent men equated "country life" with "peace and morality".

"Rennels owns the lease to Baxter's villa. All seems friendly between them. Rennels examined Baxter's corpse and decreed it natural causes: Heart strain from infection resultant to untreated injury."

"You disagree."

"Yes!" Hopkins had been dreading this moment. He pulled a scrap of paper out of his pocket. It wasn't a bad drawing, but as to the subject matter . . . .

Lestrade scowled. "What am I looking at? Are those . . . *teeth punctures* in the sole?"

"That's why the locals say he was bit by a monster in the marsh," Hopkins said wearily. "He allegedly limped to The Proud Host (that's their only establishment) this past fall and pulled off his stocking to show everyone where a monster bit him through his shoe while walking down the estuary, and when the story got twisted, as it was bound to do, it became 'monster in the swamp'. (Lestrade groaned.) Aye, a strange joke at your own expense! His leg was red and puffed up like bee stings, and for days he demanded a bucket of hot water for soaking as he held court before the taps. The regulars fretted that his limp worsened and he more easily tired, yet he didn't complain. Everyone was shocked when he died."

"Yes, I saw that, Hopkins. 'Passed away in church.' That isn't at all in-depth."

"It was his usual custom to come to the little chapel – Blackfenn's only house of worship – on Saturdays for supper with the Reverend Jude once his clericals were finished. The vicar told me that the captain came at four o'clock as usual, looking exhausted and sweating heavily. He rested at his usual pew. Reverend Jude finished some paperwork within twenty

161

minutes and went to collect his friend, but instead found him slumped against the back of said pew, dead."

"Which Dr. Rennels attributes to natural causes." Lestrade blew out his breath, drained from the lack of useful evidence. "This is absolutely a case for Mr. Holmes."

Dr. Watson

The train from the seaside made good time, and we found our platform already occupied by two familiar figures: Inspectors Hopkins and Lestrade, along with two large country constables. Hopkins spied us first and waved.

"By Jove, it's good to see you both!" the young man cheered, "I apologize for the rude accommodations. This sort of spiteful weather is rare in the lowlands."

"Can you stand a hot meal at the public?" Lestrade wondered. "A little time to thaw and learn our news might be of use."

"It would indeed," I reassured them. "Inspectors, would it be appropriate if I were to take on the medical portions of this examination, and leave the rest to Holmes?"

"Yes!" was the resounding answer, and Holmes chuckled merrily around his travelling pipe. No one could ignore the relief in the policemen's eyes.

Within minutes we were hustled to a large public house. The bobbies stood watch against interruptions as Lestrade and Hopkins passed over their written notes of the case, verbally expanding when we had questions. I didn't need long to conclude and slapped my papers on the table. "Dr. Rennels may be correct in a layman's verdict, but that is all. Thank you for summoning me."

Holmes added his file to mine. "I at first thought this a possible waste of time, but this is *outré* enough to raise questions. I presume this is the same Dr. Rennels, MRCS, who has achieved a modest fame with his papers on the sustainability of gamekeepers?"

Hopkins paled. "I don't know. His profession outside of medicine never came up. When I interviewed him, he said he was a bit of a scribbler and liked to take notes of the marsh. No one here told me different when I asked about it."

Holmes scoffed. "One of those men." He shrugged at their embarrassment. "Not a poor scientist, but inept in society. He proclaims himself a base amateur, and then is outraged when people take him at his word. I'm sure you would have discovered his false modesty soon enough."

162

"I believe I recall a few of his writings," I mused. "My friend Mortimer described them as precise but short of content, the refuge of a man who doesn't spend a lot of time in-depth on his subjects."

"Is it important?" Lestrade wondered uneasily.

"Perhaps," Holmes mused, tapping his long white fingers upon our table. "We should settle our accommodations and speak with him. Watson, it is your responsibility to examine the body and support or deny Rennels' original statement."

"Exactly. I perform an initial, simple examination with a policeman as witness, but I cannot perform an in-depth autopsy without proper facilities. As a certified board surgeon and trained military physician, I am qualified to go further in my discretions than Rennels."

"What happens if you say we need a more thorough examination?" Hopkins asked.

"I shall ask it regardless."

"Thank you. That is most reassuring."

"A second examination isn't so unusual in the medical field," I assured them. "Indeed, it shouldn't be considered remarkable in winter, when there could be the slightest hint of an epidemic. I saw the nostrums were hawking influenza cures at the station. That suggests the disease is a concern here."

"The marshlands are always suffering one ague or another," Hopkins admitted. "You do make good sense, Doctor – eh?" the young inspector twisted in his chair, for a bobby approached with a paper in his glove.

"Messenger boy, sir."

The policemen leaned together to read the paper, and twin expressions of surprise and annoyance crossed each face.

"Speak of the devil and you see his horns," Lestrade smiled through his teeth. "Dr. Rennels received our notification, and is asking us to bring you to him. Cheek."

"Better sooner than later," Holmes assured us.

Hopkins grumbled. "We'll use the cab and add your luggage. We're staying at the captain's villa, gentlemen, unless you object. It is the only roof available."

We had no objections. Before long we were trotting along a well-cleared dirt road that showed us a rushy landscape laced with tendrils of fenland before draining to the sea. Only the skirr of winter waterfowl, cottage, and once, an old Catholic chapel on high ground broke, the smooth monotony of watery earth.

"The soil must be very fertile." I lost count of the long, exposed hills and mounds of black earth, exposed to collect the nitrites in winter snow.

"True," Hopkins laughed, "though the sulphur stink of the summer isn't nice. Part fen and part marsh thanks to the convoluted drainage. When it's drained, they grow just about anything they please here. Rather than turning fallow, they open the dykes and let it rest under water, collecting the nutrients and making it pay as a hunting field. Plumpest ducks in the isle, I'll be bound, and coarse fish. It provides, and no mistake.

"The water monster fable started when the Roundheads and Winstanley's Diggers were running amuck. The Blackfenners are even today haymakers and lathe turners, and they've always depended on the marshes as they are. They cut the water-meads for reeds, withies, and greenwood, and to speak nothing of the fishing and fowling. Even a child can collect money for clothes or school by harvesting the plants they find to the right market.

"The landowners wanted everything drained so they could rent farmland. As you may imagine, there were acts of violence to man and machines, and when questioned the marsh men shrugged and blamed it on the Blackfenn Beast. Time has passed, but while circumstances have settled, change comes slow. They still grow skirrits instead of carrots here, so don't be surprised at the pies you order." The carriage surprised a flock of widgeons: Hundreds took to flight over their heads, whistling as they landed on the other side of the fields. Hopkins laughed. "There's a familiar sight. They're efficient grassclippers, gentlemen. My advice is let them do the work if you don't want to pay a gardener for the task."

Lestrade laughed too. "I forgot you're fen-bred."

"Some things you never forget." Hopkins' good humour melted as we neared a small line of shops and services perched tightly between the train lines and a cluster of tenant housing. "Oh, dear. There he is."

Dr. Rennels was taller than Sherlock Holmes and even more skeletal, but funereally grand in an expensive suit, its grandeur slightly spoiled by snow stains on his trousers – the weather is forever ruining the vanities of a proud man. He awaited us as he adjusted a beaver hat the same sable as his fur-trimmed coat, a ring of heavy brass keys chiming at his waist.

Hopkins jumped out and hailed him. "Hello again, Doctor," he said merrily. "I've returned as promised. Dr. John Watson, this is Dr. Alain Rennels, our usual examiner for the region, and the primary landlord for the properties about. You'll find him an authority on the marsh."

Rennels clucked self-depreciatingly, and we shook hands as he was introduced to Holmes. "Dreadfully sorry for your trouble," he said softly. "Bad weather for visits. Still, I can't fault the police for being thorough. I understand military matters require more attention."

"It is often the case."

"Well, he died of natural causes, as far as I could tell. He wasn't my patient, strictly, just my tenant, and we shared our fascinations for the moss."

I nodded to show I understood. "You determined heart failure?"

"Oh, yes, he had all the signs. Constantly breathless, chest congestion, easily fatigued, edema, and sporadic fevers that never quite went away. Resisted my offers to treat him."

To our amusement, Lestrade was writing this down behind Rennels' back.

"That is most helpful, sir. I will make my examination post haste, and of course give you a copy of the report." These delicate negotiations were necessary to prevent the open warfare that lurked in the potential rivalry between two doctors in overlapping territories.

"I've no objection. The remains are in our morgue – that old Catholic chapel put to practicality."

Holmes smiled. "I too am fascinated with Blackfenn Marsh. Are there any historical accounts or guidebooks?"

"Bah, nothing worthwhile. I shall personally remedy that in the spring with my treatise."

"Had the captain any projects when he died?"

"Why, yes. He was helping me with lifting the water table to its original level."

"I should like to see."

"You are enthusiastic, sir."

"Learning is my passion."

"Well, it shan't take you long." Rennels nodded down the road where we could just make out a sliver of ice peeking through a maze of weeds and leggy willows.

"Excellent! Watson, Inspectors?" Holmes quickly drew the doctor down the road, leaving us struggling to catch up. Lestrade was bringing up the rear when I grabbed his arm.

"Lestrade," I whispered, "can you confirm if Baxter truly refused Rennels' treatments?"

"I can," he whispered back. "You think differently?"

"You would be astonished at the gaps in understanding between doctor and patient. I can hardly request all of his records if he wasn't the doctor."

"You need proof of a professional relationship if we are to search his files."

"Exactly."

"We'll be cold as poor Baxter before long."

Inspector Hopkins kept his countenance, but Lestrade's resignation made it difficult.

"This is a lot of trouble," the older policeman muttered under his breath, and winced as his own words wrapped icy mist over his face.

With finely honed instincts, the professionals hushed and fixed their gaze upon their (unwanted but self-appointed) tour guide. Dr. Rennels was astoundingly fit for his fifty years, though the police could spot artifice in his black hair a mile away. It was as dark as the man's ten-pound suit – more suited for a professor about to give a lecture before the Great Exposition than the wind-blighted bulrushes of Blackfenn. A physician should wear the cloak of his field, but it was impossible not to contrast this sleek, tautly groomed and puffed rusticator against Dr. Watson. That Rennels was aping the physicians who saw to the needs of Royalty was obvious, and his confidence matched it well.

Dr. Watson, who by default was "their man", scorned his grey hairs and stood with the simple posture that becomes a part of a soldier who loves the life, and if his old war wounds were suffering against the icy wind – why, he was man enough to dress sensibly in good clay worsted.

It didn't escape the four policemen that Rennels ignored them the way a host ignored his furniture. They were well used to the puzzled social conflict of gentlemen (policemen were an awkward problem to have with one's social fluency), and really, it saved a lot of time to just give Holmes and Watson the lead. Both men had proved their worth to the Yard long ago. Holmes shrugged at his country squire roots, but his carriage and language – indeed, his every atom – advertised his equality to their host, and as a physician Watson had no need to demand respect. If Rennels were to let something slide, it would be before these two, and not the common policemen.

"You see before you the reservoir that holds much of the water in the Marsh," Dr. Rennels swept his hand several times at the flat, elongated pond about three square acres in size, a sleeping white serpent of ice feathered with faded bulrush and clumps of spiky-looking dead reeds. "It is chained by a series of ancient dykes, but for years the operations were low. The main dyke has been broken since 1650. Since I repaired it, we haven't lacked for water! This has brought in considerable revenue to the people who live here."

Hopkins and Lestrade traded cynical blinks. They knew landlords.

"This is an excellent feat of engineering," Holmes commented as if this wasn't the most boring thing to happen in a fortnight. "It must have cost a considerable sum in time and labour."

Rennels laughed, his blue eyes chips of metal under the clouds. "Less than ten shillings, and it was finished in the season. Captain Baxter was my overseer."

That got their attention. Everyone's gaze arrowed to Rennels, the reservoir, and back to Rennels.

"Allow me to introduce you to the engineers!" Dr. Rennels stepped upon the ice and began walking in a straight line across the reservoir.

Lestrade gulped as Dr. Watson followed. A high-pitched squeak split the air – an effect of friction between shoe and ice that Hopkins knew as a fen skater. He whispered the particulars of this phenomenon to the older policeman, but Lestrade's sallow face stayed pale as Rennels marched across the pool.

"This is much stronger than it looks," Hopkins whispered. "I know – perfect skating ice." Hopkins was very proud of his skating trophies.

Lestrade flinched when a slow-swimming loach wobbled by, literally under his feet. Through the distortion of ice, it was a pale, wrinkled thing.

"You needn't worry," Rennels called. "The ice is quite thick!"

"It isn't just the thickness," Dr. Watson muttered, but he and Holmes followed suit. The doctor held his stick like a baton, level and horizontal, waist high.

"I've never seen him do that before," Lestrade was puzzled at the doctor's mannerisms – and how he glared at Holmes until his friend did the same.

Hopkins was doing it too. "It's to help catch you in the ice if it gives way. Dr. Watson's being proper cautious. It also helps you keep your balance if you fall. A hard, fast fall to the ice can be like a hammer – the force out of proportion to your weight and mass."

Lestrade swallowed hard enough to be heard in the thin winter air and imitated the pose. "And you skate competitively," he accused. "Why?"

"The prizes," Hopkins said succinctly. "Anyway, see how the water is flush against the ice?"

"I don't want to, but yes."

"That's good. The water level's stable. The water reinforces the ice, just like buttress. The colder the water, the denser it is. Believe you me, if there were any largish air bubbles sliding past, I'd screech like an owl until we were all off the ice."

"Screech away, Hopkins . . . ."

The inspectors quieted to concentrate on their steps. Their shoes weren't as practical as the bobbies' boots, but more flexible. Lestrade gulped again when, without warning, Dr. Rennels stopped in the middle of the reservoir and waited for everyone to catch up. Hopkins' lips thinned in disapproval.

"Our engineers are at home!" Dr. Rennels gestured at a lump of sticks on the bank of the pool. It was half-a-storey in height, and powdery snow had wedged into the crevices. A thin thread of steam or mist was rising from the centre of the lump. The men blinked and squinted in the overcast light, looking for the riddle that must be within.

Sherlock Holmes lifted a single eyebrow into his hat brim. "A beaver lodge?" he asked quietly.

Lestrade had rarely seen him so surprised.

"Very good!" Dr. Rennels clapped his gloves together. "The captain brought them here from France, and they have done much to restore the moss."

"Aren't beaver vermin?" Lestrade spoke up, because while he would probably be cut down for it, not knowing the answer would be more galling.

The doctor smiled at Lestrade the way a ringmaster would at his well-trained pony.

"A popular fallacy. True, they damage property if unchecked, but they also fulfil one last service to Man with their pelts." Rennels tapped his hat smugly. "Look downstream and you can see the fruits of their labours," He pointed to what looked like a ragged log jam of flotsam across a break in the old dyke. "They repaired the hole in this dyke faster and more efficiently than any man. Dams slow the water flow to the point that it has time to freeze, thus sealing in even more water."

"They would appear to have no shortage of bolt holes," Holmes mused. "The maintenance of your engineers must be exhausting."

Hopkins would agree with the assessment. The lodge pressed up against a short slope – all Blackfenn roads were well above marsh level – and the snow and ice showed smooth tracks around the lodge. All else was a confusion of bulrush and dead reed.

Dr. Rennels laughed again. It sounded better with practice. "Nothing insurmountable – but forgive me, you look frozen to the bone. You should get out of the wind. The inn at the station can set you up with a hot drink in a trice!"

No one argued. Nor was anyone (save Rennels) particularly surprised when Holmes walked all the way to the lodge and gave it a long, hard look before rejoining their retreat. His thin face was well hidden in his pipe smoke, but they thought they could see a strange expression on it that looked like . . . satisfaction?

Dr. Watson

Dr. Rennels begged our leave on *terra firma*. He must, he explained, return to his duties. I thought him a strange sight, a formal crow in a muddy hamlet. Lestrade bought everyone hot tea and bade the constables fill their cans before they relieved their mates guarding the little morgue holding the remains of Captain Baxter.

Hopkins looked unhappy. Lestrade poked him in the ribs and nodded at the table where Holmes had already commandeered the corner. "That's the first time I've ever seen Mr. Holmes sit without his face to the doorway," he marvelled.

"He looks like he's already thinking hard. Something's gotten his attention." Hopkins blushed as he looked at me. "What? We all saw the same thing he did." I think he knew he sounded peevish but couldn't help himself.

"I don't know if anyone sees the world the way that man does," Lestrade mused. "I've learned a lot simply watching him, but I'll never learn it all."

"There is no sense trying to prise the information before its time," I reminded them. "He would rather wait and give correct facts before a hasty guess."

The Inspectors

Watson cleared his throat when they were alone. "I have some thoughts about the matter, but I should put to rest my irritation at my colleague first."

"Whyever for?" Holmes's surprise was comical to the policemen, for he precisely echoed their thoughts. The detective had been caught in the act of lighting his pipe. He made a new attempt and puffed hard to gain ground. "Watson, my new definition for vanity shall now be, 'A man with ambitions'."

Anger added decades on Hopkins' unfortunately youthful face. "Everyone for miles around fears Rennels. He's loaned a lot of money out to many a marsh-man, and he buys up the notes of those who fall behind. I'd heard he had 'stolen' work from some of the families by having outsiders repair the dyke but . . . beavers? The truth is stranger . . . ."

Watson grimaced. "Do you suspect him of Baxter's death?"

Hopkins hesitated. "He's so unpleasant I want to believe him guilty of something. Yet I haven't found a true motive for wanting the captain dead. He was a source of income, and if we are to believe that demonstration, Baxter was doing the work for his research."

Watson hummed and stroked at his moustache. "My friend was a merry soul, and I cannot imagine them partnered. Rennels is very . . . different."

Sherlock Holmes brightened slightly at Watson's observation, but, maddeningly, said nothing.

"I am glad you called me, gentlemen," Watson quietly thanked the policemen.

Hopkins remembered to breathe. "How may we help?"

"I will visit the morgue. An assistant would speed matters."

Lestrade lifted his hand. "It isn't the first time I've held a dissection tray."

"And I should be glad to help you, Mr. Holmes, if you need some assistance." Hopkins turned to the tall, thin man digging industriously away at his tobacco. "Your observance might help clear up some of my questions."

"Oh?" Holmes's thin lips picked up a quick smile. "You have me curious, Hopkins."

"I don't know if it is worthy of your time," Hopkins warned, "but since we have permission to quarter ourselves at the villa, I would like you to verify assurance there are no clues to be found in the rooms we shall be using. I did search thoroughly, but you are fresh eyes in a strange case."

"I approve of your thoroughness," Holmes chuckled. "If no one objects, I shall order up a supper for everyone tonight. Our day is liable to be a long one."

A time-blistered statue of a young saint with a frog in her hand still sat in crumbling decay at the deconsecrated chapel: St. Ulphia, patroness of watery lands. The inside walls were thickened with blocks of ice and packed moss. Three corpses rested on their slabs, dressed only in canvas sheets and identification cards with the dates of expected collection for burial or transferal. Watson consulted the chart, nodded his satisfaction, and found Baxter's remains.

"Heavens!" Lestrade stamped his feet. "You'll have some trouble with an examination, Doctor. He must be stiff as a plank."

"Almost," Watson agreed. "If you would please record that I have positively identified Captain Baxter? And now, let us see these mysterious marsh monster wounds – " He flicked the canvas off the lower half of the body and Lestrade looked up in time to see his eyes grow wide with shock.

Baxter's villa was a small two-storey affair often rented for hunting parties, for its back was to the reservoir and the front faced a fine field currently alive with teal, widgeon, and pintails. Hopkins admired its whitewashed, simple elegance and heavy thatch roof, but Sherlock Holmes stopped before it and frowned. "Inspector, are you aware someone slipped inside earlier?"

"What?" Hopkins gasped. His glare was for the wide-eyed bobby guarding the front door. "Henders! What is this?"

Holmes lifted his hand to forestall the flurry. "He wouldn't have seen. An entry from the back, I suspect. The curtain in the top is twisted. It would have slowly corrected itself over the course of the day for those look like heavy winter-weight drapes. Shall we?"

Hopkins followed as Holmes dropped his bags on the porch and quietly walked around the house to where a staggering, lurching trail made its way from the slim cover of a spindle-tree copse and across the broad flat plate of the frozen reservoir.

"Common ice-walking clogs," Hopkins groaned as he recognised the rounded prints around which depressed four divots at the corners. "We'll be lucky to find a match."

"Perhaps," Holmes murmured. His lips kept curling up in a smile – something was amusing him. "He didn't find what he sought. See the length of the strides? More calm and even from the footpath to the step, but on his return to the path? He is angry and hasty – foolishly so with the loose snow and ancient ice crusts under the new crust. He fell there, which has reminded him the value of caution." The detective glided down the slope and stopped at the edge of the ice, hands on his hips, thinking hard as the wind blew golden drops of poisonous spindle berries about his feet.

"Rennels," Hopkins growled. "His left knee was darker all the way up the thigh. Like snow had packed in the cloth and then was brushed out. And yet I cannot prove that was he, and anyone could have walked over that ice and out of sight!" He groaned out loud.

"Do not lose hope!" Holmes clapped his shoulder. Pure wickedness glowed in his eyes, and the inspector belatedly recalled that nothing stirred the man's hunting instincts than someone who tried to be cleverer than he. It was a challenge he couldn't resist. "Let us see what secrets the house still keeps."

It never failed to impress Hopkins how Sherlock Holmes could sweep a room like a beam of light, his grey eyes chips of curious stone. They returned to the front of the house where a stingy fire kept the frost away. The furniture was simple and smooth – a local latheturner's artistry.

The walls groaned under books. Shelves lined every inch and even stretched over the doorway, Holmes grunted his approval, and for the next twenty minutes Hopkins had all he could do to keep up with the tall, long-limbed man as he leaped from room to room. At times he thought Holmes knew what to look for. Other times he did not. The window sills were barely glanced at, even the one with the twisted curtain.

"Look, Hopkins!"

The intruder had entered through the kitchen. Its door faced the marsh, a dull keyplate hanging loosely on one screw. Someone had been opening it and the elderly mechanism had failed – a common hazard for cast-iron in very cold weather. Holmes dropped to his knees before it, his fingers digging into a gap in the planks where generations of stepping in and out had worn the wood weak. Hopkins wouldn't have sworn it possible, but the detective slipped his entire hand through the thin gap, skilled as any pickpocket or thief. He pulled out that hand to show a scratched skeleton key tweezered between his fingers.

Holmes turned his head to share in the triumph, but something over Hopkins' shoulder caught his eye. The other man saw his face grow slack in utter astonishment, then,

Holmes burst into laughter.

Hopkins stared, astonished, but the detective was absolutely helpless. He leaned against the wall, hugging himself in delight like a child as a waterfall of mirth escaped. Hopkins tried to track the direction of his gaze for clues.

In the east corner sat a small nook once devoted to rising of loaves and lardy cakes. It caught the sunrise where the late captain enjoyed his morning tea with correspondence. A fine walnut desk ruled this small space, and Hopkins blinked at the incongruity of that deeply loved piece so awkwardly pressed against the rude, unvarnished country hutch holding the wooden dough bowls and moulds.

Holmes wiped his eyes. "Forgive me. I haven't seen one of these desks in years."

"A . . . *desk*?" Hopkins blinked, but Holmes was rushing to the hutch. "Mr. Holmes, that is a hutch. A cupboard, not a desk."

Holmes deftly pulled the woodenware away and, to Hopkins' shock, yanked off the two legs holding the top shelf up. It, plus the entire back of the piece, folded down like an accordion on a series of hinges. The piece was now a writing desk.

Holmes stepped aside so Hopkins could see blue pasteboard-backed journals, neatly stuffed with looseleaf paper, letters, a German publication, and an expense book. "I recognised the handiwork, Inspector. A carpenter who made props for magicians and illusionists. By day he was a proper gentleman and a private clerk. Before he died, he made quite the fortune creating . . . confidential furniture."

172

It was difficult to dismiss two days of painstaking and fruitless searching through the cottage for clues, much of which had been on his hands and knees crawling under tables and peering into musty corners. Eventually, Hopkins recovered his breath. "I hope he was paid due worth."

"Unknown. He hid his wealth in his house."

Hopkins strangled a little at that. "Well, if the captain used this, perhaps he had something to hide." His fingers itched for the books.

"And what needed hiding?" Holmes agreed. "The light is still clear and there are two journals. Let us find what we can before our friends join us."

Dr. Watson

After the morgue, I accompanied Lestrade to the living chapel where the reverend confirmed his testimony, but disagreed that Rennels wasn't Baxter's physician. The publican gave similar witness as he packed our ordered supper.

"Not an expert on gentlemen's ways, you understand," he assured us in a voice that seemed to be comprised mainly of rounded vowels, "but when the agues came about, he walked himself to the doctor's same as anyone here and suffered as much as we did on the price. Not that the price is so bad, mind you, if the rents weren't even higher and we're paying our own money to keep these rattletraps over our heads."

It was long past sunset when Lestrade and I were driven to the Villa. We were hardly prepared for the sight before our eyes: Through the open window we saw the living room, converted into a library or study. Open books and papers rested on every inch of the tables and over them Hopkins and Holmes were scampering back and forth, arranging and reading.

"May as well advertise police business with flaming letters across the sky!" Lestrade scolded in high dudgeon as he swept inside.

Hopkins blanched but jerked his head to Holmes, indicating it was his idea.

"Ah, you remembered supper! Come to the fire, gentlemen." Holmes cheered us in. "Watson, you'll be interested to know we found a bread hutch by our old friend Noah Oliver."

I laughed out loud. "That old devil? What contraband did you find? Lestrade, did you ever meet the man? He made secret compartments for the strangest clients!"

"No," Lestrade scowled like a thundercloud. "I never heard of him."

"Captain Baxter was cautious, Watson." Holmes poured hot chocolate and we soon began a meal. "How were your hunts?"

173

"Baxter may not have been murdered, but his death was needless. The puncture wounds you saw in Hopkins' drawing were from a large weever fish. It must have been lying disguised in the estuary sands, as they so often do, and when he stepped on it all unknowing, those wretched spines pierced the sole of his boot and filled him with venom."

"Heavens!" Hopkins blurted. "Those fish hurt worse than a stabbing! But I haven't heard of them killing anyone in years."

"They typically kill the very weak or elderly. Baxter leached out the venom with hot water – the only effective treatment. However, the spine fragments were caught deep in the flesh. I would have strongly urged him into surgery before they introduced the infection that killed him." I felt the anger rise in my throat and stopped for a moment. "Gentlemen, I insist we move the body to the nearest professional coroner's office, wherever that may be, and I should like an investigation on Rennels' relationship with the captain."

Lestrade added, "And Reverend Jude assured us Rennels was examining the captain over the injury, but both men were keeping mum because the captain was attending some sort of important conference in late spring, and he didn't want anyone to know about his 'silly injury'."

"'Pride goeth'," I finished sadly. "I hope the reverend's word is enough."

"Oh, but we have our own tale to tell!" Hopkins beamed. "Mr. Holmes, would you care to do the honours?"

Holmes summarised how an intruder – unconfirmed to be Rennels – had compromised the villa and the discovery of the hutch. "This spring conference is the crux. Baxter writes much of it in his diary. He was working with many scientists in a tandem project across the globe that was funded by agencies in Ontario, Germany, France, and New York State. Each scientist was introducing and monitoring a population of beaver for observation, in hopes of proving they would be a profitable solution to restoring lost moss or creating them where they weren't currently thriving."

"Moss," Lestrade repeated flatly. "All this for . . . moss."

"Moss concerns governments plagued by the limitations of supply and demand." Holmes held up a booklet dated from 1882 that had seen hard use. I could barely see *Arch. für Klin. Chir*, or *Archive for Clinical Chirugery*, on the cover. "Modern bandages are heavily reliant on cotton, which isn't always available. Eh, Watson?"

"Cotton is a necessary evil," I agreed. "Our Empire needs it as much as food and drink. Its rare ability to protect wounds and drain is essential to saving patients. In times of war, our supply lines are disrupted. Cotton farmers are lost, impressed to service . . . a small shift in weather that could be alleviated by a little extra labour or water during peacetime can be insurmountable during the rationing of war. Man has enslaved other men for cotton, yet ironically the masters are enslaved too."

"Well put, Watson. This consortium hopes to give the world a workable option during times of low cotton supply. Sphagnum moss is their darling. The beavers were chosen because they can easily create marshy ponds in the most difficult of places.

"Beaver work tirelessly building dams and don't take bribes nor demand days off with wages. Regardless, the success of the project meant all the researchers would get a monthly stipend and at the conclusion and shared fame in the fully published study, with guaranteed publication for each separate paper. Scientific interest was high enough that each contributor was expecting a comfortable sum in prearranged sales, and full publishing rights to the author. Despite some missing letters, there are references to Rennels' work by Baxter. Rennels pretended the reservoir was his project when it was Baxter's.

"From the papers, we construe that Rennels was initially enthusiastic about his friend's work, but grew bitter when he wasn't allowed to join. He felt he should be more than a footnote. Baxter allowed him a few limited tasks because he was a sloppy researcher – easily distracted, and impulsive."

"I've no reason to doubt you," Lestrade was perplexed, "but . . . Beavers are destructive! Look, if you have a problem with rats, you get a cat or a dog to control them. But beaver in a wild marsh? How can you control that?"

Holmes saluted Lestrade with his cocoa. "Excellent! How indeed? You may be closer to the solution than you know, and more answers may reveal themselves. Soon, if I'm not mistaken."

"Soon? Oh . . . ." Lestrade stared at the open window helplessly. "Baiting traps again, are we?"

"Effectively, if we are to believe Constable White's impression of being watched from the spindles. I asked him to pace around the house as slowly as possible. It takes him a good quarter-hour to complete his circle, and I daresay that will be enough opportunity for a man desperate to walk in and walk out."

The Inspectors

The men doused the lights with a show of yawning and moved upstairs to bed, drawing the curtains almost absently. After a few minutes they quietly crept down the stairs and spread themselves, guarding the only two entrances – Hopkins and Watson to the living room, Lestrade and

Holmes the kitchen. The entire night felt like a heavy breath about to release.

The fire burned low. Icy chill slipped into the house. Hopkins heard a low, crisp sound as of a branch snapping under pressure. A faint squeak – something moving in dry cold air.

Holmes glided over the floor, signalling Lestrade to stay and nodding to them as he paused at the front door. He opened it and moved outside. He and PC Hughes split in opposite directions from the porch.

It was a little eerie, thought Hopkins, to see Watson with his stiff leg and shoulder move so silently. He slipped from the shadowed corner with one hand by his revolver pocket. Icy air rolled like the tides across the floor and over their feet. Moonlight glittered the motes of ice that came with it.

Without a word the two crept to the kitchen, bodies pressed against the wall where the floor was least liable to betray them with a squeak. Lestrade was crouched by the stove, his dark eyes fixed on the scratchings and scrapes squeaking from the outer door. Hopkins was just barely discernible in the gloom by the writing desk.

A shoulder pressed slowly against the frame. The door squeaked open and Rennels stepped inside. He wore ice clogs and the wooden nubs clicked quietly on the rough floor stones. One hand clutched his keyring and the other hung low. Hopkins knew the shape of a knife when he saw it and this was a brute, a rough-hammered rectangle of scrap iron used for everyday use from cutting to prizing and wedging.

"Hello again, Dr. Rennels."

Sherlock Holmes's low voice from outside sent a gasp through the intruder. He whirled, his keys jingling in his upraised fist as he stared out to the yard he had just left.

"If you are looking for your missing key, I fear it was confiscated as evidence. Luckily I see you have others."

"What are you implying?" Rennels blustered. "This is my house! I have the right to enter or leave it as I see fit!"

"I think not," Holmes explained almost gently. "You left too much of your personalia. What do you hope to find? The medical bills that prove you were treating – or pretending to treat – Captain Baxter? Or his papers you planned to co-opt for your own research? He never completely trusted you, despite your efforts to win him over. He disliked being a patient and you were a shoddy scientist – eager to take another's ideas and sell them as your own. I don't believe you meant him to die. You hoped he would be weakened enough that you could take over the work for him . . . but you couldn't stop once you'd started. You were committed by your own ambitions, and the greed for fame and fortune."

176

The others stepped out of the shadows as Holmes spoke – a single footfall, a heavy boot proclaimed at least one bobby was sliding around the house.

Rennels ought to have done the sensible thing and surrendered, but when he saw the circle of men closing, he lost his head, and his impulse sent him flying against Holmes and a startled PC Hughes. Hopkins wouldn't have sworn in court a man could run with ice-clogs on his feet, and yet he did, slipping and sliding but staying upright somehow, down the slope through the hedge of spindle trees, and out of sight.

Lestrade and Watson leaped to follow, only for Hopkins to grab them with all his strength. "No!" He cried hoarsely. "He's headed for the ice! Never cross ice at night! Not ever!"

They gnashed their teeth but saw the sense. Holmes and Hughes stood, snow-spattered and breathless, but none the worse for wear. Over their breaths they could hear the eerie tap of clogs hammering into the ice, until distance and the wind swallowed him up.

The manhunt went on for hours. Lanterns and manpower were a struggle with the moon slipping in and out of the cloud cover, and the terrain was no safer. The roads were sealed first. Rennels could only be headed to the small town or the open rails. He was trapped like a fish in a net. The night welkin aged and blackened to ink with scraps of thin starlight in the hours before dawn. During the shift switch, the inspectors found themselves together and walking downstream to the reservoir on a treacherous little footpath popular with fowlers. Rennels' only hope, slim as it was, was to reach the low dykes downstream, and Hopkins didn't like trusting the bobbies with their dangerously heavy uniforms for the walk. "A mile downstream at most. Then the first dyke is below that beaver's dam. He wouldn't dare walk over that – not if he's been studying the beasts!"

The men were silent, absorbed in the unpleasantness of the walk for a long time.

"I still can't believe I saw him run like that."

"So you keep saying, Stanley," Lestrade reminded him wearily. "It – Oh!" The older man saw a tiny lamplight on the other side of the marsh flashing back and forth. "That's Watson. He says . . . 'No sign of R' . . . ." He held up his own bullseye and flashed back an affirmative. "Continue on or join them?"

"Continue on," Hopkins quoted from the book of procedure, and peered about in the hopes of seeing something through the winter-dead shrubs. He wasn't sure if Rennels had broken this slim trail, or a wild animal or even a poacher.

Lestrade's brows rose as his companion slowly stopped walking, his gaze fixed upon something in the distance. "What is it, Hopkins?"

"The moonlight," Hopkins murmured absently.

"Eh?"

"The moonlight on the ice. It isn't right. The reflection's . . . lower."

"Lower?"

Hopkins grabbed the other's arm and hurried downstream. "I'd rather be certain than sorry later!"

"Certain? Sorry? Hopkins, I don't – " Lestrade gave up and allowed the tow. They were getting close to the dam, he guessed without being sure. He couldn't look up. The white-clad earth was dangerous and their walking sticks couldn't be more priceless. Hopkins had that unerring ability to manoeuvre the hazards, a true child of the fens. His feet were featherlight, testing the slippery ground just before committing his full weight upon each step. Lestrade wisely copied this to the best of his abilities, and they gained speed.

He heard Hopkins gasp and nearly ran into the younger man's back for he had stopped stock still. Peering around him, he saw the smooth, icy mirror of the reservoir was ruined. A crater of black water lapped back and forth over shattered planks of ice in the middle of the lip where water drizzled into a waterfall. A single log topped the rim, but a large hole yawed where the willow stakes and branches had been yanked out and tossed downstream. Here and there, tooth-sharpened stakes poked up like knives, and flotsam bobbed sluggishly in the murk.

"Good Lord! The dam's broken in half! We walked that!"

"See why I told you the water needed to be right under the ice?" Hopkins' voice shook. "The water level dropped when the middle of the dam was broken, and the crust broke under its own weight. Wonder how deep it is now?"

"Would it matter? You'd have to find where you fell through and try to climb out. There's no hope of breaking through those slabs!"

"Lestrade, are you certain you aren't enough of a cynic for this work?"

"Not by half," Was his gloomy answer. "At least we know Rennels couldn't have done it. A man couldn't rip out those stakes like that – Eh? What's that?"

Hopkins squinted as a dark shape slithered over the ice with a flopping fish in its jaws. "Why, that's an otter! What do you know? I didn't know they'd survived in these parts!"

A second sleek head popped out of the weeds and, despite the depression of Rennels escaping, the men choked down a laugh when the little beast barked like a disapproving dog at them. It was a ridiculous night. This was a ridiculous moment.

Meal completed, the first slithered merrily down the slide of smooth ice and dropped in, only to climb out and repeat the fun. A third joined the others, a long, fish dragging from its mouth like a child with a ribbon.

"Suppertime." Lestrade found himself smiling at their unabashed joy. "It's like children on a picnic."

A fourth tiny head peeped over the surface of the ice, looked from side to side, and dipped down with a strong, tapered tail in the water. The men laughed softly as the head popped back up a moment later with a fat loach. Strong, squat tusks gleamed in the moonlight. The men heard the crunch of bones over the ice. "He eats like my brother-in-law," Lestrade mused. "You should see him with a pike under cream sauce."

"A fine night to be an otter if not a man," Hopkins said at length. "White and Burns are below us. They'll see Rennels if he tries to slip through the bulrush . . . ."

The same thought trickled through their tired minds at the same time. A chill of horror bounced back and forth at they met each other's eyes. The stared back at the hole in the ice. Lestrade's face drained of colour. He hated drownings even more than he hated dogs.

Hopkins cleared his throat. "Lestrade, would you mind signalling the rest?"

"No." Lestrade swallowed his relief. "I'll go right now."

Dr. Watson

Rennels' body was difficult to retrieve from the reservoir, but the police persevered. The unpleasant chore was completed before noon. By all appearances he had drowned, but I satisfied myself with an autopsy first.

Holmes and Hopkins had searched his office. There was enough to see why Rennels had acted so stupidly. He was courting on paper several women of standing and wealth. He was also deeply in debt, both to lawful and unlawful agencies. Many men would have fled to Australia or resumed a new identity, but a man of his character would rather murder than fail to present himself less fashionably than the cream of society.

"He risked everything because he had everything to gain," Hopkins shook his head. "Mr. Holmes, we would have caught him surely, but I believe you saved us days, if not weeks of grueling work. I don't know how to thank you for this."

Holmes scoffed lightly. "You may thank me, but my powers were low. I believe my recovery on the coast muddled my processes." He cheerfully ignored the fond exasperation huffing from Watson's face.

"But how could the dam break?" Hopkins fretted. "That makes no sense. It was working fine earlier in the day."

"The dam did not break, Hopkins," Holmes said quietly. "Rennels' arrogance killed him."

"That I wish to believe," Lestrade grumbled. "Do explain?"

"I believe you gentlemen thought my wits had left me when I walked to the beaver's lodge during our tour."

"Er," Lestrade flushed as Hopkins looked away. "We didn't understand why you were so interested . . . but you often do things we don't understand."

"Why, thank you! Do you recall the smooth planes of snow and ice around the lodge?"

"It looked like animal trails to me," Hopkins shrugged. "And there were beaver in the lodge, so why not beaver trails?"

Holmes selected a small leather folio with *J. Baxter* inked on the front. "I once vacationed in the Broads and learned some of its ecology on the duck hunts. It suited the Trevors to keep their lands as they saw fit and were quite fond of its creatures. Beaver and otter were permitted to swim freely in their waters, for they were effective in keeping open the weed-choked water channels. They also kept their identity secret. Others would have killed them for their furs, or from outrage at an animal going after 'their' rightful fish."

"Beaver do not slide on their bellies, nor are they the only residents in their winter lodge. Captain Baxter did more than study *C. fiber*. He also added its best population check: The otter. When beavers take up too much room, otters prey on the young."

"I'm glad they were just animals," Hopkins had to laugh. "When those little heads popped up, I first thought about the Marsh Monster."

"You wouldn't be the first. A family of otters often swim in tandem, and their shapes have spawned many legends about giant water serpents. I should imagine this is the current guise of local myth."

"Good heavens!" Lestrade stared.

Holmes opened Baxter's folio and paged to a simple watercolour of otter swimming in the reservoir. "The captain was overall pleased with the beaver, but frustrated that they kept expanding the reservoir by adding to the dam, affecting drainage. Since he was using the methods of nature to improve the marsh moss, why not use another natural method to control the beaver?"

Holmes turned the page and read aloud:

180

The use of the common otter ought to be fruitful, for I often saw them in the wild cheerfully reducing the hard work of the beaver, removing the top levels of their dams. This never wholly ruined the structure, but lowered the water levels, trapping the fish they sought into a smaller pool.

"This is ironic, Holmes," I concluded. "Rennels was so focussed on stealing the work of my friend that he didn't play attention to the thing he was stealing!"

"Ironic, yes, but hardly unusual," Holmes mused. "He wanted to claim fame from the Natural World, but not to the extent that he wanted to gain its wisdoms. A common-enough mistake for even the most advantaged men. Watson, I regret not meeting your friend, but I shall personally see to it that his writings get their just due with his project. There should be no reason why his portion of the award cannot be allocated to the protection of Blackfenn Marsh, a place he loved so clearly."

The Disappearance of
Little Charley
by Tracy J. Revels

"Y ou see before you the most miserable creature on God's earth," Mr. Cullen Hart muttered. "My life, it seems, is nothing but a series of misfortunes and tragedies. First my Annie, then Christopher, and now Charley. If you can shine no light into my darkness, I swear to you I shall leave these rooms, go immediately to London Bridge, and throw myself into the Thames."

These words, spoken with great earnestness, were countered with a flurry of soft, matronly objections. The gentleman who sat upon the sofa looked like a soul teetering on the abyss, his face ashen, his eyes raw and bloody, and his chin covered in several days of stubble. He was well-dressed but his clothes hung loosely on his frame, and his dark brown hair stood about wildly on his head. He was perhaps thirty-five, though his haunted expression made him look older than his natural years. Seated next to him was an elderly lady clad in black, her soft chin quivering while her plump hands fluttered in distress.

"You must not say such things, Cullen," the lady gently chided. "Please, gather your strength and recall what the inspector told you – you must have faith in Mr. Sherlock Holmes."

My friend had been standing before the fireplace and studying this strange tableau silently. I knew he was taking in every detail of both his visitors

"I am not surprised to see you, Mr. Hart. I only expected you to come sooner."

I flinched inwardly at Holmes's comment. My friend's nature, to those who did not know him, could at times seem cold and unfeeling, and indeed the pair on the sofa looked up with expressions of shock. Yet I understood his words, for Holmes had been following the case through the newspapers for almost a week, as had the rest of England.

Sadly, the world has changed so profoundly since the passing of our good Queen and the dark depths of the Great War, that readers of these narratives may not realize that there was once a time when the possibility of a child being kidnapped was a remote one. It was a fate that one might, if possessed of an evil imagination, envision for the son of a lord, but not for the offspring of some solid *bourgeoise*. The details of the case were therefore a feast for the more sensational press, which Holmes avidly devoured with his morning coffee.

"I should have, sir. Inspector Gregson advised me to seek your assistance and told me that you have had much success in your endeavors. But you must understand that the matter is so delicate – so shameful – that for days I couldn't stir myself to come to you. Even now I fear that when you hear my story you may refuse to help me."

Holmes settled into his armchair. "The life of a six-year-old child is endangered. No scandal could dissuade me from bring all my powers to bear to find him. I shall state to you all I have learned from the papers and you may correct me if I err." He paused with one eyebrow slightly raised. "Mrs – ?"

"Cassidy, sir."

"You are the neighbor lady."

She nodded eagerly. "I have lived next to Mr. Hart for three years. I am the one who saw the strange men in the landau."

"Then we shall come to you in due time, Madam. I have gathered that Mr. Hart is a solicitor of great promise, having worked in the city for seven years. There was a Mrs. Hart who sadly died just after giving birth to twin sons. You have been a widower ever since, raising your boys with the help of a small staff. Is this correct?"

The man licked his lips nervously. "Yes."

Holmes frowned. Even from my position at the desk, where I was taking notes, I could sense how disingenuous the answer was.

"This is perhaps a point we should return to. All was well until six months ago, when young Christopher sickened and then perished."

Again, the man gave a jerk of his head. Holmes wove his fingers together.

"Since that time, your staff has been reduced to a housekeeper and a nursemaid for the remaining child. Both are mature women of unimpeachable character. Charles – known affectionately as little Charley – was kept strictly at home. No neighborhood children were allowed to play with him, nor was the nursemaid permitted to take him to the park or on any other outings."

"It was a cold day in the park that killed Christopher," the father muttered. "Our garden was good enough for Charley."

"Yet it was from this garden that the child disappeared, five days ago, at approximately one in the afternoon. The nurse had been outside with the child but was called inside to receive a package delivered by a commissionaire. As this man proved to be a former neighbor of hers, some idle chatter was made, and perhaps five minutes passed before she returned to the garden to find the boy missing. No immediate alarm was raised, as the nurse assumed her charge was in the kitchen with the housekeeper, and she was grateful to have a span of time to do some tidying in the nursery. When she learned that the boy wasn't with the housekeeper, a rapid search commenced. The child wasn't found, you were summoned from your office, and soon the entire neighborhood was turned inside out in a quest for the missing lad."

"That is all correct, sir."

"And there has been no message – no note or demand?"

"None, sir. It is as if Charley has vanished into thin air."

Holmes shook his head. "Let us not immediately leap to impossibilities. As I understand it from the quite comprehensive diagram in one of our London dailies, your home is on a corner lot. An eight-foot-high wall protects the garden on the street side, and Mrs. Cassidy's home, which borders yours, has a similar garden. Your rear lawns are separated only by a whitewashed wooden fence. The back of the garden consists of another stone fence, though this one is lower, perhaps only six feet in height. A tree just at the wall would also make it quite easy for an active lad to escape confinement in his own yard."

"That is true, sir, but the property behind my house, which commands an entire block, is patrolled by three of the most savage mastiffs you have ever seen. They can be set into a ruckus merely by hearing Charley's laughter on the other side of the wall. I assure you my boy was terrified of them, and under no circumstances would have climbed into the neighbor's property."

"Is it possible, Mrs. Cassidy, that the child might have come into your garden?"

The lady shook her head brisky. "I was outside, puttering about with my flowers, when I heard the cry being raised. Charley is such a dear, sweet child – of course I would have seen him had he come over."

"Did you hear him with his nurse?"

"Oh yes. Until she was called inside, I heard him pretending to be a pirate. She was, I think, the English sea captain he was about to capture."

"And afterward?"

The lady shook her head. "I heard nothing. But that's Charley's way. He always plays quietly when alone."

"Is he a shy child?"

I noted that the lady looked to her companion before answering. "More so since his brother passed away. But he has a great imagination and is much taken with ideas of adventure in faraway places."

"Too much," Hart abruptly snapped. "Mrs. Cassidy, if you wouldn't mind stepping out. Perhaps the lady who admitted us – "

"Mrs. Hudson will no doubt be delighted to entertain female company," Holmes said, "especially of the respectable, genteel type. Our good landlady finds her halls too often filled with criminal characters, as well as two somewhat disreputable boarders. But before you go, Madam, I would like you to tell us what you told the police about the strangers in the landau."

The lady had already risen, clutching her little velvet bag to her chest. "I saw them three times before Charley vanished, always in the middle of the day. There was a driver, and two men who sat facing each other. One was an Indian, in a white costume with a great black beard and a blue turban with a red feather sticking up. The other was a Chinaman, wrapped in yellow silk, with his shiny hair all in a long train."

"And the driver?"

The lady shrugged. "An Englishman, I supposed, in a black coat and a high hat. I could see little of him, but I had the impression that his skin was pale, and he had just a hint of a red beard, kept short and neat. The horses were very beautiful, both of them pearly gray and perfectly matched."

"No coat of arms or markings on the vehicle?"

"None that I saw."

"And how did they behave?"

"They drove very slowly down our street. The first time, I only noticed them because they were strange. The second and third time, I noted that they had stopped before Mr. Hart's carriage step and appeared to be talking with Charley. I saw him wave his arms as if he had given them directions, and I saw the Chinaman hand him something in reward. I assumed it was a shilling, for he put it into his pocket very eagerly."

"Did you hear of these visitors?" Holmes asked Hart. The man groaned.

"Not a word, until after Charley disappeared. He was only allowed to play on the walk immediately in front of our door, so it would have been easy to hail him from the street. But he had been warned not to converse with strangers, and the nurse should have been watching him."

"A small boy is difficult to watch every moment of the day," Holmes said. At a nod from him, I rose and escorted the good Mrs. Cassidy down to the kitchen, where she began to chatter with Mrs. Hudson. By the time I returned, the atmosphere of the room had changed. Holmes had lit his pipe, and Hart was smoking a cigarette. Hart's face was even paler than before.

"And there you have it, sir – all that the newspapers could print. The police told me that I must hold some things back, so that if a demand was received, we could sort the true villains from the pranksters. No one knows that when he was taken, Charley was wearing a silver locket with a picture of his grandmother in it, or that he has a strawberry-shaped birthmark in the small of his back."

"These were wise precautions," Holmes agreed. "But now you must tell us the rest – the aspects you are unwilling to share with your motherly neighbor."

The man dropped his head. "It is most shameful, and if there was any way I could avoid speaking of it, I would. But I fear that it may have a bearing on my son's disappearance.

"I married when I was barely a week out of the university, before my prospects were clear. My parents, God rest their sainted souls, warned me against tying myself to Annie Reddon, but I was young, rash, and convinced that they held her humble origins against her. Annie was beautiful and, I thought, spirited – it hardly mattered to me that she had been a barmaid. At first everything went well for us when we moved to London, but soon Annie became frustrated. She had no flair for housekeeping, she bored easily, and she missed the free companionship of the public house. Then, when she found herself in a family way, things seemed improved. I was certain that motherhood would change her.

"But it did not, sir. She suffered greatly giving birth to twins, and for weeks she would do nothing but lie in the bed and stare at the walls. She showed no interest in our infants, wouldn't even rouse herself enough to nurse them. They were nearly a year old before she finally seemed well again, but instead of being a loving mother, she returned to her disreputable ways. She began to drink heavily. It was all I could do to retain servants when their mistress stayed intoxicated. This went on for almost two years. At last, I had enough, and I threatened to have her committed to an asylum. There was a terrible row, and it ended with her packing her bags and storming out of the house. I thought she would return when her temper cooled, but she did not. It was shortly after this terrible event that I hired Mrs. Waverly and Mrs. Brown, my housekeeper and nursemaid, who have been with me ever since. It was also just a month or so later that Mrs. Cassidy moved into the house next door.

"God forgive me, but I didn't know what to do. I was still up to my eyeballs in debts, working almost around the clock, and my boy Christopher was sickly. There was no money to hire a private agent to track Annie down. When a year passed and I didn't hear from her, I began to tell people that she had gone to America, to visit a relative, and had died during the voyage. This was the story I told my boys, when they grew old enough to ask why they had no mama."

"But you have seen your wife again," Holmes said.

"Yes. I remember it well. It was the week after the boy's fourth birthday. I had a client who was interested in buying some property in Whitechapel and wanted my opinion on the investment. We were riding through that neighborhood in the middle of the day – it is hardly a place a decent person would visit after sundown – and as we passed by in a cab, I saw her, standing with a half-dozen other slatterns, all of them washing their linen in a horse trough. For a moment I didn't believe my eyes. Her hair, coal black on our wedding morning, was now streaked with gray, her figure was coarse, her front teeth were missing. Indeed, I might not have known her if not for her tattoo. She has the image of a fiery bird, a phoenix, upon her right arm. She has possessed it since before our marriage. It was one of the many things that my parents held against her. I must have given some cry or incoherent shout, for she looked up and saw me, and though she didn't speak, I was certain I had been recognized.

"I don't know who put the idea of blackmail into her head, for Annie was never particularly intelligent. Perhaps it was one of those other drabs standing at the trough. A few days later, I received a letter, very poorly written, stating that she needed money. I would have done anything to protect my boys from learning the truth about their horrible mother, and indeed I began to send money to her, on the sole condition that she never show herself at my door."

"How did you send the funds?"

"A rough man named Sully was our go-between. He came once, sometimes twice a month. I never gave him much, but he seemed satisfied, and each payment bought silence. One occasion, however, gave me a fright. I happened to be at home, laid up with a sprained ankle, and when I looked through my window, I saw a heavily veiled woman watching the boys play on the walk. I called them in immediately and gave orders that they never be allowed outside again without their nursemaid by their side. The woman vanished, and I haven't seen her since, nor has the man, Sully, presented himself again in almost a year."

"Tell me about Christopher," Holmes said. "What claimed his young life?"

"The doctor told me it was a weak heart, a condition he was born with. The boys weren't identical – Charley was always larger and healthier. One morning Christopher complained of a pain in his chest, but before the doctor could even be summoned, he had slipped away."

"And in the six months since his passing, has your life been altered in any way beyond your sad loss? Has there been an inheritance, a sudden shift in fortune – anything that might tempt an evil man's jealousy?"

187

"No, Mr. Holmes. My cases have increased, but I haven't been promoted, or handled business for nobility, or come into any especially confidential information."

Holmes gave his pipe a few meditative puffs. "Then, Mr. Hart, we must face another rather unpleasant possibility. If your soon wasn't kidnapped, he ran away."

Mr. Hart leapt from his chair. "Impossible! Charley is a good and obedient boy!"

"I wasn't implying that the problem lies with Charley's character."

The man's face turned scarlet as he digested Holmes's meaning. He wasn't a large or physically imposing specimen, but his hands immediately curled into fists.

"How dare you insinuate that – "

"If you don't wish me to assist, the door may be found directly behind you."

Hart gasped, and then exhaled in a long, shuddering breath. Slowly, he resumed his seat.

"I didn't mean what I said to my son – it was only an angry retort. Surely Charley wouldn't have acted on it."

"Be precise, Mr. Hart."

The man nodded. "After Christopher's death, Charley was very glum and morose. It was sad to see the little fellow so blue, but after a month passed, he seemed to rally, even enough to complain about his mourning jacket being 'itchy'. I resolved to treat him not as a child, but as a little man, to show more interest in his lessons. But, Mr. Holmes, I confess I wasn't created to be a schoolmaster. I have no natural talent with children. I lost patience as Charley worked over his letters. I was too critical when he took up his pen. I tried to teach Charley how to sit with me at dinner, to use proper manners. But he taxed me with his constant talk, his foolish prattling. He was always making up stories, wild tales, and I am more for practical things.

"A month or so ago, he became obsessed with stories of America – of the Red Indians and the cowboys who fought them. He would talk of nothing else at the dinner table. Much to my annoyance, he began to build castles in the sky, fantasies that we would leave England, travel together, become cattle rustlers or bandits on the great frontier. I had a terrible headache the other night, when he suddenly abandoned his chair and jumped up beside me, tugging on my sleeve in a crazed, animated fashion.

"'Oh, we must go, Papa! Now, we should pack and leave, before the next cattle drive begins!'

"Mr. Holmes," the man sobbed, "I didn't mean to be so cruel, but I had been worn thin with work, with the loss of my other boy, with the fears that my estranged wife might appear on my doorstep. Without thought, I slapped Charley's face and told him that he was too old for foolishness, and that the only place he was going was to Eckardt's School, in the north, as soon as the winter term began. His eyes grew wide, his lips trembled, he turned and fled up the stairs. I am ashamed to say it, but that was the last time I laid eyes upon my son, for I didn't see him at breakfast and, just after noon that day, he vanished."

Holmes's expression made his contempt for the situation clear, but his voice remained even and neutral. "Had he ever spoken of running away?"

"Never."

"The strange men that Mrs. Cassidy mentioned – were they ever an object of conversation?"

"Not that I can recall, though . . . in truth, I only half-listened to most of Charley's prattle."

Holmes rose and knocked out his pipe. "You have heard nothing from the former Mrs. Hart since your son disappeared?"

"Not a word."

Holmes reached for his coat. "Very well, Mr. Hart. I will accompany you to your house. I could have made more of the field had I been called in immediately, but perhaps even now there is some detail which may have eluded the official forces. Will both of your servants be home?"

"My housekeeper will. Mrs. Brown, the nursemaid, went out to visit her invalid mother, but she should return shortly."

"Very well. If you will retrieve Mrs. Cassidy, I will be down momentarily." Holmes waited until Hart had slipped through the door before taking my arm. "Watson, I must deputize you. I am expecting a report from Wiggins."

"On another case?"

Holmes shook his head. "I knew about the missing wife, Watson. Gregson sent me a note yesterday, asking for help in finding her. The police have nothing as efficient as the Irregulars, and I wouldn't wish any news that Wiggins might bring to go astray. I honestly expect nothing to come from this journey, but I feel I must make it. There's a good fellow."

And so, an hour later, I wasn't surprised to hear the ringing of the bell and light footsteps on the stairs. I was shocked, however, when the person who appeared in the doorway wasn't the disreputable little leader of Holmes's street urchins, but a sensible-looking middle-aged woman in a tweed walking dress.

"Mr. Holmes is not in?"

"No, Madam, but he may return shortly."

The lady shook her head. "I cannot wait, I am overdue already, and they must never know I have made this call. When I learned that my employer was seeking Mr. Holmes's help, it gave me hope, but I know that Mr. Holmes can only work if he has the truth."

"You are the Hart family nursemaid?"

She nodded tightly. "My name is Eleanor Brown. I was widowed young and have worked for several families, taking care of children until they were old enough to go to school. I have been with Mr. Hart for three years. I loved the boys dearly." She gave herself a tight shake. "But I will not screen anyone, not even Mr. Hart, especially if there is any chance that Charley might yet live."

I sat down across from her. "You think that Mr. Hart has harmed his own child?"

"I don't know what to think! I only know that he was a harsh and cold father. He much prefers to be with his law books and papers than with his boy – that is the nature of many men, I suppose – and he blames everyone but himself for Christopher's death."

My blood ran cold. "He killed the other lad?"

"Not directly, but he was hard on him. The child was thin and frail. Something was wrong with his heart, but Mr. Hart insisted that he take hard exercise and eat more than he wanted. He was often ill as a consequence, and that only annoyed his father more. I think Christopher broke down under the pressure, poor tyke. I will not accuse Mr. Hart of willful murder, though he was infuriated when he couldn't force his son to grow and thrive simply because he willed it. But – I must speak quickly! – it is what happened to Charley that is so upsetting."

I had grabbed up my notebook and was feverishly scratching in it as she spoke.

"After the funeral, Mr. Hart came into the nursery and began gathering up all of Christopher's toys, his tin soldiers, and his books. When I asked what he intended, he said he couldn't bear the sight of anything that reminded him of Christopher. He carried off the boy's clothes, stripped the linens from the bed, took away the little pictures on the wall. I protested that these things might give Charley comfort, especially as the boys had shared everything. Charley is a precocious boy. He can already read very well, and he loves the books that were filled with tales of American outlaws, pirates, and the Arabian nights. Mr. Hart wouldn't be moved – by the time he finished, the room was nearly barren. I assumed he would bring Charley new books and presents that would help make up for the loss. But he never did. I saved a few pence and was able to buy Charley some little toys and books myself. Otherwise, he would have had nothing.

190

"At the same time, Mr. Hart forbade me to take Charley on walks, or let him play in the park. He ordered that Charley was to have no friends, and that no company might visit. Charley's entire world was the house, the garden, and, on occasion, the pavement before the door. Mrs. Cassidy, who had become like a grandmother to the boys, was the only ray of kindness. She let us come over on some mornings, and Charley enjoyed playing in that big old rambling house of hers. She knows what it is like to lose a child, and when she heard how cruel Mr. Hart was being, she brought out her late son's playthings and storybooks. That is all I know. Everything else I have told to the police.

"I don't wish to speak harshly, sir. Mr. Hart has been good and fair to me, though I did fear he would dismiss me when Christopher died, as he wanted someone else to blame."

The clock chimed, and she rose. "Do tell Mr. Holmes this – the housekeeper and I, and even Mrs. Cassidy, know about the wife in Whitechapel. Mr. Hart thinks we are ignorant, but we have learned the story. We all have some sympathy for the woman, even though we have never met her, for among us we agree that while Mr. Hart might appear a respectable gentleman, he would be the devil himself as a husband."

She departed, and I was just getting my notes on her remarkable narrative into order when Holmes reappeared, looking profoundly weary. He slumped into his chair and listened to the nursemaid's story, occasionally giving a nod.

"I have no doubt as to the veracity of her statement. The entire house speaks of meanness and a kind of pettiness, the way a youthful Ebenezer Scrooge might have lived, had he married before his instructive evening with the ghosts. Young Charley's room looked more like a monk's cell than a nursery. An inspection of the grounds reveals that he could hardly have climbed over any of the fences, and the mastiffs on the back neighbor's property rival any hellhounds of legend. There is a little gate that connects Mrs. Cassidy's yard to the Hart's garden, a detail that wasn't mentioned, but the old lady was very pleased to talk about how the child enjoyed romping around her domicile." A smile flickered on Holmes's face. "I can understand the child's natural curiosity about the old lady's house – do you recognize the address?"

I stared at the card that Holmes had flipped upon the table. "Why – surely this is the old Sutton Hospital for the Insane!"

"Indeed. The Hart's home once belonged to the caretaker, while Mrs. Cassidy's house made up the main complex of the private hospital."

"If those walls could talk!" I said, shaking my head in amazement. I looked toward my friend. Holmes's eyes were suddenly bright, and he surged forward in his chair.

191

"What was that, Watson?"

"I am only imagining the stories that building might tell. It was quite the infamous place until it closed a decade ago. They said one of the Queen's deluded, would-be assassins was given the cold-water treatment there."

Holmes was about to speak when there was a sharp rap on the door. It flew open a moment later, revealing young Wiggins.

"Ah, good lad! You have found her?"

"Yes, Mr. Holmes – but you won't like where!"

The St. George in the East Mortuary was surely one of the grimmest places in London. Many have described it as the antechamber of hell. They do not exaggerate.

The attendant showed us to the innermost chamber, where a young doctor in shirtsleeves was washing the corpse of a woman. Immediately, I spotted the telltale tattoo on her bruised and battered arm. It was fortunate that this mark remained, for her skull had been crushed and her face so badly broken that it was hard to realize she had ever been human.

"What happened to her?" Holmes asked.

"Fell from a rooftop is all I know. There's a policeman in the next room, talking with her fellow lodger."

We followed his gesture and found, of all people, Inspector Lestrade. He loomed over a ragged, frightened woman, and was uttering threats about Brixton Prison and the rope. Holmes touched his shoulder and drew him aside.

"Lestrade, are you accusing this woman of murder?" he asked, his voice lowered.

"No, no – half-a-dozen folks saw the suicide. But I think she knows where the boy is! The dead woman is – "

"Charley Hart's mother."

"How the blazes did you know? Wait – Gregson told you!"

Holmes sighed. "Still rivals after all these years? If you will give Watson and myself five minutes alone with the lady, I think we can provide you with clues that might give you an edge upon your opponent."

Lestrade snorted, but promptly left the chamber. Holmes offered the sobbing woman a drink from his flask, and his handkerchief to absorb her tears.

"Bless you, sir. I thought that man would slap the cuffs on me, and I've done nothing but share a room with Annie Hart all these years."

Holmes nodded, seating himself beside the woman. "Annie's husband was cruel to her."

"Yes. Lord, the nights we've laid awake, after our paying gents were gone, she telling me all the things he's done. That's why she left him. She thought maybe he'd be better to the boys if she was gone. She knew she was weak for the gin, she couldn't change. Why do people say we have to change when we can't, and no one will help us?"

"A mystery beyond my feeble skills to unravel," Holmes said, his voice so soothing it was almost a purr. "Was it Annie who demanded the payments from her husband?"

"At first it was. But then she felt bad about it, said it was 'soul money' and she wouldn't write to him no more. But that rascal Sully, he kept it up – until he got coshed in a brawl at the King and Key, more than a year ago. Hasn't been able to strong-arm anyone since."

"That explains a good deal. How did Annie react when she learned about one son's death and the other son's disappearance?"

"When Charley went missing was the first she knew of Christopher being dead, sir. Oh, how she wept and took on. She kept saying she should go to the house, but I told her 'If you do that, they'll arrest you.' Who would believe she hadn't stolen him away, maybe in revenge or something? But she just got worse every day, and this afternoon she swallowed half a bottle of gin and then she climbed onto the roof and before I could get to her – "

"No, no, keep the handkerchief," Holmes instructed. He reached into his pocket and forced several coins into the woman's grubby hand. "There is enough here to see that Mrs. Hart is decently buried. When her body is released, you must take care of the arrangements. I will make sure that rather unpleasant policeman troubles you no more."

"What do you propose to do?" I asked Holmes, as he closed the door on the weeping woman.

"I will send Lestrade to Mr. Hart's house to collect the grieving husband and bring him here for the essential identification. Gregson must remain behind to guard the home in case any further tips arrive."

I eyed Holmes. "That is not the real reason."

"You are far too astute today, Watson, so I must play my cards close to the vest," Holmes said, hailing Lestrade as we turned a corner. He rattled off the instructions, and I could see that Lestrade was none too pleased with the thought of a trip across London.

"I should file a report first. Clearly, the dead woman kidnapped her son, did away with him, and then killed herself in remorse."

"That is your theory of the case?"

"It makes sense!"

"There is no harm in giving such a theory a few more hours to percolate," Holmes replied. "Do bring Mr. Hart here – an inaccurate identification would be dangerous. And make sure that you do not allow the solicitous Mrs. Cassidy to return with you, no matter how much she volunteers. This is clearly no place for a respectable lady."

Grumbling, Lestrade set off. Holmes hailed the next cab and directed the driver to Baker Street.

"There is no more to be done?"

"On the contrary, there is much to be done, but I shall require a tool. It will take only a moment to procure. Do wait in the cab for me when we arrive."

Holmes was as good as his word, dashing up to our rooms and lingering no more than five minutes. I had assumed he would hurry back to the location of the crime, but instead he insisted that we pause at a small shoppe and have a cup of coffee.

"Let us review the key elements of the case," he said. "We know that the boy went missing just after his lunch on Monday, and no one has seen him since. There have been no demands for ransom, or threats directed at his father, who is an unlikely target of vengeance. Let us therefore dismiss the kidnapping for ransom scenario from our deck."

"The child's home was a sad and rigid one," I said. Holmes nodded.

"Indeed, the father hints at his own cruelties and failures, even if he refuses to take full responsibility for them. I was able to have a private moment with the housekeeper earlier this afternoon, and her story corroborates that of the nursemaid. The house is sad and lonely – a torturous place for a spirited little lad to live."

"So, the child ran away."

"A much more likely possibility."

I snapped my fingers. "The Indian and the Chinaman that Mrs. Cassidy saw. Two such exotic figures would easily have temped him to fly with them."

Holmes shook his head. "It won't do, for several reasons. What would a wealthy Indian and a silk-clad Chinaman want with an ordinary English boy? If they needed a child, for whatever vile purpose they might concoct, it would be far easier to pluck up a street Arab than to risk snatching a well-dressed youth from a suburban street, especially as their striking appearance would be memorable to all the bored ladies glancing through lacy curtains."

I understood Holmes's point. "No one else saw them. Yet according to Mrs. Cassidy, they had appeared more than once." A chill ran across my skin. "Mrs. Cassidy is lying."

Holmes smiled as he settled the bill. "I think enough time has passed. Let us pay the good lady a call."

When our cab deposited us before the Cassidy home, I was immediately stunned that a widow with no family would choose to live in such a large dwelling. It had indeed been a former asylum and bore all the sinister markings of such a place, including that most famous phrase from Dante, "*Abandon Hope All Ye Who Enter Here*", engraved upon the lintel.

"How many servants does such a pile require?" I whispered, as Holmes sounded the knocker.

"Half-a-dozen – all of whom, according to the Hart housekeeper, were sacked about two weeks ago as an economy measure. As the housekeeper is a cousin to Mrs. Cassidy's cook, she found the explanation most unsatisfying. As do I."

The door opened. Mrs. Cassidy was red-faced, her hair damp and her sleeves pushed back. She clearly appeared to have been dragged away from some strenuous activity.

"Mr. Holmes, Dr. Watson – has there been some news?"

"Might we come in?" Holmes asked, with a furtive glance down the street. "I wouldn't wish to be overheard."

"Of course, of course! This way." She ushered us into a parlor that was in a state of disarray. Wooden boxes were everywhere, carpets were rolled up and stacked against the wall, pictures were resting in a pile. "Please excuse me, sirs, I have been doing a bit of sorting, in preparation for selling a good deal of my furniture. At least there is somewhere to sit. Would you like some refreshment?"

"That would be delightful," Holmes said.

"I will need to get it myself," she said. "Do make yourselves comfortable."

The moment her black skirt whisked through the doorway Holmes leaned over to me.

"Drink nothing that she brings, but in a few moments ask her to show you something in the house – stay there and allow her to return to me."

"Why?"

There was no time for Holmes to answer. The lady had reappeared with glasses of water. A slight elbow nudge from Holmes sent me into action.

"Mrs. Cassidy, I understand that this was once the home of Dr. Sutton, the great alienist?"

"Yes, it was. I made modifications, of course, but his office with his splendid collection of books is still on the first floor."

"Might I trouble you to see it?"

She looked wary. "But if there are any new developments in the mystery . . . ."

"Do show him up and allow him to knock about, Mrs. Cassidy," Holmes said. "Watson asks such inane and stupid questions that I find it much easier to speak to important clients alone. I will wait here."

With a slow, hesitant nod, the lady rose, and I followed her up a twisting staircase. She almost shoved me through the office door, pausing only to light a single lamp before hurrying back downstairs. The office was oval in shape, a magnificent sanctum filled with books, cabinets, and antique medical devices. There was one rather unexpected item in the room – a small black and white puppy with pert upright ears. It was tied to the doctor's desk with a leash, which it strained against, whimpering piteously.

"Hello, pooch," I said, petting its soft coat. "What's wrong? I see you have food and water here. Why are you so unhappy?"

"Watson!"

I spun around and raced down the stairs at the sound of my friend's shout. Our hostess was sprawled on the floor. Holmes quickly slid a pillow beneath Mrs. Cassidy's head.

"The lady has fainted?"

"No, the lady has been drugged." Holmes waved a rag over his head, and I caught the odor of chloroform. "Thus the detour to Baker Street. A thousand apologies for my unkind words earlier, but it was quite essential that the lady leave the room long enough for me to take up a post behind the door, from which I could easily seize her."

"Holmes!"

"This is no time for chivalry, Watson. Her intentions are clear – she will be departing soon, for heaven knows where. Look at that trunk – note that it has unusual holes in it. She has the lad and intends to transport him with her."

I stared down at the motherly face. "Why?"

"She can explain later, once we have freed the boy." Holmes removed a silver chatelaine from her belt. "The only question is, where could Charley be? A home this size, that had once been an asylum, must have cells and padded, even soundproof rooms. It was simplicity itself to keep Charley confined, but it may take us hours to locate his prison."

I snapped my fingers. "I can take us there directly."

Holmes lifted an eyebrow. "You have a clue?"

"I have a puppy."

"The breed is known as the European toy spaniel," Holmes said, as he gently stroked the silken ears of the small dog. "But it is more commonly known as the Papillon, or 'butterfly dog', and was a favorite gift among royals in the sixteenth century. You may see a number of this

196

little gent's ancestors in the paintings of Titian, and the most famous of the breed was rumored to have accompanied Marie Antoinette to the scaffold."

Mr. Hart turned his head, looking at Holmes with great, red-rimmed eyes, clearly confused by this delightful narrative on canine heritage. He had barely ceased weeping since we carried his son into his home and placed him back in his nursery bed. Gregson had taken the chore of escorting the semi-conscious Mrs. Cassidy off to Scotland Yard, while Lestrade now hovered in the corner of the room, making notes. The nursemaid and the housekeeper also lingered, warmly embracing each other, overjoyed that their young charge was unharmed. The child was sleeping, for he had been drugged with laudanum, but otherwise he bore no physical injuries.

"Why?" Hart croaked. "Why would she do this?"

"Perhaps she considered herself a heroine," Holmes said. "No doubt she saw herself as rescuing a child from a cruel father. I regret the frankness of my words, sir, but too many sources – including your own confession – paint a picture of a household from which a child would wish to escape. No one blames you for your wife's sad demise, or the loss of your other child, but if you wish to retain the love and respect of little Charley, you must examine your own soul."

"She seemed so kind."

Holmes nodded. "A quick inspection of her papers told me that she was the relic of Captain James Cassidy, commander of the *Fair Maid,* a vessel in the China trade that was wrecked off the coast of New Zealand a decade ago. All hands perished, including the captain and his child, the couple's only son, a lad of just fourteen. The vessel was well-insured, and there was a substantial settlement for the widow, but nothing could mend her heart for the loss of her boy. She invited Charley into her home, she watched the deterioration of his life, and finally – wickedly – she acted upon it, stealing the child, locking him in one of the padded and sound-proof rooms in the mansion. She intended to flee the country with him at the first opportunity. It explains why she abruptly dismissed her servants, and the packed baggage that we found.

"And, most pathetically, young Charley tried to save himself before he was ever taken."

At this pronouncement, all eyes turned to Holmes. "What do you mean?" Lestrade asked.

"I mean only that Mr. Hart told us how his son begged for the two of them to go away and have adventures together. What would have planted such an idea in the child's mind? I find it likely that Mrs. Cassidy did – that she lured Charley with tales of adventure in foreign lands. A number

197

of pictures in her house are of American scenes. Indeed, we may learn that the lady was originally an American, or spent time there in her youth. Be that as it may, the boy naturally thought such adventures would be more delightful in the company of his father than with an elderly widow. But when his father reacted to the invitation by threatening to send the child away to a dull boarding school – that sealed the bargain. Charley slipped through the gate the next day. Now the lady had only to restrain him until she could make arrangements to leave."

"Remarkable," Lestrade breathed.

"Ah, but such deductions must be tested, and I think the quickest way to verify them would be to awaken Charley, assure him of his safety, and let him tell his story. Afterward, a long holiday in America with his father might prepare the lad for a bright future." Holmes rose from his chair. "No injection of stimulant will be necessary, Watson. I think our Papillon pup may do the trick. Ah, see how readily he licks the child's face. No doubt they were the best of friends in imprisonment. The lady probably procured the puppy as an additional enticement to the lad to cast his lot with her. Taking the dog away was surely an act of discipline, once she had Charley in her snare. When we arrived, we found that the puppy wanted nothing more than to return to the child, leading us to the hidden room that we might never have found otherwise. Ah, the dear faithfulness of dogs – see, Charley awakens. Watson, I believe our work is done, so let us retire from the scene."

The Adventure of the Impudent Imposter
by Josh Cerefice

The summer of 1898 was a busy period for my good friend, Sherlock Holmes. In no more than a single month, he had unraveled the cryptic riddle of Hilton Cubitt and the dancing men, thwarted the nefarious schemes of his nemesis Brigadier Benjamin Horrigan, and solved the perplexing puzzle of champion pugilist Tommy O'Lonaghan and his pet orangutan. He had little time to celebrate these triumphs, however, for no sooner had he bidden goodbye to one client than another would come drumming at our door, invariably in a state of some distress, and challenging my friend with a new conundrum.

Our next visitor, it so happened, arrived at our rooms on what was a mild evening in early August. My friend and I were just finishing our desserts – a delicious almond pudding prepared by our diligent and doting landlady, Mrs. Hudson – when a stranger appeared on the threshold before us.

He was a tall man of early middle age with a tangle of curly, dark hair and a few faint pockmarks covering a broad, swarthy face. Though I didn't possess Holmes's extraordinary powers of perception, it was plain to see, from the way the man's eyes darted restlessly about the room, that he was severely stricken for some reason.

Holmes moved forward and proffered a polite hand before inviting him to sit down.

"How can we be of assistance, Mr. – ?"

"Crockford," he answered. "Emerson Crockford, Junior."

I recognized the name. The gentleman's late father had been, by all accounts, a man of some distinction, known as one of the wealthiest individuals in London – a fortune he attained, according to *The Daily Telegraph*, during the Californian gold rush of the late 'forties and early 'fifties. There were also rumours, just as plentiful, that Mr. Crockford, Junior was something of a philanderer.

"I'm sorry for disturbing your meal, gentlemen," said our guest, "but the matter I've come here to discuss is of a pressing nature and couldn't wait any longer. I hope I haven't inconvenienced you."

"Not at all," I said before Holmes could sweep another glance at his pudding.

"What is the reason for your visitation?" prompted my forthright friend.

Mr. Crockford drew in a deep, bracing breath. "I have recently become the victim of a perverse and cruel deception, one which has shaken me to my very core. I didn't know where else to turn."

"We will do our best," Holmes said with a civil smile.

It was at this point that Mrs. Hudson came bobbing in and bestowed cups of steaming hot coffee upon us. "Thank you," I said as she placed mine beside me.

Crockford took a satisfying sip and commenced his tale. "I haven't long returned from Africa, where I've spent the last twenty-seven years of my life working as a plantation holder. It was on the foothills of Mount Kenya that we harvested and brewed the finest coffee and sold it to the furthest corners of the globe in what, it transpired, was a terrifically profitable enterprise."

Indeed, everything about Mr. Crockford's appearance distinguished him as a man of handsome means, from his attire – he wore an elegant beige suit and Italian leather shoes – to the assortment of paraphernalia that adorned his person, chief amongst which was a glimmering gold pocket-watch that swung lazily from his left breast.

Holmes arched an eyebrow. "A coffee connoisseur, eh! I hope Mrs. Hudson's offering isn't offensive to your refined tastes."

"Not at all," he replied, taking another draught as if to demonstrate his approval. "Quite the contrary. It's rather pleasing to the palette. Not a patch on Kenyan, mind, if it isn't churlish of me to say that. Have you ever tried my own? It's the volcanic soil, you see. Gives it a flavour quite unlike anything else."

"I'm sure it does," Holmes said indifferently, eager to press on. "If the coffee trade was so lucrative for you, why have you come back?"

"Kenya is a beautiful country, but the blistering African heat wasn't always to my liking. I intended to come back years ago, but work detained me there. Since then, however, business has slowed down, so I decided now was the opportune time. I'm glad I did, too. There's nowhere quite like London, is there? The history. The hubbub. The people."

"The crime," said Holmes.

Crockford ignored him. "Frustratingly, though, I haven't been able to enjoy it fully, for business has confined me to my London rooms and has barely afforded me opportunity to revisit my old haunts and reacquaint myself with former friends." He stirred his coffee. "Ten days ago, however, I treated myself to lunch at the St. James Club in Piccadilly, where I used to accompany my father in the late 'sixties. Much, of course, has changed since then, and no one even recognized me as the spotty and

200

socially introverted young man who always seemed shackled to the furthest corners of any room.

"It was at St. James that I met a man of similar age who went by the nick-name Spinner, on account of him being a champion billiards player. I learned that he's there every day. We chatted amiably for several hours and discovered that we had much in common – not least our love of horse-racing and backgammon – and the two of us became fast friends. That would quickly change, however, when, the following evening over drinks, he told me his real name." He paused, struggling to shape his words. "It was *Emerson Crockford*!"

I couldn't for the life of me believe what I had just heard, and threw a fleeting look towards Holmes, who, by contrast, appeared wholly unperturbed by this incredible revelation. Few things ever seemed to surprise him.

"It was in this moment of cold shock that it dawned upon me that this man may not have just stolen my name, but also my life. I was so stunned that I didn't want to confront him on the matter, or tell him my own name, which he had never asked. Feeling nauseous, I returned immediately home. There, I telephoned my country residence in Bishop's Waltham, where I've yet to visit since my return, and learned from my butler Trumble that 'Mr. Crockford' was in London but would be home in a few hours. Apparently, 'Mr. Crockford' has since been living at the house since returning from abroad two months ago!"

"The scoundrel!" I said. "But how did your butler mistake this imposter for you?"

Holmes answered on behalf of our guest. "Mr. Crockford has been away for nearly three decades, Watson. People's appearance can alter a great deal in that length of time. Any physical differences between the young man who left and the middle-aged one who returned, therefore, can be attributed to the passing years. Naturally, the butler would consider this a more probable explanation than a lookalike usurping the identity of his master, which conversely, is highly improbable – though not, it would seem, an impossibility."

"That makes sense," I admitted.

"My manor wasn't the only thing he took from me," Crockford continued. "Next day, I left for the bank, where I learned something even more disconcerting. Someone claiming to be me has been making regular withdrawals from my account there. I asked for them to say nothing until it can all be sorted out.

"And so, bereft of all but my person, and thoroughly shocked, I wandered the streets for several hours until finally folding into a chair at St. James's, where a stiff brandy began to restore my battered senses.

"However, no sooner had I sat down than I was asked to leave by the secretary, who accused me of using someone else's name to enter the club. I did my damnedest to convince him that I was Emerson Crockford and that the other man was the fake. I even invoked my father's name, thinking it would add validity to my assertions. Unfortunately, it was to no avail and the man, steadfast in his convictions, wouldn't be swayed. Even those who were once my closest friends wouldn't listen to my vehement appeals."

Throughout his narrative Crockford had, to his credit, remained calm. Now, however, he surrendered to shame. "I can't believe what a fool I've been!" he said, shaking his head. "How did I not see him for the charlatan he was?"

Holmes attempted to appease him. "Do not punish yourself. You made an error of judgement, but you weren't to know what he was up to. The person you have described sounds like an expert dissembler capable of deceiving even the most discerning of men."

"But why me? He could have chosen anyone."

"This was no indiscriminate crime. He picked you, and for a very simple reason: You are a man of immense influence who once inhabited the upper echelons of society. By stealing your name, he can now walk into any private members club in London, as he indeed did, without anyone questioning his right to be there. This, in turn, allows him to rub shoulders with the social elite who frequent such places, people who may have spurned him in the past. He likely had no idea that you would return to London. And then there's your sizeable wealth and comfortable lifestyle to consider, all of which make you an alluring target for such an unscrupulous person."

Crockford was crestfallen. "I just want my life back. Is that too much to ask?"

I pitied the poor fellow. Not only had he been robbed of his money and usurped from his home, but to make his downfall steeper still, those who had formerly regarded him as a friend now looked upon him as a social pariah.

"We will retrieve what is rightfully yours," Holmes assured him, "but you must be patient. Whom else have you approached? Your attorney? Business agents?"

Crockford shook his head. "None besides the bank."

"Then wait for a few days before doing so. In the meantime, I will do everything I can to find out who this man is and make him answer for his crime. Only then can you reclaim the life that has been taken from you."

"It's comforting to know that I have someone like you on my side, Mr. Holmes."

"And you haven't reported it to the authorities yet?" I asked.

"I've been to Scotland Yard, but the detective there – an Inspector Toller, I think his name was – said they can't make an arrest because there is no tangible proof that a crime has been committed." He sighed. "As things stand, they only have my word for it."

"Unfortunately, the inspector is correct on that score."

There was a pregnant pause. "So what do you propose we do now?"

"First, Watson and I will meet this man at St. James Club tomorrow morning and try to learn as much about him as possible, particularly anything in his appearance that sets him apart from you. That will be a good starting point, I think." Holmes stood up to signal that the consultation had come to an end. "For now, though, please try not to worry yourself."

"That, I fear, isn't going to be easy," said Crockford, rising. "Should you need to contact me, you can find me at No. 56 Wimpole Street." He asked for a pen and paper, on which he scribbled the address down. "Here," he said, handing the note to Holmes. "In case you forget."

"We'll notify you if any developments arise."

"I'm much obliged to you, Mr. Holmes," he said with a bow of the head before taking his leave.

"I can't accompany you to the St. James, I'm afraid," my friend said once our client had gone. "The death of Professor Alexander Snow and his stolen Majorian gemstone has come to a head. That's why you must be my eyes and ears."

I felt flattered that Holmes entrusted me to undertake such an important assignment. Equally, I was concerned that I wouldn't be up to the task. What's more, a multitude of misgivings began to take root in my mind: How would I get into the club without being a member? What if the man recognized me? Would I fail to spot something crucial to our investigation?

Once I had given utterance to these qualms, Holmes began to address each one in turn, enumerating them on his thin fingers. "As far as getting into St. James is concerned, I'll ask Mycroft to pull a few strings and sign you in as a guest."

Indeed, Holmes's brother was a man of not-inconsiderable influence, largely owing to his standing as co-founder of the Diogenes Club, an establishment we'd had occasion to visit innumerable times since the foul affair of Mr. Melas and his covetous captors.

"Secondly," he continued, unfurling a forefinger, "it is highly unlikely that the man will recognize you. As a physician and author, you are largely invisible to the public eye. You should probably use a *non de plume* though, just to be safe."

"From one pretender to another," I said glibly.

The irony wasn't lost on Holmes, who smiled wryly at the remark. "You are also afraid of overlooking something significant. You have observed my methods for many years now, have you not? I would like to think at least some of them have rubbed off on you."

"Well, I hope your faith in me isn't misplaced," I said dubiously, despite Holmes's best efforts to dispel my doubts.

"Nonsense! You will do splendidly. I'm certain of it." His eyes fell upon the mantel clock. "It's getting late. It would be wise to get some rest. You shall need it for tomorrow."

The following morning, rejuvenated and refreshed after a restful night's sleep, I made my way to the St. James Club without delay, electing to travel by hansom cab instead of going on foot. It was a decision I immediately regretted, however, for the busy traffic compelled the cabbie to take a circuitous route through Seymour Place and Brook Street, which prolonged our journey by no less than fifteen minutes. Eventually though, after a lengthy detour, I arrived at my destination at 106 Piccadilly, where I paid my fare and headed inside the building, an imposing structure built in the neo-Palladian style.

The interior of the club was even more ostentatious than its exterior. Enormous pillars supported a frescoed ceiling depicting scenes from the Old Testament. Magnificent staircases swept majestically from one grand gallery to the next, and portraits of barons, dukes, and lords hung haughtily from every wall, serving as timeless monuments to the prestigious individuals who had paced its hallowed hallways throughout the centuries. Being in so luxurious a place amongst such exalted company was, I'm unashamed to admit, a humbling experience.

Finding the person in question was no easy feat either. The club was a labyrinth of lounges, libraries, and bars that seemed to blur into one another, making navigating my way around the building an onerous task. Mercifully though, after combing every nook and cranny of my lavish surroundings, fortune finally favoured me.

After a discreet inquiry, I found my quarry secreted in one of the building's well-appointed parlours, reading a newspaper and smoking a pipe. Mindful not to attract too much attention, I positioned myself in a chair adjacent to him. A waiter came over and I ordered a cup of tea, then took a broadsheet off the table in front of me and perused the columns of *The Pall Mall Gazette* as I waited patiently for an opportunity to strike up conversation.

"It's awful," I said, tutting aloud and shaking my head in exaggerated disgust. "Just awful!" I was remarking upon a recent spate of robberies in

High Holborn perpetrated by a notorious female gang known as The Forty Elephants. "And I thought women were the fairer sex."

This contentious comment piqued the gentleman's curiosity, causing him to peer up from his paper. "They aren't as virtuous as they seem," he opined.

Rather fortuitously, I had turned up an ace.

"Prison is too good for these degenerates," he added peremptorily. "Bring back public hanging, I say."

I found the man's hypocrisy to be utterly risible, yet I had no choice but to nod in assent. "Douglas Weaver," I said, holding out my hand.

He pressed my palm with a firm grip. "Emerson Crockford. But my friends call me 'Spinner'."

For the next hour or so we spoke cordially about current affairs – particularly the latest news concerning Captain Alfred Dreyfus and his captivity on Devil's Island – before drifting over to the billiards table on the other side of the room, where a small group of members were drinking in companionable silence.

"How about a wager?" Spinner asked, chalking his cue. "Twenty shillings to the winner?"

I was no stranger to the game, having played it with my friend Charles Thurston on countless occasions before. As such, I felt confident in my own abilities and willingly accepted the high stake.

Without further ado my opponent broke off, sending balls flying furiously around the table and colliding into each other with a clatter. One of them, by sheer serendipity, disappeared into a corner pocket.

"Bravo! A fine shot," I conceded, tapping the table sportingly as a monocled man in the corner applauded in appreciation.

Although the man standing in front of me looked like our client in several significant respects, the light hanging above the billiards table brought his features into sharper focus and highlighted a number of notable differences between the two. Spinner's hair was a shade lighter – more of a chestnut brown than black – and his jawline longer, while he bore none of the blemishes that flecked the face of the real Mr. Crockford.

"What did you say you do for a living?" he asked casually.

I lined up a shot. "I'm a stockbroker," I said, striking the ball. A red dribbled over a pocket, but refused to roll in.

"Oh. Business good?"

I nodded. "Very. In fact, I've just negotiated a deal between George Cadbury and a client of mine."

"Impressive!"

"You?"

"I'm in business too," he replied. "The coffee trade to be exact. It's very profitable. And Kenya is a magnificent place. In fact, I would still be there now if . . . other things hadn't lured me back here," he added, bending over the table to take his next shot, which missed its mark by a considerable margin.

My silent celebrations were short-lived, however, for it wasn't long before he recovered his focus and found a second wind, doling out a drubbing to me in what was a dazzling display of potting prowess.

I congratulated him on his victory and grudgingly handed over the winnings. "The best man won," I said, trying to save face.

Spinner, in fairness, was magnanimous in victory. "That's very generous of you, but you were a worthy opponent. It was only a slice of good fortune that gave me the edge in the end."

I couldn't help but admire his good grace, even if it was all a cynical charade, and I knew now why Mr. Crockford had been so easily taken in by him. How, I wondered, could someone as depraved as he play the part of one so dignified?

"A rematch?" I proposed, hoping to reclaim my money.

Spinner smiled apologetically. "I'm afraid I can't. I have a business meeting this afternoon. Another time, perhaps."

"Of course."

"Well, thank you for the game, Mr. Weaver." He shook my hand. "It was a pleasure."

"The pleasure was all mine," I lied.

I returned to Baker Street later that afternoon to find my friend in a state of profound meditation. Knowing better than to disturb his musings, I took a silent seat opposite him and sought temporary distraction in the pages of a book while I waited for Holmes to emerge from his reverie. The adventure of Edmond Dantès and his crusade of bloody vengeance proved to be a thoroughly absorbing read and served as the perfect diversion to pass the time. In fact, so engrossed was I by its swashbuckling tale of romance and revenge that I forgot my friend was still there until he next spoke.

"So how did your little *tête-à-tête* go?" he asked, pulling me out of Napoleonic Paris. "Did you discover anything of note?"

I placed the book down with a puff of the cheeks. "There isn't a lot to tell, really. All I learned is that the two Mr. Crockfords look quite similar but aren't a spitting image. But that doesn't prove anything, does it? Aside from the obvious fact that they are two different people, which is self-evident."

"But by attesting to that, you have corroborated Mr. Crockford's story. We now know beyond any reasonable doubt that there is a man impersonating him."

"I suppose so."

Holmes folded his legs. "As well as the physical differences you observed between the two Crockfords, you may have also noticed that Spinner was a left-handed player."

I nodded. "But how could you kn – " It suddenly dawned upon me. "You were there?"

His lips curled into an impish smile as he gestured at an eyeglass lying on the mantel, and suddenly I remembered the monocled man who had spectated our game of billiards. "That was you? But I thought you trusted my judgement?"

"Come, come, Watson. Don't sulk. It wasn't a question of faith, but probability. Two pairs of eyes can see more than one. What I may have missed, you would have spotted. And vice-versa."

Despite feeling affronted, I thought it best not to pursue the issue further. "What's next? The trail seems to have run cold. How on earth are we going to find out who this man is?"

"Don't despair. As I told Mr. Crockford yesterday, we must be patient. All in good time, my friend. All in good time."

"But we have no more leads," I said, wondering whether Holmes, as was his wont, may have been keeping his cards close to his chest.

"Not so. This morning, when you first departed for the St. James to get acquainted with our fraudulent friend, I telephoned Mr. Crockford's butler at Bishop's Waltham and apprised him of the situation."

"Presumably he gave little credence to what you told him."

"He was . . . unconvinced, to say the least, and firmly believes that the man living there is none other than his master. Despite his doubts, however, he has agreed to speak to us in confidence just in case – albeit reluctantly."

"But won't *he* be there?"

"According to the butler, he stays in town late on Wednesdays for business and isn't back until late."

I was less than enthusiastic. "It sounds like a shot in the dark to me. But I see no better alternative."

"It's certainly worth a try. If we learn nothing, what have we lost? 'Mr. Crockford' has been living there for several months. If there's anywhere that we can hope to unearth evidence of his identity, it will most assuredly be there." His brow suddenly darkened. "A snake in the grass cannot hide forever. Soon enough, we will flush him out."

With this solemn pledge, he sprung up from his chair and took his inverness cape from the hook. "Come, Watson. We should make haste to Waterloo Station. The next train to Hampshire will be departing soon."

Our journey passed without incident. While Holmes spent most of it immersed in a brown study, his mind firmly focused upon his purpose, I, for my part, whiled away the time by admiring the glorious view outside the window. However, as the pleasant Hampshire pastures passed by us in a blur, tedium and tiredness soon began to set in. I was relieved, therefore, when, after what felt like an interminable amount of time, we eventually came to a juddering halt at our final stop.

From the station we took a dog-cart through the quaint medieval market town of Bishop's Waltham, past the local clay pits and strawberry fields, and over rutted rural tracks until we reached Emerson Crockford's country residence, a prepossessing Georgian property surrounded by acres of dense woodland.

We knocked on the door, which was promptly opened by a wizened old man with an aquiline nose and balding head, from which a few remaining clumps of wild white hair sprouted like snow-covered weeds. He was, I surmised, Mr. Crockford's manservant, Trumble.

"Welcome to Crockford Manor," he said croakily, beckoning us into the hallway with a stooped bow. "I trust you've had a comfortable journey?"

"It was certainly a long one," I said with a weary sigh.

"Then please allow me to fetch some refreshments for you both," he said, squinting at us through a pair of horn-rimmed spectacles. "A cup of tea, perhaps?"

We politely rejected our host's hospitality and, with pleasantries duly observed, the man wasted no time in getting to the pith of the problem. "Regarding our conversation earlier today, Mr. Holmes: Frankly, it has left me puzzled. An imposter? Under this roof? It's rather far-fetched, isn't it?"

"Nonetheless, that's what we suspect."

The butler was skeptical. "Forgive me for speaking out of turn, but do you have any evidence to support what you're saying?"

"At present, we have nothing concrete. However, yesterday evening we were visited by Mr. Crockford, who alleged that another man had stolen his name and was living in his home. That's why we're here."

Trumble chuckled incredulously. "I've known Emerson since he was a child. Do you not think I wouldn't recognize him from a stranger?"

"I realize it sounds absurd. But if you would humour us."

"Very well," he said grudgingly. "What do you wish to know?"

Holmes came straight to the point. "Have you noticed anything unusual about your master – by which I mean the man presently living here – since he returned two months ago? Anything different in the way he has been behaving?"

"Nothing that comes to mind. Although . . . ."

"Yes?"

"It's just that . . . Oh, it's probably nothing."

"I'll be the judge of that."

"Now that I think about it, Emerson hasn't been himself lately."

"In what way?"

"With the exception of myself, he has been treating his staff appallingly. A few weeks ago, for instance, he berated the cook over a trivial matter and subjected her to a string of bitter vituperations before rudely dismissing her. The Emerson I knew would never talk to someone in such a ghastly manner. It wasn't like him at all."

"In short, then, he has been acting out of character."

The butler was obdurate in his convictions. "He has been behaving strangely – I admit that much – but to suggest that he is someone else entirely . . . I'm sorry, that isn't something I can countenance."

Holmes, it seemed, thought it futile to dispute the matter further. "If you would be so kind, may we look around?"

"I don't see what you hope to find, but as you wish," said our unwilling host, who proceeded to escort us through the large house until we found ourselves in an elegantly furnished drawing room.

"Souvenirs from your master's travels?" Holmes said, pointing to a collection of African tribal masks mounted to the far wall, each of their faces contorted into all manner of hideous expressions.

The butler nodded. "I don't see their appeal, personally. They're ugly things."

"He clearly has a predilection for the grotesque, that's for sure." Holmes then gestured to a framed photograph lying on the mantel above the fireplace. "And this must be Emerson."

The picture depicted a considerably younger Mr. Crockford than the one we had met the night before. He was standing in front of a billiards table, wearing a boyish beam upon his thin face and a stylish waistcoat around his scrawny frame, clutching a cue in his hand.

"He was only eighteen at the time," said the old man, wistfully. "It was the first tournament he ever won." A proud smile grew upon his lips. "He was quite the talent."

It was clear that his relationship to the younger man went far further than that of a master and servant. Indeed, he spoke about him with the fondness of a father.

"Shall we continue?" Holmes said, rousing the man from his reminiscences.

"Oh, sorry! I was miles away. Yes, of course . . . follow me."

Moments later, we found ourselves in a study filled with the overwhelming smell of tobacco smoke and tanned leather. It was there that, with the butler's reluctant permission, my friend began rummaging through the contents of Mr. Crockford's writing table.

"Now this is interesting," Holmes said, waving me over to the bureau. "Watson, come and have a look."

There, lying in plain view, were two letters, both penned in stylish handwriting by Mr. Crockford, and addressed to the same recipient. The first one read:

My dear Helena,

I cannot bear this any longer. Father is keeping a close watch on me and has forbidden me from seeing you. He treats me like a child and thinks he can govern my life. The tyrant! I feel like a bird in a gilded cage. But soon, we will fly away together, my love. Soon, we will be free.

Yours eternally,
Emerson

"They were barely older than children when they planned on running away together," the butler said, reflectively. "Emerson's father never approved of the match, of course. Said they were too young. He even confiscated some of the boy's letters. That's why this one is still here, I imagine – never sent. In the end, his influence was too strong, and Emerson was forced to call off the engagement. Not long after that, he moved to Kenya. Broke the girl's heart, he did."

I then picked up the second letter, which read:

My Dear Helena,

Time has done nothing to extinguish the fire of my love for you, and though an ocean has kept us apart all these years, you have never left my thoughts for a single moment. I was a fool to have deserted you – not a day goes by that I don't regret it – and I'm truly sorry for the pain I caused you. But there's no point ruing what might have been. Let's look ahead to what may, perhaps, still be.

210

Yours eternally,
Emerson

"He wrote this one after he returned," said Trumble. "He never stopped loving her, it seems."

"It is the signatory, not the sentiment, that interests me," Holmes replied.

It didn't feel right to be prying into the man's private business, but Holmes appeared to have no such compunctions. While the butler was looking in the other direction, he folded the two letters and tucked them into his breast pocket. "Thank you once again for your time. We will show ourselves out."

Much to my surprise, we revisited Crockford Manor the next day after spending the night at the Barleycorn Inn, a charming tavern in the centre of town. On this occasion, however, we were accompanied by Inspector Toller and Mr. Crockford, who answered my friend's summons post haste and rendezvoused with us at the train station.

"Thank you both for coming on such short notice," Holmes said to the pair once they had disembarked and jostled their way across the crowded platform.

Inspector Toller looked entirely inconvenienced by the whole thing. "I hope it isn't a wasted journey," he said. "I don't like to be pulled away from my desk for no good reason."

My friend essayed a conciliatory smile. "As I said in my wire last night, your presence here is invaluable, Inspector."

A train went thundering past, producing a tremendous gust of wind. "I'm pleased to hear it," he said, brushing specks of dirt off his peaked cap, which had blown to the ground.

Not since the curious case of the malevolent mesmerist had we worked alongside Inspector Ralph Toller, a towering bull of a man with a craggy face and coarse manner who, more often than not, preferred to mete out justice using a baton rather than his brain.

"And it's good to see you again, Mr. Crockford," said Holmes, addressing our client. "You look well."

It had only been two days since he had visited us at Baker Street, yet something about him had imperceptibly changed for the better. Perhaps, I mused, it was because he was no longer weighed down by the worry of it all, knowing that his dreadful ordeal was coming to an end and that within a few short hours he would be back at his manor house sipping contentedly on a brandy.

211

"Come on, then," Toller said tetchily. "The sooner we get this done, the sooner I can get back to London."

After an uncomfortable cab ride over bumpy country lanes, throughout which the inspector complained ceaselessly about being beckoned to an "uncivilized backwater in the middle of nowhere", we soon found ourselves, once again, in the dining room at Crockford Manor, where the other "Mr. Crockford" was eating his breakfast and reading the morning columns in a crimson dressing gown.

He sensed our presence on the threshold and lowered his paper before standing up. "What is the meaning of this?" he stammered, bewildered our unexpected. Then he narrowed his eyes at me. "Mr. Weaver?"

I wasn't sure whether to come clean or keep up the ruse, so in the end, I did neither and decided to remain quiet.

Our client, however, wasn't so reticent. "Inspector, arrest this man!" he commanded. "Or I may not be accountable for my actions."

"Mr. Crockford" retreated as Toller advanced towards him. "This is preposterous!" he cried. "I've done nothing wrong!"

"That won't be necessary, Inspector," said Holmes, holding out a hand. "The man you are about to arrest is an innocent man. The same, however, cannot be said for *him*." And he aimed an accusing finger at our client. "You've treated us all to a fine performance, one worthy of Henry Irving himself. But I'm afraid it's your final curtain call, Mr. *Gribbon*."

The man in the nightgown was growing impatient. "Someone had better explain what is going on – and quickly!"

"We're sorry for the intrusion, Mr. Crockford. My name is Sherlock Holmes, and these men are Dr. Watson and Inspector Toller. The man who just ordered your arrest is called Vincent Gribbon. He's a professional con artist who has recently been released from Newgate Prison."

"Good heavens!"

"He came to us the other night, claiming that his name was Emerson Crockford and spinning a yarn about a stranger who had stolen his name and money and taken up residence in his home. That stranger was you. He attempted to use me as an independent witness to verify his account so that he could have you arrested for fraud. You had been out of the country for decades, and he hoped to get away with it – at least for a little while. When you were in prison, he planned to finish stealing your identity."

Crockford was stunned into incredulous silence by the astonishing revelation.

I stole a glance at Gribbon, who was smirking insolently. "Where's your proof? Until you have that, none of you can touch me."

"Unfortunately, he's right," conceded Toller.

"My suspicions were first aroused by the coffee," began Holmes. "You told us you had spent twenty-seven years working on a coffee plantation in Kenya. Yet your complexion suggested that you have been mostly indoors – in prison, as it turns out. Then there was the matter of the coffee. When you sampled Mrs. Hudson's offering, I distinctly recall you saying that it was 'not a patch on Kenyan'. Unbeknownst to you, however, our coffee was from that same country."

Gribbon sneered. "That doesn't prove anything."

"Other than the fact you were lying. After that, I began to question the veracity of your entire narrative. All I needed to do then was ascertain the identity of your would-be victim." Holmes faced Crockford. "During your game of billiards with Watson at St. James', I observed that you were a left-handed player."

He went over to the mantel and picked up the photograph of the young Crockford. "In this picture you are also holding the cue in your left hand. I spotted it when I came here yesterday. That was the first thing that distinguished you from our client, who happens to be right-handed." He now addressed Gribbon. "When you visited Baker Street, you wrote down your address for me – a fake one, no less – and also used your right-hand," he explained, before turning back to the real Crockford. "But it was these," he said, reaching into his breast pocket and pulling out the letters he had taken the previous day in the man's study, "which proved your identity for certain."

"What are they?" asked Toller.

"They are missives of a romantic nature, the first of which was written by Mr. Crockford before he went away to Kenya – the butler attested to that fact – and whose authorship, therefore, is indisputable. There is no way it can be a forgery."

Crockford looked puzzled, and then outraged, but before he could speak, Holmes continued.

"The second letter, however, was penned after Mr. Crockford returned – again, confirmed by the butler – which, conversely, means it might have been counterfeited by an interloper living here. Thus, I had to compare it to the first to authenticate its provenance." He showed Toller the documents. "Notice how the penmanship is identical in both, Inspector – both written by a left hand."

"Even the most adept forger couldn't imitate the handwriting so accurately," the Yarder acknowledged.

"That told me, beyond any reasonable doubt, that the man living here was in fact the real Mr. Crockford."

Gribbon clapped his hands in mock applause. "You really are as clever as they say, Mr. Holmes," he said with a sardonic smile. "I'm impressed. It seems that there's no fooling you, is there?"

"Get him out of my sight!" barked Crockford, whose incredulity had now become indignation. "Before I do something I'll regret!"

Within an instant, the tall, burly figure of Inspector Toller was looming over Gribbon, brandishing a pair of handcuffs in his spade-like hands. "Your fellow inmates at Newgate won't even notice you've been gone," he said, clicking the cuffs in place before marching the prisoner off the premises.

"I can scarcely credit what has just happened," said Mr. Crockford, pouring himself a drink in his study. "It's all so incredible."

"It must be a lot to take in," I said sympathetically.

"Am I correct in thinking that you had never met Mr. Gribbon before today?" asked Holmes, as pragmatic as ever. "He said you spoke to him at the St. James Club."

He shook his head. "I've never seen him before in my life."

"I suspected as much."

"And yet, his face was familiar to me . . ." There was a prolonged pause, during which Crockford looked lost in thought. "That's it!" he said at last. "He was here a few weeks ago during one of my *soirees*. I didn't recognize him, so naturally I simply assumed one of my friends had brought him along as a guest. He was acting very oddly, though. He spent most of the evening loitering about in the garden and drinking my wine, and he barely made any effort to talk to anyone. I also got the distinct impression that he was watching me. Whenever I turned around, he would be there." He picked up his glass with a tremulous hand. "I didn't think anything of it at the time. But now, given what I know, it makes my hairs stand on end."

"He has probably been stalking you for weeks," Holmes said, "studying your mannerisms and movements so that he could better imitate them when the time came to put his plan into action."

Crockford looked deeply disturbed by the sinister notion. "And to think that he nearly succeeded. It doesn't bear thinking about."

It was at this point that our host began riffling through a drawer, from which he produced a pile of notes. "A token of my gratitude," he said, slapping them down before my friend.

Holmes raised a hand in protest. "I cannot accept that, though I appreciate the gesture."

"I must insist," he said. "If it wasn't for you, I'd be languishing in a jail cell while another man would be sitting in this seat, enjoying

214

everything I have spent the last three decades to build – at least until he could be sorted out."

Holmes was adamant. "Nonetheless, you never solicited my services, so you aren't technically a client. But," he added, "Watson here is due reimbursement for his own expenses at the St. James Club as part of the investigation." And he reminded Crockford of our wager over the billiards table. I started to protest – I had been beaten honestly – but Crockford insisted that I take the money. Then he again offered to pay Holmes, who refused.

"Well, if you're sure," Crockford relented, re-depositing it in the drawer. "I just wish there was some way I could repay you."

"There is," said Holmes. "You can answer one more question for me."

"Of course. What is it?"

"It's a rather delicate matter, I'm afraid."

"Don't spare my blushes, Mr. Holmes. I'm not easily embarrassed."

"The woman in the letters . . . She was the reason you came back, wasn't she?"

After a moment, with a melancholy sigh, he said, "Business wasn't what it was, so I was planning on returning anyway. But yes, the prospect of seeing Helena again was what decided it for me. I missed her as much as I missed home. I don't think I ever truly got over her."

"But twenty-seven years is a long time," I said.

"Too long, apparently." He shook his head sadly. "She has since moved on."

"How do you know?"

"I saw her in town the other week, holding another man's arm and with a small child by her side." He smiled weakly. "I'm glad she has finally found happiness."

"Which is why you didn't post the second letter," Holmes said. "The one in which you hinted at a reconciliation, and perhaps more."

"It wouldn't have been appropriate. She's a married woman."

"Though you are philosophical about it now, at the time you must have been feeling all sorts of emotions. Sorrow. Jealousy. Anger."

"It was an upsetting sight to behold," he admitted. "I was in quite the funk for a few days afterwards."

"And your staff bore the brunt of your ill-temper, didn't they?"

He dropped his head in disgrace. "I'm not proud of it, Mr. Holmes. There is no excuse for my behaviour."

"It isn't for me to pass judgement, though, in my humble opinion, I think your cook deserves a second chance."

"Yes . . . yes, you are quite right. I will recall her immediately."

Holmes checked his pocket-watch. "Watson, we must go. We have a long journey ahead of us and the next train will be leaving shortly." He stood up. "I wish you a happy and prosperous life."

Our host raised a grateful glass. "And to you, gentlemen," he replied as we made for the door. "And to you."

"So how did you discover name, *Vincent Gribbon*?" I asked as the train left the station.

"Not long ago, I read an article in *The Illustrated Police News* about a notorious con man who, after a lengthy hearing, had been released on parole from Newgate after serving a sentence for posing as Baron Sebastian Braithwaite."

"But surely there are other swindlers in London."

"True. But very few, I wager, hadn't long come out of prison. Fewer still, would have shared a *modus operandi* with our supposed 'client' – he, too, targeted wealthy individuals who spent prolonged periods of time overseas. What's more, the illustration in the newspaper showed a striking resemblance to the man who visited us the other evening. It wasn't a certainty, I grant you, but it was a strong likelihood."

"And his guilty reaction confirmed your hypothesis."

"Precisely. It's likely that Gribbon consulted parish records to search for prosperous individuals who had made their fortunes abroad," he elaborated, "and in whose absence he could pull off his sordid masquerade. Once he had drawn up a shortlist of potential targets, it's probable that he did a spot of house-hunting, gaining access to his victims' country piles by pretending to be a guest at their social gatherings. That's why he was at Crockford Manor a few weeks ago. While he was there, he saw Crockford and realized that they weren't too physically dissimilar."

Despite Holmes's elucidation, I was still mystified. "I wonder why he didn't put his plan into motion while Crockford was in Kenya?"

"In all likelihood, that may have been his original intent. However, he spent some unexpected time in prison, and he didn't anticipate the real Crockford returning so soon. As a result, he had to devise an alternative means of getting him out of the way. That's why he used me to have Crockford arrested."

"But claiming that someone else was pretending to be him wasn't enough to warrant an arrest, was it?"

"That's true," Holmes said. "Doubtless Gribbon planned to fabricate evidence to incriminate the man further, evidence he would have made sure I found."

"But if he hadn't yet done that, why was he so willing to believe that you were ready to arrest Crockford?"

"I simply told him we had enough to arrest the man and hold him in custody for a few days until further proof came to light. That seemed to satisfy Gribbon, who was probably intending on using that time to plant the fake evidence in Crockford's home, or to strip his accounts."

"It was a risky ploy on your part."

"But a successful one. He took the bait."

"You pulled the wool over the inspector's eyes as well," I said. "He almost arrested the wrong man."

"I couldn't tell him everything. He might have given the game away before we even got to Crockford Manor."

"I still don't understand . . . Even if Gribbon's plan worked, wouldn't people have realized that the real Crockford was in prison and that he, therefore, was a fraud?"

"Not so. Gribbon was willing to go to great lengths to convince everyone – including the police – that the man in jail was a fraud. Consequently, everyone would have believed that the person walking around London was Emerson Crockford."

"I didn't consider that," I admitted. "Gribbon seemed to know a great deal about the man's life, didn't he?"

"It isn't inconceivable that, while at the *soiree*, he befriended someone close to Crockford, someone who knew him intimately, and could serve as a reliable source of information."

"It was certainly a cunning scheme." Then something suddenly occurred to me. "Why didn't you tell me this sooner?"

"For the same reason I didn't tell anyone else. I couldn't risk you possibly giving it away before I had determined all the facts. If Gribbon was apprehended at that stage, the police wouldn't have been able to charge him, not without conclusive proof. Not only would he have gotten off scot-free. He would also have known that we were hot on his heels. Added to which, it lends your future narrative a certain suspense, does it not?"

"What are you insinuating?" I said in mock offence. "That my chronicles are so lacking in all other facets that they need to rely upon unnecessary tension to hold my readers' attention?"

He smiled archly. "I would say nothing of the sort."

"I hope his sentence will be a long one," I said after the conductor had collected our tickets. "The punishment for attempted fraud is, dare I say it, not a particularly strict one. Gribbon will probably be out in a few months, scouring the capital for his next unsuspecting victim."

"He almost destroyed a man's life. If I had my way, he would never see daylight again."

Throughout our adventures over the years Holmes and I had crossed paths with the very worst of humanity, be it the brutish Jack Woodley or tyrannical Jephro Rucastle. And yet, even in the company of such wicked malefactors, Vincent Gribbon was, in my estimation, one of the most detestable creatures we had ever encountered.

"Regrettably," added my friend, "his fate is beyond our control."

"At least Mr. Crockford still has his freedom," I said, clinging to a consolation.

"It would have been a terrible injustice if an innocent man had been sent to prison. In all good conscience, I couldn't allow that to happen."

Some of my friend's more vociferous critics have, in the past, condemned him for lacking compassion and accused him of treating his clients' problems as nothing more than cold, hard data to be analyzed and deciphered for his own intellectual amusement. I, however, knew him better than that. Beneath the cool and callous façade he presented to the world, there was a generous soul who cared profoundly for his fellow man and took immense pleasure in seeing the people he had helped come to something good. Perhaps, in his own peculiar way, Sherlock Holmes was the greatest pretender of them all.

The Fatal Adventure of the French Onion Soup
by Craig Stephen Copland

"It's a beautiful May morning, Watson. Fancy going for a brisk walk?"

"Thank you, but no," I told Holmes. "Rather busy with my writing."

"What would you say to a walk that included a fine lunch at our local pub?"

"Sorry. I'll make do with whatever Mrs. Hudson provides. I am under a deadline to get this over to *The Strand*."

"Then what about a lunch not only with me but also with a beautiful, rich woman who wants to purchase my services?"

I put down my pen and turned and faced him.

"Holmes, almost all of your female clients are rich and beautiful. If they weren't, they most likely wouldn't be in trouble and needing help from a detective. Why doesn't she just come here and state her case like all the others do?"

"Because she is convinced that she's being followed and would be in even greater danger of being murdered if she were to be seen coming here."

"You don't say. Is she truly in danger, or are her thoughts merely muddled and her fears unfounded?"

"I don't yet know, and that is why I need your medical opinion to help me decide. Here's your walking stick. You will not require a coat."

"Fine. Where is she?"

"Waiting for us at The Beehive Pub."

It was indeed a splendid morning in May of 1901, and I have to admit that I enjoyed the stroll down Baker Street and three streets south of Marylebone to one of our better neighborhood pubs. As soon as we entered, the publican stepped out from behind the bar.

"Ah, Mr. Holmes, a word, if I may?"

"By all means, Mr. Pinchback. What is it?"

"The lady at the back of the room said she was here to meet you. That right, sir?"

"I am indeed here to meet with a lady. Why do you ask?"

"Well, sir, don't quite know how to put this, but she's acting more than a bit odd, and I just wanted to make sure."

"What do you mean, *odd*?"

"Well, sir, as my American patrons would say, she's as nervous as a long-tailed cat in a room full of rocking chairs. Can't hardly sit still. Keeps shifting herself and looking all over the room. She already asked my barmaid twice if you'd arrived. You've got yourself a strange one, Mr. Holmes. No offense, sir, but if she becomes a problem, I may have to ask her to leave. Try to keep her still and settled, all right?"

"We shall do our best to calm her down and keep her that way. Won't we, Watson?"

"What? Oh, yes, yes," I assured the publican. "We'll do that."

As we worked our way through the pub, I asked Holmes, "Who is this woman?"

"She signed her note to me only as *Lady F.T.*"

"That isn't much help."

"It was sufficient. She is Lady Frances Tribble. The letter was postmarked in Chipping Ongar, and the only estate near there inhabited by a young rich woman is that of a Lady Frances Tribble."

"How do you know she's young?"

"Her handwriting is sloppy, a product of the educational reforms of the past two decades."

"That's hardly enough to decide on her age."

"Her picture in the society pages was also useful."

Lady Frances Tribble was indeed as described by Holmes. Young and beautiful would be an understatement. With her radiant red hair, flawless milk-white skin, and perfect proportions, she was as singularly beautiful as a woman around thirty years of age can be – at least in England.

When she observed us approaching, she beckoned us with an elegantly manicured index finger and pointed at two empty chairs across the table from her.

We exchanged rudimentary greetings and sat down. She took a generous swallow from her glass of wine, which was already almost depleted.

"Did anyone follow you?" she asked.

"No, Madam," said Holmes. "Did anyone follow *you*?"

"Not today. No one knows I'm meeting you here. I told everyone that I would be spending the entire day shopping on Regent and Bond streets."

"Excellent," said Holmes. "I see you've already been served your soup course. Shall Dr. Watson ask for three orders of fish and chips?"

"Good heavens, no. The French onion soup here is passable, but anything else isn't fit for human consumption." She took another swallow of wine and ignored her soup.

"Pray, proceed."

It occurred to me that if she launched straight away into stating her case, my lunch would never appear, and I was about to give Holmes a kick under the table. I lost the opportunity to do so when she began to speak.

"Someone is trying to murder me."

"Why do you say that?" said Holmes. "More specifically, what has happened that has led you to that conclusion?"

"Listen carefully, Mr. Holmes. My time with you is limited. I have to be back on Bond Street in half-an-hour, or those watching me will know that I have gone. Very well then, I shall begin with the recent attempts on my life."

"A very good place to start. Pray proceed."

"Two weeks ago, I was driving by myself in my trap with my best harness horse, Viscountess Kaydance. We were speeding along merrily near the edge of our ravine when the wheel fell off the trap, and it went tumbling. Had I not been able to jump free, I would have been thrown over the precipice. I could have been killed."

"And you believe that someone tampered with the wheel?"

"Well, of course, I do. They don't just fall off all by themselves."

"If you say so. Was that all that happened?"

"No. A week ago Sunday, someone tried to poison me."

"Oh, dear, what happened?"

"I was a few minutes tardy coming down for my lunch, and the maid had left a tureen of rabbit stew on the table. Its aroma was utterly delectable, and I put a spoonful of it on a saucer and shared it with my dear Countess Evelyn."

"With whom? Is she some relative of yours?"

"No. She is my precious little puppy. She gobbled it, walked twice around the table, and fell over dead. The stew was poisoned."

"How dreadful. Did you keep a portion of it so that it could be analyzed?"

"No. I was so terribly upset at the loss of my puppy, I hurled it out the window. That dear little doggy has been my constant companion for the past eleven years. I was utterly distraught with losing her."

"My sympathies. Was that all?"

"No. Last week, I went for a ride on my lovely mare, Marchioness Meadowlark. We were galloping over the north trail behind the house and my saddle slipped, and I was flung from my horse. I could have broken my neck. Had it not been for my considerable athletic skills that allowed me to leap free, I would have died. Clearly, someone had loosened the saddle."

"Oh, yes, quite clearly. Now then – "

221

"I'm not finished. Two days ago, I was out for a walk with my little Baron Xerxes – "

"Another pet?"

"Heavens, no. He's my son. He'll be four years old come June. Well, we were walking along the east side of the house, and I observed that one of the gargoyles had fallen from the roof. Had we been passing under it at the time, it would have killed us both."

"Did you look up? Did you by chance happen to see anyone up there looking down on you?"

"No, of course, not. He was long gone."

"Are you certain?"

"Certainly, I'm certain. It must have fallen during the night when whoever it was tried to loosen it so he would be ready to drop it on us as we passed."

Holmes appeared to begin to roll his eyes but caught himself and offered a condescending smile instead.

"Lady Tribble, these events have no doubt been disturbing, but unless someone has a strong reason to want to murder you, they amount to no more than – "

"How many reasons do you need? I can give you a half-dozen. And since you asked, you can start with my husband, Marcus. He is trying to sell several of our farms, and as they are half-owned by my family trust, he will only receive half the income. If I am dead and gone, he gets it all, and that amounts to well over five-thousand pounds."

"If he is desperate for cash, that could be – "

"And then there is the entire local theater guild. They hate me with a passion."

"And why is that?"

I noticed that Holmes had started to tap his fingertips on the table, ever so slightly.

"Because I am a consummate and accomplished actress and said to be stunning on stage, even now that I am expecting a child. They have no more presence on stage than a . . . than a pregnant hippopotamus. I'm awarded all of the leading roles, and they hardly get their names on the playbill."

"Actors are known for the intensity of their – "

"I mustn't forget my brother. He has threatened several times to end my life because of the book I'm writing."

"A book? And why – "

"Because of its contents, of course. I will be speaking to the editors at *The Strand* so they can issue it in monthly installments. I expect it will sell thousands of copies. I mean, really, Mr. Holmes, if the public will buy all those stories about you, then surely they will gobble up a revelation of an entire dynasty of scandal after scandal."

"Your brother, you say, has threatened you over this."

"He said, several times, that he would wring my neck if I aired our century of dirty laundry to the public."

"Such an action has been known to cause friction within a family and spoil a Sunday dinner, but – "

"And last but not least, there is Siegfried, my former suitor. He has a consuming passion for me, and it is patently obvious that he has decided that if he cannot have me, then no one will. He will most likely take his own life when he takes mine. Germans are inclined that way. They're all like young Werther, every one of them. Now, if I think about it for a moment, I might come up with one or two more who wish me dead."

"I'm quite sure that is sufficient. However, before I continue with my questions, I fear I'm feeling somewhat parched. Allow Doctor Watson and me to obtain some cold cider before we continue."

Before she could say anything, he was on his feet and tugging at my arm. I followed him over to the bar, where we asked for three glasses.

"Your thoughts?" Holmes asked.

"I must say that you've won the sweepstakes with this one. She strikes me as one who is, shall we say, beyond the pale. Wheels do fall off, and saddles slip of their own accord. Eleven-year-old dogs have a habit of dying. The woman does indeed exhibit a rather questionable mental state."

"By which I take it you mean she is barking mad and more in need of your services than mine. Shall I find a tactful way to get rid of her and let us go home?"

"No, you shan't."

"What? Why not?"

"Get rid of her by all means, but you still owe me lunch."

We started back to the table with the cider. I had a glass in both hands, and he carried the third. Lady Tribble was watching us intently, tapping the toe of her foot on the floor as we started toward her.

We had only taken two steps away from the bar when a loud bang like the crack of a rifle split the air. Several of the patrons screamed, and Lady Tribble's upper body crashed downward, her face splashing into the bowl of French onion soup.

Holmes was a step in front of me, and he dropped the cider he was carrying and ran toward her. I placed my two back on the bar and raced after him.

Blood was pouring out of the back of her head, through her hair and into the soup.

"She's been shot!" said Holmes. He glanced around and put his finger on a hole in the wainscoting where a countersink plug had been removed.

"Tend to her!" he shouted as he rushed out the back door of the room.

There was nothing I could do. She was dead. I removed her head from the bloodied bowl of soup and laid it on the tablecloth. I pressed my suit jacket into service and used it to cover her head and shoulders. Then I stood between her and the rapidly gathering crowd of the curious and prurient.

Holmes returned a few moments later, holding a rifle, the barrel of which had been shortened, and he put it down on the table.

"This," he said, "was in the alley behind the pub. Tossed aside when he fled."

He looked at the covered torso now lying on the table.

"Dead?" he asked.

"Dead."

He pointed to the hole in the wainscoting. "Someone was hiding in one of the stalls in the men's lavatory on the other side of this wall. There was a hole in the tile, and he shot through it."

I looked at the modified rifle on the table. "A Winchester," I said. "Cut off so it could fit inside the lavatory stall?"

His heavy breathing had diminished and he nodded. "Precisely."

"He was gone?" I asked although the answer was obvious.

"I ran down the alley and back and forth. There was no sign of anybody. I questioned two people who were standing out there, but they both said they had seen nothing unusual."

"So someone truly was intent on killing her. It would appear that she wasn't crazy after all."

"Let me get this straight, Mr. Holmes," said Inspector Lestrade. He had been summoned immediately and had been told what took place. "You say she was in the middle of wanting to secure your services and telling you that someone was trying to murder her when she up and got herself murdered right in front of you. Is that right?"

"That is a concise summary of what took place, Inspector. You can see the hole in the wall through which the killer held the end of the rifle. At the moment her head was directly in front of it, the shot was fired."

"Right. Well, you better not go letting the Press know what happened. If everyone reads that Sherlock Holmes's clients was shot in the head while chatting with him, it might throw cold water on any more of them wanting to pay for your help."

"That is an interesting observation, but doesn't help us advance this case."

224

"Right, maybe not. Well, seeing as you already have your finger in this, you can keep on trying to find out who spoiled the soup. But please keep me informed."

"As always."

"It's rather clear that one of those people up in Chipping Ongar who she said wanted her dead must have followed her to London, seen his chance when she sat down, and shot her. I suppose that you're going there and start asking questions."

"An excellent suggestion. As always, I am grateful for your advice. But may I ask for your insight on something that is troubling me?"

"Go ahead, Mr. Holmes. Always happy to help."

"Are you suggesting that it was by chance that her killer happened to be carrying a cut-off rifle, noticed the hole in the wall, and it was her sheer bad luck that she was sitting in front of it?"

Lestrade looked down at the table and pushed his lips out into a duckbill. "Of course not. Someone must have known in advance about the hole."

"Ah, yes, thank you. But then how was it that she ended up sitting in exactly the right spot for the back of her head to be directly in front of that hole?"

His lips emerged again, and he moved them back and forth while scowling.

"Well, it's clear to me that was no accident. Someone must have directed her to the chair. And now that I think about it, he must have made sure the chair was in precisely the right spot for her to get shot."

"Ah, yes. An excellent deduction. Any insight on who that might have been?"

"You mean whoever likely showed her to that spot and placed the chair in the right place? Right. Go fetch the publican," he told a constable, "the one who said she was nervous." Turning to us, he added, "I'll bet it was him. I'll let him know he's about to be charged with accessory to murder if he doesn't sing loud and long. Watch me hold his feet to the fire."

"Now look here, Inspector," said an agitated Mr. Pinchback. "It's nonsense to think I had anything to do with her getting shot. In case you hadn't noticed, having women murdered in one's establishment isn't exactly good for business."

He gestured with a sweep of his arm to the now empty pub. The site of a bowl of French onion soup with a mixture of blood and cheese and dripping off the table, had a deleterious effect on the appetites of the patrons, as did the sight of a corpse being carried out to the pavement by a couple of chaps from the hospital.

"But you admit," said Lestrade, "that you led her to the chair in which she was sitting when she was shot. Right?"

"Like I said, this bloke came in this morning and told me that some beautiful redhead was coming here for lunch and that she was meeting Sherlock Holmes. He offered me five pounds to sit her where I sat her and say nothing. Put some chalk marks on the floor so the chair would be in the exact right spot. Five pounds is five pounds, so why not?"

"Why not, Mr. Pinchback?" said Lestrade. "Because she is now dead and wouldn't have been had she been sitting elsewhere. That's why not."

"And how was I supposed to know that? He said he was from some newspaper and wanted to take her picture when she was meeting with the famous detective, Mr. Sherlock Holmes."

"Why did he want to take her picture? Did he tell you?"

"No, and it's none of my business. Society photo, scandal rumor, advertisement? How should I know?"

"And was that," asked Holmes, "why you asked me to keep her calm?"

"Right. He told me he'd give me another five pounds if he got a good picture of the two of you and it got in the newspaper."

"Which newspaper?" asked Holmes.

"*The Evening Star.* Look. Here's his card. See? He set his camera up behind the curtain over there. Look. It's still there. But he isn't, all right. That's all I know, and it would be appreciated if you could catch him and hang him so he doesn't ruin my business ever again."

"It would help," said Lestrade, "if you could give us an accurate description of him. What did he look like?"

"Him? Well, average height. Average weight. Talked like any other chap from London. Maybe around thirty to forty years old. Brown hair. Dressed like any other bloke who comes in here. Blue jacket and trousers. White shirt. Blue tie. Not shabby, but not looking like a toff either. No scars. Didn't look in his eyes, so can't tell you what color. That's what he looked like."

"And you noticed no signs that someone had drilled a hole in the wall? No dust or suspicious noises?"

The man simply shook his head.

"Thank you, Mr. Pinchback," said Lestrade. "You have been so very helpful, Mr. Holmes. Why don't you take a look at his card and the camera and tell me what you notice, if anything."

A tripod with a camera mounted on it was indeed set up behind one of the window curtains. The card gave the name of Mr. Norman Henson from *The Evening Star.* Holmes examined both the camera and the card.

"These are deceptive. The card isn't one used by any reporter at that newspaper. The camera appears to be rented from a Horaczko Photography in Marylebone Street. The photography request was a blind to keep the woman in place so that she could be shot through the wall. However, before Dr. Watson and I travel up to Chipping Ongar, we shall return the camera to the shop. Possibly the proprietor has a better memory of the man who rented it."

The name above the photography shop read, *Antoni Horaczko, Photographer,* and the windows showed several attractive photographs of weddings, funerals, debutantes, and the receiving of knighthoods. We were greeted with a broad smile as we entered, bearing the camera and tripod.

"*Dobry wieczór!* Welcome. I was hoping that you would never return that old thing."

"Are you the owner of this camera?" asked Holmes.

"That I am. Your friend rented it from me yesterday. And now you bring it back, and I have to give you back the twenty pounds you left as a deposit. I was hoping he would steal it. It's falling apart and not worth more than a few shillings now. I haven't used it in years. But wait here, and I will get you your twenty pounds."

"That won't be necessary," said Holmes.

"What do you mean, not necessary? Your friend gave me the twenty pounds. You are returning the camera. I have to give it back to you. Saint Casimir would never forgive me if I were to be dishonest. My wife would never forgive me either, and that would be worse."

"I fear, sir," said Holmes, "that the news I have to give you is far worse than anything your wife or saint could impart."

Holmes introduced himself and, over the next few minutes, he informed the man about the use to which his rented camera had been put. The poor chap paled, and his face became a portrait of dismay. He crossed himself and then left us and entered the back of his shop. Two minutes later, he returned, accompanied by his wife. She was holding onto his arm and trembling.

"Whoever has done this terrible thing, sir," she said, "please, we beg you to believe us, we never suspected that we were being used by a murderer. Can you tell us anything about this poor woman? If there is something we can do for her family, we will do our best. Never has such

227

a terrible thing happened to us, not since our mothers and fathers came to London thirty years ago. What can we do?"

"The most useful thing you can do straight away," said Holmes, "is to give me the best description you can of the man who rented this from you."

"*Tak,* that I can do," said Mr. Horaczko. "I take people's photographs, and I must look closely at their faces and bodies. This man, he had blond hair, blue eyes, and a large mustache. He was tall. Taller than you, sir and thick too. Thicker than the doctor here. He had a scar on his left cheek. Not a big one but whitish. It stood out on his face. On his right hand, there was a tattoo. It said *Mother.* He wore a heavy coat even though it was a warm day. A black coat, so I couldn't see what his clothes were like. What have I missed, my dear?"

"His boots," the wife said.

"Ah, yes. His boots. Thank you, my dear. They were unusual. When they were new, they must have been light in color, almost yellow. Now they were well- worn and darkened. Quite unusual."

Holmes nodded and thanked them and gave them his card.

"If there is anything else you remember about him, pray let me know."

"We will, sir, but what shall we do with the twenty pounds? We cannot keep it. It has evil attached to it."

"Give it to Saint Casimir. He will know what to do with it."

Once we were out on the pavement of Marylebone, Holmes lit a cigarette and stood looking off into the eastern sky.

"Someone has thoroughly plotted this murder, Watson. I suspect that the man who rented the camera and possibly the one who came to the pub may both have been plants. The villain could be some other man entirely, and he has taken care to put several layers between himself and the evidence. Very clever."

"I must say, I think you're right. Well then, what now?"

"A journey to Chipping Ongar. It is just inside Essex, and we can catch a train from King's Cross and be there within an hour."

The Tribble estate was located a few streets east of the town center, just beyond the Mulberry House rectory. Its appearance was singularly striking, as if it had only been uncrated and assembled a few days earlier. The design was utterly *avant-garde,* along the lines promoted by the Parisian *École des Beaux-Arts* and eagerly copied by the emerging class of wealthy English merchants and financiers. The grounds had been splendidly laid out with trees and shrubs that were of the size that might have been transported here and planted less than a year ago.

"What do you know about this fellow?" I asked Holmes as we stepped out of a local cab and walked toward the entrance of the impressive house.

"I haven't yet had the opportunity to look him up and can only go on what I can remember."

"That is usually more than enough. What of him?"

"Sir Marcus Tribble came from a farming family here in Ongar. As a young lad, he was hired by one of the railway companies. He worked his way quickly up through the ranks and became the youngest manager ever of the division that serviced Essex. He invested every farthing he earned in railway stocks, first in England and then in America and Germany, and made a fortune by the time he was thirty-five years old. He returned to his home village ten years ago, married the most beautiful woman available to him, and recently built this busy red-brick monstrosity of a house. He now owns many of the farms in this corner of Essex and lives quite handsomely off the rents. Beyond that, I cannot remember anything of importance about him."

"That isn't a bad start. I gather he was several years older than his wife."

"About twenty."

"He must have done something to receive his knighthood."

"He bought it."

"Come now. You cannot be suggesting that he bribed our dear Queen. She is – "

"To be more specific, he made a large donation to the trust that maintains and improves the Royal Albert Hall and the Prince Albert Monument in Kensington. In gratitude for his unselfish and patriotic action, she bestowed a knighthood on him."

We had reached the front door of Tribble House and were welcomed by a young woman. I was struck not only by her remarkable dark hair, dark eyes, flushed cheeks, and stunning beauty, but also by her condition, which was obvious to a doctor. She was in the first flush of early pregnancy, and approaching the date when most mothers-to-be remove themselves from any form of employment.

"Mr. Sherlock Holmes and Dr. Watson?" she said with a hint of a French accent.

"That we are," said Holmes. "I take it you have been informed of the reason for our visit."

"We have, and we have been expecting you. Our constable came to the house a half-hour ago and told us of the tragedy. Please come in."

"Thank you," said Holmes, and the two of us followed her into the spacious front parlor. The interior of the home was in keeping with the exterior in that everything – the furniture, the paintings and *objets d'art,* the carpets – was in the latest fashion and still bore the faint odor of being new.

"Madam," said Holmes, "if you might be so kind, would you please introduce yourself, as you don't appear to be a member of the household staff."

"That I am not, Mr. Holmes. I am Mrs. Alvin Beeman, and I've recently been appointed as the governess to Sir Marcus's son. The staff were so terribly upset by the horrible news of Lady Tribble that Sir Marcus excused them from service for the rest of the day. I, however, couldn't abandon the child, and will have to care entirely for him now that he has lost his mother. Please wait, and I shall let Sir Marcus know you have arrived."

"Madam," I said, using my most empathetic medical voice, "you shouldn't be running around the house in your condition. Please, my dear, why don't you just sit down and put your feet up, and I'll go and find Sir Marcus."

She smiled back at me. "I have months to go before the expected birth of my child, and Sir Marcus is a thoroughly modern and enlightened man who believes that there is nothing to be hidden away when a woman is expecting a child. Please wait here."

I sat in one of the elegant armchairs but, to my surprise, Holmes tiptoed after her down the hall. He returned a few moments later.

"What are you doing?" I said.

"Nothing important. Merely eavesdropping."

I was going to ask him what he had heard when Mrs. Beeman returned.

"Sir Marcus is in his study. Follow me."

She led us to the back of the house and ushered us into a large room that served as an office and library and introduced us. A man of about fifty years of age was seated behind the desk and didn't look up as we entered. A child sitting in the corner of the room who had been playing with his blocks did. With his curly dark locks, he was remarkably adorable, and I returned his spontaneous smile.

Holmes started to speak but was interrupted by Sir Marcus Tribble.

"No need to explain, sir. I know you have a job to do, and I shall do whatever I can to be of assistance regardless of how difficult it may be for me. Please. Proceed."

He gestured to a set of chairs at a nearby meeting table, and Mrs. Beeman immediately walked over to them and carried one to a place directly in front of the desk. I hurried to fetch and place the second one. Then the governess took the child and stepped out.

"Sir," said Holmes, "I regret that I have to ask such a question, but did your wife have any enemies that might wish her death?"

"Enemies that would murder her? No. Cannot think of any."

"Your wife is dead. Clearly, she had at least one. If you wish to assist us in apprehending her killer, please answer my question truthfully."

Tribble sighed and laid his pencil on the table and leaned back.

"I know, I know. One mustn't attempt to hide the truth from Mr. Sherlock Holmes. Very well then. My wife may not have had murderous enemies, but she most certainly did not have any friends either."

"I must ask you to explain," Holmes responded.

"Frances could be somewhat trying at times. No, I must admit, Frances was severely trying *all* of the time. No one liked her and, I confess, that includes me, and I was married to her for several years."

"And what, sir, do you mean by *trying*?"

"She was – no, before I answer that question, I must give credit where it is due. She was a kind and affectionate mother to our son, little Baron Xerxes. He is going to miss her awfully, and is too young to understand that his mommy is dead."

"Duly noted, sir. Now, about her unlikeable behavior."

"Oh, how can I describe her? She was convinced that everyone she met was her enemy and treated every one of them as if they were indeed her enemies. But I must give credit where it is due. She did have some exceptional abilities. She was a stunning actress and had a brilliant head for business. I wouldn't have this house and all the rents I now have had it not been for her."

"Are you saying," asked Holmes, "that she had a better head for commerce than you?"

Sir Marcus sighed again. "Yes, you could say that. She was an irresistible force when it came to driving a contract or purchase. I wasn't at all poor when I asked her to marry me, but my estate has tripled in size since then, and it was all due to her."

"And didn't that create enemies?" asked Holmes,

"Well, yes and no. She was detested, but every business transaction she carried out was fair and honest to the farthing. She never crossed anyone, and no one dared cross her."

"And was she well-known in Chipping Ongar?"

"Oh yes, when she was here and not enjoying her visits to Paris or London or the coast of France. She was always here for our local theater

231

season. It wouldn't do to miss her chance to play the lead in yet another production. You might wish to speak to the manager of our theater about that."

"I shall, but a delicate question, if I may," said Holmes.

"Of course."

"She informed me that you were arranging to sell some of the farms. Is that true?"

"Yes and no. It was she who had put them up for sale at prices far higher than she had me pay for them seven years ago. They would have turned a fine profit. It was all her doing. As I said, she was rather good at managing our finances."

"Is it not true, sir, that if she were still alive, half of the profits would be paid to her family trust, but with her death, all of it will now accrue to you?"

"Oh, goodness, no. How I wish that were true. No, the family trust reverts back to her father, dear old Hamish MacFadden. To be honest with you, Mr. Holmes, I would far rather have to deal with Frances than her father any day. If she was frugal – well, he is an utter skinflint."

"Is that so? I thank you for your forthcoming answers, sir. You have been most helpful. Before I leave you to your business, may I ask if you have a gun room in the house? I've heard that you are quite the outdoorsman."

"Well, yes, of course I have a gun room. But I can't see what that has to do with Frances being shot. My guns are kept in a locked room and in secure cases. But come and take a look if you want. You won't need me to take you there and I am frightfully busy. Let me call Adelane and have her show you."

Mrs. Beeman was called and appeared almost immediately.

"Let me show him," she said, moving toward the door. "Come, gentleman, this way."

"You'll need the keys," said Sir Marcus.

"But of course," she replied, walking over to his desk, where she was given a ring of keys he had procured from the center drawer of his desk.

"This way, please, gentlemen."

She led us down the hall to the third door on the left, undid the lock, and opened it.

The room was small and windowless. Once the lamps had been turned up, I observed that three of the walls were lined by cases with glass doors. One entire wall of cases had nothing visible behind the doors, but the other two held racks of rifles, shotguns, revolvers, and pistols. Holmes walked past those walls, gazing through the glass doors. About two-thirds of the way along the first wall, he stopped.

"Would you please open this case for us, Mrs. Beeman?" he said.

She fumbled with a cluster of small keys, trying several in the latch before the door opened. Holmes quickly reached into the rack of hunting rifles and lifted one of them out and tossed it to me. Instinctively, I caught it and couldn't help but register my surprise.

"This is a drill parade wooden replica," I said.

"Precisely," said Holmes. "Mrs. Beeman, would you mind asking Sir Marcus to join us."

The woman nodded and departed, returning a couple of minutes later with her employer in tow.

"I regret having to drag you into this," said Holmes, "but please look at this item and its place in your gun rack."

He responded straight away. "My Winchester is gone. Someone has taken it and put this toy in its place."

"I expect, sir, that you will be able to retrieve it at Scotland Yard – although, you may find its usefulness somewhat shortened."

Holmes explained the finding of a Winchester rifle with a portion of the barrel cut off. Sir Marcus shook his head vigorously.

"That's impossible. That would mean that someone from this house took it and used it to murder Frances. That's unthinkable. All of my staff are decent people who would never dream of committing such a vile deed. And I'm the only one who has access to the keys for this room."

"Sir," said the governess, "may I remind you that everyone on your staff knows that the keys are kept there, and in keeping with your democratic principles, you don't lock the doors of the house. Anyone from the village or beyond could have entered and taken the gun."

"Well, Holmes," I said to him as we walked away from the house, "at least you can assume that it was someone from Chipping Ongar and not some mysterious killer from goodness knows where."

"An excellent observation, my dear Doctor. Yes, I have now limited my list of suspects to no more than six-hundred. Thank you."

"You're welcome. So who's next? The brother? The theater manager?"

"The brother lives in the village and runs the local post office. We shall pay him a visit."

As we approached the town's small post office, an elderly woman was emerging from it. She took one look at us and quickly turned around and went back inside, closing the door behind her. A moment later, she came back outside, studied us up and down, and walked away.

We gave each other a look.

"It couldn't have been anything you said," I said.

He smiled, shrugged, and opened the door.

The postmaster was standing behind the counter, busily stamping a stack of letters. He was a tall, well-made fellow with bright red hair and a matching mustache.

"Good afternoon, Mr. Holmes," he said without looking up or interrupting his task.

"Good afternoon, Mr. MacFadden. I regret having to bother you so soon after you heard about the death of your sister."

"You're just doing your job, sir. I have mine to do as well. Work is a far better treatment for sorrow than liquor. How can I help you?"

"You appear to have been expecting us?"

"Your picture has been in *The Strand* and the newspapers. When you arrive in a village, you are noticed. The entire village comes to the post office. I had a dozen or more of them tell me that you were here and on your way to Tribble House. And two more who let me know that you were on your way here. So how can I help you?"

"You can start, sir, by telling me about your sister. Did she have any enemies who had reason and motive to kill her?"

He put down his postal stamp and looked up at us.

"No."

"Clearly she did, or she wouldn't have been murdered."

"All right, then. None that I know of. Franny was a very difficult woman – always was since she was twelve – but we all tolerated her. She was the most self-centered person anyone could imagine. But she was scrupulously honest, exceptionally hard-working, and clever. That's enough to get any beautiful woman disliked – but not murdered."

"Did she offend other people? Was she mean-spirited and nasty to any of the local people?"

"No to either question. She was utterly oblivious to the needs and values of anyone other than herself. The rest of the village may as well not have existed."

"Could you please be more specific? What did she do that so rubbed people the wrong way?"

He spread his hands out on the edge of the counter and lowered his head, shaking it slowly.

"Where do I start? She was – Doctor, you will correct me if I use the wrong term – what they call a 'hypochondriac'. If she wasn't complaining about one malady or pain somewhere in her body, it would be another."

"Did she suffer from poor health?"

234

"Goodness no. She enjoyed it, absent though it was. We both grew up on a farm. We did hard physical work since we were five years old. Franny was as healthy as a horse and as strong as an ox."

"Her complaints would no doubt be annoying, but – "

"It wasn't so much her complaints that were annoying. It was her criticisms. Anytime she thought anyone was doing something badly, she let them know. She did it with her fellow actors and actresses, with the village's shopkeepers, and, ever since her son arrived, with every other mother. Even when her advice was good, she was intolerable. But again, sir, everyone tolerated her. No one would ever want to kill her."

"What can you tell me about your family trust. I understand it owned half of the property of the Tribble estate."

"What do you want to know about it?"

"Your father was a local farmer. Where did the money come from?"

"Have you ever owned or worked on a farm, Mr. Holmes?"

"No."

"That, sir, is obvious. Farming can be a highly profitable business if you work hard and manage your crops and livestock shrewdly. My father inherited a substantial farm when he was twenty years old. For the past forty years, he has repeatedly bought other farms in the area to the point that he owned well over one-thousand acres of productive land before he set up the trust."

"And he entrusted half of it to your sister?" asked Holmes. "That was rather generous."

"He didn't entirely trust Marcus Tribble, and he wanted to be sure that Franny was financially independent of him, just in case. You understand?"

"I do. And with her death – forgive me for having to ask – will the entire trust now come to you?"

"It will . . . in about twenty years when Father finally dies. He is only partway into his sixties, has never indulged in tobacco or liquor, eats copious servings of fruit and vegetables, and could run circles around me . . . or you, sir."

"Well good for him. Now, what about this book that your sister she was writing. You told her you would wring her neck – her words, sir – if she ever published it."

"Of course I would, and for good reason. It isn't her book. It's *mine*. I have spent the past two years writing it. I showed it to her and, without my permission, she had it copied and was intending to pretend that she had written it. *Wring her neck*, sir, is a figure of speech. What I had told her I would do was to hand the matter over to a solicitor and to notify every magazine and publisher in the country that any submission they might receive from her was fraudulent. That put a stop to that nonsense."

We thanked the postmaster for his time and candid answers and departed. Once we were standing outside, I queried Holmes.

"Are you prepared to strike him off your list?"

"Yes, for the time being. The same goes for the husband."

"Who's left?"

"Next we visit the theater crowd. Come, the manager is quite likely in the theater office. We can ask him about Madam Tribble's dramatic relationships."

We found the local theater building at the far end of the High Street. The entrance was open, and we knocked on the door marked "*Westcot Summerville, Manager*". A tall, thin man who was dressed in a manner one would associate with the playwright Oscar Wilde opened the door and bade us enter.

"Ooh . . . my . . . *Gaawd*, it is the great detective himself. Ah, yes, do come in. And welcome to the humble home of the Chipping Ongar theatrical assembly, famous throughout Essex for our brilliant renditions of plays both ancient and modern. I *assume* – I *deduce* – nay, I *perceive* that you have come to ask about the tragic, the horrible, the devastating death of our beloved Lady Frances Tribble. The terrible news of her death has only just recently made its way to my ears, and my heart is stricken. Torn asunder! Dear me, what can I say? Indeed, it has been a heart-rendering day."

"All I need," said Holmes, "are some concise answers to a few of my questions."

"Concise, you say? Well, my advice would be that we must all be *precise*, and that surely would *suffice* and be an excellent *device*. So what do you want to know?"

With every word he spoke, his hands moved as if he was on a stage.

"How long have you been the manager of this theater?"

"Ah, some days it seems like a lifetime. But, in truth, not quite a year has passed since I accepted this noble responsibility. Before that, I was the assistant manager in Aylesbury. Those were the times that try men's souls. But fortune smiled upon us and I accepted the position here, and our productions since my arrival have been stellar, if I do say so myself."

"Good to know. Now then, who amongst your troupe of actors hated Lady Tribble enough to murder her?"

"Ooh . . . my . . . *Gaawd*. How could anyone have harbored such feelings in the darkest corner of their souls? It is beyond human comprehension. What can I say? How can I begin to answer such a question? But since you ask . . . nobody."

236

"Somebody murdered her. And your actors are one of the few groups in the village with whom she associated."

"Oh my, well, if you insist, sir. I have only been here in Chipping Ongar for a year, and I already disliked her. We all disliked her intensely, by, my *Gaawd*, the woman could act. I read all the past reviews. Anytime she was in the leading role – Lady Macbeth, Estella, Milady DeWinter, Carmilla, the Wicked Stepmother . . . and she played them all – the house would be sold out. She could strut and fret her hour upon the stage like no one in the history of our beloved playhouse. So we put up with her."

"And will your business suffer now that she has gone?"

"I suppose it will, but – no. A brilliant idea has just now come into my mind. Yes, oh yes. We can create an original drama about her. That would draw the crowds. What do you say, Mr. Holmes? We will give you a cut of the profits. Dr. Watson will write the first draft, and I will enhance it and prepare it for production. Oh . . . my . . . *Gaawd* . . . it's brilliant! How soon can you find her killer? We will need at least a fortnight for rehearsals. Can you have it ready for us by the end of June, in time for the summer season?"

Holmes rolled his eyes up toward the top of the wall behind Mr. Westcot Summerville and started to sigh, but then he stopped. His eyes were fixed on a small, framed certificate almost hidden amongst the photographs of past productions.

"Mr. Summerville?"

"Yes, Mr. Holmes. I do trust I have been – "

"Who is Alvin Beeman?"

"Me."

"You?"

"Yes. Westcot Summerville is my stage name. My birth name is Alvin Beeman, but who would ever come to see Al Beeman perform, or a play directed and produced by Al Beeman? Even since I entered the theatre, I have been known far and wide as – "

"What is your relationship to Mrs. Adelane Beeman, the governess of the son of Sir Marcus Tribble?"

"She's my wife, my dearest love. I adore her beyond all words. She was brilliant, utterly brilliant, as an actress, a role she has now abandoned in exchange for her new calling as a force of nature, molding young minds as the finest governess a family could ever dream of having. I worship the ground she walks on." He clutched his left pectoral muscle with his right hand as he spoke.

For a moment, Holmes said nothing and then nodded slightly and turned toward the door.

"Thank you, sir," he said. "We may have to return for a repeat performance. My best wishes for your summer season."

He walked out of the theater, but I stayed behind for a minute.

"I couldn't help but notice," I said, "that you and your wife are expecting a child."

"Indeed, indeed we are, Doctor. This autumn we shall be blessed to participate in the miracle of the creation of a new life."

"Mrs. Beeman appears to be in excellent health."

"Oh, yes, she is that. First-rate, outstanding, brilliant health! Mind you, she is somewhat nervous, but that is to be expected."

"Ah, your first?"

He stopped gesticulating with his hands.

"No, Doctor, our second. Our first – our son – died in infancy. That was four years, ago but it's something a mother never forgets. So both of us are rather tense. I'm sure you understand."

"I do. Just make sure that her life is relaxed and free of anything that could harm the baby, and everything will be fine."

He thanked me in a quiet, sincere voice, and I departed to join Holmes out on the High Street.

I caught up to Holmes as he found a bench in the copse of trees that bordered a portion of the High Street. He was looking off into the sky and puffing slowly on a cigarette.

"Can we strike the impresario off the list as well?" I said.

"Again, for the time being. The connection between him and the governess is curious, but I cannot see any connection to the murder."

He resumed his silence, and I could almost hear the wheels turning and spinning inside his unusual mind.

He tossed his cigarette onto the ground and ground it with his heel.

"Mrs. Tribble may have suffered from an over-active imagination, but the ones she named as wanting to kill her are indeed the only prospective murderers we can find. There appears to be universal agreement that she was quite unliked, but never a cause for murder. I fully expect that if we were to interrogate other members of the village, we would get the same answer as we did from the villains she accused."

"Might I make a suggestion?" I said.

"By all means. As usual it will likely have no intrinsic merit, but it might stimulate my mind to consider alternative possibilities."

"Her doctor – the one here in the village."

"She likely made use of one on Harley Street, not here."

"But, I would wager, only after she married Tribble. Before that, I expect she went to the local chap just like every other girl in the village. Shall I have a chat with him? Doctor-to-doctor and all that."

"You may as well. It can't hurt. I'll wait for you here. Your absence will give me the peace and quiet I need to concentrate."

Dr. Nelson Reese's surgery was also on the High Street, less than one street away from where I left Holmes. Then town clock had recently struck five, and I hoped I would find the local doctor still at work but having bade goodbye to his final patient of the day. To my good fortune, I was right on both counts.

My luck prevailed, and the man was nearing the age when doctors should retire, which meant that it was almost certain he attended to the MacFadden family for the past several decades.

"Good heavens! You aren't *the* John Watson who writes those stories about that detective – what's his name?"

"Sherlock Holmes."

"Yes, that's him. What brings you to some out-of-the-way place like Chipping Ongar? Oh, good heavens, have you come because of what happened to Franny MacFadden? I heard about it from every one of my past five patients. Is that it?"

"It is indeed, Dr. Reese. Sherlock Holmes has been asked to investigate, and I am assisting him."

"My goodness, awfully decent of you to stop by and say hello, but I cannot imagine how I could help you. Franny abandoned me three years ago for some costly doctor on Harley Street. Goodness knows, she had the money by then to hire whatever doctor she wanted, so she left me. I'm in the dark about anything significant in her life since then."

"No detail is too small when one is investigating a murder," I said, doing my best to sound like Holmes. "What can you tell me about her during the years she came to see you?"

"Goodness gracious, that was since she was born. I delivered her, you know."

"I assumed you had, but perhaps we can start at some time later in her life. Anything? Serious illnesses, injuries, secrets only known to her doctor?"

"No. Nothing. She grew up on her father's farm, and he worked her and her brother like they were slaves and made them eat properly and get to bed on time. Both of them were as healthy as the day was long. Of course, that didn't stop her from finding some imagined ache or deadly disease to complain about. During her teen years, she came to see me once every month or two convinced that she had acquired whatever latest illness she had read about."

"And did that continue up until she stopped seeing you?"

"It did. As soon as she knew she was expecting, she sent me a note thanking me and saying that she was off to France."

"To France?"

"Goodness, yes, France. I still have the note in her file, but I can tell you what it said. She said that she was feeling very poorly and feared she would miscarry, so she was taking herself off to some spa on the coast of France and would stay there until the baby was delivered. She came home several months later with the babe in her arms. I only saw her once after that, but her behavior had changed. She stopped complaining. I asked her about her stay in France, but she refused to say anything about it."

"That is an odd change of behavior."

"It was. As you know, most women, when they become mothers for the first time, have good reason to complain. They complain about being exhausted, about their tummies that will never be flat again, about cranky infants who will not sleep more than three hours at a time, and most of all about their husbands. But she did the opposite. I felt that something strange had taken place in France, but it was only a feeling. And, of course, it was France and, my goodness, no end of strange things take place there."

We chatted for a few more minutes, and I thanked him and hurried back to Holmes to relate what I had been told. He listened, saying nothing until several minutes had passed after the end of my report.

"Well done, Watson. Did you happen to get the name of the spa in France?"

"I did. It isn't far from Calais, in Dunkirk – the *Maison de Pompadour*. I've heard of it. Quite the famous place to relax and recover from whatever ails you."

Again, he said nothing and puffed on yet another cigarette. He crushed that one out and turned to me.

"Fancy a short trip to France?"

The following morning, we rose at four o'clock and hurried through the pre-dawn to Victoria and from there to Dover. By half-past nine, we were on the ferry to Calais.

"Come now," I said as the two of us stood by the rail, looking out over the Channel. "What do you expect to find in France?"

"I'm not sure. All I know is that the first piece of data I've heard that indicates anything out of the ordinary about this woman is what the doctor told you about her time there. Beyond that, I'm in a fog. If it turns out that nothing significant took place there, I shall have to start again."

As soon as we disembarked in Calais, we rushed through the port town and across the canal to the *Gare de Calais Ville.* There we boarded the train up the coast to Dunkirk.

The *Maison de Pompadour* is a jewel of gardens, stone patios, fresh and saltwater pools, and lavish accommodations. It has a reputation for delectable French cuisine and wines, and is patronized by the self-indulgent rich of England, France, and, of late, America. The cheerful young woman behind the hotel desk welcomed us.

"*Bonjour messieurs, bienvenue chez nous.*" As soon as she determined that we were from the other side of *La Manche,* she effortlessly switched to somewhat-accented English.

"Please, permit me to ask your names. So I may to retrieve your reservation."

"We aren't here as guests," said Holmes, handing her his card. "We come on behalf of Scotland Yard and wish to speak to your general manager."

"But of course. Please to assist here, and I will go to find him."

The gentleman who soon appeared looked awfully French. He bore a trim mustache and a cravat, and his trousers and jacket were far too tight to be tolerated by an Englishman.

"*Oo-la-la*, we are paid a visit by the famous English detective! And are you, sir? His amanuensis, the writer, Dr. Watson?"

I confirmed that I was indeed he, and the fellow then introduced himself.

"I am also a doctor, sir. My name is Arnaud Bombardier, and it is my esteemed privilege to serve as the director of this excellent establishment. Do come into my office. A little cognac to celebrate your visit, perhaps?"

We followed him into his elegant office with its magnificent view out to the sea. He went straight away to his credenza, upon which sat several bottles of brandy. He reached for a select cognac and poured three glasses and served two of them to Holmes and me. I must say, it was a stretch better than any brandy I had ever tasted in England, but we all know that the French keep the best for themselves.

Holmes wasted no time getting to the purpose of our visit.

"Several years ago, sir, you had a guest who stayed with you for several months – a Lady Tribble. Lady Frances Tribble."

"But of course. Lady Frances was our guest about four years ago. One cannot forget such a woman. Nor can one forget her little dog, the Countess Evelyn. Has she committed some terrible crime? It wouldn't surprise us. She wasn't given to abiding by convention."

"No, Doctor. We're here because she is dead."

Holmes proceeded to give a concise report of what had happened to Frances Tribble. As he spoke, the manager's face contorted in grief, and tears began to roll down his cheeks. By the time Holmes ended his account, the poor man was dabbing his eyes and wiping his nose constantly.

"*C'est absolument* horrible," he muttered. "So very sad."

"You appear to have been rather fond of her."

"*Bien sûr*. Lady Tribble was a goddess. So tall, so beautiful, so perfectly made, so . . . so *magnifique*. When she walked through our dining room or beside our *piscine*, everyone – men and women alike – would look at her and feel blessed by being so close to such beauty. She was – *comment dit-on* – good for business. When she was away in Paris or Cannes, it wasn't the same. Her presence was *un grand plaisir*."

"Did you not find her occasionally arrogant or demanding?"

He gave a Gallic shrug.

"*Bien sûr*. Of course she was, but *monsieur*, these things are – how shall I say – *relative*. Most of our guests are French. We . . . we invented arrogance. It is our birthright. When one is born into a country that is the pinnacle of civilization, *un pays sans egal* – nonpareil is word you English use, *n'est-ce pas*? – one is entitled to be arrogant. Compared to the women who come here from Paris, Lady Tribble was almost humble."

"I had been informed that she was inclined to be difficult and demanding."

"Demanding, *monsieur*? This is also a relative thing. Recently we have had many guests from New York City. *They* are demanding – much more so that Lady Tribble ever was."

"Then was there no one who disliked her? Had she no enemies here?"

"*Non, monsieur*, not a one."

"Did any enemies come to visit her?"

"Enemies? No, there were never enemies who came to visit."

"Ah, then there were other visitors?" said Holmes.

Another Gallic shrug.

"From time to time, people came to visit, *oui*."

"Who?"

"*S'il vous plait, monsieur*, this I cannot tell you. We guard the privacy of all of our guests."

"Dr. Bombardier," said Holmes, "may I remind you that the woman is dead. She will not object to your telling me. It may help in our finding who killed her and keep him from killing anyone else."

"If you put it that way, sir, yes. There was one man who came a few times, indeed *plusieurs fois*. *Un Allemand*. A man from Berlin. An officer in the German army. A colonel."

"His name, sir?"

242

"If I remember, I believe it was Colonel Siegfried Hecker. *Oui, je suis certain,* that was his name."

"And did this man go back to Berlin after his visits?"

"Sometimes, yes. But when her stay with us was over, I believe he accompanied her back to England."

Holmes paused for a moment as if rehearsing his next question.

"It is a delicate matter, sir," he said, "but is it possible that this German was the father of her child?"

"What child?"

"The one she was carrying when she came here. The one who was born here. You were the doctor. Did you not assist in the birth?"

M. Bombardier looked at Holmes as if he had grown a second head.

"Sir, *c'est de la folie.* She wasn't pregnant when she came here. She was never pregnant, and *sans aucun doute,* I never delivered her child. We don't provide such services, not even to rich, beautiful English women."

Holmes's face went blank.

"You are telling me that Frances Tribble didn't give birth to a child while in France?"

"No. She was slender when she arrived and the same when she departed. She never had a baby – at least never when she was here."

For another moment, Holmes was speechless. Then he quickly stood up.

"Thank you, Dr. Bombardier, you have been very helpful. Watson, come – we have to return to England."

Holmes nearly ran me off my feet as he hurried back to the Dieppe station and on to the first run back to Calais. Once we were inside a cabin, I had to speak up.

"Holmes, that woman is a spy. She was having an affair with some German colonel. I'll wager she double-crossed him, and he shot her. Or at least he had her shot, probably by one of his underlings. The Germans are rather like that and – "

"My dear Watson, you have a grand gift of silence. It makes you, as I have said before, quite invaluable as a companion. Pray exercise that gift now and leave me in peace to think."

I assumed he was racking his brain to recall the names and whereabouts of every known German agent in England. I left him alone, quite certain that by the time we reached England, he would have deduced who was behind the murder of Lady Frances Tribble.

At the Calais train station, he made a beeline for the telegraph office.

"Watson, your French is passably decent. I may require your help to help convince these French chaps that I need utmost urgency in sending off a wire."

There is no more obnoxious a person on earth than a government official who possesses a modest degree of power. The most infuriating of all are those low-level officials who are also French. Regardless of our protestations, we were made to wait our turn in line while three men and one woman wrote out their telegrams at the counter and then waited while the chap in charge perused them. Slowly. As we waited, Holmes began to dictate his message, and I struggled to write without the aid of a desk.

"Write this down, coming from Sherlock Holmes: '*To Scotland Yard. Attention Inspector Lestrade. Regarding* – '"

"Scotland Yard?" I said. "Holmes, if this is a matter of espionage and international intrigue, should you not be alerting someone in Whitehall?"

"No. Murder takes precedence."

I wrote a message to Lestrade telling him to meet us the following morning in Chipping Ongar. By the time we had placed it with the Frenchman behind the counter, evening had descended, and we hurried to the docks to catch a night crossing back to Dover.

Holmes was remarkably placid on our journey across the Channel. It was a lovely late-spring night, and he stood by the rail of the deck with that look on his face to which I've become accustomed. He seemed serene, bordering on smug, and I knew that he was about to pounce on some unsuspecting spy, or perhaps an entire ring of German spies who had arranged the murder of Lady Frances Tribble.

"So, Mr. Holmes, you think you've solved this," said Inspector Lestrade the following morning as the three of us stood together in the small railway station in Chipping Ongar.

"I have reason to believe that the solution is at hand. However, I've need of you to exert your legal authority and assist me in acquiring the last necessary pieces of data."

"Always happy to come to your aid, but if this is a matter of German spies and such as Dr. Watson has said, why did you drag me up here and not some toff from the Foreign Office?"

"And let the Press give all the credit to some snob from Whitehall who fancies himself a diplomat and not to the hard-working policemen of Scotland Yard? That would never do."

"Well, yes, right. Only proper that virtue and hard work be acknowledged. What do you need me to do?"

"We need to pay a visit first to the town Registry Office, and then, I expect, the local constable."

Holmes led us on a forced march down the High Street, and then a short distance west to the singularly modest office of the Ongar Town Council. Once we were inside, Lestrade demanded of the clerk that he produce the registry of the citizens of the town for the months before and after June 1897. The poor fellow behind the only desk in the room appeared to be thoroughly incommoded, but he scrambled down to the basement to find the records. A few minutes later, he reappeared bearing several large ledger books.

"Is this what you're looking for, gentlemen?"

"It is," said Holmes as he opened the one with the earliest date.

For the next ten minutes, Holmes scanned page after page of the register while Lestrade and I stood and waited for him. At one point, the inspector looked at me and mouthed the words, "What's he doing?"

I shrugged and mouthed back, "I have no idea."

"A-ha!" exclaimed Holmes as he snapped the second registry ledger shut. "Now, on to the constable's office."

The local office of the Essex Constabulary was another two streets south on the High Street, and the constable on duty leapt to his feet when we entered. It appeared that he recognized both Inspector Lestrade and Sherlock Holmes and had likely been warned by several observant villagers of their presence in Chipping Ongar.

"Good morning, sirs. Constable Tyler Tiklarik at your service, sirs. I was told that Sherlock Holmes himself was here a few days ago asking about Lady Tribble. Terrible thing that was, right? And it looks as if someone local snuck into the Tribble house and stole one of his rifles, right? That's what I heard. Can't imagine anyone from the town ever doing such a terrible thing. But I have a list of all the strangers and visitors to our town over the past fortnight. Prepared it just in case it might be useful to Mr. Sherlock Holmes, and now here you are, and so is Scotland Yard. If you will just wait here a moment, I'll be back with my list in two shakes of a dead lamb's tail."

"Don't bother," said Holmes. "Instead, kindly bring us your log of incidents from May 1897 through July of the same year."

The poor fellow looked utterly crestfallen.

"You don't want my list, sirs? But it has the complete record of anyone who could have broken into Tribble House and stolen his rifle. I'm certain the killer must be on that list, sir."

"Of course, Constable Tyler," said Lestrade. "By all means, fetch your list. I will examine it closely, but while you are at it, kindly bring the incident logs Mr. Holmes has requested as well."

Constable Tiklarik grinned and vanished into the back of the constabulary station.

"Now look here, Mr. Holmes," said Lestrade, "I know what it's like to be a constable in a village. Miserable. Doing diligent work and then being deflated by Sherlock Holmes isn't what this lad needs. And if you

245

do solve this case, you will jolly well make sure that this constable gets credit for his work."

"As always, I am indebted to your experience and insights. But here comes your diligent young chap. Let's see what we can find."

"These are the logbooks, Mr. Holmes. I wasn't stationed in Ongar at the time, so I cannot help much with whatever is in them. And here's my list, Inspector. Shall I go over it with you?"

"Excellent work, Constable," said Lestrade. "Yes, a quick summary of those you listed would be in order. You can give those log books to Mr. Holmes, and he can look at them while you tell me about the visitors to your town."

The young constable started in somewhat enthusiastically while Holmes pored over the pages of the incident logs. I looked over his shoulder and noted paragraph after paragraph of accounts of fights in the pub, missing cats, and misplaced bicycles. Part way through the month of July 1897, he stopped and smiled, again that satisfied smug smile of assured accomplishment. He was about to interrupt Constable Tiklarik's account to Lestrade when I put my hand on his forearm and mouthed the words, "Just wait."

The moment the constable completed his testimony, I spoke up.

"Well done, young man. Now, Inspector, I do believe that Mr. Holmes has something to say."

"What is it, Mr. Holmes?"

"Do you wish to make an arrest, or don't you? If you do, then follow me." He turned and headed for the door and called back. "Constable, come along with us. We may need you."

I fell into line behind him, and Lestrade took a second to thank the young constable before we departed, leaving his cherished list on the counter.

"Enough of your secrets, Mr. Holmes," said Lestrade as we marched up the High Street in the direction of Tribble House. "Out with it. What did you find that makes you so cocksure?"

"Ah, let me see . . . I found the absence of the birth of one baby, the presence of the birth of another one, and an account of the theft of an infant. Come, now. I shall identify the murderer, although it will be up to you and the Crown, Lestrade, to build a case that will stand up in court."

Upon arriving at the door of Tribble House, Holmes turned to Lestrade and smiled.

"The door will be answered by a maid or the butler. I expect that they have recovered from the loss of their not-so-beloved mistress. You will demand to see Mrs. Adelane Beeman, the governess, and you will arrest her for the murder of Lady Frances Tribble."

"Holmes!" I said. "You cannot be serious! That poor woman has already lost one child. Arresting her could easily cause her to – "

"To deny everything, but the evidence is compelling."

"Yes, gentlemen?" said the lovely governess. "I understand that you wish to speak to me."

"I fear we do, Madam," said Holmes. "Dr. Watson has rebuked me and made it clear that we aren't too upset you, as it might harm the child you're carrying. You certainly suffered greatly when you lost your first baby, and we wouldn't want to imperil this one."

"Well, thank you, sir, that is very considerate. It was a very trying time. My little boy died when he was less than a month old, as my husband has told the doctor."

"Yes, and both of you have lied repeatedly. Your infant did not die. He was born well and healthy, and the police logs report that he was stolen from you when you left him unattended for over an hour in the local theater. The Aylesbury theater troupe was on tour and gave a performance here in Chipping Ongar of *Lady Windermere's Fan*. That is the truth, is it not, Mrs. Beeman?"

A flash of fear swept across her face and dark eyes, but she recovered straight away.

"Yes, Mr. Holmes, it is. Our baby boy was stolen from us and it happened here."

"And you never found him? Correct? Not even a whisper of where he might have gone?"

"Yes. It was a horrible soul-destroying event. The constable at the time conducted a search. Flyers were sent out all over Essex. Alvin and I went door to door asking – *begging* – everyone we spoke to for any shred of help. But nothing. We were devastated. After year had passed, Alvin and I did the only thing we could. We agreed to believe, or to act as if we believed, that our son had died. That may have been foolish, but it was the only way we could get through the night without weeping. Am I now supposed to congratulate you, the famous detective, on discovering our charade? Is there some reason you bringing this painful memory up at this time?"

"Yes, there is, and I suspect that you know the reason. A year ago, your husband was offered his position here in Chipping Ongar, and the two of you agreed to accept it with the faint hope that you might yet find a clue concerning your son. Is that correct?"

"That is possible, yes."

"And six months ago, as fate would have it, you were hired by Lady Tribble to serve as governess to her son. Your mother's instincts told you, quite correctly, that the child, little Baron Xerxes, was in truth the one to whom you had given birth. That is not only possible, it's the truth, isn't it? You knew that the boy is your son, not hers. If his parentage can be proven, Mrs. Beeman, it might be possible to restore the boy to you and Alvin. Do you want your son back? Tell me the truth, Mrs. Beeman."

"Yes! I did suspect that he was my child, and that Lady Tribble had arranged to have him stolen from me."

"And you are French, and you have friends and family in France, and they were able to confirm that Lady Tribble wasn't pregnant during her sojourn in Dunkirk and hadn't given birth to a child while there. Is that also the truth?"

She nodded. "It is. She was a horrible, evil, utterly self-centered woman, and I knew she stole my baby from the theatre and passed it off as hers."

"And as soon as you became pregnant once again, she also announced that she was with child, and you suspected, most likely with good reason, that she might do the same thing again."

"I wouldn't put it past her."

"And so you murdered her."

"No! I did not. I couldn't have. I was here in Ongar, here at the house when she was murdered in London. I may have hated her with a passion, but I didn't kill her."

Holmes turned then to Lestrade.

"Inspector, did I by chance overhear the constable giving you the name of a Siegfried Hecker who paid a visit to Chipping Ongar recently? Is that correct, Constable Tiklarik?"

"Right, yes, that was one of the names. German chap. Big blond fellow. Had the look of the Kaiser's army all over him. Right, he was on my list."

"And you, Mrs. Beeman," said Holmes, "met with him. I'd wager that you speak German as well as French. You spoke to him. You discerned that he was furious with rage at Lady Tribble, and paid him to murder her. He would wreak revenge for both of you. And you would be free to raise your son. The truth, Mrs. Beeman."

She glared back at Holmes.

"I met with him, yes, but you have no proof whatsoever of your accusations. That is nothing more than your conjecture."

"Is it? Very well, Madam, you have a choice: Inspector Lestrade will find this German fellow within a few days. He will be identified as the man who rented the camera and paid the publican in London, and he will be charged with murder. Now, either you can cooperate with the police and the Crown and give evidence against him, or he will cooperate and give evidence against you. The court will be more favorable to whomever cooperates. What will it be? The choice is yours."

She started to say something, then stopped. She took a deep breath and continued.

"He . . . he hated her. He had been passionately in love with her – utterly smitten. And she used him for her amusement. He used to visit her any time he had leave from the army. Two weeks ago, he came and demanded that she leave Marcus and go away with him. He threatened to tell Sir Marcus about them if she refused."

"And what did she do?"

"She laughed at him. She ridiculed him. She told him that Marcus put up with her amusements and that he was only one of several and not as good as the others. He was furious with rage. You don't laugh at a German colonel. It drives them mad. Germans are like that. I overheard it all and saw my chance. So yes, I encouraged him. But I didn't pay him. It wasn't necessary. All I had to do was to inform him of her itinerary, and he took it from there."

A faint smile appeared on her lovely face. She had a look of smug satisfaction, of grim accomplishment.

"Did you provide the gun?"

"Of course not. That would implicate me in whatever he was going to do. He took it himself."

"Using the keys you led him to find?"

"More conjecture, Mr. Holmes. You cannot prove that I'm not telling you the truth."

"If you are telling the truth and the court believes you, you will escape the gallows. Your withholding evidence makes you an accomplice after the fact, and you will be sent to prison. Given the circumstances and your present condition, your sentence will likely be short. Now, is there anything else you wish to tell us?"

"Yes. My husband does not know anything about this. He is entirely innocent. Please let me be the one who tells him. He will be devastated."

Holmes looked at her, and a flicker of an ironic smile crossed his face.

"Mrs. Beeman, if you promise your husband that while you are in prison, you will write up this entire story as a tragedy in three acts to be performed exclusively at the Chipping Ongar local theater, he may be inclined to adore you even more than he now does."

Inspector Lestrade instructed the constable to lead Adelane Beeman away and have her charged, but to let her stop for as long as she needed that the local theater. One of the maids was told to make sure the boy was looked after, and a note was left for Sir Marcus, who was somewhere on his estate shooting at pheasants.

The three of us strolled back toward the railway station.

"I suppose," said Lestrade, "we should pay a visit to the pub and let the owner know that he is off the hook. If we make good time, we should be there in time for supper."

"A brilliant suggestion, my dear Inspector," said Holmes. "The fish and chips are excellent, but I would stay away from the French onion soup if I were you."

The Adventure of the Subversive Student
by Jeffrey A. Lockwood

August arrived with a heat I last endured during my time of service in Afghanistan. So while my constitution was adapted to sweltering conditions, Holmes was miserable. Although the drapes kept the mid-morning sunlight from turning our Baker Street sitting room into an oven, my companion was stretched listlessly upon the sofa, poring over the agony column in *The Daily Telegraph* in what I presumed was an effort to seek relief in the suffering of others. I was perusing a tedious article on the treatment of asthma in *The Lancet*. Occasionally, we broke away from our reading to pursue a desultory conversation that lurched from the techniques of single-stick, to the application of Abbe's Equation in microscopy, to the origins of human violence.

All at once, Holmes sat up with an energy I hadn't seen in days. "We have a visitor," said he. I hadn't heard anyone coming to the door, but my observations were as dull as a butter-knife compared to his razor-sharp senses. Following a clang of the front bell, the boy-in-buttons escorted the visitor upstairs. Holmes rose languidly, belying his relief at having our morning lassitude disturbed, and greeted the dapper, clean-shaven fellow who I placed between thirty and forty years of age. He held himself with an affecting combination of confidence and obsequiousness.

"I apologize for arriving unannounced to the home of England's most famous private detective," he began, "but I am in need of your consultation." Holmes nodded approvingly. "And Mr. Holmes, your reputation at Scotland Yard is unparalleled."

"You are a rather fresher version of the detective corps that those who often drop by," said Holmes, an eyebrow arching in curiosity and pleasure. He disdained popular notoriety, but relished expressions of respect from friends, including a select few at the Yard.

"I'm supposing that you might be referring to Inspector Lestrade, as it's my understanding that he's a frequent visitor. And indeed, he directed me to you," the young man smiled. "I am Inspector Jonathan Foyle."

"You seem a bit young for such a rank," remarked Holmes, "but perhaps it helped to know the likes of Lestrade."

The fellow lifted his chin indignantly. "I rose from constable, through sergeant, to become the youngest inspector at Scotland Yard on my own merits, I assure you."

Holmes gave a brief nod of acquiescence. "My friend, Dr. Watson, and I are pleased to make your acquaintance. But pray tell, what brings you to our apartment?"

"I have been given my first case and I am under great pressure to deliver. But I admit that I don't have a clear sense of how to proceed from the single piece of evidence that has come to me," he said, pulling from his coat pocket a long, blue envelope. He shook the contents onto our table and assembled the scraps of a torn telegram:

> *Plan to gain their freedom is developing. Trusted and capable band being assembled. Your assistance crucial for their escape from cruel imprisonment, as they have done nothing to deserve such inhumane confinement. Watch* The Times *for further instructions as to where and when to meet.*
>
> Z

"How did this come into your possession?" inquired Holmes, leaning over the fragmented document.

"A landlady brought it in, as she thought it hinted at pending criminal activity by one of her lodgers. Evidently, Mrs. Thurlow so savours nosing into the doings of others that she isn't averse to digging into a waste bin to discern the private affairs of her boarders.

"Does this busybody know who received the telegram or who 'Z' might be?" asked Holmes.

"She finds all of her boarders to be boorish, but hasn't any reason to suspect one over another. And she knows nothing of the sender."

"What is your assessment, Inspector?"

"I think that a criminal gang is plotting a prison break to release a number of their confederates," he said, staring intently at the telegram such that he didn't see Holmes flash an amused smile, suggesting that he knew the inspector was exhibiting the impulsiveness of youth. "But foiling this escape isn't possible without knowing the location or the timing of the operation," Foyle continued despondently. "What would you advise?"

Holmes straightened himself, and his eyes took on the hard, dry glitter which was a sure sign of keen interest. "I would advise that it is a capital mistake to commit to a theory before one has the facts. And the most relevant facts at this time are to be found at Mrs. Thurlow's lodgings, while

252

those of greatest value are to be found by watching for personal advertisements in *The Times*."

"I can take you and Dr. Watson to the boarding house immediately, if you're available," said Foyle.

"Tell me, Watson, would you prefer to roast here like a side of beef, or venture into the scorching streets of the city?" asked Holmes. I replied that I quite favored the latter.

The boarding house was at 43 Queen Anne Street, a fifteen-minute walk from our quarters along pavement crowded with slow-footed Londoners made surly by the heat. Mrs. Thurlow was a buxom woman well into her sixth decade and evincing the irascibility of her years, but Holmes's gallantry soon put the landlady at ease. She led us to the dining room, which was a source of pride in a house otherwise furnished in a random assortment of threadbare sofas, rickety chairs, and mismatched lamps. Mrs. Thurlow swept her beefy arm above the expansive dining table and lifted a corner of the soiled tablecloth to show us the gleaming, maple surface that her late husband had spent his last years polishing to perfection. She was in the midst of an impassioned description of the matching chairs which were upholstered in a vulgar Jacobean pattern when Holmes gently interrupted to ask about her tenants. Her countenance transformed from ruminative rapture to severe judgment.

"They are six," she began, "and not a virtue among them. Mr. Wilborn is a timberman prone to heavy drinking and sinful language. Mr. Jenkins is a ribston-pippen of a man with breathing problems and allergies which have grown more severe of late, even though a chimney-sweep's work diminishes during the summer when less malignant and better-paying labour can be found. Then there's Mr. Graham, who's studying medicine, and while you might think a college fellow would have social graces, he's utterly lacking in discretion when it comes to the ladies." Her litany was cut short by the arrival of a deliveryman who required her attention.

While Foyle and I watched, Holmes undertook a meticulous inspection of the room, passing his powerful magnifying lens over the chairs, pressing his nose to the tablecloth, and crawling beneath the table. Upon the landlady's return, Holmes picked up where she'd left off and described not only the employments of the other three men, but indicated where every individual sat at the table. Mrs. Thurlow confirmed each of his deductions and gasped as if in the presence of a sorcerer.

"But how?" Foyle stammered while the landlady lowered herself heavily into a chair.

"My train of reasoning is quite elementary," said Holmes. "To begin, as Mrs. Thurlow was describing the first three residents, her eye movements indicated she was recalling a linear arrangement of individuals at the table. From there, I ascertained that the timberman sat at the near corner, based on the smell of Scots pine from freshly sawn wood at his place. I knew the location of his labors, which Mrs. Thurlow affirmed, from the colour of the dried soil beneath his chair which is unique to the area where the Twopenny Tube tunnel is being excavated. That the chimney sweep was in the next place was evident from marks on the floor indicating that he pulled his chair very close to the table, as would be expected from a man of a slight build.

"The medical student's presence in the next seat was evident from the faint odour of ether and chloroform residues on the tablecloth. I would also note, Mrs. Thurlow, that your chimney sweep's allergies might be aggravated by the adjacent student having been in contact with a cat, as I inferred from the flakes on his seat which were identifiable as cat dander by their sharply irregular shape."

"Having traced those individuals to their chairs, pray tell how you determined the seating and employment of the other three men?" asked Foyle.

"Given they couldn't afford finer accommodations than a common but well-kept lodging-house," replied Holmes, nodding felicitously at Mrs. Thurlow, "the possibilities were somewhat constrained. I deduced that one of the men is a coster based on the faint green-and-purple stains on the tablecloth from his hands, and by knowing that August is the month for greengages and plums. The coal heaver was reasonably simple given that his place emitted a sulphurous odour, along with his wobbly chair being consistent with the wear caused by a very large man. And finally, the bricklayer was given away by the fine, red dust on his seat."

We thanked Mrs. Thurlow, who was still looking mesmerized, for her time and started back. During our stop together for a quick lunch of coffee and sandwiches, Foyle marveled, "I would have thought you were some sort of wizard, Mr. Holmes, but your explanations made it seem strangely both simple and remarkable to reach your conclusions."

"Indeed," said Holmes. "Once a magician reveals his secrets, the audience is often unimpressed by what had enchanted them moments before."

"*Omne ignotum pro magnifico est*," I mused, to which Foyle cocked his head in perplexity but he was soon deeply engaged with Holmes in planning their next move. For my part, I enjoyed seeing my friend reanimated by the promise of a challenging case.

The following day, Holmes had settled into his well-worn armchair with his favorite clay pipe and a copy of *The Times* while I savoured a second cup of morning coffee. My reverie was broken by his shout. "Halloa! We have our next clue."

"Indeed," I said. "What have you discovered?"

He handed me the paper, indicating the cause of his excitement with a long, thin finger. The entry read:

> *Meet at Albert's on our street at 2 p.m. on the 25th anniversary.*
>
> *Zoop*

"Do you surmise that *Z* and *Zoop* are the same person, given their alphabetical convergence?" asked I.

"A plausible if thinly drawn inference, my dear Watson. However, the more compelling evidence," he continued while tapping the stem of his pipe on the newspaper, "is that the newspaper message from *Zoop* provides instructions exactly as the telegram from *Z* indicated. Precisely when the red-letter day occurs remains to be solved, along with the location of Albert's. However, I'm confident that these can be ascertained through diligent inquiry." He rose and selected one of his scrap-books from a shelf beside the fireplace and began paging through the volume.

"Perhaps you ought to inform Foyle of this development?"

"Ah, yes," said Holmes with a hint of annoyance. "I doubt he will prove of much use, but I'll telephone him as soon as I've had a look through my clippings for 1876 to see if I can identify an imprisonment of any nature that year which might beget an escape attempt on its silver anniversary."

When Foyle came by in the afternoon, Holmes had covered every surface of our sitting room with newspaper clippings, scrap-books, and volumes of his encyclopedia. With the heat wave abating, my companion had been sitting comfortably for some time with eyes closed while breathing deeply. He cocked an eyebrow when the young inspector came into the room with a burst of excitement and declared, "I've cracked the case, Mr. Holmes! I know what is to transpire."

Holmes offered an indulgent smile as Foyle explained that he had scoured police records and found that in 1876, burglars had cut through a solid brick wall to break into the safe of a bullion merchant. The case went unsolved for many years until the gang's leader, a Mafia scowerer, tried to sell gold sovereigns with distinctive markings to a law-abiding merchant. Alberto Venucci was sentenced to an extended prison term.

"You see, Mr. Holmes," said Foyle, "tomorrow is the twenty-fifth anniversary of the theft, and Alberto's gang must be preparing to break him out of Newgate Prison, perhaps with his cellmates. That's why the private message in the newspaper referred to 'Albert', and we can be sure that the bricklayer at the boarding house would have had the skills to cut through the wall."

"What is your plan?" asked Holmes with a twinkle of amusement in his austere grey eyes.

"I'm going to follow that bricklayer tomorrow, nab the gang, and foil their plot."

"I wish you well. If you succeed, your career as an inspector will be made."

Foyle dashed from our apartment. Holmes lit an Alexandrian cigarette and blew wavering rings of smoke up to the ceiling.

"You doubt his success," said I.

"The bricklayer is Irish or Scottish, given the strand of red hair left on the tablecloth at his place. I doubt that he would be in close league with the Sicilians."

"But you didn't share information about his nationality at the boarding house."

"A capable investigator would have noticed such an obvious clue on his own. A wild goose chase will provide Foyle a valuable lesson in humility."

As for wild creatures, Holmes sent for Wiggins, the captain of the Baker Street Irregulars, who were his unofficial police force comprising a ragged pack of street Arabs. When the lead urchin arrived, Holmes handed him a shilling and directed the scoundrel to track down Mr. Graham at the medical school, follow his every move, and report back the next day. The little beggar scampered downstairs and into the street.

"And now," said Holmes, "I will ponder my next line of research, if you will exhibit the capacity for silence which makes you such an invaluable and pleasant companion. I must concentrate on the nature of the imprisonment, as this is key to the case but remains ambiguous."

"You suspect something other than the normal confinement of criminals then?" I asked, to which my companion raised a finger to his lips in gentle remonstrance.

I held my tongue thereafter and spent the next day quietly catching up on correspondence with a couple of mates from my days in the Fifth Northumberland Fusiliers. Holmes was fully absorbed in his research until our tranquility was broken that evening when a deeply chagrined Inspector Foyle came to our rooms to report that the bricklayer had done nothing all day except to build a sturdy wall. Holmes feigned sympathy and with a wink to me offered the fellow an Irish whiskey.

All the following morning Holmes was absorbed in indices until Wiggins appeared at our door to report Mr. Graham's activities. Standing at attention, the grimy youth reported, "Well Guv'nor, the man you described met a pretty girl outside a big building with a dome and columns."

"And then?" asked Holmes.

"And then they walked to the Albert," at which point Holmes arched an eyebrow of recognition at the name of place. The urchin continued, "That's where they spent the evenin' drinkin'. After that, he kissed her a good one, put her in a cab, and went home by hisself."

"Well done, Wiggins. Now be off and keep out of any trouble that would make you unavailable for further service to me," said Holmes, who returned to his scrapbooks until Mrs. Hudson delivered lunch. She brought up a tray of buttered bread, thick slices of cold beef, and her special concoction of cheese mixed with cream and chopped walnuts for making sandwiches, along with a third pot of coffee for the day. I was delighted, but Holmes was so possessed by his investigation that he couldn't be bothered with eating.

Looking up from his cup of coffee, he asked me to retrieve a copy of *Laws and Legislation: 1870-1880* from a top shelf, which I did at some not-insignificant risk to myself by balancing on a crate that I retrieved from the lumber room. After paging hurriedly through the volume, he leapt to his feet, sending his chair crashing backwards.

"Great Heavens, what a blind beetle I've been!" he cried. And dashing to the door he shouted, "Come Watson, we must hurry to have a chance of catching them." Reaching the street, he hailed a cab and told the driver, "Take us to The Albert in Victoria Street and drive like the devil. There's half-a-crown in it if you get us there in fifteen minutes." Turning to me, Holmes explained, "I made the unpardonable error of being distracted by Foyle's inquiries when I knew from the beginning that he was misguided. So, it wasn't until just now that I realized today marks the anniversary of the passage of 'The Cruelty to Animals Act of 1876', which sheds light on the confinement that motivates those who are planning what our young inspector surmised was a prison break."

"The timing of that legislation accounts for the allusion to the twenty-fifth anniversary in the personals, and I assume that young Wiggins's report led you to deduce that 'Albert's' referred to the pub of that name rather than a man's home or business."

"Yes, that was helpful, along with the reference in the newspaper to meeting at 'our' street."

"I'm afraid I don't understand."

"The legislation was the result of political pressure brought by a group that now call themselves the National Anti-Vivisection Society."

"How does that pertain to a location?"

"These reformers originally called themselves the Victoria Street Society which is, of course, the avenue on which The Albert is located. And as you noted, this is also the location of Mr. Graham's evening with his fair lady, according to the finest of Baker Street's Irregulars."

"Very clever," I averred, "but who is '*Zoop*', and what escape is afoot?"

"As to the former, I have suspicions but lack substantive evidence at this time. With regard to the latter, the details of their plan may become apparent if we arrive in time to eavesdrop on the conversation, but one can reasonably infer that their interest lies in the release of guileless captives."

"I remember that the anti-cruelty sorts staged a public protest last summer. Some of them were arrested and convicted of assault for having injured two of the faculty in the melee that transpired when they forced their way into the Royal Veterinary College to disrupt a course purportedly involving vivisection. Perhaps they intend to engineer the escape of their imprisoned members, although they are hardly blameless."

"Indeed. Purity of soul isn't a human condition."

As I pondered my companion's obtuse meaning, we arrived at our destination with the driver having earned his bonus. We descended from the cab and entered The Albert, named in tribute to the late Queen's husband. The distinguished pub was faced in yellow brick with attractive red-brick dressings and ornate iron balconies. Upon entering the cool, dark interior, Holmes immediately drew the attention of the aproned waiter, a corpulent fellow with bushy, gray side-whiskers.

"My good man," said Holmes looking about the mostly empty pub, "I am hoping to connect with a small group of people who suggested that we meet in this fine establishment."

"There's no group here at the moment, although a half-dozen people engaged one of our private rooms earlier."

Being a master of putting humble witnesses at ease and knowing the value of compensating individuals for their assistance, Holmes slipped half-a-sovereign into the waiter's vest pocket and asked, "What might you remember about them and the nature of their conversation?"

"I can tell you there were five women and a young man," the waiter said, giving his pocket an appreciative pat. "The ladies included an extraordinarily pretty girl who sat next to the fellow and seemed much taken by his flaxen hair and lean jaw. The other women were matronly and very intense."

"Intense?" asked Holmes to draw forth further details.

"They didn't seem to be having a good time, unlike the lass who smiled at the fellow whenever she caught his eye."

"Can you describe any of the older ladies?"

"They weren't particularly notable, except perhaps one," the waiter said and then paused. Holmes waited patiently while the man plumbed his memory. "She was strikingly similar to Queen Victoria. Not meaning any disrespect, but this woman was quite rotund, with substantial jowls, generous ears, and the bluest eyes, which I've been told were a distinctive feature of Her Majesty."

"And might you have overheard the nature of their conversation?" asked Holmes.

"I am discreet but attentive in my duties," said the waiter with a slight wink. "For the most part, they fell silent when I was present. However, when I brought in a tray of drinks during an animated exchange such that they didn't notice my presence at first, one of the old ladies was saying that they shouldn't reveal their plan to '*FBC*'. Another one replied that they ought to hew to the principles of Lordess. I think they were speaking in code to keep outsiders from gleaning the content of their meeting."

"Indeed," said Holmes. "And did you manage to overhear anything further in the course of fulfilling your professional obligations?"

"When I returned with their food, which they insisted could include no meats and thereby quite annoyed the cook, a shrill woman was disparaging someone named Henry for instilling weakness in their movement. But I don't think she was referring to the young fellow at the table, because he didn't look at all offended by this judgment."

"You have been most helpful," said Holmes. "Might you allow us brief access to the sitting room that they vacated?"

The waiter nodded, took us to the chamber, and retired to his work as thirsty customers sought respite from the summer heat which had ameliorated but hardly vanished. Holmes inspected each of the upholstered chairs and nodded knowingly when he passed his glass over the backs of an adjacent pair. Having completed his perusal, we each had a glass of beer to refresh ourselves.

"What did your inspection of the chairs reveal?" I asked, leaning against the bar.

"The pieces of this most intriguing puzzle are beginning to fall into place. The man at the table had been in recent contact with chloroform and ether, while the woman next to him left behind several flakes of cat dander."

"Do you mean to say that the medical student at the boarding house is our culprit, and that he has been spending time with the young woman who owns a cat?"

"Your reasoning is consistent with the evidence, and we might well take this to be our provisional theory. But keep in mind the danger in becoming too fond of either a hypothesis or a woman upon an initial glimpse."

"But what more is needed to apprehend this man and deliver him to Foyle for questioning?"

"My dear Watson, your instinct is always to do something energetic. But suspicion isn't proof, and he would merely proclaim his innocence. I believe he is involved in an escape plot of a kind markedly different than what our young inspector anticipates. The evidence points to the escape of mongrels rather than malefactors. However, it is imperative to ascertain the identity of this *Z* or *Zoop*. And there is likely to be one person who can describe this individual."

Having finished our drinks, we made our way to Printing House Square and the offices of *The Times*. Holmes had developed a valuable relationship with the newspaper's editor by sharing elements of particularly newsworthy cases with his reporters on occasion. Charles Frederic Moberly Bell was a balding and severe man, but his countenance warmed immediately upon Holmes's arrival. Moberly Bell called in the clerk who took advertisements for the paper. In the presence of his superior, the man trembled noticeably, but Holmes quickly put him at ease in the way he had with common folk.

"Please take a seat," Holmes began, guiding the mousy clerk to a chair and putting a reassuring hand on the man's shoulder. "Now tell me, my dear fellow, can you recall who gave you the wording of the advertisement that was signed '*Zoop*'?"

"I do," the clerk said, looking anxious toward Moberly Ball, who nodded for his employee to continue. "It was an older woman, rather short and plump, I might say. She initially had written a longer signature but crossed out part of it before she handed it to me."

"Did you keep the handwritten version?" asked Holmes.

"I always do, just in case someone claims that we've misprinted their words," said the clerk. "I can retrieve it from my files, if you'd like."

"Indeed, I would," said Holmes. The man scampered off and quickly returned with a sheet of paper which he handed to Holmes. The signature read, '*Zoophilist*', which meant nothing to me but my companion seemed intrigued.

"One more thing, if I may," said Holmes, "Did you notice the color of this older woman's eyes?"

"I can't say that I did," the clerk began. "However, with her severe temperament and pale complexion, she struck me as Germanic, so I suppose her eyes might've been blue."

We thanked our journalistic comrades and returned to our flat, where Holmes had Mrs. Hudson prepare two pots of strong coffee for his dinner. I couldn't guess what he had in mind, but his deeply furrowed brow indicated that he had lapsed into intense concentration. This disposition carried him through evening as he pored over his reference books. When I retired for the night, Holmes had changed into his dressing-gown, gathered up an ounce of shag tobacco, lit his old briar pipe, and sat motionless in the glow of the lamp.

In the morning, I found my comrade looking no worse for an all-night vigil fueled by caffeine and nicotine. Amid a formidable stack of scrap-books and compendiums, he looked up with a clear-eyed focus. Our good Mrs. Hudson deduced in a maternal way that her charge would be famished and, in addition to toast and coffee, she provided a platter of ham, eggs, and curried fowl. From Holmes's voracious appetite, I inferred he had made substantial progress on the case and was ready to proceed with a day of energetic investigation.

"Tell me," I began, while filling our cups, "what did your night of research and reflection reveal?"

"I will begin with the identity of Z," said he.

"You mean *Zoop*?"

"One and the same. The alias is an allusion to '*Zoophilist*' as became evident yesterday from the handwritten advertisement. I've since learned that this is the title of the Anti-Vivisection Society's journal, a publication binding together those committed to all things humane when it comes to animals. And the woman using this *nom de guerre* is Millicent Stopes, a fervent feminist and anti-vivisectionist. Your recollection of a riotous protest last summer at the Royal Veterinary College that resulted in the arrest of several activists was most useful in my research. That incident was reported in *The Times*, along with a photograph of the woman who spoke on behalf of the protestors. Having filed that clipping under '*Hooligans*', I found the image of Millicent Stopes, who does bear an uncanny resemblance to the late Queen Victoria and who is undoubtedly the ring-leader of the incipient plot to release captive animals."

"Did you make headway with what the waiter at The Albert overheard?"

"Indeed," he replied, taking a sip of coffee and stabbing a slab of ham, "although this line of inquiry was more challenging since our informant wasn't particularly accurate in his account. The waiter recounted one of the women warning the others not to reveal their plan to '*FBC*' which led me down blind alleys until I realized that the initials were surely '*FPC*' and belonged to Frances Power Cobbe, who published numerous articles opposing animal experimentation. She is quite extreme in her views, but less strident anti-vivisectionists drew Queen Victoria to their cause."

"Surely Her Majesty wasn't the Lordess who was mentioned in the conversation," said I, thinking that such would be terribly disrespectful.

"Although that term is used by American feminists as the counterpoint to *Lord*, rather than *Lady*, what the waiter heard as '*Lordess*' was undoubtedly '*Lord S*', which was a reference to Lord Shaftesbury, an avid supporter of animal rights."

"They are evidently well-connected and highly committed reformers of a rather militant inclination."

"Indeed. Their contempt for someone named Henry was almost surely directed at Henry Stephens Salt, who published a seminal work on animal rights and formed the Humanitarian League a decade ago. But as a staunch pacifist, he is opposed to violent tactics which, we can infer, are part of the plan being developed and, if we aren't too late to intervene, implemented."

"Have you deduced the particulars of their scheme?"

"I have a good idea of what is afoot," said he reaching for the remaining coddled egg, "and for the escape to be foiled, I require your assistance."

"I am, of course, at your disposal in pursuit of these miscreants, however well-intended their endeavors might be."

"We will need access to your *alma mater*, where I have good reason to believe the plot will unfold. The logical intersection of our medical student, the anti-vivisectionists, and the release of innocents from 'inhumane confinement' is the University of London, where the medical faculty keep animals for teaching and studies."

"Access to the facilities can be readily obtained, as I remain a familiar face in the halls even more than twenty years after graduation. Indeed, I lunched with my former professor of anatomy, Dr. Ferguson, last month, and I recently dropped in on the Dean to garner his opinion of Kolle's cholera vaccine, as he had been the chair of infectious diseases during my studies."

"Then swallow your coffee with all due haste," he said having washed down the last piece of buttered toast with his third cup, "for the sooner we start the better."

We took a hansom to the University of London and stopped at the stately Wilkins Building housing the Faculty of Medicine. The colonnaded portico evoked a Greek temple and afforded an appropriately solemn entrance given the weightiness of training students to battle suffering and death. The massive stonework inside provided a cave-like respite from the rising heat of the morning, and we headed down the south cloister to the offices, lecture halls, and laboratories. Although no one questioned our presence, there was a palpable tension in the hallways. Rather than their usual hearty greetings, the faculty flashed polite smiles and gave sidelong glances at my companion.

I explained to my friend that something felt amiss, so we should move confidently and briskly to minimize suspicion. Holmes replied that he knew of no other way to comport himself. He wanted to begin his investigation by visiting the kennels where the dogs used for physiological research and teaching demonstrations were kept. As I led him down a staircase into the basement, the air grew decidedly cooler and the lighting dimmer.

"Now look here, Guv'nor," said the kennel boy as we reached the rows of cages, "the dean tol' me no one is to be down 'ere 'til the situation is worked out."

As Holmes slid past him with a genial smile and a graceful movement, I drew the fellow's attention. "I was just paying a visit to my old college to show a friend where the finest medical training in the world takes place, thanks to brilliant professors and dedicated chaps like you." He gave a slight bow while over his shoulder I saw Holmes pull a flannel from his coat pocket and wipe it along the bars of the empty cages. "So, my dear fellow," I continued, "what is this situation that has everyone unsettled?"

"I can't rightly say," he replied and dropped his voice, "but you'll notice that there's nothing to see down here. And that's all I can say without making trouble for m'self."

"For my part, I would say you do a splendid job of maintaining a first-rate facility," said Holmes, drawing forth an appreciative grin, "and I imagine that you clean these cages between the departures and arrivals of animals, eh?"

"Indeed, I do," the kennel boy answered with evident pride.

We thanked the fellow and went back upstairs, where Holmes asked me to take him to the teaching venue. As we headed along the cloister, I whispered to my companion, "The kennel is typically filled with barking dogs being readied for demonstrations."

"Indeed," said Holmes. "It seems that we have arrived too late to thwart the plot, but if you could lead me to wherever the students are gathered, we may yet have an opportunity to settle the case beyond all doubt."

I quietly opened the door to the surgical theatre with its steep rows of seating where I expected to find the medical students. The room was empty. The class was meeting across the hall in an auditorium where a professor had drawn a diagram of the lingual nerves of the salivary glands and was explaining that salivary pressure was independent of blood pressure. Based on their slouched postures, I could guess the medical students were daydreaming about their future, lucrative practices along Harley Street.

The young men had hung their coats outside of the room on a row of pegs. To my eye, the linen jackets were identical, as lads collectively gravitate to whatever fashion is deemed stylish. Holmes inspected each garment, then acquired a roll of surgical tape from a table inside the door of the surgical theatre, wrapped a few lengths around his fingers with the sticky side outward, wiped the sleeves of one of the coats, and put the tape into his trousers pocket. Just as we started to take our leave, he turned back, took out a penknife, and cut a button from the coat.

Back at our quarters, Holmes pulled one of his unfinished manuscripts from a shelf dedicated to ongoing projects, set up his low-power microscope on the acid-stained, deal-topped table, and spent the afternoon bent over the instrument examining the samples he collected from the kennel cages and the student's coat. Just before dinner, he leaned back, rubbing his hands together with satisfaction.

"Someday, I must complete my monograph on identifying the hair of mammals. The methods are rather less challenging than distinguishing the brands of cigars based on their ashes, but no less useful to a detective."

"I would venture to guess you have made a breakthrough with the materials you acquired from the university, although surely the kennels simply held dogs."

"My dear Watson, I would have been able to discern if the cages had housed one of nearly seventy species, including the wombat and the giant rat of Sumatra, along with the cheetah and baboon, thanks to hair samples that I acquired from Dr. Roylott's estate some years ago."

"So the kennels held exotic animals?"

"Not at all. The truth is most often commonplace, and my analysis revealed only hairs with the vacuolated medullae and spade-shaped roots typical of canines. The cages held four mongrels and a Blenheim spaniel, based on the characteristically silky red-and-white hairs of one to two inches in length, with the exception of a few much longer hairs from the animal's ears."

"And the student's jacket – "

"Had hairs shed from all five dogs that were held in the kennel. The strands were quite abundant across the inner arms and lapels. Given that the cages are cleaned between animals, we can infer that the fellow carried each of the dogs shortly before they disappeared."

"What is our next step?"

"After I telephone and tell Foyle to meet us at the boarding house betimes in the morning, we shall have dinner at Simpson's."

The next day, we arrived at Mrs. Thurlow's as the boarders were finishing their breakfast. Holmes instructed Inspector Foyle to detain Mr. Graham, the medical student who bore a striking resemblance to a young Johannes Brahms, Germany's most dashing musician of the last century. The young man looked put out but had little choice but to meet with us in the parlour where he took a seat on the horsehair sofa. Foyle stood in the doorway, appearing officious to mask his perplexity with Holmes's proceedings. The inspector would eventually learn that my friend was lothe to communicate his full plans until the instant of their fulfillment, which was trying for those working alongside him. For her part, Mrs. Thurlow hovered in the hallway in an effort to overhear the conversation. Holmes settled into a velvet-lined armchair, crossed his long legs, and began his questioning.

"Mr. Graham, would you be so kind as to tell us the name of the comely young lady with whom you conspired to release the dogs from the university kennel?"

"I have no idea of your meaning, sir," he replied defiantly.

"Come now, surely her name is easier to recall than that of Mrs. Stopes and the other matrons who were also involved in the caper," said Holmes. Graham cocked his head as if confused, so Holmes continued. "Or perhaps Inspector Foyle could undertake an investigation of the Anti-Vivisection Society and discover the identities of all the conspirators." At this, the young man's attempt to appear baffled was belied by a deep furrow of worry forming between his eyebrows.

"My personal life is none of your concern, as it involves nothing of interest to the police. And I resent your having followed me without cause," he added.

"I didn't follow you, Mr. Graham, although one of London's grimy two-legged strays did so and reported to me. For my part, I followed the cat dander that you left behind as a trail leading to and from the young lady. Then there was the trail of ether and chloroform vapors that you deposited while dining here and at The Albert with your associates. But the more revealing evidence was the dog hair from the cages which precisely matched that which I found on your coat. You unwittingly

265

acquired these hairs in the course of transporting the animals out of the building last night and into the waiting arms of your confederates."

"How do you know that it was my garment? Many of my classmates have similar coats."

"Ah, but yours is missing this," Holmes replied, taking a button from his own pocket.

Graham fingered the missing spot on his coat and fell silent. Holmes leaned back, put his finger-tips together, and assumed a judicial expression. Foyle shifted uncomfortably from one foot to the other but knew better than to disturb the interrogation. At long last, Graham sighed deeply, directed his unfocused gaze toward the far end of the room and told his story. A month earlier, he had been profoundly disturbed by having observed the vivisection of a small brown mongrel, stretched out on its back on an operating board with its head clamped and mouth muzzled. The creature had been inadequately anesthetized and struggled in an effort to lift its body off the board as Graham's classmates joked and laughed. The following day, he reported the incident to the Anti-Vivisection Society and conspired with them to orchestrate the escape of the dogs being held in the kennel and their placement in suitable homes.

"There you have it," he concluded. "I did what my moral sense required as a man devoted to reducing suffering of all creatures – both human and lesser beings."

"But the medical school will just replace the dogs you stole," said I.

"Of course, but does a doctor not save one patient because another is sure to arrive?" he replied. Graham looked at Foyle, then turned to Holmes and asked, "What are your plans for me, now?"

"The inspector has considerable discretion in cases such as yours, where the English and moral laws are entangled. He could rightfully arrest you for the theft of property," said Holmes and Foyle nodded affirmation. "However," Holmes continued, "a clever lawyer could argue that dogs gathered from the streets are hardly anyone's possessions. What is more, little would be done to advance the inspector's career by nabbing a man who transported stray animals into the company of compassionate people. Indeed, a trenchant newspaper reporter might well make a mockery of Scotland Yard devoting its energies to such trivialities." Holmes turned to Foyle and continued, "Instead, I think the inspector could tell his superiors that rather than an escape from Newgate Prison, as he had initially theorized based on keen investigative skills and which he was fully prepared to foil, what transpired thanks to his professional acumen was only a minor offense that was best handled quietly."

"Would that account not suggest that the inspector prevented a serious felony without saying as much?" I asked.

266

Holmes cocked an eyebrow and Foyle gave a wan smile, saying, "Alas, there are far fewer commendations for preventing crimes, even imaginary ones, than for solving them."

"Indeed. But yours wouldn't be a poor outcome for the first case assigned to a newly minted inspector," said Holmes.

Foyle directed his gaze at Mr. Graham. "I would insist in the strongest possible terms that no more dogs go missing from the faculty of medicine, or you can be assured that less-forgiving consequences would ensue." The young man nodded solemnly, and I wondered just how he would resolve his aspirations to relieve human afflictions with the desire to alleviate animal suffering.

Upon leaving the boarding house, Foyle went his way and Holmes and I decided to walk back to Baker Street, as the morning hadn't yet become sultry. "I presume you have no reservations in condoning the deception of Scotland Yard in this case," said I.

"British law," he said, "recognizes the so-called necessity defense, in which a person may commit an offense if doing so prevents a greater harm. Perhaps this principle applies to both Mr. Graham and Inspector Foyle."

Still fixated on what amounted to my friend encouraging the police to ignore a well-orchestrated criminal enterprise, I continued after several moments of consideration. "But does harm to a stray dog in the course of advancing knowledge among future doctors justify theft?" asked I, as a wiry mongrel breakfasted on garbage in the gutter.

Holmes, who rarely showed much compassion toward animals but sympathized with those least able to defend themselves, simply replied, "I had rather play tricks with the law of England than with my own conscience."

The Adventure of the
Spinster's Courtship
by Tracy J. Revels

"**L**et me be perfectly clear, Mr. Holmes – I do not approve of this consultation, although I will indulge my wife by covering whatever fee you may charge for your advice. Mine was offered for free but rejected as being insensitive. I counter that my dearest Corinna is the one being insensitive to the future happiness of her friend. This sudden concern for Miss Emily's welfare is misplaced. For Heaven's sake, the woman has little enough joy in her life. Why spoil things for her now? But I have been overruled. I shall putter around Regent's Park for exactly an hour, and then I will return. Let us hope, Corinna, that your mission is completed by that time."

This speech, delivered in the coolest and most patronizing of tones, was punctuated with sharp cane taps from the deliverer, a tall, thin, raven-haired man in an Albert coat, with a golden *pince-nez* highlighting the blueness his eyes. His card proclaimed him Lord Chester Winthrop, and surely readers of these chronicles will recall him as one of the great esthetes of the age, a man whose trendsetting was the talk of three continents. But on this morning in Baker Street, he was no more than a greatly aggrieved husband who had learned, as most husbands eventually do, that his opinion mattered little when it clashed with the ideas held by wife. His spouse, Lady Corinna, a mesmerizingly beautiful blonde woman in a fashionable mauve dress, merely nodded a dismissal at him. He departed our suite with a mocking bow. Holmes's amusement tugged at the corner of his lips.

"Dear me, I suspect he also disapproved of the draperies. Or was it the rug?"

Lady Corinna offered a thin smile. "He disapproves of most everything, sir, though usually not of me. It is uncomfortable for us to quarrel – and undignified to do it before strangers – but I couldn't sleep another night without putting my problem before you, especially as it concerns the life and future happiness of one so dear to me, who lacks any family to advise her or – let me be frank – any decent gentlemen to defend her."

Holmes chuckled as he settled into his armchair. "Never let it be said that Dr. Watson is anything less than a true *chevalier*. I am merely his meager squire. But as your husband seems the impatient type, please give us a succinct statement of the case. What crime has been committed against your friend?"

"None, yet. However, I fear – oh, Mr. Holmes, that is the worst of it! To have a sense of doubt and dread, to be so sure that something is amiss and to not know why. But enough! You have asked me for a statement, and I will seek to give it to you clearly.

"Before I was Lady Corinna Winthrop, I was merely Corrina Bray, of Brayford Castle," she began. Holmes interrupted her.

"Then yours is a heritage much older and richer than your husband's," he said. "There have been Brays in Surrey since the time of Richard III. Your husband's title is of Georgian extraction, bestowed by a German-speaking king in dire need of funds."

The lady half-raised her finger to her lips. "I am grateful for your knowledge of history, Mr. Holmes. Indeed, my family is an old one, loyal retainers of the Crown, though never ennobled for our services. Our home – calling it a castle is rather pretentious, though it does date back to the fourteenth century and has the requisite high walls and moat – has been well-preserved for generations. It is perhaps one of the finest medieval castles outside of the royal collection of estates. There were once many Brays in the countryside, but the Bray line sadly dwindled over the past two centuries, due to misfortunes in war and a tendency to contract consumption. Of my family there was only my father, Anthony Bray, my mother, Julia, and my young siblings, Marion and Ashton.

"An ancient castle is a far from pleasant place to grow up in, despite what fairy tales imply. There were no modern conveniences in the house, and it was perpetually cold, damp, drafty, or oven-like, depending on the weather. Over the generations, much of the estate had been sold, so we lacked any kind of deer-park or woodlands to play in. Indeed, there are now much finer houses on either side of the small estate. Our castle suddenly appears like something ghostly and haunted, dropped down on its little hillock from another era in time.

"Father attended medical school and became a noted Harley Street specialist. He felt it best that his children be brought up in the country, in the family home, despite the fact he could rarely be with us because of the needs of his patients. Mother much preferred city life, so we were raised principally by nannies and tutors, but we felt the closest connection – almost familial in nature – to Mr. Crow and his daughter Emily.

"Mr. Crow was an old retainer, a combination of steward and historian. He was a rather queer-looking gentleman, with a long, hooked nose and a shiny bald head. He always wore black, and with his hunched back and his strange, hopping gait, he truly reminded everyone of his namesake. He was a widower and dwelt in a small cottage just behind the castle, along with his daughter, who is ten years my senior. Crow, as we called him with childhood familiarity, was the dearest old fellow, full of tales of adventure and the great accomplishments of our ancestors. It was from Crow that I learned how Mistress Alice Bray had been a 'tiring woman' to Queen Elizabeth, responsible for handling and cleaning her gowns and jewels. There was an old, dark portrait of Mistress Alice in the hall that I loved to admire, and as a young girl obsessed with her dresses and ribbons, I used to stand before the ancient silver mirror in the castle and imagine that I was Good Queen Bess, and that my sister was Mistress Alice, who had to serve me.

"But it was Emily Crow who was my dearest companion. I was much closer to her than I ever was to Marion. It was Emily who taught me my letters – she never grew impatient with me, even when I proved the dullest of students. I don't know why, Mr. Holmes, but sometimes the letters that I see aren't in the same arrangements that others see them! It makes it most difficult for me to plough through a book or an essay. Emily alone seemed to understand, and for that I loved her!

"But I must leave off this childhood reminiscence and come to my point. Some three years ago, Father passed away. Sadly, he had more of a brain for infectious diseases than for investments, and my family was facing financial embarrassment. Mother, however, came up with a most unusual scheme: Both my sister and I were recently wed, and my brother was just beginning his studies at Oxford, so there was no family member in residence at Brayford Castle. Mother turned the entire estate over to Crow, instructing him to convert it into a kind of architectural and historical attraction, and to charge admission. When Mother first told me her plan, I thought it was fantastical. Imagine, people parting with hard-earned shillings to see our old house! But Crow immediately went to work, and soon Brayford Castle had become the talk of the Surrey countryside. Crow was the chief tour guide, and I think it was the combination of his amusing appearance and his great enthusiasm that people appreciated."

"Did Miss Emily serve as a hostess as well?" Holmes asked.

A sudden shadow came over our guest's lovely features. "No, Mr. Holmes. Crow forbid it. You see, Emily isn't an attractive woman. She has a golden heart, a sweet voice, and a compassionate character, but she is sadly formed, low and squat, and her hair is the color of a pumpkin. She suffered from smallpox as a child, and later had a great deal of blemishes, which left her skin pitted and scarred. Her teeth are uneven, and her eyes – I don't have a name to put to the condition, but they seem permanently crossed. All her life, she has been the victim of cruelties. Wicked boys have been known to throw stones at her. Now in her middle years, she is pitiful, a woman who deserves to be loved, but whom nature has given no favors that might spark romantic devotion in a man. So you see, Crow didn't wish her to 'turn away' any paying customers. Instead, he hired a very attractive young man – I believe his name was Copper or Craft something, and I only met him once, and for less than an hour – to help with the tours.

"All went very well until last winter, when Ashton returned to Mother's London house for the holidays. He has become quite the student of history and, according to my sister, who was there for dinner that night, he began to ask Mother many questions about some of the old bits and baubles in the castle. The next day, my mother and brother spent time in the British Library before embarking for a visit to the castle. Much to my surprise, they were away for three days, and when they returned, both were in sour moods.

"'What has made you so irritated?' I asked when they dined with us.

"'I have sacked Crow and that young scamp who worked for him,' Mother said. 'He'll never see another penny of Bray money, not as long as he lives. And I've served him notice, that he had best be out of the old cottage by Boxing Day, or I'll have him thrown into the streets, along with that ugly baggage of a daughter.'

"I was horrified, of course. I begged Mother to tell me what had happened, but she refused – Mother can be quite haughty that way, and because I was so slow at learning my letters, she presumes that I am too stupid to be entrusted with any family secrets. I took my brother aside and tried to twist his arm, but Ashton would say only that Crow had endangered the Bray family honor. Ashton bragged that when he completes his studies at Oxford, he will return to the village and operate the castle himself. Mr. Holmes, my brother may have the makings of an excellent historian, but he is so slothful I know he will fail to keep our family business afloat. I tried to impress this upon him, but he was most insistent that Crow was no longer welcome on the estate.

"'Then think of Emily!' I said to him.

"'I would prefer not to.'

"'Be ashamed! She was kind to you, a good nurse when you needed care and Mother was too busy with her society friends in London to be bothered by a sickly boy. How dare you talk of throwing Emily into the streets!'

"But nothing would move him. At last, I turned – reluctantly – to my husband for help. He agreed to give me enough money to help Crow and Emily establish themselves in a little home in the village. I found them a small house with a good garden, for I knew Emily took great pleasure in growing roses. She wept at my kindness but could say nothing of what had

271

caused such a row between my mother and her father. I could only guess that she, like me, was kept ignorant of the situation. Meanwhile, Mother hired a small troupe of actors to serve as tour guides at the castle. Actors, sir! As if people of that ilk could be trusted not to steal the silver!

"Not even a month passed before this terrible and mysterious event exacted a heavy toll. Crow died suddenly in his sleep, leaving poor Emily all alone. I wanted to bring her to London as a paid companion, but my husband refused. Ashton and Mother wouldn't assist, but my sister and I pooled some money to provide the poor woman with a small annuity. She also mends and does fancy needlework for ladies in the village, so she isn't entirely destitute. Which brings me, I suppose, to the reason I have come to you."

Our client drew a deep and dramatic breath.

"You see, Mr. Holmes – a gentleman is making love to her!"

I confess that I looked up from my notes with a start. My friend's eyebrows were fixed into their most astonished angle. His voice was low and sardonic.

"Indeed?"

"Yes. It is the scandal of the community. This man – Professor Alexander Whipple by name – is old enough to be her father. He arrived two months after poor Crow was lowered into his grave and took lodgings in The Hart and Crown public house. He is bent nearly double, has the most ludicrously thick spectacles, and wobbles along with the help of a heavy cane. He wears long black frock coats and a thick scarf, even though the weather has warmed. He made Emily's acquaintance at church and claims that he fell in love with her at first sight. Can you imagine!"

Holmes seemed to be struggling not to smile. "From your description of the maiden, it seems that a man might be struck with horror rather than with *amour*."

"Exactly, sir! Only a blind man might be able to make such a statement, that he was 'taken with her beauty' and 'worshipping at the altar of her fair face'. Those are exact quotations!"

"So you have been taken into Miss Emily's confidences."

"Yes. Right from the start, she wrote to me and told me of her swain. She begged for my help, for she has no experience in such matters. I raced home immediately and spent a few days with her. Why, Mr. Holmes, I thought nothing short of a broom would chase the man from the house. When I arrived, he was holding yarn for her to roll, staring up into her face with the devotion of a dog. It was horrible."

I cleared my throat. "Is there something suspicious about the man?"

"Beyond his choice in lovers?" Holmes added.

"He claims to have been a professor of biology at a small college in America, and that he has returned to his native country in retirement. He revealed to the men at the pub that he is an old bachelor, has a good pension and some investments, and now wants a 'charming lass' to make his home complete. In and of itself, there is nothing objectionable to him. He was dignified and polite to me during our visit, and he has slipped a darling little ruby ring upon Emily's hand. They plan to marry on Sunday."

Holmes shook his head. "Madame, as much as it grieves me to say this, perhaps your husband is correct. As strange as your friend's romance may appear, if she is happy and the gentleman is besotted, then what legitimate objection can you make?"

The lady's face turned red. Her fingers curled into fists.

"But it is wrong! Oh, Mr. Holmes, if you could only feel the certainty of my intuition. Women understand these things. Emily would understand them too if she hadn't been so sheltered. She is far too innocent. She actually believes these things he scrawls on his chalkboard and – "

Holmes held up a hand. "Scrawls on a chalkboard?"

"Oh – oh, did I forget to mention it? That is the oddest bit. He is mute! He isn't deaf, but he cannot speak. He claims to have been that way since birth. He carries around a small board, upon which he marks his words."

"Ah . . . that is indeed an intriguing detail," my friend agreed. "How, might I inquire, did he manage a successful academic career with such a handicap?"

The lady frowned. "I don't know. I suppose his students were as enamored of him as Emily is. He can be very charming – he is quick to bow and kiss one's hand, and some of the things he writes are so witty and expressive. Indeed, even I felt drawn to him, as if by a magnet, and yet – it is wrong! He has some vile intention, I am certain." She leaned forward, dropping her voice. "Emily told me that he has plans to change her garden – that after the wedding he will replant it with a 'better variety' of flowers. And she has the finest roses in the village. Tell me there isn't some evil there, when he is so eager to destroy the things she loves the most?"

Holmes took out his pocket-watch. "Your tale intrigues me, but your husband will return in a moment. Indeed, that may be his tread I hear upon the stairs."

"Will you investigate?"

My friend smiled. "The countryside is so charming this time of year. Watson, I do believe we could amuse ourselves for a day or so, could we not?"

The next afternoon we found ourselves in the quaint little village of Brayford. It was one of the most picturesque destinations in the district, alive with flowers and budding trees. A short drive took us to Brayford Castle, which Holmes insisted on exploring after we placed our overnight cases at The Hart and Crown. As Crow and his daughter had been dismissed from their jobs, and the castle was now under the control of a new set of guides, I didn't see the purpose in this excursion. Still, it made for a pleasant two hours as we rambled around the old stones and listened to the docent – a young actress in a replica of a Tudor maid's costume – describe the dwelling's history.

"In this hall," she said, rather breathlessly, and with her eyes fixed on a handsome young gentleman who had arrived with his elderly parents, "are relics from the time of Roger and Alice Bray. Roger held several stewardships, but his wife was the more favored of the pair, as she was a tiring woman to Queen Elizabeth. Here – " She gestured to a gown, one displayed on a mannequin which had been roughly painted and bewigged to resemble England's most famous monarch. " – is a dress from the period. Family lore says that it was given to Alice by the Queen herself. Now, if you come this way, I will show you the room where King Charles . . . ."

She had already slipped through the doorway, but I hung back with Holmes. Much to my surprise, and some embarrassment, he had taken out his lens and was using it to inspect the details of the antique garment. He fingered the elaborate ties and twinkling stones.

"Holmes! The party will miss us."

"But this bit of history is quite intriguing." Holmes straightened, his eyes roaming the gallery, with its wealth of poorly executed paintings. "This display suggests a theory to me, but I must wait until I have more data."

"Sirs, if you will step this way?" the girl called. Holmes gave me a playful shove.

"I fear my friend has fallen in love with the Queen!" he said, and laughter erupted all around us. I shot him a sideways glance and got a wink in return. As annoying as Holmes could be at times, to see him in such a rare high humor was a pleasure, and so I took up my role to the point they were all assured that I was a blundering idiot before the tour ended.

Afterward, we enjoyed a leisurely stroll back to the heart of the village. Lady Corrina had given us the number of Miss Emily's home, and we found it to be a sweet little cottage at the end of the westernmost street, not far from the little church where the lady planned to be wed. The garden was one that might put even Hampton Court to shame, for its rich assortment of roses. Holmes hesitated for a moment at the low brick wall that surrounded the lovely flowers.

"Dear me. This is as troubling as it is suggestive."

"What do you mean?"

Holmes gave a quick shake of his head and moved on. I took another glance over the wall, my mind now racing. What had Holmes seen that I had missed? The garden looked so charming, but now I began to imagine that every petal was poisoned and that venomous vipers lurked in the shadows of the blossoms.

A notice on the church door announced a children's musical recital that afternoon, and – much to my dismay – Holmes insisted that we attend. Two hours of poorly performed songs and screeching violin solos must have been torturous on my friend's sensitive ears, but just after the event began, I deduced his reason for coming: Miss Emily Crow and her suitor, Professor Whipple, had slipped inside and silently occupied two chairs in a corner. As this was the only social occasion of the day, and Miss Crow was a devout member of the church, it was natural they would attend, and Holmes could covertly assess their relationship.

Sadly, the lady was exactly as her friend had described. I have rarely seen a more ill-favored woman, and her choice in attire – a red checkered dress and a bright yellow hat with a stuffed bird mounted atop it – did little to improve her appearance. Her fiancé was also rather odd, with his great mass of unruly white hair, tiny peering eyes behind thick spectacles, and a heavy black coat which might have been fashionable in the days of the Sailor King. He carried a schoolboy's slate, and from time to time he scrawled upon it and showed it to the lady. I couldn't read the words from my position, but they were amusing to his beloved, who blushed and giggled and once even daringly planted a kiss on his check.

Following the recital, the crowd made its way onto the lawn where a treat was being set up. Holmes waited until the couple had collected cake and lemonade, then trailed them to the secluded spot they had chosen within an arbor. Asking me to stand back, he charged forward.

"Professor!" Holmes cried. "Can it be? Professor Whipple! I am so happy to see you, sir!" Holmes thrust out his hand. The little man nearly fell backwards from his chair, he was so startled. I, meanwhile, was astonished by the ease at which my friend adopted his posture and accent to fit the look and sound of a brash American. "Don't you remember me, sir? John Sherrinford, from your class on invertebrates? It was the best class I ever had at the old college."

The gentleman gasped for breath and then pulled up his board. He wrote out, "*I don't recall you.*"

"Really, Professor? But you said I was one of your finest students. Why, you even gave me credit for discovering a new *genus* of roaches."

The man frowned, then scratched out another line that read, "*Of course, but you have changed.*"

"Indeed, I have, sir! I'm not the scrawny, callow youth I was back then. But I am being rude – Please, Professor, introduce me to your lovely companion."

At this compliment, Miss Emily blushed. Holmes took her hand and kissed it. For almost ten minutes he stood and chattered to the professor, referencing old friends at the school, and reminiscing about amusing incidents in the classroom, including one in which the "naughty boys" set the professor's trousers on fire.

"But I am taking up too much of your time, sir. I am staying at The Hart and Crown – You are there as well? Excellent! Perhaps you will stop in and drink a class of port with me tonight, for old times' sake. Here's to the old school motto – *Conquer and prevail!*"

I caught up with Holmes just outside of the churchyard. "That was amusing," I said.

"Indeed, I can rarely recall having so much fun watching a villain squirm. But let us dismiss the cad for the moment, give our battered ears a rest, and enjoy a good dinner and a cigar. I expect we will have company this evening."

The food at The Hart and Crown was uninspired but substantial, and by the time we retired to our suite, Holmes was in a relaxed and talkative mood. He conversed on a variety of subjects, including fox hunting, the mythic origins of the Druids, and the artistic sensibilities of the pre-Raphaelites. At last, I was able to guide the discussion back to the case at hand.

"I will never completely dismiss a woman's intuition," Holmes began. "For what we males call 'female intuition' is often a careful, though unconscious, set of observations. Women have honed the skills of making deductions from clues, even if they give the results a different designation. Lady Corrina was quite right to observe that Miss Emily Crow is as unappealing as her family name. Her beauty is of the interior sort, and few men are willing to seek out such hidden gems as kindness and compassion. We males are, by and large, a shallow lot when it comes to the qualities we desire in mates. The former Miss Mary Morstan was the exception to the rule – as beautiful in face and figure as she was in soul. You were a very lucky man."

To this I wouldn't disagree. Holmes waved a hand airily.

"It was incomprehensible to me, from the start, how a man who couldn't speak could control a schoolroom. Not impossible, perhaps – there are many talented academics who labor under handicaps – but rather improbable. Thus, I needed to see for myself if all the things that smacked so heavily of a disguise were, indeed, a façade. Surely you recall the unfortunate Miss Mary Sutherland, also an unattractive maiden lady, who was made love to by her own stepfather incognito."

"So this man is someone known to Miss Crow."

Holmes nodded. "Yes, but he is someone who lacks the confidence of the odious Windibank, who blamed swollen glands for his whispery voice. This fraudulent gentleman felt it best to remove his voice all together."

"But Windibank, if I recall, wanted to prevent his stepdaughter from leaving the household so he could keep control of her money. Does this false lover also intend to abandon his betrothed at the altar?"

Holmes snuffed out his cigar and moved to look out of the window. "No. I think there is a more dangerous evil at work. How fortunate we are that Lady Corrina recalled Whipple's intentions to dig up the garden! The devil plans to wed her and then – Ah, he returns. He has but two choices now: To pack his bags and flee, or to come to me and offer a partnership in his crime. Unless, of course, he intends to kill me. That would prove entertaining."

"Holmes!"

"Fortunately, I am well protected. You have your revolver, I trust? Excellent. We shall give him five minutes to decide his fate."

Within seconds of Holmes speaking these words, there was a rapping at the door of our small suite. Holmes rose and opened it, bowing as he ushered the bewhiskered man into the room.

"Professor, how good of you to join us. We have so much to discuss. Please, take the easy chair, I know your old bones are tired. Let me relieve you of all unnecessary burdens."

As deftly as a magician, Holmes snatched the slate from his guest's hands. I stepped beside my friend, folding my arms across my chest and twisting my features into a menacing scowl. Whipple threw up his hands and then, after a moment's consideration, dropped them with a sigh.

"You have me, sir." His voice was shockingly youthful. "Might I ask if Sherrinford is your true name?"

"It is not, just as Whipple is not yours."

"Shall we be honest with each other then?"

"I find honesty is usually the best policy," Holmes said smugly, "but as I have a certain advantage, I am loathe to surrender it. Neither one of us is what we seem, yet perhaps we can use that to our mutual advantage." Holmes settled into the opposite chair and casually lit a cigarette, then offered one to our visitor who, with a shaking hand, took it. Holmes even did the honor of lighting it for him, as if they were two businessmen about to settle into comfortable negotiations.

277

"Tell me," Holmes said, "why this elaborate charade? Surely if a man loves a woman, he has no need to play such a preposterous game."

Our visitor removed his hat and then his wig. He peeled away the beard, pulled putty from his nose, and scrubbed roughly at his face with his handkerchief. These actions revealed the young and rather handsome youth who had hidden beneath the mask of age.

"My name is Randall Collins," he said. "Five years ago, I was a university student, down on his luck, unable to afford another semester's tuition. Old Crow, Miss Emily's father, hired me to help him manage Brayford Castle. I was a combination clerk, tour guide, and custodian, and Crow treated me more like a son than a hireling.

"Crow loved history, especially the legends and lore of the castle. The Bray family showed little interest in their heritage, beyond how they could use it to finance their life in society. Crow had a theory: That one of the Bray ancestors had been a thief, and had stolen gems and baubles from none other than the Virgin Queen herself!"

"Alice Bray, the tiring woman," Holmes interrupted. Collins started. "Why . . . yes. But how could you have known?"

"A close inspection of the dress in the castle," Holmes said. "It was obvious to my lens that some of its adornments had been snatched free, leaving aged threads dangling and unravelling. The paste replacements were poorly and very recently sewn in. But even before I saw the frock, the knowledge that an ancestor had served as a dresser suggested a person with great opportunity for – shall we say – *personal enrichment?*"

The young man nodded eagerly, caught up in the story despite his awkward position. "Yes, yes, you understand! Queen Elizabeth had so many jewels – more than any monarch before her – and she was a careless person. Pins, pearls, broaches, sparkling things were always going astray. A cunning tiring woman could easily pocket a fortune, if she dared, and this woman did. Crow deduced from her portrait that she was wearing pieces that also appeared in a lesser-known image of the Queen. Mistress Alice did have the good sense to wait until after her mistress's death to have her own picture painted, however."

"And I take it that these gems had never been found."

"No – and then, one day while searching amid the castle's archives, Crow found the journal kept by Edwin Bray, the tiring woman's son. In the entry dated on the day of the lady's funeral, Edwin noted that it had been his mother's last wish to be buried in the '*great dress*' given to her by her mistress the Queen. I don't know if Edwin didn't realize the dress was decorated with precious stones, or if he simply was determined to honor his mother's last request, but he noted that Alice had been buried wearing the gown." Collins grinned. "Crow speculated that the request had been a way to spite Mistress Alice's daughter-in-law, whom Mistress Alice loathed, and who might have inherited the jewels if they hadn't been placed on the lady's corpse."

Holmes arched an eyebrow. "And so you and Crow sought to validate this theory with a bit of grave-robbing."

Now the young man offered a guilty nod. "We were mad with curiosity, and what harm could it do? The lady was buried in the vault of the family chapel. Imagine our astonishment when we pried open the sarcophagus and found some strange atmospheric conditions within the chamber had preserved the lady and her gown. It was like viewing the body of an incorruptible saint. But once we exposed the corpse to the air, it quickly became obvious that such a miracle wouldn't last for long. We removed the gown and wrapped the body in a fine silk shroud. I assure you there was no disrespect intended.

"Crow mounted the gown for display. Since no one knew its provenance, it was simply another artifact for Crow's little museum. He took the jewels from the gown, but the damage was too evident, so he replaced them with paste replicas. Miss Emily could have done a much better job on the gown, as she is a talented seamstress, but Crow was determined that she would know nothing of our crime. He warned me that she was 'too religious' and 'too honest' for what we were doing, and I was sworn to tell her nothing about it."

"But your perfidy was discovered."

"Yes, by Ashton Bray. While poring over his books at Oxford, he caught the resemblance between the jewelry in the portraits of the Queen and Alice. He turned up unexpectedly one day and examined the gown, demanding to know where it had come from. Crow wasn't a good liar. He babbled something about having found it in a trunk. The Bray heir was having none of it, and when he brought in his mother, things only got worse. They were certain we had stolen from them but lacking the key document – which Crow had wisely put into my keeping – they couldn't prove where the dress had come from, or the jewels gone off to. Still, we were given the sack in disgrace."

"And Crow pawned the gems," I said. The young man snickered.

"Clearly, you aren't a detective," he said to me.

"Crow kept the jewels," Holmes countered. "And now his daughter has them in her possession, without her knowledge."

"Now *you* are the clever one," Collins laughed. "Crow couldn't overcome his love of history. Not even the thought of immense wealth could tempt him to part with items that had once been caressed by the greatest monarch of our isle. He kept them in an iron box, and when he and his daughter moved to the little cottage in town, he planted them beneath her roses. He assured me that when some time had passed, he would begin to pawn them and divide the proceeds with me. I was loathe to wait that long, as his health was poor, but he gave me one large pearl as a show of good faith. I left the village, sold the pearl in Edinburgh, and set myself the task of finishing my degree. Just a few weeks later, I received word that Crow had perished.

"You can imagine my conundrum. Miss Emily had no idea that a treasure lay beneath her roses. But what would happen if she changed her lodgings? Or if, in digging about, she found it? She was too innocent and naive, she would no doubt turn the box over to the authorities, and what would happen then? I thought about sneaking into town and digging up the box by moonlight, but the village is so small and folks so nosey that I dared not. The woman is such a homebody, luring her away seemed impossible. At last, I hit upon the scheme of making love to her. Poor soul, she is ugly and lonely, I knew she would respond – jump at the chance to alter her spinster status. As I had lived and worked with the Crows previously, I knew my disguise had to be an impenetrable one. An actor friend suggested the character of the mute old man, so that I wouldn't struggle to conceal my voice as well as my face. It all worked very well until . . . I suppose it was her friend, the older Bray daughter, who must have become suspicious."

"So you planned to wed Miss Emily and – " I shook my head. As a formerly married man, I saw some difficulties with maintaining his illusionary character past the ceremony itself.

"Some poison placed in the nuptial wine would no doubt have solved the problems," Holmes said. Collins's face went white.

"No! No – I may be a rogue and a grave-robber, but I am not a murderer!" the man insisted. "My plan was to insist that we spend our first night together in the cottage. I would drug her – I had the powders ready – and that night retrieve the treasure. I would depart in the darkness, leaving behind a note claiming that I had been recalled to America by the sudden death of a wealthy relative. I planned to send her a portion of the proceeds from the sale of the gemstones, just enough to keep her comfortable. She could have the respectability that came with marriage, even if she never saw her strange little husband again!" Collins leaned forward, rubbing his hands together. "Now you have it. We three are the only men who know where a treasure – which Crow estimated at over ten-thousand pounds – lies buried. I am supposed to escort Miss Emily to the church in less than forty-eight hours. What is there to prevent my plan from proceeding if I include you gentlemen as partners?"

His greedy smile was sickening. Holmes rose and flung his cigarette into the fireplace.

"Nothing, perhaps, except my name. Do you still wish to know it?"

Collins's lips began to twitch. His grin faltered. "Well, yes, it is always best to know who one is working with."

"My name is Sherlock Holmes."

The man's cheekiness collapsed into terror. He gasped, choked, and then made an awkward attempt to bolt for the door. Holmes tripped him easily, leaving him sprawled on the carpet.

"Rarely have I met a more cunning sneak and villain," Holmes said. "Your participation in the desecration of the dead is repulsive, but your plans for robbing rightful heirs and breaking a poor woman's heart is even more disgusting. Crawl back into that chair, you worm. My experience of women is intellectual, not emotional, but I am sure the good Doctor Watson – yes, you recognize my chronicler now, I take it – is far more insightful. Watson, do you think our friend's plan would have pleased Miss Emily Crow?"

"No," I said, sharing Holmes's sense of utter loathing. "It would have torn her apart, and probably killed her."

"Then what should we do with her intended murderer?"

Collins began to weep and beg for mercy. Holmes considered him with cold grey eyes.

"If we bring the police into this matter, it will only cause more heartache and scandal. There is some paper on the desk. Watson never travels without both his trusty revolver – " At this the man's eyes widened in alarm. " – and his best pen. We shall begin with a complete confession, in your handwriting, with which your fiancée is undoubtedly familiar."

It was a delicate business, but Holmes had a more than capable ally in Lady Corinna, who had arrived in the village to attend the wedding. After a consultation the next morning, the three of us arrived at Miss Emily's cottage, where the lady was excitedly putting the final items into her honeymoon trousseau. I shall spare my readers the painful reception of the hurtful revelation, and how copiously the lady wept when she read the confession and learned she had been cruelly deceived. With her permission, Holmes and I shed our jackets, rolled up our sleeves, and went to work with spades in the garden, digging in the precise spot where Crow had buried his loot. We were soon rewarded with the ringing of the tools against an iron box. We removed it from the soil, cleaned it, and brought it into the kitchen, placing it upon the table. Miss Emily, leaning on her friend's arm, tottered in to watch as Holmes broke open the lock.

Within was a jumble of Tudor era jewels – loose diamonds, pearls, rubies, and garnets, a golden broach in the shape of a phoenix, and another in the likeness of a snake biting its tail. Beneath some tattered velvet was

281

a string of jade beads that alone would have purchased a mansion in London. Holmes opened two books, one with a portrait of Queen Elizabeth, another with the picture of Mistress Alice from Brayford Castle. It was clear that the former tiring woman had rather boldly worn her ill-gotten gains sewn into her gown.

"Oh, Corrina, I am so sorry!" Miss Emily sobbed. "How could Father have done such a terrible thing?"

The lady shook her head. "Do not apologize. In fact – I am grateful to Old Crow."

Miss Emily dabbed at her eyes. "Whatever can you mean?"

"Why, he discovered my ancestor's perfidy. She didn't deserve to spend eternity with these jewels. These precious stones once adorned the woman who famously and gloriously put duty above love – and they should once more."

With that pronouncement, Lady Corinna pushed the box in her friend's direction.

"This belongs to you, Emily. No, say nothing, I want you to have all of it! Mother and my brother need never know the missing jewels were found. Take them, Emily, and live well. You can come to London, join me in society, and if anyone asks how you came into your fortune, you may rightfully tell them that you discovered it in your own rose garden."

Even now, so many years after the fact, it warms my heart to think of Lady Corinna's goodness and Miss Emily's innocence. Holmes and I took a vow of secrecy and left the ladies plotting as to how to best change antique jewels into modern pounds. A year later, I noted Miss Emily's appearance in the society pages, where she was hailed as one of the most fashionably dressed women of the season. Later, I saw that she had embarked on a world tour. And perhaps two years after that, I saw a wedding announcement – that the former Miss Emily Crow was now Lady Emily Lawson. Holmes and I were inspired to visit the photographic studio on Oxford Street where images of celebrities and beauties were displayed. To our delight, we found the wedding portrait of the couple. Sir Richard Lawson was a large, stout man, balding with sizeable muttonchop whiskers and slight crossed eyes. The pair stood with arms linked, his huge, flipper-like hand laid with great delicacy over hers. The newlyweds focused on each other, mirror images of devotion and love. Holmes smiled as me as we turned away from the window.

"I think it is fair to say, Watson, that I have rarely seem a more splendid couple, or known a happier end to a story!"

The Politician, the Lighthouse, and the Trained Cormorant
by Mark Wardecker

I take a good deal of pride in my discretion and the trust my friend, Sherlock Holmes, places in me as a chronicler of our various adventures together. He always assured his clients of my trustworthiness, and I have never with my pen betrayed anyone who agonised over the reputation or honour of a family member or friend. Nevertheless, recent attempts to get at and destroy my records of our cases may force my hand, as I stated in my recent tale of the Abbas Parva tragedy and its aftermath. If you are reading this now, please know that I do not take this step lightly and have been all but compelled to expose Sir Clive Blackstead as the first-class villain he is. This formal account has only been prepared by me with Holmes's approval as a last resort to finally defend both him and myself against this unscrupulous bounder and the various blackguards with which he freely associates.

It was on a brisk autumn afternoon when I, after the cancellation of my only remaining appointment for the day, decided to make a trip to Baker Street and pay Sherlock Holmes a visit. I pitied the poor hansom driver as a cutting, blustery wind seemed to blow right through my overcoat and threatened my hat as I sheltered inside his swiftly rollicking cab. Upon reaching my destination, I was immediately warmed by Mrs. Hudson's reception as she greeted me at the door of 221. After catching up for a few moments and relentingly agreeing with her that I *did* understand that "he just wasn't the same when we weren't living under the same roof," I made my way up the steps to the old sitting room.

As I approached the door, he yelled from within, "Ah, Watson! Please come right in and help yourself to whatever's on the table." I immediately entered upon a scene so familiar it was as though I had never left. Holmes was leaning on the mantel by a roaring fire, reading a telegram while trays containing the lunch that Mrs. Hudson had prepared for him lay neatly untouched upon the table. As I poured myself some much needed coffee and began assembling a sandwich, he walked across the room and joined me.

"As ever, your timing is impeccable. Though I still find it hard to forgive you for deserting 221b for matrimonial bliss, I suppose I should at least take comfort in the fact that you still seem to be able to join me at the beginning of so many of these little puzzles. But I jest, my good fellow. Tell me, does this not seem promising?"

He handed me the telegram he had been studying, which I then read aloud:

> *I should like to come this afternoon at four o'clock to discuss with you an extraordinary thing I found in a fish my Cassandra disgorged. Please reply.*

Andreas Georgiopoulos

I then read it again and shook my head, "How extraordinary."

"Isn't it just? What do you make of it?"

"I have to admit that I'm having a hard time thinking about anything other than a woman 'disgorging' a fish. A woman named Cassandra, apparently," I added as I began chuckling.

Holmes threw back his head and laughed. "It does conjure a definite image at first glance, does it not?" After we had settled down, he continued, "But what else? Surely you noticed the sender's name is a Greek one? Does that and the reference to the fish and its 'disgorgement' not suggest anything else to you?"

I have to admit I looked at him blankly and chuckled some more.

"Greek fishermen are known for sometimes enlisting birds, specifically cormorants, as assistants. A snare is tied around the trained bird's throat – that way it can still devour smaller fish, but not a larger catch. When it does land a big fish that it cannot swallow, it returns to the fisherman and *'disgorges'* it. There isn't much to go on here, but I think we are much more likely to encounter a cormorant named Cassandra when we meet Mr. Georgiopolous than a gluttonous spouse or daughter. We'll find out soon enough, as he's due here in about five minutes."

Not wanting to take the bet, I finished my sandwich while Holmes discarded his mouse-colored dressing gown for a frock coat. Within a few moments, we were addressing one of the most astounding pairs of visitors to have knocked upon the sitting room door.

"Greetings, Mr. Georgiopoulos," said Holmes. "I see you have brought Cassandra with you. I am Sherlock Holmes, and this is my friend and colleague, Dr. Watson. Please take a seat.

"I see too that you are an avid fisherman and a shipbuilder. In fact, you seem to have been involved in almost every aspect of the craft. Note the calluses from the caulking mallet upon his right hand, Watson, not to mention those on the fingers of the left created by sewing sheets of canvas.

284

Yet there are also shiny marks upon the rather expensive wool coat sleeves that suggest long hours at an angled drafting table."

"And of course, Mr. Holmes, you noticed the state of my favourite hat, the band of which has been sorely taxed, having had one too many lures stuck into it. I am overwhelmed that you have taken in my entire career at just a glance, but there's no denying it. I've been in love with ships and fishing my entire life, from my childhood in Greece to my autumn years in London. You see, I married an Englishwoman and moved here when I was a young man. Cassandra is the latest addition to the family."

Cassandra gurgled but remained perched on his shoulder as he sat down in the basket chair near the fire. She was a truly magnificent creature with dark gray plumage, interrupted by white patches upon her head and breast and a yellow band near her beak. She seemed perfectly comfortable in her new surroundings.

"It was Galanis, the tobacconist, who recommended you to me. He also suggested how I should phrase the telegram to get your attention."

"Ah, yes. I've spent many hours and a good deal of money in his excellent shop. But please, tell us your story," encouraged Holmes as he sat down in one of the easy chairs with his fingers steepled and eyelids beginning to droop.

"Certainly, Mr. Holmes. There really isn't much to tell. Cassandra and I like to fish along the coast when we can get away for a few hours, and last Sunday, I was fishing off Canvey Island while she ranged further afield. In fact, later on, she was out of sight completely for quite some time before returning with a large catch lodged in her mouth. Between you and me, it's just as well she couldn't swallow it. It was a sea bass, and they go through her, as you English say, like . . . well, you know the expression. After we returned home, as I was cleaning it, I found these lodged in its mouth and throat."

He reached into his vest pocket and retrieved two small brilliantly glittering objects and handed them to Holmes, who made a long arm for a looking glass.

He let out a low whistle. "Two cufflinks made of eighteen-karat gold," he observed as he examined them. "The letters 'C' and 'B' entwined on one and filled with diamonds and sapphires of the very best quality. The other is a match with the letters 'A' and 'T'. These are worth a small fortune," he added as he handed the cufflinks to me. "You are a very honest man, Mr. Georgiopoulos. I wonder if the owner will appreciate it."

Indeed, they were bonny things that seemed to emit gleaming sparks of white, yellow, and blue. Cassandra turned her head to look at them and gurgled again.

"Cassandra would most certainly tell us more if only she could, but I am afraid that's all I know, Mr. Holmes. I was on my way to place an ad in the newspapers about them when I stopped by Galanis's shop. He thought you might be interested. If you are, I can offer a small fee. Given the circumstances, I wouldn't want to pay too much."

"What sort of person would I be if I charged an honest man for such an unselfish deed? We shall look into this, Mr. Georgiopoulos, and will hopefully soon be able to tell you the whole story. May I keep these until then? Excellent. I assure you that I'll return them to you if we cannot ascertain the owner. I shall also credit you with their discovery if it turns out a reward has been offered. Then we shall be in touch with you. Good day, sir."

After obtaining his address and showing Mr. Georgiopoulos out, I tried to get Holmes to divulge his next steps, but all he would say about the matter was that he needed to do a bit of fishing, too. When I left him, he was still staring at the cufflinks and thinking. The next week went by with no word from him, and over the weekend my curiosity got the better of me. I visited Baker Street late Sunday afternoon and, even though Holmes hadn't yet returned, waited for him in the sitting room. I was comfortable in the familiar old surroundings – the Persian slipper by the mantel filled with his noxious tobacco, the correspondence affixed to the same with a jack knife, the gasogene which prepared many a brandy-and-soda for a sorely tried client, and the deal table with all his chemical apparatus. I had just begun to doze off over the afternoon paper when Holmes arrived.

"Ah, Watson, I'm glad you've come," he said as he hung up his overcoat and hat. "I believe I've figured out who's been so careless with his cufflinks. Help yourself to one of those cigars." Warming himself by the fire, he resumed, "I've been secretly shadowing our Mr. Georgiopoulos. No, not because I suspect him of anything. It's Cassandra I'm interested in, but they're a package deal. I wanted to see if the bird has any favourite fishing holes. Georgiopoulos clearly only works part-time now at the Samiday Brothers Shipyard, which leaves him free to fish in the afternoons. That one spot on the coast in particular that he mentioned is an obvious favourite, and Cassandra seems to favour it, as well.

"We travelled along the Thames Estuary to Canvey Island last Tuesday, Thursday, and today, and while Georgiopoulos was taking his place upon the shore, I lingered on a tall dune in the background with my best binoculars. Every single time, after about an hour, Cassandra made a beeline to what is obviously her favourite spot far off shore. That is because two out of those three times, there was a large sailboat anchored there, and the owner was always generous about sharing some of his catch

286

with her. Last Tuesday, she alighted on the stern of the boat, the *Persephone*, and waited for the man fishing there to come over with a couple of fresh herring. Cassandra is apparently extremely bright and well-trained. Normally, cormorant fisherman keep hold of the leash they tie around the bird's neck, but Georgiopoulos evidently trusts her enough to let her roam freely most of the time. She tried the same gambit again on Thursday, but the boat wasn't there. Today, she struck gold again. I wonder if there isn't a more direct route for determining a bird's wanderings?

"What is even more interesting is the name of the *Persephone*'s owner: Sir Clive Backstead, MP for Wormesly Central, who is almost certainly the owner of the cufflinks."

"But how would his cufflinks wind up inside a fish?"

"It is hard to imagine such a thing occurring by accident, is it not? I'm currently following six lines of inquiry to ascertain the identity of '*AT*', but haven't had any luck as of yet."

"You could simply ask him when you return the jewellery to him."

"Yes, but having gone this far, I would like to be able to see the complete picture. As you implied, it's odd to find one's cufflinks in a fish."

"This coming from a man who keeps his tobacco in a slipper," I chided.

"What is this?" he asked as his gaze rested upon the front page of the paper I had been reading: "'*Unmanned Lighthouse Nearly Causes Ship to Crash upon Rocks Near Southampton.*'"

"Yes, I was just looking at that. It will be of special interest to you," I added before reading aloud:

> The group of passengers had chartered the yacht, SS Paradiso, *from Mssrs. Eastham and Cheswick for a day at the casinos in Deauville and were returning to Southampton when they found themselves almost dashed upon the crags at Pike Rock. According to both passengers and crew, the Pike Rock Lighthouse was both dark and silent. Had the captain been less capable, the results could have been disastrous. Fortunately, Captain Feargal Smiley knew the waters well enough to sense their danger in time and divert the yacht before disaster struck. As it stands, the ship only sustained some light damage to her hull.*
>
> *The real mystery is the absence of the lighthouse's crew. According to Trinity House, the three keepers that had been working there came into the offices on Saturday to complain about having been replaced by a new crew without warning.*

287

The Brethren at Trinity House knew nothing of the substitution, but the original crew produced official paperwork they had been given by their relief indicating that they were all being reassigned elsewhere. This would be highly irregular, since it is customary for only one keeper at a time to be relieved when such a situation is necessary. The whereabouts of the relief crew are still unknown and the Brethren at Trinity House have pledged to get to the bottom of this mystery.

"What do you make of it?" I asked when I saw the keen look on his face.

"Can your practice and Mrs. Watson spare you for a day or two? It appears Providence has offered us another line of inquiry."

"Yes, I can contact Anstruther today to see if he can step in as a *locum*, but what could this possibly have to do with Sir Clive's cufflinks?"

"Probably nothing, but it is worth exploring. Sir Clive is one of the Elder Brethren of Trinity House."

I only dimly began to grasp the significance of that simple statement and, as is usual, could get nothing more from Holmes that afternoon. After agreeing to meet at Baker Street in the morning, we parted company with him heading out to run an errand and me to make my arrangements and excuses.

The continuing frosty weather confronted us again as we hailed a cab the following morning. As we made our way south and then east through the tangled crowd of pedestrians, carts, buses, and other cabs along the Strand to Tower Hill, Holmes mentioned that he had paid a visit to his brother, Mycroft, the previous evening at the Diogenes Club in order to obtain an introduction to the Brethren. I have mentioned elsewhere that Mycroft ostensibly audited the books for several government departments, but in actuality, sometimes *was* the British government. His word would no doubt grant us an ingress denied to many. The Brethren, three-hundred Younger and thirty-one Elders, preside over Trinity House. Most come from maritime backgrounds and provide nautical advice to the government and administer charitable funds for the benefit of retired seamen, in addition to managing all the lighthouses of England, Wales, the Channel Islands, and Gibraltar. Our hansom soon entered the iron gates and deposited us before the arched doorway of the stately stone building overlooking the Tower.

A doorman in uniform greeted us and led us across rich Oriental rugs through the hall filled with paintings of famous sailors and glass cases containing exquisite wooden models of famous ships. After passing through an arched opening flanked by shiny green marble pillars and alcoves containing model lighthouses that were actually lit, we entered another smaller hall with a wide staircase that branched to both left and right from its first landing. Our guide directed us to the right and, upon reaching the next landing, down a long corridor with oak doorways and Romantic paintings of nautical scenes at regular intervals. At one of these, he stopped, opened the door, and motioned for us to enter. A fastidiously dressed man with wavy hair and a rakish mustache rose from a large desk and approached us.

"Mr. Sherlock Holmes and Dr. Watson, welcome to Trinity House. My name is Abelard Fanthorpe, and I'm one of the Elder Brethren. Your brother and I both frequent the Diogenes, Mr. Holmes. Please, have a seat."

We both sank into luxurious leather armchairs by large wooden globes, one terrestrial and one sidereal, on each side of Fanthorpe's desk. After lighting our cigarettes, Fanthorpe asked what he could do for us.

"I would very much like to see the mysterious paperwork that was given to the original crew of the Pike Rock Lighthouse when they were relieved."

"Certainly. I had it retrieved earlier. Here you are," he said as he opened a long drawer in the middle of the desk from which he retrieved a slim packet of documents."

"Do you yourself see anything suspicious about these?"

"No, Mr. Holmes – other than that we have no record of the three crewmen that arrived at the lighthouse that day. Everything else is in order and, I have to say, bureaucratically routine."

"And the official signatures appear genuine?"

"Yes, but neither of those men recall having ever signed them."

"And this stationery with the House's letterhead and watermark is available to all the Elder Brethren."

"Naturally, Mr. Holmes."

"Is Sir Clive Backstead in today?"

"No, but why do you ask?" he said, raising an eyebrow. "He isn't one of the signatories."

"Is there an office that he uses when he is here? May we see it?"

Fanthorpe was obviously confused but rallied quickly.

"Yes, it's just down the hall," he replied and proceeded to lead us back out into the corridor. As we walked back toward the stairs, he stopped by one of the doors and unlocked it with a key from his waistcoat. The empty office was small with two green curtained windows, two desks, a small bookshelf, and wooden filing cabinets. Upon one of the desks sat an L.C. Smith typewriter, which Holmes began to examine, plucking at the strikers with his fingers and running his fingers over the reversed letters. Pulling a piece of stationary from a pile, he fed it into the machine and began to type.

"A-ha! Watson, do you recall my mentioning that monograph I've been meaning to write on typewriters?"

"Yes, you said once that the type from a typewriter is as unique as an individual's handwriting. I'm guessing that this is the machine that typed those documents."

"It is indeed. Note the blurry bowls in the lowercase *e*'s and *a*'s and those faint finials. There's no doubt it's the same.

"Mr. Fanthorpe, I'm afraid I must impose upon you. I need to turn these documents over to my brother's office and insist that no one enter this room until he has said otherwise. I apologise for any awkwardness this may cause."

"Please don't mention it, Mr. Holmes, but would you mind telling me what it all means? That the documents would've been typed here hardly seems significant – in fact, that's precisely what I would expect. Did Backstead do something . . . dubious?"

"They were typed in his office, and yet he wasn't one of the Elders who signed the documents. Is that customary?"

"Well, no. I would have expected Rogers' secretary to have typed them. But why is that important?"

"Are there a limited number of typewriters in the building?"

"No, most administrative offices are equipped with one, but I must ask again – "

"As of right now, I don't have enough data to draw conclusions, but if I can eventually shed any light on this mystery for you, Mr. Fanthorpe, I assure you I will do so. Thank you for your invaluable help."

And with that, we took our leave of the bemused Mr. Fanthorpe and returned to our cab. As he climbed in, Holmes shouted the address of the nearest telegraph office and struck the ceiling twice with his stick. As we drew up to the curb, it seemed he bounded out before we had even stopped moving. In a few minutes he emerged, flourishing a telegraph.

"'*A.T.*'!" he shouted to me, smiling and then showed the cab driver the telegram. As soon as we were on our way, he explained.

"Yesterday, I telegraphed the office of Eastham and Cheswick, the firm that owns the *Paradiso*, to ask them if there was a passenger in the manifest with the initials '*A.T.*', and if there was, to send me the name and address. Knowing this telegraph station was nearest to Trinity House, I asked for the reply to be directed here and held for me. This is their timely answer. We're now on our way to the West End to meet Miss Andrea Thesselthwaite."

Our driver stopped before a neat red three-story row house on a fashionable street in Mayfair that sat back from the pavement behind a short brick wall with an iron gate. In answer to our knock, a butler opened the door for us and took our cards.

"Please tell your mistress we would like to talk to her about the *Paradiso*," said Holmes.

The man disappeared into the house and soon reemerged to lead us into the drawing room, which was warm and cosy despite the gray weather outside. A fire burned in the grate and fresh flowers adorned the various tables and piano. Miss Thesselthwaite was wearing an enchanting teal silk tea gown. Putting her knitting aside and sitting up from her couch, she greeted us cordially enough, though her apprehension was clear.

"Please, Mr. Holmes and Dr. Watson, take a seat, though I'm not sure how I can possibly tell you anything more about the accident than the crew of the yacht."

Holmes sat down in a wingback chair directly facing the woman, while I sat off to one side in an easy chair.

"It must've been quite terrifying."

"I really didn't know what was happening at the time. I was talking to my friend, Phyllis, on the deck when the ship made a sudden lurch that knocked both of us off our feet. Sailors who had started running across the deck helped us up before running off again. Then there was another lurch and a horrible sort of grinding noise. It was only at that moment that I realised something was truly wrong. But within a moment, the noise stopped and we were proceeding along just as before. I hardly had time to be afraid."

"You were very lucky," said Holmes as leaned forward in his chair. "Then, again, I suppose, if you'd been truly lucky, the lighthouse would've sounded its horn and lit your way far from those rocks. It is that which concerns me. That and the identity of '*C.B.*'."

She paled a little at this and only said, "I'm not sure what you mean."

"Those initials are on this cufflink. We discovered Sir Clive Backstead trying to get rid of it," said Holmes as he held up the jewellery. "Here is its mate – '*A.T.*' – '*Andrea Thesselthwaite*'?"

The colour had now gone from her face completely, and she replied, "Yes, Mr. Holmes, I am ashamed to say you are correct. I gave those cufflinks to Clive as gift."

"Watson, I think perhaps a little brandy? Please Miss Thesselthwaite, you can rely on our discretion completely. Nothing will come out that isn't absolutely necessary. I'm very much afraid that your life is in danger and need for you to tell me the whole story."

Taking a couple of sips of the brandy I offered her, she composed herself enough to speak.

"When I met Clive at Phyllis's party – that's my friend, Phyllis Dredgerton that I just mentioned – I thought he was the most charming and interesting man I had ever met. There seemed to be no end to his accomplishments, and over the next three weeks, I accompanied him to dinner, the theatre, the opera, and a variety of social gatherings. Finally, Phyllis's husband, James, thought it was necessary to put me fully in the picture. I had no idea that Clive was married, Mr. Holmes. He wore no ring. I'm embarrassed to say that, at this point, I was rather infatuated and reluctant to break things off. No real harm had been done. But it was also at right about this time that things began to change. I had seen how cruel he could be to his staff and how little he thought of other people. He became more and more controlling: Insisting I wear certain clothes, act a certain way around his friends, and he was always trying to coerce me into doing things I'd no desire to do. When I committed what he deemed an infraction, he would become quite vicious. There was nothing for it then but to break it off. Still, that wasn't the end. He would show up unexpectedly and threaten me to keep quiet, always accusing me of gossiping behind his back. Then, last week, he didn't appear at all. It is a habit I hope he never breaks, and I now understand why his wife doesn't come down to London."

"Did the darkened and silent lighthouse suggest anything to you?" asked Holmes.

"Yes, Clive is connected to Trinity House."

"Holmes," I interrupted, "are you saying this was an elaborate attempt to murder Miss Thesselthwaite?"

"Given that she knew of Sir Clive's influence over the lighthouses, his intention was probably only to threaten, but it could have conceivably ended with several deaths."

Miss Thesselthwaite shuddered and drank the rest of the brandy from her glass.

"A pretty Byzantine scheme to cover up an affair, is it not?" I asked.

"For a career politician? No. This scheme was probably no more complicated than any other for Sir Clive. A typed form and some signatures set all the wheels of bureaucracy turning, and people's lives hang in the balance."

"It wasn't just to hush up our relationship, Mr Holmes. Sir Clive was often indiscreet, particularly when he was drinking. Please do not ask me to be any more specific. I should only say that what I know involves government business."

"Please say no more and do not worry. Watson and I now have what we need to ensure that he never threatens you again. I'll come around again in a few days to confirm that Sir Clive has been taken care of. Thank you for talking to us."

The next day found me returning to Baker Street, having imposed upon Anstruther yet again. Holmes was hoping Sir Clive's routine from the previous week would hold and that we might be able to confront him. He had received a letter from Mycroft the day before with what he said were a few guidelines. I had picked up a yellow-backed novel at a newsstand that morning, and was still reading it by the fire while Holmes sat in his chair and engaged in some rather hectic and impatient violin playing. At about three o'clock in the afternoon, Mrs. Hudson brought in a telegram, and Holmes had jumped from the chair and plucked it from her hand before she had a chance to say a word.

"It's from Georgiopoulos. I asked him to notify us and Mycroft if he spotted Sir Clive's sailboat in its usual spot. We should head to the docks."

We reached the bustling marina within the hour and had another hour's wait before Sir Clive's boat hove into view. Fortunately, a warm front had blown in with a light rain the previous night, and the sun was shedding a welcome, though still somewhat anaemic, warmth upon the docks while Holmes had been scanning the waters with his binoculars. The boat soon docked, and while the crew went about securing the vessel, Sir Clive, dressed in a pea-coat with gray flat cap and flannel trousers, began to gather his catch and other gear. Holmes and I walked along the dock until we were beside the stern of the vessel.

"Sir Clive Backstead, I am Sherlock Holmes, and I would like to have a word with you about the business at the Pike Rock Lighthouse."

Sir Clive started, then scowled.

"I've heard of you. The other son. Some sort of detective, right? Well, I recommend you have a sniff around Trinity House or let your brother look into it. I don't know anything about it, aside from what was in the papers."

"Oh, but I *do* know something about it," said Holmes as he held up one of the bejewelled cufflinks in each hand, "and it would be in your best interests to discuss it."

Sir Clive's eyes widened briefly, but he quickly regained his composure. He then hastily descended from the boat to the dock and walked over to us.

"What do you have there, Holmes? They're very pretty, but I'm not sure why you're flashing them at me in such a dramatic fashion."

"It won't do, Sir Clive. I know they are yours, partly because they bear your initials, '*C.S.*'. It was an eccentric way of disposing of the evidence of your affair, but you stuffed them into the mouth of a sea bass, which you then fed to a cormorant, from which I was able to recover them. I've also shown them to Miss '*A.T.*', who confirmed that she gave them to you."

"B-b-but how?" he sputtered. "If it were a different time, you'd be accused of witchcraft! No one could've observed me that day – not even the crew!"

"It is my business. I also examined these forged documents from Trinity House and found out they were typed on the typewriter in your office there. The police are still searching for the three fake keepers, which should make this chain of evidence so complete that even the most inept prosecutor can obtain a conviction."

Sir Clive was visibly shaking, and I half-expected him to either start running or hurl himself at us.

"But we shall leave that for now. Please restrain yourself, sir. We aren't here to clamp you in irons. I'll settle for your word that you'll never bother Miss Thesselthwaite again. Do I have it? Good. Though Trinity House won't have anything more to do with you, I know that several of our friends in Whitehall will soon be in touch. You may be able to evade what I'd consider justice this time, but you have earned the constant scrutiny of both myself and my brother."

We all followed Holmes's gaze as he looked over his shoulder at the hulking man regarding us from a park bench further down the dock.

"Were I a criminal, such as yourself, I would fear that much more than the police."

I followed Holmes as he turned his back on the MP and walked away.

"Come, Watson. There is a pub around the corner that does an excellent Tweed Kettle. We can celebrate the end of this case there."

"But should we really have let him go like that?" I asked, trying to hide my disappointment.

"I don't like it either, but I'm afraid a higher authority has taken the matter out of our hands, my friend, and Scotland Yard's, too, no doubt. Evidently, an embattled Sir Clive would be a political liability, but a compromised Sir Clive is a potentially precious asset. Cheer up. I sincerely doubt Sir Clive will ever be a threat to anyone again."

"What about Mr. Georgiopoulos?"

"I shall return the cufflinks to him and tell him that he's welcome to them. A bad end to a torrid affair. The owner wants nothing to do with them, *et cetera*. Perhaps if we're lucky," he said with a sly smile, "he'll reimburse us for our luncheon."

The Gillette Play's the Thing!
by David Marcum

Chapter I

"**I** trust," said Sherlock Holmes over the last half of his pint, "that you've satisfied your commitment – that there will be no more of your little tales in *The Strand*." It was a statement, not a question.

His comment was unexpected at that moment, but not atypical in general.

I gave a quarter-turn of my own glass while I silently considered my reply.

Not long after the gales had assailed the eastern coast in early January 1905, when the pier at Scarborough washed away and Great Yarmouth flooded, I journeyed down to visit my friend at his Sussex cottage. Just weeks earlier, he'd been invited up to London to spend Christmas with us in Queen Anne Street, but my wife and I had known that it was very unlikely he'd make the trip, and we'd been correct. We both understood that he wasn't the type to feel lonely during the holidays, and he was quite able to entertain himself without any feelings of self-pity, but there is always a concern that arises, especially during that particular season, when thoughts turn to those we care about and we wish to have them close by.

I had set off that morning, driving south through the blue-gray twilight that had gripped the nation for a number of days. The countryside looked so different than in the warmer months when I usually made the journey, either by train or in my own automobile. When the sun was high over the vibrant summer fields and forests, it was more beautiful than could be expressed. Now the fields lay fallow and empty, with the ragged stalks of last year's crops silhouetted against the low sky, awaiting the return of spring. Often I would see distant cottages across the vacant pastures, with one or two lights showing in their windows and smoke rising from the chimneys. Sometimes a dark figure would be visible near a building, or perhaps a few animals might be silhouetted against the horizon, but mostly there was a sense of emptiness as everyone hid away from the dark day.

In spite of the bleak aspect, however, there was still an unmistakable charm and stark beauty to it too. Since Holmes's retirement a little over a year before, and move to the southern edge of the Downs, I had seen him quite a bit, both in Sussex and when he came up to London, but I realized how very little I'd made this journey during the colder parts of the year. I resolved to do better.

I arrived in early afternoon to find him researching a chemical question in the cozy little laboratory he'd set up in one corner of his study – specifically, he was analyzing which compounds were toxic to the ergot fungus, and which left it to survive. As if we were carrying on a conversation that had begun just an hour before, he explained that there were certain medico-legal aspects to his research, relating to the forced suicide of Lord Woodford the previous week. I had apparently arrived at a crisis, but within moments he had the result he'd sought and, after he'd recorded his results neatly in his laboratory notebook, he shut off his Bunsen burner, washed his hands, and settled me before the fire with a restorative whisky.

Our conversation, as it usually did, ranged from current events to past cases, and encompassed news about those whom we'd known over the years. Holmes would be turning fifty-one the following day, and I was a year or so older, so we'd arrived at that age when mortality was beginning to creep up on us. Still, it was always something of a surprise to hear that this or that person with whom we had been long acquainted had passed from natural causes – especially as we'd known so many who died over the years from violence.

After an hour we decided to adjourn to the nearby village for a pint or two. As the day was cold and the chance of rain still likely, I drove my automobile. (Typically we would walk the mile or so across the pastures behind Holmes's small farm.) We exited Holmes's property and joined the road running east-to-west along the base of Beachy Head, which was highlighted against the gray southern light and fast-scudding clouds. Within a few thousand feet we were passing below the Belle Tout Lighthouse, abandoned a couple of years before, and high above us on the left. Not much further and we reached Birling Gap and the Coast Guard houses. A right turn there, and then in less than a mile we had arrived in the small village of East Dean. Parking the vehicle, we walked into the grassy village square and so into The Tiger Inn. As we entered, familiar faces offered greetings, and soon we were in a warm corner, continuing our earlier discussions.

Holmes told me that he'd recently had a visit from Trevor and Edith Bennett, who happened to be staying in nearby Eastbourne. They brought the sad news that Edith's father, Professor Presbury, had finally succumbed to the madness that slowly overtook him following his personally detrimental experiments of a year or so before. "Apparently his undiagnosed dementia was seriously exacerbated by those injections," explained Holmes. "Bennett said that during the professor's final months

– spent alone, as his engagement to his young lady had ended – he had to be restrained completely so as to avoid doing violence to himself or harming others."

We fell silent as I considered the fate of the professor, whom Holmes and I had always referred to as "the creeping man". I doubted that his injections of monkey gland derivative had actually caused any true deleterious effects on him. The instances when he crept about displaying simian behaviors – the reason that Holmes was initially consulted – were more likely related to his declining mental condition than anything he'd put into his body. As I continued to chase these thoughts, Holmes spoke again.

"I trust that you've satisfied your commitment, and that there will be no more of your little tales in *The Strand*."

I was abruptly returned to the present with the realization that I'd been thinking of publishing those very same singular facts connected with Professor Presbury, if only to dispel once for all the ugly rumours which still agitated certain learned societies of London and the university with which he'd been associated. Of course, perceiving my thoughts had been mere child's play of deduction for Holmes.

"I'm uncertain," I replied noncommittally. "With the publication of 'The Second Stain' last month, this series is complete – but Doyle wants to keep the door open."

Holmes shook his head. "He's certainly changed his tune. As I understand it, it was he who wished to cease your joint publishing venture a dozen years ago after you'd made public the events of my encounter with the Professor at Reichenbach."

"This is true. At the time, he felt that his own works were being eclipsed by the effort he was making to get your adventures published."

"You mean to publish *your* writing – *your* efforts," Holmes countered. "He has taken advantage of you, Watson. For years he's done it. From the beginning, and all the way down the line." His tone was peeved, and he had made this familiar argument before. "For heaven's sake! He offered to be your 'Literary Agent' – a job which you could have done yourself, especially in those early days – and then it's his byline over your story! You do the work – after you lived the actual events and faced the dangers! – and he reaps the credit and takes his substantial financial cut."

It was a conversation that we'd had in countless variations over the years, and would doubtless have again. The question of my 'Literary Agent' was one of those rare situations when I felt that I did not have Holmes's full respect. His opinion of my actual published works themselves waxed and waned, and I was never quite certain where he would land on the question at any given time. He was sometimes willing to admit that the stories had helped make him more well-known than he might have been otherwise, and while he didn't like having a reputation built on "that character in *The Strand*", as he sometimes disparagingly referred to it, he did agree on rare occasions that some interesting clients had found their way to his door who might not have otherwise have done so except for knowing about him by way of my stories.

The entire topic was something of a sore spot with me. When I'd first met Doyle – Sir Arthur to everyone else, but always Doyle to me – we'd both discovered that we each had ambitions to be writers. He drifted toward historical novels, hoping (I believe) to be the modern Sir Walter Scott. I had always simply been a writer – a keeper of journals recording my own experiences. In the mid-1880's, after making records of Holmes's cases for several years, I'd finally had the gumption to polish the narrative of the Lauriston Gardens mystery, as I'd promised Holmes to do not long after we met. I'd let Doyle read it, and he noted that it needed something more – a central section that he offered to write, detailing the long-ago and far-away historical events leading to the London murders. By then I was attempting to build a medical practice, and as such I had the notion that putting my name on such a sordid little tale might somehow damage my professional credibility. Doyle, who handled the arrangements of the sale of the story to a small holiday periodical, ended up placing his own name on the cover. He made an explanation about it at the time – something about liability and perceptions and a misunderstanding with the publisher – and I accepted it – which laid the groundwork for more of the same in years to come.

Just a few years later, I finished up a second story concerning another old vengeance brought to England's shores, and it was easy enough to rationalize along the same lines. I had a practice and a reputation to consider, and even though I had written the entire second book without assistance, Doyle again did the work of placing it for publication, attending a dinner with an American publisher when I was too busy to do so myself. Afterwards, we followed the same arrangement as before, and in hindsight, I was quite naïve in allowing him to again put his name on the cover instead of mine. (The second time seemed more deliberate.)

My wife was certainly unhappy about it, stating that it was as if Tommy Ryan had fought and won the fight, but his manager was given all the credit. And she was no happier when we repeated this method the next year after that, publishing shorter versions of Holmes's investigations in a new monthly periodical, *The Strand*. Sadly, she passed away some months before the last of them appeared, so when Doyle indicated that was ready to move on to something else and disassociate himself from any more of

Holmes's adventures, I agreed, no longer having any interest in publishing further – or in much of anything, for that matter.

But at the turn of the century, Doyle had visited the West Country, where he'd run across a few people who told him of one of Holmes's more *outrè* investigations there in the autumn of '88. He came back asking me for additional details, and before I knew it, he'd talked me into writing up the affair of the Baskervilles for publication. I'd checked with Holmes about this, of course, as he'd refused to allow any further publication of his cases following his return to London in 1894 after his supposed death. By the time *The Hound* began serialization in late summer 1901, Doyle had actually achieved his goal of becoming a famous author, and we agreed to continue the previous arrangement, as his name was so associated with the stories by that point, and he could also negotiate a much larger sale based upon his reputation.

In late 1903, Holmes had chosen to move to Sussex, part of his supposed retirement to give the impression that he was no longer in active practice, as in fact he'd transitioned into something of a specialized agent for his brother Mycroft's governmental department. It was in the best interest to spread the word that he was retired, and part of this was accomplished with the publication of thirteen more tales in *The Strand*, some with discreet references to Holmes having left London. But as of December 1904, the last of these had appeared, with no firm plans for additional efforts. Doyle, however, was suddenly pressing for more of them – I suspect the money was a factor – and hearing about the late Professor Presbury had reminded me of that. It was just the sort of thing that Doyle, with his growing and unhealthy interest in the occult, might appreciate – although I was sure that he'd want to emphasize the horror of it, to the diminishment of describing Holmes's methods.

When conversing with Sherlock Holmes, one never knew when this topic might rear its head, and I certainly hadn't expected to be defending my writing, yet again, in the warm and comfortable corner of The Tiger Inn. I tried to think of a new topic to discuss, but all that entered my mind was my other reason for visiting Sussex that day, in addition to celebrating Holmes's upcoming birthday on the morrow. I took a sip and, with a deep breath, tentatively broached the subject, aware that it was just as likely to elicit a similar response from my friend as that brought about when considering my recent publications.

"I have been asked," I explained, my tone neutral, "to attend the theatre tomorrow tonight. In Eastbourne – the Royal Hippodrome."

Holmes raised an eyebrow. "I do still read the newspapers, you know. It hasn't escaped my attention what is premiering there tomorrow night, and then playing for the next two weeks – a touring company's version of

Gillette's play." He said it with the same tone that a titled lady might use to describe an East End slattern marrying her precious son.

I nodded. "I was invited by the actor playing . . . well, playing *you*. Brian Singer. And he asked if you would join me. I believe that he has a problem and needs our help."

"Really, Watson," Holmes said as he leaned back. "You could have mentioned this earlier. When were you planning on bringing it up?"

"Soon. Later this afternoon. But then we ended up talking about publishing – "

" – And only then did your thoughts turn to this appointment, which has a loose connection with your other published works, by way of that drodded play." He turned up his glass for a sip. "What is Mr. Singer's complaint? Are you certain that he doesn't simply want to lure us to the theatre in order to have our presence bestow some sort of approval upon his performance?" His voice took on a rolling theatricality. "'Ladies and gentlemen, we are *honored* tonight to have with us Mr. *Holmes* – Do rise and take a *bow*, sir! And also here is Sir Arthur's scrivener friend – You too, sir! Don't be shy!'" He finished the remains of his ale and then said, his voice returned to normal, "Will a member of the press, perhaps a friend of Mr. Singer's, be lurking in the shadows to leap out and take our photograph, standing alongside the costumed actor? Will we continue to see it when least expected for years to come as it's used for his personal publicity, until both the photograph and we too have faded beyond visibility or interest?"

I thought he was being unnecessarily sarcastic, but I bit my tongue, hoping that he might be lured into accompanying me. But perhaps that was the wrong approach.

"Here is his letter," I said, pulling the missive from my pocket. "You can decide his veracity for yourself."

Holmes took is and, as expected, he first examined the envelope. I had long ago learned to do the same thing when receiving a letter, and while I generally don't see a fraction of what he does, I knew that what he observed was fairly straightforward. Apparently Holmes agreed, because he quickly pulled out the single sheet without comment, looked it over front and back, and then read it to himself.

"Singularly uninformative," he concluded, dropping it onto the table. "He identifies himself, apologizes for the intrusion on your time, indicates that he is in some unspecified danger, and then asks if we can meet with him tomorrow afternoon in his rented lodgings before the performance. Have you had no other communication with him?"

"I telephoned the theatre yesterday after receiving the letter. He was in rehearsal but broke away to speak with me. He didn't provide any more information than what he wrote, instead preferring to discuss it in person. He's being harassed, he said, by someone he knows. He believes that several attempts have been made on his life, but the incidents may have been accidental. When pressed, he wouldn't provide any further details. He simply hopes that we will meet with him tomorrow."

"If he's in danger, why not sooner?"

I turned over a hand. "I informed him that I planned to drive down here today, and asked about meeting with him this afternoon, but he seemed to feel that tomorrow would do just as well. The play doesn't open until tomorrow night, and apparently they're busy with rehearsals, and also becoming accustomed to the theatre."

Holmes shook his head. "A drowning man doesn't typically ask to wait and have the rope thrown to him tomorrow. I reiterate my fear that this is just some ploy to get us to the play."

"Possibly. He did say that after we met, he'd make sure we had tickets for the best seats in the house."

Holmes nodded and leaned back. "That's it, then – We'll meet and talk, and it will be some contrived excuse that amounts to nothing. We'll reassure him – all part of his plan – and then, when we're in our seats and least expecting it, a spotlight will find us and, before you know it, we'll be bullied into coming onto the stage."

I finished my ale and, after a moment of silence, said, "We will meet with him, of course."

Holmes's mouth tightened, but in good-humored resignation rather than irritation, and he nodded. "I suppose so."

"And I do wish to attend the performance," I added. "I haven't seen it in four or five years – since Gillette finished up at the Lyceum. I'm curious to see how it plays in the provinces."

"Why not? If we're singled out for special attention, it can only reinforce the notion that I'm permanently rusticating here, and no one will expect to find me anywhere else. Perhaps I'll dodder onto the stage and shock everyone with my feeble helplessness." And he then gave that silent laugh of his which so often boded ill for someone.

I nodded, took our glasses, and went to the bar for refills, considering what Holmes had just said.

In late 1903, a combination of circumstances – which I do not propose to recount here – had led Holmes, then only forty-nine years old, to announce his retirement. Some of what happened then was personal, but a great deal of Holmes's decision was also related to the perceived threat, understood particularly by his Holmes's brother Mycroft, that the European situation was becoming more and more tangled, and thus fraught with peril for England. Many politicians refused to comprehend this, while others in the government understood all too well what might possibly occur in the coming years.

For quite a while, Mycroft had been urging Holmes to turn his attentions from those "petty problems of the police courts", as he liked to call them, and focus his energies and talents on the plots and plans devised by the British Government to prepare for upcoming threats. It must be admitted that Holmes had a special skill in such areas, as demonstrated by his recovery of the Bruce-Partington submarine plans, or more recently, the capture of the deathbed visitor to the woman whom we'd spent a lifetime believing to be our Queen, and the subsequent retrieval of the two items removed from the woman's personal lock-box – one of which had the absolute power to immediately topple more than one European kingdom. (I'm believe that it was the latter case that finally turned Holmes around to Mycroft's way of thinking, and it's a narrative that I'm absolutely and forever forbidden to record.) When certain personal matters occurred in 1903, Holmes realized that he must assume new obligations. The die was cast, and he threw himself into his new life.

I believe that he was happy during his times in Sussex, and he certainly stayed busy – keeping his bees with a passion I wouldn't have expected, delving into various scientific researches, accepting Mycroft's urgent missions, and continuing to take on the occasional private investigations for the occasional someone in need – often with my help when I could manage to get away, or when he happened to be in London. Our invitation to the Royal Hippodrome on the morrow would be one such affair.

After another half-hour or so, we departed from The Tiger Inn and returned to Holmes's cottage, where a warm meal awaited us. We had further discussions regarding old cases and new, and a little ongoing matter that would require Holmes to visit London within the next few weeks. He indicated that while he was there, he planned stay for a time in the old rooms in Baker Street, which he had retained following his decampment to the coast for when he needed a temporary base from which to carry out his inquiries in the capital. We didn't make further mention of our meeting tomorrow with the actor playing the part of Holmes, because without data, what reason did we have to speculate further?

It was still early when I went up to my room. Holmes had turned his attention back to his chemical researches, with no indication that he planned to stop for the night – very much like old times.

Chapter II

The next day passed quietly enough, and I took advantage of my holiday to relax, sleeping late and then sitting and reading by the fire in Holmes's study. He was up early, as usual, taking care of various chores around the small farm, and then resuming his research.

He was already outside when I arose, so it was only later that morning when I was able to wish him Happy Birthday and present the small gift I'd brought from London – a package of his favorite tobacco, the strong shag from Bradley's that he so favored. He acknowledged it with simple but sincere thanks. He packed some to take with him just before we set out for Eastbourne and our meeting with Mr. Singer.

We departed about half-an-hour before our scheduled appointment, driving east along the coast road past The Gables, the well-known coaching establishment, and then circling Bullock Down to our left. Upon reaching Holywell I turned right, just before Warren Hill, and so entered the maze of Eastbourne streets, working my way steadily toward our destination. We stayed just inland, going straight when we could. Luckily, pedestrians in early January are quite scarce, and not long after we passed the pier, we reached the theatre. I gave it a glance as we went by, but almost immediately Holmes advised me to turn left into a winding warren of lanes and alleys, and within moments we found ourselves before a small but tidy house just a couple of streets away. This, then, was where Singer was staying for the time that the play would be rehearsed and performed.

The street was empty, with nary a vehicle or pedestrian in sight, so I pulled to one side and shut off the engine. We exited and stood for a moment, looking at the plain two-story brick building, adjoined to similar-looking structures up and down the narrow lane. Then Holmes pulled his coat tighter, glanced at me, sighed, and stepped the short distance to the door.

Seconds after he had rung the bell, we were greeted by a beaming lady no more than four feet in height, and nearly as round as she was tall. She looked to be in her sixties, and her white hair contrasted with her prominent cheeks, resembling red apples. She looked up at us with her round pink face wreathed in a welcoming smile and wheezed, "It *is* you!" Then she stepped back and invited us in. "Young Mr. Singer told me that Mr. *Holmes* and Dr. *Watson* were planning to call. I had no idea he knew such noted figures, but I supposed that since he's the star of the play . . . Such an honor, gentlemen! Such an *honor!*"

She bustled around us to shut the door while indicating where we could hang our coats and hats, all the while chattering about how the neighbors would be so jealous, and then pivoting effortlessly to inform us

303

of the other visitors of note she'd entertained over the years, all apparently actors of one sort or another – Edward Righton and Wybert Reeve, Arthur Wontner and William Henry Pennington, to name a few that I recall her mentioning. Though we'd been there less than a minute, she was already deep into a reminiscence of one Henry Spry when Holmes raised a hand.

"If we may, Mrs. – "

"Spence," she replied. "Eula Spence. Widow of Mr. John Bennett Spence, formerly of London, gone these twenty years. He trod the boards as well. Who knows what heights he might have reached before his untimely passing? One of the greats, gentleman! Even from a young age, he was one of the greats! Thanks heavens we had set up this lodging house before his illness began, and before he departed. I can't count the times that – "

Holmes glanced at a nearby wall clock. "Our appointment with Mr. Singer is overdue," he said. "Might you direct us to him?"

"What? Oh, certainly. He wasn't feeling well, the poor lad, and came home early from the rehearsal to take a nap. I sent for the doctor – he didn't want me to, but I insisted. After the passing of my husband, Mr. Spence, I'm ever-so careful, you know. Gone twenty years! One never knows, does one? In any case, Mr. Singer said that when you arrived to please join him in his room. Upstairs, one floor. Middle door on the right."

We thanked her and she continued talking, but this time to herself as she turned and moved off toward a closed door beyond the foot of the stairs.

The house was very quiet, and the sound of the squeaking steps as we ascended seemed excessively loud. Upon reaching the first floor, we found a dim hallway stretching toward the back of the house. It was lit only by a window behind us, over the stairs we had just climbed and facing the street, and another at the far end. In between were just six closed doors, three on either side. From the overhead transoms, I could see that all the lights were out, except for our destination. We stepped to the middle door, as directed, and Holmes knocked. There was no answer.

A second knock resulted in the same non-response. Holmes, being who he was, had no compunction at reaching for the door knob and turning it. It was unlocked. He pushed it open and I involuntarily gave a small cough as the faint smell of smoke, unmistakably from a recent gunshot, wafted out.

Holmes glanced at me and then stepped inside. I joined him, pushing the door softly shut. Then I locked it with the key that was protruding from the keyhole on the inner side.

I knew that Holmes would prefer to examine the room first before others disturbed any clues, but I had a duty to perform as a physician. "I need to check him," I said. "There's a chance he's still alive."

"Step carefully," Holmes replied. Then, as an afterthought, he asked, "Do you think she'll bring tea?"

"Likely so." I walked carefully in a straight line to the narrow bed, where the body of a man was lying on his back. I knew that Holmes would be able to identify the marks of my footsteps as he sorted the various telling signs in the room, but I didn't want to add any more confusion than necessary to his task.

The room was illuminated by a gaslight on the wall near the door, and another above the bed. It was a humble space, and the fact that Singer had stayed here, instead of somewhere nicer, indicated to me that his stature in the theatrical community, despite his role as the leading man, had been rather small. There was a bed and small table holding an empty glass, and I leaned to sniff it. The scent was unmistakable. Nearby was an open wardrobe with several bureau drawers in the lower half, a small table suitable for eating, and two straight chairs beside it. There was a low bookshelf near the door, with just a couple of shelves filled with what had looked to be darkened and old volumes from many decades past. There were no windows, as the building was squeezed between two others of identical construction on each side. A small fireplace was on one wall, its chimney no doubt shared by the adjacent room farther from the stairs toward the rear of the building. The room was warm, but the small coal fire had gone out.

Beside the bed were a pair of patent leather shoes, apparently removed by the man when he lay down. He was on his back and a quilt was pulled up to his chest, with his arms lying relaxed on top. A pillow was under his head, and another lay across his upturned face, hiding it from us. The white linen of the top pillow was marred by a dark irregular stain, sloping down to a small darker indentation. In Holmes's company I had seen this before: A gun had been fired through the pillow, muffling the sound but blackening the pillow cover with a powder burn. I glanced at the man's chest. There was no movement. He was most certainly dead.

While Holmes stood on the other side of the bed, leaning over to watch carefully in the stance of a predatory bird, I carefully lifted the pillow to reveal the awful site underneath. The man's features were horribly marred by a bullet hole over his right eye. Death had certainly been instantaneous. From the lack of blood on the pillow beneath his head, the bullet had remained in his skull, no doubt ricocheting multiple times and doing massive damage to the brain. The right eye itself had been terribly expelled from its socket by the sudden expanding pressure of the

305

entering projectile just above it. It was nearly unrecognizable, while the left eye stared into eternity, its surface having that peculiar and final flat film.

"How long?" Holmes asked softly.

The skin was cool. "Hard to tell, since the fire has gone out."

"That wasn't long ago," Holmes said. "The coals are still warm." I hadn't seen him examine them – but then, the sight of the body had taken much of my attention.

"Possibly an hour. Mrs. Spence or the doctor can confirm when they last saw him."

"Go down and seek her out – prevent her from coming in here, and have her send for the doctor. Tell her that Singer's condition has worsened – a fair assessment – but share nothing else."

I nodded and left him to his further examination of the room. Downstairs, Mrs. Spence was in fact completing the assembly for something approaching a high tea. She began to babble once again, something about a recent visit by the noted Thomas Weldon Anderson, and she was able to talk for far longer than I wanted when I was forced to interrupt her and ask that she send once more for the doctor.

"Dr. Honner?" she asked. "But aren't *you* a doctor?"

"I wish to consult with him about Mr. Singer."

"Oh – Isn't he getting better?"

"No. Is Dr. Honner very far?"

"Not far at all – just two houses up." She wiped her hands and pushed the tea makings back from the edge of the counter. "I'll be back as soon as I can."

I followed her to the hallway, noting that she had suddenly become very quiet. As she put on her coat, I went back upstairs, pausing halfway to look back and verify that she had left the house. I wondered if I'd just spoken to the murderer and then requested that she leave the premises.

I found Holmes in one of the chairs by a table. He looked up. "I've already checked – all of the other rooms on this floor are currently empty. Four appear to be completely untenanted, and the resident of the fifth hasn't been in since last night – the accumulated dust, though insignificant, is enough."

He nodded to a small and sturdy strongbox open on the table beside him. He was thumbing through a stack of letters, apparently retrieved from it.

"Singer was being threatened," he explained, waving one of them. "There are over two-dozen of these, stretching back several months, and all mailed to Singer in care of different theaters in different cities – no doubt wherever he was appearing at the time." He set the letters down on the table. "They're quite vague – simply demanding the return '*of what is mine*' or '*what you stole from me*', and promising punishment."

"He likely thought of asking for your help when the play moved to Eastbourne," I added. "After all – he was playing you on stage, so he may have taken the time to find out a bit about you, including that your 'retirement' is located nearby."

"Very possible."

"And the strongbox?" I asked.

"That tells its own tale," he said. "It has a very good lock – it took me nearly a half-a-minute to open it." I knew that he rarely went anywhere without his lock-picking tools. "Apparently it defeated the person who previously tried to get in – I wasn't the first to try. There were very fresh scratches on the lock, showing that someone recently tried to retrieve the box's contents – almost certainly right after the murder."

"Was there anything else in it besides the letters?"

"Yes. A number of bearer bonds and deeds for properties in the north which will need sorting when we have more time. The box was hidden in that drawer at the bottom of the wardrobe. The drawer's lock also had scratches in the keyhole – fresh ones, and that time the intruder was more successful, as the drawer was opened to reveal the box."

"It isn't very big – no more than eighteen inches long. Why didn't he – or she – simply carry it away after the murder?"

"Perhaps it was still too bulky, and the murderer was afraid it would be seen, or raise questions. Possibly the killer panicked and fled when the box wouldn't easily open, before obtaining what he came for. And I see you've jumped to the assumption that the person who sought the box and its contents was the murderer."

"I think it's a safe leap to make."

"I would tend to agree – provisionally."

I looked around. "Where are the keys – to the wardrobe and the box?"

"I made a quick search while you were downstairs. They aren't in any obvious locations, and they weren't in the Singer's pockets. They're likely hidden somewhere here in the room – he wouldn't have left them at the theatre."

"Are you satisfied that the dead man *is* Singer?"

"I think it's a safe assumption. He looks the part."

I glanced toward the body on the bed, the head now uncovered, while the blood-stained portion of the pillow that had been lying against the dead man's face was turned upward beside him. From this angle, without the terrible distraction of the bullet wound or the distended eyeball, I could see that there was indeed a strong resemblance to my friend. Singer was tall and lean, and the angularity of his skull, along with a strong jaw and high forehead, gave him quite the resemblance to a reclining Sherlock Holmes. He would have been a good choice to portray the detective on stage in Gillette's play.

"Has the doctor been summoned?" Holmes asked, interrupting my study.

"He has. I'm told he only lives two houses away, so he should be here soon. You haven't found the keys – did you discover anything else of interest?"

"Several things. You will have noticed that the empty glass on the table smells of medication – likely something given to Singer related to his sudden illness."

"Laudanum," I agreed.

Holmes continued. "I believe that the killer entered quietly and that Singer simply never woke up, probably due to the medication. The pillow was quickly placed over his head and the gun was fired. It's very unlikely that the killer then lifted the pillow to look at the dead man, or to verify that he was dead. The blood stains on the underside of the pillow are completely centered around the bullet hole in the pillow covering. There is no smearing, meaning that the pillow was left to lie where it had been during the murderous shot. Death was instantaneous, and there was no excessive bleeding. This fact might be of use to us.

"Other than our footprints, I've identified four other individuals who have been in this room of late: The dead man, as matched by the shoes beside his bed, and his other pairs in the wardrobe. A woman with small feet and a very short tread – clearly the landlady, Mrs. Spence. There is another who has walked around both sides of the bed – This was certainly the doctor – randomly dropping Trichinopoly cigar ashes, such as those produced by our friend Thorndyke. Then he tossed the stub of his cigar into the fireplace, overpitching the grate."

He reached into his pocket and removed one of the small glassine envelopes he always carried for the placement of evidence. "From the marks on the cigar's remains, this man's front right central incisor is shifted slightly ahead of the matching left tooth. Identifying him will be child's play. This man left ashes on the bedside table, probably when preparing the medication, and he seems to have been on both sides of the bed, back and forth, occasionally treading across the ashes he dropped – probably as he carried out his examination. When he arrives, we can confirm these facts."

"And the fourth person?"

"Almost certainly the murderer – for his curiously small footprints and right inward twist appear to have approached the bed directly from the door. He then went to the wardrobe, and nowhere else. Those footprints are the most recent, treading across all the others. The dead man and the landlady were here first, followed by the doctor, who treated Singer after Mrs. Spence's departure. Then the doctor left, having conveniently dropped ashes throughout the room, and sometime later the murderer arrived, leaving his footprints over the top of the other three. Possibly not since the Biblical Daniel scattered the ashes to trap the priests and diminish the dragon have ashes been so useful – they help to establish the order of what happened here."

I considered pointing out that he had also made use of ashes in a similar way just a decade or so before, when he'd used them to locate the hiding place of Professor Coram's estranged wife. But before I could speak, we both heard a subtle and nearly imperceptible noise, as if a door had shut somewhere in the big quiet house. Holmes glanced my way. "She's back with the doctor. Go and bring him up, but keep her downstairs. Let her think Singer is simply ill. I have an idea – quite a long-shot, but if it works . . . ."

I left the room and was halfway down the steps when I met a grizzled fat man carrying a doctor's bag on his way up. Just behind him trundled Mrs. Spence.

Introducing myself, I truthfully explained that Mr. Singer seemed to have taken a turn for the worse, and asked if Mrs. Spence would mind waiting downstairs while we carried out our medical examination. I could see that she wanted to continue upstairs with us, and to assert her rights as the landlady, but my firm expectation that she would comply with my request seemed to convince her, and she nodded and she exited the stage, muttering.

"I'm Dr. Honner," explained the man as he moved up the steps to where our eyes were at a level while offering his hand. He looked to be in his late sixties, with shaggy iron-gray hair and matching bushy eyebrows and beard. He was about five-and-a-half feet tall, and plump. As expected, the front of his suit had evidence of cigar ash spilled across it. "I'm not sure how he could have gotten worse." His voice was rough, and I soon determined that he had a habit of clearing his throat often. "He seemed to have nothing more than the beginnings of a head cold. He was rather stressed – opening night nerves, I gathered – so I gave him something to relax."

I didn't like to judge Dr. Honner's medical skills on such scanty evidence, but I had to consider that the young man had been prescribed a strong-enough dose of medication to sleep through his own murder. Additionally, the smell of liquor hanging about my fellow medico tended to bias my thinking quite a bit. I introduced myself and asked, "What did you give him?"

A quick look crossed his face, as if suddenly cautious because questions were being asked. Then, apparently recalling that I too was a physician, he replied, "A bit of laudanum mixed with water. He seemed to be a stressed," he repeated. "I thought it would be just the ticket."

To myself, I questioned whether it was just a "bit", and also the man's judgement and the efficacy of his treatment, as the actor, expecting visitors momentarily and then needing to be at the top of his game for his opening-night performance just a few hours later, probably hadn't wanted something that would put him to sleep to such an extent – so soundly that his murderer could enter the room unnoticed and carry out his fatal task.

By that point we were outside the door to Singer's room, and as Honner reached for the knob, I laid a hand on his arm. "I want to let you know, Doctor, that Singer is dead."

His eyes widened, and I felt his stance stiffen. "*Dead!*" he hissed, and I knew that he was wondering if his treatment had killed the actor. If I'd been the attending physician, I might have done the same, instantly recalling the prescribed medicine and wondering what factors I might have missed. I nodded but hurried to clarify.

"He's been murdered. You're the first to be informed, before we call the police."

"We?" he asked. "Who is 'we'?"

"Sherlock Holmes is inside. We discovered the body when we arrived to keep an appointment."

He nodded. "He mentioned that someone was stopping by." He glanced at the door. "Can I see him?"

I reached and opened the door, letting him precede me inside.

Holmes was standing by the wardrobe, holding one of Singer's suits. I assumed that he was looking for the missing keys, but I was to learn that I was incorrect. He was checking its size.

Dr. Honner glanced that way, but then he stepped to the bed and leaned over. I heard him gasp at what he saw.

Holmes hung the suit back in the wardrobe and turned toward the doctor. "What time did you see him?" he asked with any preamble.

"What?" Honner refocused his attention and turned our way. "What? About two hours ago."

"And we've been here for nearly half-an-hour," said. "The murderer was here between your departure and our arrival." I had Honner repeat what he'd told me concerning his summons and subsequent treatment.

"Did he give any indication what was causing him stress?" Holmes asked.

310

"Not a thing – but it's not unusual, you know. For these actors. They work themselves up into such states. I'm able to help a great many of them."

I could only imagine how many actors found themselves addicted to laudanum after being *helped* by Honner – but this wasn't the time to address that question.

"I have an idea," said Holmes, speaking more to himself than the two of us. "I noticed from the wires outside that Mrs. Spence has a telephone. I'm going to notify Inspector Bardle. In the meantime, could the two of you wrap up the body in the quilt?"

Then he slipped out of the room, leaving me and a very confused Eastbourne doctor. I started to explain that Holmes had his methods, which often only he initially understood, but the man raised a hand. "I've read your stories, Doctor. I once worked with a man of similar temperament – Dr. Bell in Edinburgh. I believe you know him as well. Men like him and Mr. Holmes have minds that race far ahead on faster tracks than the rest of us. I have no fears that what he's doing is for the overall good. I simply have one question: Why am I so immediately included in your councils? Why am I not a suspect as well?"

I indicated that we should begin wrapping Singer in his temporary shroud, and as we did so, I explained about the evidence of the cigar ash, and how Holmes had determined that another man had entered the room following the doctor's departure. Honner nodded. "Thank God I'm a cigar smoker, then," he said. "Something good has finally come of it."

At that moment Holmes returned and, seeing our progress, nodded. "I've taken time to quickly re-examine this floor now that I've identified the killer's footprints. He isn't the other tenant – that man's feet are much larger. The killer didn't go anywhere else on this floor except from the top of the stairs to this room, and then back again to depart."

"Do you think that Mrs. Spence let him in?"

Dr. Honner started to protest the lady's innocence, but Holmes raised a hand. "It seems that he was being very quiet. Some of his footsteps in the hall and here in the bedroom show that he walked on tiptoe, and he took care to fire the gun through the pillow. If the landlady had helped him, she could have told him that no one else was home besides Singer, and there would have been no need to be so careful."

He stepped to the wardrobe and turned to face us. "I managed to use the telephone without Mrs. Spence overhearing me. I spoke to the inspector, and he's in agreement with my plan. Place Mr. Singer's body under the bed, along with the bloody pillow, and re-make the bed to look as if it hasn't been used."

"To fool the killer if he returns for the strongbox?" I asked.

"No, simply to hide the body away for a while so that Mrs. Spence won't find him and summon the authorities, causing a distraction from our other plans."

"Which are?" I said with effort, as by then we'd placed the body on the floor and were pushing him underneath the bed.

"The killer didn't get what he wanted," said Holmes. He then summarized for the doctor the evidence of the strongbox and the papers within. "It's likely he's watching the house to see if he can get another chance – or to see if the body has been discovered. Instead, I intend to decoy him elsewhere."

As he spoke, Holmes began to change out of his own clothing and into one of the dead man's suits – the one that he'd been holding when we entered. Within two minutes, he had not only donned the new outfit, but seemed to have acquired a new personality as well.

"Of course I never met Mr. Singer," he explained, "or saw him in life, but I know the type. He looked to be in his thirties and, as an actor, he would have always projected a certain energy and attitude." Holmes then practiced strolling around the room with a vim and vigor that I hadn't seen from him in several years. I always thought of him as rather ageless – and he certainly seemed to be aging at a slower rate than me – but seeing him display this new vivacity, looking so much like the young man in his mid-twenties that I'd first met nearly a quarter-century earlier, reminded me of just how much time had passed.

"Conspicuously carrying the box, I shall make a show of departing for the theatre in time for my call, and with any luck I'll lure the killer to follow me into our trap."

I did not miss what he'd said.

"Your 'call'? Do you intend to take Singer's place on stage – *playing yourself?*"

He nodded. "If necessary – depending on how long it takes our killer to make his move."

"But Mr. Holmes," countered Honner, "what makes you think that you can fool the murderer into believing that Singer is still alive?"

Holmes explained how he'd determined that the pillow was never raised after the bullet was fired through it – and thus the killer hadn't confirmed Singer's death. "Or so it seems. We shall use that to our advantage. And if he does know somehow that Singer died, it will unnerve him to see the man walk out – and carrying the strong box that he killed to obtain."

"If he's watching," I said, "he will have seen the two of us arrive – and also Mrs. Spence go to summon Dr. Honner."

"But he won't know what any of that means. Two strangers entered – possibly tenants. A man with a doctor's bag – to treat the actor who didn't die after all. All he'll know for sure is that Singer – the man whom he thinks he killed – will depart for the theatre in just a few minutes, carrying the box that he'd kill for. Since I arrived as Sherlock Holmes and will leave as Brian Singer, that should be enough to fool him."

"But what's to stop him from shooting you in the street and taking the box?" asked the doctor.

"I will lure him," replied Holmes, "but I don't intend to let him catch me!"

Then, satisfied that the body was hidden and the room reasonably restored to normality, he ushered us quietly into the hall. Pulling out his nipper from his lock kit, he carefully inserted it through the keyhole and, using it to grasp the end of the key which was still in the lock, he turned it so that the room was locked from the inside. Entry, if attempted, would be that much more difficult.

And so it was that I was dispatched downstairs to keep Mrs. Spence, whom I found in the kitchen at the back of the house, distracted while Holmes would be let out of the front door by Dr. Honner, who would remain in the shadows. As I tried to hold her attention, the little landlady was clearly curious, as what was supposed to have been a simple visit by two middle-aged gentlemen to one of her lodgers had escalated into a summons for the neighboring doctor – his second visit of the day – followed by Holmes's use of her telephone, and then the conversation which she'd been unable to overhear. I vaguely informed her that Dr. Honner had given the actor additional medication to ready him for his performance, and that he was departing even as we spoke.

We heard the thump of the closing front door and I nodded. "Mr. Singer must have just left for the theatre. I should be going too. Thank you very much for your hospitality."

She glanced toward the tea tray, still in the process of elaborate assembly, with a look of disappointment. Without waiting for the chance of further conversation, I nodded and left the kitchen.

I feared that she might trail along behind me, but she remained where I'd left her, and I found Honner at the front door. Beside him, the curtain covering the small window beside the door was pulled slightly back, as if someone had been looking through it. He nodded and whispered, "Mr. Holmes set off with a brisk stride, and in mere seconds, a man revealed himself in the areaway across the street – his head popped up and he watched intently until Mr. Holmes reached the corner. Then he came out and set off down the street in the same direction."

I nodded. The bait was taken. Pulling on my own coat and hat, and also retrieving Holmes's Inverness and fore-and-aft cap from the stand, I indicated that we should depart. We slipped quietly outside, pulling the door shut without any noise.

I started to thank the doctor and say goodbye, but he held up a hand. "If you don't mind, I'd like to accompany you. I . . . I feel a bit of responsibility for my poor young patient."

He might have said more, but I simply nodded in agreement, and we set off for the theatre in silence.

Chapter III

Dr. Honner and I walked through several short streets, and I was always alert for signs of Holmes or the man who was following him – along with the possibility of sudden violence if the man tried to attack Holmes and steal the box from him. Yet we encountered nothing, not even other pedestrians on that cold January afternoon, and in just a few minutes we had reached the theatre.

I had seen it before during other trips to visit Holmes, but had paid little attention to it. Rather inauspicious, it might have been a long storefront. The street before it was narrow, and the building, possibly a hundred feet or so long, was only three stories. The upper floors were represented by plain uninteresting windows, and along the street were four or five entrances to small shops. At the center of the building was another door, this one to the theatre's box office. It was to this that we walked at a steady pace. We were thirty feet from reaching it when Honner whispered, "There. In the shop entrance two doors down on the left. It's the man who just followed Mr. Holmes."

In the dim evening light I couldn't see much, except that he was in some sort of cream-colored coat and that his bald head, looking much the same color as his outer garment and giving the illusion that they were all of one piece, was unprotected by a hat. I had the sense that he was tall, but I only had a glimpse, and then we had entered the theatre.

At that time, it was slightly over twenty years old, but the previous year, it had received quite a bit of attention in the form of new improvements and judiciously applied paint. Originally opened as the *Theatre and Royal Opera House*, in 1904 it received its new name, *The Royal Hippodrome Theatre*, as well as a new focus in the type of entertainment presented. I was sure that having a performance of Gillette's play in January, when the tourist season was at its ebb, was part of the management's new strategy to encourage visitors during the colder months of the year.

Inside, Dr. Honner seemed quite familiar with the layout, and he took me through the building and along several winding passages that seemed to double back on themselves until we reached a dim hallway containing a row of dressing rooms. He paused at the first on the right and knocked. "This would be Singer's," he explained. "He was the star, you see."

The door opened to a narrow gap, and then, when we were recognized, wider to allow our entry. Sherlock Holmes nodded as we passed and shut the door behind us. There were two other men in the room. One I recognized: Inspector Bardle of the Sussex Constabulary – a steady and solid man who watched the world with thoughtful, if bovinian, eyes.

The other man was introduced as Mr. Pilsbury, the theatrical company's manager. He had a most troubled look on his face. "We don't have an understudy," he complained. "The cast is already doubling some of the parts. I suppose that Hinkle, who plays Moriarty, might be persuaded to be Holmes, and Willis, who plays McTague, can take on Moriarty, but – Oh, that won't work! We'll have to cancel the show!"

"That won't be necessary," said Holmes. "I can take the lead."

This was met with silence – and a raised eyebrow on the part of the inspector. I myself had long maintained that the stage lost a fine actor when Holmes became a specialist in crime. More recently, I recalled the night before Old Baron Dowson was hanged, when Holmes and I had been summoned to his cell so that he could provide the final pieces that helped explain his motive for murder. After he'd extracted a promise to keep the truth from his granddaughter, he'd relaxed, and even praised Holmes, stating that what the law had gained when he became a consulting detective, the stage had lost.

"Mr. Holmes," said Pilsbury, apparently not quite sure how to respond, "do . . . do you think you could? The curtain rises in less than an hour. It's a long script, and Sherlock Holmes – that is, your character – is on stage for a substantial amount of time."

"I've seen the play before," said Holmes, "and I was an actor once, long ago. I perfected the trick then of quickly memorizing lines. I was in the Sasanoff Company twenty-five years ago. We only performed Shakespeare, and we frequently changed from play to play, with very little time to learn the next one."

"Then . . . then that would be exceptional!" cried Pilsbury. "The publicity will be wonderful. I'll just have time to notify the newspaper – "

"You misunderstand," Holmes said, cutting him off. "My participation must remain unknown. I will be playing the part of Brian Singer, who just happens to be portraying Sherlock Holmes. We hope to lure the killer into the theatre to obtain the strong box – apparently the motive for the murder. Hopefully he believes that I'm here – as Singer –

315

and he will be confused as to why the man he murdered is still among the living." He glanced toward me, and I nodded.

"A man was hiding across the street. He surfaced as soon as you left, and he's now across from the theatre, lurking in a doorway."

"Presumably," added the inspector, speaking for the first time, "he's more interested in the contents of the box you brought than in killing Singer for a second time – so he'll be back here where we'll set our trap, instead of trying to kill you while you're on stage, Mr. Holmes."

"But what will I tell the cast?" asked Pilsbury.

"Let them know that Singer is indisposed, and that I've agreed to step in. You can say my name is – "

"Presbury Roylott," I interrupted.

Holmes smiled. "Presbury Roylott – Exceptional! But whatever you do, don't announce the substitution to the audience."

It seemed a simple-enough plan, and Pilsbury went to inform the cast that there would be a change for the night. In the meantime, Bardle set about placing his plain-clothed officers in different spots in the theatre, each briefed on what to expect and whom to be watching for. Holmes used what time he had to make a quick but intense study of the script. However, he took a moment to discuss the matter when I brought him a cup of hot coffee.

"Did you find Singer's keys?" I asked. "When I went downstairs to meet Dr. Honner?"

Holmes nodded. "He'd made a small incision at the bottom of the bedspread and hidden them there. I've seen the same thing done at times where something small was hidden in the bottoms of window drapes – but that room had no windows, of course."

"I wonder what would have happened if the killer hadn't followed you here," I said. "After all, he was likely watching when he saw us enter – followed a short time by the doctor." I nodded to Holmes's coat and hat, lying on a nearby table where I'd left them. "You do cut a rather distinctive figure. Surely the killer would have been suspicious seeing us visit there."

"Ah, you perhaps give too much credit to our supposed fame," was the reply. "Why should the murderer suppose that we were there to visit Singer? There are other rooms for rent. We could have been there to see any one of those tenants, or to visit the landlady herself. The killer might have been aware that Singer was playing me, but he wouldn't necessarily know that he was actually *seeing* the real Sherlock Holmes when we arrived at the house."

Something else had been bothering me. "Holmes," I asked, "are you certain of the footprint evidence? It occurred to me that Dr. Honner says he saw the man across the street when you left the house – but I didn't.

316

And then, when we arrived at the theatre, it was him again who pointed out a man standing in a distant doorway and identified him. We only have his word that there *was* a man across the street from the house. Might Honner have been the killer after all? For some reason unknown to us, he may have been writing the threatening letters. He saw his chance today when summoned by Mrs. Spence. He tricked Singer into drinking the too-strong laudanum, and then he shot him. Afterwards, he tried to get into the strongbox and failed."

"And the other set of footprints?" asked Holmes with a smile. "The ones overlaying those of Honner and the rest?"

I realized that my theory, never very strong, was breaking down. "Perhaps he obtained another set of shoes to make fake footprints?" Even as I said it, I understood that it was ridiculous.

"You're right to question, Watson," said Holmes. "It never hurts to pull every thread. But in this case, I believe that the doctor's veracity can be accepted." He finished the last of his coffee. "No, the last set of footprints were real."

Then he went back to his studies. Soon he would need to apply makeup – to look like Brian Singer's version of looking like Sherlock Holmes. I excused myself and went to confer with the inspector.

"He's here," he whispered. "Based on the doctor's description, just such a man bought a ticket and entered ten minutes ago."

"Where is he now?"

Bardle looked suddenly sheepish. "We lost him when he came inside. He slipped backstage, and could be anywhere. But we believe that he'll head for the dressing room as soon as Mr. Holmes takes the stage – and that's when we'll have him."

There was nothing to do but wait for it. A search through the theatre might alert our prey long before we found him, spooking him into fleeing before we could take him. With the approach of the curtain, I had no choice but to take my own place, hidden behind some flats near stage right, not far from the entrance to the dressing room passage.

Long before I met Sherlock Holmes, I'd had some familiarization with the theatre. As a medical student in London of the 1870's, I became something of a stage-door lurker – not something I'm proud of, to be sure, but nevertheless a formative part of my young adulthood. As such, I was often backstage, so the inner workings of the theatre, and the off-stage behaviors of the actors and actresses, was no surprise to me. Of course, through my long association with Holmes, there had been many calls to theatres, ranging from interviews to the investigation of terrible and bloody murders.

I'd come to know a great many actors as well, so it was no curiosity when I'd been approached by William Gillette, the famed American performer, writer, and producer, about his interest in presenting a play about Sherlock Holmes. Sometime in the mid-1890's, unknown to me, Doyle had taken it upon himself to write a five-act play about my friend (and me, I presume), and had been in touch with the famed American producer, Frohman. The latter apparently didn't care much for Doyle's finished product, and suggested that William Gillette rewrite it – as well as play the lead.

Gillette was a handsome fellow, but he didn't look much like Holmes, whose likeness was so well captured in the illustrations by Sidney Paget in *The Strand*. (When Doyle and I first began publishing with the magazine in mid-1891, I was adamant that Holmes be correctly portrayed in the *Strand* illustrations. I had no such influence when the later American illustrator, Frederic Dorr Steele, began using Gillette's visage to represent Holmes in the American magazines.)

Gillette apparently did a revision of Doyle's play, but both works were lost in a San Francisco hotel fire in 1898, and Gillette began anew. That's when I first learned of the matter – when he wrote me a letter indicating that he was going to be in London and would like to meet. He arrived in May 1899 and we had lunch at the Langham. I didn't know until then what had been in the works for years, and that he'd already met with Doyle the week before, upon his arrival in the capital.

I read the play and was unhappy with several aspects. However, considering how much money I was offered, I was willing to set that aside. Of more concern was Holmes's possible reaction. After his return to London in the spring of 1894, he'd absolutely prohibited further publication of his adventures – and now a drama melding aspects of several of his cases was going to be premiered, not only getting some things incorrect, but worse – abandoning his pure reasoning approach to provide a romantic conclusion wherein his character and the leading lady are in an affectionate embrace, implying that he has abandoned all of his principles for her.

I should have known that Holmes was aware of the matter long before I told him, and curiously, he was indifferent. Or so he implied. At that time he was involved in a series of extremely complex affairs, and I believe that rather than waste energy or thought on combatting the play, he simply placed it into a separate box in his brain attic and hid it away.

Although the play premiered in the United States in the fall of '99, it didn't come to England until September 1901. Holmes and I were in the audience on opening night, although Holmes was well-disguised, and I went mostly unrecognized. Doyle was certainly willing to soak up the attention – a fact that I attribute to his interest a couple of years later in once again publishing more of my stories about Holmes.

Holmes and I rarely discussed the play. I believe that he didn't blame me too much, since so much of the initial preparation of it was accomplished without my knowledge. I didn't know for sure, but I was always fairly certain that he'd read the script – either to codify his thoughts on the matter, or simply because he had once been an actor. In any case, he intended to draw on what he'd previously seen on the stage and subsequently read in order to carry out his performance, and I wished him well, even as I shifted in my hiding spot, waiting for something to happen.

I was aware when the audience's rustling and conversation silenced and the play commenced. Holmes wasn't immediately on stage. The first of the four acts has a long scene involving the conspirators' discussion before Sherlock Holmes ever makes an appearance. After that, his appearances are intermittent but effective through the first half of the play. If the killer were to make his move, he'd need to do so during those times when Holmes was on stage and out of the dressing room – and unless he knew the play quite well, picking those times might be a matter of luck for him.

I heard the first act roll along, and then I was aware when Holmes took the stage. His voice was distinct and clear, and he spoke his lines with confidence. I dearly wished that I had the opportunity to be in the audience and see this unforgettable moment, but alas, my duty was elsewhere. I redoubled my efforts to perceive anything unusual in the dressing room hallway – and I didn't have long to wait.

There is always something going on backstage, as preparations for upcoming scenes are made, things used in old scenes are removed and sets are struck, and actors and technicians with time to kill move from here to there. But during a lull, I saw a movement from behind some stored flats – it was like a ghost hovering about a foot above the floor, moving quickly to the door of the star's dressing room. I realized that it was the killer's bare head and cream-colored coat had merged into a ghostly shape, while the floating illusion occurred due to the man's black pants legs and shoes underneath. Even as I comprehended what I'd seen, the man reached the star's dressing room and slipped inside. As I emerged from my hiding place, so did Bardle and four of his men.

Sometimes the capture of an insidious villain is memorable or dramatic. After "Killer" Evans shot me in the leg, Holmes whipped him across the head with his pistol. We found Grimesby Roylott dead from a snake-bite, with the vicious serpent coiled nightmarishly around his head. Rodger Baskerville had died after being swallowed into a Dartmoor mire – or so we had believed at the time. Lord Blackwood had managed to hang

319

himself amongst the construction atop the Tower Bridge. And Fenton Cable, in attempting to electrocute both Holmes and me, was instead grounded himself in the pool of his last victim's blood and had been left a smoking husk, unable to fall until the current was turned off.

But other criminals were taken with a minimum of fuss. Such was the case for Dale Warriner, the man in the cream-colored coat. We opened the door to the dressing room to find him trying and failing to open the strongbox which Holmes had placed in an easily spotted location. He looked up and saw us blocking his escape, all with guns drawn, and with a sob he simply sagged to the floor, a beaten man. He wept quietly for the next couple of hours as we left him alone, with two officers close by on either side should he unexpectedly decide to do himself an injury.

Bardle and I had agreed that Holmes should be there when we questioned Warriner, who had provided his identity without any resistance. During his first respite from the performance, Holmes had slipped back to the dressing rooms and seen that his plan had succeeded. However, before he could do much more than get a look at Warriner, and be seen in return by the surprised and weeping fellow, he had to return to the stage – this time for the scene where he was visited in Baker Street by Professor Moriarty, stylistically dramatized from the true events as related in "The Final Problem".

Seeing as how the prisoner was well-guarded and subdued, I took my chance to edge my way into the theatre. In spite of the January off-season performance, the show was sold out, and I was only able to find a place standing along one of the side walls.

There was silence from the stage, but there was tension nevertheless, and I saw that everyone in the audience was tightly focused on Holmes as he moved with purpose from a listening pose to retrieve a revolver from a nearby table and then slip it into his dressing gown pocket. Afterwards, he seemed to relax, facing a door which slowly opened. A man walked through – tall, thin, and with a high shining dome above his eyes. He was dressed all in black, and even though the man was simply acting a part, he managed to convey the evil that had always exuded from Professor James Moriarty – curiously and incorrectly renamed "*Robert*" by Gillette for the play.

Moriarty and Holmes simply faced each for a moment, and someone in the audience hissed, while another gasped in apprehension at what might occur.

In a low voice, Moriarty stated, "It is a dangerous habit to finger loaded firearms in the pocket of one's dressing gown."

Holmes responded, his voice also low-pitched, but with unmistakable authority. "You'll be taken from here to the hospital if you keep that hand behind you."

Moriarty lowered the hand in question and grasped it with the other.

"In that case," said Holmes, taking the revolver from his dressing gown, "the table will do quite as well."

As he placed on the table beside him, Moriarty sidled a step forward. "You evidently don't know me."

Holmes nodded toward the revolver. "I think it quite evident that I do. Pray take a chair, Professor. I can spare you five minutes – if you have anything to say."

What followed was much the same conversation that I'd heard told to me that long-ago day in April 1891, when Holmes, his knuckles bleeding, had managed to sneak into my medical practice in order to enlist my aid in the affair that would terminate just days later atop the Reichenbach Falls.

I had an interest in the play as a whole, and which parts of the narrative still made me wince. My thoughts on the chap playing "Dr. Watson" are best left unrecorded. In general, I noticed which actors were more successful than others, but in truth, I was most interested in Holmes's performance. Of course I was in awe of his ability to perform the role so well, having only seen it once years before – at least that I was aware of – and also with just a couple of read-throughs, one just a few hours earlier.

He moved with the vitality of a man half his age, and under the lights he seemed to be an even more intense version of himself. I would not have missed that performance for the world.

He held the audience in the palm of his hand. When he played his famous trick with the cigar in the Stepney gas chamber, some in the audience applauded or cheered. And they cheered again, over the thunderous applause, after Holmes stated, "There is every reason – " to the actress playing Alice Faulkner before pulling her to him in an embrace just before the lights darkened and the curtain swung shut.

The curtain calls were met with great enthusiasm and cheers, and none more so than for the man playing Sherlock Holmes – whom the audience believed to be the unfortunate late actor, Brian Singer. When curtain finally came down, the cast were just as enthusiastic. I felt sorry for them when they learned that Holmes's performance was a one-time thing.

Finally Holmes and I were able to return to the dressing room, along with a beaming Mr. Pilsbury. Holmes sat down across from Dale Warriner and introduced himself. The man seemed to have no idea who Holmes was, and appeared to assume that he was another policeman. As Holmes succinctly laid out his observations as to how the murder was committed, almost as if he'd been there and watched it, Warriner's eyes widened, and he agreed.

Then Holmes finally removed the various letters, deeds, and bonds from an inner pocket.

"My bonds," Warriner said, his words slurred. I wasn't sure if he was unhealthy, or simply spent from a day that ran from murder to capture.

"How is that?" asked Holmes.

"Brian and I – we were half-brothers. His mother married my father when we were boys. He was always clever – much more than me. He was told to help me. To help take care of me. But he never did. He would smile and lie, and they would believe him, no matter what I said.

"We – my dad and me – had some lands in York. Family lands. My dad was always careful, and saved, and invested, and bought the bonds. It was all supposed to be mine, from my father, just as the lands had come down to him from his father. When Brian's mother died, he was nearly grown, and he felt no ties anymore, and he left to become an actor. Dad and me, we got by, but then he died too, and he passed the land to me. But there was something wrong. The lawyers said there was something wrong, but they couldn't make me understand, and just then Brian came back for a visit. He understood – something wrong about the way the documents were set up. He said he'd help, but then he took them and left, and the lawyers said there was nothing that I could do.

"Brian owned everything now – I don't know how – but I kept living there because I had nowhere else to go. Then I found out where he would be as an actor and wrote letters – telling him what he'd done was wrong – but he never wrote back. Finally I was running out of ways to pay the bills, and the lawyers were saying I would have to leave soon, so I decided to find Brian, and visit him, and make him give back what he stole."

"How did you get into the house today?" I asked. "Without being seen?"

"It was easy," Warriner replied, noticing me for the first time. "I'd watched for several days. Only one other person besides Brian and the old woman were living there. They came and went all the time. The front door was never locked – they would just open it to go in, and pull it shut to leave. I always followed Brian to the theatre and tried to work up the courage to speak to him, but I never could. Today he left the theatre and went back to the house early, and I decided that this was my chance. I was about to go in when the old lady walked out. She was back in just a few minutes with an old man – *You* – " He nodded to Doctor Honner. "That spooked me, and I hid until the old man had left again. Then I figured I'd best take my chance, so I slipped across the street and went in."

322

More tears were rolling down his face now, but he didn't bother to wipe them away. "It was dark inside, and so quiet. I didn't know where Brian was, but I figured it was upstairs. I went up, and there was only one room with a light on. I went to it and knocked on the door but there was no answer, so I looked in, and he was asleep on the bed.

"I went over, intending to wake him and ask him to give back what was mine, but there he was, and an anger welled in me like I'd never felt before. Everything thing he'd done to me since I was a boy was in it, along with feelings about what he'd taken from me – what he'd *stolen!* – and how bad my life had been since then. It was almost like I was watching someone else from an audience as I took out my old gun. I knew that the bang would call up the old lady, and I would lose my chance to search, so I put the pillow over his head and . . . and then I . . . ." He broke down sobbing and couldn't continue. But it didn't matter, as we already knew what happened after that.

Holmes stood and handed Bardle the packet of letters and papers, and then he his men shepherded Warriner from the room. Honner, shaking his head sadly, silently shook our hands and departed with them. The theatrical manager, Pilsbury, remained behind, looking pale and numb.

"I cannot . . . Life is so *desperate* sometimes," he said. "Why does fate play with us in such ways?"

I had heard Holmes, in some of his darker moods, ask the same question. I have never found an answer.

Holmes removed himself to the makeup table, where he sat and leaned forward in order to remove those additions and enhancements that had simply served to make him look more like himself.

"I thought it went well," he said, changing the subject. "The gas chamber scene wasn't as effective as Gillette's version, although in writing his script, he deviated quite a bit from the actual fact. Some of the actors were thrown by my timing – which is understandable – and they were all clearly curious about me, since they'd barely been introduced to 'Mr. Roylott' before the play began. One chaps eyes widened when he heard the name – no doubt one of your readers, Watson, who recognized the association." He finished his task and leaned back. "All in all, it was a tolerable experience."

"*Tolerable?*" asked Pilsbury. "Mr. Holmes, you were brilliant! I realize, sir, that you were playing yourself, so to speak, so your interpretation is bound to be the definitive one, but still, you were miles past whatever Mr. Gillette was ever able to convey. Certainly better than Brian Singer – God rest his soul. I know it's too much to ask, but would you be willing – ? I mean, is there any way that I might entice you . . . ?"

Holmes rose, turned, took a step forward, and offered his hand to the manager, who wordlessly took and shook it.

"No, thank you, sir," replied Holmes. "I am retired, and this curious detour back to the days of my theatrical youth is a very-much one-time thing. I do appreciate the unexpected though tragic opportunity, and also your faith in allowing me to assume the helm of your production."

"Mr. Holmes, based on what I saw tonight, I'm offering you a partnership! As an actor – "

"No, no, my decision is final. But again, thank you. Good evening."

I wished the manager the same as Holmes retrieved his coat and hat from where I'd earlier left them, and then we departed.

Outside, the temperature had dropped considerably, and only then did I recall that my automobile was still parked near Mrs. Spence's house, several streets away. Pulling my coat tighter, I said with a rueful smile, "Faces to the north, then, and quick march!"

Only later, when we'd driven halfway back to Holmes's villa (as he liked to call it), did he speak again, pulling us both from our various thoughts. "I suppose," he said, "that in some round-about way, your writings cannot be blamed for this occurrence."

"Hmm?"

"The murder would have occurred regardless. In fact, without the connection forged by way of your stories and Gillette's play, and the character portrayed by Singer, we might not have been involved at all."

I shook my head. "These questions of fate are too deep for me. It's late, and I'm hungry."

He was silent for a moment, and then he continued. "What I'm saying is that, in the great tapestry of events, your recording and publication of my cases has not been completely objectionable."

"Kind of you to say so."

"And," he added, "should you choose to do so again in the future, I would not be averse."

"It's likely up to Doyle," I said. "He may have lost interest again."

I sensed that he nodded. It wasn't until we'd rattled past The Gables and were approaching Holmes's farm that I spoke again. "I enjoyed seeing your performance, and I sense that you enjoyed being able to give it." I glanced toward him. "Happy Birthday, Holmes."

"Indeed," he replied. "Forgive me for saying so, but, in spite of the tragedy, it *was* a happy birthday." He shifted into his seat as I turned into his drive, noting that the front window was lit and there was every indication that something appetizing awaited us.

"I wonder," he added, "what tomorrow will bring?"

As it turned out, quite a lot . . . .

Devize's Divisive Devices
by Kevin P. Thornton

"I see we are off ballooning," I said as I walked into our old rooms in Baker Street. Although Holmes had encamped to his bee farm nearly three years since, he had kept our old rooms as his London base. He still received mail there, and such was his fame that even mail addressed to *Sherlock Holmes, London* was delivered by the Royal Mail to Number 221b.

I was hoping for the same reaction from my friend that he usually engendered in me. I was disappointed. Holmes instead greeted me with a warm handshake and, surprisingly, a smile. For a man whose normal demeanour ranged from indifference at the one end to outright scorn at the other, such charm was a like a shock to my system – a pleasant one, but no less surprising. I examined him insofar as I could in the dull light struggling through the windows. He looked as healthy as I had ever seen him. He could still use an extra stone in weight to his lean frame, and an hour in the sun would benefit his complexion, but by his standards my friend Sherlock Holmes looked hearty, healthy, and almost hale.

"What gave it away?" he asked. "Was it the book about the theory of flight on the landing that I must return to the library? Have you been following all the newspaper tales about the need for a military presence in the air, or was it the way I asked you to dress for our excursion? The combination of warm yet easily cast-off clothing along with protective eyewear must have suggested to you that we would be outdoors, and our destination, Brighton, has two notable geographic points of interest. It is by the sea and there are advantageous cliffs nearby. As the attire I suggested was aimed at warmth without waterproofing, did you conclude our investigation would be into airships by a process of deduction?" All this was said as he ushered me back out the door, down the steps, and outside.

Then he saw the charabanc stopped in front of the door.

"I may have had a little help," I said. Our awaiting transport had a sign attached to the carriage door: *Devizes Dirigibles* was followed underneath by the qualifier *Our Future is Above Us*.

Holmes looked at me for a moment as if I was a foreign particle on his dinner suit before he smiled, a rare occurrence, and clapped me on the back. "By Jove, the biter bit, eh? Well done!" He stepped back and looked at me closely as if seeing me for the first time. "I have missed your company, my friend. I'm glad you've been able to come with me today, even though your ingrown toenail isn't healing as you would like it to and is causing you some discomfort. Did you consult a colleague for a second opinion? You did not, did you? You never do. In this case, as in all involving your own health, '*Physician heal thyself*' is misguided advice."

We pulled out into the road and turned left twice, passing by Hyde Park as we headed to Victoria Station. There was an envelope on the seat next to Holmes. He perused it and said, "Baron Devizes wishes to impress us. He has booked an entire compartment for our journey to Brighton. More importantly, there is a return ticket, so we may travel back in comfort, regardless of the results of our investigation." He looked at me, the look on my face no doubt one with which he was familiar through our years of shared accommodation.

"The biter who bit now has more to chew on," he observed. "Before you splutter and curse me, let me explain how I knew of your injured foot. I could tell you that as a man who shared lodgings with you for many years, there isn't much I don't know about your health. I could always see when you suffered the pain from your Afghan injuries. I remembered the gout you inflicted upon your joints after Mary died, and the self-control you exerted to wean yourself away from the port soon thereafter. I know of your arthritic twinges. I can hear your footsteps grow heavier with each passing year, and sadly I know that you suffered from bunions and ingrown toenails alike all through our time together."

"Please, let us not rub salt into the wounds of my incipient dotage."

"Indeed," he said. "I could also tell you that you took great delight in telling me your bunions were cured some months back, yet you have a limp today. It was slight, too slight for a sprain or a strain. All that was left was the possibility of an ingrown nail. They are a constant curse to you, and once you treat yourself as gently as you treat your other patients, they will be less so. As I said, I could tell you all of that, but in truth Mrs. Hudson bumped into your wife yesterday and was told all about your wounded toe, which is exacerbated by your rough thereof." He stopped there as he saw the look on my face.

"Holmes," I said. "You cheated."

"I assessed all the evidence and came to the correct conclusion. I would in all likelihood not have said anything until you tried to play me at my own game. Tell me, had there not been a garishly labelled charabanc outside 221, would you have concluded anything from all the available information?"

Sadly, I admitted I would not.

"Then it's a good thing we are a team, because where we're going warrants some keen investigation." And for once in his life, he promised to tell me all. "Once we are entrained, Watson, once we are entrained."

Our tickets gave us a level of treatment we weren't used to as we were led past the lines of people waiting and up to the first class carriage where a conductor showed us to a private compartment booked under the Duke of Norfolk's seal.

"Is he your client?" I asked. Norfolk was the premier non-royal Duke in the land, and his castle at Arundel wasn't far from Brighton.

"Not officially," said Holmes, "although he is an investor with Baron Devizes. Have you heard of the Baron, or are you merely trying to get the verse of that name out of your head? It is popular in rugby clubs and the like, is it not?" [1]

He must have seen the look on my face. "Come now. I have told you before that you should never play any game where bluffing is involved. I have on occasion heard you returning from your reunions, singing about the man from Nantucket, the Bishop of Birmingham, and the lad from Devizes. Puerile, to be sure as limericks are wont to be, but you are often in fine voice, my friend, and occasionally the rhymes are quite clever. The maid from Aberystwyth is a match in poetic agility for any Shakespearean line."

"That's all very amusing, and to be sure I shall try to curtail any future carousing whenever you are near."

"Quite. To answer your question, the Government has become enthused at the possibility of air warfare, as if the land and sea forces cannot cause enough carnage. The Wright Flyer three years back proved the possibility of powered flight, so there are several tenders out to supply the military with British-made air superiority over any future battlefields. The Baron formed a consortium of like-minded members of the House of Lords to develop a flying machine."

"And it is not going as well as planned?" I ventured.

"That depends on whom you ask," said Holmes. "According to the Baron, everything is proceeding as expected. However, at the behest of the Duke of Norfolk, one of senior Mandarins of Whitehall was asked to investigate further."

"And what did Mycroft say?" I asked. "'I am too busy. I will send my younger brother, the whippersnapper Sherlock Holmes, who doesn't have a real job anyway.' Is that why we are off to Brighton?"

Holmes permitted himself an infinitesimal grimace at my attempted humour. "It isn't merely Mycroft's doing. Baron Devizes managed to raise a large amount of money from his ennobled brothers in the House of Lords. He has spent the money quickly, but whether it has been spent wisely is a matter of some doubt. It is also feared that two of the Lords

327

involved will face certain bankruptcy if Devizes' plan doesn't work, and that is looking more likely."

"And this government, like all governments elected since the dawn of time, doesn't wish for a scandal to taint their record."

"Precisely," said Holmes. "If the Baron is incapable of satisfying the requirements of the government, Mycroft needs to know. We shall, as always, wait until the evidence is available, but it doesn't look good. For a start, all the other bidders for the contract are developing heavier-than air machines of the type that is known as an 'aeroplane'. If reports on the development of these are true, an aeroplane will one day soon be able to fly at speeds in excess of one-hundred miles an hour, and manoeuvre like the most-expert of equestrians."

"What is the Baron doing instead?"

"As the name of his company suggests, Baron Devizes believes that inflatables are a preferable solution. He has convinced his investors that his newly designed airships can equal the speed and manoeuvrability of an aeroplane, will be easier to build, and cheaper to maintain."

"If what he says is true," I said, "then why can't a farm chicken dart about the skies like kestrel or a hawk?"

"That is an apt analogy. We shall see what the good Baron has to say for himself."

"He can't be happy that his inventions are being subjected to scrutiny by one such as you," I said.

"On the contrary, he seemed to be delighted to hear I was coming. He had heard that there is doubt about his designs, and his reaction was that my testimony as to the efficacy of his work will keep his investors happy."

"Hmm. Maybe he knows what he's doing."

"Maybe indeed," said Holmes. "In any event, when I was given a list of the investors, I saw an opportunity to secure anther opinion. The Earl Russell is, next to The Duke of Norfolk, a significant partner in the consortium, and his brother is a scholar of some note. I have invited him to join as at Baron Devizes' demonstration."

"I'm surprised at you," I said, trying to draw him out. "It's a rare occasion when you admit you need help of any sort." But on that matter he remained silent.

Our fellow traveller was waiting for us at the station. I knew the name Bertrand Russell, but I was unfamiliar with his work. There had been an article in *The Times* about his recent paper on mathematics a precursor to a more detailed work, and *The Economist* had mentioned how his theories were changing the way scientists looked at problem solving. I knew he was a mathematician then, and a philosopher, and I was therefore prepared

328

to be bored to tears. Holmes by contrast was delighted to meet Russell, who was a slender young man of medium height and striking angularity. He had the look of a Roman Emperor, yet when he spoke, his manner was one of gentility and shyness. Holmes seemed disappointed that Russell took a separate carriage out to the demonstration. He apparently had another engagement later and could not delay. I felt that Holmes had been looking forward to talking with him, and this was confirmed as we left Brighton station.

"He is a most brilliant man. Truly he may be one of the finest minds of this generation. There is one other I can think of who is his equal – a Swiss-German whose papers on relativity and Brownian motion have been fascinating to read, but other than that, Russell is in a field of one."

"What is Russell's specialty?"

"Brilliance," said Holmes. "He has recently suggested that he and Whitehead will be able to prove that one plus one equals two in their upcoming work. It will be seminal, truly seminal." He no doubt enjoyed the look of astonishment on my face.

"That hardly seems startling," I said.

"It doesn't, does it?" agreed Holmes. "Yet its intellectual importance is almost incalculable. It is in many ways the foundation for all scientific thought of the future." I had rarely seen Holmes so galvanised, and while I was glad for him, the theories of the Honourable Bertrand Russell had already passed me by.

"So what will he do for your investigation?" I asked.

"I hope that he will provide a sounding board for the theories behind Devizes devices, and sort the wheat from the chaff."

"And maybe," I said, "there will be a moment or two for the two of you to talk about sums."

Just outside of Brighton, the white cliffs rise up from the sea in a fortified boundary compatible with and comparable to those at Dover. The splendid school for girls, Roedean, had been open for less than twenty years, and extant at the location on the edge of the Sussex Downs for less than ten. As a new institution, it had grounds to spare and no doubt some debts at the bank, so Baron Devizes had been able to rent a parcel of property next to the cliff so as to test his flying machines.

As we rode up to the school, we were directed away from it by a sign pointing to the grounds near the cliff. Devizes Dirigibles had taken over a field the size of Sussex County Cricket Ground, and we were pointed to an area where at least a dozen other personages and their carriages had already gathered. I hadn't seen so many expensive means of transport in one place since my last visit to the carriage show at the Earl's Court

Pleasure Grounds, and I commented on the perceived importance of all the witnesses.

"Even the serfs are a better class, Watson. When one reports to a Duke or such, one is used to speedy transportation, although I fear their disappointment once they cast their eyes yonder."

I looked in the direction of his gaze. At the far end there was a glass hanger, as impressive on its smaller scale as The Crystal Palace in London. Tethered outside it was torpedo-shaped lighter-than-air contraption. It looked to be a descendant of the airships of the nineteenth century – I remembered occasional pictures in the papers – but was smaller and appeared inelegant in comparison to designs I had seen by Santos Dumont and Zeppelin.

Holmes, unable to spot Russell, walked over to the carriage he came in. We found him still sitting inside, notebook and pencil at hand, staring through the roof. Holmes hushed me in a pantomime of silence and we waited until his focus returned and he frantically wrote his idea down. Then he seemed to return to our earthly boundaries and saw us at the door.

"I apologize," said Russell.

"No need," said Holmes. "Did you recall your fleeting thought?"

"Half," he said. "I had two things to fetch on my way home, and I can only remember the one." He saw our collective frowns and he gave a slight giggle. "Oh dear, you thought I was thinking something profound. My apologies for disappointing you, but sadly, most profundities are the result of hard work and analysis, not leaps of fancy."

"It is much the same in my world, no matter what Watson writes. Pray tell sir, what do you think of the flying contraption?"

Russell stared across the field. "This isn't my field of expertise, Holmes, and I would certainly like to get closer to it to examine it more carefully, but it seems out of proportion. Others that I have seen appear to need a larger airbag to fly. The Devizes dirigible looks sleek, though impressive. It has the requisite parts needed: The crew compartment below, motor at the back, propeller. However, unless he has found a gas that is lighter than Hydrogen, I think he has made some design errors that are going to cost the Duke, my brother, and all the other investors dearly."

I looked around the gathered people. They seemed to be gentlemen of business, not nobility. Holmes saw me and said, "The Ducal class does not get their hands dirty. They send their representatives: Business managers, household factotums, trusted representatives – "

"Philosophers, detectives, and doctors," I murmured.

"There is something else you should know," said Russell. He was staring out to sea, watching the birds swirl above. "I don't know if he has chosen this spot on purpose, but that strong wind we feel now will help in

330

propelling him outwards and upwards, until he reaches the height of those gulls."

"At which point he will be aided back towards land," said Holmes, also watching the birds. "It appears that Devises has picked the perfect sport to display a machine that seems unlikely to fulfill the requirements of the tender. His design seems as if it will be slow and unstable, and I hope the other watchers aren't taken in by the show we are about to see. It's all very well launching with favourable winds, but I wonder how it will do on the dry plains of Afghanistan or the Transvaal."

"I think we're about to find out," I said as a carriage came in from the road and, instead of stopping in an orderly manner next to the rest of our transport, pulled up in front of us. A man dressed as if heading to the city climbed out and stood on the top step.

"My dear friends," I said. "I am Baron Devizes, your pilot to the future. In a moment I shall demonstrate my invention, Devizes' Dirigible Mark I. I ask you please to be patient until I return, when I shall answer any and all questions you may have. Believe me, once you have seen it fly, I believe that most of the queries will be resolved."

There was a mumble of disenchantment among the group, but it was very slight and very English. Devizes rode off across the field to the hanger while we waited to give him his chance.

"What do you think, Russell?" said one of the men to our companion. "He puts on a good show, does he not?"

"If that thing does all it is supposed to do according to government requirements," said Russell, "we shall offer him a job at Cambridge so he can explain to how he bent so many laws of physics."

There was a slight guffaw from the man before he realized what Russell had actually said. He turned away and spoke *sotto voce* to the others, and in a matter of a moment the mood had changed from one of optimism and fair play to the gloom of pending undoing.

In the meantime, we continued to watch the display across the field from us. The carriage dropped Devizes on the near side of his contraption, and then pulled round the far side next to the hanger. Devizes climbed into the crew compartment, and from within he started the motor and released the mooring ropes. The flying machine rose slowly in the air, the motor seeming almost to lose its battle with gravity before it caught the swell of the wind and headed out to sea. We watched it for what seemed a long time, but when I looked at my timepiece again scarcely five minutes had passed. I wasn't alone with this feeling. Thereafter one of the other observers took it upon himself to toll the time, minute by excruciating minute as we watched the failure of the Devizes dirigible. Its speed was non-existent, its manoeuverability as paltry as a wallowing walrus, and its ascent so slow it may as well have a painted target on it. I mentioned as much and Holmes said, "Indeed. Then why?"

I must have looked puzzled, but before Holmes could explain, Russell said, "Precisely, Holmes. Devizes had to know his design would fail. Why then would he invite one of the finest minds in the country to invigilate this examination? He knew he was going to be found wanting." Then he saw the look on my face and realized what he'd said. "I wasn't tooting my own horn. I was referring to your colleague, Sherlock Holmes."

"Thank you, Russell. You are too kind, and your point is most valid. Even if Devizes has no plan to return and is escaping to Le Havre, why invite an audience?"

Holmes was interrupted by an acclamation from one of the watchers. "It's turning," he said. "Look, it's coming back."

And indeed it was. "Do you think he has changed his mind?" I asked. "Or maybe his intention all along was to try and bluff his way past the poor performance."

"I think he was caught by the crosswind we observed earlier," said Russell. "He doesn't have enough power to fight it, and the only way to lower it and get away from the wind is to let gas escape from the inflatable balloon above him. That requires a lot of faith if you know you're flying a substandard piece of equipment."

We watched another minute. It was faster returning, the wind from the sea gave it a momentum added to by the sudden loss of altitude as Devizes seemed almost to want to dive his machine into the earth. So far it was the only impressive part of the display, and it quickly became obvious that when he landed it would be a solid one. The tube above the crew compartment was deflating rapidly – too rapidly it seemed. At the last second, when it seemed as if the landing would be a crashed one, the contraption was caught by the same prevailing wind at sea level that had helped to launch him and stalled to a shuddering halt. Several among the gathered witnesses hurried to help tether the machine lest it get caught by the wind again.

"I should like a close look," said Russell. Holmes was already striding across the field, and the two of us followed in his wake. We were halfway across when we heard a shout. One of the helpers had opened the door to the crew compartment. "It's empty!" He looked around him, his head bobbing like a meerkat at London Zoo, and just as wide-eyed.

"At last," said Holmes.

"You were expecting this?" I said.

"I was expecting something. No disrespect to you and the others, Watson, but the machinations behind why Russell and I are here to have to do with our being irreproachable witnesses to the events. A missing flier becomes an even bigger mystery if the country's finest mathematician and its leading detective, both irrefutable masters of logical thought, cannot explain the conundrum."

"And has it beaten you?" I asked mischievously, awarded with his famous look of disdain normally reserved for members of the police.

"No," said Russell. "And it won't."

"You seem certain," I said.

"He is Sherlock Holmes," said Russell, with a certainty that heretofore I believed only I had ever felt. For a second I felt displaced by a younger smarter man. Then Holmes inadvertently came to my rescue.

"Watson, if you would please exert your authority and remove all the factotums from the landing before they trample away all the evidence. Find one with a smattering of common sense and ask him to go over to the school and message the local police. We have to inform them, but he may take his time. Then ask all of them if they noticed when Devizes' carriage departed." I looked over at the hanger, which now looked more like a cheaply made greenhouse that an offshoot of the Great Exhibition. Although glass-walled, the effect out in the fields was one of opacity from reflected images. I had thought the carriage to be behind the hanger, but there was a path leading away down to the main road which assumed the explanation.

The gathered witnesses were men used to taking orders and I had them moved to the side in no time. I was thus able to return to Holmes and watch more of his investigation. Both he and Russell were in the crew compartment, which had a ceiling and width of eight feet and a length of forty. The whole was made of wicker. There were two seats at the front, behind a glass window, the only means of exterior view. In between the seats there was a stout cable that ran to the back.

Holmes watched as I looked around. Both he and Russell were standing at the rear, next to a contraption that looked like a large hopper.

"What do you think?"

"There is but one cable. If it is, as I expect, attached to the rudder, then it is for steering only. There is no mechanical means to raise and lower the contraption."

"Precisely. This falls so far short of the requirements of the government tender that Devizes must have known he would be found out today. Russell, do you think what I said is possible?"

"There are crude markings down the inside of this hopper that suggests it to be so. If that is the case, it solves half the question. The other half I leave to you." With that, Holmes exited from the other side of the compartment and I followed him through. As I trod on the wicker floor it gave alarmingly.

333

"Surely there is a smarter way to build than using basket weavers." I said.

"I agree. Although the early lighter-than-air inventions were nothing more than a basket under a balloon, wicker isn't a product made for a quick turn-around in time of war." He paused to look more closely at the walls. "I can think of only one reason why he would use such a compartment for his demonstration, and Russell will soon prove if I am right."

He walked rapidly over to the balloon, now emptying rapidly as gas spilled from a ruptured wall in the side of its canvas. "A-ha!" said Holmes. "Here is the final proof of what happened." He turned as he heard a rustle from the door of the compartment and the mathematician joined us at the gasbag.

"It is as you expected, Holmes. If a man were familiar with the power-to-weight ratio of the dirigible, it would be fairly easy to calculate the sand that would be required and its flow rate from the hopper."

"Which is why the floor had to be porous," said Holmes. "All that is needed is to discover how the canvas was torn to reverse the process."

'I may have that answer as well," said Russell. "There was a lever attached to the bottom of the hopper. I haven't proved it yet, but at a certain point in the proceedings it would have swung shut, causing a counterweight to fall. If that weight was attached to the emergency cables on the canvas, they would be torn free."

He stopped and looked at me as my face must have betrayed my confusion.

Holmes also saw and said, "I am afraid we have mystified my friend. Perhaps if we explain ourselves, he may yet make another of his tales about this. In a way it is one of Watson's favourite investigations: A locked room mystery, I believe you would call it?"

"I have no idea what you're talking about, but if you're going to explain yourself, you should do it for all the other watchers so that they may go back and tell their Lords and Masters how their money was spent."

Holmes agreed and, after dispatching one of them to the school with another message, this time to Mycroft, he said, "He will know which arms of government are needed to bring this mess to a conclusion," Then he allowed me to gather the rest in the hanger. As they walked in, Russell pointed out several large bags of sand in one corner and Holmes nodded as if it meant something.

I would be glad when Russell returned to his College. It had taken me years to understand some of how Holmes's brain worked. It would be too much to have to deal with another such intellectual giant. They understood and presupposed each other in conversation in a way that would soon become irritating.

Holmes looked around at the gathered men. "You are all here as the representatives of the investors in Devizes Dirigibles, yet what we were actually invited here for today was to witness the disappearance of the Baron as he took his airship out for a test run. Most of you already suspected something was wrong. It didn't seem possible that it would fly at speed, manoeuvre with agility, and be available for all forms of battle. He wasn't even dressed for the occasion, looking as if he had somewhere else to be. In fact, the machine is quite the opposite to what we expected. It barely made it off the ground, nearly didn't turn around, and almost crashed on landing. And when it did, the Baron, who we had all seen get into the flying compartment, was no longer there."

"So where is the Baron?" I asked

"Probably on his way to the Port of Southampton, heading for parts foreign and far," said Holmes, "carrying with him the rest of the investors' money." There was a restlessness among the men as they heard this and realized that they would each have to report back this news to their employers.

"I have already sent word to my brother, Mycroft Holmes, who many of you know by reputation. He will be shutting down the ports and harbours instantly until Devizes is found." He paused for a moment, devilment in his eye. "I'm sure he will be delighted to entertain individual queries from the investors, so you may rest assured he will be delighted to see them all in his visitors' chambers."

"Holmes," I whispered in an aside to him. "Are you mad? You know how much your brother values his privacy."

"He will not attend," said Holmes, "but the numerous requests will irk him and may teach him that I'm not his bidding boy. This could all have been solved within the confines of 221b, but Mycroft was asked to dance attendance on Norfolk and his lackeys, and instead chose me to be at the Ducal beck and call."

Turning back to the assembled party, he continued his explanation. "Eventually, an investigation into the Baron's affairs will turn up why he did what he did. I know not, nor do I care. Devizes decided to run, and when he heard who would be here as witness to his failure, a sense if unearned hubris must have overcome him as he tried to create a mystery of his disappearance. But I, Sherlock Holmes, know how this was done."

He ignored the questions and continued to talk. "We all saw the Baron get into the dirigible, and we all know he wasn't there when it returned. There are three possibilities. He stepped into the compartment and stepped out again. He flew it to a height and then fell out, or he escaped in the mangled landing."

"He didn't fall out," said Russell. "We would have seen if this was an accident. It isn't possible we all would have missed it. In any event, I watched it the entire time and he didn't fall."

"How can you be so sure of that," asked one of the others. "You may have looked away, relaxed your neck muscles, possibly closed your eyes for a second."

"I didn't," said Russell. "My ability to concentrate is quite finely honed. You may be sure that whatever happened, Devizes didn't fall."

"I believe you," said Holmes. "I also don't believe that he escaped on landing. If he truly wanted to get away, we would have wanted as much time as possible."

"He may have made it to his carriage and ridden off," said another.

"It wasn't there," I said. "He rode it over at the beginning, then his driver either stopped behind the hanger or rode off immediately."

"It is a hanger made of glass," he said. "We should have seen through it. And why, if he was bilking his investors, did he build such an expensive hanger?"

"He didn't," said Holmes. "On closer investigation, which you may do if you wish, you will see that it's nothing like the Crystal Palace built for the exhibition. It is a worn old building, put together from several old greenhouses. From afar it gives the illusion of respectability and affluence. The nearer one gets, the more obvious it is how old the structure looks. Even the glass is tired and opaque so that it acts as effectively as a stone wall. It is mere artifice."

"You are saying then," I asked, "that he climbed in and climbed out immediately, went to his carriage, and rode off down the path hidden by hanger?"

"Yes," said Holmes.

All too often I have fallen into his trap of pleading for the answer, allowing him the sense of superiority he wore on occasion like a smug cloak. Not today. Today I had allies in the form of people who needed the story to tell their employers. They didn't let me down and their cacophony of questions rose in a crescendo that took Holmes by surprise. He looked to me for help in quelling the queries, and I will state that I wasn't proud of how I behaved. But that was later. I left him to it, and it took him several moments to be heard above the noise. Eventually I felt guilty and helped him.

"Gentlemen," I barked in my best parade ground voice, "if you must howl like beagles at the hunt, then I am afraid we will leave, and you may read the solution to your masters from the news pages of tomorrow's *Times*."

That silenced them. "Please," I said to Holmes. "If he climbed in and out so rapidly, how did it fly out and return. Were there secret wires?"

"In a manner of speaking," said Russell. The younger man was obviously thrilled at the events of the day. This was more exciting than mathematical proofs of simple sums.

He stopped when he looked at Holmes, as if he had overstepped his mark. "Carry on," said Holmes generously. "The calculations were yours."

"Thank you," said Russell. "When we looked inside the compartment, there was only one control, for steering the machine right or left. There was nothing to guide the air in such a manner as to raise or lower it while flying. It could only ascend by reducing the weight, and it would only descend by reducing the gas that kept it buoyant."

"Someone had to be in it then," said one of the chorus.

"Not necessarily. The hopper at the back, in all likelihood, held a large quantity of sand. When Devizes climbed in, all he need to do was start the engine, open the hopper, and let the sand begin to trickle out. Then he climbed out the other side and back into his carriage. When enough sand had fallen out to the ground through the wicker floor, the dirigible would rise and move forward over the cliffs and out to sea. Devizes was already disappearing down the track behind the hanger. "He carried on quickly before the questions began. "For those of you who understand something of aerodynamics, you will know that air machines are designed to slice through the air. Hence when Devises' device reached the upper winds above the coast, it was unable to propel itself forward, the engine power being pitiful. It was turned around and shortly thereafter the second part of Devizes sand hopper came into play."

Holmes had been quiet for long enough. "Thank you, Russell. The emptying of the sand in the hopper triggered a lever that dropped a counterweight attached to cables stitched into the canvas doors of the gas buoyancy bag. As these ripped open the dirigible, powered by the higher altitude wind and the effects of gravity, returned to land."

"It sounds fantastical," said one. "How did it return to the same spot?"

"That was a singular fortuity," said Holmes, "and is irrelevant. Regardless of where it landed, we would have followed it and ascertained that it was empty. That it came back to the same place it started merely maintained the charade thirty seconds longer for those with clarity of thought and purpose, while befuddling the rest of you even further."

"I could replicate what Devizes did." said Russell, to the interest of all. Even Holmes perked up. "Much of what he managed to do is calculation based on estimation and experience. Say he flew his airship several times, taking detailed notes as to constant deviations. He could easily measure wind speed, the amount of sand ballast needed, the size of

337

the hole in the airbag. After some attempts, he would have known how the rudder needed to be set approximate a landing. Of course things could have gone wrong. It might have been a windless day. His sand in the hopper may have become wet and clumped, changing its rate of flow. His engine might have failed."

"It sounds like anything could have gone wrong," said another.

"Nothing that would have changed what he was trying to do," said Russell, "which was to disappear in a mystery."

"He would have been better off with a smarter plan for his escape and lesser witnesses," said Holmes, "and left the clever mathematics to those best suited."

Russell nodded his head slightly at the compliment, then said to us, "I would like to hear more of this. If you don't mind, I shall return with you. Maybe your brother will have news of Devizes capture." He asked one of the others to send a telegram excusing himself from his previous engagement. The messenger's eyes nearly bulged through his spectacles. "Sandringham?" he said. "But that's, that's . . . ." Words failed him.

"Quite," said Russell, "and I tire of being their party piece. The last time I was invited, I was asked to explain to the King's eldest grandson why my proof of mathematics was so important. He isn't a boy of great intellect, young David [2], and he told me that one plus one has always been two, and I should do something more important with my life."

Russell sighed and shook his head. "I don't wish him harm, but I do hope his reign is brief." He pulled out a handkerchief from his trouser pocket, found it was a pocket square that matched his tie, and blew his nose with gusto.

I watched him, begged his pardon, and reached into his top pocket. "This is yours," I said to him as I handed him his missing shopping list.

Russel looked at the list in his left hand and the pocket square in his right and burst into laughter. "My word," he said, "isn't that the best trick of the day?"

In the distance, a lone policeman rode towards us, answering Holmes's earlier call. To a man, the gathering of witnesses and managers and accountants and factotums converged on him, happy to have a focus for their ire.

"There is nothing as English as complaining to the authorities," said Holmes, "regardless of their ability to resolve anything. We must leave now, before we become embroiled in the clamour."

As we rode out, I almost felt sorry for the lonely policeman, bravely trying to take notes without any idea of what had occurred. Russell was also watching. In the small time I'd know him, he had displayed an impish humour which he unrolled once more before us.

"When you come to write about this tale, Watson – and by the way, I am a devotee of your work – remember this moment. It lends itself to the title *The Mystery of Devizes' Divisive Devices*, does it not?

Holmes erupted with a snort and a "Ha!" as if it was the funniest thing he had heard. For once though, I wasn't insulted. The Honourable Bertrand Arthur William Russell, philosopher, scientist, and premier mathematician, had just said he liked my stories.

I leant back into the plush leather, luxuriating in its wonderful feeling and silently agreeing with him. It was indeed a fine title.

NOTES

1. The rugby ditty to which Holmes refers, "Sing Us Another One", is an old favourite wherever sporting men gather and imbibe. The chorus links any number of verses which are whatever limericks can be remembered by all who have congregated in the bar. *"There was a young man of Devizes . . ."* was a popular early starter to the singing, and does not bear repeating in this genteel collection.
2. David, christened Prince Edward Albert Christian George Andrew Patrick David, was the oldest male grandson of King Edward VII, and he would indeed reign briefly. He was considered rather dim by all who knew him, and many say he did the Kingdom a favour by giving up his crown to marry Wallis Simpson, leaving his brother King George VI to lead the Empire through the Second World War.

The Ambassadors'
Skating Competition
by Tim Symonds

It was a Monday morning and I was in my surgery. England's Capital lay under a lacklustre sky, the elegance of the Edwardian Era, and *Art Nouveau*'s emphasis on greens, browns, yellows, and blues confined to the interiors of the great Town Houses of Mayfair and Belgravia. Discouraged by the unpromising weather, only two patients had so far drifted in. Pensively, I stared out at the London traffic. I had heard nothing of late from my former comrade-in-arms Sherlock Holmes, some three years into retirement on a bee-farm in the South Downs.

The Mansion House wall clock struck eleven. I sent the receptionist off for medical supplies and reached for the day's *Times*. Militant Suffragettes had disrupted the State Opening of Parliament. An Anglo-Russian Convention relating to Persia, Afghanistan, and Tibet was about to be signed in St. Petersburg. Geologist Richard Oldham was proposing the Earth has a molten interior.

I decided to shut the surgery for the day and set off on foot for a meal at one of my clubs. I would leave it to Fate which one. Boodle's was enticing. It had been a while since I had tasted their wonderful Orange Fool dessert. The cream of the Clubland crop was located along St. James's Street, including Boodle's, Brooks, and White's, the latter the most prominent of all, or on Pall Mall, such as the Army and Navy and The Travellers – the latter's Pall Mall elevation inspired by Raphael's *Palazzo Pandolfini*. A principal qualification for membership in the club was at least one journey of five-hundred miles from England. The Club was a haunt of several old Army friends from my time on the North-West Frontier with the 66th Berkshire Regiment of Foot. I glanced at my watch as I came to Pall Mall. The Travellers was nearest. I should be just in time for the excellent *déjeuner à la fourchette*.

I was wending my way to the dining room when my attention was caught by a small group of men in the Billiards Room. They were deep in conversation, standing at the table with their cues raised like lances. "Why, it's the Sungazers!" I blurted out, my heart pounding. I recognised three of them immediately. The German-born Sir Julius Wernher was reputed to have the staggering personal fortune of some £12,000,000, and who, through his activity in the Kimberley diamond market, held the greatest financial power in the world. Next to him was the Earl of Cromer, an Orientalist known for his belief in the "white man's burden".

England's duty, he held, was to act *in loco parentis* to the less advanced peoples of the world. The third was the famous "Poet of Empire" and story-teller, David Siviter, with eye-glasses as thick as gig-lamps, who lived in a Jacobean iron-master's house deep in the Sussex countryside. Rumours abounded that Siviter was in the running for the Alfred Nobel Prize in Literature, in consideration of his remarkable talent for narration. The award would come with 138,000 Swedish Krona. A fourth person seemed hazily familiar. The fifth I had never seen before. "So the Sungazers and the Kipling League still live," I breathed.

There was a good reason for my pulse to race. Holmes had suffered one of the most humiliating defeats of his illustrious career at the hands of the mysterious Kipling League, a case I recorded against his will. * The League at that time consisted of Siviter, Sir Julius Wernher, Sir Alfred Weit, and the Earl of Cromer. Holmes and I had dubbed them "the Sungazers" because of their South African connections. The Sungazer is the heavily armoured dragon lizard *Cordylus giganteus*, the largest of the cordylids. It lives in underground burrows in the boulder fields and rocky outcrops of the high veldt of the northern Free-state and southern Transvaal – where the goldmines are. "I tell you, Watson," an angry Holmes had warned at the time, "notwithstanding that some deem them the greatest subjects of the Crown, no crook and loafer in all the underworlds of New York or London has the edge over them."

A billiard room steward came out of the stock room carrying boxes of *Romeo y Julieta* cigars. I reached out as though to engage him on the subject of cigars but instead said *sotto voce*, "Steward, I have a question. The gentlemen at the billiard-table . . . I recognise Evelyn Baring, now Earl of Cromer, recently Britain's Consul-General in Egypt. The slight fellow next to him is the story-teller and poet David Siviter. On his right is the Randlord Sir Julius Wernher, but who are the other two? And do you have any idea what they're discussing so intently? They appear to have forgotten why they're standing at the table."

The steward asked, 'And you are, sir?"

I told him. "Did you say Dr. Watson, sir?" he exclaimed "Dr. John Watson, Mr. Sherlock Holmes's biographer?"

I inclined my head in assent.

He stood for some seconds looking at me speculatively. "Even so, sir, what happens at The Travellers doesn't happen, if you know what I mean. I *did* overhear some of their conversation, but you know that my job would not be worth – "

342

" – A Lady Godiva?" I interrupted, using Cockney slang for a five-pound note. I reached toward my pocket.

The steward broke open the top box of cigars and held it out to me, whispering, "The man leaning on the table, the one with the round head – that's Sir Otto."

"Sir Otto who?" I whispered back, selecting a cigar and sniffing at it.

"Sir Otto Weit," came the reply. "You must remember his older brother, Sir Alfred, sir? A Randlord just like Sir Julius. Sir Alfred died last summer."

I held the cigar up as though to determine the price. Instead I asked, "And the other fellow at his elbow? There's something familiar about him."

"Lord Minto," came the reply. "Governor-General of India."

"Ah yes," I said. "He served with Lord Roberts in the Second Afghan War. He's a lot older now."

"You were in that war too, weren't you, sir?" the steward remarked. "I remember you saying so in one of your stories."

"I was," I nodded, "until we took on Ayub Khan west of Kandahar and a marksman got me with a ten-rupee Jezail. Ended my Army days."

The steward told me he too had been in the British Army. "Served in the Anglo-Zulu War, under Lord Chelmsford."

We were now on sympathetic terms. I bobbed my head towards the billiard room. "The subject of their conversation?" I murmured. "They look very conspiratorial."

The steward's hand came forward and took the five-pound note.

"Hardly, sir. Mr. Siviter was telling Sir Otto all about a lily-pond he plans to dig in his gardens in Sussex."

"A lily-pond?" I queried.

The steward nodded. "Yes, sir. He was explaining it in detail. Seems Sir Otto also plans to dig a lily-pond at his country estate. Lord Minto seemed very interested in ponds too, except not particularly for lilies. Something about his old days in Canada – ice-skating during their dreadful winters."

My dubious expression showed how little I felt I was getting for the five-pound note now in the steward's clenched hand. I would keep the cigar for my next dinner at Simpson's. The steward started to turn away. He stopped.

"There *was* something else, sir," he continued. "A Russian name came up. That's when they went into a sort of huddle. Made it much harder for me to hear what they were saying."

"What about this Russian?" I asked.

"Well, sir, it seems they're going to invite him to Tewin Water."

"Tewin Water?"

"Sir Otto's country house. It's in the same part of the country as Sir Julius's estate, Luton Hoo, but even bigger."

He went on. "I'm trying to remember the Russian's name . . . Yes, it's beginning to come back . . . ." Expertly his hand took the second "Lady Godiva". "Now I remember – Count somebody or other. Something like Beckerdorf."

"Count Aleksander Konstantinovich Benckendorff?" I asked. "The Tsar's Ambassador to the Court of St. James?"

My companion snapped the cigar box shut.

"That's the one, sir. Alexander was his first name, without a doubt. Same as my brother, Alex."

I had now missed the *déjeuner à la fourchette*. I walked on into the well-populated Outer Morning Room. I would bring the fact of the meeting to Sherlock Holmes's attention. With Alfred Weit dead, it seemed the mysterious League had recruited replacements in the form of Alfred's younger brother, known for his impetuosity, and Minto, both likely members of the Imperial Federation League. Sir Otto was as fanatical in support of the British Empire as his older brother had been. Under the spell of Cecil Rhodes's imperialist vision, it was Otto who had encouraged the ill-fated Jameson Raid ten years earlier, attempting to annexe The Transvaal for Britain.

If this assembly of the richest and most powerful men in England was up to something, Holmes might be tempted to come out of retirement – not least to seek revenge. Forgive and forget was not a virtue I readily associated with him. But why would such men meet in the sanctity of The Travellers' billiard room simply to discuss digging lily-ponds? Did inviting Count Benckendorff to Sir Otto's country house mean anything in particular? Why would anything to do with the Russian diplomat be of special interest or concern to the Sungazers?

On the walk back to Queen Anne Street, I stopped at a post office and scribbled a note to Holmes. A dismissive letter came by return:

Dear Watson, [he wrote]

As far as I understand, it is not yet considered unlawful assembly if a gaggle of extremely rich men meet in the billiard room of a London club. If something more substantial about the conclave comes across your path, let me know.

344

A fortnight went by. I was at work in my surgery, following the departure of Lord -----, whose predilection for show girls had led to certain complications. The second postal delivery of the day dropped with a clatter inside the entrance. A large square envelope with a Marylebone postal marking jutted out from among bills and circulars. I took it outside to a favourite bench under the branches of a London plane tree. It contained an ornate invitation card headed: *"Winter Merry-Making at Tewin Water, Welwyn, Hertfordshire"*, followed by:

> *Sir Otto Weit invites you to attend a Winter Festival champagne and beefsteak reception at his country estate to celebrate the inauguration of the Minto Skating Club. This will be followed by a tripartite ice-skating competition between the Ambassadors of France, Russia, and the United Kingdom. France and Russia will be represented on the ice by His Excellency Monsieur Paul Cambon and Count Aleksander Konstantinovich Benckendorff, the United Kingdom by Sir Arthur Nicolson, 1st Baron Carnock GCVO, Her Britannic Majesty's Ambassador to St. Petersburg. The prize will be awarded by the 4th Earl of Minto, whose skating expertise derives from six years as Governor General of Canada.*

> *RSVP Lady Lilian*

The date was *"to be set soon after the first heavy frosts of the winter"*. Guests would be informed suitably in advance. Neither my name nor any other of a guest-to-be had been inscribed. Instead, in large letters in lurid red, someone had scrawled: *"It will have blood, they say. Blood will have blood."*

I put the card away and set off for my afternoon constitutional. Despite the dramatic reference to blood, I was disinclined to bring the matter to Holmes's attention after his cool reaction when I had alerted him to my sighting at The Travellers. Or ought I to tell him? He said if something more substantial came across my path I should let him know. This card had arrived only two weeks after spotting the Sungazers at The Travellers – sheer coincidence, perhaps?

I entered the Regent's Park and settled on my favourite bench by the lake. I came to a conclusion: I would inform Holmes but underplay it. *"Holmes, it may be of no interest whatsoever, and completely coincidental, but . . . ."* I would quote word for word the two obscure hand-written sentences. I left the park and made my way to a nearby post office.

The next day brought an urgent knocking at the front door. I flicked a sixpence at the expectant telegraph messenger boy and took the small envelope. The wording was brief. I was to come down to Holmes's Sussex farmhouse at once. I was to bring the envelope, as well as the invitation card.

The motorised cab from Eastbourne Station rumbled into Holmes's yard and halted alongside the verandah. My old friend was waiting for me. Together we went into the sitting room where, to judge by the warmth and the deep pile of glowing embers, the housekeeper had laid the fire at dawn. Holmes held out a hand with an eager look.

"The card, please, Watson. '*It will have blood, they say. Blood will have blood*'," he read out, adding "'*Stones have been known to move, and trees to speak*'. Macbeth's Lament, Act 3, Scene iv."

"What do you make of it?" I asked.

"There's a saying: 'The dead will have their revenge.' One death foreshadows more deaths to come. Whoever sent this is telling us there's a conspiracy to murder. He sent this card with the aim of thwarting the intrigue. I'm inclined to take up the challenge. We have the 'when and where' it will take place – in a few weeks' time at Sir Otto Weit's Estate, and in broad daylight, before a considerable throng to boot. We must visit the scene well beforehand. In case we are apprehended, we shall go equipped like men from the National Mapping Agency. Bring a camera and a book of mathematical tables. Remind me what the steward told you about the Sungazers' conversation in the billiard room."

"Not the most gripping exchange you'll ever have heard," I replied apologetically, recounting what I'd heard. "Siviter was describing a lily-pond he plans to construct in his garden in Sussex. Mostly he was addressing Sir Otto. This skating competition indicates Sir Otto will by then have his own pond. Also, the Russian diplomat's name came up. The steward gathered enough to know they planned to invite the man to Sir Otto's country house."

"The Russian turns out to be the Count on the invitation card?"

"He does. Count Aleksander Konstantinovich Benckendorff."

"Now the envelope," Holmes ordered. He looked at the postal mark. "Marylebone," he muttered. "Remind me, who else was present in the billiard room?"

"Besides Siviter and Sir Otto, there were the Randlord Sir Julius Wernher, Lord Minto, and Evelyn Baring, 1st Earl of Cromer."

My companion crossed to a shelf and pulled down a copy of Debrett's *Peerage and Baronetage*. "Marylebone," he repeated to himself several times, flipping from name to name. "Belgrave Square, no." Then, "Bath

346

Street . . . that's Piccadilly, not Marylebone." Finally there came "Ah, good! Wimpole Street is within the Metropolitan Borough of St. Marylebone."

"Hardly a five-minute stroll from my own premises," I confirmed. "Why do you ask?"

"Because the Earl of Cromer's townhouse is at Number 36 Wimpole Street. The lackey dispatched to post the card was too lazy even to stroll down to a post office in Mayfair. One last thing: In your Army days, in addition to your medical work, did you engage in such activities as military sketching and so on?"

"I did," I replied. "Attachments on the North-West Frontier required training in map reading and field sketching. I still have my old sketching board designed for use on horseback. It came with compass, inclinometer, ruler, a roll of paper, and an arm buckle."

"What constitutes a good field sketch?"

"It should show the north arrow, then the scale – how many inches to the mile. Ridges, valleys, saddles, isolated farmhouses or even villages. Why this sudden interest in my Army days?"

"Ponds too?" came the query.

"Yes. Lakes and ponds too."

At King's Cross Station, I purchased a copy of *The Strand* to read on the journey to Welwyn, and joined Holmes in a first-class carriage of our own. We reached our destination just after dusk. Under a half-moon, we emerged from a thick windbreak of Scots Pines on the edge of the Weit estate, looking across a small river at the attractive Regency-style building set in formal gardens. Every room was ablaze with electric lighting. At our feet was a freshly-dug pond, almost the size of a small lake. Three small poles, each carrying a national flag, had been placed at predetermined places at the far side from a small wooden jetty. The nearest to us displayed the vertical bands of blue, red, and white of the French Tri-colour. The next had the three equal horizontal fields – white on the top, blue in the middle and red on the bottom – of Imperial Russia, and beyond it the Union flag, the red cross of Saint George edged in white, overlapping the Cross of St. Patrick, the two superimposed on the Saltire of Saint Andrew.

Holmes raised an arm. "The pile of earth across there from digging the pond," he asked. "Does anything about it strike you as unusual?"

"Quite a lot of clay in it," I pointed out. "That's what you'd expect from any large excavation around the London Basin."

"I didn't mean its geology."

"Then what?"

347

"The sheer quantity of soil. It must have occasioned an awful amount of work on the part of farm labourers, yet even the largest waterlilies prefer a depth of no more than thirty inches."

It was time to start to work. I took a bearing on geodetic North with my old army compass and sketched in silence. Holmes stood by, preoccupied with the pile of excavated soil and the flags. Suddenly he asked, "You must have dealt with situations where someone topples into icy water – crossing foaming rivers on rope-bridges in the Afghan mountains in winter, perhaps? What's happens within the body?"

"Blood is immediately redirected from surface tissues to the brain, lungs, and – not least – the heart."

Holmes responded, "I meant, what happens to the human who happens to be in the body at the time?"

"Perfectly straight forward," I replied. "Cold shock can bring on cardiac arrest. Death quickly ensues."

"How quickly?"

"Often within a minute."

This was followed by silence. Then, "Those flags. The Russian flag – it's between the other two. What do you make of that?"

I studied the positioning for a few seconds.

"What do I make of that?" I repeated. "Nothing."

Holmes continued, "I presume the winner is the one who skates across the pond, retrieves his nation's flag, and gets back to the finishing line before the others. Count Benckendorff is the only one required to skate across the very middle. Why are the flags so far apart? They could easily be clumped much closer together. Ambassadors are very likely to know which flag's theirs."

I returned. "If you want to me finish this sketch, Holmes, do keep any such inquisition for our return journey."

The moment we took our seats in the train for London, Holmes commenced with, "We shall need a few inconspicuous auxiliaries. Resourceful. Daring. About half your weight. Suggestions?"

"I've no idea what you're up to," I replied, "but you're describing to perfection our old ragamuffin friends, the Baker Street Irregulars. They were daring and resourceful. As to weight, they never had a decent meal except when you employed them for a day or two. I doubt if even their leader, Wiggins, weighed more than seven stone."

The street urchins in question were Holmes's unofficial force during our Baker Street days. Holmes paid them a *per diem* of a shilling with a handsome bonus on providing a vital clue.

"Exactly who I had in mind!" Holmes exclaimed. "We'll see if Wiggins or Simpson's successor is at the old haunts. Meanwhile, we'll make use of our old sitting room at 221b. We need waste no time in arranging a meeting there."

After moving to Sussex, Holmes had purchased the lease of 221 Baker Street from Mrs. Hudson, and he retained the property for those times when he needed a base in London. Two days later, and promptly at two o'clock, the street door received a hammering. Mrs. Hudson could be heard expostulating, her words drowned of any meaning by the clamour of high voices. A swift pitter-patter of naked feet was followed by a half-dozen ragged little street-Arabs rushing into the room. One of their number, taller and older than the others, gave a sharp order. Despite the rough and tumble of their entry, they instantly drew up in line and stood with expectant faces. The leader stepped forward with an air of lounging superiority, disarming in such a disreputable little scarecrow. "At your service, Guv'nor," he said, a mock left-handed salute knocking his dark grey flat cap to one side.

"And your name is – ?" Holmes enquired.

"Nick, sir," came the response. "Wiggins and Simpson and that lot gave up the street, sir," he explained. "They've gone into proper jobs, bless 'em, sir." He waved a hand proudly at his companions. "We're the new Baker Street Irregulars, Guv'nor, at your service. That is," he added, looking hopefully from Holmes to me and back, "if there's money in it."

"There is," Holmes assured him. "We'll offer the old scale, a shilling a day each, one day's pay in advance. You'll get your orders now. Be ready to execute them the moment you hear there've been a few hard frosts in Hertfordshire. Post one of the Irregulars at King's Cross. Anyone arriving on a Great Northern train will know about the weather in Herts. Understood?"

"What about a bonus?" Nick pursued, taking the unusual commission in his stride. "I heard you gave a guinea each for anything 'ceptional."

"Guineas there will be," Holmes agreed. "Watson, give Nick here the sketch you made so they can find their way to the pond at Tewin Water. Now, Baker Street Irregulars, listen carefully . . . ."

As we left the building, I turned to my friend, my cheery smile to Mrs. Hudson turning to a frown. "Now look," I expostulated, "I know you like to keep me in the dark until the very last moment, but surely I'm entitled to an explanation. For example, why did you give the Irregulars money to go to the ice-rink in Westminster and learn to skate."

349

"My dear fellow," came the amused reply, "surely it shouldn't be left just to aristocrats and Ambassadors to enjoy recreation on frozen ponds?"

"That I can agree," I replied, "but why order Nick to purchase – or more likely steal – a supply of waterproof gloves and buckets? And why order his 'aide-de-camp' Fred to buy a six-foot pole – and an auger. Where is he about to drill holes?"

"Ah, Fred and the length of bamboo and the auger. Yes, life does have its little mysteries. You must wait a while before you learn the reason for those."

"Holmes," I retorted, "I must warn you, no one should confront such rich, powerful, and ruthless men head on. We learned that lesson a few years ago. We are not of their ilk. They'll ride rough-shod over us again. We don't have the tools their wealth provides. You have a fine reputation – the finest in fact – but as a *Consulting Detective*, not a Randlord whose worth exceeds that of many a state, or someone who has spent a life-time governing subcontinents like India or countries like Egypt. Country squires and one long-forgotten French artist are numbered in your ancestry. You have had to make your way to considerable fame solely on your wits and deductive powers. By contrast, the Kipling League have pedigrees miles wide, and bank-balances miles deep. They not only know the system in which we guppies swim, they are the very ones who *created* the system."

I saw Holmes to his Sussex train. Back at my own premises, I propped the invitation card against the mirror on the hall table. I stared at it, arms akimbo. What was the sender up to? What was Holmes up to?

New Year's Day came and went. *The Times* reported the lowest temperatures on record across Britain over the past week. A communication (again anonymous) arrived, giving me a date for the Tewin Water skating gala. I let Holmes know. A reply came:

> Have instructed Irregulars to prepare for their mission. Beforehand, I want to play you a piece on the violin. Come down soonest."

"'Play you a piece on the violin'," I repeated aloud. The words generated a pang of nostalgia. On occasion during our Baker Street days, he would play a Mendelssohn's Lieder on his Stradivarius. The age-hardened wood resonated wonderfully. By contrast, left to himself he would seldom produce any music or attempt a recognised air. He would throw the fiddle across his knee, close his eyes, and scrape away.

I would make arrangements for a *locum* and take the morning train to the Sussex coast.

Holmes's housekeeper cleared away the lunch plates. The remains of the pork joint were earmarked for Tallulah, her much-loved prick-eared Norwich terrier. Holmes stood up. He gave the already-blazing fire a further poke before reaching for his violin. "Now," he explained, "I asked you down because I'm about to play you a piece from Mozart's *Magic Flute*. Note the position of my fingers . . ." He held the violin forward. ". . . and especially the note produced when I hold these two fingers down on the third string."

"Holmes," I protested, amused, "It's not my intention to take up the violin. I have enough on my plate treating aristocratic patients for syphilis. Bedsides, my hearing has nowhere near the auditory quality of yours. It seems you have the heaven-sent gift of perfect pitch."

"Nevertheless," Holmes commanded, "do pay particular attention. There's a special reason for this little exercise. Tomorrow we shall be returning to Tewin Water."

Once more we emerged after dark from the thick line of Scots Pine on Sir Otto's Estate. Holmes placed a violin case against a tree. It was a cheap instrument that he had specially purchased for our mission. I kept an ear open. Rustling from behind us would announce the approach of Nick and the Baker Street Irregulars. Temperatures across the country had remained freezing even by day, reflected in the pale layer of ice on the surface of the pond.

The half-dozen small figures appeared at our side like dragon's teeth rising from the damp soil. They emanated an air of collective expectancy, staring at the pond and then beyond at the well-lit Regency house. The troupe shook our hands in a surprisingly formal manner. Three had pails at their unshod feet. Two of them were struggling with a thick wooden plank. Their leader Nick held a claw hammer. The smallest had skates dangling from their necks. One of the latter carried the auger and the length of bamboo. In the starlight, the dark clothing Holmes had ordered for them combined with thick daubs from burnt corks across their foreheads and cheeks made it impossible to spot them against the scaly orange-brown bark of the wind-break behind us.

"Like you asked, Mister 'Olmes," Nick said, pulling one of the skaters forward, "this'n's the musical one among us – not much more than four stone neither. Used to sing treble in a boys' choir until his mother and father got run over by the Great Northern coach. Died on the spot."

With the Irregulars at our heels we retreated some hundred yards into the Scots Pines. Holmes opened his violin case and pointed the bow at the musical urchin. "Listen carefully," my friend ordered. "Memorise the highest notes."

The beautiful *Queen of the Night* aria filled the glade.

We returned cautiously to the woodland edge. The musical urchin strapped on the skates. With surprising facility, the tiny creature glided away from us. His arms remained at his side until quite suddenly, nearing the middle of the pond, his right hand shot up. "Excellent!" Holmes exclaimed. "Mark that spot on your sketch. He's telling us the ice is producing a High C."

"Holmes," I whispered, "I've gleaned from all the palaver with your violin that High C is important in all this, but what does it mean? What does it matter if the ice produces a note equal to Lilli Lehmann singing "*Casta Diva*" – or if it just rumbles?"

"Something I learned from the King of Scandinavia," Holmes whispered back. "Skating radiates a tone whose frequency depends on the thickness of the ice. A low rumble means the ice is thick, it can easily support your weight. The thinner the ice, the higher the tone. High C means the ice is barely three inches thick. Anyone even slightly heavier than our young friend would already have crashed through into the freezing water."

A few minutes later I passed the sketch-pad to Holmes. The area of the pond outlined by the skater whenever he raised his hand revealed an extraordinary fact. Through the middle of the pond there was a single patch some twenty feet in length and six feet wide where the ice was dangerously thin.

"Why," I asked, "would the water freeze in that particular pattern? Surely – "

"Left to Nature it wouldn't," came the reply. "The Sungazers have arranged it so." His bony forefinger tapped at the pad. "They must have covered this patch with matting of some sort while the rest of the pond was hosed with water, ensuring the ice on the outer areas grew thick enough for a man's safety. It means they've earmarked just the one skater for an unpleasant death. You look doubtful. Well, with young Fred's help, you shall have your proof.'

On Holmes's nod, Fred picked up the auger and the bamboo and eased his way on to the frozen pond. He began to drill a succession of holes, plunging the cane through each, raising an arm whenever it failed to touch the bottom. Almost exactly under the patch of thin ice lay a trench more than eight feet deep, extending in a straight line towards the flag of Imperial Russia.

"As I thought," Holmes said. "How else could you explain the sheer quantity of earth over there? The only skater obliged to cross the very middle of the pond – precisely where the ice is thinnest – is the Russian Ambassador. Weighed down by skates and winter clothing, his veins charged with champagne, the Count will plunge into freezing water right where the pond is deepest and rescue within several minutes least likely. Except," he added, "the mighty Kipling League, for all their miles-wide pedigrees and miles-deep bank-balances, will now be thwarted by Nick and the Irregulars. If the Kipling League are bent on murder, it is our obligation to prevent them. If it was Cromer who forewarned you, he has achieved his aim – the Russian Ambassador's survival – even if for reasons we cannot divine."

Taking his cue to commence, Nick broke open a hole in the thicker ice "off-piste" with the claw hammer just large enough for the buckets to draw water. Rhythmically the tatterdemalions took turns sending already near-freezing water swirling across the patch of ice overlaying the trench, thickening it with each inundation. Satisfied neither we nor the Irregulars had left any clue to our presence, we returned en masse to the railway station where Holmes paid of the motley crew with a "Well done, Irregulars!" and the gold guinea promised to each.

On the day following the festival at Tewin Water, I went through *The Times* with a tooth comb. A short report on the event said a fine time had been had by all. The Russian Ambassador had won the skating competition.

A week later a most curious incident occurred. At dusk my receptionist saw the last patient to the front door and went home herself. Within seconds a sharp rap came at the front door. I walked past the hall stand where the card still lay and opened the door to find a most unexpected visitor: Sir Julius Wernher. He said, "Dr. Watson, as Francis Bacon tells us, '*If the mountain will not come to Muhammad, then Muhammad must go to the mountain*'. May I come in?" He pre-empted my acceptance by stepping past me. I pointed to the consulting room. The Randlord settled himself on the settee while I took a comfortable chair and looked at him with some apprehension.

"I should mention that my doctors give me less than five years to live," he began. "Nevertheless, I'm not here on medical matters. It cannot go on, Doctor, it really can't. There must be a truce between the Kipling League and you and Sherlock Holmes."

An expression of incredulity must have passed over my face because he quickly continued. "If not friendship, then understanding. If not understanding, I really don't know what to say without sounding menacing, which is not my present intention by any means. Three or four years ago, we were challenged by your friend Holmes over the matter of a corpse at Scotney Castle * and we came out on top. Hands down. This recent matter at Tewin Water had a reverse outcome. In both instances, our goal was of the utmost significance to England and her Empire.

"At Tewin Water, our aim was to prevent the proposed an Anglo-Russian Convention from coming into being later this year, a pact which aims to overturn centuries of enmity between St. Petersburg and London. Sir Edward Grey and Count Benckendorff have just announced it'll be signed in a few months' time.

"When you and Holmes prevented us from removing the Count from the negotiations, it meant we will fail in that aim. By our own failure, we failed the British Empire. Despite the blandishments of the Tsar's foreign minister, Izvolsky, we believe the Convention will act as a fig leaf to mask continued Russian activities against England's interests in Persia and Afghanistan. Worse, St. Petersburg will continue to make every effort to wrest control of your immense trade with British India, the Jewel in England's Crown, the fabulous land which supplies your traders with pepper, raw cotton, Chinese silk, porcelain, fine spices, tea, and coffee – and gains you your world prestige. Lord Curzon said as long as England rules India, she is the greatest Power in the world, but lose her and you drop straight-away to a third-rate Power."

I remained silent. I had no idea how to respond to his words. Then, as though from nowhere, he asked, "Doctor, I believe you were at the Battle of Maiwand? You will know David Siviter penned some verses to the men who fell there?"

At once the opening lines came back to me.

There was thirty dead an' wounded on the ground we
    wouldn't keep –
No, there wasn't more than twenty when the front began to
    go;
But, Christ! along the line o' flight they cut us up like sheep,
An' that was all we gained by doing so.
I 'eard the knives be 'ind me, but I dursn't face my man,
Nor I don't know where I went to, 'cause I didn't 'alt to see,
Till I 'eard a beggar squealin' out for quarter as 'e ran,
An' I thought I knew the voice an' – it was me!

Yes, I reflected. That was Siviter, poet of Empire. I could hardly bear to recall the poem, so deeply did I pine our losses in the face of Ayub Khan's unstoppable onslaught. In vivid dreams, I would still see the graves dug so hastily of the soldiers we left behind on that lonely plain – even wish myself with them in the dusty ground.

My visitor continued, "Do you remember how great were your losses?"

"The 66th was worst hit," I replied. "We lost sixty-two percent of our strength."

"What did that mean in numbers of men," he pursued remorselessly, "Grenadiers, Indian troops, and so on?"

"Nine-hundred-forty-eight soldiers, and twenty-one officers dead."

My forehead furrowed. "Sir Julius," I went on, "I don't wish to be impolite, but your presence here disturbs me. If it isn't for medical reasons, please explain why you've come to my surgery. It's hard to believe it's to reminisce about a defeat so tragic for my Regiment and for me personally."

"On the contrary,' came the reply, 'that *is* why I'm here, Doctor. Do me the kindness to respond to one or two more questions on the men who paid so dearly. Wouldn't you agree those Tommies' lives were utterly wasted? Didn't you leave the majority of their corpses to rot in the dust, the flesh open to predation by wild dogs while your Regiment fled?"

I felt my face reddening with anger.

"Look here," I retorted, pointing towards the hallway, "you may retrieve your hat and gloves, sir, and leave. Those men were among the bravest and most patriotic – "

My words came to an abrupt halt. My uninvited guest made no move to leave. Instead he was nodding sympathetically.

"Indeed," he said. "They stood and died because the British Empire called on them to do their duty, am I correct?"

"You are," I replied, mollified.

"And they responded magnificently," Sir Julius continued. "Without their willingness to die for the British Empire, your country's influence in the East might have come to an end. Every officer and every Tommy Atkins knew if you were pushed back, the Great Game between the Russian Empire and British Empire might be lost. Tell me, Doctor: Is there any Power to rival you for control of the Indian subcontinent, keen to undermine your control of much of the Black Sea and Persia?"

"Still only the one," I returned. "The Russian Bear."

Sir Julius got to his feet. "Thank you for your courtesy in receiving me," he said, bowing slightly. "As I expected, on certain aspects of Weltpolitik we are in complete agreement. I hope I have given you my reason for being here this evening. I wanted to express my admiration –

355

Yes, as a German – for the British Empire. It is the Kipling League's primary motivation. Above all others across the span of human time, your Empire conducts itself with majesty. It is a force for good in a benighted world. It fosters peace and prosperity, innovations in medical care, education and railways – civilisation itself. By contrast, behind the mask of friendship, Russia remains a predator, the Russian Bear sitting on the tail of the Persian cat while the British Lion looks on. She will continue to eye Persia and British India like the hot-eyed wolf eyes the lamb. Those of us in the Kipling League shudder at the very idea of an Anglo-Russian Convention. It will not halt Russian expansion – it will encourage it. In Central Asia, it will hinder rather than further the British quest for security for the overland routes to the East. As to Tibet and Korea – The Kipling League sees no reason to trust Petersburg one *diuim*."

The Randlord stood at the hall table for a moment, pulling on a pair of fine leather gloves. I accompanied him to the door. We halted, facing each other. I was uncertain whether to offer him my hand.

"Dr. Watson," he continued, "We have agreed the British Empire is a magnificent civilising force, its physical integrity in need of protection at all cost. Tewin Water was meant to be the *pièce de résistance*. You lost nearly a thousand men at Maiwand. We would have accomplished far more with the death of just one slippery diplomat, Count Benckendorff. If you had let the Count fall through the ice, the Convention might have been postponed *sine die*."

"Sir Julius, before you go – the ingenious plot?" I asked. "Who came up with it?"

"I did," came the reply. "On 15 January, exactly forty years ago, the ice cover on the boating lake in the Regent's Park collapsed. Over two-hundred people plunged into the lake. Forty died."

"One last question," I added, pointing back to the invitation card on the hall table. "What reminded at least one of the Kipling League of mine and Holmes's existence?"

"We Germans have the word *Ansatz*," Sir Julius answered. "It means an 'educated guess'. Siviter recognised you at The Travellers, speaking to the Billiard room steward. A few more Lady Godivas, plus the threat to have his job taken from him, convinced him to relate the conversation. Nevertheless, your involvement in the Ambassadors' skating competition came as an unwelcome surprise."

A gloved hand rose, pointing behind me at the hallway stand.

"As to *'at least the one of the League'* . . . That card. I recognise Cromer's hand. I should have had my suspicions. Imperial Russia is the foremost debtor country in Europe. Cromer's brother, Lord Revelstoke of the Baring Brothers and Company, is leading secret negotiations with St.

Petersburg on a very large loan by an international syndicate of bankers. The proposed terms are fifty-million pounds at 89.25, commission 3.875. Barings wouldn't want that wrecked. At all costs he would want the Tsar's foreign minister Izvolsky and your Sir Edward Grey to sign the Anglo-Russian Convention. I should have realised Evelyn wouldn't be with us on this one."

With that he was gone.

NOTE

* Holmes and Watson's previous encounter with the Kipling League was published the title *Sherlock Holmes and the Dead Boer at Scotney Castle* (2016, MX Publishing)

What Came Before
by Thomas A. Turley

For Daniel D. Victor

Should any of my readers wonder, I can assert with perfect truthfulness that all the stories I have written of Mr. Sherlock Holmes are firmly based on fact. It may have been required upon occasion to disguise a well-known person's identity or alter details of a case, but the events behind such necessary changes were presented as they happened. If my tales have strayed at times from "the dictates of pure reason," including "romantic" or "sensational" elements that my friend deplored, it was because I sought to entertain as well as to instruct. The verdict of the public has vindicated this approach, for my most successful book to date concerned a spectral hound. The story of Sir Henry Baskerville would be poor stuff indeed without its atmosphere of thwarted love and evil legend.

So far as I am aware, only one case in which we were involved was ever turned into a fiction, and that fiction originated with our client. Although I write "our client", strictly speaking she was only mine, for Holmes refused to meet the distressed lady and soon removed himself from my attempt to help her. Yet, in the end he solved the case, at least to his own satisfaction. When an account came to be written, it was not me who wrote it, but rather a novelist whose literary reputation far exceeds my own. Many years have passed since Mrs. Wharton published her imaginative rendition, and the principals in the case are now deceased. With the author's kind permission, I shall reveal the facts behind her story "Afterward". – J.H.W.

In the year before King Edward died, I was invited to join a late spring gathering of Anglo-American literati. This summons, as I was aware, owed less to my own modest literary eminence than to the fact that Sir Arthur had been unable to attend. Nonetheless, my wife and I made the short journey to Queen's Acre, a country house near Windsor Park, belonging to a gentleman named Howard Sturgis. The scion of a wealthy Bostonian who had headed Barings Bank, Sturgis *fils* lounged in dilapidated comfort at "Qu'acre". His younger housemate, William

Haynes-Smith, was an acquaintance of Priscilla, as their fathers had served together as colonial administrators. Himself an "Old Etonian", Sturgis had kindly advised my wife's son Peter on gaining entrance to that public school. Only afterwards did we learn that he once anonymously published a novel, set in Eton, which unblushingly depicted "the love that surpasses the love of women". Such was our host's *entrée* into a literary circle that included Henry James and Edith Wharton. Happily, the merits of his eccentric hospitality far outweighed this minor bygone scandal.

After a delicious luncheon, we regressed to a low-ceilinged, white-panelled drawing room, seating ourselves in chintz armchairs around a table piled high with novels and picture magazines. Qu'acre's sedentary owner reclined on a settee, his legs covered by a shawl while his hands occupied themselves with knitting needles. Although his eye occasionally wandered to the French windows that opened on his weedy lawn, Sturgis followed our discussion in attentive silence. [1]

The readings that afternoon were singularly unremarkable, considering the fame of my companions. I bored the company with "Wisteria Lodge", which had recently been published in *The Strand*. James (whose verbosity exceeded even that of Mycroft Holmes) plodded through "The Married Son", his contribution to a collaborative novel, with frequent parenthetical asides and explanations. Rather than *The House of Mirth* – which Priscilla and I had very much admired – Mrs. Wharton read from her latest book, a tome that harped quite tiresomely on questions of labour relations and industrial reform. [2] As a literary afternoon, therefore, the occasion was less scintillating than we had expected.

Afterwards, Sturgis's visitors (less their host, who remained inside knitting) ambled companionably through Qu'acre's neglected rose garden, where a marble faun cavorted jauntily beside a blue-tiled pool. Haynes-Smith and I were commiserating with each other on the Derby, where we had fluttered against the King's colt Minoru and paid for our disloyalty. My wife and Mrs. Wharton walked ahead of us: Two handsome, titian-haired ladies, although the author's face in middle-age retained more character than beauty. She was describing to Priscilla a motor-tour of the southern counties from which she and Henry James had just returned.

"In fact, my dear," she said, "there's a matter related to the trip I'd hoped to mention to your husband." Turning back in our direction, she smiled sweetly at Haynes-Smith, who recognised his cue and vanished. I assumed an expression of polite enquiry.

"I am very fond of old houses, Doctor – I have even, as you may know, written on the subject [3] – so when Henry and I passed through Dorsetshire, I made a point of calling on an old acquaintance from New

York, now Mrs. Edward Boyne. Lyng, her country house, is a virtually untouched Elizabethan manor." [4]

"Indeed?" I murmured dutifully.

"Oh, yes. It is a large, impressive place, but much too antiquated for either comfort or convenience. How poor Mary can go on living there alone, after what happened to her husband, I cannot understand."

"What happened?" asked Priscilla.

"Why, he simply disappeared! In December of last year, it was. Someone – a young man Mary had never seen before – called for him at Lyng, and they went off together. Ned Boyne never returned! Mary has had no word of him from that day until this."

"Wait a moment. . . ." I remembered something of this mystery. The search for Edward Boyne, a retired engineer from the American Midwest, had lasted several weeks. Though Scotland Yard had been called in, no trace was found of him or his companion. Nor had the latter ever been identified. It was the sort of case my friend Sherlock Holmes would undoubtedly have taken had he still been in practice, but by then he had long since retired to the South Downs. While his so-called "retirement" was by no means complete, lost husbands, abandoned wives, or other "petty puzzles of the police court" (as Mycroft once described them) no longer fell within Holmes's ken.

As I suspected, however, his ken was precisely what Mrs. Wharton sought. A lady of considerable determination, she was unfazed by my assurance that the Great Detective would be unlikely to oblige her wish.

"Yes, I know he is retired, but I shall trust you to persuade him, Dr. Watson. You see, I'm very worried about Mary Boyne. Mr. Holmes lives now in Sussex, does he not? Taking a train from Eastbourne to Weymouth shouldn't unduly inconvenience him."

It was, in fact, a considerable journey, but a few hours on the train wouldn't deter my friend should he agree to take the case. I asked my interlocutor, "What, specifically, concerns you regarding Mrs. Boyne?"

"Oh, she has developed a very odd idea about Ned's disappearance, based upon a foolish legend associated with the house. I was subject to such fancies in my youth, and it distresses me to see my friend succumb to them. [5] But I shall say no more, lest I prejudice you and Mr. Holmes against poor Mary. I expect that he would rather judge the situation for himself."

"Surely, John," my wife put in, "Mr. Holmes will not be so ungallant as to refuse this lady. Were I in her position, I should be at my wit's end. I hope you will do your best for her!"

Both ladies were regarding me with steely expectation. "Of course, my dear," I said, "but you know how unyielding Holmes can be. I'm afraid, Mrs. Wharton, that I can make no promises."

Conversation on the subject ended, and Priscilla and I left Queen's Acre soon thereafter. Our drive home to Queen Anne Street was a mostly silent one.

The next morning, I prudently honoured my non-promise by telephoning Sherlock Holmes. Initially, his response was much as I had feared.

"I am sorry, Watson, but a trip to Dorsetshire is impossible at the present moment. I must complete the preparation of my hives before the summer is upon us."

Nevertheless, my friend recalled Boyne's disappearance and admitted to taking an interest in the case. He had even retained the newspaper accounts.

"So I already have the public facts. Do you visit Mrs. Boyne and obtain the private ones. Lay them before me upon your return, and I shall do my best to advise you and this unfortunate American lady."

As this result wasn't entirely negative, my report to Mrs. Wharton – and my wife – received their guarded approbation. The author vowed to write her friend and schedule a time for me to meet with her. I also pleased Priscilla by inviting her to accompany me on the trip to Lyng. Mrs. Boyne, I hoped, would be reassured and comforted by the presence of another lady, while a feminine perspective on the case might be of value. Holmes would have pooh-poohed such an idea in the early years of our detective partnership, but after meeting Irene Adler he developed a sounder understanding of the intelligence and capacity of women. I never doubted it in the case of my third wife.

Prior to leaving London, I decided to visit Scotland Yard and interview the detective who had handled the Boyne case. This (as I remembered from the press reports) was none other than Inspector Stanley Hopkins, who had first worked with Sherlock Holmes on several cases in the middle 'nineties. [6] By 1909, "young Hopkins" was no longer young. He was an experienced detective in his prime, a mainstay of the force as our old stalwarts Gregson, Bradstreet, and Lestrade approached the end of their careers. Hopkins received me in his office overlooking the Embankment, removing from the chair before his desk a mounted stag's head with bloodstained antlers.

"Evidence," he explained briefly. "Sit down, Doctor. I'm very glad you've come." Aside from the grey in his mustache, the inspector looked much the same as ever. "This Boyne case ought never have been discontinued. I only wish I'd had you and Mr. Holmes along to help me at the time."

"It seems a most mysterious affair," I noted. "Unfortunately, after nearly six months I've forgotten the details."

"Then let me fill you in." Hopkins took from his desk a thickish file and started leafing through it, cogently outlining what little was known of the fate of Edward Boyne. I shall quickly summarise those facts.

Boyne and his wife Mary, a wealthy young couple from Waukesha, Wisconsin, had arrived in England in the spring of 1908. After purchasing Lyng, a decrepit Elizabethan manor, they had repaired the house but done little to modernise it, apparently preferring its "authentic" lack of electric lighting, hot running water, and other innovations to mere comfort or convenience. Once in residence, the Boynes "kept themselves to themselves" and made few friends among their neighbours, although they maintained good relations with the tradesmen employed to restore the house and grounds. They were also well-liked by their servants.

"The house has a modest staff: The butler, Wilson, Trimmle, the parlour maid-*cum*-housekeeper, two younger maids and a footman, the cook Mrs. Dockett, and a part-time gardener. Trimmle and Wilson sleep on the premises. The rest come in from the village. I interviewed Trimmle at some length. She was fond of Mrs. Boyne. 'A very genteel lady, sir,' she told me. 'She's brought this old 'ouse back to life. A painter she is, too, an *artist*, if I'm any judge. You wouldn't think she were *American*, if you 'adn't 'eard 'er tawk.'"

"What about the husband?" I enquired, after we had shared a chuckle.

"He was a rather different type. Kind enough as an employer, Trimmle said, but distant and preoccupied. Spent most of his time in his library, writing a book. I examined the manuscript: *An Economic Basis of Culture*, he was calling it. Often took long walks alone, but tended to avoid going out in public. 'There wore something *wrong* about 'im, sir,' so Trimmle thought – and perhaps she had it right."

The inspector handed me a photograph of Edward Boyne. He was aged no more than forty, fair-haired, lean, and handsome, offering the camera a genial smile. Yet was there not a certain wariness behind the eyes, a touch of insincerity in the curve of the thin lips? Or was I merely "theorising in advance of data," as Sherlock Holmes would charge? Boyne, after all, may well have been the victim of a crime.

"That photograph," said Hopkins, "was circulated throughout the British Isles and on the Continent, along with Mrs. Boyne's vague description of her husband's visitor. There was the usual plethora of rumours and false sightings, but every lead we followed up came to a dead end."

"Could you establish any motive for Boyne's disappearance?"

"Barring an actual kidnapping – and there was never a demand for ransom – when a man takes flight it's usually over money or a woman. We found no indication of another woman in Boyne's life. It would have been odd to leave with a *male* visitor had a secret romance been involved. Unless, of course – " The inspector stopped as though a new idea had struck him: " – his visitor *was* the other party in the romance! I must admit, Doctor, *that* thought hadn't occurred to me."

"Far more likely to be money," I opined, but Hopkins shook his head.

"Not on the face of it. Boyne's bank account in Dorchester holds just over £20,000. There was no large withdrawal in the days before he left, nor has any significant amount been taken in the six months afterwards – only the sums his wife required to run the house. That money was handled from a separate account."

"It certainly begins to look as if the man is dead. Otherwise, that's quite a fortune to have left behind. Had he access to any money elsewhere?"

"Not according to Mrs. Boyne or our sources in America. Their wealth was of quite recent origin – A sudden windfall from a mining venture. But the lady claims that she knew very little of her husband's financial affairs."

"*Claims,* you say?" I noted. "Did you have grounds for suspecting Mrs. Boyne?"

Hopkins sighed and shook his head. "Not as such," he muttered, rising and gazing at the looming clouds outside his window, which on that drizzly afternoon were even greyer than the Thames. "But in the end her attitude disturbed me, all the same.

"You see," continued the inspector, "late in February, after three months of wheel-spinning, we'd finally begun to make some progress on the case. Edward Boyne had been writing a letter in his library on the morning that he disappeared. It was addressed to '*My dear Parvis*' and mentioned the death of somebody called '*Elwell*'. The local constabulary had traced this Harold Parvis – he was a lawyer in Waukesha, where the Boynes had come from – but he professed to know nothing of the matter.

"Then, on my last visit to Lyng, Mrs. Boyne showed me an old news article she had received by mail on the evening before her husband left. Why she hadn't done so earlier I cannot say. Perhaps connubial loyalty came into it, because the article – which had been clipped from *The Waukesha Sentinel* – told of a lawsuit against Boyne by a Robert *Elwell*, almost surely the dead man mentioned in Boyne's unfinished letter.

"Well, after returning to London I was prepared to follow up this clue, but two days later I received a telephone call from Mrs. Boyne. She was most insistent, Doctor, that we drop the case! Wouldn't give her reasons – except to say that she was now convinced her Ned was gone, and that no one would ever know what happened to him. Until then, the lady had seemed heartbroken at our lack of progress. It was an amazing change of front."

"It would certainly appear so. How did you proceed?"

"I took it to Gregson, and the two of us went straight to the Commissioner. You can probably guess the result of *that* conversation. 'Three months wasted, Hopkins, searching for a lost American? And you want to devote *more* time to such an unproductive case, against the wishes of the subject's wife? Quite out of the question, I'm afraid. The Yard, Inspector, has other fish to fry.'"

I smiled with rueful sympathy, long accustomed to the indomitable inertia of the official mind. "But there would be no objection from the Yard to *my* investigating further, and referring the case to Holmes for his opinion?"

"Not if you keep me – and no one else – informed," Hopkins replied sagely. "I only hope, Dr. Watson, that you'll find enough new evidence to justify reopening the case. There's more to Ned Boyne's disappearance than has so far met the eye."

I rose to go, pausing in the doorway with a query that might help me to determine the best approach to Ned Boyne's wife. "In your last conversation with her, Hopkins," I enquired, "how did Mrs. Boyne *sound* when she spoke to you? Like a murderess afraid she would reveal her guilty conscience? Or a grieving wife unable to continue waiting in false hope?"

Inspector Stanley Hopkins gave me a long and thoughtful look before he answered. "Like neither of those women, Doctor, I should say. My strong impression was that the lady was afraid. And not of Scotland Yard," he added quietly.

It was with a sense of oddity that I departed Waterloo Station on the seventh day of June, in company with my dear wife instead of Sherlock Holmes. I, for once, was the detective on the case, while Priscilla took my old part of "second fiddle". This wasn't a role for which she was ideally suited, and I expected a more even-handed partnership than mine had been with Holmes. Naturally, I couldn't claim to fill the Great Detective's shoes, so I was very glad to have my wife's assistance.

The morning of our journey was a pleasant one. Sunny, clear-blue skies prevailed once we left behind the smoke and fog of London. Having previously visited only the coast of Dorsetshire – with its towering rock cliffs, sand-strewn beaches, and quaint harbours – I was delighted to see green, rolling hills and pastureland as we approached Dorchester from the north. The village of Lyng was several miles from town, so after luncheon at a local inn I hired a trap to drive us to the house. We arrived just after our scheduled time of two o'clock.

Contrary to Mrs. Wharton's description, Lyng wasn't a large house by Elizabethan standards. Built of grey stone, it had the high chimneys and wide, mullioned windows of that glorious age, with a walled courtyard and a gated lodge adjacent to the village. We were admitted by the butler and taken to the library. Once indoors, it was obvious that Lyng had been lovingly restored, with admirable concern for authenticity and little for expense. Its oaken-shelved and panelled library, as implied by Hopkins, was Edward Boyne's *sanctum sanctorum* and from what I understood, the last place he was seen alive. Priscilla and I seated ourselves in two of the three chairs beside his desk and waited for his wife to join us.

The lady who entered was about Priscilla's age – that is to say, in her mid-thirties. Mary Boyne was tall and statuesque, with dark hair, deep-set eyes, and a rosebud mouth that would have held a lovely smile. Only an arched and pointed nose detracted slightly from her beauty. However, shock and grief had added ten years to Mrs. Boyne's apparent age. Her brow was furrowed, her lips drooped sadly, and her face wore in repose a look of dazed incomprehension. The greeting she offered as we rose was less than warm.

"I agreed to see you, Dr. Watson, at the insistence of my old friend Edith Wharton. Nevertheless, I consider her intervention presumptuous and your visit most inopportune. I have already consulted both the local police and Scotland Yard, and they were able to accomplish nothing. Edith tells me you are acting on behalf of *Sherlock Holmes* – whom I had thought as fictitious a character as Long John Silver! If he really lives and breathes, could he not be bothered to put in an appearance?"

I began haltingly to explain Holmes's retirement, but Priscilla came to my defence. "My husband, Mrs. Boyne, has worked with Mr. Holmes for many years. John has been thoroughly briefed by Inspector Hopkins and knows the basic facts. He wishes to hear the details from your own lips, and he will report to Mr. Holmes when we return to London."

Mary Boyne regarded my wife with bemusement. "I must admit, Mrs. Watson," she replied, "that I hadn't expected to consult a *lady* detective on the case!"

With the ice broken by her laughter, we resumed our seats, while Mrs. Boyne took the third chair. "Where would you like me to begin?" she asked.

"Why not at the beginning?" my wife suggested. "John, as I mentioned, knows the background of your case, but I have heard almost nothing of it. For instance, how did you and your husband come to live at Lyng?"

Priscilla smiled disarmingly, and Mrs. Boyne returned her smile. I was pleased to see that the two women had established a rapport. From that point on, our client told her story willingly, and no doubt more freely than she would have had I come alone. Again, I shall summarise large parts of it.

Mary Boyne's family had occupied the same exalted stratum of New York society as Edith Wharton's, although the two friends were years apart in age. She had married at twenty to Ned Boyne, a rising young engineer, whose firm soon despatched him to the American Midwest. Our hostess dwelt briefly on the "soul-deadening ugliness of *WAW-kuh-shah, Wis-KAHN-sin*" – (Here Mrs. Boyne's cultured East Coast accent lapsed into a nasal twang.) – where she and her husband had lived for fourteen dreary years. Their exile appeared likely to continue for another decade before Boyne (who "ground on doggedly" with his engineering work) would be in a position to retire. Then, "with a suddenness that still makes me blink" had occurred "the prodigious windfall of the Blue Star mine," in which her husband had invested and reaped a massive profit when he sold his shares. Armed with their new-found wealth, the couple fled Waukesha to fulfill Ned Boyne's fondest dream: Starting a new life in The Old Country, including ownership of "a genuine Elizabethan manor" to call his own.

It was Mrs. Wharton who had introduced the Boynes to her friend Alida Stair, from whose cousin they had ultimately purchased Lyng. Despite its antiquated inconvenience, the house had been everything that they could wish. They had delighted in the successful outcome of its restoration, and Mary Boyne had especially enjoyed making something of the long-neglected garden. The villagers, to her surprise, had been most welcoming. She found no difficulty in recruiting an adequate staff. During their "spare time", Mary had returned to her girlhood love of painting, while Ned began work on the economic treatise he had planned for years. In short, the first months of their life at Lyng had been idyllic.

"When did things begin to change?" I enquired quietly. "Was there no indication of impending trouble before your husband disappeared?"

Mrs. Boyne glanced at me distrustfully, but Priscilla offered her a reassuring smile. "Ned *had* seemed . . . troubled in the weeks before," she answered finally, "just as he was during our hard times in Waukesha. He had been sublimely happy in our first days here, so I thought his book must be going badly. But, no, he said it was progressing well. . . . I remember something strange he said last fall. We had climbed up to the belvedere on Meldon Steep and were looking down on the house and the green hills above the village. It was the same day – " She broke off, hesitated, and went on.

"'You know, Mary,' Ned said to me, 'they're lucky people, these English. Living on this little, compressed island, where a few miles can be a distance. With so much contrast of scenery in a pretty small space. So small a man could find it hard to get lost in.'" [7]

"Did you know what he meant?" my wife asked softly.

"I didn't then." Mrs. Boyne's eyes had filled with tears. "I only wish I didn't now.

"You see, Mrs. Watson," she went on, as Priscilla and I exchanged a guarded look, "after Ned left, I found out he had done something . . . wrong. It was nothing illegal or criminal, nothing for which he could be prosecuted. Why, even the lawsuit that came out of it was soon dismissed. My husband had merely played – " (It was here that her voice quavered slightly.) " – a very shabby trick."

I recalled the case notes Hopkins had provided. "Did it have to do with a man called Robert Elwell?"

"Yes, Doctor." This time, Mary Boyne turned to face me calmly. "Mr. Elwell was a junior member of Ned's firm. It was he, I found out afterward, who advised my husband to invest his money in the Blue Star mine – although this was *not* the account that Ned had given me. I learned the truth from Harold Parvis, a Waukesha lawyer, who came to Lyng in February, nine weeks after Ned had disappeared."

"Parvis?" I repeated in surprise. "But Parvis had told the local authorities that he knew nothing of the matter."

"Oh, *he knew!*" Again, our client's voice was trembling. "He told me everything: How my husband had known the Blue Star mining shares were greatly overvalued, and an adverse engineer's report was on the way. It's how Ned made our fortune, don't you see? He sold his own stock at exactly the right moment. But he never passed on the news to Robert Elwell, and Elwell and his family lost everything they had."

Here Mrs. Boyne succumbed to tears. My wife went to kneel beside her chair and take her hand. "I'm so sorry. Could it have been his guilty conscience that made your husband decide to disappear?"

"Oh, no!" Boyne's wife answered bitterly. "He was pleased to put it all behind him! The afternoon before, you see, both of us had received letters from Waukesha. Mine was only a clipping from the *Sentinel* that told of Elwell's lawsuit against Ned. It was the first I'd heard of it, so naturally I asked him for an explanation. Ned assured me that the suit had been withdrawn – not that it would have stood a chance in court – so the whole affair was over. He kissed me, laughed, and told me not to worry.

It was as if the worry I'd seen in *his* face for the past weeks had vanished in an instant!

"What I didn't know then was that my husband's letter from Waukesha had told him of Robert Elwell's death. I didn't find *that* out until I read the letter he'd begun to Mr. Parvis on the morning that he left. In the end, of course," she added with a sudden laugh, "his leaving wasn't entirely Ned's decision!"

Her merriment presaged an attack of near-hysteria. For perhaps half a minute, Mary Boyne sat sobbing helplessly, while Priscilla kept a protective arm around her shoulders and I fetched a glass of whisky (which had the fine aroma of Kentucky bourbon) from the decanter on the sideboard. Once she gulped it down, our client gradually recovered. She smiled gratefully at my wife, who had resumed her chair, then turned to me.

"I apologise, Doctor – and Mrs. Watson – for that unseemly outburst. Since all this started, I have had no one 'unofficial' to confide in, except for Edith Wharton. And *she*," Mrs. Boyne added with a momentary smile, "does not encourage weakness. I fear that when you've heard what I have next to tell you, you'll agree with Edith in deciding that I'm mad!"

Just at that moment, the library door opened. A gaunt, middle-aged woman, dressed as a parlour maid, entered and gingerly approached her mistress. "Shall I serve tea now, ma'am?" she enquired anxiously.

Our hostess took a moment to respond, but she had regained her composure. "Tea? Yes, please, Trimmle, but give us fifteen minutes, would you? First, there is something I should like to show my guests." She turned to Priscilla. "Would you and the Doctor care to see more of the house, Mrs. Watson?"

"Why, certainly," my wife answered, as determined as our hostess to restore an air of calm. We dutifully followed Mrs. Boyne into the lofty entrance hall and up two flights of stairs onto the second floor. Along the way, she asked me, "Dr. Watson, do you and Mr. Holmes believe in ghosts?"

"Holmes says not," I answered briefly. As for myself, I recalled an uncanny incident that had occurred when my first wife, Constance, died. [8] However, it was not a tale I had ever told my present wife, and now wasn't the time for it. I said nothing more.

"All these old houses have them," she assured me gaily, "but ours is rather special!" We had entered a cramped bedroom. Behind a table in one corner hung a faded tapestry. Mrs. Boyne pushed it aside to reveal an ancient wooden door.

"You'll never guess where this leads!" she promised, with the same air of slightly manic cheerfulness. "I was *so* pleased when I found it."

Once opened, the door revealed a spiral stairway that led into the attic. After we arrived there, Priscilla and I waited beneath the steeply-angled, oaken beams as Mary Boyne ascended a ladder into an alcove that opened onto the roof. Again we followed and found ourselves in a secluded coign, the narrow ledge beneath us facing a stone parapet. From this vantage point, we could see Lyng's grounds and gatehouse, as well as the church, most of the village, and the tree-lined hills beyond. "What a delightful prospect!" I enthused.

"Yes, isn't it?" agreed our client. "Do you see there?" She pointed to a portion of the lawn below us, where the drive emerged from an intervening corner of the house. "That's where we saw it first."

"Saw what, Mrs. Boyne?" This from Priscilla, who had come to stand beside me.

"Why, the Ghost of Lyng! Of course, we didn't know it *then*," she went on quickly. "That's the marvellous thing about our ghost. You never know you've seen it until long, long afterward. At the time, Ned told me he thought it was a man who'd come to fix the stable drains. But from that morning, he was never easy in his mind again, not until the night before he went away." She smiled hopelessly, her face newly streaked with tears.

"Perhaps we ought to go inside, my dear," my wife said gently. "Surely it is time by now for your maid to serve the tea."

We returned to the library, where the tea indeed was waiting. As our hostess poured with steady hands, an atmosphere of near-normality descended. "This visitor who came to see your husband that last morning," I enquired when we had finished the last morsels. "Can you tell me more about him than was in the police reports?"

"I can indeed, Doctor." Mary Boyne offered me a serene smile. "The man who took poor Ned away was Robert Elwell."

I stared in absolute bewilderment. Hopkins had said nothing of such madness.

"But . . . Mrs. Boyne," Priscilla faltered, "Robert Elwell was dead by then."

"Oh, I have no doubt he was. I didn't know him *then*, you see. Remember, here at Lyng, one doesn't realise one has seen the ghost until long *afterward!* In this case, I had to wait nine weeks."

"I don't expect you to believe me," she said sadly as we sat in silent consternation. "Mr. Parvis didn't, when I recognised Elwell's photograph in *The Waukesha Sentinel*. He had shown it to me in the hope that I'd contribute something to the Elwell family."

"And did you?" Priscilla asked distractedly.

"Well, naturally. With my husband gone, it was only I who could make restitution. I cannot touch Ned's capital, of course, until he's . . .

369

declared *legally* dead. Nor have I any money of my own. So I wrote to Father. Although he disliked Ned and had opposed our marriage, he did agree to help Ned's victims, just as I had known he would. [9] I'm sure that seeing me humiliated in that way gave Father a certain satisfaction." Mrs. Boyne's voice had grown eerily calm.

"You're *quite* sure the man you saw was Elwell?" I reiterated, hoping for a response I could believe.

"Oh, yes, Dr. Watson. I had been in the greenhouse that morning with Cooper. We were waiting for a man from Dorchester to come and fix the pipes. At first, I thought that Elwell was that man. He was standing in the gateway to the garden, with the sun behind him, so I couldn't clearly see his face. But he was young, and dressed *exactly* as in the *Sentinel's* photograph: An American grey suit with a wide-brimmed hat. He looked just as he did the first time we had seen him."

"The first time?" my wife echoed.

"From the roof," our client patiently explained, "the ledge where we were standing earlier. Ned and I watched a man in grey walk down the drive toward Lyng, but he had vanished by the time that Ned ran down to meet him. It was October twentieth, the same day we climbed up Meldon Steep.

"It was also," Mary Boyne went on bleakly, "the day Robert Elwell shot himself. He didn't die for several weeks, however. He didn't die until the day before I saw him in my garden. It was only after he was *dead* that our Ghost of Lyng could take his form and come again. The ghost had come for Ned, you see. It asked me quite politely to see 'Mr. Boyne', so I told it he was working in the library. I sent it to this very room, to take my husband from me for the rest of time."

It was shortly afterwards that Priscilla and I took our leave. When we declined her obviously reluctant dinner invitation, Mrs. Boyne offered her manservant and carriage to convey us to the station. I promised to report our interview to Sherlock Holmes, and even said I hoped that he would soon communicate with her. While she expressed gratitude for our endeavours, our client stated firmly that she wanted or expected nothing more.

"No one, not even Sherlock Holmes," she said, "will ever know what happened to my husband. That's what I told Inspector Hopkins after I had met with Mr. Parvis. There seemed little point in telling Scotland Yard about the Ghost of Lyng, so I simply asked the Inspector to give up the case. I shall make the same request of you, Doctor. You've heard my tale, as Edith wished, but there is nothing you or Mr. Holmes can do. Please

370

respect my wishes and let this be the end of it. Thank you both, and now good-bye."

After a quiet night in our hotel, Priscilla and I took an early train to London. We sat silent as it left the platform. Watching the hills of Dorsetshire recede into the distance, I found myself musing on the Ghost of Lyng. This spectre – given the mad assumption that it was more than myth – seemed to derive its power from the guilty consciences of those it haunted. What form, I wondered, would it assume were I to encounter it? The brother I abandoned, years before, to despair and suicide in San Francisco? [10] The friend and fellow doctor who became my bitterest enemy when Mary died, himself dead now for fifteen years? [11] Or would Lyng's ghost, like that of Hamlet's father, assume some new and even more horrific shape? Given the Great Detective's probable response to Mrs. Boyne, it seemed one mystery, thank God, that I wouldn't be called upon to solve.

I was rescued from these idle speculations when my wife asked suddenly, "John, if we should be able to persuade her, do you believe that Mr. Holmes will help that poor, distracted woman?"

"I think not," I answered honestly, "once he learns of her obsession with the ghost."

"Then what *good* is he?" Priscilla demanded sharply. And she said no more of the case, the Boynes, or Sherlock Holmes for the duration of our journey.

I must admit that I was of Priscilla's way of thinking, several days thereafter, when I spoke to Holmes. I had posted to his home a careful but complete report of our afternoon with Mrs. Boyne, asking my friend to telephone as soon as he had read it. When Holmes did so the next morning, it was to declare his refusal to participate further in the case.

"You might, for once," I growled at him, "summon up a little human feeling."

"Human feeling can be of little practical assistance so long as Mrs. Boyne persists in her delusion," the detective replied imperturbably. "I have read your admirably thorough and cogent memorandum, but I decline to waste my time in searching for a ghost."

Perhaps my irritation radiated through the telephone, for Holmes condescended to explain. "As you know quite well, Watson, Stanley Hopkins is a competent detective, and these days the Yard's resources are far superior to mine. If Edward Boyne was still within these isles, then Hopkins would have found him. It isn't England but America that holds the solution to this case, and I have neither time nor inclination to undertake that journey now. You may inform Mrs. Boyne," he sarcastically concluded, "that should I ever find myself in Waukesha, Wisconsin, I shall be happy to investigate her husband's fate."

This ill-meant message was destined to remain undelivered. Aside from a curt reply expressing her displeasure, it was six months before Priscilla and I heard again from Mrs. Wharton, to whom I had regretfully reported Holmes's dereliction. However, two weeks prior to Christmas, we were dismayed to receive from her the following note:

> *My Dear Dr. Watson,*
>
> *I am sorry to inform you and Mrs. Watson that my friend Mary Boyne is dead. Her body was found yesterday on the drive in front of Lyng, a year to the day from the date of her husband's disappearance.*
>
> *From all indications, Mary had fallen from the isolated rooftop coign where (according to her) she and Ned first saw the ghost of Robert Elwell walking up the same drive toward their home. Whether she again witnessed this spectre or some fresher horror, or whether her death was simply accident or suicide, you and I will never know.*
>
> *One thing seems certain: The legendary Ghost of Lyng (in which, I admit, I now believe) has claimed another victim. Let us hope poor Mary is its last.*
>
> *Yours sincerely,*
> *Edith Wharton*

The following year, I was surprised to read in *Century Magazine* a new ghost story, entitled "Afterward", which Mrs. Wharton wrote regarding the tragedy at Lyng. Whether intended as a tribute to her friend or simply as an exercise in fiction, it followed almost to the letter the events of the case as Mary Boyne perceived them.

However, "Afterward" was not to be the final word, for the story had an unexpected epilogue. In 1912, Sherlock Holmes *did* find himself in the American Midwest, during the momentous mission Sir Arthur and I have recorded elsewhere. [12] "Having a couple of days free," (as he jocularly told me later) my friend decided, "purely on a whim," to take the relatively short train ride from Chicago to the town of Waukesha, Wisconsin, located just south of Milwaukee. "There I solved the Boyne case in a single afternoon."

I didn't learn the details until the following spring, when Holmes made one of the periodic returns to England required to preserve his own well-known identity and distract the attention of his foes from "Altamont." In late March, I travelled down to my friend's Sussex cottage, and we traced a well-worn path above the chalk cliffs near Beachy Head. Although Priscilla had long ago forgiven Holmes for deserting Mrs. Boyne, the subject of our conversation wouldn't have been a welcome one in Queen Anne Street.

"Needless to say," the Great Detective began his exposition, "the idea of a ghost was always inadmissible. I took as my starting point, therefore, the thesis that the person Mrs. Boyne encountered in her garden on the day her husband vanished was *not* – as she so foolishly believed – a ghost, but was, in fact, *the living Robert Elwell."*

Holmes raised a hand to quell my scepticism. "If this was true – and it seemed the only logical conclusion – then it was surely obvious that Elwell and the attorney Parvis had conspired together. My task, therefore, was to locate Harold Parvis."

I nodded briefly to show that I had followed.

"Waukesha, as your client once complained, is a most depressing burg – I beg your pardon, Watson. My vocabulary has been defiled by my need to adopt American lingo. Its sole claim to distinction is its healing waters. The local citizens pridefully deem their city 'the Saratoga of the West'. You will observe, however, that Saratoga's occupants seldom refer to that charming New York resort as 'the Waukesha of the East'. But I digress . . . ."

"Harold Parvis," I reminded him.

"Indeed. I found his law office through the simple expedient of consulting the local telephone directory. Mr. Parvis was in his forties, balding but heavily black-bearded. His keen eyes squinted at me from behind thick spectacles. He had a colourful manner of speech – the very epitome of the 'hot-shot, small-town lawyer'. Let me resurrect my rusty acting skills to give you an impression of the man: 'Well, gosh all fish-hooks, the famous Sherlock Holmes, right here in my office! Welcome to Waukesha, sir!'" [13]

I laughed aloud, for Holmes had matched exactly the annoying nasal twang that Mrs. Boyne employed to mock the denizens of her despised former home. "Well, I expect you made short work of *him!"* I chortled.

"By no means, Doctor. Despite his bumpkin-ish exterior, Harold Parvis possessed both a shrewd intellect and a good deal of nerve. He wasn't intimidated in the least on learning the object of my visit.

"'The Boyne case? Well, now, I'd thought Scotland Yard had given up on *that* one long ago, but I suppose you're investigating privately. No,

I don't mind telling you the whole story, Mr. Holmes. I don't believe I can be convicted of anything illegal, and both Ned Boyne and Bob Elwell are well beyond your reach. Take a chair, then, and I'll give it to you straight.

"'The thing you have to realise,' began Parvis, 'is that Bob Elwell was a really well-liked guy. When the local engineering firm had hired Elwell, the more experienced Ned Boyne had acted as his mentor. Bob always had an eye for a good thing, (as Parvis put it). It was he who had advised Boyne to buy the Blue Star mining stock, although the latter had reversed their roles when lying to his wife. Unluckily, Elwell also discovered that his mentor routinely engaged in petty graft. You know – padding hours and expenses, skimming a little off the top. Nothing a lot of other guys weren't doing. Being young and idealistic, he threatened to report Boyne to the company's managers unless such irregularities should cease.

"'When Ned saw his chance to make a killing and skip town,' Parvis informed me, 'he got his own back on Bob Elwell by not warning him about the overvalued mining stock. Bob had put in every cent he had, so when Blue Star collapsed, he and his family were absolutely ruined. The poor guy tried to shoot himself, but he made a mess of it – thank God! – and only spent a few weeks in the hospital.'

"'Thank God, indeed,' I murmured piously.

"'Well, by this time a lot of Bob's friends here in Waukesha were pretty mad. We've got a saying on this side of the water, Mr. Holmes: *"Don't get mad – get even!"* So I got to talking with Ben Miller and Bill Colwell – Ben edits the *Waukesha Sentinel*, and Bill had retired the year before as police chief – and we put our heads together. By the time Bob got home from the hospital – (The bank allowed him to skip payments on his mortgage, so he hadn't lost the house.) – we had a plan ready to present to him – and Bob went for it like hotcakes. This was in the late summer of '08.'

"'I see.' With his reminiscences flowing smoothly, I was required to provide Parvis only minimal encouragement. I was, however, taking careful notes.

"'Obviously, the first thing we had to do was find Ned Boyne. He'd sold up and left town without even saying "Bye!", but anyone who knew Ned had heard him gab about his lifelong dream of retiring to Olde England. So your country seemed the place to start. We thought about calling in the Pinkertons, but involving them was just too risky. We even considering hiring *you*, Mr. Holmes, until we found out you'd retired. In the end, Chief Colwell decided to do the job himself. He located the Boynes' home in Dorsetshire in mid-October, a week from the day that he'd arrived in London.'"

"Good heavens, Holmes," I laughed. "Please don't mention *that* fact if you ever tell this tale to Stanley Hopkins!"

My friend smiled ruefully and resumed his account by describing the conspirators' next steps. Robert Elwell's failed lawsuit had been merely an invention designed to worry Boyne. "'We got Dan to print a few fake *Sentinel* articles to send to Ned,' Holmes continued, quoting Parvis, "'holding them while we raised the money to send Bob to England. You might think *that* took a lot of doing, but practically the whole town chipped in. In the end, we put Bob Elwell on the *Lusitania* early in December and sent him over there in style.

"'Meanwhile, I'd mailed Boyne a real article from the *Sentinel* about Bob's suicide attempt, as well as a couple of bogus ones reporting the fictitious lawsuit. They bothered Ned enough to show his hand and write to me. Finally, I sent one of the lawsuit articles to *Mrs.* Boyne, timing things so she'd receive it at the same time we expected Bob to get to Dorsetshire. I also wrote again to Boyne, giving him the sad news that Elwell (who – so far as *he* knew – had been languishing in the hospital for the past two months) had passed away. As I learned later from your British police, Ned had been writing to thank me on the very morning Bob showed up on his doorstep.'

"By now, the course of subsequent events seemed clear. I enquired whether Parvis was acknowledging his role as an accessory to murder.

"'Hell, no!' The startled attorney leaned back in his chair and glared at me. 'Murder was never in the plan. All we intended was to scare Boyne enough to sign over part of his fortune to save the Elwell family. Otherwise, we'd expose him for the crook he was! The idea was restitution, Mr. Holmes, not murder.'

"'But murder – or kidnapping, at least – apparently took place,' I reminded him.

"'Yeah? Well, you can't *know* that, and even if you did you'd never prove it.' Parvis gave me a speculative glance, no doubt considering how much of the truth could safely be revealed. 'Look . . . *we don't know* what happened when they met. Nobody here in Waukesha ever heard another word from Bob. He had a pistol with him, so I expect he forced Boyne from the house at gunpoint. But they never got to the bank in Dorchester, because no money was withdrawn from Ned's account. Even Scotland Yard got that far.'

"I elected to ignore the unjust aspersion on friend Hopkins. 'Then what do *you* think occurred, Mr. Parvis?'

"'I don't know, Mr. Holmes,' he sighed, 'and after all this time, I don't really care! Maybe Ned Boyne murdered Bob and fled to China. Maybe it was the other way around. After all, neither of them had much to go home to at that point. My only concern, once it was clear Bob Elwell wasn't coming back, was providing for his family.'"

"Because the conspiracy had failed to secure the money for that cause, Harold Parvis had been forced to solicit charity from Mrs. Boyne, whom he visited two months after her husband's disappearance.

"'I felt sorry for his wife,' the lawyer admitted to my friend. 'It was obvious that she hadn't known what Ned was up to, and she seemed like a nice lady. How she got mixed up with a rat like Boyne, I'll never know! When I showed her the newspaper, and she got that weird idea about a ghost, I tried to talk her out of it, but she just wasn't rational. Finally, Mrs. Boyne calmed down enough to discuss making some provision for Bob's family. I got a nice cheque from her a few weeks later. Not only that, but before she died later in the year – I was truly sorry to hear it, by the way – she wrote to say she planned to change her will. She would leave the Elwells Ned Boyne's whole estate, once he was declared legally dead and everything cleared probate. All Mrs. Boyne held onto was the house, which – for some reason – she said she wouldn't leave to her worst enemy. I've no notion, Mr. Holmes, what she meant by *that!* Looked like a nice place when I was there.'"

"Thus, Watson," Holmes concluded his long recollection, "it seems I am vindicated. Edward Boyne did *not* fall victim to the Ghost of Lyng. Rather, he fell victim to a more mundane, but perhaps more deadly, foe: Small-town America."

Naturally I had several questions, which the detective answered readily. Robert Elwell's family no longer resided in Waukesha, but if Parvis knew their whereabouts ("and I am sure he did"), he wouldn't say. Holmes was by no means satisfied with the lawyer's account, but he realised that it came as near to truth as it was possible to come. Nor, assuming any valid charges could be brought against them, did my friend see any point in prosecuting the conspirators. "In a moral, if not a legal sense, they had justice on their side. Remember also," he reminded me, "that I couldn't involve myself in a public prosecution without compromising my Altamont identity and risking the failure of my greater mission."

"May I ask one thing more?"

"Of course, old friend."

"Parvis mentioned that the Waukesha police chief found the Boynes' home in mid-October. Could the actual date have been October twentieth? Did he approach the place?"

"Well asked! I posed the same question myself to Harold Parvis. But, no, Colwell couldn't have been mistaken for the first appearance of the so-called ghost. An elderly man, he looked not a jot like Elwell. Besides, he had left Dorsetshire three days before."

"Perhaps," I could not forbear musing, "it really *was* the Ghost of Lyng."

"Fie, Doctor! Whoever it may have been, that idea was a phantom of Boyne's guilty conscience. Recall Proverbs 28:1: '*The wicked flee when no man pursueth –* '"

"' *– but the righteous,* '" I completed, thinking of Bob Elwell, "'*are bold as a lion.*'"

NOTES

1. In her memoir *A Backward Glance* (New York: Touchstone Books, 1998 [1933]), Edith Wharton had a similar recollection of Howard Sturgis in his drawing room at Queen's Acre. See p. 225.

2. *The Fruit of the Tree* (1907), one of Wharton's less remunerative efforts. Henry James's "Married Son" comprised one-twelfth of *The Whole Family*, conceived by William Dean Howells and featuring ten other authors less well-known today than him and James.
   See *https://en.wikipedia.org/wiki/The_Whole_Family*.

3. Besides *The Decoration of Houses* (1897), Edith Wharton's relevant writings at this date included *Italian Villas and Their Gardens* (1904), *Italian Backgrounds* (1905), and *A Motor-Flight Through France* (1908). See *https://en.wikipedia.org/wiki/Edith_Wharton*.

4. *"Actually, the lady's name was* not *Boyne, nor was her home called Lyng. For the sake of convenience and discretion, I have adopted here the same aliases Mrs. Wharton employed in her story 'Afterward'." (JHW)*

5. Edith Wharton discussed her youthful fear of the supernatural in a passage not included in the published version of *A Backward Glance*. Following a serious illness at the age of nine, she *"lived in a state of chronic fear,"* feeling that *"some dark, undefinable menace [was] forever dogging my steps."* With time, and her parents' patient understanding, Edith's fears diminished. *"But how long the traces of my illness lasted may be judged from the fact that, till I was twenty-seven or -eight, I could not sleep in the room with a book containing a ghost story...."* Fortunately, she recovered sufficiently to write a superb set of ghost stories of her own. See "An Autobiographical Postscript" appended to *The Ghost Stories of Edith Wharton* (New York: Simon & Schuster, Scribner Paperback Fiction, 1997 [1973]), pp. 301-303.

6. Those recorded in the Canon include: "The Adventure of the Golden Pince-Nez" (1894), "The Adventure of Black Peter" (1895), and "The Abbey Grange" (1897). However, Watson referred to there being at least four other cases in which Hopkins solicited Holmes's aid.

7. Ned Boyne's words on Meldon Steep, and other bits of dialogue from Watson's notes (but not in Edith Wharton's story) were used in Granada's ITV dramatization of "Afterward" produced in 1983. It and six other ghost stories were included in the series *Shades of Darkness*, which was later shown on PBS. "Afterward", wonderfully performed by Kate Harper and Michael J. Shannon as the Boynes, is available (at this writing) on DVD and on YouTube at:
   https://www.youtube.com/watch?v=FyML_1QEv2A.

8. Watson recorded this incident in "A Ghost from Christmas Past," published in *The MX Book of New Sherlock Holmes Stories, Part VII: Eliminate the Impossible*, edited by David Marcum (London: MX Publishing, 2017), pp. 130-152. An illustrated version, featuring an original painting by artist Nuné Asatryan, was published in *The Art of Sherlock Holmes: West Palm Beach*

Edition, cutated by Phil Growick (London: MX Publishing, 2019), pp. 196-211.

9.   Even as late as 2015, Great Britain had established no legal mechanism to allow the families of missing persons to make financial decisions on their behalf. My friend Malcolm Carmichael, a retired attorney, advised me that it would be unwise to speculate on the specifics of Mary Boyne's legal situation. Happily, the method she chose of providing restitution to the Elwells obviated the necessity.
     https://www.theguardian.com/money/2015/aug/01/ what-happens-finances-missing-legistaltion-families

10. The fate of Watson's elder brother, Henry, is recounted in "A Ghost from Christmas Past" (Note 8).

11. See "Sherlock Holmes and the Adventure of the Tainted Canister", available as an e-book or audio book from MX Publishing The story was also included in *The Art of Sherlock Holmes: USA Edition 1*, curated by Phil Growick (London, MX Publishing, 2019), pp. 94-108, paired with a painting by artist Angela Fegan.
     https://www.amazon.com/Sherlock-Holmes-Adventure-Tainted-Canister-ebook/dp/ B00J3QS5CW)

12. Most famously in Doyle's immortal "His Last Bow", but later in Watson's own "The Welbeck Abbey Shooting Party," set in 1913. It is the last of four novellas involving Holmes and Watson in events leading to the outbreak of World War I. The collection is entitled *Sherlock Holmes and the Crowned Heads of Europe* (London: MX Publishing, 2021). For "Welbeck Abbey", see pp. 222-282.

13. According to his biographer, W.S. Baring-Gould, the young Sherlock Holmes had enjoyed a brief career on the British and American stage. See Chapter V of *Sherlock Holmes of Baker Street* (Avenel, NJ: Wings Books, 1995 [1962]), pp. 47-51. Naturally, his thespian training was of assistance whenever the detective adopted a disguise – most crucially, of course, as the Irish-American "Altamont".

The Adventure of the
Art Exhibit
by Dan Rowley

"Uncle John, we're in a terrible situation, and I almost didn't know where to turn. Mr. Fry refuses to call in the police, and this could be a catastrophic turn of events for the exhibition. I finally persuaded him to allow me to come to you. I thought you could coax Mr. Holmes to come out of retirement."

These words reverberated in my head as I waited for Holmes's train. The blistering heat of summer had finally yielded to the crisper air of late October, and the steam of the locomotives pulling into the station wasn't enough to dissipate the relieving coolness. I was fairly certain that my friend would respond to my summons, but he hadn't replied. Suddenly my reverie was interrupted.

"Watson, surely you didn't for a second believe I wouldn't come. I see by your pacing and the knit of your brows that you have some uncertainty."

I turned with relief to face Sherlock Holmes. He still retained his erect posture, and he seemed younger than his fifty-six years. His lean face was offset by his aquiline nose and penetrating eyes. Although he looked as if he hadn't gained an ounce, I couldn't say the same for myself. I knew I needed to start watching my eating habits more carefully, but even if I do say so, my military carriage was not yet lost.

"It is so good to see you, Holmes. I cannot tell you how good."

"I sent a telegram from Eastbourne Station in response to yours of last night confirming I was coming. I take it by your demeanor that you didn't receive it."

"I came here very early to await your arrival, so it must have arrived after I left home. While you are correct about my anxiety, it has more to do with the situation than any doubt that you would make the journey."

"I hesitated to send the telegram for fear that the current Mrs. Watson wouldn't approve of our reunion," he replied with a wry smile.

"I admit I didn't tell her, but I will bear the consequences in due course. May I offer you a coffee at a charming café across the street while I give you the details?"

"Let us do so. I would welcome any elaboration on your cryptic, *'Please come at once. Family member needs our help. Will meet you at station tomorrow morning.'*"

We made our way across the street from the station, settled in at the table, and placed our order. "I apologize for the brevity of the message," I said, "but I felt it necessary not to divulge anything that could lead to public disclosure, just in case a careless clerk at the telegraph office said something to someone."

"Don't concern yourself, old friend. You wouldn't call me from my bees if it weren't important. Now which family member is in need of our help?"

"You recall, I'm sure, Abigail Kent, the daughter of Sheila, who was a dear friend of my Mary. She came to me as her godfather. Abigail is quite bright. She studied at the Painting School of the Royal Academy of Arts and has worked at several museums here in London as an assistant curator. She is now employed in connection with an exhibit at the Grafton Gallery."

"I take it you are referring to this collection of *avant-garde* works referred to as 'Post-Impressionism' that I've read about in the newspapers? I probably shouldn't have said long ago you were jealous that we didn't share the same views about art. My study of philosophy during my retirement has led me to explore the possible connection of art to current social conditions. My reading informs me that these Post-Impressionists focus on abstract or symbolic content, rather than the play of light or realism. That raises interesting questions about our current society. Although I'm pleased to have you and Miss Kent as my 'clients', this type of art creates even more interest for me."

"Yes, that is indeed the exhibit, which is due to open in a few weeks. I'm not sure I share your enthusiasm or interest in this type of art, but Abigail tells me that the organizers believe it will transform English public opinion. They use extravagant phrases such as 'art quake' and 'changing human nature'.

"One of the paintings has apparently been stolen and replaced with a forgery. Abigail discovered it, but the people organizing the exhibit are adamant that the police not be notified, for reasons that aren't clear to me. She was quite distraught, worried that the exhibit would be cancelled, resulting in loss of employment for her, and possible harm to her reputation due to her role as curator. She finally persuaded them to allow her to notify me, given my relationship with you, in the hope that we could discreetly solve the matter. She has assured me that the relevant people will be available to us today."

"That isn't much to go on, but let us see what we can accomplish. Shall we hail a cab?"

"I brought my automobile, so I can transport us there."

"Lead the way."

As we made our way, I asked, "How is your book on beekeeping coming along."

"Quite well. And will 'The Cornish Horror' be published soon?"

I hesitated. "Thank you for agreeing to allow that. It will be in *The Strand* this December."

"I sense by your manner you haven't used my nomenclature. Come, now, what have you called it?"

"'The Devil's Foot'." He shook his head but said nothing, to my relief.

Reaching the automobile, we climbed in and I started it. As we drove, Holmes remarked, "Every time I come back to London there seem to be more of these automobiles."

Piccadilly always reminded me of a Parisian boulevard. The market carts on their way to Covent Garden had already passed this way, as some remnants of cabbage leaves and other vegetables showed. Because it was still early, the pedestrians were mainly shop girls and clerks bustling to their places of employment. The crisp October air made everything seem sharper and clearer.

Eventually we turned into Bond Street, where the gallery had relocated from its eponymous foundation on Grafton Street. I found a place to leave the vehicle nearby, and we alighted and walked toward our destination. "Watson, I commend you on your driving skill. Perhaps it will be of use to us some day in one of our adventures."

We arrived at the Gallery which, unlike the other buildings on the street, had a two story, three-sided structure protruding from it. The ground floor of this structure contained an arched entrance that led to the main door. The other two sides had similar arches but were ornamental and didn't allow entrance, because at the bottom of each hung a glass box containing announcements of what could be seen inside. Prominently displayed was an advertisement: *Manet and the Post-Impressionists – Opening 8ᵗʰ November, 1910.*

We went through the arch and the main door, and into to a large rectangular room, with the long sides stretching from Bond Street all the way to the back of the building ending in a semicircular annex. There was quite a bit of activity, with workers carrying paintings, scaffolding, ladders, and various tools. I spied a young man of about thirty who, by the nature of his dress, clearly wasn't a worker. He was slight, about five-feet tall, with a nondescript face, a noticeable squint, and black hair parted in the middle. I called to him. "Excuse me, sir. We're here to see Miss Kent. She's expecting us. Do you know where we might find her?"

"She's in the Octagonal Gallery over there," pointing to a doorway to the right of the main entrance, his eyes downcast the entire time.

We thanked him and proceeded through the indicated door. The eight-sided room contained many paintings on the floor leaning against the walls. There was only one occupant at the moment, my goddaughter. Turning toward us, her face brightened. She was thirty-two, almost Holmes's height, slim with reddish-brown hair and pleasant features. She rushed over to us and gave me a hug and peck on the cheek.

"Uncle John! I am so happy to see you. And Mr. Holmes, I'm so sorry to have you come all this way, but I didn't know what else to do."

Holmes slightly inclined his head. "Please think nothing of it. When your 'Uncle' told me a family member needed my assistance, I was on the earliest train I could catch."

"Would you care for refreshments, or would you like to commence?"

"Let us get started. I understand other relevant people will be available, but I would prefer to start with your discovery of the forgery."

"Of course. As you can see, the paintings leaning against the walls are in the tentative placement they will have when hung for the exhibit. They are uncrated in the back and brought to the appropriate location in the Gallery."

"How is the location determined?"

"That's part of my task. I make a preliminary sketch of where the paintings will be placed and review that with Mr. Fry. My goal is to have each room demonstrate a commonality among the paintings, whether by artist, theme, technique, and so forth. This room contains mainly paintings by Edouard Manet and Paul Cezanne. I decided on these because they show people in various settings and nicely illustrate the similarity and differences between the artists as they deal with such themes. They also display the artists' use of structure, and often distort the normal play of light.

"Once the paintings are placed in a room, I can concretely visualize how the exhibition will look. It also allows me to move paintings around physically to determine if there is a better arrangement."

"Very concise and helpful. How exactly did you uncover the forgery?"

"As I was examining and rearranging the paintings, I noticed that the canvas for one of the Manet paintings was thicker than all the others. Here, I'll show you." We walked over to an unframed painting that showed a man and two women sitting side by side at a table with steins of beer in front of them. They were dressed very fancily, with the woman on the left wearing a hat with a silk ribbon. The man had a top had and a very large mustache. The woman on the right, who might have been a young girl, was looking directly in front of her, while the man and other woman were looking in different directions. The lighting was odd, as the two women were in the light but the man was shaded.

Abagail continued. "This is Manet's *Au Café*. It is one of a series he did of people sitting in this café. They showed a mix of social strata, including middle class, working people, and Bohemian types, which is very characteristic of his work.

"Once I noticed the canvas anomaly, I removed it from the frame to examine it more closely. As you can see, the canvas is stretched over a wooden frame. The canvas goes into the back of the frame. The front of the canvas is held in place in the picture frame by a lip around the picture frame called the *rabbet*." She then placed the canvas inside the picture frame. "Because this canvas frame is thicker than the distance between the *rabbet* and the back of the picture frame, the canvas frame isn't flush with the picture frame. Manet was very particular about how his paintings were framed, always insisting that the thickness of the canvas frame exactly match back of the picture frame. All of the Manet paintings for this exhibit, except this one, are framed in that manner."

"Excellent, Miss Kent. You not only see, but you observe." So saying, Holmes glanced at me, but had the decency not to embarrass me in front of my goddaughter by reminding me of his many admonishments to me to that effect. "Was that the only clue?"

"No. I then went and retrieved my magnifying glass to examine the painting more minutely. I quickly determined that the brushstrokes weren't exactly like Manet's typical technique. It also seemed to me that the paint appeared fresher than it should from a painting executed in 1878. And the way the light struck the man's top hat wasn't quite right."

At this point, Holmes positively beamed with delight. "Miss Kent, if you ever decide on a different career, I would suggest a position with the Metropolitan Police."

Before he could continue, a man appeared in the doorway. He had a long, thin, clean-shaven face. His cheeks were a bit sunken, and he was wearing a top coat, battered fedora, and wire-rimmed glasses. He looked us over. "Ah, Abigail, there you are. I see our visitors have arrived. Allow me to attend to one matter, and I'll be right back." He turned quickly and went off toward the rear of the building.

Abigail turned to us. "That was Mr. Roger Fry."

Holmes nodded. "Yes, I have read about Fry." He clearly was familiar with the painter and critic who was a member of the notorious Bloomsbury Group in London, consisting of Bohemian artists, painters, writers, philosophers, and academics. "Am I correct that he is the driving force behind this exhibit?"

"Yes," replied Abigail. "He's responsible for obtaining the loan of most of the paintings here. I went to him as soon as I discovered the forgery of *Au Café*, and he agreed with me it wasn't a Manet. He didn't want, however, to call in any other expert. I'm sure he will explain his reasons for that to you."

"Good. Watson, we'll want to explore with him who owns these paintings and how they came to be here, as that could provide valuable insight about the motive for this forgery."

At that moment, Fry returned to the Octagonal Gallery. He strode over to Holmes, extending his hand. "Sherlock Holmes, I presume. I recognize you from the pictures in *The Strand*. And Dr. Watson. I cannot express my appreciation for your arrival on such short notice. I'm blessed with having Abigail as my curator, but had no idea her value would include the ability to have you come here to help us."

Holmes gave a wry smile. "You're correct sir. I wasn't aware that members of the Bloomsbury Group read Dr. Watson's stories."

"Please don't reveal my secret passion," he said with a smile. "One cannot subsist solely on a diet of Virginia Woolf and Maynard Keynes. Now, how can I help"

"Let us start with why you don't want to call in the authorities but prefer to have Dr. Watson and me investigate."

"Of course. There are two reasons, one general and the other specific. In general, one doesn't desire any scandal related to an exhibition, especially one as potentially controversial as this one. I anticipate some harsh criticism, as many of my fellow aficionados don't share my enthusiasm for these works. As you may know, I coined the term 'Post-Impressionism'. This exhibit has the potential to revolutionize the art world, and even a hint of a forgery would allow those lying in wait to pounce on me with glee."

This last was said a little smugly, but Holmes ignored the tone and nudged Fry on before he could regale us with more along the same line. "Quite understandable. What is the specific reason to which you allude?"

"Ah, yes. You may have heard of Auguste Pellerin, the entrepreneur and art collector. After making his fortune by making margarine, of all things, he began collecting works by Manet and Cezzane, among others. He is rumored to have some ninety paintings, some of which he has loaned us for this exhibit. In fact, he is on the committee for the exhibit, along with many other notables."

"I see. So it would be a major embarrassment to have someone so closely associated with this exhibit connected to a forgery."

385

"It is worse than that. Earlier this year Auguste sold thirty-five Manets to a consortium of art dealers. The price was one million francs, and there was a fair amount of controversy over the valuation."

"And that transaction could be thrown into doubt if a forged Manet comes to light."

Fry sighed. "Indeed. Moreover, the dealers in the consortium have loaned to the exhibit some of the paintings they purchased from Auguste. In fact, *Au Café* is one of the paintings so purchased. I haven't informed Auguste of the forgery, and it is imperative that we discover the truth and find the original before he or any of his purchasers learn of this outrage."

"I see the need for discretion. I have some questions about other matters, such as the ownership of the paintings, how they were gathered, the procedure for preparing them for display, security here at the Gallery, and so forth."

"I have to attend a meeting, but we can summon a few others who can answer your questions. Abigail, would you fetch Neil so that he can find who Mr. Holmes needs to talk to." As she left, Fry said, "In the meantime, the draft catalogue of the exhibit may be of use to you." He handed Holmes a printed brochure, which he began to inspect as I looked over his shoulder. The first page contained a list of members of the committee, which was quite impressive. In addition to a number of members of the gentry and minor aristocracy, it included an earl, a French count, and a princess. The next page listed a much smaller executive committee of which Fry was the chairman. After an essay of some thirteen pages concerning the nature of Post-Impressionism, the listing of all the paintings began. There also was a notation that prices of paintings could be obtained from the Secretary of the executive committee.

As we were perusing it, Abigail reentered with the young man who earlier had directed us to the Octagonal Gallery. Just as they came in, I remarked, "There isn't a single English painter in this exhibit."

The young man looked up at me. "Yes, I think – "

Before he could continue, Fry interrupted. "That will be enough, Neil. If we desire your opinion, we will ask for it. These gentlemen need you to bring some people here for them to interview. Mr. Holmes, do you have a preference."

"I should like to start with the Secretary of the exhibit mentioned in the catalogue. Then the manager of the Gallery. In that order, and one at a time if you please."

Fry dismissed the hapless Neil. Abigail gently remonstrated. "Mr. Fry, you and Mr. Nicholson could treat Neil a bit more kindly. He is more experienced than you credit him. He is fairly knowledgeable about art, especially painting techniques. As an employee of the Gallery, he has been

386

very useful to me as an outsider working for you. He knows everyone here and can accomplish much."

Fry shrugged. "Abigail, he is a dogsbody. You are the mind behind this, and please don't forget that. Mr. Holmes, I must take your leave. Is there anything else you require?"

"One question. Is either of these gentlemen with whom we're about to speak aware of the forgery? They might be curious as to why I am here, as many people are aware of my profession."

"Yes, I took both of them into my confidence on the assumption you would wish to speak to them. They understand the need for absolute secrecy. MacCarthy, our Secretary, has the same devotion and interest in the Exhibit as do I. Manager Nicholson doesn't want his Gallery involved in a scandal, so we also can rely on him."

"Very well. I would prefer to keep Miss Kent here, as she is fully familiar with the workings of the Exhibit and has already demonstrated to me her powers of discernment. We'll let you know when we need to speak again."

As Fry was leaving, another man entered the room. He was dressed neatly in a grey suit. His eyes showed intelligence, and he was well-proportioned, if not handsome. His hair was receding, and his oval face fit well to his body. He and Fry had a brief whispered conversation, and then he came over to us.

"Hello. I'm Desmond MacCarthy, Secretary of the Exhibit. I understand from Roger you have some questions for me, and that I'm to cooperate fully."

After introducing ourselves, Holmes commenced. "Please explain how the paintings were selected and who owns them."

"Roger has had this exhibition in mind since the beginning of the year. He has been conversing with collectors and dealers for some time. When the Gallery asked him to create this exhibit, he used his many connections to obtain the paintings that will be included.

"There basically are three types of owners. Some of the paintings are owned by wealthy, private collectors with whom Roger is acquainted. They are a disparate lot, and include an American heiress and museum directors and fellow critics. A few of the paintings were provided by the artists Matisse and Picasso. But the bulk of the paintings have been lent by Paris art dealers."

"How did Mr. Fry communicate with these dealers?"

"He and I travelled to Paris in September and met with Robert Dell, our agent for the exhibition. He had a list of dealers and a corresponding list of approximately fifty paintings, if my memory serves. We met with all those dealers and made arrangements for loans. Roger made a second trip later that month with two friends and made more contacts."

"So it sounds as if most of the exhibitors are dealers?"

"Yes. Roger is worried that critics will say this is a sale, and not a proper exhibit. I believe he's mistaken, but my entreaties fall on deaf ears."

At this point, I asked, "Are the paintings insured?"

"Well, it depends on the underlying insurance policy held by the owner. The artists who have lent paintings are unlikely to have any insurance. I suspect most of the dealers rely on the Gallery's insurance. As to the collectors, I'm afraid I cannot say."

Holmes stood in thought for a few minutes. "One last question, Mr. MacCarthy: Who would be harmed if word of this forgery became well known?"

"Again, it depends on when the substitution was made. If it occurred before the painting arrived here, either the owner or the party from whom he obtained it could suffer. If after arrival, most likely the Gallery. But in either event, Roger would incur acute embarrassment." He then looked deprecatingly at Abigail. "And any of those associated with him could be tarred with the same brush."

"Thank you very much. That's all for now. If the Gallery manager is out there, please send him in."

MacCarthy left us, and a few moments later a man of about fifty years, and of medium height and weight, entered. His hair was turning grey, and the monocle and goatee he sported gave him a somewhat pompous air. He cleared his throat. "I am David Nicholson, the manager of this establishment. I have been informed you are Sherlock Holmes and Dr. Watson. I'm not cognizant of how a private sleuth – a retired one no less – can assist us. But proceed with your questions.

Holmes ignored the barb and didn't correct him that the proper term was "Consulting Detective".

"Can you describe for us how the paintings arrive and are stored?"

"There is a service delivery in the rear along an alleyway. The paintings are brought in there and placed in a storage room. Normally they're in crates and remain so until ready for placement out here in one of the gallery rooms."

"When did the paintings for this exhibit begin to arrive?"

"In October. We have had daily consignments, at times as many as ten or more a day."

"How long did they remain back there?"

"We grouped them according to Miss Kent's instructions. She specified which paintings would go to which Galleries. She also gave us the order in which she wanted paintings brought to each gallery. Pursuant to those instructions, the afternoon before paintings were desired, we uncrated them and took them to the relevant room."

"Who performed the uncrating?"

"I, of course, don't bother myself with such menial matters. We hire temporary workmen for these tasks, and Neil Hammond, who I believe you have met, oversees the uncrating and moving of the paintings to the respective galleries."

"What are the security arrangements you have made here?"

"During the day, we have two guards. One patrols the rooms and the other either attends the front door when we are open to the public or stands at the back door when deliveries are being made. During the night, we have one guard who is posted at the back door but also makes regular rounds every hour. In addition, I've made arrangements with the local constabulary to check the building on all sides every sixty to ninety minutes. Before I leave for the night, I examine all the windows and doors. Then I lock the back door once the night guard is in place."

"Was there any sign of forced entry once the paintings began to arrive?"

"Absolutely not. We've never had a single such incident either here or at our former location. No one enters or departs without us knowing it."

Holmes stood staring as if the popinjay wasn't there. Realizing that he was done, I thanked Nicholson and bade him depart, assuring him we would summon him again when we had anything to report.

After a short while, Sherlock Holmes broke his reverie. "Miss Kent, who assists you in arranging the paintings?"

"Neil does. He's quite helpful to me, as I mentioned before."

"Please ask him to join us." She left and shortly returned with the nondescript young man. I refer to him as young, but that was more his appearance, as I realized he was about the same age as Abigail.

Holmes smiled at him. "I understand you have been assisting Miss Kent with her preparation of the exhibit."

"Yes, sir."

"Is that normally the type of duty you perform?"

"I generally do whatever Mr. Nicholson asks. I run errands for him as needed. Make sure that hired workers are performing their tasks, keep records, take care of Mr. Nicholson's appointments – really anything he needs."

"Were you involved in deciding to make the invitation to Mr. Fry to create this exhibit."

Neil's eyes brightened. "Yes. I was able to accompany Mr. Nicholson to Paris this spring to see some of the potential works that might be useful. He had me along to take notes. He even hired a photographer there so that he could show the Gallery owners the potential for the exhibit. It was quite exciting, as I have never been outside of London before. I only wish we had taken time to see some of the sights."

"Yes, that sounds like quite an adventure. Do you recall when *Au Café* arrived here?"

"I do not, but I could look at the records if that's important."

"Do you remember when it was uncrated and moved into this room?"

He looked at Abigail, who replied, "It was two days ago in the afternoon. I recall looking at the paintings before I left that day as I was going to work on them the next morning, which was yesterday."

"Did either of you notice anything odd about the painting before yesterday morning?" Both shook their heads. "Well, then, that's all I have. Miss Kent, your Uncle John and I are going to go outside for a bit as I feel the need for some tobacco. Could you assemble everyone that we've talked to in this room in forty-five minutes? It might be more comfortable if chairs are brought in. Thank you."

Holmes and I left the Octagonal Gallery and went back out the front door. The sky already was darkening, and the air had taken on more of a chill. We both lit cigars and I waited for Holmes to speak, as I had divined that he wished to converse in private. We smoked for a while in companionable silence, as only long-time friends can do.

"Well, Watson, what do you think of this matter?"

"I must say, I don't quite find my way to a solution as yet. But I'm beginning to perceive an outline of a path to one."

"Do continue."

"I see two primary issues: Motivation and method." He nodded encouragingly, so I continued. "As to motive, I should think it is the oldest of all, money. I paid close attention to your questions about the financial arrangements of those who loaned the paintings. Based on the answers, presumably the thief either wants to collect insurance or sell the authentic painting to a collector.

"Now with regard to method, it's unclear whether the painting was switched before arrival here or after. Given the tight security arrangements here, I lean toward the substitution taking place before arrival. So it would seem we have more investigation in front of us."

"Watson, you certainly have been exercising acuteness today. It's an excellent exposition, quite clear and lucid. You have correctly identified the two key issues – motive and method. But I believe there is no need for further inquiry."

"You mean to say you have deduced the answer?"

"Yes. In fact, you gave me the vital clue that started my chain of though in the most fruitful direction. It's always a joy to have you at my side, and not least for that reason. Come, let us return to the Gallery. And be on your guard."

It was with a mixture of pride at his praise, and I confess some puzzlement as to what clue I had uncovered, that I followed him. We reentered the main door and turned once again to the Octagonal Gallery. In our absence, someone had arranged a semi-circle of armchairs upholstered with red leather seats and backs. The various people we had met earlier were milling about. Fry rushed over to us. "Mr. Holmes, do you have an answer?"

"If you will kindly join the others, it will be clear in due course." After everyone was seated, Holmes solemnly surveyed them in silence for a few moments and then began. "While we were outside, Dr. Watson correctly identified the two questions that must be answered here: Who had a motive to substitute a forged painting for the authentic Manet, and how did he or she accomplish it?" At the mention of my name, Abigail glanced at me and smiled.

"It will be fruitful to begin by considering the nature of this exhibit. Although some collectors and artists have been kind enough to supply paintings, the bulk of them have been loaned by art dealers – all of which suggests that a primary purpose of the exhibition is to sell paintings. Yes, Mr. Fry, I acknowledge your passion to educate and astound the world with the marvels of Post-Impressionism that have so captivated you. And I will concede that your motive isn't so much financial gain as it is furtherance of aesthetic standards." Mollified by this, Fry, who had appeared to be ready to object, settled back into his seat.

"You may, however, concede the point that others, while perhaps sharing your passion, also hope to accrue financial gain if the exhibit is the success you wish for. The artist can make more money if there is more demand for his work. The collector's paintings would rise in value. And the dealer could command a higher price for his inventory.

"But how to translate that rise in value to the substitution of a forgery for the genuine *Au Café*? What did the forger, assuming for the moment that the forger is working alone, hope to accomplish? We can leave the artists loaning paintings out of our calculations, as Manet is no longer with us. The painting in question was owned by a consortium of dealers that acquired it early this year, so let us set aside the collectors as well.

"Dr. Watson again correctly identified two possible financial motives for the substitutor – namely, collection of insurance proceeds, and sale of the authentic painting." Abigail again smiled at me, and I was grateful that my friend was mentioning me to this extent. He undoubtedly had been impressed with Abigail earlier, and was graciously crediting me to her gratification.

"Collecting insurance proceeds doesn't seem a viable motive for any dealer in this situation. I have had the fortune – or misfortune as you may call it – to have had numerous dealings with the insurance industry in my many investigations over the years. While the dealer may purchase insurance for his inventory of paintings, that typically only applies to objects under his possession and control. Once on loan to a gallery such as this, the object then becomes covered by the policy of the gallery."

Nicholson blustered. "That is quite true, but I resent any implication that I had anything to do with this."

Holmes made a slight bow. "I intended no such implication. You are the manager and wouldn't benefit from any insurance proceeds. And as Mr. Fry noted earlier, your primary interest is in having the exhibit succeed. Moreover, if your contract with the lending dealer requires turning the proceeds over to him, there is no financial benefit to the Gallery."

"Some of the contracts do so require. Does that not bring us back to the dealer as the financial beneficiary?"

"Perhaps. But the dealer stands to gain more by having the exhibit succeed, thereby increasing the value of the painting. The dealer would hope to receive more funds from a profitable sale than the insurance money, which would have set the value at the worth prior to the exhibition.

"That leaves as financial motivation sale of the original to some willing buyer. There are a number of objections to this. Foremost, whether or not the forgery is discovered, the dealer would have to admonish the buyer to remain clandestine. If the forgery isn't discovered, the dealer would have to explain the sale of two copies of the same painting to the non-public buyer. That would lower its value considerably, as the buyer would be unable publicly to boast of having the original. If the forgery is discovered, the same considerations would apply. Although there may be unscrupulous people in the world who are willing to have a secret original of a painting, the sale of such items is quite difficult and could come to the attention of the authorities. The dealers in question here are quite reputable and are unlikely to take such a risky course." At this, Fry, MacCarthy, and Nicholson vehemently nodded.

"So I conclude financial gain isn't the motive. We will return to motive, but let us focus now on method. *How*, and, as Dr. Watson correctly noted, *when* did the forger make the substitution? Miss Kent, in a quite brilliant manner, detected the forgery fairly rapidly when she first saw it. It had passed through numerous similarly expert hands before arriving here. It stretches credulity to believe none of those experts would have detected the forgery. That means the substitution was made either after shipment from Paris and before arrival here, or after arrival here."

"Substitution after shipment and before arrival was impossible," Nicholson reluctantly admitted. "The paintings were placed in individual crates and the locked in strong boxes to which I had the only key. Also, the boxes were under continual armed guard from Paris to here by a bonded agency. There was no evidence of tampering with the boxes upon arrival, as I unlocked each one personally."

"I appreciate your candor. That means the substitution was made here at the Gallery."

Fry interjected. "But Nicholson has the highest standard of security in the art world. How could a substitution be made?"

Holmes smiled. "There is one person who had both the motive and opportunity to make the substitution. Dr. Watson uncovered the motive when he mentioned that there were no English painters in the Exhibition. The perpetrator began to agree, but you, Fry, cut him off."

At this, Hammond began to stand, but I also arose and motioned him back to his seat. Holmes nodded to me. "It was clear you and Nicholson treat Mr. Hammond with disdain. I sense he is more intelligent and egotistical than you credit him, as evidenced by his enthusiasm in describing his trip to view paintings. He also is a painter himself, which was suggested by Miss Kent's remark that he is quite familiar with painting technique. Further confirmation can be found by an examination of his fingernails, which show traces of paint. There also is wear on his hands that is normally associated with use of turpentine. I have made a study of the effect of various substances on the skin, and his hands are quite characteristic of that use."

Turning to Hammond, he asked, "You were offended by the absence of English artists, hurt by being treated as a menial, and decided to show everyone that an English artist could create a painting as good as any done by Manet. Am I correct?"

Hammond glared defiantly at the assemblage. "Yes, I have always had a passion for painting. I had applied to study with Vanessa Bell and Clive Owen, but they rejected my samples as, in their words, 'pedestrian'."

At this mention of two fellow members of the Bloomsbury Group, Fry was quite startled. It was clear he had no idea this young man had any contact with his Group.

Hammond continued. "So I had to settle for working in one of the damnable art factories in Chelsea that churn out cheap paintings for the middle class who have no taste, but simply want something gaudy that they can brag about rather than appreciate. I could barely make a living there and despised the work. I decided to come to work here at the Gallery for more money, but at the cost of devoting my time to my painting."

"So when you accompanied Nicholson to Paris, you saw a chance to demonstrate your superior talents and at the same time show up the misguided judgments of all who treated you so shabbily."

"Yes. That is when I decided to create a copy of the Manet painting. You all are so taken with these French artists that it would never cross your elevated minds that a mere English factotum could create such a work of art. Nicholson, you never had a clue. Had Fry not brought Miss Kent here, you and he would still be crowing about your French masterpiece."

Holmes looked at him knowingly. "And you concocted this idea on your trip to Paris. You mentioned that photographs were taken, one of which undoubtedly was of *Au Café*. You must have started the forgery soon after you arrived back here, because Miss Kent noted paint was new. When no one was observing me, I touched the painting and it was dry, which means you finished it more than a week ago.

"Your substitution was so simple that I almost would say I admire it. You oversaw the workers uncrating the paintings, so it would be easy to have them uncrate *Au Café* before it was needed. They would have no idea you had changed the order. Then you probably laid the painting aside until you could go on one of your errands that you mentioned, which I assume includes taking and bringing paintings from and to the Gallery when Nicholson needs to borrow or return something here in London. You could easily bring in your forgery, remove the original painting frame from the picture frame, and replace it with yours. Then when it came time to bring the paintings into this room, you simply added the forged painting to the group being conveyed here by the workers. One question: Did you notice the painting frame wasn't flush with the picture frame?"

"So that's what put you on to it. It must have been Abigail who noticed. None of these other dolts would have."

"You scoundrel!" exclaimed Fry. "What have you done with the original? If you have harmed it – "

"Have no fear. While Hammond believes he is the equal of Manet, nonetheless he is an art connoisseur by his own lights. He probably has it somewhere safe so that he can admire it."

"Yes. It's in my flat. I would never harm it. Only a cretin could imagine such a thing."

Nicholson's fury was palpable. "You are fired effective immediately! I will have a guard accompany you to pack up your things and then go with you to your flat to retrieve the true Manet." He left the room to get a guard. Hammond sat glowering, fully aware that while he might not be arrested and prosecuted in order to protect the gallery's reputation, he also wouldn't receive a recommendation, and that he might have some great difficulty finding other employment.

Fry came over to Holmes with an envelope. "We cannot thank you enough. Please accept this as a small token of our appreciation."

Holmes gave a slight bow. "I am quite comfortable in my retirement. I would prefer you give it to Miss Kent, as we never would have discovered this without her perspicacity."

Abigail blushed. "Oh, thank you, Mr. Holmes! May I at least buy you and Uncle John a drink with this money? There's a charming public house just around the corner."

We readily agreed, took our leave of the others, and repaired to The White Stag. We settled ourselves in a booth near the back. Once Holmes had his claret, me an ale, and Abigail a shandy, she implored, "Mr. Holmes, is there not something I can do for you?"

"Miss Kent, I will accept one thing: A private tour of the exhibit guided by you, so that we can discuss the impact of society on art. You see, I have in mind a monograph . . . ."

The Adventure of
Peter the Painter
by David MacGregor

If there is one truism that transcends all of human history, it's that a knock on the door at four in the morning never bodes well. So it was that in mid-December of 1910, I found myself being summoned from the arms of Morpheus by a distant rapping sound that was growing more frantic with every passing second. Emerging from my bedroom, I almost ran headlong into Holmes, who was in the process of putting on his dressing gown. As we locked eyes for a moment, there was no need for either of us to express our mutual understanding that we were about to learn of some kind of terrible event that could not wait until morning.

In theory, Holmes had retired to Sussex Downs some years ago, but research at the British Museum and various other affairs brought him up to London on a regular basis, where he always stayed with my wife and me in our cozy little abode in Queen Anne Street. Thankfully, my wife was off visiting her sister on this eventful morning, and moving down the stairs as rapidly as my still-stiff limbs would allow, I couldn't help but speculate upon who or what I might find upon opening the door. A moment later I found myself gazing upon the pale complexion of Inspector Stanley Hopkins. Holmes made a habit of letting Scotland Yard know whenever he was in the city, and it was Hopkins who made the most use of Holmes's consultation services. In the present instance, he didn't say a word, but proceeded inside as I followed in his wake. Upon entering the sitting room, I saw that Holmes had already poured a snifter of brandy and was holding it out towards Hopkins, who reached for it eagerly.

"I suspect you need a drink, Inspector," said Holmes.

"Indeed I do." Hopkins took the glass and drained half of it in one gulp before sitting down and taking a long, shuddering breath. As I busied myself stoking the fireplace with fresh coal, Holmes took a seat opposite Hopkins and eyed him closely.

"It's a bad business," began Hopkins. "What on earth is the world coming to?"

"How many casualties?"

Hopkins looked up in surprise at Holmes's question, then nodded as he understood the logic behind it. "Of course. I wouldn't be here otherwise, would I? Five officers. There's been nothing like it. Not in the entire history of the Force."

Hopkins drained the rest of his glass and, as I moved to refill it, I could see him gathering himself to give Holmes as clear and concise a description of events as possible. For his part, in an effort to fully awaken himself and focus his mental faculties, Holmes stood up and gazed into the fire.

"Details," said Holmes curtly.

"There was an attempted robbery this evening at a jewelry store on Houndsditch," began Hopkins.

"The shop owned by Henry Harris?" enquired Holmes as I handed Hopkins more brandy.

"Precisely," answered Hopkins. "And this was no smash-and-grab operation, Mr. Holmes. Clearly, considerable time and planning went into it. The gang had apparently determined that Mr. Harris kept over £20,000 worth of jewels in the store's safe, and so they proceeded to rent No. 11 and No. 9 in the Exchange Buildings, which are only separated from the back of the jewelry store by a small yard. Just how long they have been planning this robbery we haven't yet determined, but we did recover a cylinder of compressed gas, a sixty-foot length of India rubber gas hose, and some diamond-tipped drills from the scene."

By now I had brought out my notebook and was rapidly scribbling down Hopkins's words as he took a sip of brandy and continued.

"We don't know how many people are in the gang, but last night they began to break through the back wall of the jewelry shop. They were overheard by one of the neighbors, who reported it to Constable Piper, who was walking his beat in the neighbourhood at the time. Piper also heard the noises, considered them suspicious, and walked around the block to knock on the front door of No. 11 in the Exchange Buildings."

"What made him choose that particular address?" asked Holmes.

"He noticed that it was the only property in the vicinity that had a light on in the back."

"Good man," answered Holmes. "Please go on."

"The door was opened, but only an inch or so, which immediately made Piper suspicious, and so he made an innocuous enquiry asking the man if his wife was in, and the man answered in a foreign accent that she was out. Piper said he would call back, then walked around to Houndsditch, where he saw a man acting suspiciously in the cul-de-sac. As Piper approached him, the man scuttled away into the shadows, and at this point Piper quite sensibly determined that he needed reinforcements. He was able to locate Constables Woodhams and Choate on their respective beats, then went to the Bishopsgate Station to report what was occurring. By 11:30, Piper returned to the scene with Sergeant Bentley and some other constables.

"Sergeant Bentley proceeded to knock on the door of No. 11 and asked the man who answered if anyone was doing work inside. The man didn't answer, but disappeared back into the building, prompting Bentley, Sergeant Bryant, and Constable Woodhams to follow him into the hall. Seeing another man standing on the stairs, Sergeant Bentley asked him to accompany them through to the back of the building.

"At that moment . . . ." Hopkins faltered, then reached inside his coat for a small notebook. Opening it, he referred to his notes and continued in a halting voice.

". . . at that moment another member of the gang opened the back door and began firing a gun. The man on the stairs began shooting as well. Sergeant Bentley was shot in the shoulder and neck. The second shot severed his spine. Constable Woodhams was shot in the upper leg and appears to have a shattered femur. Sergeant Bryant was shot in the arm and chest. The three men from the gang then attempted to escape, accompanied by a woman, but they encountered Sergeant Tucker in the cul-de-sac, who was shot through the heart and died instantly. Constable Choate managed to get hold of one of the gang, but his accomplices came to his assistance and Choate was shot twelve times. By this point the officers were able to return fire and wounded one of the gang, but he was carried away by his accomplices and they made their escape."

"I take it that the constables received firearms at the Station?" I asked.

Hopkins nodded, closed his notebook, and put it back inside his coat. "Constable Choate was taken to London Hospital and Sergeant Bentley is at Barts, but the doctors despair for both of their lives."

"And this gang," said Holmes, "I take it they were wholly unsuccessful insofar as their planned jewel heist was concerned?"

"They got nothing. The safe was unscathed."

"But who are they?" I asked. "Who would attempt such a bold and reckless crime?"

"Given the accent of the man who answered the door," returned Hopkins, "we suspect we're dealing with a group of criminals from Eastern Europe."

"Ah," I nodded. "That makes perfect sense."

"How so?" asked Holmes.

"A crime like that . . . well, let me just say that in my opinion it's entirely out of character for the typically phlegmatic British nature."

Holmes turned to look at Hopkins. "You say your men were able to wound one of the perpetrators?"

398

"Yes, sir. He cried out when he was hit and needed the help of his associates to flee the scene."

"It's unlikely they would take him to a hospital, so he may already be dead, or if the wound isn't that serious, the gang may have him hidden away until he can recover."

Holmes paused to light his briar pipe. "Tell me something, Hopkins: Do you have any officers who speak Russian or Yiddish?"

Judging by the inspector's expression, Holmes might just as well have asked him if he was hiding a polecat in his trousers. "Why no. Not to my knowledge. Do you happen to be familiar with either of those languages, Mr. Holmes?"

"I may possess a smattering," answered Holmes. "Enough to get by, at any rate. I'd like to examine the site, if I may, and speak to any witnesses."

"Thank you," said Hopkins. "I was hoping to get your opinion. But if you don't mind – "

"By all means visit your wounded comrades, Hopkins," said Holmes. "I would do the same in your position, and I know where the jewelry store on Houndsditch is."

"Shall I accompany you?" I asked.

"No need," answered Holmes. "I'm arming myself simply as a precaution. Whatever danger there was has likely passed and the perpetrators are now holed up somewhere licking their wounds. For the moment, I shall work better and more quickly on my own."

With that, Holmes and Hopkins left together, leaving me to jot down a few more notes, following which I did the only sensible thing I could think of, which was to go back to bed.

By the time I arose the following morning I expected Holmes to be back, but there was no sign of him, or any indication that he had returned while I was sleeping. Having my own duties to attend to, I busied myself with those, but as the noon hour passed I will confess to sneaking more than one glance up and down the street in the vain hope of seeing Holmes's tall, thin form striding rapidly along. It was only as three o'clock neared that I heard the front door open and the clatter of footsteps as Holmes shouted out instructions to the housekeeper.

"Hello! Food! Tea! Something! Thank you!"

A moment later the door was flung open and Holmes entered in a rush.

"Developments, Watson!" he began. "Things are proceeding apace! It is a nasty business to be sure."

Moving back to the door, he shouted down the stairs. "Sooner better than later! Thank you!"

As he turned back into the room, I brought out my notebook. "What's happened?"

He shook his head. "Regrettably, Constable Choate died early this morning. Sergeant Bentley was conscious when I spoke to him an hour ago, but when I talked privately with the doctors they expressed doubt that he would last the day."

"Does he have family?"

"His quite evidently pregnant wife hasn't left his side for a moment."

"Good God." I was lost for words as Holmes went to the window and glanced up and down Queen Anne Street.

"Are you expecting visitors?" I asked.

"No, merely ascertaining that I wasn't followed back here. I took the usual precautions to conceal my tracks, but we are dealing with desperate people, and as of the moment we have no idea how large their organisation might be."

"What have you been able to determine so far?" I asked.

"After their escape from the scene, the gang made their way to Grove Street and holed up there. Concerned for their wounded accomplice, they summoned a doctor and explained away the bullet wound in his chest by saying that he had been accidently shot by an acquaintance. The wounded man's name was George Gardstein, and when the doctor recommended taking him to London Hospital, he refused to go. The doctor gave him some pain medication and said he would return shortly to check on his condition, but when the doctor came back, he found Gardstein dead on the bed. Having no knowledge of the events on Houndsditch, the doctor followed standard protocol and reported the death to the coroner. It took another hour before he passed along this information to the police. At that point, Hopkins and I made our way to Grove Street with several constables and found Gardstein's corpse on a bed. Where is that woman?"

"What woman?" I asked, genuinely confused.

Holmes made his way back to the door and as he flung it open, there stood my housekeeper with a tray. She gave a little cry of surprise as Holmes took the tray from her, "Thank you, my dear! You are a paragon among women!"

Closing the door with his foot, Holmes had already devoured half a sandwich before he put the tray down and poured himself a cup of tea.

"But that wasn't all that Hopkins and I found in Grove Street," he continued. "There was a woman there as well, a certain Sara Trassjonsky, who was busy burning as many papers as she could."

"Surely that isn't her real name," I interposed. "She would have made something up."

"Normally I would agree with you, of course," replied Holmes, "but the look in Hopkins's eye when he spoke to her wasn't something I have ever witnessed previously. I think she recognised it would be in her best interests to speak the truth, with the hope that our judicial system will be merciful to her on account of her gender."

"But why was she even there?" I asked. "Why hasn't she fled the city?"

"An excellent question," answered Holmes. "One would suspect some kind of allegiance or intimate association with Gardstein, but then, this is no mere gang of jewel thieves, Watson. We're dealing with Anarchists who have fled Russia for our more hospitable shores and who are determined to organise and launch their revolution from England. Of course, revolutions require capital and funding – hence their attempt to rob the jewelry store of Henry Harris."

"And what happened to this Sara Trassjonsky?"

"Arrested and currently enjoying accommodations in police headquarters in Old Jewry. I was able to have a short but productive private interview with her, with the understanding that I would communicate her cooperation to the police." Holmes paused to freshen his tea. "The papers she was attempting to burn were largely anarchist pamphlets and literature. Are you, perchance, familiar with any of their rhetoric or philosophy?"

"No," I returned. "I wouldn't poison my mind with such nonsense."

"Ah, then I suppose it's a good thing that I have never invited you along on any of my excursions to the Anarchist Club."

"Surely you're joking." I looked closely at Holmes, but his inscrutable expression gave nothing away. "You mean to tell me there is such a thing? An Anarchist Club in the heart of London?"

"It's in the East End. Jubilee Street, if you fancy a visit."

"Holmes, I don't understand. Why should you choose to associate yourself with that crowd? You're likely to get yourself assassinated!"

"It's always best to keep a finger on the pulse of every segment of society, whether you happen to sympathise with its ideology or not. As for the Anarchist Club, they aren't all wild-eyed bombers and revolutionaries. It's a social venue largely made up of Jewish émigrés from Russia."

"Still," I mused, "they fairly advertise their purpose with a name like the Anarchist Club. It's hard to believe the police haven't shut it down."

"Go to any meeting and it won't be long before you spot a plain-clothes policeman or two in attendance. They sincerely believe that their presence goes unnoticed, but they're as conspicuous as scorpions crawling over a tray of scones."

Holmes seemed inclined to continue, but something that had completely eluded me had evidently caught his attention.

"Do come in, Inspector Hopkins!" he announced. Sure enough, our door opened to reveal the haggard Hopkins, who shuffled his way slowly into the room.

"Help yourself to a sandwich and some tea, Inspector," said Holmes. "I was just filling Watson in on the case and its connection to the activities of the Anarchist Club."

"There is no question that last night's crime was hatched there," remarked Hopkins as he looked over the sandwiches. "But I've had two of my best undercover men in the club regularly and they had no clue that such an elaborate scheme was being planned."

"What have your men been able to learn, Inspector?" I asked.

"Very little," returned Hopkins. "They don't wish to make themselves known, and the language barrier is an issue as well. Regardless, they both feel certain they know who the mastermind behind the crime is – a gentleman known only as Peter the Painter."

"What makes your men suspect him?"

"Because he consciously makes himself conspicuous, which is no doubt intended to deflect attention from his activities behind the scenes." Hopkins was now pouring himself a cup of tea. "He's a tall, thin, dapper fellow, with a goatee and moustache that he waxes religiously."

"And he's a painter, you say?" I asked.

"No idea," answered Hopkins. "These people change professions and names from one day to the next. However, his bowler hat is marked with a splotch of red paint for some reason. Likely nothing more than an affectation to set him apart from the crowd."

"Or to identify him to Anarchists who may be new to London," I offered.

"Possibly. My men have attempted to follow him whenever he leaves the club, but without success. He is a will-o'-the-wisp who can apparently appear and disappear as he pleases. As you are no doubt aware, Doctor, the East End is a veritable warren of dark passageways and secret places. You could practically hide a herd of elephants there if you wished."

I turned to Holmes, who had listened attentively to Hopkins's recitation. "Then you should track him down! There isn't a man you couldn't trail if you wanted to, just as there isn't a man who could follow you if you didn't wish to be followed."

"You're very kind, Watson, but if this Peter the Painter was involved in last night's robbery, I suspect he will have gone to ground for the time being. Speaking of which, may I assume that this isn't merely a social visit, Hopkins? Is Mr. Gardstein ready for his session with the photographer?"

402

"As ready as he'll ever be, Mr. Holmes."

Holmes nodded and went upstairs to his bedroom. When he returned, carrying a small leather case, I asked, "What do you mean – session with a photographer? You said this Gardstein fellow was dead."

"Indeed I did. Your powers of recollection do you credit. Coming?"

Two minutes later Holmes, Hopkins, and I were out in the brisk air of Queen Anne Street. We strolled along in silence for several streets, but then it occurred to me that this was a propitious time to get a better understanding of these Anarchists and their goals. I posed this question to Holmes and, as expected, he rose to the occasion.

"If you study human history, Watson, you will find that in almost any oppressed community there exists a burning desire to become oppressors themselves. Where they were once persecuted, they now wish to persecute. Where they were miserable, they now seek to make the lives of others miserable. I recommend the example of the Pilgrims who left this country and settled in North America as an excellent illustration of this tendency. Similarly, these Russian expatriates, having fled the brutal caress of Mother Russia, now find themselves in an England that is relatively liberal by comparison. No longer under the thumb of the Czar and his secret police, some seek nothing more than better lives for themselves and their families, but others are almost exclusively focused on the destruction of society as we know it, particularly the upper class."

"Well," I answered, "while I would never sanction cold-blooded murder or the bombings of which these Anarchists are so fond, I will say that some of the excesses of the nobility and the wealthy do need to be reined in."

"Of course," returned Holmes. "And many of your fellow citizens heartily agree with you. But then, the Upper Ten Thousand, as they are termed, are extremely adept at manipulating social opinion through the press and by other means, so that the downtrodden and indigent are more often than not set at each other's throats, with the poor Englishman pitted against the poor foreigner rather than recognising and confronting their true oppressors and antagonists. Ah, but here we are."

Looking up, I saw that we had arrived at the stone steps leading up to The City of London Mortuary. With Hopkins leading the way, a few moments later we were gazing upon the quite deceased George Gardstein. With his mouth hanging open and streaks of blood on his face, he made for quite the grisly sight. Nearby, a photographer was in the process of setting up his camera as Holmes looked over the corpse disapprovingly.

"No, no, this won't do. Mr. Gardstein must be tidied up and made as presentable as we can make him." Holmes held up the case he had brought with him. "Luckily, we have just the tools for the job."

403

Opening the case, Holmes pulled out a sponge and a hairbrush and set to work as Hopkins and I looked on. I became aware that Holmes was actually humming to himself as he cleaned Gardstein up, something that Hopkins noticed as well. Just as the inspector was about to make some remark to me, Holmes stepped back from the corpse to display his handiwork.

"Well gentlemen, what do you think?"

The effect of Holmes's efforts, I must say, was truly remarkable. With his face clean, hair neatly coiffed, and eyes open, Gardstein appeared to have been resurrected.

"Excellent work, Mr. Holmes," said Hopkins. "If I didn't know better, I would say that Mr. Gardstein was still among the living."

"Then I should say he is quite ready for his appearance in tomorrow's newspapers." Holmes nodded to the photographer to get on with his work, then turned back to Hopkins. "What is the reward for any information on the whereabouts of Mr. Gardstein's associates?"

"One-hundred pounds."

"No, no, no. That won't do. We need a figure large enough that news of it will spread quickly by word of mouth. Make it five-hundred for whomever identifies the Houndsditch murderers and their current location."

"Of course." With a glance at the photographer, Hopkins took Holmes by the elbow. "If I might have a word."

As we emerged into the hallway, Hopkins glanced left and right and, having determined that we were alone, he leaned towards Holmes in conspiratorial fashion.

"While I feel quite sure that Gardstein's picture in the paper and the reward money will soon flush the rats out, there is something with which I could use your help."

"Do tell."

"It's regarding this Peter the Painter fellow. I have it on good account that in the past six months, he has planned any number of heists and even an assassination or two."

"But how is that possible?" I objected. "There hasn't been anything reported in the newspapers."

"Because there has been nothing to report," answered Hopkins. "What this Peter the Painter has failed to realise, at least so far, is that there is a traitor in his organisation who keeps us apprised of the various crimes these Anarchists intend to commit."

"Then what happened yesterday at the jewelry store on Houndsditch?" I asked.

404

"You have me there, Dr. Watson. We had no advance warning whatsoever."

"I believe I have an explanation," interposed Holmes, "should you wish to hear it."

"Of course." Hopkins looked at Holmes with the keen eyes of a terrier who has just heard the scurrying sound of a rat across a kitchen floor.

"In looking further into the matter, I was able to ascertain that all of the perpetrators of last night's crime are recently arrived from the region of Latvia, which is on the Baltic Sea in the northwestern corner of the Russian Empire. They appear to have kept their plan to themselves and didn't share it with the larger Anarchist community – which would include Peter the Painter."

"Did you learn that from the Trassjonsky woman?" asked Hopkins. "I couldn't get a word out of her."

"English is not her strong suit, Hopkins," answered Holmes. "Fortunately, I have a passing understanding of Russian, which seemed to set her at ease to a certain extent."

"What else did she tell you?"

"That Gardstein was the leader of the gang, although she may be saying that simply because he's dead and beyond the reach of justice. She lived with him in Warsaw six years ago, until they had to flee the city when he was accused of terrorism. They then combined forces with three other revolutionaries: Yakov Peters, Yourka Dubof, and Fritz Svaars, who is a cousin of Yakov Peters. Svaars had taken part in the 1905 Russian Revolution, but then fled the country when the insurrection failed. Between them, the three men had blazed a trail of murder and robberies across Europe until finally arriving in London. It was here that they met another Russian expatriate, William Sokoloff, who had been in London for about ten years and worked as a watchmaker and jeweler, but made a habit of stealing from his employers."

"And all this to what end?" I asked.

"To finance the overthrow of the Russian government – particularly Czar Nicholas and his family, for whom they all share a pathological hatred."

"Why? What did the Czar ever do to them?"

"As Russian Jews, they were all subject to the most appalling depredations imaginable. When Yakov Peters was jailed for handing out revolutionary pamphlets, all of his fingernails were torn out. Yourka Dubof was publicly flogged by the Czar's Cossacks until he lost consciousness. As for Miss Trassjonsky herself, she too suffered the unwelcome attentions of the Cossacks, although she refused to say anything more than that."

405

"It's a sorry tale, Mr. Holmes," remarked Hopkins, "but I'm afraid it doesn't give them license to come to England to prey upon people who have never lifted a finger against them."

"On the contrary, they see all of Europe's nobility as little more than an organised criminal family who are all related to one another and a cancer to be excised as quickly and bloodily as possible. Don't forget, Hopkins, our late sovereign, King Edward VII, was uncle to both Czar Nicholas II and Emperor Wilhelm II of Germany, and George V is a first cousin to both of them."

"Well, that's true enough," conceded Hopkins, "but my allegiance is to England, and more specifically to my fellow officers in Scotland Yard. I won't rest until every one of the men involved in last night's attempted robbery is standing on the gallows."

"Well then, get Gardstein's picture in the paper, along with the reward money being offered, and I suspect you won't have to wait long for news of their whereabouts."

"Very good, Mr. Holmes. I'll be sure to keep you posted on any developments."

"Please do," answered Holmes. "I'm as anxious to get these murderers off the streets as you are."

"And in regards to Peter the Painter," continued Hopkins, "I'm not going to pretend that I understand or condone all of your methods, but in this case, if you could possibly use your powers to track this fellow down, I would be most grateful. Whatever it takes. And you have my personal assurance that no questions will be asked."

The next morning's papers featured not only the lurid details of the Houndsditch murders, but also the photograph of the late George Gardstein and the sizable reward being offered for more information on the men who had murdered three policemen. Holmes glanced only briefly at the papers, then paced about the room like a nervous cat. One moment he was at the window. Then he was attempting to read. Finally I was startled by the sound of his fist slamming against the table.

"I am not well suited to this, Watson."

"To what?"

"Waiting. Passivity. Held to a complete standstill while waiting for someone else to do something. My entire being rebels against it."

"Perfectly understandable, but you can't very well conduct a house-to-house search of every building in London for these Anarchists."

"And I shouldn't have to. I should be able to put myself in the position of the perpetrators and logically narrow the parameters. But London is no longer the city it was when we first met. New streets and neighborhoods seemingly spring up overnight. In the past thirty years, the population has swollen by nearly three million people. I fear we may have reached a tipping point where informants and investigations will no longer be enough to hold the criminal elements at bay."

"You're saying that the Anarchists may very well win the day."

"If a sufficient percentage of any population feel aggrieved and that they have nothing to lose, then the society may very well fall into chaos, yes."

"Then maybe Hopkins is right," I began. "The solution lies with Peter the Painter. If you can locate him, surely the other pieces of the puzzle will fall into place. Perhaps he has borrowed a page from Poe's 'The Purloined Letter' and you'll find him at the Anarchist Club, hiding in plain sight."

"Unlikely," replied Holmes. "You can be certain that every entrance and exit to the Anarchist Club is now under surveillance by Hopkins and his men. We won't find our quarry there."

"Then what can we do?"

"As much as it pains me to say it, we wait. Time, like water, is an irresistible force. I feel certain there will be no more Anarchist crimes in the immediate future as they lick their wounds and wait for the hysteria surrounding the Houndsditch murders to abate. Bear in mind that not only will the police be looking for the murderers, so will the public, with their appetite whetted for the chase by the reward money being offered. All the same, however, I think I'll venture out, to ease my nerves if nothing else. You stay here and hold down the fort. I expect events to start unfolding very quickly."

As much as I chafed at the thought of remaining at home as Holmes went out to pace the streets of London, I was also aware that I would struggle to keep up with him and that there wasn't much that we could do in terms of uncovering new information through investigating. Rather, as Holmes noted, that new information would come to us, courtesy of acquaintances, landlords, or observant citizens anxious to lay claim to the reward money.

Sure enough, the very next day, the police trumpeted the arrest of Osip Federoff, an unemployed locksmith who was a known Anarchist and associate of Gardstein, although there was no evidence linking him to the Houndsditch murders. There then followed three days with no further progress, and with a memorial service for officers Tucker, Bentley, and Choate planned for December 22nd at St. Paul's Cathedral. Hundreds of thousands of Londoners turned out to line the route to the cemeteries, with the London Stock Exchange closing down for half-an-hour to permit the brokers to watch the procession as it made its way down Threadneedle Street. That same day there appeared to be a major break in the case, as Yourka Dubof and Yakov Peters were both apprehended. However, when

Federoff, Dubof, and Peters were charged with the murders of the three policemen at the Guildhall Police Court, they all pled not guilty. Of the notorious Peter the Painter there was no sign at all, and the press speculation was that he had fled the city and had already made his way to the Continent.

Increasingly, it appeared as if the two prime suspects in the Houndsditch murders were Fritz Svaars and William Sokoloff, but New Year's Eve came and went with no sign of them. Then a grisly discovery connected with the crime was found on Clapham Common in South London on New Year's Day: A Russian Jewish immigrant by the name of Léon Beron was discovered by a passerby severely beaten and semi-conscious, but what sent the press into a frenzy of speculation was that the letter "*S*" had been carved by a knife into both of his cheeks. Surely, this could be nothing less than a warning from Svaars and Sokoloff to any other Russian immigrants to keep their mouths shut. That meant they were still in London, and new hope arose that they would both be apprehended quite soon.

Holmes was out more than he was in, but whenever our paths crossed and I ventured a question, I was met with a noncommittal shrug or merely a grunt of an answer. I could tell that the entire affair was weighing on him heavily and there was even some speculation that members of the Russian Secret Police (also known as the *Okhrana*) had arrived in London to deal with the Anarchists in their own fashion. Of course, the newspapers were having a field day with each new lurid detail that came to light, fanning the flames of prejudice against practically every immigrant in the East End, proposing one outlandish theory after another regarding the whereabouts of Svaars and Sokoloff, and what crimes they might be planning next. For his part, Peter the Painter was built up to be a criminal mastermind of Professor Moriarty's proportions.

Just as I was thinking of going to bed on the evening of January 2nd, a rather frantic pounding on the front door sent me scurrying down the stairs to find a breathless Hopkins standing on the front step.

"Hopkins!" I exclaimed. "I'm afraid – "

"I know Mr. Holmes isn't here!" Hopkins cut me off. "But he's done it! We know where they are! Get your coat if you want to be there when we put the cuffs on them. Just be sure to put in a good word for Scotland Yard if you decide to write this up as one of your stories."

Scarcely a minute later, Hopkins and I were rattling along at high speed in a police automobile. Anticipating every question on my lips, Hopkins filled me in.

"I told Mr. Holmes I wouldn't ask any questions regarding his methods and I won't, but late yesterday he sent a note to Scotland Yard saying that Sokoloff and Svaars were holed up at 100 Sidney Street, and requesting £500 in cash for his informant. We've had the address under surveillance all day, and there was a meeting with the City Police and the Metropolitan Police this afternoon to decide what to do."

"Why not just enter the building in force and arrest them?" I asked.

"If only it were that simple, Doctor. We feel certain that these men are very well-armed, and there are dozens of tenants in the building. We can't run the risk of any innocent people being taken as hostages, so we need to evacuate everyone without rousing the suspicions of Svaars and Sokoloff. We just started that process an hour or two ago to accomplish it under the cover of the night."

"And what of Holmes?" I asked.

"I'm sure he's in the vicinity," returned Hopkins, "and I trust him to be able to take care of himself. The same goes for you, because anything might happen when we try to arrest those men. It could go wrong very quickly."

In all candour, I will confess that I was utterly unprepared for the sight that awaited me as we arrived in Sidney Street. I was expecting a handful of policemen and vehicles, but as I glanced around in wonder at the cordoned off area outside 100 Sidney Street, I estimated there to be no fewer than two-hundred officers in the area. The building itself was three stories high, and many of the people who had been evacuated from it remained on hand to watch the proceedings. Some of them had apparently summoned friends and relatives for what they anticipated would be a memorable event. Holmes was nowhere to be seen, and Svaars and Sokoloff, the only two people left in the building, seemed to be quite unaware of what was transpiring outside. Spotting Hopkins in a heated conversation with what I took to be some governmental official, I waited until the gentleman had stalked off in high dudgeon before I approached the inspector.

"He wants us to storm the building right now, but I'm not having it," seethed Hopkins. "Those men are on the top floor, and the only way up there is a winding stairwell in which two men can barely stand abreast. I'm not about to bury any more officers if I can help it. There's nothing for it but to wait until dawn so we can see what we're doing."

"Perhaps the two of them will surrender once they see what they're up against," I offered optimistically.

Hopkins turned his face away from me and I could see him attempting to master the emotions that threatened to overwhelm him. "Look around you, Dr. Watson. All of these officers just lost colleagues who were murdered in cold blood. And the two men in that building know very well that if they make it out alive, the only future they have will be at the end

409

of a rope. This is the calm before the storm, and we can only hope that the storm passes quickly."

At that, Hopkins strode off to consult further with his men, and I became uncomfortably aware of the fact that despite the hour, the number of curious bystanders was steadily growing. By the time the first tendrils of dawn crept over the horizon, there was the general feeling that at any moment, something momentous was about to take place. At some signal that I didn't see, a single policeman approached the front door of the building and knocked loudly. The gathered crowd held its collective breath as the officer knocked at the door again, but with no response. He was then joined by another constable, and together they gathered up some stones and began flinging them high into the air and against the windows on the top floor.

It was at that moment, just as I turned to see how the crowd was reacting to this new development, that I saw a distinctive figure that had been thoroughly described to me only days earlier. He was about fifty yards from where I stood – tall, thin, with a goatee and upturned moustache, a high white collar, and a red blotch of paint on the side of his black bowler hat. It was none other than Peter the Painter. It had to be.

As I began to move towards him, there was a collective gasp from the crowd, and as I looked up at 100 Sidney Street I saw the figures of two men who had been roused from their slumber at one of the windows. Before the police could say or do anything, the two men smashed out the window and began firing down below. An instant later I saw a police sergeant fall to the ground clutching his chest, and as his colleagues ran to his aid a swell of movement in the crowd practically lifted me off my feet, and I soon found myself thirty yards from my original location through no volition of my own.

The crowd scattered for cover as the police returned fire, and as the chaos grew I lost sight of Peter the Painter, who was swallowed up in the sea of humanity. Some were fleeing for their lives, but others were more intent on jostling for a better view, and as the waves of bodies crashed against one another, I felt the very breath being crushed out of me. In my naivete, I had fully expected the whole incident to be over once the shooting began and the police returned fire, but that proved to be far from the case. As the minutes passed, it was clear that Svaars and Sokoloff had superior weapons to the police, as well as an abundance of ammunition at their disposal. Hopkins and the other authorities present were disinclined to send any of their men on a suicide mission into the building, and from my protected vantage point I was able to see them huddled together in frantic consultation at what they should do next.

410

By ten o'clock, the answer came as a detachment of Scots Guards appeared on the scene and began taking up positions in the buildings across the street from the Anarchists and at both ends of the street. I would learn later that they had been summoned from The Tower of London where they were stationed, and that it was the first time the military had joined forces with the police to end an armed siege in London. However, even these reinforcements failed to turn the tide in favor of the authorities as more and more curious citizens flocked to the area. By noon, there was at least one Pathé News camera filming the events, and Home Secretary Winston Churchill had arrived on the scene as well, much to the displeasure of the crowd, who blamed the Liberal Party's immigration policies for allowing these Anarchists to come to England in the first place.

It was just short of one o'clock in the afternoon when smoke began to emerge from the second story windows of the building, and when a representative of the London Fire Brigade requested permission to attempt to extinguish the blaze, he was promptly turned down by the police, who by this point were quite happy to watch the building burn with the two men still inside. The shooting coming from Svaars and Sokoloff soon ceased, and when part of the roof collapsed, the Fire Brigade was given permission to stop the blaze from spreading to nearby buildings. It took a few more hours, but eventually the charred corpses of Svaars and Sokoloff were pulled from the ruined building, the crowd dispersed, and I began to make my way back home, still having never caught a single glimpse of Holmes. To my surprise, as I trudged along, still trying to make sense of the events of the day, Inspector Hopkins came by in a police vehicle and offered me a lift back to Queen Anne Street.

Shaken by all of the events that we had just witnessed, we rode in silence, and when I disembarked, Hopkins did the same and we made our way inside. It was with some relief that we found Holmes in residence, smoking his cherry-wood pipe and staring into a well-stoked fire. He turned as Hopkins and I entered and remarked, "A sorry day in the history of London. I have already taken the liberty of helping myself to a brandy, and I heartily recommend that you do the same, gentlemen."

Hopkins and I lost no time in pouring two snifters, and after his first sip Hopkins observed, "A sorry day indeed, but a necessary one. I can only hope that the Anarchists learn from this and realise that they cannot escape English justice if they choose to bring their fight to these shores."

"They will take their revolution back to Russia soon enough," said Holmes. "Their failed uprising in 1905 served largely as a training exercise. If he had any wits at all, the Czar would realise this, but sadly, the nobility aren't noted for their sagacity."

"I do want to thank you, Mr. Holmes," continued Hopkins, "for all of your help. But if I may be so bold, may I ask you a question? Just between us?"

"Yes?" Holmes eyed Hopkins keenly.

"There is only one of the Anarchists that we failed to apprehend or bring to justice – Peter the Painter. Forgive me for saying so, but it leads me to believe that he was the source of your information on the whereabouts of Svaars and Sokoloff. Perhaps in exchange for that, you aided him in his disappearance?"

"No."

"I have your word on that?"

"Peter the Painter doesn't exist."

To say that Hopkins and I were both shocked beyond measure at Holmes's calm pronouncement doesn't do justice to the incredulous look that we exchanged before we turned back to Holmes.

"But he does!" I fairly shouted. "I saw him!"

"Saw him?" Holmes raised an eyebrow. "Saw him where?"

"In Sidney Street as dawn was breaking. He was just as Hopkins described him. Tall, thin, with a goatee, and an upturned moustache. And he had a splotch of red paint on his hat!"

"Are you sure that's what you saw, Watson? In the dim light of the morning? After being up all night? Would you be willing to swear to that in court? Or did you only see what your mind had prepared you to see?"

"I . . . ." Hesitating, I tried to conjure up the precise image that I had observed for a few fleeting moments before utter chaos ensued. "I could have sworn – "

"Well, then," chimed in Hopkins as I faltered, "if Peter the Painter doesn't exist, how would you explain this?"

Reaching into his coat, Hopkins removed what was quite clearly a bowler hat that had seen much better days. It was battered, muddy, and flattened, with an unmistakable blotch of red paint on it. Hopkins handed the hat to Holmes, who proceeded to push and prod it into something vaguely resembling its original shape. Holding the hat at arm's length, Holmes looked at it and pronounced, "It would appear to be a bowler hat with a splotch of red paint on it. Recently recovered from Sidney Street, I take it?"

Hopkins nodded, "And I think we may assume it was trampled in the stampede that followed the first shots ringing out."

"Not an injudicious assumption," agreed Holmes as he put the hat down.

"Mr. Holmes, I will simply thank you again for your services in this case with no further uncomfortable questions. Quite frankly, I don't

412

particularly care whether you paid this Peter the Painter off or are seeking to give him time to flee the country, but I must insist upon your assurance on one point."

"Name it."

"That I will never see nor hear of Peter the Painter in London again."

"You have my word, Hopkins."

"Excellent. Then with that let us put this entire sorry affair behind us." Hopkins turned to me, inclined his head slightly, and then he was gone, leaving me to gape at Holmes in some wonderment.

"So let me understand," I began, "you were in consultation with this Peter the Painter all along?"

"Watson, I suggest that we take Hopkins's most excellent advice and put this case behind us."

"But why? What kind of power – what hold does this Peter the Painter have over you?"

"He's gone, Watson," returned Holmes. "If that's enough for Hopkins, it should be enough for us."

"But you could find him from his hat alone!" I insisted as I picked up the battered bowler. "Do you remember the case of the Blue Carbuncle, and the astonishing deductions you were able to make regarding Mr. Henry Baker simply from examining his hat? You were able to describe his wife, his home, the decline in his fortunes. Here – " I thrust the hat at Holmes and he took it. "Take one minute to examine this closely and I feel certain that it will shed light on the whereabouts of Peter the Painter."

"Very well." Holmes picked up his lens and proceeded to subject the hat to a close inspection. "The gentleman in question would appear to be middle-aged, but in good physical condition. Given to bursts of energy, he is also capable of barely moving for days at a time – both a consequence of his somewhat unique profession, which necessitates the work coming to him, rather than him pursuing the work. Semi-retired and unmarried, he currently lives in the southeast of England, but makes regular trips to London, where he stays with a friend of his. This friend is a professional man, most likely a doctor with a literary bent and an occasional pawky sense of humour."

And as Holmes cast a glance at me out of the corner of his eye, he placed the hat on his own head. "Found him."

In the course of my association with Sherlock Holmes, I have experienced any number of bizarre and strange situations, but as those two simple words left Holmes's lips, I was so stunned that it felt as if reality itself was dissolving in front of my very eyes.

"You?" I finally managed. "You mean to say that *you're* Peter the Painter? But why?"

413

Removing the bowler from his head, Holmes turned it in his hands thoughtfully. "When I became aware of the number of Anarchists flooding into London, I realised it was only a matter of time before they embarked on a campaign of assassinations and bombings to bring attention to their cause, as they had elsewhere in Europe. Given that, the choice was between reacting to events after they happened, or to somehow be able to anticipate and forestall events before they occurred. I couldn't very well go to the Anarchist Club as Sherlock Holmes, and so I simply invented a new identity for myself – that of Peter the Painter. As you are aware, my grandmother was the sister of Horace Vernet, the French artist, and so it seemed to be a suitable role for me to play. Through the judicious use of spirit gum, I was able to apply a beard and moustache, a light application of make-up was enough to take a few years off my appearance, and a high collar completed the effect by obscuring the skin on my neck, which is always the surest way to mark an individual's age.

"Presenting myself as a first-generation Englishman with Russian parents, I was able to quickly establish my utility to their cause thanks to my familiarity with London, excellent English, and passable Russian. I was also able to take the heated rhetoric I heard inside the walls of the Anarchist Club and suggest utterly plausible schemes that somehow always ended up being thwarted at the last moment, as I anonymously passed the necessary information on to the police. The important thing was to make the Anarchists feel that they were taking action, even if this robbery or that assassination never quite succeeded. Sadly, in the case of Mr. Gardstein and his associates, they were all Latvian and distrusted anyone not in their immediate circle. They were able to plan their robbery of the jewelry store on Houndsditch with no one in the Anarchist Club having any inkling of what they were up to – not even Peter the Painter, who would, of course, have informed the police had he known."

"And I take it that it was in the guise of Peter the Painter that you found the informant who revealed the whereabouts of Svaars and Sokoloff."

"Correct. He wanted the reward money, but was afraid of going to the police directly."

"Then why on earth were you in Sidney Street earlier today as Peter the Painter?"

"Ah. There we enter the dark and troubling world of authority figures trying to exercise their authority just to prove that they have it. It was the Metropolitan Police who coordinated the evacuation of the building, but during the long night vigil, as we waited for dawn to break, the higher-ups among the City Police became convinced that Svaars and Sokoloff had somehow slipped out when the other tenants were being evacuated and

414

were no longer in the building. As you can imagine, the discussion on this point between representatives of the two police forces was extremely spirited and threatened to undermine the entire operation. Fortunately, I was able to notify my informant, and for an additional one-hundred pounds, he was able to verify that Svaars and Sokoloff were still there this morning – but he insisted upon receiving his payment in person from Peter the Painter himself."

"Very well then," I observed, "Hopkins may be satisfied, but what about the press? What about the government? I saw Home Secretary Churchill on Sidney Street watching it all unfold. There will be questions and an investigation, with at least part of it surrounding the identity and whereabouts of Peter the Painter."

"They are entitled to investigate and ask as many questions as they wish, but in this case, I'm afraid I will have no answers." Holmes stepped nearer the fire and tossed the bowler into the flames. "When the accounts of the events on Houndsditch and Sidney Street are written, Peter the Painter will remain nothing more than an enigma. After all, Watson, what's life without a little mystery?"

With that, Holmes went upstairs to his bedroom and closed the door behind him, leaving me to gaze into the fire, where the only evidence of Peter the Painter's existence was burning itself into ashes. Sure enough, in the coming weeks and months there were many things written about what came to be known as the Siege of Sidney Street, and there was considerable speculation regarding the mysterious figure of Peter the Painter. Had he fled to the Continent? Had he been murdered by his fellow Anarchists? Various very clever people proposed various very clever answers, but not one account came near to the truth of the matter – that the mysterious Peter the Painter had never existed at all.

NOTE

The events surrounding the Siege of Sidney Street (aka The Battle of Stepney) are much as described in the above story. In January 1911, London police found themselves in a pitched battle against heavily-armed Latvian anarchists, who had murdered three policemen the previous month. Winston Churchill himself came to personally view the unfolding drama, and the mysterious figure of Peter the Painter figured prominently in newspaper accounts of the time, but his real name was never discovered and he subsequently disappeared, never to be seen or heard of again.

The Valley of Tears
by Andrew Bryant

The letter was postmarked Sussex, and the handwriting as familiar as my own. The message was brief, as expected. He had the ability to simplify complexities and explain motivation and reasoning in far fewer words than most others could – including myself.

> *Meet me at Paddington. Tomorrow. Cardiff train. Man drowned in bedroom.*

It had been written the day before, so tomorrow was now today. I packed a bag and cabbed to Paddington and found Mr. Sherlock Holmes waiting on the platform reading a newspaper.

"*Sut wyt ti?*" Holmes said.

"Beg your pardon."

"*Sut wyt ti?*"

"Not Gaelic," I said.

"*Na.*"

"Erse?"

"*Na.*"

"Manx?"

"*Na.*"

"Cymric?"

"*Yess.*" Then he said, "Do you remember our previous visits to Wales?"

"Of course. The Blue Lady of Dunraven comes to mind."

"Yes. This time around Mr. Ivor Jones, a director of the Cambrian Combine, has been found drowned in his bed in Penarth, just West of Cardiff. And I – and you – have been requested to investigate, as the local constabulary have come up cold."

"Requested by?"

"The Cambrian Combine. It seems that prematurely dead directors make other directors nervous, and they would like a resolution of the death so the remainder of them can rest easy."

"Did this Combine give you any clues?"

Holmes handed me a letter. Across the top of the page was embossed the company name with crossed shovels preceding it and a shining lamp following. I read the letter to myself, skipping quickly through the self-aggrandizing sections regarding the social and moral standards of a company that ran a multitude of coal mines and employed thousands of men, and who cared for nothing more than the well-being of their employees. After this introduction the letter got to the point, which was that Mr. Ivor Jones, director, had been found drowned in his bed and the Combine wished to hire Mr. Holmes to investigate and hopefully resolve the case satisfactorily. A note added that the company doctor, D. Morris, signed the death certificate stating that Mr. Jones had drowned under unknown circumstances.

Holmes had a valise at his feet. Around us swirled people and rushes of steam, the grating of shoved baggage carts, and the constant shouting of times and platform numbers and destinations.

"How can you read a newspaper amid all this hurly-burly?" I said.

"Disassociation," he replied. "Sometimes the world needs to be listened to in every remote detail, and sometimes the world needs to be ignored in its entirety. One just needs to know which extreme needs to be applied to the situation that presents itself."

"What are you reading?" I asked.

"*Gwyliedydd Newydd.*"

"I see," I replied.

"Do you believe that the mind diminishes at a rate equal to the body?" he asked.

"Without a doubt, both mind and body. Not always equally but certainly in tandem. Show me a seventy-year-old as physically strong as a twenty-year-old. The same is true of the mind, although challenges and responsibility and stimulation, reading and puzzles for example, may help, ultimately all the exercises of mind and body will not be able to stave off the unthinkable."

"Unthinkable. No more apt word for it. The inability to think. Whatever you do, Watson, don't ever allow me to deteriorate mentally. Take my body before my body takes my mind."

"Is that the reason for the Welsh language?"

"Yes. I believe the mental discipline of learning a new language must do wonders for the connections within the mind, and it is appropriate for our destination."

"It cannot but help," I said.

Holmes looked away for a moment, lost in another thought, and then changed the subject.

"Can you imagine that a war is coming, Watson? Queen Victoria's children at such loggerheads! But perhaps that is the problem – perhaps if they weren't all related, this war wouldn't be coming. They are adult children squabbling like infants, only these adults have countries and

417

armies at their fingertips instead of an infant's toys. Strangers are often less inclined to go to war than families are."

"Do you believe it's really coming, or is it all just bluster and bullying?"

"From the look of the newspapers it appears inevitable. The Germans at Agadir. Italy and Turkey at war. Stolypin assassinated. Anger in Berlin over the Moroccan deal with France. The seemingly random events are piling up and pointing in an unstoppable direction. Why do we elect fools to govern us? Should we not elect wise men?"

"It has been said that nations get the governments that they deserve. We elect fools to govern us and so we are consequently governed by fools."

"So this inevitable war is our fault? Every citizen is culpable by engagement or culpable by lack of engagement? And does it matter which?"

"History, or at least the writers of history, are always the deciders of that," I said.

"And they can only decide when it is too late, only once the deed is done."

"Such is history," I said. "Tales told through the mists of Avalon."

Holmes folded the newspaper.

"We should board," he said.

We stepped up into the carriage, found our seats, and waited for the hammering of the cars together to let us know we were about to be underway. We travelled in silence for some time, Holmes with his newspaper and I with the view.

Finally, I broached the subject of our journey.

"Other than a director of this Combine, who is Ivor Jones?" I asked.

"A man who made his fortune from mining coal. Or more accurately, a man who made his fortune because other men were mining coal for him. Cardiff is the busiest port in the Empire, shipping nearly ten-million tonnes of coal a year, and a sizable quantity of that coal belonged to the late Mr. Jones. Ten-million tonnes of anthracite shipping out annually to help keep the rest of the world in working order. Entire villages in the Welsh valleys dedicated to nothing but that. All the men and boys over the age of ten working down there below ground, twelve hours a day for a five-pence daily wage."

"I'm sure Mr. Jones made substantially more."

"We'll find out how he lived when we get there. We're staying at his house."

"Any suspects? A maligned worker perhaps?"

"Unlikely, as no one of the miner's class would ever be allowed anywhere near him. It is improbable that Mr. Jones ever set foot in any of the valleys or villages or pits that he owned. His workers would have no access to him. Most of the miners likely don't even know the names of the individuals who control the Combine."

"A business partner?" I offered.

"Plenty of opportunity I'm sure, but very little motive. They are all greedy men and greedy men don't murder within their own circle as long as the finances are all in order. They will do practically anything else to each other, but, as you know, murder takes a different kind of cold-heartedness, and also a lack of concern for consequences."

"Consequences?"

"The upheaval within the company, the vying for position now that a director's chair is empty. The stock of the company has already dropped on the London Exchange. Business doesn't like uncertainty – no one will invest in uncertainty. Business likes the *sure thing*, as our American friends would say, and murder doesn't lend itself to the *sure thing*."

"Passion," I suggested. "Passion does not care for money or position. Passion is as irrational as business is rational."

"Yes, and passion takes many forms: Romantic, theological, political. Mania in all its shapes and causes. Our job is to identify the passion in this case and, with that knowledge, identify the murderer. You remember that several of our cases in the Land of Song centred on the *femme fatale*. And you know what the moral of that is, Watson?"

"Never anger a Welsh woman."

"Precisely. Remember your history. The Celtic woman was as fierce a warrior as the man. The Romans feared both equally. What a sight it must have been, the wild men and women charging down the hillsides at the Legions, axes raised and swords drawn, spitting out invective and Druidic rabble-rousing as they came. No wonder the Romans never fully conquered the country."

"Or the English either," I said. "We have never won the hearts of the people."

"And we never will. Our form of invasion has been more subtle. Imposing our rule through financial control and through laws forged in London to support that control. Children speaking Welsh in school are thrashed and made to wear a sign around their necks stating *Welsh Not*. The Proceedings in Courts of Justice Act forbids the use of Welsh in court cases, and don't tell me *such is Empire*. Such is social and emotional martial law. Why can't we just leave other people alone, Watson?"

I paused before answering.

"Such is Empire," I said.

"I, of course, am not one who has ever argued with reality, like it or

419

not, but yes, Empire *is* the only answer. But this looming war will re-draw borders and end dynasties and start new chapters in the history of Empires."

"Do you think it will be as serious as all that?" I said.

"The Kaiser is a serious man, and a spoiled man. He is already building up a formidable Navy, and threatens allies and enemies alike. It would be naive to assume that a man so arrogant and reckless is going to stop of his own free will. Europe will soon be in flames, worse than the Napoleonic Wars, as now we have weapons capable of monstrous destruction, and we have aeroplanes capable of sending down death from above. For the first time in human history we can wage war on land, sea, and in the air simultaneously. Imagine the carnage, if you can."

"There is no guarantee of this future."

"Yes, there is. The guarantee is human nature. The guarantee is politics. The guarantee is the egotism of power. The guarantee is the fragile shell of civility that we cultivate but which ultimately shatters under the pressure of dictators and despots of all political stripes. Fanaticism is at the root of it all, whether it be politics or religion or some other personal menu of grievances. All the ills of man come down to that – fanaticism."

"And our current case?"

"A personal fanaticism. One cannot drown someone in their bed without a great deal of malice, forethought, and planning. It isn't an easy thing to do, to drown someone in a place that has no water. But we will find out all the details when we question the Combine and the household. And, perhaps we'll have a rare bit while we are there."

"A rare bit?"

"Cheese on toast," Holmes said.

"It doesn't sound . . . rare."

"We named it."

"We?"

"The English. We named cheese on toast a *rare bit* as an insult to heap upon the existing injury of poverty. Meat couldn't be afforded, so our jocular response to poverty was to name the poor meal *rare*. Our innate superiority allows us to belittle the suffering of others, and by *our* I mean our Empire. Mercifully, it will soon be over and we will again be nothing more than a little island with a long, complex, and fascinating history. I like mine with mustard."

"History?" I said.

"Rare bit. A thick slice of coarse bread and a pile of cheddar cheese melted upon it with a dollop of Tewkesbury. The best supper in Sussex."

"You're importing Welsh cuisine into Sussex?" I said.

"Yes, and meeting with some resistance, but I'll win them over," he said, adding "Have you ever eaten laverbread?"

"No."

"It's seaweed. Wonderful with a fried egg."

At that moment we shook and jolted our way into the Severn Tunnel, the four-mile-long burrow under the River Severn that joins England to Wales. The train was noisier in the tunnel with the clatter and engine churn confined, with the smoke, in the narrow confine that seemed barely larger than the train itself.

There was nothing to see of course, and I found the noise and the surrounding darkness too disconcerting to converse or read. Most of the other passengers put their books and newspapers down and looked out the window at the pitch dark, able to see nothing but their own jarring reflections in the windows. Some people closed their eyes and didn't open them again until they heard the "*Hurrah*" when we sped out into the daylight. I thought that this must be what it is like to be born: Total darkness with only the sounds and motions of your carrier, and then, abruptly forced out into the blinding light of a new world. No wonder newborn babies cried.

Across the green of Monmouthshire, Holmes practised his new language.

"*Faint o'r gloch ydy hi?*" he said. And added "*Sut mae'r tywydd?*"

"Language or no language," I countered, "we are still English."

"*Croeso i Gymru.*"

I looked out the window until the train slowed and we entered the outskirts of the city. At Cardiff Station, we changed trains for the short hop to our final destination. When we exited the train at Penarth Station, we were met by a cab, the horse stock-still and quiet.

"Gentlemen," the driver called out. Holmes answered that we only had a brief walk to our destination.

"*Twmffat,*" the driver said.

"*Diolch yn fawr iawn,*" Holmes replied.

The driver stared at us as we passed.

"I assume that wasn't a pleasantry," I said.

"On his part, no. But I thanked him anyway."

We walked across the station approach and around the corner to Victoria Road. Shortly we came to the house. A massive grey, cut-stone place with a dark slate roof and window frames and front door painted black. We went in through the iron gate. To the side of the house a man carried sacks of coal while a girl in a maid's uniform walked beside him and chatted with him as he went. Then she kissed him on the cheek. Another man lolled against the garden wall watching them.

Holmes knocked on the front door, and momentarily an elderly man

421

answered.

"Sirs?" he said.

"My name is Sherlock Holmes and this is Doctor John Watson. We are here regarding Mr. Ivor Jones."

"You're too late. He's dead."

"Yes, we are aware. We are here at the request of the Cambrian Combine to investigate his death."

"He drowned," the man said.

"Yes, in his bedroom."

"Yes."

"How does a man drown in his own bedroom?" I asked.

"The Lord works in mysterious ways."

"As do people," Holmes interjected.

"Are you the butler?" I asked.

"No, I'm the gardener."

"Why is the gardener answering the door?"

"I was the closest to it when you knocked."

"Why is the gardener answering the door at all?"

"It doesn't matter who answers the door here."

"Why doesn't it matter?"

"Our employer is dead. The Combine will move someone else in shortly, but for now it is only us."

"Us?"

"The staff. We still perform our duties, of course, as we are still being paid, but our positions and duties are even more random now than they were before."

"There is no mistress in the house?" I asked. "No other relatives?"

"None. Our employer never married and always lived alone. Except for us, of course."

"And how many of you are there?" asked Holmes.

"Five."

"Five servants to look after one man?"

"It takes the labour of a number of people to keep some other people," he said.

"Who are you five?"

"The gardener, who is myself. The driver, the cook, and two maids."

"All are at home?"

"Yes."

"May we speak with each in turn?"

"Are you intending to come in?"

"Yes. We are staying here."

"Are you?"

422

"At the invitation of the Combine."

"No one said anything."

"Nonetheless, we are here," Holmes said, and went passed the man and into the hall beyond.

The gardener led us through the hall and into a sitting room that looked over the garden. "I would be delighted if you spoke to me first," he said.

"As you wish."

"I'll ask Liz to bring tea."

"Liz?" Holmes said.

"Liz the Scuttle."

The gardener left the room, and Holmes looked out the window at the colourful but rambunctious garden while I turned and walked the room. Landscape paintings and china plates filled the walls. Plump furniture, small ornate tapestries of rustic life, and a white marble fireplace tiled around the hearth with depictions of the seasons. Over the mantel, a sombre portrait with a brass insert in the frame identifying "*Mr. I. Jones*".

"Would you ever hang a portrait of yourself in your own sitting room?" I asked.

"What would be the point? My bathroom has a mirror."

"The place is a little gaudy."

"Barely subtle *nouveau riche*."

The gardener came back into the room. "We will have tea and biscuits shortly."

"I neglected to ask your name," Holmes said.

"John Jones, but they call me John the Petal."

"Are you related to our victim?" I asked.

"No, sir."

"You are from Cornwall," Holmes said.

"Yes, from Gwithian. How did you know?"

"I recognized a trace of Cornu-English."

"I haven't lost my accent completely, as some people do."

"How did you come to be here?" I said.

"I came to work in the coal mines, but I was ill-suited to the darkness and the grime. And I didn't like the sight of the ponies down there underground hauling trams and never seeing daylight, never seeing a green field. I felt a great affinity with them, and so I left the mine and ended up here as gardener."

"The late Mr. Jones owned the mine in which you worked?"

"Yes."

"Your treatment here was an improvement over what the miners received there," Holmes motioned to the north.

423

"Yes. At least here I can see green and growing things, and I am able to scrub myself clean at the end of a work day."

"When it came to the mines, Mr. Jones wasn't a generous employer?"

"Show me a generous man of wealth," he replied.

"Indeed, Mr. Jones."

"Call me Jones the Petal."

"To differentiate you from all the other Jones'?"

He laughed. "I'm from the Cornwall Jones-es, but there are close ties between us and here."

"As between all the descendants of the ancient Britons," Holmes said.

"Yes, we are a nation within a nation."

Liz the Scuttle came in carrying a tray with teapot, cups, and biscuits. She served us, Holmes first and then me, and left the tray beside Jones the Petal. When she turned to go, Holmes stopped her.

"May I ask your name?"

"Elizabeth Lewis."

"You clean and stoke the fireplaces?" he said.

"Among other things."

"You were here the night your master died?"

"My Master is God in Heaven, sir. Mr. Jones was merely my employer."

"You are an honourable girl then?"

"I would like to believe so," she said.

"And you are from?"

"Tonypandy, in the Rhondda Valley."

"How did you come to work here?"

"My aunt is cook at another house in town, and sent for me when she heard this house was looking for maids."

"How old were you when you came here?"

"Twelve years."

"What about school?"

"You get paid to work, not to go to school," she said.

"Did you see or hear anything on the night your employer died?"

"No, sir."

"Where do you sleep?"

"The very upstairs."

"This is a solid house," I said. "Not many creaks or echoes?"

"Not as solid as the Rock, but yes, it is solid."

"Do you attend Church or Chapel?" Holmes asked.

"Chapel, of course."

"You're a non-conformist?"

"Chapel shows the true way. Church shows only the convenient way."

424

"The true way to – ?"

"Heaven, of course."

"Thank you, Miss Lewis."

"Of course, sir."

She had used the word *Sir* throughout the conversation merely as an obligatory term. She used it in the way some disgruntled shopkeepers call their customers *Sir*, even though they may have a healthy and perhaps justified dislike of their own customers, but are obliged to refer them as *Sir* in order to retain their custom. It is rote politeness, and isn't to be believed for a moment.

Miss Lewis left the room.

"Is the cook available for an interview?" Holmes asked the gardener.

"I'm sure she is. I'll fetch her."

I walked the room again while we waited. A finely inlaid table sat in front of a window where it would be in full sun most of the day. It was bleached nearly white, and some of the inlay cracked and shrunken from exposure to the magnified light through the window.

"Some aspects of this house show a disregard for care and attention," I said.

"Yes," Holmes agreed. "A general disregard seems to permeate the place."

The gardener entered, followed by a women wearing an apron.

"Miss Mary Lewis," the gardener said.

"I am Sherlock Holmes and this is my associate, Doctor John Watson. Do you know of us?"

"Of course, sir. Word has gotten around."

"Then you'll understand that we have to ask you a few questions."

"Of course, sir."

"Are you related to Miss Lewis, the Scuttle?" I said.

"No sir. Why would you think so?"

"You have the same surname."

"There are five names in Wales – Jones, Lewis, Morris, Evans, Llewellyn – and sometimes Morgan and sometimes Thomas and sometimes Davies."

"That's eight."

"I said sometimes, sir."

"May I call you Mary?" Holmes asked.

"May Dough is what I'm called."

"Very well, May. Were you at home on the night your employer drowned?"

"I was."

"Did you hear or see anything?"

425

"Nothing. Not until the morning when Aeronwy started screaming."

"Aeronwy?"

"The house maid. She was the one who found him."

"And where do you sleep?"

"The top floor."

"Do you all sleep on the top floor?"

"Yes, sir. The scum rises."

"As does the cream." Holmes replied.

She laughed harshly, more at the irony of it rather than the humour.

"I assume you ran downstairs when you heard the scream."

"I walked. I don't run."

"And what did you find when you got there?"

"Our employer dead in bed. Cold, immobile, pasty. Much the same dead or alive."

"Then what did you do?"

"I called Glyn to contact the police."

"Glyn?"

"Glyn the Wheel. He drove to the police station to report it."

"The house doesn't have a telephone?"

"No. Our employer didn't trust telephones. He thought they were a fad, and he would just have to have it removed after the fad had run its course."

"What happened then?"

"The police came, and the company doctor came."

"What did the doctor do?" I asked.

"He felt around the body, used a stethoscope on him, lifted up his eyelids, looked in his mouth, and then stuck a big needle in our employer's chest and drew out some half-black liquid."

"Half-black?"

"Like cloudy water."

"From the lungs?" I said.

"I'm not the doctor," she said.

"What did the doctor do with this cloudy water?"

"He put the needle in his bag, said that it was a case of drowning, and left."

"Thank you," Holmes said.

After May Dough, the other maid entered, shyly in the presence of the English. Holmes introduced us.

"Your name?" Holmes asked.

"Aeronwy Jones."

"Are you related to your employer?"

"No, sir."

426

"Are you related to anyone else who lives here?"

"No."

"Your job here is?"

"Maid."

"Upstairs, downstairs?"

"All stairs. Liz and I look after the entire house."

"How long have you worked here?"

"Four years."

"And how did your employer treat you?"

"Master and servant. You must know the hierarchy, Mr. Holmes."

"Not really, no. I have an employee who looks after my rooms and meals, but we aren't master and servant."

"What are you then, sir?"

"Employer and employed. I would call us mutually dependant."

"Is your employee your equal?"

"Not in position or intellect, but if she was she wouldn't be in my employ."

"And you, Doctor?" Aeronwy asked.

"Mr. Holmes doesn't employ me. I am a – What? A volunteer, a chronicler, a willing associate, devil's advocate when necessary, and friend."

"Are you equal to Mr. Holmes?"

I paused.

I certainly wasn't equal to Holmes in intellect or in powers of observation or deduction, but I had knowledge and experience that he didn't have, and that he would never have. I had fought in a war. I had a license to practice medicine. I have experienced women and marriage. We weren't equal in all respects, but we each had our strengths and our weaknesses, we each had different fields of knowledge and experience, but it was our differences that made us what we were: Holmes and Watson, not Watson and Holmes. He had extreme feelings of certainty and self-worth that I didn't have. I did feel that I was worthwhile and that my life had purpose, and I felt that I had earned everything that I had, but I didn't think that my life went very far beyond my family and my friends and my patients. I was fulfilled by those things. Holmes was a man who drew attention both by accident and by intention, and he revelled in the action and in the endless possibilities of everything. He was, by my admission, and his own, superior.

"Somewhat," I replied.

"Meaning, sir?"

"Meaning that you can wash and iron a bed sheet and I'm certain that your employer couldn't. Does that make you inferior or superior?" I said.

"*Wedi dweud yn dda,*" Aeronwy replied.

"Well said," Holmes translated for me.

She smiled at Holmes, and they conversed briefly in Welsh before returning to English for my benefit.

"Your employer," I said. "Was he demanding?"

"Not very. The work had to be done, but he didn't really care who did it or if it was done to a high standard. He just wanted it done so it could be said that it was done."

"He didn't have a real interest in the quality of the work?"

"No. I would say that disregard was his stock in trade."

"Do you know anyone who works in the Combine's mines?" Holmes asked.

"Of course. Everyone knows someone who works in the mines. It's the largest industry in the country. The trains go from the valleys to Cardiff docks all day long. We keep the world moving, Mr. Holmes. You came here by train?"

"Yes."

"Where did the coal come from to feed the boiler to create the steam that got you here?"

"Fair enough," Holmes replied.

"This attitude of disregard that your employer possessed," I said. "Have you heard that it extended to his mines as well as his household?"

"Without a doubt. He just wanted the job done. That was all that mattered to him."

"Thank you, Miss Jones," Holmes said. "We may need to speak with you further."

"I'll be nowhere but here."

She left the room and Holmes and I were alone.

"Your opinion of the household so far, Watson."

"No one seems to have greatly disliked Mr. Jones, although they don't seem to think much of him either. I would say that, so far, the guiding emotion regarding his death is apathy."

Glyn the driver came in next.

"May I have your full name," Holmes asked.

"Glyn Llewellyn Johns-Lewis."

"Are you related to Mary or Elizabeth?"

"No, not the cook, the maid, nor the Queens."

"Where were you when your employer's body was discovered?"

"In the garage."

"That early in the morning?"

"Early, late. It makes no difference to me. I live in the garage."

"Why don't you have a room in the house?"

"Don't want one. I have the attic over the garage, and some nights I sleep in the car if the mood strikes me."

"Why would you want to sleep in a car?"

"Because who else can say that they sleep in the future? Who else can say that they sleep inside a mechanical marvel of an ilk never seen before?"

"You are mad for automobiles?" I said.

"Completely mad," Glyn replied.

"Tell us about the night your employer died," Holmes said.

"He went to bed same as normal and when he woke up in the morning he was dead."

"Did you see or hear anything during the night?"

"Not a sound, but the garage is separate from the house, so I am in human silence. I only listen for the sounds of the cars."

"You were called to notify the police?"

"Yes. I drove to Windsor Road and reported that Mr. Jones was found dead, and then I drove back."

"Did you enjoy working for him?"

"He paid me, and he left me alone when I wasn't needed to drive, so it was all right."

"How did you personally feel about Mr. Jones?"

Glyn paused to think about his answer. He had the air of a man who didn't care much about cause or explanation, or about the end results of one's actions.

"He didn't know how to drive," Glyn said.

Holmes and I were accommodated in two rooms on the first floor, and met for breakfast in the dining room in the morning.

"How did you sleep?" I asked.

"Fairly well, considering I was in a dead man's stead. But it gave me the opportunity to examine Mr. Jones' bathroom. You slept well?"

"The sheets were damp. I couldn't get warm for the life of me."

"But we have both slept in worse places."

"Without a doubt," I smiled.

After breakfast we walked across the approach to the station and caught the Cardiff train.

Within half-an-hour, we were walking into the offices of the Cambrian Combine on John Street. We were shown into the offices of a Mr. A. Llewellyn, a director of the Combine, a "Lower Upper-class gentleman". He was gracious, and had tea and biscuits brought while he and I chatted and Holmes paced about the room. On the walls were photographs of villages black from dust under the stark outlines of cranes and derricks. Portraits showed weary men, their faces black with grime.

"The photographs capture the miner's life perfectly," Holmes said. "With all its harsh beauty intact."

"Yes," Mr. Llewellyn replied. "I surround myself with them to remind myself that I am here in my office every day, and that I bathe daily, and I can sip on a whisky whenever I choose while supping at my Club. I hang these pictures to remind myself that I'm not them. To remind myself that they work for me and that their lives have nothing to do with mine. In short, I hang these pictures because I am in a position which entitles me to hang them."

"You and the late Mr. Jones were of a like mind then?" Holmes said.

"Meaning?"

"You have little or no regard for the men who labour to give you your position."

"Nothing has been given to me, Mr. Holmes."

"These photographs say differently."

"And what do they say?"

"They say that men are breaking their backs while crawling like moles in the darkness to hammer out the black rock so you can sip whisky and frequent your Club."

"If God wanted it any other way, it would be another way."

"Yes, of course," Holmes said. "God is both the cause and the solution."

"In all things."

"Do you have your company doctor's report on the drowning?" I asked.

"No. Doctor Morris has it, and I believe he gave a copy to the police."

"Where may we find Doctor Morris?"

"Newport Street".

We cabbed to Newport Street and were greeted in the doctor's office by a deranged room of chairs and tables, not one anything like the other. School desks, kitchen chairs, day beds, and the like scattered throughout the waiting area as if Dr. Morris was expecting an overwhelming influx of patients. Holmes and I were the only ones in the room. The desks and tables were stacked with ancient copies of *Punch* and years-old copies of *The South Wales Echo* and *The Times*.

Holmes approached the reception desk and asked the uninterested clerk if Dr. Morris was in house.

"Who may I ask is calling?"

Holmes introduced us, and added that it was a matter of some urgency.

"And what is the nature of your visit?" the clerk asked.

"It's a medical matter."

"Of course. Of a personal nature?"

"No, a professional nature. We are here on police business regarding the death of a Mr. Ivor Jones of the Cambrian Combine."

"Oh, him."

"May we see Doctor Morris immediately?" I asked.

"I'll see if he is available," the clerk said, rising from his desk and disappearing down a hallway.

We waited several minutes for the clerk to return. "Doctor Morris will see you in a few minutes," he said.

"Is he with a patient?"

"No."

"Then would it be possible to see him immediately?"

"No."

"Why not?"

"Because it will be a few minutes."

"As one doctor to another, it would be a professional courtesy – "

"In a few minutes," the clerk interrupted.

Holmes and I sat down in the waiting room.

"Damned infuriating," I said.

"Some people are just naturally belligerent," Holmes replied. "There may be no obvious reason for it, and it makes no sense whatsoever, but there you have it. The more you insist, the more drawn out the situation becomes."

"Our time is being wasted."

"The doctor will see us when he's ready," Holmes said, loudly enough that the clerk could hear. Then he added quietly, "That should knock a minute or two off the wait time."

I picked up an old copy of *The Times* and leafed through it to an article on Russian Czar Nicholas and his Winter Palace in Saint Petersburg. The place was alleged to have fifteen-hundred rooms, and was occupied by one family.

"What an incredible life some people lead," I said, half to myself.

"Are you referring to us?"

I laughed.

"In this instance, no. To Czar Nicholas."

"But in the modern world, lives like that cannot be lived for very long. Revolution is in the air, Watson. A population cannot be oppressed and deprived and starved without consequences. We're lucky we have a functioning Parliament in Britain – otherwise our monarchy would have been overthrown years ago. Other monarchs will not be so lucky."

"The doctor will see you now," the clerk said.

431

We followed him into a dingy room where Dr. Morris sat, lounging and smoking a pipe.

"Sorry to keep you waiting gentlemen," he said, without any intonation of sorrow. "You are here regarding the death by drowning in bed of Mr. Ivor Jones."

"Yes. You signed his death certificate."

"I did."

"Did you find it unusual that he was found drowned under such circumstances?"

"Very unusual."

"And did you investigate?"

"It isn't my job to investigate. It's my job to pronounce. And I pronounced him dead by drowning."

"In highly unusual circumstances."

"Circumstances aren't my concern. The medical results are all that interest me. The circumstances would be more your field, Mr. Holmes, if Doctor Watson's literature is to be believed."

"Were there any marks on the body," I asked. "Bruises or abrasions?"

"No, nothing. He was as unblemished as a baby. Have you spoken to the servants?"

"Yes, we have," Holmes replied.

"Do you still have the vial?" I asked.

"Yes."

"You drew it from a lung?"

"I did."

Dr. Morris stood up and went to a cabinet behind his desk. He took out a vial of dim liquid, held it up, and shook it vigorously. The contents went black.

"It's a particulate too heavy to stay in suspension. It served no purpose in his drowning. He would have drowned any way, particulate or not."

"So whatever is in the vial is a message?"

"It's your prerogative if you want to believe that."

"And you?" I asked him.

"My report states – *death by drowning* – and that is all that it states."

"May we have the vial?"

"Of course. As a professional courtesy."

I secured it in my pocket.

"Are you going to write this story down?" Dr. Morris asked.

"That depends on how it ends. Would you like to be included or excluded if I do?"

"Included, of course. A man always wants to be more storied than he

432

actually is."

"One more thing," Holmes said. "Were the bed sheets dry when you examined the body of Mr. Jones?"

"Dry as a bone."

"Thank you, Doctor," I said.

Holmes and I left the office and made our way back to the station. Once on the train, I took out the vial and shook up the sediment.

"I will have to perform one small experiment for confirmation," Holmes said.

"And once confirmed?"

"We have a house of possible suspects, but more than that, we also have a mine of possible suspects."

Back in the Jones house, Holmes poured the contents of the vial through a handkerchief, catching the sediment. He scraped this onto the hearth.

"We'll let that dry."

We went downstairs and asked for May Dough, but she had gone out for the evening. Miss Aeronwy Jones offered to make us a supper, and we sat in the warmth of the kitchen while she rattled about the stove.

"Are we having rarebit?" Holmes asked.

"No, sir. Soup with bread sop."

"How often do you go home?" I asked her.

"Not often. I only get Sunday afternoons off every week, so there's little time. And with the strikes in the valleys, my brother writes me not to come. You never know, he says, when the Devil is going to charge through Tonypandy Square."

"You are also from Tonypandy?" I asked.

"I am."

"And what form does the Devil take?" Holmes said.

"Strike-breakers protected by the Glamorgan Constabulary. They say that Churchill is massing troops in Cardiff, just waiting to go in with bayonets and guns, and all because the Combine says that the miners are working too slowly. I'd like to see them work in their own mines. They wouldn't last an hour."

"Your family works in the mines?" Holmes asked.

"Everyone's family works in the mines – that is until they can't do it anymore. Injury or sickness stops them all sooner or later."

"And the Combine?"

"Not a whit of care or compassion. There's no conscience in those people. No pension, no compensation beyond the miserly pay. Injuries have to heal on their own, and if they don't heal, the men go back to work injured. But no one goes back after the mine really gets inside them – men

433

coughing their guts out and spitting up black. Can't breathe, can't work, can't live."

"You've seen it yourself then?"

"All have. I saw my tad die of it. Forty years in the mine. Gave his life for it, and got nothing in return but a pittance, broken fingers, and a body full of dust."

She put soup on the table for us with an uncut loaf between.

"If you don't mind helping yourselves for more, I have rooms to clean."

"Of course," Holmes replied. "Thank you."

Aeronwy left the kitchen and I heard her steps on the stairs.

The soup was leek and potato with some meat in it. I cut a slice of bread for Holmes and another for myself.

After supper, I borrowed a book from the house library and we sat up late reading, Holmes with his pipe and that day's *South Wales Echo*, while I immersed myself in *The Time Machine* by H.G. Wells. I had read it before, of course, but found the concept of it just as enthralling the second time around.

"If you could go forward or backward in time, Holmes, which would it be?"

"Definitely backward," he said, "to a time before that book was published."

"It's merely speculation."

"Speculation should lead to an inventive reality, not just to further speculation."

"Nonetheless, it's an enjoyable read."

"I prefer his non-fiction."

We both went back silently to our respective reads until Holmes dropped the newspaper.

"It should be dried out by now," he said and left his chair to kneel at the hearth. He struck a match and held the flame to the top of the small heap of sediment. There was a flare and smoke and a brief smoulder giving off the unmistakable odour of coal.

"Tomorrow, Watson, we take the train to Tonypandy."

We mingled on the platform, waiting for the train, with dozens of police officers from the Glamorgan Constabulary. Holmes attempted to engage them in conversation but only received the same rote reply – *Government business.*

It was standing room only on the twenty-mile ride up and into the Rhondda Valley. The Constabulary were on edge, like men riding into war: Quiet, waiting, unsure of what was coming – and hoping that they were ready for it. I knew the feeling, but had never felt it within my own island.

At the Tonypandy Station, the Constabulary formed up on the road behind us while Holmes and I walked up through the town. We went into a chemist's shop.

"We're looking for the brother of Aeronwy Jones," Holmes said.

"Which Aeronwy Jones?" the man behind the counter replied.

"How many are there?"

"Three. Two that remain and one that went away."

"We're looking for the brother of the one that went away."

"Why?"

"Personal business."

"Are you police?"

"No, we are unaffiliated. We are taking no side."

The man looked us over and weighed us with a critical gaze. "Is Aeronwy well?" he said.

"Yes, quite well."

The man paused. Then, "Halfway up the hill. The house is *Arhosfa*." he said.

"*Diolch yn fawr iawn,*" Holmes replied.

We went out and continued up the hill, past the line of small identical houses, all joined in a long row and built by the Combine as miners' residences. At the top of the hill, a line of men stood across the road blocking access to the mine. Visible behind them, the mine was a construction of sheds and cranes and pulleys. The black dust was everywhere.

We found the house, the name roughly chiselled into the stone lintel. "It means '*Waiting Place*'," Holmes said.

He knocked on the door. Shortly, it was opened by a small dark-haired woman. "*Bore da*," she said.

"*Bore da*," Holmes replied. "I am Sherlock Holmes, looking for Mr. Jones."

"My husband is gone to the ground," she said.

"Your sons?"

She paused. "Not here either."

"We aren't constables or strike-breakers," I said.

"What then?"

"You are the mother of Aeronwy Jones?"

"Yes. Is she all right?"

"She is perfectly fine, but her employer, Mr. Ivor Jones, was recently found dead in his bed."

"The world is a better place already," she said.

"We are here to talk to anyone who had a connection to Mr. Ivor

435

Jones, and to anyone who had a connection with an employee of the house."

"Never been there and don't want to go."

"May we talk to your son?"

"Which one?"

"How many do you have?"

"Two."

"And they both work in the mines?"

"No, only one. The other left the mines after his father died."

"What is the name of the one who left?"

"Gareth."

"Where may we find your other son"

"Up at the line," she said, pointing up the hill to the grim wall of men.

"And what is his name?"

"John."

Below us, coming up from the station, was a faction of constables and strike-breakers, walking slowly shoulder to shoulder, their truncheons and clubs at the ready. Some people leaned out of their windows to shout, whistle, and jeer as the wave went by.

We walked up the rough street between the gathering sides. The miners were quickly reinforced as the breakers and constables neared. The miners were armed with their own means of resistance: Hammers, cudgels, and the long steel bars that were the drill bits they drove into the coal face to crack it apart and reap the broken harvest.

"No closer," someone shouted at us.

We stopped.

"We aren't constables or strike-breakers," Holmes said. "We only wish to talk to Mr. John Jones."

"Which one?"

"The one with the sister, Aeronwy, employed at the house of Mr. Ivor Jones, deceased."

"Ivor the Terrible is dead?" someone called out.

"Dead in his bed," I said.

"Today isn't all bad news then."

A man stepped out of the crowd. "I'm John Jones," he said.

"And I am Sherlock Holmes. I have a few questions regarding Mr. Ivor Jones."

"If you are going to ask me if I will mourn his death, then the answer is no. No one will mourn him, unless the Combine hires mourners the way they hired these breakers," John said, pointing down the street, coming up faster now, filling the road and pavement.

"When is the last time you visited your sister in Penarth?"

"Visited? Never! I will not set foot in that house or in that town. It the home of that monstrous class of people who profit from the labour of others, be them land owners or ship owners or mine owners. They all claim credit for the results of other men's labour while never doing any of it themselves. It is because of the wealthy, idle men of this country that we are here today."

"*Cymru am ddim!*" someone in the crowd shouted out, followed by a chorus of repetitions that rang down the street.

"'Free Wales'," Holmes translated for me quickly.

I looked down the street to see the strike-breakers almost upon us.

"You see?" John shouted above the increasing din. "You see how the breakers come first, ahead of the constabulary? That demonstrates even to the most naive of observers what the hierarchy is: The Combine's hired gang ahead of the law."

Somewhere a window broke, and that was all it took. The strike-breakers charged up the street, their footfalls and shouts a gathering storm. The miners tightened their line and held their ground.

"Step aside, gentlemen," John said to us. "Step aside or be in the middle of it."

Holmes and I moved towards the doorway of a house to shelter ourselves, but too late. The opposing sides met and cudgels rose and fell. I went down onto the roadway and lost sight of Holmes in the melee. All about me were boots and clubs, rising, falling. Boots kicking, and the roar of conflict, the ageless sounds of battle. Bodies striking and being struck. Shouts, cries. This was a small civil war, two sides claiming they wanted the same thing – to get the coal out of the ground and into the fireplaces and boilers of the world – but looking at that shared ideal from the opposite sides of the cause. The ones who profited, and the ones who paid the price. Meanwhile, Mr. Churchill waited in the Home Office in London to learn the outcome of today's trial run. Would the troops with bayonets be sent in or not?

My shoulders were grabbed by a pair of hands and I was dragged into a doorway, out of the vicious brawl.

"Are you injured, Watson?"

"I don't believe so. A few bruises perhaps."

"This degree of action is a young man's game," Holmes said. "I think you and I are best to sit this one out."

"I agree," I said.

We watched the spectacle unfold and disintegrate, the Constabulary moving in behind the breakers to make arrests. The strikers fought on in small groups until both sides broke it off and regrouped, tired and bloody. Those arrested were hauled off down the street, and the two factions stood apart and eyed each other.

When calm resumed, I went out into the street to give aid where needed. The injuries were consistent with the weapons used. Head wounds, broken fingers, fractured bones, cuts from broken windows. I hadn't brought my medical bag, not thinking it would be necessary, so I improvised with handkerchiefs and ties and dishtowels, and cudgels and pokers for splints. The miner's wives and younger children came out to tend their beloveds, spitting obscenities and curses at the other side. Some of the wives were first-rate field medical nurses, having no training, but possessing the vital reference of experience to stitch up wounds with sewing kits and compress blood flow with shirts and towels, and creating tourniquets from wooden spoons and string. There being no company doctor here, the wives tended the injured in the manner of poor people anywhere in the world – that is, they did the best they could with what they had.

Holmes assisted me, and we worked until near dark, until everyone who could be helped had been helped. We ended up at the home of John Jones, who had received a head gash, and badly bruised hands to the point where he could barely move his fingers. He held up his hands.

"Like many things," he said, "these will be worse tomorrow."

"Will you be working then?" I asked.

"Not a chance. The strike is full on. After today, other mines will join us, and we'll bring the coal industry to a standstill. Then, they will have no choice but to negotiate."

Holmes and I glanced at each other. After this many years together, I believe that we were often thinking the same thought: That the Combine's idea of negotiation would be vastly different from the miner's idea of it. The miners were up against the weight of an Empire that was supported by the pillars of capitalism, not by the pillars of idealism.

Leaving the Jones' house, I asked John if he had any message for Aeronwy.

"Just tell her not to come here. It isn't safe. I will write to her when I can."

With that we made our way to the station and boarded the last train with the battered strike-breakers and constabulary.

"Do you think Churchill will send in troops?" I asked Holmes.

"A noble lineage doesn't always beget noble deeds," was his terse reply.

Holmes tried to discuss the day's events with the injured passengers, but received only brief replies or silence in return. He turned to me.

"It always amuses me when secretive responses are given to simple questions. Obfuscation always reveals a palette of secrets, and the shorter

438

answer often tells the longest story. The breakers reveal by their accents and disdain that they are Englishmen hired by the Combine to not only break the strike, but to break limbs and heads in the process. Their motivation is nothing more than Combine money. And the Constabulary are all from the Cardiff region, where everyone benefits from the mines without ever having to do any of the work. Everyone benefits except the men down there crawling around in the dark, actually hacking the stuff out of the ground."

On the journey to Cardiff, I treated any injuries proffered to me. The wounds were in keeping with the miners: Cuts, abrasions, sprains, and a few broken bones.

"It won't be so pretty next time around," one of the breakers said.

We arrived late back at the Jones' house. Aeronwy was in the kitchen with Glyn the Wheel.

"There was trouble today in your village," Holmes said, "but be assured that your brother John is only slightly scathed and will recover in no time."

"You saw him?" she said.

"We did. Saw him and spoke with him."

"And?"

"It appears that the strikes will widen and things will get worse. But your brother and mother are well at the moment. They are in the thick of it, but seem well-suited to it and able to withstand it."

"We have all had lifetimes of withstanding." she said.

"He doesn't want you to visit," I said. "The situation is too unstable."

"When was your brother last here?" Holmes asked.

"Here? John has never been here. He hates the idea of this place. He says that troubles all start here and end up there." She pointed north towards the valley.

"Will you all retain your jobs now that your employer is dead?" I asked.

"We always have in the past."

"Even though your employer died under mysterious circumstances?"

"These things happen."

"Men drowning in their beds?" Holmes asked. "It doesn't happen very often."

"But it could happen," Glyn interrupted.

Holmes turned to Aeronwy.

"Miss Jones, do you have a beau?"

"Of course not, sir. The Combine rules are very strict on that. Personal relations are considered to be a serious distraction from housework."

"Indeed they are," Holmes said. "In this house and in all others."

Holmes and I took our leave of the kitchen.

Upstairs, in the hallway outside our chambers, Holmes stopped me.

"Pack your belongings in the morning. We'll be leaving on the midday train with a brief stop in Cardiff to advise the Combine of the resolution of the case."

Holmes went into his room and closed the door. I was aware that I had in my possession the exact information that Holmes had regarding this case, yet he obviously had found the solution while I had not. I smiled to myself, knowing full well that it isn't the information that one possesses that's important, but how that information is connected, aligned, and juried – in this instance, a jury of one. Everyone has a *brain*, but not everyone has a *mind*. That's what separates a brain from a mind, the ability to connect information, and to reach a logical conclusion. A doctor would call it an accurate diagnosis, assembling the hints, the clues, observations and admissions to discover just what is at the root of it all.

I went into my room.

I rose early and was down in the kitchen when Liz stirred up the banked fire and added coal to it. "What would you like for breakfast, sir," she said.

"Eggs if you have them, please," I said.

"Of course."

She went into the pantry, and soon two eggs were frying in the pan.

"Doesn't May insist on doing the cooking?" I asked.

"Why would she?"

"Most cooks are particular about their kitchens."

"It's only a job, Doctor Watson. She became cook because that was the job that was open. What we do here isn't a vocation."

"No one considers their work a career?"

"For people in our position, a career is whatever you current job is, and whatever your next job will be."

I was eating my eggs when Holmes entered. "Sleep well?" I asked.

"Very well."

"Breakfast, sir?" Liz asked.

"Not today, thank you. But could you set out tea for three in the parlour and ask Aeronwy to join us there?"

"Yes, sir."

When I finished my breakfast, we made our way to the parlour, and Aeronwy warily entered shortly after. "Am I the only one to be interviewed today?" she said.

"Yes, you are our only interest this morning," Holmes replied. "Please sit down."

She sat.

"Tea?" Holmes said.

"No, thank you."

Holmes leaned forward and began.

"Miss Jones, your employer was found drowned in his bed, but he wasn't drowned in his bed. He was drowned by two people in his own bathtub. He was then dried and dressed in his pajamas and laid out in bed as nicely as you please. The bed sheets, as you already know, were dry."

She stared at Holmes, not knowing yet whether the evidence against her was airtight or not.

"Do you have a beau, Miss Jones?" Holmes asked.

"No, sir. I told you before that it isn't allowed."

"Yes, you did tell me that. So if the young man whom you kissed on the cheek, not on the lips as one would kiss a lover, wasn't your beau, then who was he?"

"I don't know what you mean, sir."

"The young man delivering the coal. You kissed him on the cheek."

"He is a friend. An acquaintance."

"No, Miss Jones. He is your brother, Gareth. There is a close physical resemblance between your two brothers. That was the purpose of our trip to Tonypandy. Gareth left your village when your father died and vowed never to work in the mines again, and he also vowed to seek revenge against the Combine for the death of your father. As did you. Am I correct?"

She didn't answer.

"The plan was made all the easier by the slapdash attitude of your employer, which made it very easy for a variety of people to take on various positions and obligations in the house without any oversight whatsoever. This house was sorely in need of a steward, but it didn't have one. So as long as the job was done, your employer didn't care – much to his own, now unknowable, regret.

"It's difficult to wash coal dust out of something isn't it, Miss Jones, be it lungs or towels."

"I wouldn't know."

"But you would know. When your father and brothers came home from the mines at the end of every shift, you and your mother saw the black dust shaken from the clothes and floating in the air and in the water in the wash basin – black. You yourself breathed it in. You know how the dust tastes. And on wash day, the towels never could be made white, no matter how much soap and scrubbing, no matter how much hanging

441

outside in the sunlight. The towels never came white."

Holmes turned to me.

"Watson, if you were to hold a man down in a bath tub, how would you do it without bruising the man?"

"Either the victim or the murderers would need padding of some sort, something to cushion the hands so as not to leave marks on the body."

"Would towels do the job?"

"Most likely."

"Most definitely. Four towels in this case. One for each of your hands, Miss Jones, and one for each of your brother's hands. Coming from a poor family, you would be loathe to discard anything that is still of use, but you should have discarded the four discoloured towels instead of returning them to their usual place in your employer's bathroom. They will never come clean again.

"I will relate my version of events to you, Miss Jones, and when I am finished you can correct any errors if there are any."

Aeronwy looked at the floor, and seemed to become smaller in the chair.

"On the night your employer was murdered, your brother was let onto the premises by Glyn the Wheel. You let Gareth in through the kitchen door, he carrying a sack of coal dust. You both came up the stairs to the bathroom – with or without the knowledge of some or all of the rest of the staff remains to be determined. That will be for the police to thrash out.

"On entering the bathroom, your employer was surprised and shocked, and possibly cried out – not that it is relevant to his death, but it is merely an aside. He would certainly have demanded to know what the coal heaver was doing in his bathroom. Your brother then ran to the bath tub and emptied the black sack of dust into it while your employer struggled to exit the tub.

"You threw two towels to your brother who, a towel in each hand, held your employer's shoulders down against the bottom of the tub while you, with your towels in hand, held his feet down so he had no leverage to fight against his confinement. You both held him there until he stopped struggling and until the bubbles stopped frothing the surface of the water, and you likely held him down long after the struggle was over just to be certain.

"And when you were certain that he was dead, you unplugged the bath, rinsed the body, dried it, dressed it in its pajamas, and carried it into the bedroom where you tucked it under the sheets for the night. Your brother took the empty sack and left the house while you cleaned the bathroom and carried the towels downstairs to be laundered.

"In the morning, it was you who found Mr. Jones' body dead in bed,

442

and it was you who screamed to express your horror at the discovery."

Aeronwy looked up from the floor, seeming to fill the chair again now that the story was told. She looked defiantly at Holmes.

"You must have met many men in your life, Mr. Holmes, who deserved to die. And also many who did not."

"I have," he said.

"My father worked his life away in the service of the Combine, and he didn't deserve to die with lungs full of dust, choking out his last breath in front of us while Master Ivor Jones lived out his idle life in this house big enough for five families, drinking his brandy and bathing in his clean hot water after his useless day was done. Where justice cannot be found, Mr. Holmes, it must be made."

"I agree, Miss Jones, that justice can and does take many differing forms."

"Are you going to arrest me?"

"I don't have the authority to arrest you. But I will sit with you while Doctor Watson summons the police."

The Adventure of the
Tinker's Arms
by Arthur Hall

More than four decades have passed since Mr. Sherlock Holmes began his career as a consulting detective. As I've recorded before, I have been privileged to accompany him on many of his cases and often witnessed his extraordinary powers of reasoning and deduction. Since then times have changed, as they inevitably do for us all – Our dear Queen was succeeded by His Majesty King Edward VII, who has himself been succeeded by His Majesty King George V. The hansom cab has been largely replaced by mechanically driven vehicles and, of course, my friend and I have advanced in years. Overshadowing all of these things is the outbreak of a war with Imperial Germany that Holmes has long predicted, a conflict of such horror as we could never have imagined.

He and I, now considered too old to serve our country, were able to meet less frequently since his retirement. Nevertheless, Holmes's abilities showed no signs of diminishing – at least none that I could detect – and there were still occasions when our friend Inspector Hopkins of Scotland Yard saw fit to enlist his assistance to solve some puzzling case of their own.

Holmes had recently been recalled to the capital from his Sussex retirement by his brother, for reasons he would not disclose to me except to say that the matter was now concluded. Our September reunion was by arrangement, and after a great deal of reminiscing, we discussed at length the news of the recent Battle of Marne and the common expectation (shared by neither of us) that the war would be over by Christmas.

"At least," said Holmes, "the German retreat will serve to save Paris, for now."

I was about to reply when a police vehicle came to a halt as we left the Langham Hotel, a scene of some of Holmes's past adventures and our current rendezvous point, as he was staying there for the duration of this visit.

"It's Hopkins," I observed. "He has seen us and is approaching. How could he have known of your presence in London? Perhaps his passing is by chance."

Holmes shook his head. "I think not. Suffice it to say that my recent business with Mycroft had a connection with Scotland Yard. I wouldn't

444

put it past my brother to recommend my services if the official force appeared to be in need of them. Perhaps he's even involved in whatever Hopkins is bringing to us."

The inspector, looking a little older than when I had last encountered him, greeted us with great enthusiasm. After much shaking of hands and asking after the health of both my friend and myself, he appeared slightly at a loss for words. I noted that his vehicle had waited.

"Come, Hopkins," Holmes said then, "let us not continue this pretence that our meeting was accidental. I'm in London for but a short time, but I'm prepared to assist you, should that be necessary."

The official detective nodded wearily. "I would appreciate that, Mr. Holmes."

"Perhaps you would care to join Watson and myself in my room, where we can discuss this as we avail ourselves of some strong coffee."

"Thank you, sir, but I would prefer it if you gentlemen would accompany me now, if you would be so good. For reasons not made clear to me, the victim appears to be of some importance."

Holmes glanced at me, and I assented. The prospect of yet another adventure together, as in days gone by, warmed my heart. I confess to feeling extreme nostalgia.

"Very well, Hopkins, where are we bound?" my friend enquired as we crossed the street to board our transport.

The inspector signalled to the driver, who acknowledged and set off at as soon as we were settled.

"An inn – The Tinker's Arms in the Commercial Road," was the delayed reply.

"The Tinker's Arms?" asked Holmes with sudden interest.

"Do you know it?" asked Hopkins.

"I've heard mention of it before."

"I've also heard of that place," I interjected. "It has been a hostelry since the 1600's."

"A very old establishment indeed, Doctor," Hopkins agreed.

Holmes gestured for Hopkins to continue with elaboration.

"A man was found dead in bed, in a locked room. He had checked in last night. The innkeeper had noted that the fellow had remained locked in his room all night and today as well. Finally at mid-morning, they became concerned, and when there was no answer, he summoned the police. For some reason that I've yet to ascertain, the Assistant Commissioner had the local constable on that beat keeping an eye on the place, and before he did anything, he sent word to the yard. At the Assistant Commissioner's direction, I took four constables and, acting on the assurance of the innkeeper that the man was still inside but not answering repeated calls, we broke down the door."

We raced through the streets of London, clogged with late afternoon traffic, until we came upon the Commercial Road. It still seemed strange to me to encounter mechanical vehicles among the traditional horse-drawn carriages and coaches, which were now disappearing from the roads at a rate which I found to be alarming. This thoroughfare too, was changing – not yet safe, but not as dangerous as it had once been in the days of The Ripper. It crossed my mind that the London that Holmes and I had known for so long was gone forever.

"What do you know of the victim?" Holmes asked Hopkins, breaking the silence that had settled upon us.

The inspector produced his notebook. "According to items found in the dead man's pockets, he is – or was – Doctor George Higgins. He's British, but seems to have been resident in Germany for some time, and returned here only yesterday by way of the ship *Rheda*, which docked at the Isle of Dogs. As far as I could tell, the man was strangled or suffocated." Here he glanced at me quickly. "Yet there were no marks on the body. Perhaps you would be good enough to confirm that, Doctor Watson."

I nodded. "Of course."

"No marks?" Holmes persisted.

"The police doctor who attended found none."

"Very well. When we arrive we'll see what can be learned. Anything else, Hopkins?"

"Perhaps, but I'd like to hear your own conclusions, gentlemen."

By my estimation it was no more than a quarter-hour later when we came to rest outside a long low building with a thatched roof. The discoloured walls were badly in need of whitewash, and the structure was strengthened by buttresses in several places. My impression was of a building in its decline and several centuries old.

We alighted and entered through a low doorway edged with black beams. The innkeeper, a portly fellow with a sombre expression, made to approach until Hopkins held up a hand.

"We will speak to you later, Mr. Berry. For now, we must again see the room."

"A moment," interrupted Holmes. "You summoned the police?"

The man nodded. "I did."

"What made you suspicious that something was awry?"

"At first, it didn't seem unusual for him – the doctor – to be in his room for so long, and it's none of our business if a guest chooses to stay in like that. But finally, when a night and much of the day had passed, I became concerned."

"Who is employed here? Is there a Mrs. Berry?"

"No sir. Just me and a couple of girls in the kitchen. I stay close, and I don't make enough to hire any additional help."

Holmes nodded. "How were you certain that Dr. Higgins was still in his room? Couldn't he have gone out and locked the door behind him?"

Berry shook his head. "There are only two ways out of the building – by way of the rear door, which is always kept locked tight, and through the front, which is never unmanned, unless I lock the door when I step away. That's how I knew that he was still here."

"But why summon the police? Could you not have opened the door yourself and verified whether he was there without breaking it down?"

"There is only one key to the room, you see, and he had it with him." He looked at Lestrade. "The inspector saw it – on one of the tables, where he must have left it after locking himself in, and . . . ."

"Yes?"

"And before he killed himself. The glass on the table – Well, we've seen this kind of thing here before. I knew enough to summon the police before disturbing the room."

I glanced at Holmes, and then Hopkins. There had been no mention of a glass, but perhaps this was part of what Hopkins wanted us to examine without benefit of his own opinions.

The landlord looked from one to the other of us, as if seeking some sort of approval for his actions, but Holmes simply said, "We shall speak with you again, Mr. Berry. Now, it you will excuse us?"

Berry nodded and bowed his head as he moved aside to allow us to pass. I had expected to climb the short flight of rather rickety stairs that confronted us, but instead the inspector ushered us to one side of them and down a short corridor beneath. That the door had been forced was clearly evident, and I could almost hear Holmes's silent groan as he saw the plentiful signs of the police investigation within the small shabby room. With Hopkins and myself beside him, he stood on the threshold in silence, his eyes taking in every detail of what lay before us.

"See what you can learn from the body," he then instructed me.

I approached the magnificent and ancient four-poster bed that I could well imagine to have been part of the original fittings of the place, while my friend produced his lens and proceeded to examine the scuffed wooden floor while the inspector looked on.

Not long after, Holmes got to his feet. Shaking his head, he looked at our friend reproachfully.

"Dear me, Hopkins, after all these years you still haven't learned to restrain your men. A herd of cattle could have been no more successful in destroying whatever evidence this room contained. Had you called me in earlier, I could have learned so much more."

The inspector looked downcast. "I'm sorry, Mr. Holmes. I – "

"No matter." Holmes turned away abruptly and approached the bed. To my surprise he didn't immediately focus his attention on the body, but took out a handkerchief and collected a sample of liquid dregs from the glass standing on the night-table that had been mentioned by Mr. Berry. He then folded the scrap of cloth carefully and returned it to his pocket before pausing to sniff the air. I also perceived a curious medicinal smell. I leaned over to smell the nearly empty glass, perceiving the strong odours of port and opium. Then I looked back toward the dead man.

I shortly concluded my examination. "He has been dead for at nearly twenty-four hours," I announced. "Probably not long after he checked in last night. Whatever the possible effect of the substance in the glass, I can confirm that this man died of suffocation, rather than strangulation."

"Not opium poisoning?" asked Holmes.

I shook my head. "It may have been a factor in knocking him out so he could be murdered without resistance, but that isn't what killed him. There are no signs on the body of an opium overdose, in spite of Mr. Berry's theory."

"There is one other factor to consider," said Holmes. I paused to allow him to speak, but he motioned that I should continue.

"Regarding the man's death: As Hopkins mentioned, there are no marks on the body. Rather, something has been pressed against him – as if a pillow were held to his face and upper chest. Observe how his nightshirt is flattened. Also, his features, particularly the nose, have been flattened somewhat as well."

"And yet," Holmes noted, "the pillow shows no signs of being used for such a purpose – no indentations from the facial features or dried spittle, for instance, and nothing else in the room could have been used either for such a purpose."

"In any case," added Hopkins, "the room was locked. No one could have entered to smother him because the sole key had been withdrawn from inside the door." He pointed, and we saw that it lay on a small mahogany table in a corner.

"And this is the only key?" Holmes asked.

"The innkeeper assures me so."

Holmes took a step back. "So it would appear that an external cause for this man's demise is unlikely. That being so, we are left with . . . ."

He left his observation unfinished, and turned to rap upon the walls with his knuckles. Beginning at the side of the bed, he progressed around the room past the single window until he arrived at the opposite side. His face bore no expression as he finished, but a moment later he turned to the four-poster itself. He stretched his body until he could almost reach to where the supporting posts met the canopy. He then leaned into the space beneath, directly above the body and from where he could inspect the underside of the canopy, before straightening himself once more into an upright position. The ghost of a smile appeared on his lips, and was gone in an instant.

He walked towards the window, which he had already examined, and turned to face us. For a few minutes he was still and appeared deep in thought. The only sound was the murmur of activity from the bar room in another part of the building.

"This window cannot open," Holmes declared. "Centuries of old paint and repairs has sealed it forever."

"We had already ascertained that," responded Hopkins.

Holmes then went through the dead man's personal effects, meagre as they were. The small leather case contained a change of linen, a couple of shirts, a toothbrush and tooth powder, and nothing else. Holmes satisfied himself that there were no secret compartments or spaces within the case.

"Incidentally," he asked, "did Doctor Higgins have any other personal effects of any significance?"

Hopkins shook his head. "No. His pockets contained a few coins, a handkerchief, and his notecase, which only held a few pounds and a bit of German money. Nothing else." Hopkins then took a step closer. "Have you discovered anything? My men and I have already carried out most of the inspections that you have yourself, but as always, I thought it best to let you proceed with your own methods. There is nothing to be found, is there?"

"Oh yes, Inspector," Holmes replied. "There was much to be found. I know how the murder was committed, but I will not disclose my findings without enough proof for you to use in court. I also intend to find out the circumstances leading to this man's death. When I've discovered something of his prior activities in Germany, I believe all will be much clearer. You may expect an arrest to result from this incident, and I should be able to conclude my investigation within no more than a day or two. Now, before we leave, a few more words with the innkeeper, I think.

"The glass on the table," continued Holmes when we found the man in the bar. "You think that Dr. Higgins used that to kill himself?"

Berry nodded. "It wouldn't be the first time that a guest has taken his own life. It's thoughtless, sirs, choosing that way to depart, with us to find the remains."

"Did he show any indications of what he planned?"

"None. He checked in last night, saying something about having just arrived in London by ship, and went immediately to his room. He didn't come out, he didn't have any visitors, and we didn't see him again."

"With the only key. Why don't you have another? Surely that's more economical than repairs following breaking down the door."

Berry lowered his gaze. "The other was lost long ago. I just never got around to having another made. Money is always a bit tight, you see . . . ."

Holmes nodded, and then said, "You have two girls who work in the kitchen. Are they here now? Excellent. I'm sure you won't mind if I have a quick word with them." And he abruptly turned and vanished into the rear of the building, giving no indication that the inspector or I were invited or required.

Hopkins had only had time to ask Berry one other question – how long he had owned the inn – and to hear the response "Fifteen years." – when Holmes returned. He seemed satisfied, and with thanks to Berry, we departed.

Hopkins appeared a little disappointed during the return journey, but Holmes was of an unusually light-hearted disposition. We parted company with the inspector outside the Langham, with my friend giving an assurance that he would send a message to the Scotland Yard man very soon.

"What do you say to having something to eat? As you know, the roast beef here is excellent."

Although I lived just a stone's throw away on the eastern end of Queen Anne Street, I agreed at once, and we enjoyed a sumptuous meal together. Holmes said nothing more about The Tinker's Arms until we had drunk the last of our coffee.

"I miss my chemical table in our old lodgings," he remarked then. "Is it possible that Barts would allow me to use their facilities, do you think?"

I thought back to our visit to the inn. "You wish to analyse the sample you took, to confirm that it contains opium?"

"And port, and nothing else. That is my intention."

"I would imagine that even if your reputation is insufficient, my familiarity with many of the staff there would serve as a guarantee of your admission."

"Thank you, old friend. If you are agreeable then, we will proceed there at once."

On our arrival, he remarked that the laboratory section of the hospital had changed little, except for some expansion, in the years since he had seen it last. Having gained permission, he began his experiment while I chatted amiably with old friends, some of whom introduced me to more recent members of staff. Thus, it didn't seem long before Holmes reappeared and we made our farewells.

"Did the analysis turn out as you hoped?" I asked him as we descended the steps.

"The result was exactly as expected. It was a strong solution of opium. Mr. Berry made a mistake by leaving it on the table and then claiming there is only one key."

"You believe the innkeeper administered the drug?"

"I do. You recall that I said there was one other factor to consider? Do you recall our search of the room?"

I thought for a moment, and then I understood. "The opium was in the glass, which may or may not have already been in the room or brought by the doctor, but there was no bottle or container for the opium. How, if the opium belonged to Dr. Higgins with the intent to drink it, did he bring it into the room?"

"Correct. You recall that Berry said that once the doctor checked in and went to his room, they 'didn't see him again'. I confirmed this with the two girls in the kitchen – neither of whom seemed to be very likely to capably lie. Mr. Berry was emphatic that there were no visitors, so his story has painted a scene where Dr. Higgins was absolutely alone in his room, locked in with the sole key, and with a glass of opium-laced port – all meant to imply that he killed himself. But there was no bottle. That was Berry's mistake."

"Yes," I said. "That, and the key."

"Exactly. It's absurd that he wouldn't have a duplicate key – in fact, I suspect that most of the keys there are interchangeable in those ancient locks. By trying to convey that the doctor killed himself in a locked room, yet forgetting to leave a bottle to hold the port or the opium before it was poured into a glass, Berry has destroyed the credibility of his tale."

"I think that you had some sort of suspicion before we ever arrived that all wouldn't be what it seemed. You seemed to have already heard of The Tinker's Arms when Hopkins first mentioned it."

"Perhaps. We can verify my suspicions at our next stop."

I was curious, but I knew from of old that to press Holmes on that would avail me nothing. He would explain when he felt that the time was right. Meanwhile, our driver was swerving around carriages, startling the horses and other horseless vehicles at a rate that I found alarming. When we entered St. James's Square, I wasn't sorry to alight.

451

I saw that Holmes was aware of my plight – possibly my colour had faded – and that his expression was one of faint amusement.

"Why are we here?" I asked him as we entered through massive double doors.

"I need facts to confirm my theory."

"About The Tinker's Arms?"

"Precisely."

We approached a bespectacled librarian who informed us that my old friend, Lomax, wasn't working that day. I had hoped that he would make quick work of Holmes's question, but my friend was prepared to carry out the research himself. The librarian directed us to a section devoted to local history. It occurred to me that I might pass the time in the medical section, but Holmes seemed – as he sometimes did – to read my mind.

"No, stay with me. This shouldn't take long."

He was correct in this, as he usually is. By the time I had taken my seat at a nearby reading table, he had scanned the shelves and selected a thick and well-worn volume. I didn't interrupt as he seated himself and quickly turned the pages, soon to find the information he sought and to pore over it briefly. Presently he closed the book and got to his feet.

"That, I think, will suffice."

"You found something of relevance?"

"I confirmed what I recalled."

As we looked for a cab outside in St. James's Square, I quickly reviewed all that I had learned in Holmes's company. It all appeared to me as a series of facts which I couldn't yet associate with that which I knew to have occurred.

"How do we proceed now?" I asked as one of the few horse-drawn vehicles nearby came to a halt before us.

"At this moment, we cannot," he replied. "I've solved part of this mystery, but my conclusions are valueless without confirmation. This I will attempt to arrange during the evening, from my room in the hotel. As for you Watson, I suggest you use this hansom to return to your home. I'll see you in the morning as before, and I expect us to learn much then. Enjoy your dinner, and kindly convey my respects to Mrs. Watson."

With that he turned away abruptly, doubtless to seek his own conveyance to return to the Langham. As the driver urged the horse into a brisk trot, I felt some relief at travelling at a more sedate and familiar pace. The London we had known was fading before our eyes, and I understood that neither Holmes nor I would fit comfortably into the new era. I recalled that he had described me, several times during our years in Baker Street, as "the one fixed point in a changing age".

452

My wife was, as always, glad to see me. She raised no objections when I explained that I must meet Holmes again the following day, saying only that I should be careful and make allowances for no longer being young.

I intended to call upon Holmes in his room the next morning, but as I alighted from the rare hansom that I'd found, I saw that he was waiting near the main entrance to the hotel.

"Did you succeed in making your arrangements?" I asked him when greetings had been exchanged.

"I did indeed. In his reply, Mycroft indicated that he'd expected my telegram. We have an appointment in – " He consulted his pocket-watch. " – a little more than half-an-hour from now."

"I recall that you saw his hand in this from the beginning."

"It occurred to me that many of his agents must be concerned with the war. If he did involve us yesterday, it's because he's short-handed. If he confirms my suspicions about Doctor George Higgins, then only one piece of the puzzle remains." He considered for a moment. "If you can restrain yourself, say as little as is possible in my brother's presence."

We arrived at Whitehall not long after, where we were escorted to a room much different to that I remembered from previous occasions. Gone was Mycroft's former grand office and voluminous desk. His current wartime sanctum was much smaller, rather drab with two tiny but heavily-curtained windows.

"Sherlock! Doctor Watson!" He welcomed us in a most uncharacteristic manner. I hadn't thought him capable of such joviality. "It has been too long since our last visit, Doctor. I think you will find these chairs comfortable. Do sit down."

As we complied, settling ourselves around a small conference table, I reflected that his corpulence appeared greater than before. Like his brother, his hair now had more than a suggestion of grey, but beyond those things his appearance had changed little.

"Mycroft, I believe you know why we are here," Holmes began. "No, I think we will forego tea, thank you."

The elder Holmes leaned back in his chair. "Ah, yes of course. I was keeping an eye on this situation, and when Higgins was murdered, and as I knew you were still in the capital, I thought you might be able to advise Inspector Hopkins. How goes the investigation, may I ask?"

"As you know, I had returned to the capital at your bidding," my friend answered obliquely, "and concluded that other little matter that was presented to me. Vindley has already been arrested. He will be tried *in camera* and will do no more harm. My participation in that affair doesn't mean that I'm at your disposal to correct every other difficulty that your department might encounter. You will recall that I have now retired, and it baffles me that you haven't done so yourself."

"But if I did, Sherlock, what would I do with my remaining days? I myself can only spend so long at the Diogenes Club every day before boredom sets in. You, I know, find that state of mind as abhorrent, as I do myself."

"Very well. But I cannot proceed with this unless I'm better informed."

Mycroft nodded, suddenly becoming as serious as I ever remembered him. "I wanted you to initially investigate without any preconceived notions, but now I'll tell you what I can. As for discretion, I don't have to mention to you both . . . ."

The stony silence lasted for a few moments before the question was brushed aside. This wasn't the first time that Holmes and I had been questioned as to our trustworthiness, however lightly, and I thought it inconceivable that Mycroft could still find it necessary to do so. It was more likely, I concluded, that he was conforming to long-familiar and inflexible regulations.

"Who was this man, Doctor George Higgins?" Holmes asked then.

Mycroft hesitated, perhaps deciding how much to divulge. "Higgins has held a senior post in a Berlin hospital for many years. Many of his patients held a high rank in the Kaiser's armed forces, and he was able to supply us with much that he learned from them. He was an expert at interrogation, you see – top of his class in training, and spoke their language fluently. Until now, none of the Germans had the slightest suspicion of the true reason for his occasionally odd and out-of-place questions, mixed among those concerned with medical conditions. Much to my great regret he was recently discovered, however. We don't know how that came about, but he fled Germany by steamship and, reverting to his true name, hid himself within The Tinker's Arms on arrival here to await contact.

"We're not sure why he chose there, instead of coming straight to me for protection. When we learned where he was, we felt that he had some specific reason for going there, and that we should see what happened instead of charging in. He was subsequently murdered, and since we already had the place under observation, the Assistant Commissioner was able to step in almost immediately. It was at that point, Sherlock, that I brought you in as well. The war has left my department rather short-handed."

"And it will be more so, I fear," said Holmes, "before this conflict ceases."

454

"I knew of course that you would suspect that I was somehow involved. If you hadn't wired me asking for an appointment, I would have reached out to you." He adjusted his bulk in his chair, causing the leather to squeak. "It has occurred to Scotland Yard, I hope, that the innkeeper at The Tinker's Arms is undoubtedly an agent of the Kaiser."

"Perhaps not yet," my friend said, "but I certainly intended to point it out to Hopkins. After all, the evidence suggests that Doctor Higgins met his end in that supposedly locked room at the hands of the innkeeper. This will become increasingly apparent, I think, and more will be revealed before this affair is concluded."

"I look forward to hearing of the man's arrest, and also to your report, Sherlock." Mycroft struggled to his feet and glanced at the casement clock that ticked away behind us. "But now I have a meeting with the Home Secretary to attend, so I will bid you gentlemen good day."

As we walked along Whitehall a few minutes later, I could tell that Holmes's displeasure hadn't lessened.

"My 'report'!" he scowled. "Sometimes I believe that my brother believes that I'm one of his lackeys."

"He is a clever and devious man, such as his occupation requires, but it cannot be denied that he takes advantage of your kinship."

Holmes shrugged, dismissing the subject. "Nevertheless, this affair must be finished. Then I shall return for a short rest in Sussex with my bees." He looked around. "Raise your cane to summon the cab that has just appeared near the corner, and we'll repair back to the Langham for an early luncheon. On the way, I'll need to stop at a post office to despatch a telegram to Hopkins."

"To advise him about the innkeeper?"

"No, simply to suggest that he withdraw any of his men who might still be lingering at The Tinker's Arms – although it would still be well to have him and a constable or two close by tonight. You may care to inform Mrs. Watson that you won't be home until the early hours – if you intend to see this through with me."

I smiled. "As ever."

"I knew my Watson wouldn't have changed."

In accordance with his instructions, I found myself later that night crouched in an areaway near the inn an hour before midnight approached. Here, I couldn't be seen from the road, but there had been little traffic in any case during the last hour. The lights of the inn had been extinguished, one by one, and the place had been in complete darkness for some little time. I moved to relieve the cramp in my legs, causing an owl to be disturbed from its nearby roost. Startled by the outraged cry, I kept to what shadows I could as I then approached the building cautiously.

Holmes had explained earlier his intention to stay overnight in The Tinker's Arms. In disguise he would, if it were possible, occupy the same room as the murdered doctor. He seemed certain that this would bring about the conclusion of this affair but, apart from arranging to admit me through the locked door at the rear of the building, he would say no more.

I moved with stealth, entering an alley and then moving through the near blackness to the back of the inn. As I neared the door, it swung open noiselessly to reveal a tall grey-haired man with a drooping moustache. Had I not expected Holmes, I wouldn't have recognised him, as he led me along the short rear corridor and into the room where Doctor Higgins had died. Moving silently, he lit a dark lantern. Then, in the faint light, I saw that he held a finger to his lips. "Remain still as much as possible," he whispered. "It will not be long before he strikes."

"Who?" I whispered. "The innkeeper?"

"The same. When I hinted to him that I was a colleague of Doctor Higgins, following behind him from Germany, he showed me to this room at once."

"Then we will discover how the doctor met his death?"

"That's what I'm anticipating. Did you notice that the room door has been quickly repaired? And once again there is supposedly but one key, which I have in my possession. When Berry pressed a glass of port on me just before I retired, I accepted it, and it stands untouched on the night-table. You will see, if your eyes have adjusted to the poor light, that I've rearranged the pillow as a substitute for my body."

As we waited, he proceeded to restore his normal appearance, making no noise. No more conversation passed between us, and our vigil began. It wasn't as long as some I've shared with him, and after some little time during which the silence was disturbed only by the occasional cry of a night-bird, we heard a far-off clock strike the midnight hour.

Soon after, I saw a faint glow pass along the foot of the door and we heard the muted sounds of someone ascending the stairs. Beside me, Holmes stiffened like a hunting hound that has espied its prey. A few minutes of silence elapsed before a strange vibration filled the room. Surprised, I looked around but could see nothing to account for it. As the noise increased, Holmes gripped my arm.

"There!" he said excitedly. "Do you see?"

I was about to whisper that I had failed to understand what it was that he had alluded to when the faint light revealed to me that the canopy of the bed was descending. It continued to do so as we watched, emitting a harsh scraping noise before finally coming to rest flat upon the sheets.

"You would have been smothered," I said in a low voice as the sound ceased.

"Indeed, as was Doctor Higgins and others were long before him," Holmes replied.

I saw that the canopy had been forced down by a thick spiral pole of hard wood, the attachment of which was hidden when the canopy was in its normal place near the ceiling. The pole extended through the ceiling.

"Berry operates it from the room above. We must now act quickly, before he retracts it."

With that, Holmes crossed the room and to the night-table. Setting aside the lamp and the glass of port, he then quietly lifted and laid the table onto the top of the lowered canopy. After several more moments had passed – long enough to assure that whomever was trapped in the bed would be certainly dead – the canopy began to ascend, but more slowly because of the additional and unbalanced weight. In the silence that had resumed, we could hear the grunts and oaths of Mr. Berry, and the loud creaking of ancient wood as he attempted to turn the screw and restore the canopy to its usual height. The night-table was carried upwards until it met the ceiling, when the mechanism jammed, whereupon Holmes threw open the door and left the room hurriedly. I followed, and seconds later saw him as he opened the rear door by which I had entered the building. He stepped outside, and then the shrill tone of his police whistle split the silence. When he reappeared, it was in the company of Inspector Hopkins and two burly constables who, at Holmes's direction, rushed in and past us, hurrying up the narrow staircase. The house shook with their steps.

Immediately after the constables' heavy tread upon the stairs ceased there came a surprised shout, followed by angry curses, mostly in German. Mr. Berry was then half-dragged downstairs and into the dead doctor's room where we waited to confront him. His face was reddened with effort from his struggle with his captors.

"What is this?" Hopkins asked him, pointing to the disabled canopy.

"A device that kills enemies of the Kaiser," was the innkeeper's reply, in a voice quite unlike that he had used previously – much more educated and precise and cold.

"A killing machine, if I ever saw one," the official detective agreed. "It's the hangman for you, and no mistake. What do you have to say for yourself?"

"I'll say nothing except that your little victory here tonight, Mr. Holmes, is worthless against the might of my homeland. Dr. Higgins is gone, and so is the information that he carried to England."

"Possibly a list of German agents here in England? Ah, I see from your smile that I'm correct. Unfortunate, but not an insurmountable problem to recreate it. But why did he come here first?"

457

"Because I was on the list," answered Berry – or whatever his name was – "and he was arrogant enough to think that he could tie a bow on his investigation by verifying further facts about me before notifying his superiors. But he had inadvertently made his intentions known before leaving Germany, and I was waiting for him."

Then he stood straighter and said, "There is nothing left to say. You have me, Mr. Holmes, but you lose."

Hopkins growled. "Take him away, Cranwell."

The constables complied at once, forcefully, with the former innkeeper uttering oaths of increasing severity in two languages as he was bundled out of the room.

"Doubtless he has accomplices near at hand," Holmes said, "but Mycroft's people are certain to get him to reveal them, as well as the names on the doctor's lost list."

"Always supposing that Scotland Yard doesn't do so first," Hopkins remarked with a quick smile. I had no doubt that whomever made the attempt would be successful. (And in fact, they were.)

Suddenly, weariness pressed hard upon me, and I could hardly stifle a yawn.

"Forgive me for keeping you away from your bed," Holmes said.

"The police coaches that I ordered should be arriving soon," Hopkins volunteered. "Permit me to offer you and Doctor Watson transportation back to your hotel, Mr. Holmes, and you to your home, Doctor. A good night's work was done here, I think."

So it was that Holmes and I stood before the darkened Langham in the early hours. As I lived so close, I'd dismissed the driver who offered to carry me the short distance on to Queen Anne Street. The streets were silent and deserted, save for the occasional appearance of a constable on his beat.

"Holmes, I had the impression that you already knew what we were dealing with, almost from the start – from the time Hopkins told us the name of the inn. Tell me – was I right?"

In the meagre illumination of the street-lamp, he nodded.

"That's correct, and once we arrived in the doctor's room, my suspicions were verified. There were a number of indicators. You will recall that I examined the bed-posts after viewing Doctor Higgins' body. That was because I'd noticed that the varnish had worn away near their highest point. At first I thought that was because its application was insufficient, but when I saw similar marks on all four posts, I realised that it was from a common cause."

"The scraping as the canopy descended," I ventured.

"Precisely. As you know, I took a sample of the liquid remaining in the glass from which Doctor Higgins had evidently drunk, for analysis. The resulting identification of opium told me that it was intended that he should be incapable of rising from the bed. The innkeeper was therefore certain that his victim couldn't avoid a rather unpleasant death."

"I see," I said hesitantly. "But why was it necessary for us to visit the library in St. James's Square?"

Holmes acknowledged the greeting of a passing constable who evidently recognised him. "That was to gain the final confirmation of my understanding of the situation. The volume that I consulted was a historical record of unexplained events in various London locations. I recalled that there was an unsubstantiated account of the installation of a murderous device at an inn in Whitechapel during the sixteenth century. It was done by a Spanish family who purchased the inn, their intention being to cause the death of various naval commanders who habitually stayed there after their ships had docked. This, I believe, was in preparation for the forthcoming Armada."

"Monstrous!" I retorted.

"Quite. There were several other similar instances recorded over the following centuries, as certain individuals came to know the purpose of the device and used it for their own ends. It had long been rumoured that The Tinker's Arms was this inn, and even though it was never proven, the victims all died in the same manner as Dr. Higgins. When the manner of his death was described, I knew enough to be alert for anything that might relate to the inn's dark history."

He shook his head slightly, as if disbelieving of the cruelty of men to each other. "But now, Watson, It's quite late, and you can be back home within just a few minutes. Good night, my friend, and don't look so crestfallen. I'll stop around in the morning before I leave, and I'm certain that with this war continuing, we'll share more adventures before too much time has passed."

The Adventure of the Murdered Medium
by Hugh Ashton

The years immediately following the Great War were in many ways even more challenging than the war years themselves. I, along with many of my profession, found myself ministering to the spirits as much, if not more so, as to the bodies of our brave boys who had returned from France who had witnessed horrors beyond our imaginings. Added to which, the pernicious influenza that ravaged our population cast a constant gloom over the whole population, myself included.

Although I had intermittently been in contact with my friend Mr. Sherlock Holmes, the intimacy of our earlier friendship was missing, and this was an additional cause for a sense of despondency which grew on me by the day.

One of the patients at the military hospital where I was practising was a former captain of the Grenadiers who had been wounded while serving with his regiment at Arras. As it happened, I discovered through conversation with him that I had served with an uncle of his in India, and this happy coincidence cheered both him and me.

One day he mentioned to me that he was anxious to be discharged from the hospital as soon as possible. This in itself was not unusual – many of our patients were impatient (if one will pardon the play on words) to return to what they trusted would be a normal life. What stuck in my memory were the words he used to describe his wishes.

"My family, though of an ancient lineage, is afflicted by poverty, though this was not always the case. One of my ancestors was a sea captain, with rumours that he was a buccaneer, and that he came home from the sea laden with treasure, which, on account of his not trusting others, he buried in the grounds of the family home, intending to dig it up should he ever be in need of the money. Sadly, he died before he recovered the gold and jewels, and the secret of their location was lost with him."

"Many such stories exist in our older families," I laughed. "Usually they are legend without any substance."

"This may be the case here," Captain Groves ruefully admitted to me. "It is, however, a very strong item of faith within our family, and indeed many of us – my late father, Sir William included – have attempted to locate the treasure and restore the fortunes of our house, but to no avail.

460

Indeed, our family was reduced to having to sell some of our land to a neighbour about a hundred years ago, in order to clear some debts."

About a month following this conversation, I pronounced Captain Groves to be sufficiently cured for him to be discharged from the hospital, though I feared he would walk with a pronounced limp for the rest of his life.

The story of the buried treasure continued to work on my mind, as I suppose it must with any man possessed of an imagination, and I cast my thoughts back to the time when Holmes and I had chased a boat, supposedly laden with a similar treasure, down the Thames. On that occasion, we had lost the jewels to the mud of the river's bed, but I had gained a greater treasure, Mary Morstan, who condescended to become my wife, for alas! too short a time before her death.

My work at the hospital continued to occupy most of my time and energy, however, and it was with some surprise that I received a letter from Captain Groves:

My dear Doctor, [the note read]

> *I very much dislike presuming on your good nature in this way, but I would very much appreciate your assistance in a matter which is causing me considerable concern. As I mentioned to you while I was your patient, my younger brother was lost in the Somme. He was always the darling of the family, loved by all, myself included, and I fear that his loss has sent my widowed mother into a nervous decline. She has recently taken up with a younger man, a certain Lucas Klopstock, of whose antecedents I am unsure, but I suspect him to be from a nation in the east of Europe. Certainly he is not British, but that should not be any cause for concern.*
>
> *What troubles me are the beliefs of this bounder. He has persuaded my mother that he is able to communicate with my deceased brother's spirit, and that, given time, he will be able to summon the spirit of Black Jack, my supposed pirate ancestor, and reveal the secret of the buried treasure. While he is making these preposterous claims, he is staying with us, living the life of Riley at my family's expense, as my mother denies him nothing. I have caught him on more than one occasion looking through our family papers.*
>
> *I dare not throw the blighter out on his ear, dearly as I would like to do so, for I fear for my mother's very sanity were I to carry out my wish. I am aware that at one time you worked*

461

with the consulting detective, Mr. Sherlock Holmes. Would it be possible for you to pay a visit to Kidlington Hall, with or without Mr. Holmes, and discover exactly what it is that this rogue is after? You may, if you choose, care to make this a medical visit. My lower leg, despite your expert attention in hospital, is still giving me some discomfort.

As it happened, I was due some leave, and the prospect of spending a few days in Oxfordshire was a pleasant one. I dispatched a telegram to Holmes, inviting him to join me, if he was free to do so, and hinting at the promise of a mystery to be solved.

Within the hour I had received a reply from him:

Delighted to join you. Will arrive Saturday afternoon. Send details of mystery to me c/o Admiralty.

SH

It was news to me that Holmes was still engaged in work for the Government – I had privily been made aware of the nature of his work during the War with the group known as Room 40, who had been responsible for breaking the codes of the Kaiser, including that infamous telegram which hastened our American friends into joining us against the Teutonic hordes. However, I had imagined that Holmes had by now severed his links with that section of the British government, and the requested address caused me to exercise a little curiosity.

Nonetheless, I assembled the few facts that I had at my disposal, summarised them, and passed them on to Holmes, addressing the letter as directed.

I journeyed down to Kidlington on Friday morning, and as arranged by telegram, was met at the station by Captain Groves himself, driving a dog-cart.

"Glad to see you, Doctor," he greeted me. "The bounder Klopstock is still with us, I fear. Still, you will have an opportunity to see him in action for yourself tonight. My mother has invited some of her more feeble-minded friends to dinner tonight, and arranged for Klopstock to perform his trickery afterwards."

"A séance?"

"Yes, that's what he calls these sessions. And not cheap, I can tell you. He demands a fair few guineas each time he summons these spirits of his."

We drove on in silence for a while, our dog-cart accompanied by the sound of cheerful birdsong and the scent of the wild flowers along our way. At one point, Groves halted the cart and pointed with his whip through a gap in the trees to our left towards a handsome well-proportioned building in the Palladian style. "Kidlington Hall," he announced, with a touch of pride in his voice.

"A handsome building," I answered him, which was indeed nothing but the truth.

We drove on and arrived at the gate lodge in a few minutes before driving up the avenue of elms towards the Hall. A servant took my cases, and we entered the hallway to be greeted by an elderly lady who was introduced to me as my friend's mother, Lady Groves.

"I am so grateful to you for taking such care of Lionel," she said to me. "He wrote such nice things about you in his letters from the hospital."

"No more than my duty, Madam," I answered her. "Though I could hardly have wished for a more cooperative and good-natured patient."

She smiled, and turned to her son. "Dear Lucas is resting," she informed him. "He is reserving his energies for this evening." She turned back to me. "I am referring to Mr. Klopstock, who is currently staying with us." She paused, and Captain Groves leaped into the conversational breach.

"I was telling Doctor Watson about Mr. Klopstock as we drove from the station," he said in a tone that effectively precluded any further discussion on the subject.

"Indeed, that is the case," I confirmed.

"Very well, then. Lionel, why don't you show Doctor Watson to the Green Bedroom so that he can make himself ready for luncheon at one o'clock?"

Groves spoke to me in a low undertone as he led the way up the stairs. "Resting, indeed. I'll bet the wretch is ransacking my father's papers at this very minute."

"For what purpose would he be doing that?" I asked.

"Searching for a clue to my ancestor's treasure is my guess. Trying to discover exactly what we own, where it is, and how he can get his filthy paws on it." His face corrugated with rage and I feared that he might suffer an apoplectic fit. I was concerned for him, given his recent medical history, which included shell-shock.

"Steady on, old man," I said, laying a hand on his arm. "Don't get over-excited about this."

Instantly he seemed to become quieter and more composed. "My apologies," he said in a calm voice. "There is something about this man and his business that upsets me beyond all reason."

463

We arrived at the top of the stairs and I caught at his arm. "Tell me, where does this Klopstock sleep?"

"Why, in this room just here," he answered me, pointing to a door.

"Might I trouble you to stand guard outside the room while I make a quick search. If, as you say, he is engaged in some nefarious activity downstairs, there will be no danger of his interrupting me."

"What are you hoping to discover?" Groves asked me.

"I have some ideas," I told him, but I was reluctant to say more. It was not my intention to be secretive for the sake of producing mystery, but I felt it was as well for as few people as possible to know what I was about.

In fact, Sherlock Holmes had replied to my letter informing him of the doings at Kidlington Hall with a letter of his own, in which he enumerated many of the tricks that were employed by fraudulent mediums in their trickery.

I slipped through the door that Groves held open for me and started to search the bottom drawers of the dressing-table. There were one or two items of interest, corresponding to those of which I had been informed by Holmes in his letter. I left them undisturbed, but made a list of them in my notebook.

The whole operation took me a little less than five minutes, at the end of which time I left the room, closing the door behind me.

"Did you find what you were looking for?" Groves asked me.

"Indeed I did," I answered, and I confess that at that moment, I felt a sense of satisfaction, as of a job well done. The room to which Groves showed me was large and comfortable, with a splendid view over the fields towards the dreaming spires of Oxford.

After an admirable lunch, Groves proposed to show me some of the estate, and I put on my ulster to join him. He was carrying a shotgun under his arm, and I looked at it curiously.

"It isn't the season for pheasant, is it?" I asked him.

"No," he laughed, "but I might get a shot at some rabbits."

The estate, such as it was, wasn't particularly large, and a walk of only a few minutes brought us to the boundary where the Groves estate marched alongside that of the Earl of Doncaster.

"A grouchy old so-and-so," Groves chuckled, referring to the earl. "Good enough in his own way, I suppose, but too quick off the mark when it comes to defending what he sees as his rights, in my opinion.

"Now," Groves told me as we turned back, "I will show you something of interest." A few hundred yards past a small copse brought us to the brink of a circular crater, some three yards across, and two deep.

464

"We saw enough of these in France, I can tell you," chuckled Groves. "But this one isn't the work of the Boche. This was all my father's doing. He was convinced that this was the site at which Black Jack had stowed his loot." He shook his head. "Clearly, he was mistaken." He stopped suddenly, and pointed with the barrel of his gun to a spot on the other side of the crater. "Halloa! What have we here?" He indicated a spot of bare earth which by all appearances had been disturbed recently, probably within the past few days.

"Moles? Rabbits? A badger, perhaps?"

"Nonsense, my dear Doctor. You have spent too long in the consulting room and not enough time in the open air. The animal that created that excavation was of the species *homo sapiens*. Look, you can even see the blighter's footmarks."

It was true enough. There was a trail of imprints, as of a square-toed shoe or boot. From my time with Sherlock Holmes, I was also able to deduce that the wearer of those boots walked with a slight limp, the left foot being slightly twisted inwards. I said nothing, but stored away the fact for future reference.

"Most intriguing," were my words as we started to turn back towards the hall.

"Damned if I'm going to let him get away with this," my companion muttered.

"Why did your father dig there?" I asked, seeking to change the subject.

"Oh, some poppycock foolishness about '*when the Chittering spire shows between the hills, and St. Michael's tower to the west is aligned with the House*'. Some nonsense of Black Jack's. See – " He pointed in one direction, where the tip of a steeple was visible through an indentation in the low hills, and then in another direction, where a square church tower stood prominent in the landscape, almost lost in the slight mist that still clung to the land. "Take my word for it, on a clear day, the tower of the cathedral at Christ Church College, which as you no doubt know is often referred to as the House, is in line with this tower at this point."

"It seems clear to me," I said. "And yet your father found nothing?"

"A false scent," Groves admitted ruefully.

On our return to the Hall, before dressing for dinner, I wrote an account of the day's events, and addressed it to Holmes before leaving it in the post-bag in the hall to be carried to the village post office, sure that it would be delivered to Holmes before his morning departure. After making myself presentable for dinner, I made my way downstairs to the drawing room, where Groves had told me the dinner guests were to assemble.

465

Imagine my surprise as I viewed the entrance hall from the stairs as I descended, to see a figure in evening dress take up the post-bag and remove a letter from it. It was too distant for me to discern the identity of the letter, but somehow I was certain that it was my epistle to Holmes that was in the miscreant's hands.

By the time I had reached the bottom of the stairs, the letter and its taker had vanished into the drawing room. I could only assume that the unknown was also staying in the Hall – it was most unlikely that one of the dinner guests would engage in such activity – and I had no reason to believe that Groves would examine his guests' mail.

I entered the drawing room, and Lady Groves introduced me to some of the guests. Most of the women were wearing black, and many of the men sported mourning bands. I guessed that all these had lost sons or other relatives in the War, and were here to attempt to communicate with their departed loved ones.

Lastly, I was introduced to the infamous Klopstock, and a young lady, described by Lady Groves as his secretary. Lucas Klopstock himself struck me with a powerful feeling of unease. It was difficult for me to state precisely on what grounds I experienced this sensation, but neither his limp handshake nor the over-broad smile disclosing teeth that seemed too regular and white inspired confidence. His voice, when he spoke, betrayed more than a trace of a European accent. As for his secretary, though she was demurely dressed, it appeared to me that her pretty young face held more than a hint of mischief. As was the case with her employer, there was something that was indefinably un-English about her speech

Elena, for that was her name, immediately attached herself to me and began a conversation which indicated that she had an extensive knowledge of Sherlock Holmes and my association with him.

"How I would like to meet him," she sighed, laying her hand upon my sleeve.

I thought to myself that if my suspicions regarding her employer were correct, a meeting with Holmes wouldn't be entirely to her taste, and might result in a somewhat different outcome to the one she clearly had in mind.

At dinner, I found myself seated next to her, and for the first course, she managed to chat away in a seemingly innocent manner without, however, providing me with any significant information about either herself or her employer. My other neighbour was the wife of a local dignitary, who proceeded to provide me with an exhaustive account of how her eldest son had been reported as missing, presumed dead, after that terrible third battle at Ypres, which claimed so many young lives.

466

Quite frankly, it was a relief to me when the signal came for the ladies to retire, and the men to light their cigars and pass the port. To my intense disappointment, this didn't take place.

Klopstock addressed the company before any of us had even removed our cigar-cases from our pockets, or laid a finger on the decanter. "The spirits will be offended if the air is polluted by tobacco smoke," he announced in his curious accent. "Nor will they manifest themselves if alcohol is allowed to befuddle our brains."

There was an audible sigh from many of the assembled company, but no one seemed inclined to challenge Klopstock on this matter. Conversation was desultory, and lasted only a matter of a few minutes before Groves rose and led the men to join the ladies in another room, where a circle of chairs had been placed around a round table, draped with a purple velvet cloth. Lady Groves invited us all to take our places and, as at dinner, we were seated alternately men and women. The secretary, Elena, wasn't part of the circle, but remained outside it, presumably to manage the "business" of the séance.

I found myself between my companion of the dinner table and Lady Groves, whose small dry hand clasped mine as Elena dimmed the lights, and the séance began.

I had attended such gatherings before, and the show played out in a familiar fashion. Cracks and knockings were heard from the table, no doubt produced by the mechanical hammer that I had observed on my visit to Klopstock's room. Klopstock himself produced a variety of voices delivering the usual vague inanities, and the fine muslin I had seen in the drawer upstairs made an appearance as ectoplasm.

These phenomena were all received uncritically by my two female neighbours, who kept muttering phrases such as "How marvellous!" and uttering sighs of satisfaction as messages, supposedly from the spirit world, reassured them that after death there was nothing but peace and light, and that there was no pain on "the other side".

After what was probably about three-quarters-of-an-hour of this, Klopstock, using his usual voice, announced that he was fatigued, and requested that the lights be turned on.

"I will need all my strength for this next manifestation of the Unknown," he proclaimed. "Through me, the great spirit Desistra will manifest herself. And to prove that she has visited us, she will place her manifested hand into this container of molten paraffin wax – " He pointed to a container on the sideboard under which Elena had lit a spirit lamp, from which she poured a large amount of liquid wax into a smaller container, about six inches in diameter and about a foot deep. " – before dematerialising, leaving a vacant space in the wax, accessible only through the small aperture formed by her wrist when she placed her hand in there. It would be impossible for any material being to perform what is about to happen, and it should convince any of you who still, despite all the proof, harbour doubts regarding the reality of the spirit world and life beyond the grave."

Once more the lights went down, the mechanical hammer did its work, and the cheesecloth again made its appearance, this time topped by a luminous mask. The grotesque charade made its way to the pot containing the wax, whose spirit lamp had previously been extinguished. There was a hushed silence for a few minutes, at the end of which the apparition vanished abruptly from view, and Klopstock gave a low groan, as if in pain.

"My dear Lucas, are you unwell?" asked Lady Groves, breaking the silence in the darkness.

"Merely exhausted with the effort of acting as the vessel for Desistra's manifestation," Klopstock replied in a weak voice. "Elena, the light, if you would."

In a matter of a few seconds, the room was once more flooded with light. Elena was standing by the switch, seemingly having been there for the whole period of the séance, but I noticed a scrap of muslin protruding from her sleeve, which I was positive hadn't previously been there. If my suspicions had not already been aroused, I would have taken it for a handkerchief or the cuff of a blouse.

Klopstock motioned to her, and she brought the container of solidifying wax to the table. There was a deep depression in the centre, which might conceivably have been made by a wrist.

"We will wait for a while," said Klopstock, "until the wax has become more solid. Perhaps some coffee might be in order, my dear Lady Groves?"

The servants brought in coffee, and we partook. I remained where I could keep an eye on the wax.

After about fifteen minutes, Klopstock clapped his hands together, and announced that it was time to prove that the spirit of Desistra had indeed visited us. "And the proof will be provided by the eminent doctor, John Watson," he announced, handing me a large scalpel, "of whose exploits in conjunction with the equally eminent Sherlock Holmes we are all no doubt aware. If you will be good enough, Doctor, to perform a dissection that will prove to us all the undeniable truth of the spirit world."

I was naturally reluctant to proceed, but I had no option but to accept the offer with a good grace. There was a strong temptation to destroy any supposed proof of the spirit visit, but I confess to having been intrigued by the problem.

As I removed the wax around the impression, I saw that what Klopstock had predicted had actually come to pass. There was a cavity within the wax which was the shape of a hand. The only connection to the outside was a wrist-shaped tunnel, along which I was satisfied that almost no human hand, no matter how contorted, could pass.

I had had occasion to examine Elena's hands previously before dinner, and her hands, though small, would be unable to pass through the narrow opening. Furthermore, the hand that had left the impression in the wax was considerably bigger than her hands, and she was the only person who had been near the wax, as far as I had been able to ascertain.

"Puzzled, Doctor?" Klopstock's tone verged on mockery. "Remember what William of Ockham said about unnecessary multiplication of entities? Or what your friend has often said about when the impossible has been eliminated, whatever remains, however improbable – "

" – must be the truth." I completed the sentence.

"Indeed so." He spread his hands. "Lady Groves, ladies and gentlemen, surely this must convince even the most hardened sceptic. But now, let us to the drawing room. Gentlemen, I believe we may now enjoy our port, and those of you who indulge in the weed may step onto the balcony and enjoy their pleasure."

He had taken control of the gathering, and it seemed that Lady Groves had no objection to his doing so. However, I glanced over to Captain Groves, whose face bore a thunderous expression, and from what I could discern, was grinding his teeth with rage.

I swiftly moved over to him. "I fully agree with you," I said before he could utter a word. "Come onto the balcony with me. I have some fine Havanas here," tapping my cigar-case. "Believe me, he isn't worth bothering with. The time to unmask him is not now. Think of your poor mother if we do. She will be made to look weak and foolish in front of her friends. We will act later."

"By God, we will!" he exclaimed. He regarded me. "Thank you, Doctor. Without your intervention I would have made a fool of myself, and my mother too." He smiled. "Come, let me sample one of these Havanas."

A little diplomacy was enough for me to keep Groves and Klopstock apart for the rest of the evening until the guests departed.

I said goodnight to my host and hostess and made my way to bed, where I fell asleep almost instantly, and remained unconscious of any events until I woke at the unreasonably late hour of half-past-eight.

I made my way downstairs to the dining room, where the only other person was the secretary, Elena, breaking her fast with porridge. I greeted her, and helped myself from the sideboard.

"Mr. Klopstock?" I enquired.

"Out for his usual morning constitutional," she answered. "He usually arises early and walks for a few hours before breaking his fast."

"Most praiseworthy," I answered.

Our repast was interrupted by the entrance of Kerrigan, the butler, clearly flustered.

"Have you seen Captain Groves, sir?" he asked me.

"No, not this morning."

"Or Lady Groves?" His tone was almost hopeful.

I shook my head. "Excuse me, but are you feeling unwell? You appear to be shaken. Come, sit down." I pulled out a chair for him. Indeed, he was ashen-faced, and sweating profusely, despite the coolness of the morning.

"Thank you, sir, but no. It's just that – " He broke off, and looked at Elena. "Excuse me, miss that I'm the one who's breaking the news, but your Mr. Klopstock . . . ." His voice tailed off. "Well, he's dead, like. Shot in the head. Harry Jacobs – he's the keeper – came in just now and told us."

"Oh my God!" Elena screamed. Her face turned as white as a sheet, and she simply sat unmoving, with unfocussed eyes gazing at nothing.

"I have a sedative in my bag in my room," I told the butler. "Stay with her until I return. If I see Captain or Lady Groves, I'll inform them of the news."

As it happened, I didn't meet anyone on my journey to and from my room. As I administered the sedative to Elena, her eyelids fluttered and a little colour came to her cheeks. I turned to Kerrigan, who was still standing, clearly still in a state of some shock.

"Find a maid," I ordered him, "to take this lady to her room. She needs to be in bed, resting."

"Very good, sir." He left, and returned within two minutes with one of the chamber-maids. I repeated my words to her, and she left with my patient (for I now regarded her as such) in her charge.

"Who has called the police, Kerrigan?" I asked him.

"Why, no one, sir. We have been waiting for orders from Lady Groves or the Captain."

I let out a snort of exasperation. "Then I shall make the telephone call myself."

"Very good, sir."

470

I was led to the instrument, and there connected to the police station, where I explained that I was calling from Kidlington Hall, and that I was calling on behalf of the Groves family, the members of which seemed to be currently unavailable.

"A dead man, you say, sir?"

"I believe so. I haven't as yet seen him. I will do so as soon as I have finished this conversation with you. His name is Lucas Klopstock. He is – rather I should say he *was* – a guest of Lady Groves."

"And your name, sir?"

"My name is Watson. John Watson. I am a doctor, and I will be happy to act as the medical examiner in the case, should you require a police surgeon."

"That's very kind of you to offer, sir, but I'm afraid that might look like some sort of conflict of interest, if you take my meaning, sir." There was a pause, and what sounded like an embarrassed cough at the other end of the line. "Doctor John Watson, sir? The gentleman who wrote about the cases of the detective Sher – "

"The same," I interrupted him.

"Honoured to have you on the case, sir. I'm sure there will be no problem with your assisting us. We will have men at the Hall within the hour. Thank you for your cooperation, sir."

I smiled to myself as I replaced the receiver. Even after all these years, and a great and devastating war, the name of Sherlock Holmes still seemed to inspire respect.

I knew that Holmes was meant to be arriving in the afternoon, but considered that it would be of some advantage if he were to arrive earlier, so scribbled a brief note: "*Come to Kidlington at once if not sooner. Murder may have been done. JHW*", and handed it to Kerrigan, with instructions that it be dispatched immediately as a telegram to Holmes at his London address, where I guessed he would be staying.

The mention of murder would be sufficient to draw him quickly, I felt, given the enthusiasm he had always displayed at the mention of such crimes. To me, it was simply an excitement generated by the anticipation of his being able to exercise his intellectual powers, but to others, it seemed to be a morbid fascination.

I took up my bag and was met at the door of the Hall by the keeper, Jacobs, who had been informed that I would be inspecting the body.

"This way, sir," he said, leading the way towards the copse that Groves and I had passed the previous day. "I warn you, sir, that he isn't a pretty sight, but I reckon as you'll have seen worse in the past few years, seeing as how you're a doctor and all that."

"Where did you serve?" I asked him.

"Mesopotamia, sir. And hell it was, sir. I was right glad to be back in Blighty where there's a nice spot of rain and the sweat isn't pouring off a man's back the whole bloody day, if you'll pardon the language, sir."

"I've heard worse," I chuckled. "I've been known to use worse as well."

We trudged on in silence for a while. "He's over there, sir," I was told.

"Have you touched him?"

"I felt his neck, like, for a pulse. Otherwise, no, sir. He's just as he was when I saw him first. Unless someone else has been here in the last half-hour or so."

I went forward. Jacobs was right. Half the back of the man's head had been blown away. It was clear that this wasn't self-inflicted. No weapon was visible, and death from such a traumatic wound would have been instant, meaning that there would have been no possibility of disposing of the weapon.

It was clearly superfluous for me to check for signs of life, but I did so, anyway. The word of a doctor would carry more weight at an inquest than that of a gamekeeper, and it might become necessary to prove that life was extinct at the time that I first saw the body. It appeared that the only injury was to the back of the head, which had clearly not been caused by a blunt instrument, but to my eyes, which had seen many such wounds in the previous few years, appeared to be the result of a firearm, almost certainly a shotgun, discharged at close range. A further cursory examination confirmed the identity of the victim as Lucas Klopstock, and that on the body's feet were the same strange square-toed boots that matched the prints seen by Groves and me the previous day.

As I straightened up, I noticed that the ground was disturbed, and blood was present on some of the vegetation which had been flattened. Clearly Klopstock hadn't been killed in the place where his body now rested. I followed the trail, careful to disturb the scene as little as possible, and after a few yards found myself in a small clearing, in the centre of which was a shotgun, which appeared to my eyes to be the one which I had seen in Groves' hands the previous day.

As I pondered the significance of this, I heard footsteps and voices approaching. I turned back and saw the keeper accompanying a uniformed constable and a man whom I took to be a plainclothes police officer, who introduced himself with a hearty handshake as Inspector Hardwicke.

"Delighted to have you here, Doctor Watson. I suppose that there is no chance of Mr. Holmes joining us?" he enquired, with a hopeful expression on his face.

"As it happens, he should be with us later today."

"Excellent. I confess that we don't have many deaths like this in our part of the country, and competent assistance is always welcome. Now," turning to the body at our feet, "this is shocking. Do we know who he is?"

"The name I knew him by is Lucas Klopstock. He was a medium, staying as a guest at the Hall, and he performed a séance for us last night. The tricks he played were all fraudulent, I'm sure."

"Make a note of all this, Collins," Hardwicke ordered the uniformed constable. "One of these spiritualist johnnies, eh? A guest of Captain Groves?"

"Of his mother, I'm sure. Captain Groves had no time for the man."

"I see. And you are quite sure that he is dead?"

I nodded. "Death would have been instantaneous."

"You would swear to that in the witness-box at the inquest?"

"I would certainly do so. I would add that it would be impossible for a man with that type of wound which has effectively broken the spinal column to have crawled twenty yards." I indicted the trail of broken branches and crushed vegetation.

Hardwicke gave a somewhat puzzled look but said nothing, and I continued. "There is a gun at the other end of that trail, in a small clearing."

"Let us see. Collins," he ordered, "cover the body with the sheet. Jacobs," he told the keeper, "come with us."

I led the way to the copse, where the gun lay prominently on show.

"Do you recognise that gun?" the inspector asked me.

"I cannot be sure, but it appears to me to be the one that Captain Groves was carrying yesterday when we walked together."

Jacobs had bent and was examining the gun. "It's the Captain's, all right. I've seen it often enough."

Hardwicke turned to me. "And how, precisely, are you acquainted with Captain Groves?" he asked. "If he's a friend of yours, I may have to ask you to step aside from the case."

Slightly stung by the unspoken implications of this, I explained that Groves had been a patient of mine, and that to the best of my understanding my invitation to the Hall had been partly for the purpose of unmasking Klopstock as a fraud.

"I'm unsure of whether I should be asking you this, sir, but were there any symptoms of, shall we say, disturbance, in Captain Groves when you treated him as a patient? If you don't answer this question, I will not take it amiss."

I was torn between my desire to see the law take its course, and my feelings, such as they were for the man who was my host. "At present, I prefer not to answer that."

"I see. And where is Captain Groves now?"

473

"I do not know."

Hardwicke asked the same question of Jacobs, who likewise was unable to provide an answer.

"In that case," he said, "we must return to the Hall, and send two men to bring in the body. That is unless, Doctor, there are any further investigations you wish to make *in situ*."

I answered that I believed there was nothing more to be seen as far as the body was concerned, though I added that the area should be disturbed as little as possible once the body had been moved. I also suggested that photographs should be taken of the body and the surrounding area before it was moved.

Hardwicke grunted in seeming approval. "You may be right," he admitted. "I will arrange for this to be done."

On our return to the Hall, Kerrigan presented me with a telegram. "It arrived some ten minutes ago," he explained.

I read it and exclaimed, "Sherlock Holmes is on his way here. He expects to be here before midday."

"Excellent news," said Hardwicke. To the butler: "Have you seen Lady Groves or Captain Groves this morning, my man?"

"Lady Groves is in her room resting, sir. She suffered a severe shock when she was informed of Mr. Klopstock's death, and retired to her room."

"Is she in need of medical attention?" I asked.

"I believe she would welcome a visit from you, sir."

"And Captain Groves?" Hardwicke asked.

Kerrigan shook his head. "No one seems to have seen him today."

"Has his bed been slept in?" I asked.

"It appears so, sir, and his walking outfit is missing."

"I shall ask you later to provide a description of Captain Groves and this walking outfit," Hardwicke told him. "Doctor, you may attend to Lady Groves. I will telephone for a photographer."

Kerrigan coughed. "If you will excuse me, sir. Photography is a hobby of mine. I have a camera and film in my room, and if you're in need of photographs, I'll be happy to assist in any way possible."

"Good man," Hardwicke told him. "Would you be prepared to take photographs of the body of Mr. Klopstock and the surrounding area?"

"I cannot honestly say that it would give me great pleasure, sir, but I am happy to assist the law. I'm sure I've seen worse in my time when I was serving in South Africa. If you'll come this way, sir, and inform me of what is needed, I'll prepare the appropriate equipment."

They went off, and I took myself to Lady Groves.

"Has my son been found?" she asked me. I shook my head. "And Lucas Klopstock? He is dead, isn't he?" Her tone almost seemed to hold a touch of relief.

"I'm afraid so. I am sorry."

"I am *not*!" Fire flashed in her eyes. "He was a foul beast of a man, and I'm glad he is gone. There! I've said it, and I will say it at the inquest if they ask me to."

I remained silent, and she continued.

"He was blackmailing me. He knew things about my late husband that would spell ruin for us if they were made public. Oh, he wasn't blackmailing me for money. God knows we have little enough of that, but he wanted the chance to find Black Jack's treasure. He was certain it was here, and he was determined to find it. He spent hours in my late husband's study and in the library. Of course, I never believed that he was a genuine medium. I knew all about the tricks he got up to in the dark, and he knew that I knew, but he saw the chance to make money from my friends, and he took it."

I must have appeared thunderstruck.

"Now tell me honestly: Do you believe my son killed him? I have heard the facts from Kerrigan and the other servants. Now I need your opinion."

"The facts argue against him."

"But I can tell from your expression that your heart tells you that he is innocent. My boy wouldn't hurt a fly."

I coughed. "I must tell you that he won his Military Cross for killing seven Germans with an entrenching tool. There is no doubt in my mind that he is capable of killing. As to whether he would murder a man in cold blood, I cannot say. It is more than likely that he was overcome by a fit of rage and didn't know what he was doing."

"I believe he is innocent." Her face was set in a determined expression, and it was clear that I would never be able to convince her otherwise.

"One last question. Did your son know of the blackmail? Or indeed of the secret regarding your husband?"

She shook her head emphatically. "No. It was my secret, and mine alone. I had no wish to encumber . . . ."

I remembered the errand on which I had originally come, and enquired if there was any medical assistance I could render.

"Thank you, no," she smiled. "I am perfectly in control of myself and my faculties. I do, however, trust that what I have just told you will remain as confidential information, as shared between a patient and her medical adviser."

I was slightly taken aback by this, and was forced to make some kind of non-committal answer.

"Never mind," she said. "I suppose all will come out anyway, with or without you. The police these days seem to have no respect for breeding or family. Indeed, I believe it gives them great pleasure to drag us down to the level of common criminals." She waved a languid hand. "You may go."

I left the room and descended the stairs, just in time to see the front door open and Sherlock Holmes admitted. Older and greyer he may have been, and moving without the spring in his step which had marked him in his younger days, but the tall lean figure was still unmistakable. I confess that the very sight of him transported me back twenty years or more, to the extent of a lump forming in my throat, even before he spoke.

"My dear fellow," he exclaimed as he caught sight of me. "I came as soon as I received your telegram. No baggage, as you see," spreading his empty hands.

"You must have wings to arrive here so promptly," I smiled.

"Hardly that – though I fear that my chauffeur exceeded the legal speeds for most of our journey. But here I am. Where is the body? Who is the officer on the case? And tell me all you know."

"Inspector Hardwicke of the Oxfordshire constabulary is assigned to the case."

"I have no knowledge of him. Sound man?"

"Inexperienced, but sound, I would say. At least he listens to what I have to say, and he seems to be what the Americans term a 'fan' of your work."

"He is more likely an admirer of your elegant half-fictions," Holmes smiled. "And who and where is the body in this case?"

"A Lucas Klopstock. Fraudulent medium and fortune-hunter."

"Ah. There is a woman in the case?"

"There is, but not in the usual way. I'll explain later."

"And the cause of death?"

"Gunshot wound to the back of the head." I indicated on my own person the location of the wound.

"Weapon?"

"There is a shotgun belonging to my former patient some dozens of yards from the body?"

"Hmm. Hardly suicide, then?"

"Impossible, I would say."

"Very well. Let us go and examine the *corpus delicti*. I take it the inspector is there?"

"I believe so. He's with the butler."

476

Holmes raised his eyebrows.

"The butler is a photographer," I explained, "and volunteered to take photographs for the police."

"Most public-spirited," Holmes commented sardonically. "Now," as we made our way to the copse, "tell me all that has happened since you arrived here yesterday."

"I wrote you a letter, which never reached you, on account of its having been purloined before it entered the postal system."

"By whom?"

"By the murdered man. I trust that the letter is still in existence."

By now we had reached the copse, and Inspector Hardwicke introduced himself to my friend. I noticed that the butler was engaged in packing away his photographic equipment, presumably having completed his task.

"Delighted to see you, Mr. Holmes," said the police officer, extending his hand in welcome.

"And I you," Holmes replied. "This here," indicating the shrouded body, "is the deceased, I take it? May I examine the gun that has been discovered?" he asked.

The inspector showed a little surprise. "Not the body?" he asked.

"All in good time." We made our way to the gun, and Holmes, having obtained permission from the inspector, used a handkerchief to pick it up by the barrel. "You will note, I hope, that I am doing my best to preserve any evidence in the form of fingerprints that may exist," he told the inspector, before applying his aquiline nose to the muzzle.

"I don't believe this has been fired since it was last cleaned," he said. "There is no smell other than that of mineral oil. I believe that when you break the gun, you will either find an empty chamber, or an unfired cartridge. At any event, the hammer is cocked and safety is still on. If this had been used as the murder weapon, I don't believe the murderer would have re-cocked the hammer and carefully placed the safety on after firing the fatal shot."

"It has, however, been identified as Captain Groves' gun," the inspector pointed out, "and the Captain is nowhere to be found."

"Tush, man. That hardly constitutes proof, as I am sure you are aware." He stopped and looked around him.

"What is through there?" he asked, pointing to a gap on the trees on the opposite side of the clearing to that where we had just entered.

"That's the edge of our estate, sir," said Kerrigan, who by now had joined us, having packed away his camera. "That on the other side of the fence you can see is Lord Rathbroke's land – that's the Earl of Doncaster, sir."

477

"Thank you. Now to the body. Have you examined the pockets?"

"Not yet. We were going to wait until the body had been moved into the Hall."

"Very well." Holmes turned to me. "Have you seen all that you want to see here, Watson? Do you feel there would be any advantage to delaying the removal of the body?"

"I do not."

"That is a satisfactory answer."

Hardwicke gave orders to the butler to appoint two servants to carry the body, and to prepare a room in the Hall to act as a temporary morgue.

We slowly made our way back and awaited the arrival of Klopstock's corpse. Kerrigan, with what might have been a sense of irony, had prepared the very room and table around which we had sat the previous evening for the séance.

When the body arrived, the inspector methodically went through the pockets. Other than a few keys, an empty silver cigar case with the initials "*W.G.*", small change amounting to seven shillings and four pence, an Ordnance Survey map of the area, some miscellaneous papers, and four 12-gauge shotgun cartridges, there was nothing.

"I'll wager that the shot that caused the fatal wound doesn't correspond to that in these cartridges," Holmes remarked. "May I be permitted to look at the papers?"

As he took them, I noted that one was the letter I had written to Holmes and which had been purloined by Klopstock from the post-bag. The envelope had been opened.

I drew Holmes's attention to this, and he requested permission to read it, given that the letter was addressed to him. He scanned it quickly, and turned to me. "Excellent, Watson. This is of great assistance." He paused. "Where is Elena?" he asked me.

"Who is that?" asked the inspector.

I smote my brow. "My God! I had forgotten all about her. She is Klopstock's secretary – at least, that is how she was introduced to me last night. I don't know her other name. I met her at breakfast this morning, and the discovery of Klopstock's body was announced while we were still eating. She was overcome by a fit of the vapours and I prescribed a sedative and ordered her to bed."

"We must speak to her," said the inspector. "As her doctor in this case, you must go to her room and bring her down here, or obtain her permission to be questioned while she is in bed."

Burning with shame for my omission, I made my way upstairs and knocked on the door of the bedroom where I had been told Elena was staying. There was no answer. One of the maids passing spoke to me.

"There's no use knocking, sir," she told me. "About twenty minutes after she'd gone in there after breakfast, she came out again in her walking-dress, carrying a small bag. She said she was going to walk into the village."

I cursed under my breath, angry with myself that I had failed to pay due attention to a woman who might at the very least prove a source of valuable information, and at most might prove to be directly implicated in the crime.

I shamefacedly returned to my companions and informed them of the news.

"We all make mistakes, Doctor," the inspector consoled me, but I remained downcast by my failure.

In the meantime, while I had been upstairs, Holmes had been examining the other papers that had been found on the body.

"I believe I now know the place where Klopstock was killed," he said, "and who was responsible for his death, even if he wasn't the actual killer."

Hardwicke and I looked at him in astonishment. "It is all here," he explained. "Remind me, if you will, Watson, what Captain Groves told you about the location of Black Jack's treasure – a legendary treasure said to have been buried by an ancestor of the Groves family," he explained to the inspector.

I repeated the story of the alignment of the spires and towers that Captain Groves had told to me.

"Excellent," he said. "Now, look here." He spread out the map that had been discovered on the body, and pointed to a pencil line that had been drawn on it. "This line connects St Michael's tower and Christ Church in the city of Oxford. If there is any truth in the legend, the treasure is buried somewhere along this line."

"Where the Chittering spire appears between the hills," I said.

"Exactly so, according to what you were told. So here we have it," he said, pointing to another line which started at the spire of Little Chittering church, and passed between two sets of counter lines marking hills. "This line meets the other one here."

I examined the map. "That is where Captain Groves' father excavated and found nothing. So Black Jack's instructions are incorrect."

"No, they are perfectly correct," Holmes contradicted me. "See here. There are two villages with the name of Chittering. Little Chittering and Great Chittering."

"True," I said. "But look more closely. The church at Little Chittering has a spire, according to the map, and that at Great Chittering has a tower. The instructions as Grove repeated them to me definitely said the spire at Chittering."

479

"Very true," said Holmes. "But now let us take a look at this – a page torn from a book on the history of Oxfordshire villages. It says that the church of Great Chittering was struck by lightning in 1805, the year of Trafalgar, destroying the spire, which was never replaced, leaving only the tower. The village of Little Chittering, for its part, constructed a spire on its church tower in the year that Victoria came to the throne, 1837."

"And where does that place the treasure?" Hardwicke was clearly fascinated.

"Here," said Holmes, pointing to where a third line which had been pencilled on the map, intersecting the line to Christ Church some few hundred yards from the first point.

"I don't believe that lies in the Groves estate," I said, after establishing the features on the map.

"It does not," Holmes agreed. "However . . . ." He produced yet another paper, this time a bill of sale in which a certain Charles Groves made over all rights to a piece of land to a Joshua Rathbroke in 1823. "I cannot be certain, but I believe that this was part of the land sold to meet the family debts, which formed part of the Groves estate at the time of Black Jack, and it is on this land that the treasure, if it exists at all, is to be found."

We sat in silence for a while.

"This is all well and good," said the inspector, "and it is indeed fascinating. But – "

"But what has it to do with the gentleman here?" Holmes indicated the body of Lucas Klopstock. "You were informed, were you not, Watson, that the Earl of Doncaster is very keen on his rights as a landowner. My belief is that Klopstock had discovered all these facts that I have just enumerated, and believed he had located the place where the treasure was buried. Unaware of the reputation of the Earl and his zealous crusade against trespassers on his land, or perhaps uncaring, or believing that there would be no one to hinder him, he crossed the fence. He was spotted by a keeper – possibly even by Lord Rathbroke himself, who knows? – and challenged. Somehow this led to his being shot fatally, maybe without the intention to kill, but killed he was."

"Incredible," I said. "But what of the gun? Why is it there?"

"Are we certain that Captain Groves took the gun? Why might Klopstock not have taken it from the rack in the gunroom as he left the Hall?"

"For what purpose?"

"Maybe he did know about Lord Rathbroke's reputation. Self-defence? Maybe as camouflage to disguise his true motives in going out that morning? It will be useful to discover whether his fingerprints are on the gun. In any case, once he died, the killer clearly decided that the body shouldn't be found on the Doncaster estate, and dragged it to where we discovered it. There was a clear trail of broken twigs and crushed vegetation leading from the fence through that gap in the trees which I remarked, and which you appear to have overlooked."

"Our attention was held by the gun."

"As quite possibly was intended by he who placed it there. The gun may have been left there as a red herring to distract you from the fact that the death took place some distance away."

"It all seems improbable," said the inspector. "I seem to remember something you once said, though, Mr. Holmes, about eliminating the impossible.

"Please, no." Holmes waved a deprecatory hand. "However improbable my theory, it fits the facts as we know them, supported by these papers. Were we to examine this area of land more closely, we might find ourselves in possession of a fortune."

"Or of a cartridge's worth of birdshot," remarked Hardwicke, sourly. "It does all seem rather far-fetched, Mr. Holmes, but I have to admit it works."

"But where is Captain Groves?" I asked.

For answer, Holmes grinned broadly. "One last piece of paper. Read," he commanded me.

"Written in violet ink in a feminine hand. Dated last night at 11:30 pm. It is addressed here to a '*Laszlo* – '" I broke off. "The envelope is addressed to Lucas Klopstock."

"His real name. Almost certainly we are looking at what remains of Laszlo Korda, the well-known Hungarian confidence trickster and swindler. If it proves to be he, the world is well rid of him. Continue."

> *I am leaving you. I have found the man I love, and who is a better man than you can ever aspire to be. You are not worthy to lace the shoes of this noble man. For the past month we have become ever closer, and we have now made our decision.*
>
> *We have made plans and you will not be able to find him or me under the names you knew us by. Nor will you be able to find the money that you stored under your mattress. It will go to repair the fortunes of a brave and honest gentleman.*
>
> *Farewell, E.*

I paused. "It seems to me that given this relationship between Groves and this woman, she would have informed him that Korda was far from being the spiritual guide that he claimed to be. I therefore fail to understand why he should ask you or me to expose him, given that he had the means to do the deed himself."

"I believe," Holmes replied, "that indeed he may have possessed the knowledge to expose Korda. However, I feel that he wished to have corroboration of this from an authoritative source in order to convince his mother, naturally unaware of the true relationship between her and Korda – and you, my friend, and possibly I, were to play that part."

Hardwicke had been listening open-mouthed to this exchange. "Let me expand on your theory, Mr. Holmes, if you will forgive my doing so. This woman wrote this letter late last night, and slipped it under this man's door," pointing at the corpse on the table. "He awoke early, read the letter, discovered that his savings had vanished – maybe she had taken them earlier in the day – and despaired. He could, of course, have waited and had it out with her later in the day, but he believed, thanks to these documents which you have linked together most ingeniously, sir, that he was on the verge of a discovery which would offset the loss of his savings."

Holmes had been nodding in agreement during this recital. "Excellent, Inspector. I find all this most plausible."

Encouraged, Hardwicke continued. "He took a gun with him, for whatever reason only he knew. Probably also a spade or some implement with which he could dig for this treasure. I am sure we will find a spade is missing if we ask the gardeners or the park keepers. And met his end, as you have described."

"Your problem now, Inspector," said Holmes, "is how you present the case."

"It is a ticklish business, to be sure," said Hardwicke. "I know that you are a man of the world, sir. How would you handle this if you were in my shoes?"

"Death by misadventure, my dear Inspector. The man went for an early morning lone walk, carrying a gun with which he was unfamiliar. He tripped, dropping the gun, which discharged itself, and it killed him. An open-and-shut case."

"That is outrageous!" I exclaimed. "That would be a complete perversion of justice. Lord Rathbroke, or his retainer, cannot be allowed to escape his punishment."

"I have to say that I agree with Doctor Watson regarding this matter," Hardwicke said. "My duty is to bring those responsible before the courts to be judged."

"Your sentiments do you both credit," said Holmes. His face was grave as he continued. "Let us assume that Rathbroke has not discovered the treasure – the existence of which, I may tell you, I have serious doubts. Too many country families such as the Groves claim to have pirate or highwayman ancestors whose ill-gotten gains are secreted away. On a few occasions these romantic legends prove to have a foundation of proof. In most cases, they are simply that – romantic legends. If it transpires in the future that Rathbroke has suddenly acquired an unexplained source of wealth, then we may re-open the case."

He paused and looked each of us in turn full in the eye. "What I am about to tell you now must be held in the strictest confidence, at least for the immediate future. As you are aware, Watson, much of my time is now taken up with government affairs. I've taken on some of Mycroft's duties in some affairs of state. I'm sure that you both are aware of Lord Rathbroke's position in the Cabinet? Yes? The position of this government is currently in a precarious state as the result of a number of factors, not all of which are public knowledge at present."

I nodded in understanding, as did the inspector.

"Very well," Holmes went on. "Should Lord Rathbroke, or even one of his servants, be arrested and prosecuted for their part in this death, it is quite likely that other sensitive matters will be revealed. We know that Korda was blackmailing Lady Groves. It is more than probable, though I cannot confirm this publicly, that he had another 'client' in Rathbroke, and maybe even more in the Cabinet. Any exposure resulting from a trial would bring about the collapse of the government."

"I see," said Hardwicke, thoughtfully.

"That would be a matter of international consequence. The new naval treaty now being negotiated between the nations of the world depends for its success on the prestige and influence of the current First Lord of the Admiralty. Should he be replaced, as would certainly be the case . . . ." Holmes shrugged.

"The naval treaty would never be signed, and the nations of the world would once more bankrupt themselves building unlimited dreadnoughts?" I suggested.

"Precisely so. And we might be plunged into another terrible global conflict."

There was a sombre pause, broken by Inspector Hardwicke.

"And Captain Groves and this woman?"

"I fancy that his mother will not be too unhappy if he believes he has found someone to love him," I said. "I have the feeling that she wishes his happiness, whatever that may be."

"One more thing," I said to Holmes as we were driven back to London in his official motor-car. "The hands in the wax. How do mediums perform that trick? I have been puzzling over it, and I cannot work it out."

"An old trick. Three words. Inflated rubber gloves. The rest you can surely deduce for yourself, having covered yourself with glory before my arrival. Save for a few major errors in judgement, of course."

I basked in this rare praise from Holmes, and sat back contented as the powerful motor devoured the miles on the road to London.

About the Contributors

The following contributors appear in this volume:
The MX Book of New Sherlock Holmes Stories
Part XXXIII – 2022 Annual (1896-1919)

Hugh Ashton was born in the U.K., and moved to Japan in 1988, where he remained until 2016, living with his wife Yoshiko in the historic city of Kamakura, a little to the south of Yokohama. He and Yoshiko have now moved to Lichfield, a small cathedral city in the Midlands of the U.K., the birthplace of Samuel Johnson, and one-time home of Erasmus Darwin. In the past, he has worked in the technology and financial services industries, which have provided him with material for some of his books set in the 21st century. He currently works as a writer: Novelist, freelance editor, and copywriter, (his work for large Japanese corporations has appeared in international business journals), and journalist, as well as producing industry reports on various aspects of the financial services industry. However, his lifelong interest in Sherlock Holmes has developed into an acclaimed series of adventures featuring the world's most famous detective, written in the style of the originals. In addition to these, he has also published historical and alternate historical novels, short stories, and thrillers. Together with artist Andy Boerger, he has produced the *Sherlock Ferret* series of stories for children, featuring the world's cutest detective.

Brian Belanger, PSI, is a publisher, illustrator, graphic designer, editor, and author. In 2015, he co-founded Belanger Books publishing company along with his brother, author Derrick Belanger. His illustrations have appeared in *The Essential Sherlock Holmes* and *Sherlock Holmes: A Three-Pipe Christmas*, and in children's books such as *The MacDougall Twins with Sherlock Holmes* series, *Dragonella*, and *Scones and Bones on Baker Street*. Brian has published a number of Sherlock Holmes anthologies and novels through Belanger Books, as well as new editions of August Derleth's classic Solar Pons mysteries. Brian continues to design all of the covers for Belanger Books, and since 2016 he has designed the majority of book covers for MX Publishing. In 2019, Brian received his investiture in the PSI as "Sir Ronald Duveen." More recently, he illustrated a comic book featuring the band The Moonlight Initiative, created the logo for the Arthur Conan Doyle Society and designed *The Great Game of Sherlock Holmes* card game. Find him online at:
www.belangerbooks.com and
www.redbubble.com/people/zhahadun and
zhahadun.wixsite.com/221b.

Andrew Bryant was born in Bridgend, Wales, and now lives in Burlington, Ontario. His previous publications include *Poetry Toronto*, *Prism International*, *Existere*, *On Spec*, *The Dalhousie Review*, and *The Toronto Star*. Andrew's interest in Holmes stems from watching the Basil Rathbone and Nigel Bruce films as a child, followed by collecting The Canon, and a fascinating visit to 221b Baker Street in London.

Josh Cerefice has followed the exploits of a certain pipe-smoking sleuth ever since his grandmother bought him *The Complete Sherlock Holmes* collection for his twenty-first birthday, and he has devotedly accompanied the Great Detective on his adventures ever since. When he's not reading about spectral hellhounds haunting the Devonshire moors, or the Machiavellian machinations of Professor Moriarty, you can find him putting pen to paper and challenging Holmes with new mysteries to solve in his own stories.

Craig Stephen Copland confesses that he discovered Sherlock Holmes when, sometime in the muddled early 1960's, he pinched his older brother's copy of the immortal stories and was forever afterward thoroughly hooked. He is very grateful to his high school English teachers in Toronto who inculcated in him a love of literature and writing, and even inspired him to be an English major at the University of Toronto. There he was blessed to sit at the feet of both Northrup Frye and Marshall McLuhan, and other great literary professors, who led him to believe that he was called to be a high school English teacher. It was his good fortune to come to his pecuniary senses, abandon that goal, and pursue a varied professional career that took him to over one-hundred countries and endless adventures. He considers himself to have been and to continue to be one of the luckiest men on God's good earth. A few years back he took a step in the direction of Sherlockian studies and joined the *Sherlock Holmes Society of Canada* – also known as *The Toronto Bootmakers*. In May of 2014, this esteemed group of scholars announced a contest for the writing of a new Sherlock Holmes mystery. Although he had never tried his hand at fiction before, Craig entered and was pleasantly surprised to be selected as one of the winners. Having enjoyed the experience, he decided to write more of the same, and is now on a mission to write a new Sherlock Holmes mystery that is related to and inspired by each of the sixty stories in the original Canon. He currently lives and writes in Toronto and Dubai, and looks forward to finally settling down when he turns ninety.

Martin Daley was born in Carlisle, Cumbria in 1964. He cites Doyle's Holmes and Watson as his favourite literary characters, who continue to inspire his own detective writing. His fiction and non-fiction books include a Holmes pastiche set predominantly in his home city in 1903. In the adventure, he introduced his own detective, Inspector Cornelius Armstrong, who has subsequently had some of his own cases published by MX Publishing. For more information visit *www.martindaley.co.uk*

Sir Arthur Conan Doyle (1859-1930) *Holmes Chronicler Emeritus*. If not for him, this anthology would not exist. Author, physician, patriot, sportsman, spiritualist, husband and father, and advocate for the oppressed. He is remembered and honored for the purposes of this collection by being the man who introduced Sherlock Holmes to the world. Through fifty-six Holmes short stories, four novels, and additional Apocryphal entries, Doyle revolutionized mystery stories and also greatly influenced and improved police forensic methods and techniques for the betterment of all. *Steel True Blade Straight.*

Steve Emecz's main field is technology, in which he has been working for about twenty-five years. Steve is a regular speaker at trade shows and his tech career has taken him to more than fifty countries – so he's no stranger to planes and airports. In 2008, MX published its first Sherlock Holmes book, and MX has gone on to become the largest specialist Holmes publisher in the world with over 500 books. MX is a social enterprise and supports three main causes. The first is Happy Life, a children's rescue project in Nairobi, Kenya, where he and his wife, Sharon, spend every Christmas at the rescue centre in Kasarani. They have written two editions of a short book about the project, *The Happy Life Story*. The second is Undershaw, Sir Arthur Conan Doyle's former home, which is a school for children with learning disabilities for which Steve is a patron. Steve has been a mentor for the World Food Programme for several years, and was part of the Nobel Peace Prize winning team in 2020.

Mark A. Gagen BSI is co-founder of Wessex Press, sponsor of the popular *From Gillette to Brett* conferences, and publisher of *The Sherlock Holmes Reference Library* and many other fine Sherlockian titles. A life-long Holmes enthusiast, he is a member of *The Baker Street Irregulars* and *The Illustrious Clients of Indianapolis*. A graphic artist by profession, his work is often seen on the covers of *The Baker Street Journal* and various BSI books.

Terry Golledge (according to his son Niel Golledge, who provided these stories to this collection) had a life-long love of all things Conan Doyle and in particular Sherlock Holmes. He was born in 1920 in the East End of London. He left school at fourteen, like so many back then. In 1939, he joined the army in the fight against the Germans in World War II. He left the Army in 1945 at the war's end, residing in Hastings. There he met his wife, and his life was a mish-mash of careers, including mining and bus and lorry driving. He owned a couple of book shops, selling them in the 1960's. He then worked for the Post Office, (later to become British Telecom, equivalent to AT&T), ending his working life there as a training instructor for his retirement in 1980. His love of Sherlock Holmes was obviously inspired by the fact that his mother worked as a governess to Sir Arthur Conan Doyle when he lived in Windlesham, Crowborough in Sussex. She married Terry's father after leaving Sir Arthur's employment around 1918. Beginning in the mid-1980's, Terry Golledge wrote a number of Holmes stories, and they have never been previously published. A full collection of his Holmes works will be published in the near future. He passed away in 1996.

Niel Golledge was born in 1951 in Winchester, England. He retired some years ago and currently resides in Kent, UK. His last employment for over twenty years was with a large newsprint paper mill, located near his home. He is married to Trisha, a retired nurse, and they have a son and daughter who have carved out careers in mental health and physiotherapy. He is an avid football fan of West Ham and loves to play golf. He is also a keen reader – but that goes without saying.

John Atkinson Grimshaw (1836-1893) was born in Leeds, England. His amazing paintings, usually featuring twilight or night scenes illuminated by gas-lamps or moonlight, are easily recognizable, and are often used on the covers of books about The Great Detective to set the mood, as shadowy figures move in the distance through misty mysterious settings and over rain-slicked streets.

Arthur Hall was born in Aston, Birmingham, UK, in 1944. He discovered his interest in writing during his schooldays, along with a love of fictional adventure and suspense. His first novel, *Sole Contact*, was an espionage story about an ultra-secret government department known as "Sector Three", and was followed, to date, by three sequels. Other works include seven Sherlock Holmes novels, *The Demon of the Dusk*, *The One Hundred Percent Society*, *The Secret Assassin*, *The Phantom Killer*, *In Pursuit of the Dead*, *The Justice Master*, and *The Experience Club* as well as three collections of Holmes *Further Little-Known Cases of Sherlock* Holmes, *Tales from the Annals of Sherlock* Holmes, and *The Additional Investigations of Sherlock Holmes*. He has also written other short stories and a modern detective novel. He lives in the West Midlands, United Kingdom.

Jeffrey Hatcher is a playwright and screenwriter. His plays have been produced on Broadway, Off-Broadway, and in theaters throughout the U.S. and around the world. They include *Three Viewings*, *Scotland Road*, *The Turn of the Screw*, *Compleat Female Stage Beauty*, *Mrs. Mannerly*, *Murderers*, *Smash*, *Korczak's Children*, *The Government Inspector*, *A Picasso*, *The Alchemist*, *Key Largo*, *Dr. Jekyll and Mr. Hyde*, and his Sherlock

Holmes plays *Sherlock Holmes and the Adventure of the Suicide Club*, *Sherlock Holmes and the Ice Palace Murders*, and *Holmes and Watson*. His film work includes the screenplays for *Stage Beauty*, *Casanova*, *The Duchess*, *Mr. Holmes*, and *The Good Liar*. For television, he has written episodes of *Columbo* and *The Mentalist* and the TV movie *Murder at the Cannes Film Festival*. He has received grants and awards from the NEA, TCG, Lila Wallace Fund, Rosenthal New Play Prize, Frankel Award, Charles MacArthur Fellowship Award, McKnight Foundation, Jerome Foundation, and a Barrymore Award for Best New Play. He has been twice nominated for an Edgar Award. He is a member and/or alumnus of The Playwrights Center, the Dramatists Guild, the Writers Guild, and New Dramatists.

Roger Johnson BSI, ASH is a retired librarian, now working as a volunteer assistant at the Essex Police Museum. In his spare time, he is commissioning editor of *The Sherlock Holmes Journal*, an occasional lecturer, and a frequent contributor to *The Writings about the Writings*. His sole work of Holmesian pastiche was published in 1997 in Mike Ashley's anthology *The Mammoth Book of New Sherlock Holmes Adventures*, and he has the greatest respect for the many authors who have contributed new tales to the present mighty trilogy. Like his wife, Jean Upton, he is a member of both *The Baker Street Irregulars* and *The Adventuresses of Sherlock Holmes*.

Naching T. Kassa is a wife, mother, and writer. She's created short stories, novellas, poems, and co-created three children. She resides in Eastern Washington State with her husband, Dan Kassa. Naching is a member of *The Horror Writers Association*, *Mystery Writers of America*, *The Sound of the Baskervilles*, *The ACD Society*, and *The Sherlock Holmes Society of London*. She's also an assistant and staff writer for Still Water Bay at Crystal Lake Publishing. You can find her work on Amazon. *https://www.amazon.com/Naching-T-Kassa/e/B005ZGHTI0*

Susan Knight's newest novel, Mrs. Hudson goes to Paris, from MX publishing, is the latest in a series which began with her collection of stories, *Mrs. Hudson Investigates* of 2019 and the novel Mrs. Hudson goes to Ireland (2020). She has contributed to several of the MX anthologies of new Sherlock Holmes short stories, and enjoys writing as Dr. Watson as much as she does Mrs. Hudson. Susan is the author of two other non-Sherlockian, story collections, as well as three novels, a book of non-fiction, and several plays, and has won several prizes for her writing. She lives in Dublin, Ireland. Her next Mrs. Hudson novel is already a gleam in her eye.

Jeffrey Lockwood spent youthful afternoons darkly enchanted by feeding grasshoppers to black widows in his New Mexican backyard, which accounts for his scientific and literary affinities. He earned a doctorate in entomology and worked as an ecologist at the University of Wyoming before metamorphosing into a Professor of Natural Sciences & Humanities in the departments of philosophy and creative writing – hence, insect-infested nonfiction and mysteries. He considers Sherlock Holmes a model of scientific prowess, integrating exquisite observational skills with incisive abductive (not deductive) reasoning.

David MacGregor is a playwright, screenwriter, novelist, and nonfiction writer. He is a resident artist at The Purple Rose Theatre in Michigan, where a number of his plays have been produced. His plays have been performed from New York to Tasmania, and his work has been published by Dramatic Publishing, Playscripts, Smith & Kraus, Applause, Heuer Publishing, and Theatrical Rights Worldwide (TRW). He adapted his dark comedy, *Vino Veritas*, for the silver screen, and it stars Carrie Preston (Emmy-winner for *The Good Wife*).

490

Several of his short plays have also been adapted into films. He is the author of three Sherlock Holmes plays: *Sherlock Holmes and the Adventure of the Elusive Ear*, *Sherlock Holmes and the Adventure of the Fallen Soufflé*, and *Sherlock Holmes and the Adventure of the Ghost Machine*. He adapted all three plays into novels for Orange Pip Books, and also wrote the two-volume nonfiction *Sherlock Holmes: The Hero with a Thousand Faces* for MX Publishing. He teaches writing at Wayne State University in Detroit and is inordinately fond of cheese and terriers.

David Marcum plays *The Game* with deadly seriousness. He first discovered Sherlock Holmes in 1975 at the age of ten, and since that time, he has collected, read, and chronologicized literally thousands of traditional Holmes pastiches in the form of novels, short stories, radio and television episodes, movies and scripts, comics, fan-fiction, and unpublished manuscripts. He is the author of over ninety Sherlockian pastiches, some published in anthologies and magazines such as *The Strand*, and others collected in his own books, *The Papers of Sherlock Holmes*, *Sherlock Holmes and A Quantity of Debt*, *Sherlock Holmes – Tangled Skeins*, *Sherlock Holmes and The Eye of Heka*, and *The Complete Papers of Sherlock Holmes*. He has edited over sixty books, including several dozen traditional Sherlockian anthologies, such as the ongoing series *The MX Book of New Sherlock Holmes Stories*, which he created in 2015. This collection is now over thirty volumes, with more in preparation. He was responsible for bringing back August Derleth's Solar Pons for a new generation, first with his collection of authorized Pons stories, *The Papers of Solar Pons*, and then by editing the reissued authorized versions of the original Pons books, and then several volumes of new Pons adventures. He has done the same for the adventures of Dr. Thorndyke, and has plans for similar projects in the future. He has contributed numerous essays to various publications, and is a member of a number of Sherlockian groups and Scions. His irregular Sherlockian blog, *A Seventeen Step Program*, addresses various topics related to his favorite book friends (as his son used to call them when he was small), and can be found at *http://17stepprogram.blogspot.com/* He is a licensed Civil Engineer, living in Tennessee with his wife and son. Since the age of nineteen, he has worn a deerstalker as his regular-and-only hat. In 2013, he and his deerstalker were finally able make his first trip-of-a-lifetime Holmes Pilgrimage to England, with return Pilgrimages in 2015 and 2016, where you may have spotted him. If you ever run into him and his deerstalker out and about, feel free to say hello!

Sidney Paget (1860-1908), a few of whose illustrations are used within this anthology, was born in London, and like his two older brothers, became a famed illustrator and painter. He completed over three-hundred-and-fifty drawings for the Sherlock Holmes stories that were first published in *The Strand* magazine, defining Holmes's image forever after in the public mind.

Tracy J. Revels, a Sherlockian from the age of eleven, is a professor of history at Wofford College in Spartanburg, South Carolina. She is a member of *The Survivors of the Gloria Scott* and *The Studious Scarlets Society*, and is a past recipient of the Beacon Society Award. Almost every semester, she teaches a class that covers The Canon, either to college students or to senior citizens. She is also the author of three supernatural Sherlockian pastiches with MX (*Shadowfall*, *Shadowblood*, and *Shadowwraith*), and a regular contributor to her scion's newsletter. She also has some notoriety as an author of very silly skits: For proof, see "The Adventure of the Adversarial Adventuress" and "Occupy Baker Street" on YouTube. When not studying Sherlock, she can be found researching the history of her native state, and has written books on Florida in the Civil War and on the development of Florida's tourism industry.

491

Dan Rowley practiced law for over forty years in private practice and with a large international corporation. He is retired and lives in Erie, Pennsylvania, with his wife Judy, who puts her artistic eye to his transcription of Watson's manuscripts. He inherited his writing ability and creativity from his children, Jim and Katy, and his love of mysteries from his parents, Jim and Ruth.

Alisha Shea has resided near Saint Louis, Missouri for over thirty years. The eldest of six children, she found reading to be a genuine escape from the chaotic drudgery of life. She grew to love not only Sherlock Holmes, but the time period from which he emerged. This will be her first published work, but probably not her last. In her spare time, she indulges in creating music via piano, violin, and Native American flute. Sometimes she thinks she might even be getting good at it. She also produces a wide variety of fiber arts which are typically given away or auctioned off for various fundraisers.

Tim Symonds was born in London. He grew up in the rural English counties of Somerset and Dorset, and the British Crown Dependency of Guernsey. After several years travelling widely, including farming on the slopes of Mt. Kenya in East Africa and working on the Zambezi River in Central Africa, he emigrated to Canada and the United States. He studied at the Georg-August University (Göttingen) in Germany, and the University of California, Los Angeles, graduating *cum làude* and Phi Beta Kappa. He is a Fellow of the Royal Geographical Society and a Member of The Society of Authors. His detective novels include *Sherlock Holmes And The Dead Boer At Scotney Castle*, *Sherlock Holmes And The Mystery Of Einstein's Daughter*, *Sherlock Holmes And The Case Of The Bulgarian Codex*, *Sherlock Holmes And The Sword Of Osman*, *Sherlock Holmes And The Nine-Dragon Sigil*, six Holmes and Watson short stories under the title *A Most Diabolical Plot*, and his novella *Sherlock Holmes and the Strange Death of Brigadier-General Delves*.

Kevin Thornton was shortlisted six times for the Crime Writers of Canada best unpublished novel. He never won – they are all still unpublished, and now he writes short stories. He lives in Canada, north enough that ringing Santa Claus is a local call and winter is a way of life. This is his twelfth short story in *The MX Book of New Sherlock Holmes Stories*. By the time you next hear from him, he hopes to have written his thirteenth.

Thomas A. (Tom) Turley has been "hooked on Holmes" since finishing *The Hound of the Baskervilles* at about the age of twelve. However, his interest in Sherlockian pastiches didn't take off until he wrote one. *Sherlock Holmes and the Adventure of the Tainted Canister* (2014) is available as an e-book and an audiobook from MX Publishing. It also appeared in *The Art of Sherlock Holmes – USA Edition 1*. In 2017, two of Tom's stories, "A Scandal in Serbia" and "A Ghost from Christmas Past" were published in Parts VI and VII of this anthology. "Ghost" was also included in *The Art of Sherlock Holmes – West Palm Beach Edition*. Meanwhile, Tom is finishing a collection of historical pastiches entitled *Sherlock Holmes and the Crowned Heads of Europe*, to be published in 2021 The first story, "Sherlock Holmes and the Case of the Dying Emperor" (2018) is available from MX Publishing as a separate e-book. Set in the brief reign of Emperor Frederick III (1888), it inaugurates Sherlock Holmes's espionage campaign against the German Empire, which ended only in August 1914 with "His Last Bow". When completed, *Sherlock Holmes and the Crowned Heads of Europe* will also include "A Scandal in Serbia" and two additional historical tales. Although he has a Ph.D. in British history, Tom spent most of his professional career as an archivist with the State of Alabama. He and his wife Paula (an aspiring science fiction novelist) live in Montgomery, Alabama. Interested readers may contact Tom through MX Publishing or his Goodreads author's page.

Mark Wardecker is an instructional technologist at Colby College, and has contributed Sherlockian pastiches to *Sherlock Holmes Mystery Magazine* and *The MX Book of New Sherlock Holmes Stories – Part XIII*, as well as an article to *The Baker Street Journal*. He is also the editor and annotator of *The Dragnet Solar Pons et al.* (Battered Silicon Dispatch Box, 2011), and has contributed Solar Pons pastiches to *The New Adventures of Solar Pons*.

Emma West joined Undershaw in April 2021 as the Director of Education with a brief to ensure that qualifications formed the bedrock of our provision, whilst facilitating a positive balance between academia, pastoral care, and well-being. She quickly took on the role of Acting Headteacher from early summer 2021. Under her leadership, Undershaw has embraced its new name, new vision, and consequently we have seen an exponential increase in demand for places. There is a buzz in the air as we invite prospective students and families through the doors. Emma has overseen a strategic review, re-cemented relationships with Local Authorities, and positioned Undershaw at the helm of SEND education in Surrey and beyond. Undershaw has a wide appeal: Our students present to us with mild to moderate learning needs and therefore may have some very recent memories of poor experiences in their previous schools. Emma's background as a senior leader within the independent school sector has meant she is well-versed in brokering relationships between the key stakeholders, our many interdependences, local businesses, families, and staff, and all this whilst ensuring Undershaw remains relentlessly child-centric in its approach. Emma's energetic smile and boundless enthusiasm for Undershaw is inspiring.

Marcia Wilson is a freelance researcher and illustrator who likes to work in a style compatible for the color blind and visually impaired. She is Canon-centric, and her first MX offering, *You Buy Bones*, uses the point-of-view of Scotland Yard to show the unique talents of Dr. Watson. This continued with the publication of *Test of the Professionals: The Adventure of the Flying Blue Pidgeon* and *The Peaceful Night Poisonings*. She can be contacted at: *gravelgirty.deviantart.com*

The following contributors appear
in the companion volumes:
The MX Book of New Sherlock Holmes Stories
Part XXXI – 2022 Annual (1875-1887)
Part XXXII – 2022 Annual (1888-1895)

Ian Ableson is an ecologist by training and a writer by choice. When not reading or writing, he can reliably be found scowling at a clipboard while ankle-deep in a marsh somewhere in Michigan. His love for the stories of Arthur Conan Doyle started when his grandfather gave him a copy of *The Original Illustrated Sherlock Holmes* when he was in high school, and he's proud to have been able to contribute to the continuation of the tales of Sherlock Holmes and Dr. Watson.

Wayne Anderson was born and raised in the beautiful Pacific Northwest, growing up in Alaska and Washington State. He discovered Sherlock Holmes around age ten and promptly devoured the Canon. When it was all gone, he tried to sate the addiction by writing his own Sherlock Holmes stories, which are mercifully lost forever. Sadly, he moved to California in his twenties and has lived there since. He has two grown sons who are both writers as well. He spends his time writing or working on the TV pilots and patents which will someday make him fabulously wealthy. When he's not doing these things, he is either reading to his young daughter from The Canon or trying to find space in his house for more bookshelves.

Thomas A. Burns Jr. writes *The Natalie McMasters Mysteries* from the small town of Wendell, North Carolina, where he lives with his wife and son, four cats, and a Cardigan Welsh Corgi. He was born and grew up in New Jersey, attended Xavier High School in Manhattan, earned B.S degrees in Zoology and Microbiology at Michigan State University, and a M.S. in Microbiology at North Carolina State University. As a kid, Tom started reading mysteries with The Hardy Boys, Ken Holt, and Rick Brant, then graduated to the classic stories by authors such as A. Conan Doyle, Dorothy Sayers, John Dickson Carr, Erle Stanley Gardner, and Rex Stout, to name a few. Tom has written fiction as a hobby all of his life, starting with *The Man from U.N.C.L.E.* stories in marble-backed copybooks in grade school. He built a career as technical, science, and medical writer and editor for nearly thirty years in industry and government. Now that he's a full-time novelist, he's excited to publish his own mystery series, as well as to write stories about his second most favorite detective, Sherlock Holmes. His Holmes story, "The Camberwell Poisoner", appeared in the March-June 2021 issue of *The Strand Magazine.* Tom has also written a Lovecraftian horror novel, *The Legacy of the Unborn*, under the pen name of Silas K. Henderson – a sequel to H.P. Lovecraft's masterpiece *At the Mountains of Madness*.

Mike Chinn's first-ever Sherlock Holmes fiction was a steampunk mashup of *The Valley of Fear*, entitled *Vallis Timoris* (Fringeworks 2015). Since then he has written about Holmes's archenemy in *The Mammoth Book of the Adventures of Moriarty* (Robinson 2015), appeared in three volumes of *The MX Book of New Sherlock Holmes Stories*, and faced the retired detective with cross-dimensional magic in the second volume of *Sherlock Holmes and the Occult Detectives* (Belanger Books 2020).

Alan Dimes was born in North-West London and graduated from Sussex University with a BA in English Literature. He has spent most of his working life teaching English. Living in the Czech Republic since 2003, he is now semi-retired and divides his time between Prague and his country cottage. He has also written some fifty stories of horror and fantasy and thirty stories about his husband-and-wife detectives, Peter and Deirdre Creighton, set in the 1930's.

Arianna Fox is a triple-published and bestselling author, keynote speaker, actress, professional voiceover talent, award winner, and public figure whose passion is to inspire, educate, and entertain others through her work. From modern stories that connect with a teenage audience to classical-style works of literature, one of Arianna's foremost passions has always been writing. An avid Sherlockian and lover of all things Victorian, Arianna disliked reading for years until she read the first few paragraphs of *The Return of Sherlock Holmes* in a bookstore and immediately fell in love with classic literature and the intricate themes woven into its messages. As a whole, Arianna's ultimate goal is to empower others to achieve maximum success and rock their lives. Arianna can be found at *www.ariannafox.com*, Facebook: *@afoxauthor*, Twitter: *@afoxauthor*; LinkedIn: *Arianna Fox*; and Instagram: *@afoxauthor*

Mike Fox is a CEO, entrepreneur, multi award-winning filmmaker, director, producer, writer, designer, creative professional, actor, voiceover talent, and illustrator. His professional work is known across the U.S. and has received numerous accolades and awards. In addition, Mike has been named "Top Pioneer & Entrepreneur" by *K.I.S.H. Magazine*, and named "Local Business Person of the Year" by Alignable. Mike and his films and creative designs have been featured numerous times in many media channels. Mike can be found at *www.splashdw.com* and *www.crystalfoxfilms.com*; Facebook: *@splashdw*; Twitter: *@splashdw*; LinkedIn: *Mike Fox*; and Instagram: *@officialmikefox*

James Gelter is a director and playwright living in Brattleboro, VT. His produced written works for the stage include adaptations of *Frankenstein* and *A Christmas Carol*, several children's plays for the New England Youth Theatre, as well as seven outdoor plays co-written with his wife, Jessica, in their *Forest of Mystery* series. In 2018, he founded The Baker Street Readers, a group of performers that present dramatic readings of Arthur Conan Doyle's original Canon of Sherlock Holmes stories, featuring Gelter as Holmes, his longtime collaborator Tony Grobe as Dr. Watson, and a rotating list of guests. When the COVID-19 pandemic stopped their live performances, Gelter transformed the show into The Baker Street Readers Podcast. Some episodes are available for free on Apple Podcasts and Stitcher, with many more available to patrons at *patreon.com/bakerstreetreaders*.

Hal Glatzer *also has stories in Parts XXXI and XXXII*

Terry Golledge *also has stories in Parts XXXI and XXXII*

Arthur Hall *also has stories in Parts XXXI and XXXII*

Stephen Herczeg is an IT Geek, writer, actor, and film-maker based in Canberra Australia. He has been writing for over twenty years and has completed a couple of dodgy novels, sixteen feature-length screenplays, and numerous short stories and scripts. Stephen was very successful in 2017's International Horror Hotel screenplay competition, with his scripts *TITAN* winning the Sci-Fi category and *Dark are the Woods* placing second in the horror category. His two-volume short story collection, *The Curious Cases of Sherlock Holmes*, was published in 2021. His work has featured in *Sproutlings – A Compendium of Little Fictions* from Hunter Anthologies, the *Hells Bells* Christmas horror anthology published by the Australasian Horror Writers Association, and the *Below the Stairs*, *Trickster's Treats*, *Shades of Santa*, *Behind the Mask*, and *Beyond the Infinite* anthologies from *OzHorror.Con*, *The Body Horror Book*, *Anemone Enemy*, and *Petrified Punks* from Oscillate Wildly Press, and *Sherlock Holmes In the Realms of H.G. Wells* and *Sherlock Holmes: Adventures Beyond the Canon* from Belanger Books.

Paul Hiscock is an author of crime, fantasy, horror, and science fiction tales. His short stories have appeared in a variety of anthologies, and include a seventeenth-century whodunnit, a science fiction western, a clockpunk fairytale, and numerous Sherlock Holmes pastiches. He lives with his family in Kent (England) and spends his days taking care of his two children. He mainly does his writing in coffee shops with members of the local NaNoWriMo group, or in the middle of the night when his family has gone to sleep. Consequently, his stories tend to be fuelled by large amounts of black coffee. You can find out more about Paul's writing at *www.detectivesanddragons.uk*.

Mike Hogan's early interest in all things Victorian led to a university degree in English and research on nineteenth century literature. He taught English and creative writing at colleges in Japan, the Philippines, Libya and Thailand. He is settled now for much of the year on the island of Mersea in Essex, UK, where he writes novels, plays, and short stories, many set in Victorian London and featuring Sherlock Holmes.

In the year 1998 **Craig Janacek** took his degree of Doctor of Medicine at Vanderbilt University, and proceeded to Stanford to go through the training prescribed for pediatricians in practice. Having completed his studies there, he was duly attached to the University of California, San Francisco as Associate Professor. The author of over seventy medical monographs upon a variety of obscure lesions, his travel-worn and battered tin dispatch-box is crammed with papers, nearly all of which are records of his fictional works. To date, these have been published solely in electronic format, including two non-Holmes novels (*The Oxford Deception* and *The Anger of Achilles Peterson*), the trio of holiday adventures collected as *The Midwinter Mysteries of Sherlock Holmes*, the Holmes story collections *The First of Criminals, The Assassination of Sherlock Holmes, The Treasury of Sherlock Holmes, Light in the Darkness, The Gathering Gloom, The Travels of Sherlock Holmes*, and the Watsonian novels *The Isle of Devils* and *The Gate of Gold*. Craig Janacek is a *nom de plume*.

Kelvin I. Jones is the author of six books about Sherlock Holmes and the definitive biography of Conan Doyle as a spiritualist, *Conan Doyle and The Spirits*. A member of *The Sherlock Holmes Society of London*, he has published numerous short occult and ghost stories in British anthologies over the last thirty years. His work has appeared on BBC Radio, and in 1984 he won the Mason Hall Literary Award for his poem cycle about the survivors of Hiroshima and Nagasaki, recently reprinted as "Omega". (Oakmagic Publications) A one-time teacher of creative writing at the University of East Anglia, he is also the author of four crime novels featuring his ex-met sleuth John Bottrell, who first appeared in *Stone Dead*. He has over fifty titles on Kindle, and is also the author of several novellas and short story collections featuring a Norwich based detective, DCI Ketch, an intrepid sleuth who investigates East Anglian murder cases. He also published a series of short stories about an Edwardian psychic detective, Dr. John Carter (*Carter's Occult Casebook*). Ramsey Campbell, the British horror writer, and Francis King, the renowned novelist, have both compared his supernatural stories to those of M. R. James. He has also published children's fiction, namely *Odin's Eye*, and, in collaboration with his wife Debbie, *The Dark Entry*. Since 1995, he has been the proprietor of Oakmagic Publications, publishers of British folklore and of his fiction titles. He lives in Norfolk. (See www.oakmagicpublications.co.uk)

Susan Knight *also has a story in Part XXXI*

John Lawrence served for thirty-eight years on personal, committee, and leadership staffs in the U.S. House of Representatives. A visiting professor at the University of California's Washington Center since 2013, he is the author of *The Class of '74: Congress After Watergate and the Roots of Partisanship* (Johns-Hopkins, 2018) and *Arc of Power: Inside the Pelosi Speakership 2005-2010* (Kansas, 2022). His collected "history mystery" Sherlock Holmes pastiches have been published in *The Undiscovered Archives of Sherlock Holmes* (MX Publishing, 2022), in numerous volumes of *The MX Book of New Sherlock Holmes Stories*, and in Belanger Books' *After the East Wind Blows*. He blogs at *DOMEocracy* (johnalawrence.wordpress.com). He is a graduate of Oberlin College and has a Ph.D. in history from the University of California (Berkeley).

Gordon Linzner is founder and former editor of *Space and Time Magazine*, and author of three published novels and dozens of short stories in *F&SF, Twilight Zone, Sherlock Holmes Mystery Magazine*, and numerous other magazines and anthologies, including

Baker Street Irregulars II, *Across the Universe*, and *Strange Lands*. He is a member of *HWA* and a lifetime member of *SFWA*.

David MacGregor *also has a story in Part XXXI*

David Marcum *also has stories in Parts XXXI and XXXII*

Kevin Patrick McCann has published eight collections of poems for adults, one for children (*Diary of a Shapeshifter*, Beul Aithris), a book of ghost stories (*It's Gone Dark*, The Otherside Books), *Teach Yourself Self-Publishing* (Hodder) co-written with the playwright Tom Green, and *Ov* (Beul Aithris Publications) a fantasy novel for children.

Will Murray has built a career on writing classic pulp characters, ranging from Tarzan of the Apes to Doc Savage. He has penned several milestone crossover novels in his acclaimed Wild Adventures series. *Skull Island* pitted Doc Savage against King Kong, which was followed by *King Kong Vs. Tarzan. Tarzan, Conqueror of Mars* costarred John Carter of Mars. His 2015 Doc Savage novel, *The Sinister Shadow*, revived the famous radio and pulp mystery man. Murray reunited them for *Empire of Doom*. His first Spider novel, *The Doom Legion*, revived that infamous crime buster, as well as James Christopher, AKA Operator 5, and the renowned G-8. His second *Spider, Fury in Steel*, guest-stars the FBI's Suicide Squad. Ten of his Sherlock Holmes short stories have been collected as *The Wild Adventures of Sherlock Holmes*. He is the author of the non-fiction book, *Master of Mystery: The Rise of The Shadow*. For Marvel Comics, Murray created the Unbeatable Squirrel Girl. Website: *www.adventuresinbronze.com*

Tracy J. Revels *also has stories in Parts XXXI and XXXII*

Roger Riccard's family history has Scottish roots, which trace his lineage back to Highland Scotland. This British Isles ancestry encouraged his interest in the writings of Sir Arthur Conan Doyle at an early age. He has authored the novels, *Sherlock Holmes & The Case of the Poisoned Lilly*, and *Sherlock Holmes & The Case of the Twain Papers.* In addition he has produced several short stories in *Sherlock Holmes Adventures for the Twelve Days of Christmas* and the series *A Sherlock Holmes Alphabet of Cases.* A new series will begin publishing in the Autumn of 2022, and his has another novel in the works. All of his books have been published by Baker Street Studios. His Bachelor of Arts Degrees in both Journalism and History from California State University, Northridge, have proven valuable to his writing historical fiction, as well as the encouragement of his wife/editor/inspiration and Sherlock Holmes fan, Rosilyn. She passed in 2021, and it is in her memory that he continues to contribute to the legacy of the "*man who never lived and will never die*".

Dan Rowley *also has a story in Part XXXI*

Geri Schear is a novelist and short story writer. Her work has been published in literary journals in the U.S. and Ireland. Her first novel, *A Biased Judgement: The Diaries of Sherlock Holmes 1897* was released to critical acclaim in 2014. The sequel, *Sherlock Holmes and the Other Woman* was published in 2015, and *Return to Reichenbach* in 2016. She lives in Kells, Ireland.

Robert V. Stapleton was born in Leeds, England, and served as a full-time Anglican clergyman for forty years, specialising in Rural Ministry. He is now retired, and lives with his wife in North Yorkshire. This is the area of the country made famous by the writings of James Herriot, and television's *The Yorkshire Vet*, to name just a few. Amongst other things, he is a member of the local creative writing group, Thirsk Write Now (TWN), and regularly produces material for them. He has had more than fifty stories published, of various lengths and in a number of different places. He has also written a number of stories for *The MX Book of New Sherlock Holmes Stories*, and several published by Belanger Books. Several of these Sherlock Holmes pastiches have now been brought together and published in a single volume by MX Publishing, under the title of *Sherlock Holmes: A Yorkshireman in Baker Street*. Many of these stories have been set during the Edwardian period, or more broadly between the years 1880 and 1920. His interest in this period of history began at school in the 1960's when he met people who had lived during those years and heard their stories. He also found echoes of those times in literature, architecture, music, and even the coins in his pocket. The Edwardian period was a time of exploration, invention. and high adventure – rich material for thriller writers.

Tim Symonds *also has stories in Parts XXXI and XXXII*

DJ Tyrer dwells on the northern shore of the Thames estuary, close to the world's longest pleasure pier in the decaying seaside resort of Southend-on-Sea, and is the person behind Atlantean Publishing. They studied history at the University of Wales at Aberystwyth and have worked in the fields of education and public relations. Their fiction featuring Sherlock Holmes has appeared in volumes from MX Publishing and Belanger Books, and in an issue of *Awesome Tales*, and they have a forthcoming story in *Sherlock Holmes Mystery Magazine*. DJ's non-Sherlockian mysteries have appeared in anthologies such as *Mardi Gras Mysteries* (Mystery and Horror LLC) and *The Trench Coat Chronicles* (Celestial Echo Press).
DJ Tyrer's website is at *https://djtyrer.blogspot.co.uk/*
DJ's Facebook page is at *https://www.facebook.com/DJTyrerwriter/*
The Atlantean Publishing website is at *https://atlanteanpublishing.wordpress.com/*

I.A. Watson, great-grand-nephew of Dr. John H. Watson, has been intrigued by the notorious "black sheep" of the family since childhood, and was fascinated to inherit from his grandmother a number of unedited manuscripts removed circa 1956 from a rather larger collection reposing at Lloyds Bank Ltd (which acquired Cox & Co Bank in 1923). Upon discovering the published corpus of accounts regarding the detective Sherlock Holmes from which a censorious upbringing had shielded him, he felt obliged to allow an interested public access to these additional memoranda, and is gradually undertaking the task of transcribing them for admirers of Mr. Holmes and Dr. Watson's works. In the meantime, I.A. Watson continues to pen other books, the latest of which is *The Incunabulum of Sherlock Holmes*. A full list of his seventy or so published works are available at: *http://www.chillwater.org.uk/writing/iawatsonhome.htm*

Sean Wright makes his home in Santa Clarita, a charming city at the entrance of the high desert in Southern California. For sixteen years, features and articles under his byline appeared in *The Tidings* – now *The Angelus News*, publications of the Roman Catholic Archdiocese of Los Angeles. Continuing his education in 2007, Mr. Wright graduated from Grand Canyon University, attaining a Bachelor of Arts degree in Christian Studies with a *summa cum laude*. He then attained a Master of Arts degree, also in Christian Studies.

Once active in the entertainment industry, and in an abortive attempt to revive dramatic radio in 1976 with his beloved mentor, the late Daws Butler, directing, Mr. Wright co-produced and wrote the syndicated *New Radio Adventures of Sherlock Holmes*, starring the late Edward Mulhare as the Great Detective. Mr. Wright has written for several television quiz shows and remains proud of his work for *The Quiz Kid's Challenge* and the popular TV quiz show *Jeopardy!* for which the Academy of Television Arts and Sciences honored him in 1985 with an Emmy nomination in the field of writing. Honored with membership in The Baker Street Irregulars as "The Manor House Case" after founding The Non-Canonical Calabashes, the Sherlock Holmes Society of Los Angeles in 1970, Mr. Wright has written for *The Baker Street Journal* and *Mystery Magazine*. Since 1971, he has conducted lectures on Sherlock Holmes's influence on literature and cinema for libraries, colleges, and private organizations, including MENSA. Mr. Wright's whimsical *Sherlock Holmes Cookbook* (Drake), created with John Farrell, BSI, was published in 1976, and a mystery novel, *Enter the Lion: a Posthumous Memoir of Mycroft Holmes* (Hawthorne), "edited" with Michael Hodel, BSI, followed in 1979. As director general of The Plot Thickens Mystery Company, Mr .Wright originated hosting "mystery parties" in homes, restaurants, and offices, as well as producing and directing the very first "Mystery Train" tours on Amtrak beginning in 1982.

The MX Book of New Sherlock Holmes Stories
Edited by David Marcum
(MX Publishing, 2015-   )

"This is the finest volume of Sherlockian fiction I have ever read, and I have read, literally, thousands." – Philip K. Jones

"Beyond Impressive . . . This is a splendid venture for a great cause!
– Roger Johnson, Editor, *The Sherlock Holmes Journal,*
The Sherlock Holmes Society of London

Part I: 1881-1889
Part II: 1890-1895
Part III: 1896-1929
Part IV: 2016 Annual
Part V: Christmas Adventures
Part VI: 2017 Annual
Part VII: Eliminate the Impossible (1880-1891)
Part VIII – Eliminate the Impossible (1892-1905)
Part IX – 2018 Annual (1879-1895)
Part X – 2018 Annual (1896-1916)
Part XI – Some Untold Cases (1880-1891)
Part XII – Some Untold Cases (1894-1902)
Part XIII – 2019 Annual (1881-1890)
Part XIV – 2019 Annual (1891-1897)
Part XV – 2019 Annual (1898-1917)
Part XVI – Whatever Remains . . . Must be the Truth (1881-1890)
Part XVII – Whatever Remains . . . Must be the Truth (1891-1898)
Part XVIII – Whatever Remains . . . Must be the Truth (1898-1925)
Part XIX – 2020 Annual (1882-1890)
Part XX – 2020 Annual (1891-1897)
Part XXI – 2020 Annual (1898-1923)
Part XXII – Some More Untold Cases (1877-1887)
Part XXIII – Some More Untold Cases (1888-1894)
Part XXIV – Some More Untold Cases (1895-1903)
Part XXV – 2021 Annual (1881-1888)
Part XXVI – 2021 Annual (1889-1897)
Part XXVII – 2021 Annual (1898-1928)
Part XXVIII – More Christmas Adventures (1869-1888)
Part XXIX – More Christmas Adventures (1889-1896)
Part XXX – More Christmas Adventures (1897-1928)

In Preparation

Part XXXI (and XXXII and XXXIII???) – However Improbable . . . .

. . . and more to come!

503

The MX Book of New Sherlock Holmes Stories
Edited by David Marcum
(MX Publishing, 2015-   )

Publishers Weekly says:

Part VI: *The traditional pastiche is alive and well . . . .*

Part VII: *Sherlockians eager for faithful-to-the-canon plots and characters will be delighted.*

Part VIII: *The imagination of the contributors in coming up with variations on the volume's theme is matched by their ingenious resolutions.*

Part IX: *The 18 stories . . . will satisfy fans of Conan Doyle's originals. Sherlockians will rejoice that more volumes are on the way.*

Part X: *. . . new Sherlock Holmes adventures of consistently high quality.*

Part XI: *. . . an essential volume for Sherlock Holmes fans.*

Part XII: *. . . continues to amaze with the number of high-quality pastiches.*

Part XIII: *. . . Amazingly, Marcum has found 22 superb pastiches . . . This is more catnip for fans of stories faithful to Conan Doyle's original*

Part XIV: *. . . this standout anthology of 21 short stories written in the spirit of Conan Doyle's originals.*

Part XV: *Stories pitting Sherlock Holmes against seemingly supernatural phenomena highlight Marcum's 15th anthology of superior short pastiches.*

Part XVI: *Marcum has once again done fans of Conan Doyle's originals a service.*

Part XVII: *This is yet another impressive array of new but traditional Holmes stories.*

Part XVIII: *Sherlockians will again be grateful to Marcum and MX for high-quality new Holmes tales.*

Part XIX: *Inventive plots and intriguing explorations of aspects of Dr. Watson's life and beliefs lift the 24 pastiches in Marcum's impressive 19th Sherlock Holmes anthology*

Part XX: *Marcum's reserve of high-quality new Holmes exploits seems endless.*

Part XXI: *This is another must-have for Sherlockians.*

Part XXII: *Marcum's superlative 22nd Sherlock Holmes pastiche anthology features 21 short stories that successfully emulate the spirit of Conan Doyle's originals while expanding on the canon's tantalizing references to mysteries Dr. Watson never got around to chronicling.*

Part XXIII: *Marcum's well of talented authors able to mimic the feel of The Canon seems bottomless.*

Part XXIV: *Marcum's expertise at selecting high-quality pastiches remains impressive.*

Part XXVIII: *All entries adhere to the spirit, language, and characterizations of Conan Doyle's originals, evincing the deep pool of talent Marcum has access to. Against the odds, this series remains strong, hundreds of stories in.*

The MX Book of New Sherlock Holmes Stories
Edited by David Marcum
(MX Publishing, 2015-   )

MX Publishing

MX Publishing is the world's largest specialist Sherlock Holmes publisher, with over five-hundred titles and over two-hundred authors creating the latest in Sherlock Holmes fiction and non-fiction

The catalogue includes several award winning books, and over two-hundred-and-fifty have been converted into audio.

MX Publishing also has one of the largest communities of Holmes fans on Facebook, with regular contributions from dozens of authors.

www.mxpublishing.com

@mxpublishing on Facebook, Twitter and Instagram

www.ingramcontent.com/pod-product-compliance
Lightning Source LLC
Chambersburg PA
CBHW032256020726
47495CB00001B/130